THE TRIUMVIRS REVEALED

Books 1 – 3

By Ways Unseen

The First to Forgive

The One Known

Daniel Dydek

BEORN PUBLISHING, LLC

CONTENTS

BY WAYS UNSEEN

Book 1 of The Triumvirs

Daniel Dydek

BEORN PUBLISHING, LLC

CONTENTS

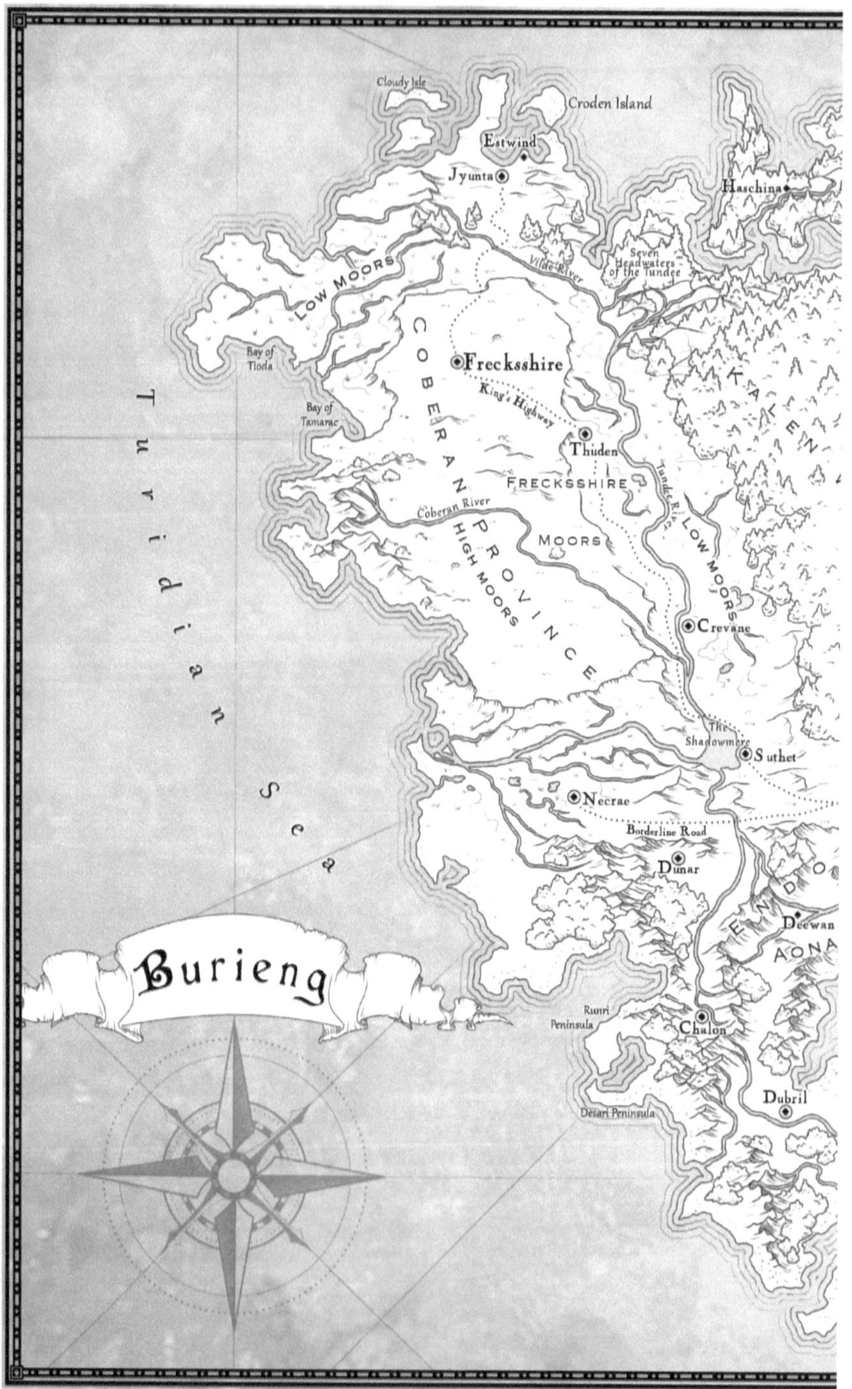

Cloudy Isle
Croden Island
Estwind
Jyunta
Haschina
Low Moors
Seven Headwaters of the Tundee
Vilde River
KALEN
Bay of Tloda
COBERAN
Frecksshire
King's Highway
Bay of Tamarac
Thuden
FRECKSSHIRE
PROVINCE
Coberan River
HIGH MOORS
MOORS
Tundee River
Low Moors
Turidian Sea
Crevane
The Shadowmere
Suthet
Necrae
Borderline Road
Dunar
Deewan
AONA
END O
Burieng
Runri Peninsula
Chalon
Desari Peninsula
Dubril

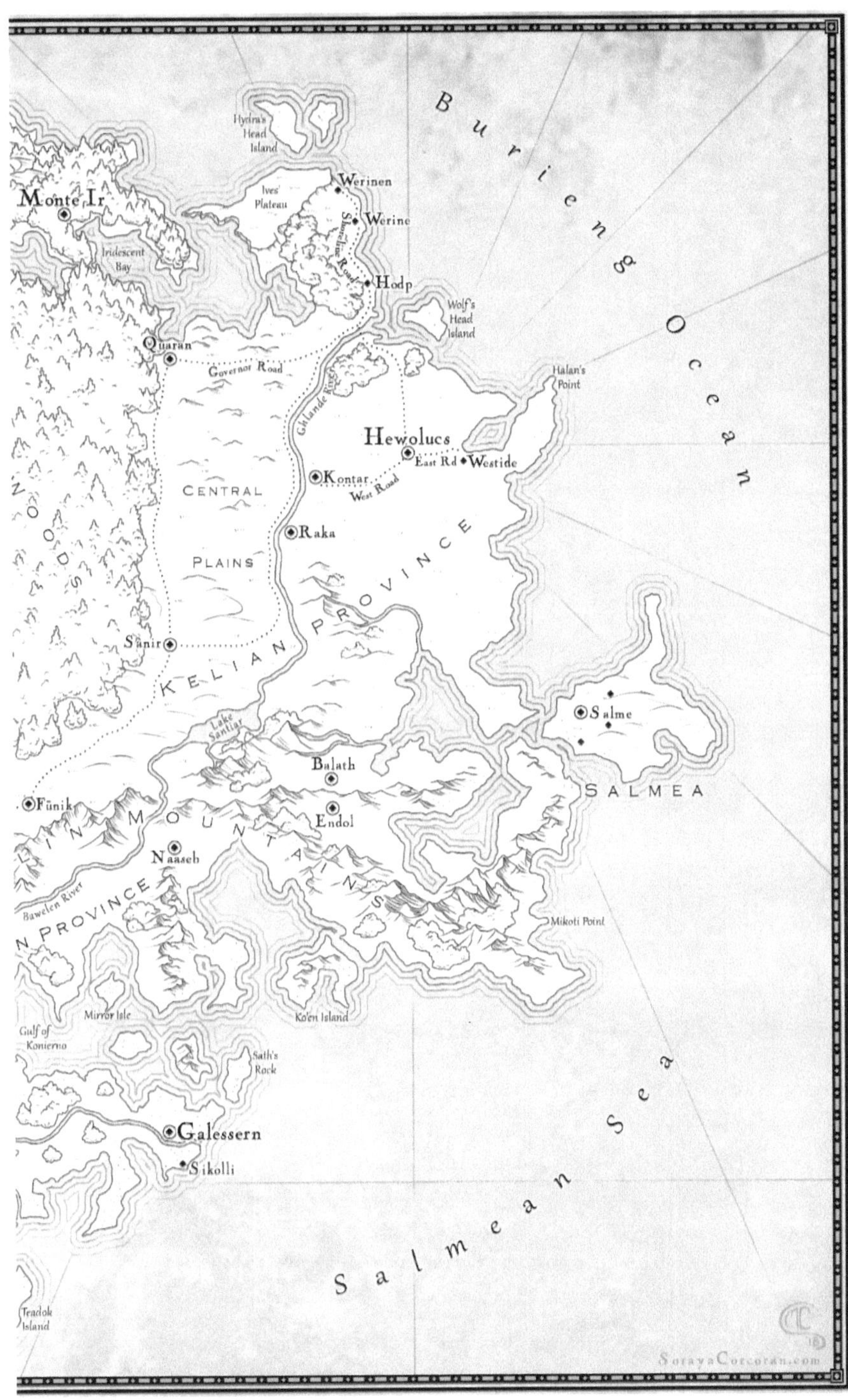

Burieng Ocean
Hydra's Head Island
Werinen
Ives' Plateau
Werine
Shoreline Road
Monte Ir
Hodp
Iridescent Bay
Wolf's Head Island
Quaran
Halan's Point
Governor Road
Galande River
Hewolucs
East Rd
Westide
Kontar
West Road
CENTRAL
Raka
PLAINS
KELIAN PROVINCE
Salme
Sanir
SALMEA
Lake Santiat
Balath
Funik
Endol
LIN MOUNTAINS
Naaseh
Bawelen River
N PROVINCE
Mikoti Point
Mirror Isle
Ko'en Island
Gulf of Konierno
Sath's Rock
Galessern
Sikolli
Salmean Sea
Teadok Island
SorayaCorcoran.com

I

FISSURES

"Have you found anything?"
"Little to give hope."
"We must move soon, though."
"Then let's hope this one isn't killed, too."

22 Nuamon 1319 [1] — Spring

Haydren stood near the middle of the classroom with arms folded, his mind tumbling through possible reasons for the students' summons at so late an hour. On the floor an ant was scurrying as though lost. It skittered down into a crack, resurfaced, and hurried into another.

It was not the entire class in the room today; only nine other boys, all nearing graduation, gathered into their little groups. Haydren stood apart, watching an ant search for a purpose.

"Say, Haydren," said Harlan, who was nearest him. "You're close to the Earl, right? What's this about?"

"I don't know," he murmured.

"I told you," the boy said to his friends as he turned back. The other boys snickered, but when Haydren ignored them they returned to their low conversation.

The truth was, Haydren did know—or rather, he hoped he knew. After eight years of dreaming of the day, devoting himself to training and

---

1. See Author's Note on Calendar for explanation of dates.

classes to prove himself a swordsman, it still seemed impossible that he might soon go outside Hewolucs. After so much delayed hope it seemed proper that it would be delayed forever.

But not after what he'd overheard from a guard while cleaning tack a few days ago.

The ant hesitated, then turned around the way it had come. Haydren drew a breath as it disappeared into a crack and didn't reappear.

"I thought I saw you here," came Kitrel's voice from behind him. He turned, his grin widening.

"I was wondering if you were invited too," he replied.

At six feet tall, Haydren no longer had to look up at most of the other students, but his eyes came barely to Kitrel's chin. And while Haydren's whipcord muscles handled a one-handed sword better than anyone in the class, Kitrel's bulk could nearly best him with a battle-axe. Haydren was glad Kitrel was one student he didn't have to worry about fighting.

They shook hands, and Haydren said, "So. How are you?"

"I'm about the same as when you saw me this morning, I guess," Kitrel said hesitantly. "Why?"

Haydren shrugged. "Well I know you had your herb exam this afternoon..."

"Oh please," Kitrel said, waving him off. "Don't even speak to me of that. What a bleeding waste of my life. I suppose you took the top score, right?"

Haydren glanced away. Kitrel punched him in the arm, laughing.

"I like the art!" Haydren protested.

"Uh huh."

"You know what?" Haydren said, returning the punch playfully. "Just because some of us are smarter than others."

"Right. Okay, school-boy, why are we here then?" Kitrel asked.

"Because we're fighting hellhounds tomorrow," Haydren replied flatly.

"We're fighting *what?*" a voice piped up near the back, with Guntsen's circle of friends.

"Nothing, Dillion," Haydren called back.

"Rumor-monger," Kitrel muttered with a smile as urgent whispers echoed among the groups. Haydren shrugged.

"I think maybe we're going on patrols tomorrow," Haydren murmured. "I overheard a guard muttering something about taking 'sprouts' on patrol soon; I don't think he meant the food."

Kitrel raised an eyebrow, glancing around the room. "We're certainly getting to the age for it. Even Harlan. I mean, if we're just talking about age."

Haydren's eyes followed his gaze, soon landing on the Earl's heir as well. He eyed Guntsen's spiced-wine-and-sweetmeats girth critically. "Yeah, but Guntsen's going to end up getting someone killed if he goes out there."

Kitrel scoffed. "I doubt he's going. They don't train his level of royalty to go on patrols, Haydren; they just want to know how to handle a sword so if they get in a huff with another lord, they can have something resembling a duel. For their honor!" Kitrel shook his head and wiped his mouth.

The door latch rattled as the schoolmaster, Sir Cullins, entered the classroom. Though he was nearing sixty, and the gray in his hair crept halfway back from his forehead, training students in swordplay and weapons history had not allowed him to age much. And it was no accident that not even Haydren could beat him in a sparring match.

Sir Cullins regarded the students as they assembled loosely before him. Haydren noted a rolled parchment affixed with the royal seal stamped in red wax.

"As most of you know, you all are nearing graduation," Sir Cullins said as the boys gave him their attention. "Within the month, most of you will be serving the Earl in one capacity or another. Since this is the case, he has decreed that you will all go with the next patrols outside of the castle."

Haydren's breath caught. Even though he had overheard the guard, something in him still had not expected it. Was he ready? Was there any way to be ready?

Haydren glanced at his other classmates, seeing the same frozen expression on their faces. Suddenly Willam cackled gleefully and clapped. The class' collective breath released, and Haydren and several others broke into smiles.

Sir Cullins glanced at Willam with a bemused half-grin. He unrolled the parchment. "You will be attached in teams of three to the three patrols. I have here the names of who is going where, so pay attention."

Three teams of three? But that would mean—he spotted Guntsen, who looked placid and a little smug. *So,* Haydren thought, *Kitrel was right.* He looked back at Sir Cullins.

"Orenius, Destis, and Gregson." Cullins paused as the three students stiffened. "You will be going to Westide at week's end. Be prepared before Dawn, at the East gate."

"Where Haydren's father used to work. You know, before he was relieved," Guntsen piped up. Haydren's gaze was steady, even as several other students snickered.

"Enough," Cullins warned. "Willam, Brahn, and Kitrel, you are going to Raka in two days." He looked at each student in turn. Guntsen's face was strangely reserved, but Cullins ignored it. "Pack enough for a long journey, for your patrol may extend to Sanir. Those orders will follow you. At the very least, you will be spending some nights in Raka. Be ready by Mid-Morning, at the west gate."

"Where Mickel works now, since he was reinstated," Haydren smirked, though he still ignored the heir to the throne.

Cullins fixed Haydren with a stern gaze. "Haydren, Dillion, and Harlan, you three ride for Hodp tomorrow. Be ready before Morning, at the north gate." He paused, then added: "Where I had all of you running in circles for an entire morning. Don't think I won't do it again simply because you graduate soon after returning from these patrols. Dismissed."

Kitrel turned to Haydren and shrugged. "I wish I was going with you," he said, offering his hand.

"To Hodp?" Haydren replied, grasping Kitrel's hand and giving it a firm shake. "Are you insane? Talk about boring."

Kitrel gave a consoling smile. "Maybe. But..."

Haydren caught the look and frowned. "Right. I guess it makes sense for me to go there, of all of us. I do wonder though." He shook his head.

Kitrel placed a hand on Haydren's shoulder. "I wish I was going with you," he repeated, then grinned. "Wouldn't be boring if we both went."

Haydren forced a smile. "That's probably why he kept us separated."

"If I don't see you, good luck. I'm going to figure out what I need to pack."

"Hey," Haydren said, suddenly serious. "Be safe. There are a lot of folks who aren't friends of non-Cariste out that way."

"Oh really?" Kitrel replied sarcastically. "Was that in class sometime?"

Haydren smiled again. "Sorry. But be safe."

"I will."

He watched Kitrel leave alone—Willam and Brahn stayed with Guntsen—then sighed as he turned toward Sir Cullins. The schoolmaster's gaze was on the students, but unfocused. Haydren hesitated, not wanting to break the master from his reverie.

But before he could decide, Sir Cullins was looking at him with a smile. "I imagine you're looking forward to your first mission?"

Haydren didn't smile. "Could I talk to you, sir?" he asked. "Somewhere that we can be alone?"

Sir Cullins cocked his head, then nodded. "Sure. I have to watch over the other students, so wait for me at my chambers. I'll be there shortly."

"Thank you, sir," Haydren replied. He bowed quickly and left, glancing back before exiting to catch the schoolmaster watching him with a clouded look. It seemed a desperate attempt. Most likely Sir Cullins would give him the 'orders are orders' speech—he had heard it before. Or something like it.

In the rotunda, he descended to the main floor where the Earl's coat was emblazoned upon the tiles, and into a hall on the east wing—the only other wing the school had aside from the Student-Quarters. Here were faculty chambers. He could never walk by without noting, and smiling at, the bright purple door of Herb-Mistress Felise's room. He turned to wait outside Sir Cullins' door with his back to the wall.

Haydren heard echoing footsteps, and Sir Cullins appeared around the corner. He said nothing as he led the way into the chamber. On the opposite wall hung a broad tapestry depicting the last great battle between Carist and Rinc Na. Of course, a goat-horned Illmali flew above the Rinc Nain armies, while a beaming but wrathful God of All sheltered the Cariste. "Have a seat, Haydren," the schoolmaster said. As Haydren politely refused the ladder-back chair in the middle of the floor, Sir Cullins lowered himself into his cloth-padded chair and leaned back, folding his hands in his lap.

"What can I do for you, Haydren?" Sir Cullins asked.

"Sir, why did the Earl train me in your school?"

"Haydren, I've been a soldier for a long time, and orders..." Sir Cullins stopped, cocking his head. "Wait, what?"

"Earl Junei expended a lot of effort, and took a major risk in enrolling me in your school," Haydren said. "He had to have known how I would be viewed by my classmates. Surely he even viewed me the same way! So..." Haydren paused, raising upturned hands. "Why?"

Sir Cullins sighed, gazing through the latticed window across the room. "Because you're skilled, Haydren," Sir Cullins replied. "Whatever else you are—or are not—you are skilled. Taeus Junei is short enough of troops that he isn't going to pass up an opportunity to train someone who may very well protect him personally one day."

"So he sends me to Hodp?"

"Everyone starts somewhere, Haydren."

"Others started in Raka."

"Haydren," Sir Cullins said, leaning forward, "bandits are increasing on the roads. Creatures are multiplying at a frightening rate in the wilds—vicious creatures, who do not hesitate to attack men. And more and more patrols are clashing near our borders with Aonan and Coberan Provinces. Swordsmen will be needed for more than patrols to Hodp."

"So why send us there now?" Haydren asked.

"Because we don't know where the enemy will strike next. Earl Junei is increasing patrols to *all* settlements under his rule; Raka and Sanir are more dangerous to soldiers, as is Quaran and the outposts to the south. But Hodp, small as it is, faces a greater risk of small raids simply because of its size. Your mission, and many after this, will be to search for evidence of the enemy's movements."

"So why would he send the more important students where there is greater danger? After all, he is sending Willam to Raka, who aside from Guntsen has the highest rank of all of us."

Sir Cullins' fist tightened, but not in anger. In the silence, Haydren's gaze moved to the square of evening light that crept toward the desk. So, he had been right. Haydren's place had been set ever since his hair had brightened from barely-tolerated commoner's brown to openly reviled Rinc Nain chestnut.

Sir Cullins let out a short sigh. Haydren's eyes focused on his, then dropped.

"I just want to be able to make my own choices, to be and do as well as the skill I have, not the lineage I do not have," he said quietly. "Is that lineage going to keep me on patrols to Hodp forever?"

"There are many units under command of the Earl, Haydren," Sir Cullins replied. "Right now, there were only three patrols going out, and nine students to send. He could not send you somewhere more important than where he sent the others. The dishonor to them and their families..." Sir Cullins paused. "Wait until you graduate, and are admitted into the Earl's ranks generally. There will be far more opportunities for you to progress then."

Haydren nodded. What Sir Cullins said made sense, but something still nagged at the back of his mind, something telling him he would forever be less than what his capabilities provided. This patrol to Hodp was a dark crevice into which he might slip and never been seen from again, and Haydren felt himself inevitably drawn into it.

"Thank you, Sir Cullins," Haydren said quietly, looking up. "I should probably begin packing."

Sir Cullins nodded graciously. "Good idea. The future is always uncertain Haydren, and you are still young; be patient: see what happens."

"Thank you, sir," Haydren said, straightening his shoulders. He paused for a moment before adding: "I will."

Haydren exited with Sir Cullins' bidding and went to his room. He packed before nightfall, then lay in bed awake till the moon had nearly set. Its broad grin hovered orange over the horizon, trying to assure him that the world was all right. But the moon was content with its lofty track over the midnight skies, and Haydren would not be content with his dusty track through the dregs of life. He rolled over, thought of his patrol, and fell asleep.

⸺◆⸺

Besides the three students were twelve mounted soldiers, and Captain Beron—a broad, scraggle-bearded man in his mid-fifties. It was a cool morning under clear skies that did not cloud over for three days as they traveled north toward Hodp along Shoreline Road. Inns were sparse in eastern Burieng, located mostly in towns and intersections. Towns were days apart: the constant threat of beasts—which had never quite diminished through the centuries—made it easier to guard wagoners' convoys than to build fortresses. Though there were farmhouses manned by stalwart Cariste here and there, more often than not the soldiers slept in tents huddled around fires. As the youngest members of the unit, the students were given guard duty with a veteran during the worst watches of the night. The only excitement came when they crossed a high arching bridge over the Ghlande River that split most of the Eastern Shores from the Central Plains. But nighttime soon came again, and by the Moonset guard shift Haydren had all but forgotten the dark ribbon meandering lazily toward a sea faintly visible on the horizon.

On the fourth morning, the soldiers chattered—whether bragging or griping, Haydren didn't care to listen. One of the soldiers, Jelleth, had recognized the coldness of Haydren's classmates on the first day, and had taken a personal liking to him. But today he was strangely silent, leaving Haydren alone to gaze at the broad plains.

Haydren stood to relieve the pressure on his backside. He longed to walk. He was a swordsman, after all, and if he wanted to ride he would have wished to become a knight. As he stood, he saw on the horizon a speck of dark on the bright plains that he recognized to be a house—another chance to pause and ask about beasts and bandits. To the east, a lone tree, gnarled and bent, poked its balding head from the otherwise treeless plain. It stood alone but unique, abandoned by the forest which must have surrounded it at one time. Hardened by time, it refused to die and stood as a monument unto itself.

"There it is," Jelleth muttered.

"I saw it," Haydren replied. "Have you ever had an chance to go look at it?"

Jelleth stared at him. "What?"

"That tree. It's strange that it stands by itself, with no trees around it. Is it a remnant of some ancient forest?"

"I meant Hodp," Jelleth said. "There's *Hodp*."

Haydren stared ahead, surprised to see the low, wooden wall about six feet high encircling the town. "That?" Then, weakly, he repeated: "That?"

Jelleth chuckled. "You've never been outside of Hewolucs, have you?"

Haydren sank in his saddle, forgetting how sore he was. Both the tree and the men around him, all were old and hardened—alone, monuments only of perseverance.

The houses of Hodp clustered on the junction with Governor Road, which ran south and west toward Quaran. There were a few outlying huts and houses. Passing one, a mother concentrated on her butter churn as Haydren and the others rode by. The father was leading a pair of oxen out to the field, and a dog bayed as it chased after a young boy. To the east, a squat windmill grazed slowly in the shifting breeze. A clamor near the north edge of the town heralded the forge.

"How...pastoral," Haydren muttered. Jelleth just snickered.

They rode through the hole in the wall that may once have held gates, but now gaped like missing teeth. On the northwest corner of the intersection stood an Inn, where Beron directed his horse. He alighted nimbly for his age and size. Before tying up his horse, he squinted north up the road. Haydren looked and saw a large plume of dust in the distance.

"We may have to quarter with the locals," Beron said, looping the reins around a pole.

One of the soldiers growled, and the rest of the soldiers looked equally displeased. The three students glanced at each other.

"Why?" Harlan asked.

"Because we can," Jelleth replied, and spat. "Those merchants can't.

And they'll fill the Inn."

"Maybe," Beron said, approaching the door. He opened it, glanced inside, then turned on his heel and returned to his horse.

"Let's go."

Muttering, the soldiers followed their captain to a nearby house. Built of wood and stucco, it rose unique as one of the few two-story houses in the village. Beron approached the door and pounded, shaking it in its frame. Moments passed before the door opened to reveal a man with close-cropped, rusty hair, who at first glance seemed stooped with age—his height would come barely to Haydren's nose. But the man's back was straight, and despite a years-worn look similar to the captain's, he retained a certain degree of vitality that Beron had lost many years ago.

"Doors are expensive," the man said calmly. "You needn't break mine just to seek my answer." Though he didn't challenge Beron directly, Haydren feared the captain's reaction to the tone.

Beron hesitated. "We require lodging," he said finally.

"The inn is across the street," the man replied. He began shutting the door. Beron thrust his foot in the jamb, and the man opened it.

"A group of merchants are approaching," Beron said. "And they have first claim to public lodging."

"How unfortunate for you," the man said, folding his hands.

"And for you," Beron replied curtly. "We are soldiers of the Earl. You cannot refuse us any less than you can refuse the Earl himself. How many beds do you have?"

The man considered Beron, then swept his gaze over the rest of the soldiers. His eyes lingered on Haydren just a moment longer than the others.

"Two," he replied.

"Very well," Beron replied. "Haydren, Jelleth, you two stay here. We regroup first thing tomorrow, right out here."

"Aww, captain, you're not going to put me up with the dissenter and the youth, are you?" Jelleth whined.

Beron glared at him. Haydren swung down from his horse and removed his saddlebags. Jelleth was behind him, moving despondently.

"Hey, Jelly, maybe you can teach him some fighting skills," said one of the soldiers.

Haydren snorted. "I could probably teach him a few things."

The soldier stared. "I meant the dissenter," he said, and turned and laughed with his comrades.

"Tomorrow morning!" Beron shouted over them. Grasping his horse's reins, he led the rest of the troop to the next house.

"I have a small stable in back," said the man of the house. "Make use as you need."

After seeing to their horses they returned to find the door still open, and the man inside near a wood-stove with his back turned. They entered, and Jelleth shut the door with a bang. The man glanced at them benignly and continued with his task.

When Haydren's eyes adjusted, his gaze wandered around a single-room lower level with dark wood flooring, a black fur rug before the stone fireplace, and a table set nearby. In the far corner, a small collection of cookware hung on pegs near the stove. To his surprise, a water pump stood against the wall, with a large basin next to it. Water pumps were rare enough in Hewolucs, he did not expect to find one in Hodp, let alone in a personal home.

"Do you live here alone?" he asked.

"Until now," the man replied, wiping his hands on a towel at his waist. His tone was still not confrontational; he spoke merely as if stating facts. A staircase near the back led to the second floor, and he moved toward it now, gesturing for them to follow.

They climbed up facing a door, and a hallway ran parallel to their right. Two more doors opened off the hallway, and Haydren could see sunlight streaming under them.

It was to the first door on the hallway that the man directed them. He opened it, and inside were two cots of straw mattresses; another, smaller fur rug between them; and a small chest of drawers centered under the single window. Jelleth glanced around dubiously.

"I thought you said you had two rooms?" he asked.

"I told your captain I had two beds," the man replied.

"What's in there?" Jelleth asked, pointing to the door that faced the stairs.

"Storage."

Jelleth stared glumly. "Can I store myself in there, then?"

"I have two beds," he repeated. "You are welcome to them, or you may sleep somewhere else. But beware, rain can come quickly upon Hodp, and the streets flood easily."

"I was only asking," Jelleth said. "Which bed do you want, youth?" he asked as he tossed his gear on the left bed.

The man opened his mouth, glanced at Haydren, and shut it. He turned to leave.

"Sir," Haydren called. The man turned back, eyes glittering beneath thin eyebrows that Haydren just noticed were dark brown. "May I ask your name? I certainly do not want to continue calling you 'dissenter.'"

The man paused. "Geoffrey," he replied. He opened his mouth to say something more, then glanced at Jelleth, who reclined with one eye cocked on him. Geoffrey shut his mouth, turned, and left.

"Talkative, isn't he?" Haydren said.

The old soldier replied with a loud snore.

⸺◆⸺

In the western provincial capital of Frecksshire, at the keep of Earl Durdamon, Sarah glanced up from the parchments before her as a messenger entered her chambers, unannounced. He stopped short, looking at the aged and curling documents before her.

"Can I help you?" she asked.

"The Earl wishes to see you," the man said, managing to lift his eyes off the table but not quite fasten them onto her eyes.

"But you do not? Or do you indeed, which is why you burst into my private chambers without knocking?"

"It's mid-day," the man replied with a disgruntled gesture to the bright windows. He flashed a quick smile. "Perhaps tonight, if you're still around."

"You've delivered your message, thank you," Sarah replied. After the man turned and left, she sighed. She could strike a man with lightning, and he would only suggest she help him take off his singed clothing.

She stood, smoothing her blue silk dress and wrapping her shoulders in a fur shawl. The Earl only and ever wished to *see* her.

When she entered the throne room, she could tell something was different this time: General Halfeng was there, as well as Thregard and Dewer, the political and historical advisors. But not Durdamon's bard.

"You requested my presence?" Sarah asked.

Earl Durdamon's gaze did not linger. "Yes; come over here and look at this," he said, pointing to the map that lay on the table. General Halfeng moved to give her space. The advisors stood gloomily on the opposite side of the table.

Her glance was swift. Most of it was familiar except a black line that traced the opposite side of the Kalen Woods, near Quaran. That it stood out immediately troubled her.

Earl Durdamon nodded gravely to her inquisitive glance. "Yes, it's a new line. According to reports, it's where the Woods are now."

"'Now'?" she echoed.

"Yes, it didn't use to be there. It hasn't been there in centuries!" replied Dewer. He glared as Thregard scoffed. "It *hasn't*. No record says it has, not since the Kalen ruled there. Perhaps before!"

"It moved?" Sarah asked.

"Grown," General Halfeng corrected. "So far as we know, the interior has not changed."

"The interior does not change, ever," Dewer muttered.

"Can magic do that?" Durdamon asked.

Sarah shrugged. "There is perhaps a way, but certainly not by air."

"Can you tell if something else could, if you looked at it?" asked Thregard.

Sarah regarded him closely. "Perhaps. Has it never grown like this before?"

"Well it didn't pop into existence fully grown," Thregard said. Sarah cast him a withering look.

"Of course it has," Dewer answered her question. "But it had been dormant for at least twenty years, just outside sight of Quaran's walls. It is said they can see it easily, now."

"It sounds like magic, but I'm not sure what kind."

Durdamon turned and leaned against the table. "Will seeing the Woods help you determine what is happening?"

"I say again: perhaps," Sarah replied. "I have affinity with air, so that is what I study."

"You also study men."

"They confuse me," Sarah said, barely managing to keep the edge off her voice. She attempted a demure smile.

"If you speak to those near it, they may have seen things to help you understand what is happening."

Sarah hesitated. "So I'm not going to this side of the Woods?"

Durdamon smiled and shook his head. "I'm afraid not."

"Is anyone going with me?" she asked, glancing around the table.

"Some," the Earl replied, turning back to the table. "But you have to look like you're on a diplomatic mission. All three are sending representatives: a squad from Halfeng, and an apprentice each from Dewer and Thregard."

"Will Junei appreciate your soldiers entering his province?" Sarah asked.

"We'll find out at Fūnik," the General replied. "I cannot imagine he is that suspicious."

"We would be," Sarah replied quietly.

"Only because of what we know," Durdamon said. "I'm honestly unsure Junei knows anything at all."

"I leave tonight?" Sarah asked, recalling the improper messenger's comment.

"If I could send someone else, I would," the Earl replied. "I hope I do not inconvenience your studies."

Sarah glanced around the circle of men. *You would send a wizard if you could, not a sorceress,* she thought. "Not at all," she said. "Some of it I can take with me. I will return as swiftly as possible."

"Return with knowledge, if not time," Durdamon replied. "Both are precious and in short supply, but I prefer the first."

"I understand."

2

REMEMBRANCES

"Do you mean we must let this happen?"
"There are many things that must happen, Teresh."
"Not things that we have the power to stop."
"A power only granted to us; it is not solely ours."

28 Nuamon 1319 — Spring

The next day, Haydren awoke with the morning already well advanced. Swearing something briefly, Haydren leapt out of bed.

"Jelleth, wake up," he said, rubbing the sleep from his eyes.

Jelleth muttered something, snorted, and continued to breathe deeply. Haydren leaned over and smacked him on the shoulder. Jelleth's eyes popped open and glared.

"Do you want to lose your hands?" Jelleth growled.

"It's time to wake up," Haydren said as he pulled on his boots. "Past time, even."

Jelleth closed his eyes. "Let me tell you something about the captain," he said. "When he says 'first thing in the morning,' he simply means before anything else *he* does; not before anything else happens in the world. We have plenty of time. So, unless you want me to cut your hands from your arms, leave me to sleep."

Haydren's foot thumped into his second boot. "Oh," he muttered. He glanced through the window.

"So, Jelleth," Haydren said slowly.

"Hmm?" Jelleth muttered.

"This angry-looking soldier on the street, looking toward our window, wouldn't be the captain, then," Haydren said. "You know, since he isn't awake yet."

Jelleth growled again as he threw the blankets aside. "The one time he decides to…" he muttered, yanking on his boots.

Haydren belted on his sword—Mickel's sword—and picked up his saddlebags from beside the bed. "I'll go out and let him know we're on our way," he said.

"And I'll castrate you!" Jelleth barked. "We go out together or you don't go out at all."

Haydren shrugged. "As you wish." He watched silently as Jelleth hurriedly dressed and gathered his gear, then opened the door for the older soldier.

As he turned to go down the stairs, he noticed Geoffrey's door open and the room empty. They walked out without seeing their host.

"Did he really leave us alone?" Haydren muttered. Jelleth was too busy cursing and still fumbling with his sword belt to hear him.

A little prophetically, it had rained and the road was thick with mud. Beron stood impatiently as Haydren and Jelleth made their way to the stables in fits of stride as they tried to show they were hurrying without admitting the need to hurry. Haydren's horse looked at them, his tongue sticking out of the side of his mouth as if laughing.

"Did you learn anything?" Beron asked when they finally approached.

"His name is Geoffrey."

Jelleth and Beron both gazed at Haydren a moment before Jelleth turned back to the captain.

"I like this kid," Jelleth said, hooking a thumb toward Haydren.

Beron snorted. "Yeah, he reminds me of you."

"You say it like it's a bad thing!"

"We're going to scout around," Beron said, turning to the soldiers as they walked up. "Did any of you find anything out from the townsfolk you quartered with?"

Flies buzzed in the captain's ear.

"Did any of you ask?" he pressed. Still silence.

"Perfect," he growled. "What did I do to deserve you guys?" He suppressed a sigh. "All right, we'll ride around and see what we can find out. We should be on the road home by mid-day."

The men brightened visibly, and all mounted their horses quickly. Beron shook his head, spat, and mounted as well.

They spent a few tedious hours around the village, but by noon they had found no townsfolk with any troubles or worries to report. True to his word, Beron had them facing their horses toward Hewolucs before the sun reached its zenith.

The journey home was as uneventful as the journey to Hodp, and by noon the fourth day the spires of Hewolucs rose over the horizon. Once inside the walls, Haydren relaxed in the familiar bustle and towering buildings of the city.

Near the middle of town, the students broke off from the column and returned to the school.

The main rotunda was strangely quiet when they entered. They were supposed to give a report, Haydren thought. He turned around several times, thinking maybe Sir Cullins was on a balcony. But the sword-master was nowhere to be seen. After shrugging at one another, Dillion and Harlan left to return to their rooms. Haydren started to follow, but heard a noise from Sir Cullins' office and turned back. He knocked at the headmaster's door.

After a moment of silence, Haydren heard a faint response. He entered; Sir Cullins was seated, a hand wrapped around his mouth as he gazed at his desk. His eyes flicked upward, his hand dropped, and he forced a grin.

"Haydren!" he said, but his voice did not echo his smile. "Your patrol is back. That's good. How was it?"

"Sir Cullins, what's wrong?" Haydren asked.

"Where are Harlan and Dillion?"

"They returned to the Apartments," Haydren replied. "We thought you would be outside to greet us. When you weren't there we assumed you would call for us."

"I am sorry," Sir Cullins replied. "I guess I wasn't expecting you back so early." He glanced out the window, noting the slant of the rays. "Or I didn't realize it was so late already."

"Sir Cullins, what's happened?" Haydren repeated.

"It's too soon to tell yet." He wiped a hand down his face. "The patrol to Raka has not sent word yet, that's all."

"Should have they?"

"It is only a little further to Raka than it is to Hodp, Haydren," Sir Cullins replied. "Think of your maps: it is perhaps two days further. And yet you have had time to journey to Hodp and back, and no word has been sent back from their patrol, at all. They were to send a falcon back when they reached the town, advising the Earl as to whether they would continue to Sanir." Sir Cullins paused, swallowing. "The Earl has received no word yet."

Haydren struggled to find his voice. "Sir, Kitrel was my closest friend."

Sir Cullins sighed. "I know; listen, there's nothing for you to do until graduation. You may return to your room, and I will send word as soon as I hear anything."

Haydren bowed his head. "Thank you, Sir."

Harlan and Dillion were both waiting for him and he relayed Sir Cullins' message to them. They stood in uncomfortable silence for some moments before breaking up and returning to their rooms. Haydren reclined on his bed, not bothering to remove his boots as he gazed out at the setting sun. It did not even occur to him, as the sun disappeared below the horizon, to light his lamps, and the room sank into darkness.

As the last of a red glow sat above his window sill, a knock came softly at his door. "Come in," he said. When Sir Cullins entered, he leapt to his feet.

"Sir Cullins!" he cried. "If I had known it was you..."

Sir Cullins silenced him with a wave. "You could not know," he said.

They stood for several moments. "What have you heard?" Haydren asked, already knowing the answer: Sir Cullins would not have brought the message himself if it were good news.

"A falcon from Raka arrived this evening," Sir Cullins replied. "The troop was ambushed before they could have been seen by the roving guard. It was not until vultures gathered that they even sent out a patrol to investigate." Sir Cullins paused, swallowing, and looked at Haydren, eyes filled with compassion—and tears. "There were no survivors," he said. "I'm so sorry, Haydren."

The darkness below Haydren yawned open, about to swallow him. Haydren sat back down onto his bed, his eyes unfocused. There had always been a slight possibility of being attacked, but he could never imagine an entire troop being slaughtered. And Kitrel was one of the best fighters in the school! It didn't seem possible.

"Who attacked them?" Haydren asked.

"The message was not entirely clear, but there were a number of dead beasts in the field. It is unlikely bandits were with them," Sir Cullins replied.

"Beasts?" Haydren asked numbly. "Is that common?"

"It is far more common recently than in the past," Sir Cullins replied. "I mentioned as much before."

Haydren gazed at the floor now shrouded in shadows, fighting a range of emotions: sorrow, hatred, fear. Mostly he wanted revenge, knowing it would not be for him to have. He looked up at Sir Cullins, his gaze hardening. "Should I expect more patrols to Hodp after graduation, Sir Cullins?" he asked.

Sir Cullins sighed, his hands clenching and unclenching at his side. "Haydren," he began, his voice a whisper.

"Never mind," Haydren said abruptly. "You don't have to say it. Thank you for coming to let me know, Sir Cullins." He meant the last part, and hoped his voice conveyed his honesty.

Sir Cullins gazed at him. "Of course," he replied. "I will send for you when we must start preparing for graduation. You are free until then."

He turned and left, shutting Haydren in utter darkness. Coming to himself, Haydren leapt to his feet, fumbling for his tinder box and taper. He extended the lantern-wick on his bedside table and shakily attempted to light it. It flared suddenly, startling him. The flame steadied, sent its diffuse glow across the table. Haydren took a long breath, and the flame fluttered as he exhaled.

He circled the room, lighting the rest of the lamps and candles before returning to his bed and sitting heavily down upon it. Kitrel had been his only friend—his only true friend. A few others had tolerated him.

Most hated him both behind and in front of his back. Now Kitrel was dead, and there was nothing Haydren could do about it. He would be on patrols to Hodp forever, because they assumed he was of lesser blood. They assumed it! They didn't know, they couldn't know. Even Haydren didn't know.

His fists spasmed in helpless frustration. Since he had come to Hewolucs, he had been visited only a few times by vague sensations of memories from before, as if standing before a locked door and knowing the sun was shining behind it without seeing it directly. Once had been in the shed when Sir Cullins' dog attacked, another on the day practicing with wooden dummies, before the Earl came in and granted him a wish. And one had been at Geoffrey's house, though he didn't realize it until now for how distracted he had been then. He couldn't place it specifically, but it was something in the way the home was designed and furnished that felt familiar.

But he grasped only at wind, or the idea of wind. Sometimes when he searched the hardest, his memories seemed furthest away.

He ran his fingers through his hair, grasping a handful and gripping tightly. He wanted desperately to be a good student, and a good swordsman, and maybe people could appreciate that—appreciate him, and realize that he was worth more. Only then could he begin to do things...

But no: he was in a box built by others, cramped together and unable to move. As hard as he might push on one side, and feel headway, he would end up only rotating into a more difficult and suffocating position. His hand dropped to the sword at his side, which he had neglected to take off. Even it could not help him, for he was unable to remove it and beat against his compressive walls. And if he managed to escape, there would be Guntsen, teeth bared in the darkness, waiting to swallow him whole.

Haydren sighed. He needed to play. The two greatest gifts he had received since enrolling in the School were a lap harp and the lessons to play. Often when he was overwhelmed the music would calm him. He reached under the bed to retrieve the instrument, then leaned back and rested his fingers on the strings. He closed his eyes, and began with a familiar slow tune as he allowed his thoughts to drift.

The song took him back to a broad plain, with the wind sweeping through the grasses. He was sitting on a newly bundled sheaf, the smell of fresh-cut hay in his nostrils. A few broken bits of straw drifted on the breeze. In his mind, beside him, a man of nearly thirty worked with a scythe. A man with bright chestnut hair, and dark black eyebrows.

Haydren opened his eyes, stilling the strings. Something was tugging at him, something about the notes he had just played. Still without looking at the harp, and as he tried to return in his mind to the images he had just seen, he played tentatively.

The notes that followed were notes he had never been taught, but that rang in him with a familiarity that brought tears to his eyes. He knew there were lyrics attached to the song, lyrics about war and grief—but he could not remember them. He played the song over and over, the notes purging him of all thoughts yet leaving him with a sense of fullness that welled in his eyes. He played until exhaustion tripped his fingers upon the strings; he stopped before the discordant notes shattered the delicate construction within him. The notes continued ringing in his ears long after he stopped playing, and they continued to echo through his dreams that night.

⸺◆⸺

Down the hall, Guntsen awoke with a start. He had not lit a candle, or left one lit: it might've burned the school down. He glanced around the room.

A man in a traveling cloak sat in a chair near the door.

"What are you doing here?" Guntsen demanded, dropping his head back against the pillow.

"Do you actually care?"

"Did you change the orders, to put Willam in danger?"

"Did you send Haydren to Hodp, to keep him out of it?"

"That's not how I want it to happen; I want it to be all my doing, not yours, and I want him to know it."

After a long silence, Guntsen twisted to look at the man. His eyes smoldered, but his body remained as still as a shadow of moonlight. "Don't look at me like that. It never works," Guntsen said, settling again into his pillow. "And don't attack my friends. I remember things like that."

"There are two ways to go about this, child," the man said quietly. "I have graciously chosen the former; I can easily make it the latter, and my soldiers will be...indiscriminate. They are very good at that." There was another silence before the man spoke again. "You are taking the next steps already?"

Guntsen gazed out of his window. "Yes."

"You question them?"

A longer pause. "No."

"Perhaps you should."

"I might fail."

"Failure at this point is the only option."

Guntsen twisted swiftly, but the candle was snuffed and the man gone.

3

VISITS

"Do we know what he plans?"
"Destruction."
"I hoped you would be more specific."
"It is a start."

33 Nuamon 1319 — Spring

Haydren woke with a start, barely catching the harp as it slid from his lap. He yawned, rubbing his eye. With a long sniff, he glanced at the harp, and the memories of last night rushed back at once. He played the song again. The haunting melody was still there, still resonating in his mind. He knew it came from his life before Hewolucs; he knew it was from his true parents.

Tucking the harp away, Haydren rose and extinguished what few lamps still burned. He needed to find more information. Hodp—complete with Beron, Jelleth, and the dissenter Geoffrey—was all he had to look forward to if he couldn't prove he was worth more. Now with a memory and the time to pursue it, perhaps he could.

He rose and threw water on his face from a basin in the back of his room. He glanced in the polished steel, the red-brown hair and black eyebrows that irrevocably set him apart from his classmates catching his attention anew. Still, it was not the contrast he had seen of the man in his vision. Closer, perhaps, to Geoffrey. Surely *he* couldn't be—Mickel and Maerie were both originally from Hodp, but they would have said something. The house *had* seemed familiar, somehow...

He leaned a little closer, trying to think. He focused suddenly, as weary green eyes inspected back frankly at him. Not green: gray. Even his eyes were not changeless. He threw a little more water on his face, and wiped it with a towel. There were too many questions. He would ask Sir Cullins for permission to see Mickel, and maybe he could find some answers.

He found Sir Cullins walking the halls alone. The schoolmaster granted Haydren permission to leave, saying he would send a messenger if he needed. After a quick breakfast, Haydren walked through the streets to a house that had never quite become a home. At the door, he hesitated before knocking. After a few long moments, the door opened to reveal his adoptive mother. She stood, gazing at him, smiling, her eyes glistening.

"You've finally come," she said at last.

"I'm graduating soon, Maerie," he replied. "We have some time to ourselves before the ceremony, and I was hoping to speak to you and to Mickel."

Maerie blinked each time Haydren referred to them by their proper names, though she said nothing. He knew what she wanted. But even as a small child, "mother" and "father" never felt right coming out of his mouth.

"Of course," she said, her smile as persistent as her love. "Mickel hasn't gone to the towers yet. I'm sure he would love to see you."

Haydren stepped inside. Maerie closed the door and gestured for him to sit while he waited. Haydren glanced around the room as he moved to a chair. Since Mickel had been reinstated to his position within the Guards, the conditions of the house had certainly improved: the floor had been scrubbed bright recently, and a padded chair near the brick fireplace was new. The looming, dark portrait of Mickel's father still slanted away from the yellow wall, as if the patriarch were leering down at whomever Haydren's adoptive family was entertaining. It was clearly one of the more inferior pieces by one of Hewolucs' many alley artisans.

His adoptive father entered, a broad smile on his broad face. "Haydren!" he boomed, grasping his hand and pulling him from his seat into a massive embrace. "Good to see you back, son. Maerie tells me you're graduating soon?"

"Uh, yes, indeed," Haydren replied, smiling awkwardly in Mickel's clutches. "I was hoping to talk to you, if, you know..." He gestured, indicating the predicament Mickel put him in.

Mickel released him, still grinning widely. "Of course! Any time you need me, son—"

"I was wondering what you could tell me about when I arrived here."

Mickel's grin faded just a little. "Anything in particular?" he asked, glancing at Maerie. She had taken a chair against the wall. Haydren spread his hands, finding his own seat again.

"Anything that might help, that might tell me who my true parents were, where I come from..." He sighed. "Anything."

Mickel cleared his throat, and lowered himself onto the creaking chair.

"I'm not sure how much there is to tell, Haydren," he said. He enunciated the name, perhaps a little more than he'd wanted to. He continued without a pause. "We had heard about the ambush against the caravan, but you arrived long after that last survivor straggled in. We—or, I—am not entirely sure that it was your caravan." Mickel's eyes clouded over. "I don't know how you could have survived for that long."

"Where was the caravan from, though?" Haydren asked.

"Westide," Mickel said heavily. "Which means it carried passengers and produce from Gintanos, Salmea, Andelen, the Clanaso Islands—if you were even part of it, it wouldn't help in determining where you were from. You might have come from even further away, from Rinc Na or Carist. You would have had to come through any one of those other countries to get here."

"But not Hodp?"

Mickel cocked his head. "Why there?"

Haydren explained his questions. Mickel shook his head slowly.

"That house must have been built after we left..."

"I think they were starting to work on it," Maerie said quietly. "But I don't know whose it was."

"And we've never gone up there?" Haydren asked.

Mickel shook his head emphatically. "Once I joined the Guards, we've been here."

Haydren sighed, gazing out the window. "What about what I had on me when I got here? Was I carrying anything significant?"

When Mickel did not answer, Haydren glanced at him. Whatever expression was there was gone before he could read it, and Mickel shook his head slowly. "Nothing really; just the clothing you were wearing, which was badly tattered. You were covered in blood, though it wasn't your own. That's why we assume you were in the caravan. But still, none of the other survivors who were still in Hewolucs recognized you."

Covered in blood, just as he had been after killing Sir Cullins' dog. Haydren rubbed his nose and sighed. This was not giving him any help. He gazed at the floor for several long moments. Mickel cleared his throat, and Haydren looked up.

"Why this sudden interest, Haydren?" Mickel asked, his eyes hedged with concern.

"A friend of mine was..." he paused, biting his lip in thought. "I will be stuck on patrols to Hodp for my entire service to the Earl, because they only see me as an orphan," he said. "I was hoping, if I could prove I was more than that..."

"Mickel," Maerie whispered, leaning forward. "What about that letter?"

"Of course!" Mickel exploded, slamming his palm on the arm of the chair. "He jumped right into questions about his past, and I completely forgot about it!"

"What letter?" Haydren asked, straightening.

"Someone delivered a letter the other day for you," Mickel said. He paused, scraping his chin with trimmed fingernails. "In fact, it almost looked like my old friend, from the old Guard. But it couldn't have been him."

"What is this letter?" Haydren asked.

Mickel looked at Maerie, who got up and left the room. She returned with an envelope and gave it to Haydren. The seal in red wax bore a crest Haydren was unfamiliar with: a circle quartered, with a flame and a tree in opposite corners, and flowing lines which were nearly similar but uniquely different in the other corners. Haydren's first name only was in flowing script directly above the seal, which he now broke as he unfolded the letter. The body of the letter was in the same writing as the address:

My Dear Haydren,

Twelve years ago, when our caravan was attacked, I thought we were done for; when we couldn't find you even a week after, and were pressed to continue on without you, I couldn't imagine how. I never thought, so many years later, I would be sitting, composing a letter to the student I thought was long dead. I still cannot believe it. And yet, I don't have time to sit and wonder.

We are in dire need, Haydren. It is a difficulty we cannot trust to anyone, nor is just anyone capable of handling it. I can only hope your training continued, there; I would not normally hope for such a thing, but what I know to be true is already beyond belief, so why not? That, and I pray you still have your extraordinary possession. You must bring it with you.

Please hasten, Haydren. The enemy moves soon, perhaps too soon. Come to Frecksshire with all haste. Even by waiting for you, we are endangering the country; but there seems no other way. Please hurry! More will be explained once you arrive.

Yours in gratitude,

Lintasur Guinad

Haydren lowered the letter. Frecksshire: capital of Coberan Province, home to the Rinc Nain on Burieng. Mistrusted enemy to Earl Junei, whom Haydren was supposed to serve. In Frecksshire was his former instructor, the reason he had such skill when he arrived. There lay his answers, a link to his past and a key to his future.

There, beyond his reach.

His fist gripped in a spasm. "I'm about to graduate," he mumbled with a sigh. "I doubt the Earl will let me go to Frecksshire. He would probably try to send someone else, if at all."

"What's that?" Mickel asked. Haydren handed him the letter. He read it and gave it to Maerie, his eyes cast in thought. She read it, and looked up.

"You might ask Sir Cullins," Maerie offered, handing him back the letter.

Haydren shook his head. "They won't even let me go on a real patrol," he replied.

"Didn't you say you saved the crops from destruction?" Mickel asked. "And this is how they repay you?"

"I'm afraid that debt has been paid, Mickel," Haydren replied drily.

"My reinstatement?" he asked quietly. Haydren glanced sideways at him. Mickel sagged. "Haydren, about that..."

"Please," Haydren said, holding up a hand. "You don't have to say anything about it."

"But, Haydren..."

"No! Because you don't...just..." Haydren paused, rubbing his forehead as his eyes gazed blankly at the page. "Don't worry about it," he said. His brow furrowed, and he looked up suddenly.

"How did my instructor find out about me? How would he know my name and that I was still alive?"

Mickel paused, scratching a finger. "Well, if it was Jeyetna who delivered it," he said slowly, "he might have come across this...Lintasur...in Frecksshire—he went out there a few years ago. And Jeyetna liked stories; he might have told the right story around the right ears, and this Lintasur asked him to deliver the letter."

Haydren scowled. "That sounds like an awful lot of coincidences."

"The God of All can do far more than that," Mickel replied.

Haydren rolled his eyes. "But why wouldn't he use my real name? Surely it's different now."

"Haydren is not a Cariste name, though," Maerie said, "which is what we wanted to give you. But it is the Teacher who gives names to the adopted, and he whispers to the God of All on what to name the child."

"So you're saying the God gave the Teacher the same name I had before?" Haydren asked, his voice thick with scorn. "If the God is even real, I hardly believe the Teacher does more than act on his own thoughts."

"But the God is real, Haydren," Maerie said, softly pleading.

"Then he has certainly abandoned Burieng," Haydren shot back. "And he certainly cares nothing about orphans!"

"He works as he sees best, not as we do."

Haydren's lips grumbled, and the room grew silent. "I should be getting back," Haydren said finally. "There are still some things I should do to prepare."

Haydren folded up the letter and stood, and Mickel and Maerie stood as well. He hugged them, promised to come more often once he was officially a swordsman, and left before they could press him further.

Haydren could neither fathom nor accept the idea that his life might be in the whimsical hands of some controlling force. Not to mention he had almost come out and told Mickel, the man to whom he owed his entire life, a secret he had kept to himself for over two years. But Haydren was far from ready to admit aloud why he had wanted Mickel reinstated.

He sighed. What was he supposed to do with 'an extraordinary possession' which he didn't still have? Even as a free soldier able to act on such a claim, it was ludicrous: even Earl Junei, with generals and armies, could not seem to stop the enemy.

No, the best thing he could get out of the letter was the possibility of finding his parents, or at the least finding out who they were. He would cling to that only, and seek the opportunity to pursue it.

He went first to see Sir Cullins.

"I wanted to let you know I'll be back in my room," he said.

"You went to see your parents?" Sir Cullins asked. "How are they?"

"They're fine," he said. "I received a letter, it came last week sometime." He paused, considering. "What are the chances of my going to Frecksshire any time soon?"

Sir Cullins smiled until he realized Haydren was not joking. He cleared his throat. "You know the two earls are not on good terms, Haydren," he said. "The Earl of Frecksshire seems to feel he is the new king of Burieng, even though he controls less land and has been in power far fewer years—and that beside the fact the west is Rinc Nain—which, I guess, is why they want more land: even centuries—" Sir Cullins cut off with a tight grin. Everyone had heard it all before.

Haydren nodded. "I thought as much," he said.

"Why do you ask?"

"The letter is asking me to come to Frecksshire," Haydren replied. "It seems to be from someone who knew me before Hewolucs, who might know my true parents."

"That's great news, Haydren!" Sir Cullins said. "I will speak to the Earl. I can request some time for you, say it's for trying to determine your lineage, which every vassal has a right to prove. The Earl is also not unsympathetic to your situation: he may permit you, even as one of his newest swordsmen. However, he may wonder why I am requesting as much time as you would need to travel to Frecksshire. If I must tell him where you are going..."

"I'm sure you'll do what you can," Haydren said. "Thank you, Sir Cullins. It would mean so much to me."

"It's the least I can do for you, Haydren," Sir Cullins replied, smiling. "I will send someone for you as soon as I know anything."

Haydren departed, a little lighter.

There was plenty to do before he could officially become a swordsman of Hewolucs. That life was, he had to admit, far more than an orphan should expect. Surely, with such fortunes as he seemed to have, the Earl would grant his request to go west.

Evening came with no word from Sir Cullins. Haydren extinguished his lamps slowly, save for one candle which he left to burn as he went to sleep. Despite the tramp of thoughts in his head, he quickly slipped into dreamless rest.

He awoke some time later. The candle had gone out. His breath caught, and a hand clamped on his mouth. He flailed at it, but before he could dislodge it, a voice whispered in the gloom.

"Haydren, calm down." He found himself obeying as his eyes strained to see, but the darkness was too deep.

"Will you be silent, and hear me?" the voice rasped. Haydren nodded. "Very well." The pressure left his mouth as the voice continued to breathe from lampless secrecy.

"There is a plot to kill you, Haydren," it said. "One in *fact*, not in idea or threat. I do not know how he intends to do it, specifically. But know he is planning to do it, and your life is in danger as long as you stay here."

Finally, Haydren could be silent no longer. He still kept his voice in a low whisper. "Who are you? How do you know this?"

"I am a friend," the voice replied. "One you may not know you have."

"And how do I know you are not telling me these things just to set me up for Guntsen, set me up to be vulnerable some way?"

"Do not be silly!" said the voice, rising almost above a whisper. "First, I told you I am a friend. Second, I do not care where you go, or even if you stay at your own peril. I came only to warn you. But if you need proof, go and speak to Dillion. He may verify my words."

"How do I know you are not Dillion yourself?" Haydren shot back. No answer.

"Or perhaps you worked together with Guntsen and Dillion to conspire against me?"

Silence. Haydren rose, fumbled for his tinder box, and lit the lamp on the table beside him. The light flared, quickly filling the room. He was alone, and his door was shut fast.

Sleep did not come so quickly, this time.

The next morning, the steward of the apartments arrived, summoning him to Sir Cullins office—Haydren presumed it concerned his request to go to Frecksshire. He dressed quickly and made his way down the hall. But as he passed Jurian's room, he heard voices coming from behind the cracked door.

"Did you put Willam on that patrol, too?" Jurian's voice came, thick and loud with smoldering rage.

"Would you be quiet?" Guntsen replied. "No, I did not. Someone must have changed it after I did. I only wanted Haydren's festering friend on that patrol."

"So what do you plan now?"

There was a brief moment of silence. Had they heard Haydren's sudden gasp?

"Friend . . . Just be . . . patrol."

Haydren moved closer, but the voices were still too low.

"When?"

". . . father . . . I gain . . . throne."

"Haydren will be dead?" Haydren jumped back as Jurian's voice cackled suddenly.

"Would you please be quiet!" Guntsen hissed.

"Sorry. Are you sure you can do it?"

Haydren didn't wait to hear more. Keeping his steps light, he continued well past Jurian's room before trotting to Sir Cullins' room. He pounded on the door. Sir Cullins answered it quickly, and Haydren glanced behind him before ducking swiftly inside.

Sir Cullins gazed at him, then shut the door. "Haydren, the Earl will not let you leave. I spoke to him late last night, and was waiting until this morning to tell you."

Haydren's head dropped for a second. "Are you sure there's no way for me to leave? Even for a little bit?"

Sir Cullins glanced quizzically at him. "'A little bit' wouldn't be enough, Haydren, to go all the way to Frecksshire."

As Sir Cullins sat behind his desk, Haydren bit his lip, his mind knocking with Guntsen's overheard threat. He had to find a way out of this box. Guntsen's teeth were growing larger every day. "If I could just take a little time, even if I stay in Kelian, to try to find out more..." *Enough time to make it to the border, at least.*

"Haydren, why is it suddenly so important for you to have this time?" Sir Cullins asked.

Could he tell him? Could he know what Guntsen planned, and help Haydren?

"It's just...something I overheard Guntsen say this morning," Haydren said, afraid to look at Sir Cullins too closely. Afraid to seem as if he were only trying to get Guntsen in trouble. "Just as I was coming to see you, he was in Jurian's room. He said...he said he put Kitrel on the patrol intentionally, because it was dangerous."

Now that it was out, Haydren looked at Sir Cullins. The sword-master looked back at him gravely, his hands folded in front of his chin, but said nothing.

"He also said he had another plan...to kill me...when his father—when Earl Junei was dead," Haydren concluded.

"You are certain both of what you heard and that it was Guntsen and Jurian who said it?"

Haydren nodded emphatically. "It was them."

Sir Cullins took a breath. "Then pack what you need for a long journey, and meet me back here tonight, after the moon rises, and I will help you flee."

Haydren cocked his head, gazing at the sword-master quizzically.

"It is not because of the ambush that your graduation has not yet taken place, Haydren," Sir Cullins said, his voice low. "But because the Earl is ill. We did not want word to get out." The sword-master leaned closer, and Haydren took a step forward to hear him better. "His illness has taken a turn for the worse. The Earl is not expected to last the week."

4

BLADES

"Will he go with him?"
"Of course not; that is not his work."
"But, then..."
"Much is yet to be done. I will return shortly."

34 Nuamon 1319 — Spring

Haydren stood, thunderstruck. The Earl was not old or prone to poor health, so what could this mean? The timing with Guntsen's plan was remarkable, but surely he would not poison his own father.

Would he?

Sir Cullins broke the silence. "Go gather what supplies you need," he said. "I'll give you a horse to make the journey. You must get as far away as possible! Guntsen will surely send word to Sanir on the border with Frecksshire. If he does, you will not make it through to the west alive. I will keep him satisfied until he ascends the throne." Sir Cullins paused, sighing. "My allegiance is first and foremost to the Earl, Haydren, whoever holds that position—including Guntsen. Earl Junei would not want you needlessly dead, and it is under that understanding that I may help you escape. As soon as Guntsen ascends, however..."

"I understand," Haydren said numbly.

"All right. Go, get packed. Leave your armor here: its weight will not be a benefit, and I have something else I can give you. Do whatever you must today, but be back here when the moon rises. Understood?"

"Yes, Sir Cullins," Haydren replied. "Thank you."

"You can thank me once you are in Frecksshire, Haydren," Sir Cullins replied. "There will be much to overcome before you are truly free from this castle. Now go! Return tonight."

Haydren lay for a long time after he had finished packing and tucked his bag away. He sometimes plucked his harp to the tune he remembered the night before. He knew, deeper and more surely than he knew anything else, that there was more to the song. But no words came to him, and nothing he tried to come up with fit properly. But he held on to it: except for the letter—which told him little—it was his only link now to his past. By the end of the day he would be uprooted and cast adrift, with no knowledge of the outside world except what he had learned at this school. He needed to get to Frecksshire, but it was not as simple as riding: physical and cultural barriers both, not to mention the Earl's soldiers, would stand in his way. He kept recalling histories and geographies, hoping to find some clue that would help him in the coming weeks. He did not find much.

Haydren sat up. The lowering rays of the sun glinted off his sword—but it was Mickel's sword. Haydren set his harp aside and rose. He picked up the weapon, gazing over its lustrous surface. Might it be stained with blood before the week was done? Before the day was done?

A sudden desire to see Mickel and Maerie seized him, and he gripped the hilt in determination. But should he tell Sir Cullins? The day was drawing to a close: there might not be time. He buckled on the sword and threw a cloak around his shoulders. He shouldn't be long.

His hurried this time, and when he arrived he knocked without hesitation. Mickel opened the door, and Haydren entered.

"You are back early," Mickel said.

"I know," Haydren replied. "I'm leaving the castle tonight, I—" He paused: should he say specifically why? He did not want Maerie to worry. "I'm being sent on another mission. Far away. I won't be back for a long time."

Instead of prying him with questions, Mickel looked at him silently, until he seemed to arrive finally at some conclusion.

"Come with me," he said, moving toward the stairs. "It's time for you to have something."

Curious, Haydren followed him to a dark room, where he lit a candle and set it atop a large chest of drawers. He opened a lower drawer and began pulling out several thick bolts of cloth.

"When you came here, ten years ago," he said, still unpacking, "you did have something on you; something I had kept hidden from everyone, including Maerie. I couldn't risk it being found. I didn't want to tell you yesterday because by my guess you were still in the Earl's ranks." He paused then, straightening. "But you aren't any more, are you? Or won't be for long."

Haydren's jaw went slack. "How—?"

"Take my advice: leave my sword in your room," Mickel said quietly. "If you do it well, they may not know you are gone for a day or more."

"I will need a sword, Mickel," Haydren whispered.

Mickel's jaw firmed, then he bent down and reached far into the drawer. "So take this," he said. "It's yours anyway."

He rose, holding a sword sheathed in black leather, with a mouth of crystal that sparkled in the candlelight. Etchings on the mouth and silver stitching on the leather were in the form of reptilian scales. Haydren took it. The hilt was in the likeness of a dragon, forged from a metal that he did not recognize: it shone like the mirrored surface of a deep lake under moonlight, though it was tinged with its own pale red that did not come from candlelight. A curled dragon's tail formed the pommel. The handle was black leather like the scabbard, also with silver stitching in scales, modeling the body. The guard was formed by thin, foreshortened wings. As he drew the sword, he gasped. The head of the dragon dipped into the blade, the lower jaw protruding through the other side. Body, head, and blade were of the same liquid-pale-red metal, and from the mouth of the dragon, spreading down the length of the blade until it formed the tapered tip, were gleaming flames in pitted red like ruby rust. As he held it, it seemed to shine with a deeper luster than he had first noticed.

"This was mine?" Haydren whispered. Could this 'possession' be what the letter meant?

"It *is* yours," Mickel corrected. "You had it on you when you got here, like I said. Even without drawing it, I could see it was unique. I knew someone would try to take it from you if they could. So I hid it until a proper time. A time when you would be able to keep it." He paused, gazing down the length of the sword. "I think that is now. Though I have often looked at it, it never shined like this. There is something very special about this sword, Haydren." Mickel's voice echoed the awe that Haydren felt vibrating inside of him. "It is yours, and no one else's, and I don't mean by your possession of it. It knows when you hold it, and it knows you are supposed to hold it."

"How—How is that—?"

"I don't know, Haydren," Mickel replied. "But I know when I look at that sword now." Mickel blinked once, closed his eyes and shook his head as if to clear it of something. When he opened his eyes, he was looking at Haydren alone. "But come," he said, his voice normal. "You must say goodbye to Maerie before you go. She would never forgive either of us if you left without telling her."

"Mickel," Haydren said quietly, halting him as he turned. "I believe Guntsen poisoned his father..."

"But the Earl is in good health!"

"No, he isn't, and I think it's Guntsen's doing, and I think it's because he wants me dead..."

"He wouldn't do that because he only wants *you* dead, Haydren," Mickel said with a glance he had used before to remind Haydren to be less prideful.

"Well, okay, fine. But he's ascending the throne soon, and he wants me dead after he does that. Which is why I'm leaving." Haydren looked earnestly at his adoptive father. "Which means you and Maerie will be in great danger after I leave. I can't assume you can go with me, but if there's any way for you two to leave..."

"And go where?" Mickel asked practically, but not sadly. "As soon as we try to leave, he'll know something is wrong. But, if he doesn't find out until he ascends the throne, it will go much better for you. We'll stay. And you won't order your father around, adoptive or not," he added with an eyebrow raised to silence Haydren's look.

Haydren nodded. He sheathed the sword and wrapped it in a gray wool blanket that Mickel gave him.

Though Maerie took the news far better than Haydren thought she would—she only cried a little, and hugged him no longer and no tighter than he wished she would—she did insist that she make him one last meal.

"If you're going to be gone as long as you say, then you're going to be going for a while without a home-cooked meal," she said. "The least I can do is to give you something to remember me by."

Haydren relented, and though he kept a wary eye on the light outside, he ate heartily. When they finished, he said goodbye, insisting he had to be back at the apartments before the moon rose.

When he returned, he replaced Mickel's sword and buckled on his own. He gazed down at it, at the silver and crystal as it caught the candlelight. He went to the door, took one last look around the room, then turned away.

Before his knuckles lifted from the last knock on the headmaster's door, Sir Cullins yanked it open.

"You're late, Haydren," he whispered, pulling him inside. "Come with me."

Sir Cullins grasped a torch from a sconce in the wall and exited a door in the back of the chamber, which opened on a long, dark corridor of smooth stone blocks. Speechlessly Haydren followed, walking swiftly to keep astride of the hurrying sword-master. The hall turned several times, and they ducked left and right through a dizzying maze of heavy doors. Haydren wondered that Sir Cullins could find his way at all. Long after Haydren lost count, Sir Cullins faced a final door, inserting a key and turning the lock easily before pushing it open.

"What is this place?" Haydren asked as Sir Cullins locked the door behind them.

"Storage," he replied curtly. He opened a box and removed several cloth-wrapped bundles. "Put these on, swiftly," he said. "It's basic armor," he continued as Haydren began to unwrap the bundles. "The bracers are leather with metal plates, but the chest-plate is solid steel."

Haydren finished removing the shrouds: the armor was quite light, and had already been dulled.

"I would recommend wearing it underneath your tunic," Sir Cullins advised. "Now hurry!"

As Haydren obeyed, Sir Cullins moved several deceptively light boxes, took a large iron rod that stood against a wall, and inserted it into a hole in the floor. With a grunt, he levered open the concealed trap-door. A breeze wafted from below, smelling of wet stone and cold water.

Haydren tied the laces of the armor, snugging it tight. It fit him far better than he expected, and he barely noticed its weight. He pulled his tunic back on, and refastened his cloak. Sir Cullins gestured Haydren to the hole, and then came behind, lowering the trap-door and shutting them inside. A flight of stairs took them downward.

"What is this place?" Haydren asked again. The stairs ended, leaving them on a long stone walk beside a slow-moving stream.

"Escape route," Sir Cullins replied. "If we are ever hopelessly besieged, the royal family can escape through here. It lets out in a rock pasture outside the castle walls, well beyond where any encamping army would have outposts. As guardian of royal students, I have access to it as well."

Sir Cullins led the way, telling him about the forming of the tunnel—that the stream had begun it, but the walk was hewn by laborers, and the ceiling had been raised.

Finally, as they rounded a bend, torchlight shone in the distance. "Sir Cullins?" Haydren said apprehensively.

"There are stables built inside the tunnel, at the end," Sir Cullins replied. He turned and glanced at Haydren. "You will finally be treated as a royal, Haydren: you will have the Earl's horse on which to fly. But we will have to work quickly. The stableman I drugged may wake up at any time."

As they neared, Haydren could hear the horses stamping impatiently. Sir Cullins slowed, then stopped and turned.

"Something's wrong," he whispered. "Draw your sword. I left the man outside, asleep in his chair, but he is not there."

Haydren swiftly drew his sword, which flashed in the blazing light of the torch. Sir Cullins' eyes widened.

"Where had you been keeping that?" he whispered.

"I had it with me when I arrived at the castle," Haydren explained. "Mickel hid it at first, but gave it to me tonight."

"Haydren," Sir Cullins said with a sigh. "I will do what I can to protect your parents, but it would have been better for them not to know you were leaving,"

"I told Mickel to try to leave Hewolucs. He refused," Haydren replied. "But I thank you for whatever you might be able to do for them."

Sir Cullins nodded and drew his sword, placed the torch on the path, and crept forward. As they neared the nickering horses, still nothing moved and no more noises were made. The stalls, except for the horses, were empty.

"Saddle your horse quickly—the black. I will keep watch," Sir Cullins said, moving deeper down the tunnel. "Lead him out when you are ready, and I will open the door for you."

Haydren obeyed, and when he approached, Sir Cullins moved to a large boulder that sealed the end of the tunnel and set his shoulder against it. With a grunt of effort, he rolled the boulder once, and Haydren could feel a fresh breeze wafting in. Turning left out of the exit, Sir Cullins led Haydren into the night.

Instantly, the alarm rose: "There they are! Move now!"

"Stay where you are!"

"In the name of the Earl!"

"Haydren, ride!" Sir Cullins shouted as the night erupted around them. Men approached from all directions, swords gleaming in the moonlight.

Haydren's horse reared, its shriek piercing the gloom. Great rock monoliths that were to screen the royal family's escape now crowded Haydren, and he quickly pushed further away from the tunnel as the soldiers closed in. Sword rang on sword behind him as Sir Cullins protected his escape.

Before Haydren could swing into the saddle, a soldier appeared from behind a large boulder. Dropping the reins, Haydren's sword flashed in a brilliant arc, seeming to come alive in his hand. The soldier faltered, and the blade struck home. Another soldier appeared; dragon and metal whirled, and a clear ringing rolled across the plains. The dragon was victorious again, and Haydren turned and mounted.

"Run!" echoed behind him, and Haydren recognized the sword-master's voice, followed by a cry. Gritting his teeth and holding back tears, Haydren spurred the horse and sprang into the night. The horse's hooves echoed sharply among the stones. Haydren knew Sir Cullins would have to hear him escaping.

"I am fleeing! Save yourself!" he shouted. The wind ripped the words into the night, denying him comfort that they had found their target. "Run, Sir Cullins!" he shouted.

Behind him was silence, and before him was darkness, and into this darkness he fled.

———◈———

Pladt awoke with the sun streaming in his eyes. He winced, groaned, pulled the blankets over his head, and sighed. A rare chance to sleep a little later than normal, shot as a hydra's eye.

He flopped the blankets off his head and sniffed. The scent of warm cakes pierced his mood. His mother was preparing breakfast downstairs. His father, then, would be sitting at the table going over whatever it was he looked at every morning before going to the warehouses.

Pladt sat up, gazing out of his window. On the horizon, its thick roots washed in the surf of Burieng Ocean, Mount Thoret burned red as its spiked peak gleamed in the morning light.

Pladt sighed. Fully awake now, he decided he might as well eat with his parents.

They were exactly as he had imagined. Though nearby houses crowded the windows, sunlight found its way in and amplified against white walls. A soft breeze, scented by the sea, sent the edges of the pale curtains dancing and waving good morning. When Pladt entered, his mother Fiora twisted around and smiled.

"Good morning, sleepy one," she said cheerily.

"Hmmm," Pladt mumbled. He was not nearly as sleepy as he wanted to be.

"I fried you some cakes," Fiora said, turning back to the large wood-stove. "Molasses is on the shelf—you know where it is," she added with a sly smile. He grinned in return, and retrieved the jar.

"So what do you want to do with your free day?" Fiora asked, pushing a plate loaded with cakes toward him.

Pladt glanced at his father, Kerrik. "I thought I might go see Mount Thoret," he said quietly.

"Oh?" Fiora said, glancing too at her husband.

Kerrik did not look up, or even appear to stop reading the manifest before him. "You can't," he said flatly.

"The hydras have not attacked in over a week, father," Pladt said. "I want to see what makes the mountain turn red, that's all."

Kerrik looked up. "Do you think their prolonged absence makes the hydras less likely to attack now, or more?"

"Do you know what makes it shine red?" Pladt asked, picking at a corner of a cake. The molasses sat unopened before him.

"Should I? Will it benefit me to know?" Kerrik returned. "I want no more discussion. This town needs you to protect it, and if the hydras are going to attack, today is more likely than yesterday."

Fiora had returned to the stove. Pladt wished she would say something, but knew she would not. Kerrik had returned to his manifest, content that the argument was over. And, Pladt realized, it was.

"You're right," he said, gazing down at his breakfast. "If they attacked, I wouldn't make it back in time to help the town. I'll probably just go talk to Naek, for now."

His father and mother remained silent. After several moments, Pladt stood, leaving his plate untouched and the jar of molasses unopened.

He left the house, turning away from the tavern where Naek worked and heading for the edge of town. Naek was not truly a friend, he was Kerrik's friend. All of Pladt's "friends" were his father's friends, or did business with one of the three warehouses Kerrik owned. They humored him occasionally, nothing more.

Pladt shook his head as he tried to brush away such unpleasant thoughts on such a beautiful day. The streets were already beginning to fill with travelers and traders. Situated between the port of Werinin and the rest of the country, Werine saw nearly a third of the people and goods coming into Burieng. Rarely was there nothing interesting to see, if he looked to appreciate it.

Sitting deep in the Mydop peninsula, the thick stone wall that protected most cities in Burieng was absent from the town. No human army could attack from the sea, and if Galessern made it that far north the city was doomed anyway, or so it was deemed. So as Pladt neared the edge of the town, instead of passing through a gate, the number of houses simply thinned until he stood on the edge of the broad grassy plain that extended to Hodp over a hundred miles away. A contingent of roaming guards passed by with curt nods. Pladt acknowledged them, and returned his gaze southward. One of the forest cuts that broke the landscape here extended to the edge of Werine. It was this cut to which Pladt enjoyed retiring after a long day. From here, he could sit back against a tree and watch the sun set among the foothills of Ives' Plateau.

But now, with the sun on the opposite horizon, nothing interested him to the west. Instead, as Pladt rested, he faced south. An early departing convoy made its way noisily down the road, a plume of dust rising behind it.

The dust soon settled. The convoy was gone, and the land empty. But glimmering in the corner of Pladt's eye, Thoret tried in vain to recapture his attention. It couldn't know that no amount of his attention would change his situation.

5

DIRECTIONS

"This is, of course, in the plan?"
"Should he stay in Hewolucs forever?"
"But, alone..."
"He is not alone. We are with him."

34 Nuamon 1319 — Spring

The silence behind him did not last. Horns sounded, and the thunder of many hooves echoed faintly. He pressed onward, crouched low behind the horse's snapping mane. His one hope was that it was bred and chosen as the fastest in the land.

Glancing back, he saw torches spread from the castle. He tried to track their progress, but rising and falling along the dark undulations of the land, he could not.

Ahead of him, against the stars, he saw a tall rise. He reined in atop it. As the horse danced beneath him, he turned and opened his eyes wide to the south and east. He could see one long line of torches moving north along the road. The other detachment was moving swiftly west toward Kontar.

But no one directly pursued. Was it possible they were making so much noise they could not hear his own thundering horse? Or did they track him without light, hidden below?

No answer for the latter. The greater problem was how to escape what he *could* see. If he stayed north of the road, those heading west might cut him off at the river before he got there, fast horse or no. He could not delay to try to cross it south, for that would guarantee failure. He was caught between two precipices: too near either side and he would fall into oblivion.

As he watched, wishing Sir Cullins was there to help, the torches to the south winked out. Eastward, the detachment spread in a long line and moved toward him. Horns echoed through the night.

It was not subtle. Clearly they hoped he was too busy running to see the southern detachment and were trying to drive him toward them. Perhaps he could use that to his advantage.

He dismounted and untied his saddle bags, throwing them over his shoulder. A bridge across the crevasse had appeared, but would not stay for long. He turned his horse to the south, gently nuzzling it.

"I need your help, friend," he whispered. The horse swiveled its ears toward him. "I need you to lead them south. Go!" He slapped the horse on its haunches. It bolted forward, galloping south.

The horns were sounded louder, and the thunder of their horses rolled over the grasses. Haydren turned north and ran.

Sir Cullins often made the students run circles in a large grassy field—usually for punishment of some sort, though often they ran simply because he said so. It was not until he ran now that Haydren was truly thankful for the discipline.

Though he ran with all the speed he could muster, his pursuers were closing. He grit his teeth and charged, but when he glanced up he knew it might still be in vain. Cursing, he threw his saddle bags behind a large clump of tall grass, took several steps further, and sprawled behind another large clump.

The horses charged nearer, and Haydren could hear the men shouting. Horns rang in his ears, echoing and pounding till he thought his skull would burst into powder. He ducked, cradling his head in his arms, hoping first he would not be seen by the riders, then hoping he *would* be seen by the horses, and not trampled. He could feel the ground shaking beneath him, and he held his breath.

The pitch of the roar changed, and the cries and horns turned. He uncurled and saw the nearest horse begin a sweeping turn to the south within a few feet of his head. The soldiers, now well-lit by torchlight, were intent on their trap, unaware it had missed. He could not believe his luck.

As soon as the last horse showed Haydren his rump, he leapt to his feet, snatched up his saddle bags and quickly tied them together with his scabbarded sword and lashed them against his back. He turned north and ran, keeping a swift but easy pace.

They would soon discover that his horse was alone, and would continue their movements north and west. Now, though, he had no horse and no chance of outdistancing them, or of reaching the border without resupply. His escape was far from assured.

His mind raced as fast as his feet. Tracking would be difficult in the broad, largely uninhabited expanse of prairie around him. To the north, away from roads and towns, the Ghlande River ran toward Hodp. But upstream, it flowed from Lake Santiar. South of that, the Bawelen River flowed from deep within the Endolin Mountains. But before then, it crossed into the mountains within sight of the border with Coberan Province—in the depths of which he would find Frecksshire.

Glancing up at the stars, Haydren corrected his course west. If he was lucky—and, all things considered, he had been so far—he might be able to make something of a boat and pole it up the waterways until he neared the border. He would come dangerously near both Kontar and Raka. But if he traveled at night, he just might make it.

He eased his pace, taking a careful sip from his water skin. Food would not be an issue in the Plains. But water would be scarce until the Ghlande.

He continued running, long after shouts and horns and thundering hooves to the south indicated his horse had been discovered. The torches flared again on the road, and both detachments turned westward. He saw one torch moving back toward Hewolucs.

What he did not see, just before he paused to rest, was another detachment of horses leaving Hewolucs toward Hodp.

⸻◆⸻

The messenger glanced warily at the advisor, garbed strangely in a traveling cloak, then back at the Earl's expectant face. "He had dismounted, your Grace. When we caught the horse, it was riderless."

"Any supplies still on it?" Though he trembled, he kept his voice neutral. He could not give away his determination, not yet.

"No, your Grace. No saddlebags were left on it."

"Perhaps he left with none," said the advisor.

Guntsen smirked. "Not with the help he had," he said. He gestured the messenger away, who bowed and left. Guntsen turned and took a seat on his father's former throne, settling into it casually.

"It looks good on you."

"Does it?" Guntsen asked with a self-assured smile. "You don't believe this is my first time sitting in it, do you?"

"In your dreams? Or when your father's back was turned?"

"You don't think I did it while he was looking at me?" Guntsen asked, pricking a little as he lifted a goblet from a servant's tray.

"No, your Grace, I don't believe you did. Why else would Haydren still be alive?"

The goblet rang against the far wall. "And what would you have me do now? Can I pursue him myself?"

"Of course not. As one who so cleverly escaped your men, a far wider net must be cast to capture little Haydren."

"What do you propose, then?"

"Would you leave this task to me?"

"You may not take my province yet, Lasserain," Guntsen said.

"Nor do I want it, yet," the mage replied.

Guntsen scrutinized him. "Use only what resources you have already in place," he said. "I want this done and over with, and no more destruction than is necessary."

"As you wish, your Grace," Lasserain said with a bow. "It is encouraging to see you care so much for your people."

Guntsen's eyes smoldered, but he held his tongue until the mage had exited the throne room. He glanced around the empty space, a flickering smile trying to enjoy what he had waited so long to attain.

"I have my throne," he whispered, and glanced ruefully at the goblet that sat against the wall. Its contents puddled around it and seeped slowly into the cracks of stone.

———◆———

Haydren continued walking and running by intervals until the horizon glowed with the faint orange streaks of approaching dawn. He found a thickly-grassed knoll from which he could see much of the surrounding countryside, and made a quick bed.

But sleep did not come. Weary, he lay listening to the plains beginning to wake. It struck him just how quickly things had changed. Two days ago, he had been looking forward to induction as a swordsman, whatever that future might bring. He had been trained for it, and he would have had leaders over him—like Captain Beron—to instruct him.

But now, as the sun rose, the prairie stretched everlastingly around him. The horizon lay unbroken, a featureless line separating sure footing from blue nothingness. He could not know what lay out there. A goblin might be crouched a hundred paces away. His knees drew reflexively upward, his innards turning back for the nearest city, the nearest human being, the nearest brain to help him know what to do. Could he make it all the way to the Ghlande River? Would there be trees, could he build a raft? Were there rapids that might overturn him and drown him? Was there a better route? How far from the road would the soldiers ride? How far from the road would bandits rest?

His knoll shrank, inverted, threatened to close around him and swallow him. His knuckles whitened on his sword as he tried to slow his breathing. He had been trained, for years. He could handle himself with a goblin, and probably with several bandits. He closed his eyes and breathed deeply. He was alone, yes: so much the better to avoid notice. He was responsible only for himself. If he grew hungry or thirsty, only he would suffer. If he reached the river and did not find what he needed, he could press on toward Quaran. He had a straight line to reach that city, while the soldiers would have to approach at right angles along the road. If he focused on one day at a time, rationing his supplies as best he could, he would survive better than an untrained commoner.

His breathing deepened, and sleep came.

For two more days and nights he traveled. On the third day the skies opened, and he was able to fill his water skins from various puddles that sprang up as he stayed huddled under his cloak. It was not the freshest water, but it would allow him to keep moving.

The next day the weather cleared and he rested under high blue skies and a cool westerly breeze. By the time the sun was bidding the land farewell he was moving again, anxious to put as much distance behind him as he could. In the last light of dusk he spied the Ghlande far to the north where it began its final, gentle turn toward the sea.

Ahead of him, a fire flared up. He could see four men huddled around it, preparing a meal. He watched them, wondering how to avoid them. Crowding out the warning of danger were four days of cold meals, and a day of cold, lashing rain huddled under a pitiful excuse for a tent. There was no doubt in his mind these four men were not simple travelers—those kinds of people stuck to the roads. But though they were most assuredly bandits, they might not assume he was wealthy. And if they did, he had nearly been a swordsman in the Earls ranks, and surely he could surprise four overconfident men.

The smell of the roasting meat reached him, and his mind was made up. He moved toward the fire. Just before stepping into the light, he inspected them once more. On each of their waists hung the unmistakable form of a scimitar, the preferred weapon of the bandits roaming the country. But before he could change his mind and slip back into the night, one of them looked up from the fire and spotted him.

They did not jump to their feet in alarm, as he expected them to. Instead, the one who spotted him smiled, nudged the man beside him, and motioned Haydren forward.

"Come have a seat," the man called. "There's plenty for a lonely traveler."

"I thank you," Haydren replied, stepping into the firelight, his hand resting on his sword. He was, he thought, just hungry and cold, not stupid. "It's been many days since I've eaten a warm meal," he said, still keeping a respectful distance from the four until he determined their intentions.

"Caught in that storm, too," the man said. "Come, warm yourself beside the fire."

"You heard him," a deadly voice whispered behind Haydren. "Move."

Haydren's veins froze, but his muscles did not. He freed his sword, turned, and struck the bandit behind him. He whipped around to face the four by the fire, who stared at him in surprise. Haydren couldn't help but smile as he held his sword in practiced grip.

But they were hardened men, and scimitars quickly slid from their sheaths. Haydren's smile faded, and he rushed forward. In the back of his mind, he remembered Kitrel. Sir Cullins had said it was only beasts that had attacked the patrol, but he also said many people believed both beasts and bandits were linked. Even if Kitrel's death was not by these men, the slaughter that made him an orphan most certainly was. Haydren stalked among the bandits, his blade dancing and ringing against their pitiful scimitars.

Before five breaths, the solitary camp was silent except the crackling of the fire and the hissing of juices from the spitted meat. Haydren lowered his sword, the rush of energy still pumping through him as he surveyed the bandits who now lay lifeless.

With a sigh, he pulled a rag from his pocket, wiping the blood from his sword. The rust flames were still charged, the same as when he had first held the weapon. The blade, once cleaned of blood, seemed in the firelight to flow within its edges like water.

A second too late, Haydren heard the footsteps. White light exploded in his vision, and his head swam. Out of reflex alone he swept his sword backward as he fell, and felt a slight tug against the tip. He pitched against the ground, and knew no more.

⸺⸺⸺◦○◦⸺⸺⸺

Haydren's eyes fluttered open, and he drew a breath. The fire had waned, and the meat was charred black on the bottom. The camp was silent except a light whisper as the wind washed through the grass. He pushed himself up to his knees. His sword was still beside him, blood-stained at the tip. Gingerly, he felt the knot on the back of his skull as he surveyed the camp. Five of the bandits he remembered. Behind him, though, was a new corpse. The ground around the bandit's legs was drenched in blood, though he had barely a mark on him save for a small slash on the inside of his thigh. The man was ghostly white, and his chest was still. Haydren held a hand above his mouth to feel for breath. The man was dead.

Haydren sat back on his heels as his mind churned. He remembered feeling the blade hit something, enough to make the cut on the man's thigh. But enough to kill him because of it? He looked closer. Of course: the main artery of the man's leg. In a half-dazed motion, he had managed to hit the one spot that would end the bandit's life and save his own.

Haydren shook his head, and winced. Placing his hand back on the knot, he considered. He had nearly died, except for some amazing luck. But it was a long way to Frecksshire, dangers hidden all along the way. He needed help. On the knoll a few days ago he thought he might avoid that need. Not now.

He retrieved the rag and resumed cleaning his sword. Even before finding help, though, he knew he needed a place to hide until he could figure out what to do. Perhaps he might even wait out Guntsen's search parties. But where could he hide?

Geoffrey.

Haydren paused as he considered the thought that had suddenly whispered in his mind. Geoffrey had been generous enough the first time, and had showed some measure of kindness toward Haydren. But would he do the same now, when Haydren approached him alone?

He continued wiping, taking some of the bandits' water to moisten blood that had dried while he was unconscious. He thought of Kitrel. *There* was someone he wished to have beside him now. Stalwart Kitrel. Despite Haydren's ribbing, he'd had a good head above those broad shoulders, too.

Haydren pressed his lips together, staring toward the edge of the fire's glow as he swiped the rag down his blade one final time. He had to stop thinking like this. He had no one to turn to. He was responsible for his own decisions now. He sheathed his sword and rose. What choices did he have? He knew absolutely no one else outside of Hewolucs, and he couldn't go back there. It was Geoffrey, or no one. Even if the old man refused, Haydren might find somewhere in Hodp to stay.

Haydren drew a knife to carve some meat to take with him. And how many people, did he expect, lived in Hodp who would help him without being paid to do so? How could he expect Geoffrey to help him without promise of the same?

Haydren bit off a chunk of meat. It was horribly gamy and more than a little overcooked, but it was warm, and he was starving. He wrapped another large chunk in some cloth and tucked it into his saddlebags. He rummaged through the bandit's belongings, but found little of worth.

He closed his eyes with an abrupt sigh, recalling his map. Hodp was a long distance away—probably over 150 miles. He desperately needed a horse. With a grimace, he remembered that on his first journey to Hodp, he had lamented having a horse and wished he could walk instead.

"Good work, Haydren," he muttered, hitching his bags higher onto his shoulders and striking north-eastward. "Next time, be thankful for what you have, would you?"

It would be eleven long nights before he would see the first farmhouse outlying Hodp. The weather was his only adversary along the way, and with weary legs finally becoming used to walking, he curled up in a small grove of trees to the south-west of the village. In the morning, he would test the luck which had served him so amply over a week ago in the bandit camp.

He was not very hopeful.

⊷◇⊶

Geoffrey rose before the sun. Another night filled with nightmares roused him to another morning before daylight. He woke from one darkness into another, with barely a blanket between him and his sins.

With a heavy sigh he rolled out of bed and tugged on his boots. He threw a cloak around his shoulders and went out into the crisp morning, leaving Hodp behind for the solitude of a lonely and gnarled tree he had discovered shortly after arriving at the village. In the quiet of early dawn he could be alone with his thoughts. As the birds awoke and twittered their conversations, his memories would slide away, allowing him to face another day.

It was the first night like this in a while. The last was when the soldiers from the Earl had come. Perhaps it was the soldiers who had awoken the memories. Perhaps it was the young man, the kind young man who had reminded Geoffrey of his own youth and the foolish mistakes he had made.

As many times as he had stood by the tree and watched the sun rise, it always surprised him how quickly it sprang over the horizon. The moments dragged by as the east gradually brightened, sluggishly bringing the day. Then, in one swift moment, the sun appeared and climbed the sky, leaping over the distant treetops and blazing forth, announcing to the world that it had returned.

Whatever he might have expected after a night of sleep such as he had, Geoffrey was not prepared for what awaited him at the door when he finally returned home.

6

DEPARTURES

"Did you know this even before?"
"I believed, yes."
"You never tell me these things."
"You assumed you knew."

10 Tetsamon 1319 — Spring

Haydren stood with head bowed, listening to the village as it awoke. But there was only silence behind the door before him. He raised a fist to knock when motion caught his eye: coming around the corner of the house was the man he knew as Geoffrey.

The two studied each other. They both looked older than what they remembered, and both wondered why that might be so.

"I'm not sure if you remember me," Haydren said.

Geoffrey flashed a wry grin, then nodded solemnly. "If I remember your captain correctly, your name was Haydren."

"It still is," Haydren said, the jest surprising even himself. Geoffrey grinned.

"You came directly to my door," Geoffrey said. "Do I still owe something to the Earl?"

Haydren paused, considering. It would make his request far easier to ask, though much harder to explain.

"I came to ask...may I speak to you inside?" Haydren asked.

Geoffrey nodded hesitantly and ushered Haydren through the door. There was still that odd familiarity to the room. Geoffrey went to the table, gesturing for Haydren to sit down.

"May I get you something to drink?" he asked.

Haydren lowered his saddlebag to the floor, but did not sit. "Could I have some water?" he asked.

Geoffrey nodded, filled a pewter mug from the sink, and handed it to him. "Do you have any other questions?"

Haydren took a long swallow. "Please understand how difficult this is for me to ask," he began. Geoffrey gestured for him to continue as they sat down. "Please also know that I have no one else to ask. I have thought long and hard about this, and you are my last...I have no idea where else to go."

"Haydren, do you have a horse outside of the village?" Geoffrey asked.

Haydren blinked quickly. "N-no, I don't," he replied.

"You have walked here?"

Haydren swallowed. "Nearly from Hewolucs," he said, losing his voice in a whisper. He cleared his throat and took another drink.

Geoffrey sat back. "That is far to walk."

"It was unavoidable, believe me," Haydren replied.

"Who pursues you? The Earl?"

"His son."

Geoffrey gazed at him a moment. "You have been walking for some time, I see," he stated. "The new Earl has no son; he is only eighteen."

Haydren gripped his mug. So, it was done; the Earl he had known, would have sworn his sword to, was gone. And a bully reigned in his place. He brought the water to his lips, but could not drink.

"Why does he pursue you?"

Haydren smirked. "Because I defeated him in every sword fight," he replied. "Because..." he paused. How much did he want to tell Geoffrey? Certainly not everything. "Because I was an orphan, and in Guntsen's view should not have been a swordsman in the first place."

"And you have a duty to serve in his ranks now, correct? That would be his legitimate claim," Geoffrey said.

Haydren nodded. "Presumably."

Geoffrey sat silently, then drew a deep breath. "You can use your former room for today. No one should bother you. But I do not know how long you might stay here."

Haydren glanced at him quizzically. Something in Geoffrey's voice gave Haydren a sense there was more to that statement than met the eye. Ignoring it, he said: "Thank you, Geoffrey. If that is all you do for me, it is far more than I could expect."

"Think nothing of it," Geoffrey replied. "I did as much without knowing you."

Haydren grinned. "But under the threat of the Earl," he said.

"Perhaps. I will leave some food, and a basin of water to refresh yourself. Remain in your room until I return. And don't answer the door."

It was impossible for Haydren to tell when Geoffrey was joking. "I can never repay you for this," he said.

Geoffrey's gaze went distant. "I do not seek repayment from you," he murmured. Haydren gazed at him quizzically, and a little worried. Geoffrey smiled. "Do not concern yourself with it," he said.

⸺◈⸺

After Haydren retreated upstairs, Geoffrey threw on a brown cloak and exited. He walked a measured pace to the smithy, and went inside. He hung his cloak on a peg in the back.

"A little warm, idn'it?" the blacksmith, Wesla, drawled.

Geoffrey rolled up his sleeves, regarding the smith sideways. "I am accustomed to warmer climates," he said. He pulled the broad blade of a plow from a nearby shelf, thrust it into the fire, and worked the bellows till the metal glowed. He tied his apron, grasped a hammer, and set to work.

He enjoyed the smithy, enjoyed the simple, hard work. Mostly he enjoyed making plows and wagon parts instead of swords and halberds. The sparks flared, and settled against the stone beneath the anvil with the rhythmic blows. Heat it, beat it, repeat—he could almost hear the song in his head.

There was a rush of movement, and he looked up to see a raven perched on the window. It peered at Wesla before its head fidgeted a moment and fixed Geoffrey with a soul-searching gaze. It knew him, somehow, and nodded in solemn recognition. They shared something, Geoffrey and the raven; they shared spilled blood, and the picking apart of near-dead victims. It knew Geoffrey as close kin, long ago.

"Will you never let me forget it?" he whispered.

"*What?*" it screeched at him.

Wesla gave a start and glared at the raven. "Git!" he shouted, throwing a rag at it. With another cry, the raven took off, leaving a feather behind. Geoffrey glanced at it, then returned to his work. He had been chased from every roost between Burieng and North Pal Isan. Always something was left behind at each home, a part of him he could not retrieve. Eastern Burieng had proved no safe haven, as he had hoped so long ago in Andelen. Chased too much longer, there would be no feathers to help him fly, and predators would pick him apart bit by bit: poetic justice, the writers called it. Geoffrey only called it death, with no more chances for salvation.

Unless.

Unless his chance for salvation had already come. Unless with one last flight he would be free of those who pursued, free to roost not as a raven, but as a gull, a bird welcomed for its guidance and the hope of land to sailors lost at sea. He had heard much about Frecksshire, and the Earl there. Any words spoken in contempt were spoken by those who daily proved to be Geoffrey's enemies. There would be some price to pay the

Earl, that much was assumed. But it might not be his life, through either death or servitude. It would be a terribly long flight, with danger pressing on each side. Far more than feathers could be lost. But what might be gained!

The hammer renewed its strokes as embers flared from the forge, and from the glowing steel. He was not bound to wield only a hammer just yet, though the hammer had kept him alive and young. He would need it all in the coming months.

⸻ ◆ ⸻

Haydren awoke to a sharp knocking on the door below. His eyes snapped open, but the room was dark. Every fiber of his muscles strained to reach for a light. Every thought in his mind warned him a lamp's glow might give away his presence.

The knocking came again, and Haydren jumped. His breath came in strained gasps. He heard boots crossing the floor downstairs, and the door opened.

"Yes?" came Geoffrey's muffled voice.

"Sir," a much stronger voice returned. "We come from the Earl."

What if they want rooms? Haydren's mind screamed. As the voices continued, Haydren rose slowly, picked up his boots and sword, and moved toward the door.

"We are searching for a man, a swordsman of the Earl's ranks named Haydren Loren. He's—do you have it? Yes: this man here. Have you seen him?"

Haydren eased open the door, stepping quietly into the hall. He knelt beside the railing, listening to the conversation below.

"Yes, I have," Geoffrey replied.

Haydren gritted his teeth, and grasped his sword. There was a clink of armor below, and a whispered question Haydren could not make out.

"My dear boy!" Geoffrey exclaimed, laughing. Haydren jumped, and his sword slipped halfway from his sheath. "That was weeks ago," Geoffrey continued. "He came with several others of your fine soldiers, and two other young men. Took up my only spare room and beds, too. They said there might be some kind of recompense?" Geoffrey added meekly.

Haydren sighed, easing his sword back. The soldier below grumbled something, then said: "Of course not, old man. The Earl doesn't pay men like you for services. It is your honor to serve him."

"Oh, I'm sorry. I am new to this country. The God bless your search."

The door closed below, and Geoffrey's footsteps crossed the floor. He ascended a few steps and stopped.

"Awake?" Geoffrey asked.

Haydren's eyes blinked open. "You scared the life out of me, just there."

Geoffrey nodded. "I must leave," he said. "Tonight. You may accompany me if you still wish to escape the Earl, though you do not have to."

Haydren straightened, staring at Geoffrey as he continued up the stairs and toward his room. Geoffrey paused there, glancing at Haydren before stepping inside. Haydren followed him.

"Where are you going?" Haydren asked from the doorway.

Geoffrey began packing a small bag with various items from his room. "Much like you, I am not sure," he replied. "Though I have heard Frecksshire is more friendly to...outsiders, than they seem to be here."

Haydren swallowed hard. Was the whole world fleeing to the west?

Geoffrey paused and straightened. "Is that further than you were hoping?" he asked.

Haydren shook his head. "No, that is exactly where I am trying to go," he replied. "I would just never have considered asking you."

"Now you don't have to." Geoffrey rummaged through a chest at the foot of his bed. "I hope I still know how to use this thing." He removed a scabbarded sword, and blew some dust off it. When he drew the sword, Haydren thought it must have dulled over the years. But as it flashed in the light, he sucked in a gasp.

It was Follus steel, the sword of the Knights of Galessern, the same Knights who swore allegiance to the King. The same Knights now controlled by Lasserain.

If Geoffrey noticed Haydren's reaction, he did not comment on it. He sheathed the sword and laid it on his bed as he laced armor onto his torso and forearms. It was similar to Haydren's armor, though it appeared stronger and heavier. Over that went a light tunic, then a cloak.

Haydren glanced to the window. Stars twinkled in the west. Geoffrey's words were so often ambiguous, otherwise Haydren might have plied him immediately with questions. Now, he had a strange sword that should never be possessed by one Haydren could trust. But he needed Geoffrey. This was his only hope.

The old soldier was looking at him. Haydren raised his eyebrows, trying to push away his thoughts lest somehow Geoffrey read them on his face. "Ready to go?" he asked.

Geoffrey nodded solemnly. "Get your bags. We'll need them."

Once they reached the front door, Geoffrey paused. "I will go first, to make sure there are no soldiers about. We cannot have you getting caught by these men," he said, and Haydren detected no insincerity. "If it is within my power, I will get you to the west. And may we both find safety there."

Haydren stood back as Geoffrey slipped outside. *What safety did Geoffrey need?* Not for the last time, Haydren wondered what sort of companion he had acquired.

A light knocking sounded against the wall, and Haydren stepped outside, moving toward the noise. He met Geoffrey on the southern side of the house, and together they vaulted the low wall surrounding the town and struck off into the fields.

"We'll get away from the village before circling around," Geoffrey explained. "We may be able to cross the road safely a few miles north."

On through the night they walked. Geoffrey remained silent, and Haydren remained lost in thought. After several hours, Haydren glanced up and found The Jewel in the sky directly ahead of them. He increased his pace and came alongside Geoffrey.

"Where are we going?" he asked.

"I was following you."

Haydren could see the pale gleam of Geoffrey's teeth in the moonlight, and grinned. "From the front?"

"How many strands does a rope have, Haydren?" Geoffrey asked.

"Um, hundreds?" he replied hesitantly.

"But they are bundled. How many bundles are there?"

"Three, usually," Haydren replied. "Why?"

"Did you ever wonder why they do not use two strands, or just one?"

"I suppose three is stronger," Haydren said.

"Hmm. Probably."

They continued in silence. Finally, Haydren blurted: "Geoffrey, where are we going? And don't answer me about ropes again."

"We are only two strands, Haydren," Geoffrey replied patiently. "We will be stronger with three. So, we go to Werine."

"What's in Werine?"

"Many things," he said. "Have you ever heard of an archer—"

"Pladt Grecce?" Haydren asked, stopping short as the grass brushed his legs. "Sir Cullins spoke of him when some of us ridiculed the bow. Even though he's barely older than I am, his fame spreads far and wide across Kelian Province. We all wondered why the Earl had not pulled him into his ranks. What makes you think he will come with us?"

"I had not realized he was so famous," Geoffrey said. "I met him when I passed through the port-town almost a year ago. I would presume the Earl has not recruited him because he's important right where he is."

"Exactly," Haydren replied. "So why would he come with us?"

"People can be complex, Haydren," Geoffrey replied. "You never know what may motivate one person to do one thing and not another. Some people are the hare, others are the fox."

"I don't understand."

Geoffrey paused as his gaze went distant. He looked up. "You leave because the Earl chases you, true? The hare runs because the fox chases. The fox runs to pursue the hare. People move because they are either chased or they pursue something. The fox may change, but the hare is often the same."

And what if someone is both the fox and the hare? "I see," Haydren said aloud. "Interesting proverb."

"Besides," Geoffrey said finally, his voice becoming light. "It cannot hurt to ask, can it?"

Haydren's brow furrowed as they walked. Suddenly, he asked: "Geoffrey, where did that proverb come from?"

"The histories," he replied.

Haydren's eyes narrowed. "Histories of what?"

"The histories of The God of All, Haydren."

"I knew it." Haydren's hand fell to his sword and he shook his head. Geoffrey's pace checked a moment, but quickly resumed.

"Is there something wrong with that?" Geoffrey asked quietly.

"Wrong with what? A supposedly all-knowing, manipulative deity who takes away the ability to choose for yourself, yet allows the orphaning of children and the death of good men? No, there's nothing wrong with that."

Geoffrey ducked his head with a thin, wary smile. "It doesn't exactly work like that, Haydren."

"Certainly not if I can help it," Haydren muttered.

"Haydren," Geoffrey began slowly.

"Forget it. Let's just not worry about it."

Haydren fumed as they continued in silence. The hope of trusting Geoffrey, of looking past the sword and wishing Geoffrey could help guide his decisions, maybe ease some of the doubt that clenched his heart, was gone. Just like Mickel and Maerie, this man trusted in something that Haydren could not. Could he not gain one friend in whom he could truly confide? One friend who would not be killed by beasts, while Haydren could do nothing? Must he spend an entire journey across the breadth of Burieng with barely an acquaintance? It seemed like something the God of All would do, if he existed. Haydren set his jaw.

The next few days were spent in vast amounts of silence. So as Werine appeared on the horizon, Haydren did not expect—nor necessarily want—much comment from his tight-lipped companion.

Yet, suddenly, Geoffrey gestured toward a stand of trees that pointed toward the city. "There he is," he murmured. Haydren squinted at the base of one of the trees, barely making out a bulge which looked vaguely like a person sitting down.

"You have amazing sight," Haydren commented.

"Or prior knowledge," Geoffrey replied. "I know Pladt comes out here, though usually at evening." He paused, fingering his lower lip. "Something else brings him out here this early. Let me speak to him first."

As they left the road and angled toward the tree, the figure beneath it rose and strode toward them.

"Geoffrey!" he shouted across the grasses. "I thought you weren't coming back!"

For the first time in Haydren's presence, Geoffrey broke into a full-fledged smile. "And leave you here by yourself?" Geoffrey called back.

Pladt laughed, and quickened his pace. Upon reaching them, Pladt went straight to Geoffrey and wrapped him in an embrace, pulling Haydren up short. He stood to one side in silence.

"Pladt, this is Haydren Loren of Hewolucs," Geoffrey said as they parted.

"Hewolucs?" Pladt echoed, genuinely surprised. "And no horses?"

"It's a long story," Geoffrey said.

"It would have to be."

"Pladt, I've heard about you," Haydren said, offering his hand. "It's my honor to meet you."

If Kitrel had had some native Werine in him, this archer was full-blooded. Almost a full head taller than Haydren, he was not gangly, but actually well proportioned. Sun-bleached hair sat in a slightly ragged mess atop a face neither bony nor fat, and his broad grin lit up eyes the color of a forest canopy with a strong summer sun behind it. He was, despite Haydren's caution of strangers, instantly likable.

Pladt cocked an eyebrow. "I've heard of you too, Haydren," he said. When Haydren's eyes widened, he laughed. "From Geoffrey. Just now." Pladt's eyes danced, and Geoffrey grinned.

Haydren, still shocked, didn't reply.

"Probably not best to make jokes like that, Pladt," Geoffrey said.

Pladt shrugged. "Sure. So what brings you back here?"

"That's Haydren's prerogative," Geoffrey replied, gesturing to him.

"I...we are traveling to Frecksshire, in the west," Haydren said. The request came easier each time he had to ask it. "We would like you to come with us."

Pladt's grin faded, and he cleared his throat. His flicked between them. "Come with me," he said, turning toward town.

Frowning, Haydren followed Pladt through streets now busy with merchants and vendors. They reached an impressive two-story building, better in Haydren's view than even Geoffrey's home. It was the nicest house he had seen outside of Hewolucs.

Pladt led them in, meeting a man who was clearly his father, though a little softer around the edges. Pladt turned to give introductions.

"Geoffrey, Haydren: this is Kerrik Grecce, my father," he said. "Haydren, you may ask him what you have just asked me."

Haydren blinked. "Sir, I am Haydren of Hewolucs. I am on a journey to Frecksshire and was looking to...I was hoping Pladt might come along with us. To aid us."

Kerrik glowered at Pladt. "He cannot," he said. "He protects this town from hydra attacks, and is indispensable. I am sorry."

"You have no other protection—guards—for that?" Haydren asked in disbelief.

"None that are effective against hydras," Kerrik replied. "Do you know what happens when a guard tries to kill a hydra, aside from the guard dying? The hydra's head grows back when it is cut off; if you wound it, it bites the head off so another can grow in its place. Pladt can loose his arrows fast enough to send a shaft into each brain before the hydra has time to gnaw the wounded head off. He is the only one effective enough to do that before many houses are destroyed. As such," he concluded, leaning forward, "he is indispensable to the safety of this town." Kerrik rocked back, casting another glare at his son. "I must get to the warehouses. Good day."

After his father had gone, Pladt guided Haydren and Geoffrey back outside. "We'll need a place to stay for the night," Haydren said, not sure what else to say after such a long but instantly fruitless journey.

"Naek's Tavern has good rooms," Pladt replied. "Geoffrey should remember the place."

"Wasn't that where—?"

"No, Geoffrey, except in your mind," Pladt said with a grin. "Haydren, some advice: if you plan on traveling with this old man, make sure you do nothing your mother told you not to. Because he will never—"

"Is that fair?" Geoffrey said smiling.

"He will never let you forget it!" Pladt said over him.

"So it did happen," Geoffrey said with a sly grin, pointing a finger triumphantly at Pladt.

Pladt returned the gesture, and looked at Haydren with raised eyebrows. "See? Good luck."

Haydren grinned weakly and nodded. Geoffrey still chuckled after Pladt had shut the door, and he and Haydren walked toward the tavern.

"Geoffrey, why under the skies did we come all the way up here?"

"I said people can be complex." Geoffrey replied. "I lived here for almost a year, Haydren. I got to know Pladt very early on in my stay here, and we became friends. I felt bad for him."

"'Bad for him?'" Haydren echoed.

"Despite his skill, his father fears for his safety," Geoffrey replied. "And the safety of Werine. Pladt is very important in defending the town, but hydras can arrive with little or no warning. The farther he is from town, the more likely people will die and homes will be destroyed if he can't get back to defend it."

"They can't build a wall to protect it?"

"That would make sense, wouldn't it," was the cynical reply.

"I don't see how this helps," Haydren said.

"It may not."

Haydren supposed they would need to earn each other's trust to make it all the way to Frecksshire, but he would have preferred taking a little more time doing it. What he had definitely learned was that Geoffrey would not give up his thoughts with more pressing.

"How does Pladt feel about it, what's required of him?" he asked instead.

"He doesn't like it," Geoffrey replied. "But I think he understands. Duty, though necessary, is not always fun: I believe he understands that. Here it is," Geoffrey said, pointing upward at a sign with a frothing mug in red.

"So what were you and Pladt talking about? He did something here?" Haydren asked with a grin.

"Ask him, though he'll deny it," Geoffrey replied, also grinning. "He and his father should be around sometime this evening."

<hr>

That night, Geoffrey and Haydren sat to eat. Aside from a large stone fireplace, the common room transported the guests to an ancient grove: the bar, the tables, and the chairs and benches were all of a rough-hewn wood too aged to define. The oaken posts seemed to have been taken directly from the forests, with their upper branches intact and spider-webbing with gnarled knuckles across the wood-plank ceiling. Lanterns hanging from pegs on the supports gave light to dark corners, which even at the dinner hour had remained mostly vacant.

They were each nursing a pint of beer after finishing a thick steak. Though Geoffrey had made perfectly acceptable meals during their journey, all from what he could hunt, Haydren missed a good cooked meal. And, he admitted, he missed Maerie's cooking. Even at times like these, he still thought back to the last meal she had made him, just as she knew he would.

Haydren was halfway done with his beer when Pladt entered the tavern, with his father close behind him. Pladt's eyes brightened when he saw them, and he waved in salute. With a glance from his father, he moved to a separate table and sat down with his drink. Faintly, over the murmur of the other patrons, Haydren heard Pladt ask: "Can I not say hello to Geoffrey?"

But Geoffrey did not turn to look, and Pladt remained seated with Kerrik. Haydren had hefted the mug to his lips when he heard footsteps stop behind him. Instinctively, he turned and slid his chair away from the table so as to better face the man who stood there.

"Haydren, isn't it?" the man asked. Though his speech was slurred a little, his eyes were clear, and in his slouch he appeared ready to move quickly. Haydren prepared to do the same.

"I'm afraid not. But you're close: my name is Hayden. Drop the 'r'," he said with a smile.

The man's eyes widened, and he straightened a little before catching himself. He tried drooping his eyelids to re-affect his drunkenness, but he must have realized Haydren was not fooled.

"Naw, you're Haydren," the man said with a sloppy grin. "I knew—knew your father. I have a token from him. Said you'd remember him by it."

Caution.

When the man reached into his cloak, Haydren kicked out with his foot, driving into the man's stomach and shoving him backward. Haydren leapt to his feet and drew his sword. The tavern emptied except for Pladt and Kerrik.

The man's eyes truly widened, then, as he gazed at the sword. "Th-that sword!" he cried, his hand shakily outstretched. "How did you—?"

Haydren, though dumbstruck, maintained his balanced grip. "If you knew my father, you should know this," he replied with more assurance than he felt. "He's the one who gave it to me."

The man straightened. "He will not be happy," he whispered. "The mas—" He cut off suddenly, his gaze hardening.

"What did you say?" Haydren whispered, stepping forward. "'The master'?"

Something—resolve, Haydren thought—tightened the man's features. He pulled out a dagger and held it before him.

"You may have your victory," the man said, his voice radically changed to one deep, and somber. "It is a small one, and one which will affect little."

With that, before Haydren could react, the man drew the blade across his own throat. He sputtered, fell, and died.

7

WHISPERS

"This wrecks many plans!"
"Oh? Did you not recognize the man?"
"...By the deeps of Oren!"
*"I do not appreciate your water-wizard's oath; but it is beginning, now, in
    earnest."*

16 Tetsamon 1319 — Spring

Guntsen rolled the goblet around in his hands, inspecting the jewels set into its surface. He grinned as the gems glittered in the afternoon light.

"You seem distracted," said Lasserain, entering then. The guards outside quickly shut the doors behind him.

"It's my father's drinking cup," Guntsen replied, noting his reflection in the burnished gold. "I've always liked it. He promised it would be mine, as it had been his father's, and his father's, and his––"

"It shows some wear," the mage said.

Guntsen sobered. He didn't need to look to see the missing gem that had popped loose when it struck the wall. The goblet wavered, and he set it quickly on the stand beside the throne. "What do you want?" he asked.

"Your assassin failed."

"As did yours," Guntsen replied coolly.

"Mine were not sent specifically for him."

"What do you want?" Guntsen asked again.

"Durdamon will not long be content to stay in Frecksshire," Lasserain said. "I want to make sure he does not soon invade. I believe you want that as well."

"I can seal our borders well enough, I think."

"No, you cannot. Also, my plan may capture your fugitive."

Guntsen glanced down at the empty goblet, at the socket where a large topaz had once rested but now lay pulverized against the wall. "Do whatever you want," Guntsen muttered. When he heard the doors boom shut behind the mage, he closed his eyes and sighed.

A thought struck him suddenly, and his eyes popped open. There was still one who might find Haydren first, and kill him. He gestured for a guard nearby and quickly sent his summons.

———◆———

"I told you, I didn't know him," Haydren said. "Ask anyone in here: I was finishing my meal when he approached me. He said a few things to me, and when I drew my sword, he pulled out a dagger and cut his own throat."

"We will ask the others," said the warden. "If they agree, you'll be free to go. But do not leave this tavern until I say you may."

"We're here until morning," Haydren offered.

The warden stopped halfway upon getting up. "You are here until I say you are," he said again, firmly.

Haydren bowed his head in submission, and the warden left.

"Touchy," Geoffrey commented, taking a drink.

"I didn't think Werine was so small that such an occasion would seem so important," Haydren replied. "If I had actually struck that lunatic? Then, maybe."

"Was he a lunatic?" Geoffrey asked.

"You saw him!" he said. "Do sane people cut their own throats?"

"They do if they believe they are dead anyway," Geoffrey replied. "Though not all sane people do that. Just ones under very strong coercion. Or maybe it was a code of honor." He took another sip. "We cannot ask him, I suppose."

"Geoffrey, of everything I need right now, your wit is not it," Haydren said into his drink.

"Are you sure you did not recognize him?"

Haydren's mug *thunked* onto the table. "Now you? I have no idea who he was. Though I doubt he was telling the truth when he said he knew my father. You know, that's something—!" Haydren stopped and bit his lip. He couldn't help a short chuckle.

Geoffrey arched a brow. "Speaking of insanity?" he asked.

"No," Haydren replied, running a finger around the lip of his mug. "Well, maybe: Guntsen."

"The Earl?"

"Guntsen," he repeated. "His plan, the one that forced me to leave Hewolucs, was to send me on patrol to Werine and have someone here ready to kill me. Playing on my need to find my father would be just like him." Haydren quickly buried his face in his mug to hide his slip.

"You mentioned to the man that your father gave you the sword, too," Geoffrey said.

He did not ask, Haydren realized. He merely opened the door. No matter what else, Haydren appreciated that. "He did give it to me, then disappeared when I was eight. I go to Frecksshire to seek him." There, thought Haydren: all of that was true.

"Very good," Geoffrey murmured as he returned to his drink, allowing Haydren to return to his.

———◆◇◆———

"That is why you are not going with these men," Kerrik said. The wardens were finally removing the body of the man who had killed himself in front of Haydren. "Trouble follows them, it would seem. And why should you and they pursue it to Frecksshire? Why would anyone from the east want to go west?"

"Father, please," Pladt said. "The reason I'm not allowed to go is because Werine cannot protect itself, isn't that right?"

Kerrik gaped at his son's vehemence, then glowered in annoyance. "Yes, Pladt, that is why."

"And until the hydras stop attacking, which will be never, I am stuck here, correct? Unless..." Pladt paused, a thought striking him.

"Unless what?" Kerrik asked.

"What if Werine could defend itself?"

"It cannot," Kerrik replied flatly. "We've discussed this; you are the only one who can protect us."

Pladt stared at his drink. There were plenty of men in Werine who were good with a bow: he personally knew nine—maybe ten. But why should they take up arms? Better to chain one man to a duty than ten of them. "I suppose you're right," Pladt said. "I'm feeling a little tired, father. I would like to say farewell to Geoffrey before he leaves, though."

Kerrik gestured his permission. Pladt rose and walked over.

"Before you leave in the morning," he said, "I wanted to wish you farewell. Both of you. Haydren, I'm sorry I didn't get to know you better."

"I'm sorry too," Haydren said. He smiled. "Surely if you were a friend of Geoffrey's, we could have been friends as well."

Haydren glanced at Kerrik, then back to Pladt. "We leave in the morning," Haydren said only loud enough for Pladt to hear. "We will walk just north of the road to Quaran, in order to avoid bandits."

Pladt leaned against an empty chair while he thought about what

Haydren said. "You don't have horses?" he asked.

"We don't have the money. We've walked this far; we should make it to Quaran. Then, who knows?"

Pladt smiled, and turned to Geoffrey. "I wish I could come with you two. But," he added with a shrug, "I suppose father knows best."

"He usually does," Haydren said with a nod.

"Well, farewell," Pladt said. "I suppose I won't see you in the morning; but I think you'll find Naek's beds are rather comfortable."

"And how would you know?" Geoffrey asked, his eyes twinkling.

Pladt set his jaw. "On second thought, I thank the gods I'm not going with you."

"Who do you thank?" Geoffrey demanded.

"The God, Geoffrey, the God," Pladt replied, patting him on the shoulder. "The 's' slipped. Old habit," he said with a wink at Haydren.

"Good," Geoffrey growled into his mug.

"Have *fun* on your journey, Haydren," he said with a playfully meaningful glance at Geoffrey. "And good luck."

Haydren raised his mug in salute. "Thank you. You too."

After Pladt had gone, Geoffrey gave Haydren a brief smile. "So, coming here might not have been a wasted effort?" he asked.

Haydren grinned in return. "I know. I should trust you."

As Geoffrey lay awake in bed that night, however, he wondered if Haydren ever would. He almost asked more than once, until suddenly he did not need to.

"Geoffrey," Haydren whispered.

"Hmm?"

"I've kept quiet for a long time, now," he said. "And I don't mean to intrude on your privacy, and I know I don't have much choice anyway, but I would like to know who I'm traveling with a little bit better. There's just some things—"

"What do you want to know?" Geoffrey asked.

"Your house," he said. "I did not expect to find a water pump in Hodp in the first place, let alone in the home of someone..." He trailed off.

"It was built by a Rinc Nain," Geoffrey replied. His companion walked a winding road to trust, it seemed. "The people of Hodp did not trust the technology, and didn't like the simplicity. They were happy when I took it."

"Oh," Haydren said. Then: "Earlier, you berated Pladt for thanking 'the gods' and yet...I mean the sword you carry isn't...I don't know how..." he trailed off once more with a mumbled curse.

Geoffrey turned and stared at the ceiling—that question was far closer to his heart than he knew Haydren could realize, but it pierced just as the raven's gaze had. It was too soon, much too soon. "That sword was given to me a long time ago," he said quietly. "I could not give it back, though I am a far different man now. I don't know what else to tell you."

Haydren sighed. "Then that will have to be enough."

Geoffrey's eyes fell upon a candle-flame, guttering solitarily. What could he possibly be thinking, running toward Rinc Na when for fifteen years he had been running *from* it? That niggling voice that always spoke the truth, the one he had silenced by young pride, told him it was because he had yet to truly pay his penance. Running now to the west just might force him to do what he had been avoiding for all this time.

He blew out the candle. Though his eyes stopped seeing, the images in his mind spun through endless scenarios, only rarely ending in peace.

⸺◆⸺

"Doesn't that mountain shine like the red in my sword?" Haydren asked, drawing the item partway out of its sheath to show him. Geoffrey studied it, glanced at Thoret behind them, and nodded.

"It is similar," he agreed. "Why does it interest you?"

"Well I don't know anything about the sword, I was simply left it. I would like to know more about it—where it was made and the like."

"You care much for seeking answers," Geoffrey said.

"My instructors loved me," Haydren replied with a smile.

Geoffrey grinned as well. "I can imagine."

They rode south as the day grew warmer. About midday, Haydren looked for a place they could rest for lunch. He hoped to reach Devil's Thumb, a small abutment of forest they had passed on their way north. Just as they spotted its green smudge on the horizon, they came to the base of a small rise.

Stop.

Haydren knelt, with Geoffrey beside him.

"Something's not right about these woods," Haydren whispered. They crept forward until they reached the top, then sat and watched the tree-line for several long moments.

The forest bent into a crooked point a mile or so eastward, close enough to skirt entirely if necessary, and if no bandits watched the road near its end. But it was also narrow here, and the shortest route south.

"Haydren," Geoffrey whispered. "What—"

Just then, a group of men left the tree-line, skirting it as they made their way east. Deadly scimitars swung at their hips.

"This may complicate matters," Geoffrey said.

Haydren rubbed his lip. A wind from the east ruffled the grasses just turning green with spring. Through the washing of stalks against one another, and almost borne on the breeze, came a whisper:

In the grove.

This is the fourth time since leaving Hewolucs, Haydren thought; *each time, it grows louder.* It was a whisper that had not yet led him astray. It directed him to Geoffrey, who was—he had to admit, despite contradictory beliefs—a better companion than he should have expected. It had prepared him for the suicidal man at the tavern. And it had just now kept him from leading them straight over the rise into full view of the bandits below. Inexplicable as it was, this—what, he wondered: instinct?—was the best he had.

"They'll most likely be gone for some time," Haydren replied. "They may have a camp deeper in, with supplies we might use."

"Remember when I said we were a two-stranded rope?" Geoffrey asked wearily.

"It's the middle of the day," Haydren replied, dropping his bag to the ground. "There are bound to be only a few bandits sitting at camp when there are so many caravans to rob. Shall I go to make sure alone?" Haydren asked, stealing forward before Geoffrey could prevent him.

Haydren moved down the rise, his eyes fastened on the tree-line. The grasses here were tall, and hid him well all the way to the edge. He stood and pressed his back against one tree. He leaned out, peering down a deer-trail to where he could make out a small camp. There was a line of brown tents, with horses tied nearby: four, sleek and fast, and a fifth like a draft horse. On the other side of the camp lay a large, tarp-covered pile of...something.

He glanced up as Geoffrey approached. Haydren waved him forward, and Geoffrey stood and bolted to a nearby tree.

"You are insane!" Geoffrey whispered. "If you do not get us killed—"

"Shh!" Haydren hissed. He peered out again. A silhouette detached itself from a tree within the camp and moved toward one of the tents. Three other silhouettes moved as well, circling the camp. Guards. Haydren looked at Geoffrey and held up four fingers. Geoffrey blinked, set his jaw, and slowly drew his sword. Haydren glanced at the Follus steel as it glimmered faintly. He realized that any doubts he had about Geoffrey's allegiance would be proved or disproved in the next few moments.

He bolted quietly to another thick trunk deeper in. It was old-growth forest, with deep, lush loam to pad his footsteps. But as he flattened against the trunk, a dead branch he had not seen squeezed between his back and the tree, and snapped with a loud crack. He gazed, horrified, at Geoffrey.

"Who's there?" one of the guards at the camp bellowed. "Come out! I heard you there!"

Haydren couldn't help thinking the bandit would feel fairly stupid if he turned out to be a deer. Geoffrey glared his way and shook his head.

Haydren could hear the guard approaching. This was his mess to clean up. Slowly, careful to remain behind the tree, he drew his sword. He held it pressed against his left shoulder, his arm high.

The footsteps neared. In one swift movement, Haydren stepped from behind the tree, sweeping his sword off his left shoulder and around, snapping the blade downward. Sword met flesh, and the guard pitched backward, staining the leaves at Haydren's feet.

The other guards were still up ahead, staring in mute surprise. With a yell, Haydren ran forward. He drove left, meeting his quarry with furious strokes. Behind him, he heard Geoffrey's blade ringing against the bandit's scimitar. There was a cry, and after a moment the sharp pinging of Follus on steel sounded again through the grove.

Before Haydren could close with the final bandit, Geoffrey's foe fell dead. The man facing Haydren dropped his scimitar, turned, and ran between them to the plains.

"Go after him!" Geoffrey shouted. "He will alert the others!"

Haydren started forward, but slipped on a root and fell. He pounded a fist into the ground as the bandit exited the grove and turned for the road. The bandit's head suddenly snapped sideways, and the man skidded limply. Staring forward in surprise, Haydren could see an arrow angling above the grasses. With widening eyes, Haydren looked left, and saw a figure advancing on a horse, a bow in his right hand, and a lead in his other hand with two horses in tow.

"Pladt!" Geoffrey shouted. "You just saved Haydren from a world of disgrace!"

"Oh I don't know," Pladt shouted back, cantering up into the trees. "He still has a mouthful of dirt."

"Thank you for stopping his alarm," Haydren said, standing and brushing the dirt off his knees.

"Good to see you, too," Pladt muttered, still grinning. He climbed off his horse and looped the reins over a nearby branch.

"You did save our lives," Geoffrey said. "Thank you. But how did your father ever let you go? Does he know you're here?"

"He gave me the money for the horses," Pladt replied. "He knows Werine is in good hands; I finally put together a group of archers—men I had helped train a long time ago, I don't know why we never employed them. I guess I was enough, and they weren't exactly going to put more tar on an already-seaworthy ship."

"Well, even though we prevented a messenger, bandits could still come back," Geoffrey said. "How are you at climbing trees?"

Pladt shrugged, then moved to the outskirts and quickly clambered up a tall maple, peering eastward.

Haydren turned away and moved to the the tarp-covered pile he had seen earlier. He pulled up a corner to look underneath as Geoffrey came up behind him.

"Firewood?" Geoffrey asked dubiously. The logs were a solid hands-breadth across, and nearly fifteen feet long. Haydren wordlessly held open a bag filled with rope, pulling one length out that measured at least ten feet. Geoffrey glanced at the rope, then back at the logs.

"Aha," he said, nodding.

Haydren shook his head and shrugged. "'Aha' what?"

"Rafts," he replied. "They can haul these and everything they've gathered to a river and float it that way."

"To the Ghlande?"

Geoffrey shrugged. "If that's the nearest river."

"They could float it all the way into the Endolin Mountains, then," Haydren said, dropping the mouth of the bag of rope.

"Why there?" Geoffrey asked.

Haydren gazed at Geoffrey. Either he actually was new to the country, or he was very good at playing the part of not being a Knight. "Have you not heard of Lasserain?" Haydren asked.

Geoffrey shook his head and shrugged.

"I'm surprised Pladt, if no one else, wouldn't have told you," Haydren said.

"Pladt was never overly concerned with things outside Werine," Geoffrey replied. "And neither was I, particularly. And later, I was not in Hodp long enough to overhear conversations."

"I suppose it's not talked about much, these days," Haydren admitted. "It's not new. Lasserain was a mage who appeared about twenty years ago—a very powerful mage. He leveled Quaran and several small villages as he made his way south into the mountains. When he got to Galessern, the home of the King of Burieng, he stopped. Eventually scouts were sent, and the castle is perfectly intact. About that time, the bandits and beasts in Burieng multiplied and became more aggressive toward humans—at least, humans in Coberan and Kelian Provinces. The belief is that the King made a deal with Lasserain to save Galessern. There's no proof, even that the bandits and beasts are tied to Lasserain or Galessern, but the coincidence is...difficult."

"So if these bandits are tied to Galessern, they might be stealing provisions to supply an army," Geoffrey said.

"That's the fear," Haydren replied. "And the presence of these rafts does not pacify that." Haydren flipped the corner of the canvas back over the pile of logs and moved toward a tent.

"We should not stay here too much longer, Haydren," Geoffrey called after him.

"We won't," Haydren replied, peering inside the tent.

Geoffrey sighed, glancing around the camp. He moved to the bandit that Haydren had first killed and rolled him over. The handle of an ornate dagger protruded from the man's belt. Geoffrey pulled it free. The blade was a hand-breadth long of a deep red metal—the same rough pitted metal as the flames in Haydren's sword. It was old, but not worn. And, he discovered to his chagrin, the edge was remarkably sharp. Geoffrey kissed the blood that welled from his thumb, and then pressed the cut against his thigh. He took the belt and sheath from the bandit and put the dagger in it. It rightfully belonged to Haydren: it was his kill.

But there was something else, an odd plane on the man's tunic near his chest. Geoffrey undid a few buttons, and reached inside. Stiff parchment met his searching fingers, and he pulled out a long, thin envelope with a broken seal.

"What is it?" Haydren asked, suddenly nearby.

Geoffrey straightened. "This is yours," he said, holding up the dagger. "It's a very nice dagger; sharp." He handed it to Haydren. "He must have been a sergeant or captain in the band. This," he continued, holding up the parchment, "was his."

Haydren took the dagger and quickly tucked it away, almost as if he disliked touching it. He took the letter, and was beginning to read it when a whistle shrilled across the camp. Geoffrey turned toward where Pladt was scrambling down from the tree.

"Time to go," Geoffrey said, trotting toward the horses. Haydren stuffed the parchment in his jacket. They threw the items into the saddlebags and mounted quickly.

"Out the back," Pladt said, pointing. "And they're coming fast."

"Our other bags?" Haydren asked.

"Already got them!" Pladt shouted back, several lengths along and pulling away.

With a glance at Geoffrey, Haydren clicked his horse into a trot, moving behind Pladt. Weaving between the trees, and through a few small meadows, the trio finally exploded out of the Devil's Thumb at a gallop, urging their horses to more speed. They blazed across the plains westward, angling away from the road before rounding south on their original heading. Haydren could not see the bandits enter their camp, but he hoped that what they would find there would strike a fear into their hearts they had not previously known.

8

SIGHTS

"Which will be their route?"
"I cannot predict the future."
"You come close."
"It would depend on Haydren accepting counsel."

17 Tetsamon 1319 — Spring

They pressed on, eating in the saddle as the sun marched westward. They stayed off the road, though in sight of the faint line where it cut a swath through the grasses of the plain.

Haydren shifted the dagger Geoffrey had given him, just short of the strange urge to throw it away. He glanced at it, unable to keep from melding its image into the memory of cutting meat from the spit at the first bandits' camp. He could see the bodies lying around the waning fire as he helped himself to what would have given them life. He had consoled himself, then, with revenge for Kitrel. But what might he console himself with for the Devil's Thumb?

He shook his head. They had been evil men, intending to prey on travelers with no other road south. Those left in the grove would have killed him without a second thought, if given the chance.

He took his hand off the dagger and placed it firmly on the reins: a fine swordsman he would have made, questioning every forced act of violence that fate might have dealt him.

That night, they gathered enough dead wood from a nearby grove to build a small fire. "It's almost like someone planted these on purpose, so travelers would have firewood at the end of each day," Haydren mused.

Out of idle curiosity, he was trying to chart their position and mark wherever they camped.

"Wait until we reach the West," Geoffrey said. "Good Rinc Nain country, it should be."

"Meaning what?" Pladt asked.

"I've heard they have fortified Inns a day's travel apart," Haydren said. "No one in class believed it. I think we joked about the spoiled Rinc Nain not being able to sleep under the stars." Haydren shook his head. He pulled out the note from the bandit camp and started to read.

Geoffrey snorted. "If Frecksshire is established anything like Rinc Na, it will have those Inns. And spoiled or otherwise, I won't mind sleeping in an actual bed."

"Yeah, but you're kind of old," Pladt said. "We would expect it from you."

Geoffrey shook his head with a grin that disappeared when he looked at Haydren. "What is it?" he asked.

Haydren's gaze was lost in the fire. "This...this is wrong," he replied. "This can't keep happening."

"What does it say?" Pladt asked, leaning over to see.

Haydren shook his head. "Oh, it's not what it says. It's the fact that I found it."

"But what is it?"

"It's a letter for all bandit groups to plan large-scale raids for a date to be specified three months from now."

"All at once?" Pladt asked, taking the letter and reading over it. "It's just Kelian Province," he said, furrowing his brow.

"Coberan might have gotten their own," Haydren offered.

"Why is it strange that you, particularly, found it?" Geoffrey asked.

Haydren set his jaw and reached into his pack. He had still kept a hold of: "This." He held out the letter from Lintasur. "It's the reason for my destination. But it also says: 'The enemy moves soon,' and tells me to come to Frecksshire with all haste."

Geoffrey read over it quickly. "He mentions your father," he said quietly.

"Yes, he does," Haydren said, drawing in his legs to sit cross-legged on his bedroll. "I suppose there's something you need to know," he continued. Though he had considered this moment all day, it surprised him how easily it came now. "As you know, Pladt, ten or eleven years ago the bandits roamed as widely as they do now. They weren't as violent back then, but... Anyway, Mickel, my adoptive father, was a guard-lieutenant in the Outer Towers of Hewolucs. Because the bandit raids were just beginning to increase, the Earl feared an all-out assault at any moment. Mickel and the other guards had to stay in the barracks, close by in case of attack. He and Maerie, my adoptive mother, were not supposed to see each other after evening meal. They were childless, then, and it was impossible to...change that." Haydren paused as Geoffrey stirred up the fire against a chill wind out of the south. "One day, a caravan on its way from Westide was massacred. Some escaped with their lives and managed to make their way to Hewolucs. But it was a week or two before I stumbled in." He paused as the fire snapped. "I was eight."

"Eight?" Pladt repeated with disbelief. "Two weeks it took you?"

"I was covered in blood, which the Sage said was not my own. I had this sword with me, according to Mickel," Haydren added, "and my memory was gone. I spoke my native language—which they didn't recognize—for a few months before I stopped trying, and started learning Cariste from them."

"Didn't they know who was on the caravan?" Geoffrey asked.

"Most of the survivors had moved on, and the Sage and Mickel were convinced I could not have survived two weeks without food or water," Haydren replied. "They thought I probably came from somewhere else. Since Maerie and Mickel couldn't have their own baby, they decided to adopt me. The problem was that guards were not permitted to adopt children. He did anyway, in secret. But after three years, the Earl discovered my existence, we still don't know how. Though, presumably," he added, "someone saw me going into Mickel's house. He and Maerie kept me inside most of the time. But you can't keep a small child locked up indefinitely.

"When I went before the Earl, I had Mickel's sword. He didn't give me this one until a few weeks ago, before I left. I loved Mickel's sword. It was not quite as exquisite as this one," Haydren continued, gazing down at at. "But it was the best I had ever seen. As soon as I entered the throne room with Mickel and Maerie, one of the guards took that sword. I made quite a fuss; when eventually they gave it back, to quiet me, I attacked the guard. Apparently," he said with a grin, "I shamed the guard. Even at eleven, I had some skill. It was enough for the Earl to be impressed, and to give me to Sir Cullins to train, with the understanding that I would serve in his ranks for a number of years after I graduated."

"Which is his legitimate claim, despite his ulterior motives," Geoffrey said.

Haydren nodded, then proceeded to give the rest of the details of living and training in the school, and of Guntsen's hate of commoners in royal places—that same hate which led Guntsen to seek Haydren's life even now.

"That letter came to me just before I left Hewolucs," Haydren explained as he finished his story. "I couldn't do anything about it then, of course. I was bound to the Earl. With this, now," Haydren continued, gesturing to the letter Pladt still held, "I can't help but wonder what coincidence might be pushing me toward."

"Or whomever," Geoffrey said, still looking over Haydren's first letter.

"Why do you say that?" Haydren asked. "Do you recognize something in there?"

"You might say that," Geoffrey said with a sideways glance.

"He means the God, Haydren," Pladt said, handing back the bandit letter. "I would think someone like Guntsen would antagonize you because you're Rinc Nain."

"I don't know if he knew that for certain..."

"Well you look just like Geoffrey, is all I was saying. I'm sure they recognized it."

"Is it that obvious?" Haydren asked, glancing between them. "I thought being common was enough."

Geoffrey cocked his head a little. "I am sure he suspected," Geoffrey said, then gave a nod. "You are right, it is not completely pure in you, either. But chestnut hair and black eyebrows does not get much more Rinc Nain. Mine have started to go white, which is a little more distinct," he added, running a thumb across one eyebrow.

"Your house," Haydren said, his mind beginning to work again.

Geoffrey nodded. "Simple, objective, and modern; three things Cariste hate, ironically. I'm sorry, Haydren, I assumed you knew. I might have put your mind at rest long ago."

"When did you know?"

"As soon as I saw you, of course," Geoffrey said. "I assumed your comrades treated you the way they did—and you treated me the way you did—because of who we were."

"They did," Haydren replied with a wry chuckle. "Just not for that lineage. Orphans exist primarily in Hewolucs because prostitutes do not bother to raise any accidental off-spring. They hand them to the orphanage and continue on their way. Though many partake of the prostitutes' services, including royalty," Haydren said with venom, "they are seen as the lowest members of society. Simply being branded an orphan was enough to offend every sensibility of the royalty for whom Sir Cullins' school existed, even if it was not certain I was the fruit of prostitution."

"I am surprised the Earl even put you in such a position," Geoffrey said.

"I was too," Haydren replied. "Though I guess, now, I should be thankful. I don't know what kind of life I would have had as Mickel's adopted son."

"You keep calling them by name," Pladt observed. "They are not your parents, Mickel and Maerie, are they? I mean, you don't think of them that way even after all these years."

Haydren grimaced. "Part of my going to Frecksshire is in hopes of finding my true parents. I have no other but them."

"And what of the other part of this letter?" Geoffrey asked, handing it back.

"We'll see," Haydren said with a sigh. "I suppose he meant this sword, though problems are never that easily solved."

"I think he did not mean that, either," Geoffrey agreed. "Especially against an army of bandits coordinating an assault."

"So we'll ignore that part for now, unless the two of you want something better than helping me find my parents," Haydren said, ducking his head.

"Oh, I'm not necessarily here just for you," Pladt said abruptly, then smiled as Haydren and Geoffrey both glanced sharply at him. "Just make it exciting, okay?"

"Oh, I'm sure it will be, trying to cross the border under these tensions," Haydren said, his voice in mock disgust.

"And I have already promised to help you," Geoffrey said soberly.

Haydren nodded slowly. "Very well," he replied. He took a deep breath, and smiled. "Thank you, both of you."

Later that night, as Haydren and Geoffrey traded watches, Haydren said: "Geoffrey, I was hoping you might help me."

"How so?" Geoffrey asked, sliding under his blanket and trying to find a place where a knot of grass didn't press its fist into his body.

"If I'm Rinc Nain, I would think I'd remember some words..."

"Aler tho've kam tun?"

"Not for a lot of years."

"Tho riddi leip gefe."

"I'm less sure about speaking it, though," he replied. He grinned. "I'm surprised I understand it so well. If I'd somehow landed on the other side of the continent, it never would have been a question."

"You are here now," Geoffrey said. "We'll start practicing a few times a day, at meals."

"Thank you, Geoffrey."

One shoulder shrugged. "For speaking to you in my native language without fear of being run out of town? Thank *you*."

⸺◈⸺

The next morning, rain began and fell in sheets. As they plodded along, Geoffrey focused on teaching Haydren basic words and phrases at first. By dinner, Haydren was speaking a few halting sentences. As his familiarity grew over the next several days, so did his vocabulary and confidence, until he and Geoffrey were able to discuss many things fluidly in their native language.

On the fourth morning, the road curved westward, leaving its course beside the Ghlande River and arrowing to Quaran six days hard riding away.

As they paused for an afternoon meal, Haydren pulled out his maps again, keeping the rain off with a small canopy of waxed leather. A little more than halfway to the great castle of Quaran, the road crossed the Littain River that began near Sanir. Their next hope of sleeping somewhere dry was there, at the village of Migan that had cropped up around the bridge.

Pladt leaned over, his eyes brightening.

"What's all those marks?" he asked, gesturing to the groves Haydren had sketched. Haydren shrugged.

"I thought it might be useful to remember where we camped," he said. He paused, and shrugged again. "I don't know why. I have no intention of coming back here."

If Pladt was paying any attention, he didn't show it. "What's here?" he asked, pointing to the crossing.

"A small village," Haydren replied. "Probably just an inn and one or two shops."

"Are we stopping there?"

Haydren grinned at Geoffrey. "We might—yes, probably. It'd be a good place to sleep on a bed before Quaran."

"'Quanioliae Bay,'" Pladt read, north of Quaran. "I remember that name! I always wanted to go see it when we lived in Quaran. Can we go see that?"

"Um, probably not, Pladt. We need to get to Frecksshire."

"Well, I know. But it wouldn't take that long, would it?"

"Long enough," Haydren said, starting to roll up his map.

"Wait, what about this place?" he said, pinning down the parchment with a finger.

Haydren gazed at him. "That's the middle of the Central Plains," he replied. "Now you're just pointing at random things."

"What's the point of an adventure if you only go straight from point to point?" Pladt asked, though he moved his finger and allowed Haydren to finish putting away the map.

"Maybe we aren't looking for an adventure," said Haydren and Geoffrey together.

Pladt sat back quickly. "Okay, then, I guess that's unanimous."

But they all grinned as they mounted their horses and continued westward. As the day waned, the land ran into itself as broad hillsides covered with brown scrubgrass and scattered blue junipers curved eventually to abrupt valleys. The rough terrain forced them closer to the road. But from the higher way as it kept to the tops of the hills, it would be easier to spot waiting bandits or beasts.

The land dived into a broad plain as they neared Migan, and as evening approached they could see that the junction tucked near the river was small, and posed too much risk that Guntsen's men—at least a small detachment of them—was staying at the Inn and would easily recognize them as strangers. So the small band slept off the road in a narrow vale, within view of the junction, but still in the soaking plains.

They made their crossing that night under a waxing moon that broke fitfully from under bunched clouds. Occasionally a light drizzle would fall, then pass, allowing them to walk with their hoods drawn over their heads without appearing to even disinterested eyes to be hiding.

As they went by the silent buildings, Haydren glanced over his horse's neck as a candle burned in a low window of the small inn. His hood shifted, covering all of his face but one eye. Just as he was about to turn away, he caught sight of a man bent over near the small flame as if he were reading something upon a table. The man looked out suddenly, and Haydren nearly missed a step. But it seemed his hood covered his face well, as the man swept his eyes over the party of three, hesitated, then went back to whatever had his attention before.

When they had exited the village, Haydren mounted. "We need to get further away, tonight," he said, moving his horse to a trot faster than questions could follow. His companions quickly caught up.

"What is it?" Geoffrey asked as he came alongside.

"Not what: who," Haydren said. "Semmelle, lieutenant of the Mages."

"I thought mages were just magic users who could do a little magic from all the element," Pladt said.

"They are," Haydren said. "But the Earl's Mages is the unit of magic users employed by the Earl for his army. Semmelle is the lieutenant, and they are in a tiny village in the middle of the plains. Which means they're following us, or at least looking for us."

"Well, I did say 'make it exciting,' didn't I," Pladt muttered. But no ambushes sprung on the travelers in the following days.

Two days after the crossing, though he had thought about it often and had come to no conclusion, Haydren found himself debating their next route after Quaran. He had assumed he would have to attempt to sneak through the lines around Fūnik. But as he and Geoffrey were Rinc Nain, at least enough to be recognized, open passage was possible.

But Fūnik would be a month-long detour around the southern tip of the Kalen Woods. He had as much money now as he did when he left Hewolucs: none. And once they hit the Low Moors—boggy, disgusting terrain with few creatures on which to sustain themselves, and plants that were barely better than poison—they would need supplies of some sort.

On the other hand, if they traveled through the Kalen Woods—known more widely on the eastern half as the Northern Forest because it sounded more romantic and mystical—they could come out the other side only half a day's journey from the High Moors, and its abundance of edible foods. There would be only one problem with that route.

"If you gaze any deeper inward, Haydren, you may collapse within yourself," Geoffrey said, glancing up from the pot he stirred the morning they expected to arrive in Quaran.

Haydren smiled. "Sorry, just trying to think."

"You don't have to think alone," Pladt said, behind him. The sun had finally broken through the interminable clouds, and Pladt was star-eyed as he surveyed the plains sweeping away around them. On top of a great, golden plate of prairie which rolled and curled like the sea with the wind upon it, and underneath such a grand blue bowl as the sky, Pladt was again in high spirits. "My father always said thinking alone is a great way to commit all sorts of blunders. He said it more profoundly than that, though," Pladt added with a grin.

"I was considering what route to take," Haydren said. "Both present problems. If we go south, we need supplies for which we have no money. If we continue directly west, we have to go through the Northern Forest."

Geoffrey's stirring stopped short. "You do not plan on the second option, do you?"

"Geoffrey," Haydren began; Geoffrey's raised hand stopped him.

"I have been in this country only a year, Haydren, and even I have heard those rumors: no one who enters comes out. And you propose to cross at its widest point! Why don't you just try to find Haschina while you're in there?"

Pladt leaned over and spat, gazing at Geoffrey solemnly. "I would not say that name so easily, Geoffrey."

Haydren glanced at Pladt quizzically. "It is the name of the first month of the year," he said.

Pladt gave him a withering look. "Haschina the month is not hard to find," he replied. "You know very well what he's talking about: the mage's home, the birthplace of the evils that are killing Burieng."

Both looked at Pladt in surprise, but Geoffrey spoke first. "You never talked about such things with me!" he said. "I assumed you did not know, or didn't care."

Pladt shrugged. "It's not the most fun topic," he replied. "I assumed you would hear it from others. Why do you think my father moved us to Quaran in the first place? He thought the hydras were a result of L's campaign."

"You call him 'L'?" Geoffrey asked with a slight grin.

"I don't like speaking the full name," Pladt replied somberly. "The only reason we went back to Werine was because of the Northern Forest. The hydras had worsened, but they weren't walking through the streets of Werine on a daily basis. Besides, I had figured out the way to kill them, and Werine was my parents' hometown."

"I just don't see how we can travel south," Haydren said, bringing them back to the problem at hand.

"I brought you two horses, Haydren," Pladt said. "Did you think I brought them with empty purses?"

"You brought money?" Haydren asked incredulously. "How?"

Pladt shrugged sheepishly. "A lot of people were grateful for the service I provided," he mumbled.

"But besides that, Haydren," said Geoffrey, "we should wait till we get news at Quaran. The land is surely changing quickly, in these times. For now, we will need water before breaking camp. Would you mind, Pladt? There should be a stream just to the south."

Pladt agreed, and Haydren got up to help him carry the skins. As they made their way across the plain, Haydren strode beside Pladt with his eyes bent unseeing on the grass. "You lived near the Forest once?" he asked.

"It was many years ago, Haydren."

"I understand. But the nature of the Forest itself has probably not changed, right? Can we make it through?"

Pladt shook his head. "Not from anything I remember hearing. But can't we wait to find out until we get to Quaran?"

Haydren set his jaw, and said nothing. Pladt glanced sideways at him.

"Or were you hoping for my support in going against Geoffrey's advice?"

"Isn't this my journey?" Haydren spat, glancing quickly at the archer. "Don't I get to decide for myself when and where I go?"

"I suppose if you want to," Pladt replied simply.

Haydren let Pladt walk a little ahead. *But I don't want to,* he thought. He wanted to know he was making the right decision, to be reassured by people he trusted. But Geoffrey seemed content to ignore choices in the pursuit of his God, while Pladt enjoyed the novelty of making choices too much to worry about making a wrong choice.

"We shouldn't need much water," Haydren said. Pladt glanced back. "We're almost to Quaran; can I leave you to it? I'll head back and start breaking camp."

Pladt nodded and took the skins from Haydren, who flashed a grin of thanks and started wandering back toward camp. The more companions he gained, it seemed, the more he was abandoned to himself. That strange instinctual whisper had not even helped him since Pladt rode into the camp.

He had only just returned to their camp, the question still forming on Geoffrey's lips, when a terrific series of booms echoed across the plains. Haydren and Geoffrey whipped around as the last arc of lightning stitched the ground to the south, not far from where Haydren had left Pladt. There was not a cloud in the sky.

"Pladt!" Geoffrey called, bolting toward the stream. Haydren followed close on his heels.

When they reached it, Geoffrey did not hesitate before charging into the valley. Haydren saw Pladt on the far bank, seated, staring blankly across the stream.

"Pladt, are you okay?" Geoffrey asked, leaping across and landing beside the dazed archer. Pladt started, gazed at him, and gripped him by the collar.

"What?" he shouted.

Haydren hesitated beside one of the dead creatures. It looked like a miniature bear, furry and soft. He prodded one and its head lolled back, showing the row of jagged teeth he knew could rip through even leather armor. He whistled long and low. "What did he do?" he asked quietly.

"He doesn't seem to be able to hear," Geoffrey said, looking concernedly at Pladt.

"A little!" Pladt shouted. Geoffrey drew back and smiled.

"What happened?" he shouted back.

Haydren gave a short burst of laughter; Geoffrey ignored him. Pladt said: "I came to get water, like you said, and those weird creatures—" He turned and saw Haydren laughing. He glanced back at Geoffrey. "Why is he laughing?"

Geoffrey suppressed his own grin and shook his head. "Keep talking," he said. "What happened then?"

"I took out an arrow and shot it when it tried to attack me," Pladt said.

"Bad idea!" Haydren shouted, still laughing. "Prairie gremlins always travel in groups." Pladt turned and looked at him solemnly, his eyes wide as he nodded.

"Yeah!" he replied. "They came out of nowhere, hundreds of them. I ran out of arrows really very quickly. Then someone told me to jump."

Haydren sobered instantly. "What? Who?" he said.

Pladt shrugged, palms up. "She wasn't very happy when I was confused, though."

"She?" Haydren asked in a normal tone.

Pladt didn't hear him. "All she said was 'jump,' and she got mad when I didn't," he continued. "Like I'm used to disembodied voices telling me to do things. When I finally jumped across the stream...BOOM!" he finished, spreading his arms wide. He pressed a finger in his ear and shook his head. "It's really loud," he lamented in a more normal voice.

"That must have been the lightning we saw," Geoffrey said.

"Probably. But did it really strike all of the creatures?" Haydren wondered.

"Perhaps the spell travels along the ground somehow." Geoffrey's face twisted a little, and he spat. "Magic," he growled.

Sprinting to the top of the hillside, Haydren gazed across the plains. The land appeared empty—though, if folds like this were common, whoever had cast the spell could be hiding in one of hundreds. And given they did not immediately present themselves, they clearly did not want to be found.

"Get him back over here, and let's return to the camp," Haydren said. "I might have something to help him."

They returned to the fire, and Haydren made a quick salve and applied it to Pladt's ears. They ate quickly, wanting to be on their way to Quaran. By the time they had finished, though a ringing persisted, Pladt was able to hear normal conversation. Relieved, and with a hopeful sun high overhead, the companions covered much ground by the end of the day. Whether they were not as far along as they hoped, or Pladt's incident delayed them more than they wished, the walls of Quaran remained hidden on the horizon. By nightfall, as they despondently set up one more camp, Pladt's hearing had fully returned.

By noon the next day—the third day since crossing the river, and the ninth day since leaving Werine—the walls of Quaran finally rose over the horizon.

But something was wrong. The outlying farms were deserted, the land ravaged. Crops were burned or trampled, wells crumbled, and not even a cow or chicken could be seen or heard. The castle walls, a dark silhouette on the horizon, were dark with soot up close. As they neared the gates, a single arrow arched over the wall and buried itself in the road ahead of them.

"Halt where you—don't move one step closer!" a shaky voice sounded over the ramparts.

"Hello there!" Geoffrey called back.

A head peeped over the wall and surveyed the party. The head tilted up in an attempt to elevate the mouth over the ramparts. "Who are you?" the head asked.

"He sounds..." Haydren said, looking at Geoffrey with concern.

"Young," Geoffrey confirmed with a nod. He called back up to the youth: "We are three travelers from Werine, seeking lodging for the night."

White eyeballs rolled, searching them. "You carry swords," came the voice.

Haydren closed his eyes briefly. What could have happened here?

"We do not wish to be killed by bandits, or beasts," Geoffrey replied.

"Nattan, what are you about?" came a thin, wispy voice. An elderly head with long, thin hair appeared over the wall, gazing down at the three. "Who are you?" she asked.

Pladt rolled his eyes, and his horse fidgeted a step and snorted. When there should have been the clamor of a city, there was the silence of death, and fear was thick in the air. Pladt's horse pranced a few steps.

"We are three travelers from Werine," Geoffrey repeated. "We were seeking lodging, and news."

"I hope it's not good news you sought," the woman replied. "What are your names?"

"Haydren of Hewolucs, Pladt of Werine," Geoffrey replied, pointing to each in turn. "And I am Geoffrey of Hodp."

"Pladt Grecce?" she fairly squeaked.

Something in her voice caught Pladt's attention then, and he snapped his head upward, smiling broadly. "Hauten?" he called.

"Pladt, you—! Open the gates down there!" Hauten called with far greater strength in her voice than she had previously. "You all get your mounts in here!"

"Do you know everybody, Pladt?" Haydren asked as the gates began to grind open.

"Don't be ridiculous," Pladt replied. "I don't know who that boy is that stopped us at first."

"Well it has been some years since—"

The gates were fully open, then, cutting Geoffrey off mid-sentence.

The castle inside had been razed. Blackened pillars that once supported houses stuck up from the ground like stubble. Here and there a stone house remained.

And rising silently and singly near the center of the castle were the torched remains of the keep, and the sun shone outward through one of the upper windows.

9

SCARS

"Too much rain cancels the hunt, it is said."
"And a fire too cold makes impure the gold."
"This will not destroy him?"
"I can only hope it will."

26 Tetsamon 1319 — Spring

Hauten stood before them, acknowledging their stunned gazes. "I assume you have been on the road for some time," she said. "This is a week old, what has happened here."

"What did happen?" Haydren asked, spurring his horse through the gate. The town was now a broad field, with broken cobblestone roadways like black lace stretching from wall to wall. Not a pair of structures stood together.

"Beasts broke through in the middle of the night," Hauten replied. "Somehow a hole was cut underneath the west wall. They poured through before the alarm could be raised."

"No one saw them approaching the wall in the first place?" Haydren asked.

Hauten looked at Pladt. "Do you remember the west wall when you were here?" she asked.

"Yes, but that was..." Pladt trailed off.

"Come with me," Hauten said. As she led the three through the battle-field, she pointed out one of the surviving structures. "The Burrow Inn is one of the few things left standing. He might have a room available. There weren't quite enough of us left to fill it, I don't think."

Even before they reached the wall, Haydren could see foliage peeping over the top. Leaving their horses at the base, they climbed an external staircase. Despite glimpsing the treetops, nothing prepared Haydren for what he saw when they finally crested the walkway.

The Northern Forest butted directly against the castle, and creepers were wrapped around the crenellation. Here and there the vines had constricted and broken off some of the large stones. The treetops themselves arched over the wall like a giant mouth preparing to swallow the massive castle whole.

Pladt stared open-mouthed. "When did this happen?"

"It's *been* happening," Hauten replied. "Even while you were here, the woods crept closer. I suppose it finally reached the wall last year, and began tearing it down."

"You can't do anything to cut it down?" Haydren asked.

"We've tried," Hauten replied. "The outer edge of the forest is too thick, and even when we cut the stalks of the trees beyond, they do not fall. When we come back to it the next day, they have healed themselves, and the forest presses onward. In another two years, at most, it will surround the castle. Another ten and we may be like Monte-Ir."

"The Kingdom of the Kalen?" Haydren asked.

Hauten nodded gloomily. "The *lost* Kingdom. It can be found, if one feels up to braving the deep woods. But no one goes there now. Quaran, too, might not be lost entirely. But none would live here."

"Why have none moved away?" Pladt asked.

"We were born here," Hauten replied. "We hoped the Forest might stop eventually, or that some way might be found to defeat it. We thought hopefully the walls would defeat it. They don't. But I have nowhere to go."

"And Nattan?" Geoffrey asked with emotion.

"You saw him on the wall," Hauten replied, on the verge of tears. "He will not leave. Both of his parents—my son, and daughter-in-law—are dead, killed in the attack. He has me only to watch over him."

"He knows he will die here?" Geoffrey asked.

"Death is not foreign to him," Hauten said.

They stood in silence for several moments, surveying the woods, and surveying the castle inside. Finally, Haydren spoke.

"We hoped for supplies, and for advice on what route would be best to take west," he said. "We are traveling to Frecksshire, and speed is of importance."

"Then seek to make it less important," Hauten replied frankly, leading them back down the stairs to their horses below. "There are no swift routes to Frecksshire."

"We had thought of traveling through Fūnik," Geoffrey said. Hauten shrugged.

"You might," she said. "We have very little news here. You might ask Sarah," she said suddenly with a backward glance. "She arrived just before the attack, from the West. She must have come that way. As far as I know, she aims to go back soon."

They reached their horses. "You do not think she brought the attack?" Geoffrey asked.

Hauten shook her head. "She lost everyone who had come with her, Besides, trouble comes from north and south, not west—at least, not that kind of trouble. Betrayers and connivers. And it just might be that kind of trouble actually comes from the east." Hauten stopped abruptly and pressed her lips together. She smiled. "Forgive me," she said. "We expected a patrol by now, someone to see what has happened here."

"I might have taken more offense a month ago," Haydren replied. He shook his head. "Much has changed."

"You would most likely find Sarah at the Burrow," Hauten continued. "Whatever you decide, Kirrin should be able to help you." She gestured toward another of the surviving buildings, not far from the Inn. "He's been supplying travelers for years, even...well, if you decide to go through the Forest, you should see him. I must return to the wall with Nattan." She hesitated. "If you would go into the Forest," she said quietly. "And if you should find any way to bring it down..."

Haydren nodded. "Of course we would," he replied.

They stood by their horses a moment, watching Hauten stride away. "You still want to go through the Forest, then?" Geoffrey asked.

"Let's see what we can learn, first," Haydren replied.

"The people here have always been eager to send warriors into the Woods," Pladt said, digging a boot-toe into the dirt. "I don't know if I can blame them."

Haydren sighed, compressing his lips. He glanced back up the wall, at the treetops hovering above it. "Yeah," was all he said. He grasped his horse's reins and moved toward the Inn.

Inside The Burrow, Sarah was not difficult to find: she wore bright blue robes among a small crowd of dun, and was the only one who could have traveled from the west without dying along the way. All candles along the fieldstone walls were unlit, but generous windows sent sunbeams to every corner. As they approached her table at the back of the room, Sarah smiled in more than welcome.

"Hello, travelers," she said, her merriment poorly hidden behind her lips and eyes. Haydren cocked his head.

"May we sit down?" he asked. "Hauten suggested we talk to you concerning a journey to the West."

"Please, do," she replied, gesturing to the chairs nearby. As they moved to sit, she said, with a widening smile: "Good to see you survived those gremlins."

Everyone froze: Pladt's surprise was mixed with appreciation, Haydren's with a little confusion. Geoffrey's knuckles whitened on the back of the chair he was grasping. As Sarah enjoyed their reactions, they slowly lowered themselves into their seats.

"That was you?" Haydren asked.

"And you're...Rinc Nain?" Geoffrey asked, noting her rich red hair and glistening onyx eyebrows.

"Thank you," Pladt said, noting her gentle smile, and nose that was a little too wide to be impish, but only barely.

Sarah passed over the first two remarks, and smiled at Pladt. "You're welcome," she replied. "Definitely be more careful in the future, though. I may not be around next time."

"A Rinc Nain who uses magic?" Geoffrey said, refusing to be ignored. "A woman?"

"We do exist," Sarah replied, her eyes strained.

Geoffrey paused. "You know those are the words of the God."

Haydren glared at him. "Geoffrey, if we might? I want her help, even if you would rather argue with her."

"What do you seek?" Sarah asked, locking her gaze onto Haydren's face.

"We're going to Frecksshire," he replied. "Hauten said you might know the best way to get there."

She smiled. "There aren't many ways," she said. "Oh, if only all problems were so easily solved. Fūnik is your route, unless you want to take a boat from Werinin to Estwind."

"We can't go back to Werinin," Haydren said softly.

"Oh?"

Haydren smiled gently. "We don't know you well enough yet," he said.

Sarah considered him for some moments. "If it helps," she said finally, leaning forward, "I work for the Earl of Frecksshire."

"What were you doing here?" Haydren asked, surprised and a little suspicious.

"Scouting the Kalen Woods," Sarah replied smoothly. "We had gotten reports that the woods were nearing Quaran. Earl Durdamon sent me to investigate in case it threatened Frecksshire."

Haydren cleared his throat. "'Nearing'?"

"Well, clearly our reports were understated."

"Clearly. When do you return?"

"Within a few days," she replied. "Whether Earl Durdamon would accept some of your companions, generous as they are," she said with an appreciative glance at Pladt, "well...we have to try to get through Fūnik first."

"No one goes through Fūnik," a new, deep voice said, standing near them. They glanced up in surprise. "I'm sorry to overhear," said a tall man who carried his bulk in his chest and shoulders. "But you would make it outside Fūnik only to turn around and come back."

"What do you mean?" Sarah demanded. "I came through easily enough."

"When?" the man asked, raising an eyebrow.

"T-two weeks ago," Sarah replied, faltering. "The beasts went south, after the attack, didn't they."

The man nodded, confirming her suspicions. "Five days ago, an army of wolves, kobolds, hellhounds, and goblins cut off the border. Kelian is isolated from the west, now. Better for us, I say."

He saluted with his mug and walked back to his table in a corner. Sarah steepled her fingers against her lips. Haydren exchanged glances with Geoffrey and Pladt. If soldiers were stationed inside a border, it was because their king owned the land. But who could be king of an army of beasts?

"I need to return immediately," Sarah said, lowering her hands. "I cannot spend the time going to Werinin. Alone I might get through the lines around Fūnik, but I would not dare Kalen by myself. Will you travel with me? We might both make it through faster than any other route."

Haydren glanced at Geoffrey and Pladt. Both looks told him they had not decided. "Give us the evening," he said.

"I leave tomorrow morning," she replied, rising from her seat. "Meet me here, if you will." She dropped a coin onto the table and strode to the stairs, disappearing up to the second floor.

The three companions slid out their chairs and exited the tavern.

"I think this is the best way," Haydren said as soon as they were outside. He began walking to the shop Hauten had pointed out earlier, stopping short when Pladt and Geoffrey both remained in the street. "Do you have a better one?" Haydren asked. "Werinin? The three of us trying to sneak past a beast army that did this?" He gestured to the broken landscape surrounding them.

"They alone didn't do this," Geoffrey said. "Whatever came out of those woods was powerful enough to flatten everything that wasn't solid stone, and you propose marching into it without a second thought."

"I have—second, third, even fourth times. I just don't know what else to do," he said wearily. "Hauten said people went in."

"A lot of them didn't come back," Pladt said quietly.

"And do you know why?" Haydren asked. "For certain? Did they come out somewhere else, like Frecksshire?"

Pladt shrugged, looking off to the walls. Haydren gazed at Geoffrey with a single question on his face.

Finally, Geoffrey nodded. "Very well," he said. "If Pladt is still up for it?"

Pladt looked at the both of them. "We go straight through?"

Haydren shrugged. "Hopefully."

"See, that's what I don't like," Pladt replied, jabbing a finger at him. "The 'hopefully' part." He sighed, glancing again around the barren castle. "But I'm in."

They continued toward the shop. "Pladt, this 'Kirrin'..." Haydren said.

"My uncle," Pladt affirmed. "My grandparents were not terribly creative. Kirrin, Kerrik, and Ketter; Ketter died as a child, and Kirrin remained when my father moved us back to Werine."

"Maybe he will give us a better price, then," Geoffrey suggested.

Pladt shook his head. "I got the impression Kirrin was not pleased that Kerrik abandoned Quaran."

"Splendid," Haydren replied.

Though charred, the door to the shop opened easily. The interior was well lit, and they could hear grunts and banging coming from the rear.

"Kirrin?" Haydren called.

One final grunt and clatter. "Yeah?" came a thick voice from behind a low counter.

"We need some supplies," Haydren called back. "We're traveling through the Forest, and Hauten said you could help us out."

A tall, broad man who reminded Haydren of Kitrel plus thirty years emerged from the back room, wiping filthy hands on an equally filthy rag. He wore a heavy leather apron over what used to be a white shirt, and black trousers. He was bald, and he scowled when he saw Pladt.

"Hi," Pladt said with a wave.

"How's your father?" Kirrin asked gruffly.

"He's doing well," Pladt replied.

"What do you want with the Forest?"

"We want to travel through it, to Frecksshire," Haydren replied.

"Hmm," Kirrin grunted, and began ticking off fingers and gesturing around the shop. "Take a couple of torches, about five cans of fuel—of course Pladt already has arrows. Probably should take some dried food though, critters can come scarce in the woods. And take this tap, and a bowl."

"Why a tap and a bowl?" Haydren asked.

"When you stop to rest for a period—you might call it night, though you probably won't be able to tell—take the tap—"

Haydren held up a hand to interrupt him. "Why not?"

Kirrin's hands dropped to his side. "The foliage is thick enough that trees that are cut down don't actually fall down, right?" he said. "Anyway, pound the tap into a tree, sit the bowl under it. By the time you're ready to move, you should have collected a bit of sap. It'll burn, but not by itself. Mix it with the fuel, about three parts sap to one part fuel. There's no way you'll carry enough fuel alone to get you through. And you could still run out."

"What?" Pladt interjected.

"But it's the best you can do," Kirrin finished.

"What if we put in more sap?" Haydren asked.

"Then your flame won't light up the torch it's burning in," Kirrin replied. "Add too much, you've wasted fuel because it won't even light."

"What about water?" Haydren asked.

Kirrin blinked. "Um..."

"Travelers in the forest don't take water?" Haydren prodded.

"Sure," Kirrin said. "They're just not in there long enough to need more than they can carry. But I imagine there's streams in the woods, still."

Pladt turned and laid a hand on Haydren's arm. "So, I've been thinking about this whole plan…"

"How much is it for everything?" Geoffrey asked.

Kirrin shrugged. "Call it three hundred."

"Three hundred?" Haydren and Geoffrey chorused.

"Fuel isn't cheap," Kirrin replied flatly. "Though you're welcome to try the other shops."

"Oh, is that it?" Geoffrey asked. "As long as you can get away with it, then."

Kirrin's hand flashed upward, and he slapped the rag onto the counter. "This forest threatens my home as well!" he thundered. "Do you really think I'm concerned with profits when no one can even buy anything?"

"You said yourself fuel wasn't cheap," Haydren replied.

Kirrin glared at him. "I've already received the shipment on credit. I'm not even paying the seller back with what I'm asking for it. So do you want my help or not?"

Haydren bowed his head. Geoffrey, too, found it difficult to look Kirrin in the eyes. Haydren glanced at Pladt.

"Pladt, do you—?"

Pladt's hand lifted, and a bag of coins arced toward Kirrin. It landed heavily in his opened palms, and he bounced it up and down.

"There's more than three in here," he said.

"Is there?" Pladt asked. "I'm pretty sure I counted out what you should need."

Kirrin weighed the bag again, then tucked it in his belt. "Take what you need," he said.

After they thanked him, he returned to the back room, and the three took the suggested items. The sun was sinking over the tree-lined wall when they exited the shop and returned to The Burrow. After packing, Haydren met Sarah as she was returning to her room.

"We're going with you, through the Woods," he said. "We've already gotten supplies for the four of us."

"Very well." She paused. "I saved your friend's life, but I don't actually know your names."

"Haydren," he replied. "The one you saved is Pladt, and the other is Geoffrey."

"Does he hate women, or just magic-users?" she asked quietly.

"I have no idea who he hates," Haydren replied. "But I believe he loves the God of All."

Sarah nodded once. "Magic-users, then, at the least. Thank you, and I'll see you in the morning."

Haydren returned to the room he shared with Geoffrey. By pure accident, he was sure, their window looked out at the doomed wall. He watched as the sun lowered, its piercing rays setting fire to the malevolent forest for a time. But once the light fell behind the devouring leaves they leapt out in violent silhouette, the jagged lower jaw of of an enormous beast.

He shuddered, glanced at Geoffrey who sat chewing his lip. "What is it?" Haydren asked.

Geoffrey looked up. "Earlier, though it was just past midday, it was...lifeless. No one was picking through the ruins, trying to rebuild or salvage any part of it."

"It's a heavy blow, I guess."

Geoffrey shook his head. "But to not even send out word of what had happened? They simply wait, for what? For anonymous death? For a miracle from heaven?"

Haydren snorted as he sat on the bed. "I thought that's what you believed in?"

Geoffrey gazed out the window. "Not like that. Miracles still require motion. The God can multiply our efforts, but nothing multiplied by infinity is still nothing." He picked at his finger. "But, Haydren...why have there been no merchants in a week, as if they knew not to come here? Why did an army utterly destroy the castle, then take up defensive positions against the west—as if they worried help might come from there?"

Haydren sighed. "Yeah."

Neither of them could answer, and neither could sleep for some time.

They met in the common room next morning. Haydren was glad to see Sarah had changed into practical traveling leathers—well-made ones, at that. If the Forest was anything like he thought, loose clothing would be quickly torn to shreds.

Someone had spread the word that travelers were entering the woods, and when the four exited the strangely deserted tavern they saw the tattered remnants of the citizenry gathered to send them off. Pladt was smiling as he squinted into the sun.

"This is more like it," Pladt said. "Just like in the plays."

They started for the gates, but the people turned them toward the west wall. "Derayus," said a man—middle-aged Haydren guessed, with greasy black hair that pulled back to a short ponytail—who came up to them and shook each of their hands as they walked. "Something like the governor, but I'm not sure of what exactly. Thank you for taking this harrowing journey into the woods."

"We need to get to Frecksshire," Haydren said simply. "We couldn't see a better route."

"Of course, of course. Well said. But while you're in there, if you find anything—"

"We will," Haydren promised.

"Well done, well done. Thank you again." Derayus paused as they continued walking. "Are you sending your horses anywhere?"

Haydren bit his lip. "If you have anyone you can send to the Earl, to let him know what happened here, you may use the horses," Haydren replied.

Pladt gazed at him wide-eyed. "Just make sure they get back to Kerrik Grecce in Werine at some point."

"Brilliant. Well done!" Derayus exulted. He stopped and turned to the crowd, caught himself, and hurried to walk beside Haydren. He beamed the rest of the way to the wall.

There, Haydren found himself at a dark hole where the beasts had evidently first broken through. "You haven't covered it?"

"The beasts left, southward," Derayus replied.

"We heard," Haydren muttered.

"Well, they could have broken right back through anything we did to block it up. They bored through earth the first time."

Haydren glanced at the hole, then up, his breath catching in his throat. The wall towered over him, and above even that, the branches of the Northern Forest threatened to come down and consume not only him but the entire castle as well. To his left, a blackened spar leaned over, ready to fall and crush him and he would be powerless to prevent it. He looked down at the hole, dark as the sun was bright, and all he could see was the gaping door of a shack with a mastiff hidden inside and Guntsen behind him saying he needn't worry about anything anymore. The crowd pressed behind him, just as Guntsen had, ready to throw him into the hole for their own amusement and desperate salvation. But it was not they who pressed him, but he who must voluntarily crawl through the darkness and into the bowels of the Forest, and do it to escape the spar and the wall and the branches. He must throw himself in, and hope to be able to fight his way back out.

He rubbed his chest as he thought again of Fūnik, far to the south: it would take a month, with the Forest always looming on one side and the eastern province on the other. A beast army would likely be waiting for them. And they would have to pass, announced, into Frecksshire. But if they made it through the Forest alive, would that not raise some eyebrows, at least? Haydren set his jaw.

"We'll tie your packs," Derayus said. "Take the rope, and pull everything through once you reach the other side. And good luck."

Pladt stood by and watched as Haydren lowered himself into the hole, then Geoffrey and Sarah. He came last, grasping the end of the rope. When he reached the bottom, he had to crawl on hands and knees through a tunnel. He could almost feel the weight of the wall above him, and prayed that it would not suddenly collapse.

Ahead was pitch blackness, though he could hear the others scraping through the dirt ahead of them. "Why didn't we bring a torch?" Haydren bellowed suddenly.

"It is a straight shot through to the forest," Geoffrey replied. "Do we need one yet?"

"It would be nice," Haydren replied, his voice shaking a little.

"Haydren," Pladt called forward. "Are you okay?"

Haydren growled. "Yeah, fine. Ow!"

"What is it?" Geoffrey asked tensely.

"I found the end of the tunnel. Looks like we have to climb up and out. I can feel some sort of steps leading out, but I can't see any light from above. They must have a cover on it."

Pladt continued forward, keeping his fist tight on the rope. It went taught suddenly, ripping from his hand. He cursed quietly, feeling behind him for the end. He found it, and pulled; he could feel the packs dragging through the tunnel behind him, and he hauled on the rope.

"Pladt, are you there?" Geoffrey asked.

"The rope is too short," Pladt replied. "I'm pulling the packs through now."

"Well we're out. Come up when you're done," Geoffrey replied.

Pladt glanced up, realizing suddenly that Geoffrey's voice came from above. He reached over with his other hand, feeling the cool earthen step that was cut into the ground.

"Oh," he said. "Okay." He could not even see the outline of an opening above him.

"And hurry up!" Haydren whispered desperately.

Sarah's voice floated gently down: "Haydren, what's wrong?"

Pladt hauled faster, till finally the packs bumped into his feet. With the loose end of the rope in his fist, he crawled up the steps. He could hear Haydren breathing rapidly above him. Suddenly, when his hand sought the next step, it slammed down instead upon the firm ground of the forest floor. His companions' breathing was next to him, and he could hear the faint washing of wind over treetops.

But still he could see nothing.

IO

TURNS

"You play with this man's life!"
"I said nothing to him."
"Exactly."
"I see Haydren is not alone in his darkness, then."

27 Tetsamon 1319 — Spring

"**G**et a torch out, quick!" Haydren whispered hoarsely as soon as he heard Pladt's hand thump against the ground.

"Well hang on," came the reply from the darkness. Haydren heard the packs bumping up the stairs, and grunts of effort from Pladt.

A hand laid against Haydren's arm, and he swiped at it frantically, as at a moth fluttering in his ear. "Take it easy, Haydren," Geoffrey's murmured. "We'll be fine for now."

Haydren's hand went to his sword, and he bobbed on the balls of his feet. The smell of cedar, though softer and more sweet, filled his flaring nostrils. He could hear Pladt wrestling with the packs and the rope, and then rummaging through one.

"Aha," Pladt said. Tin rattled, and metal struck against metal. Sparks erupted, settling on a fuel-soaked ball of cloth that rested in the basket of a torch. The glow spread, but not far: Pladt's triumphant face was lit, but the shadows of Geoffrey's face gave him an eerily grotesque mask.

Pladt handed the torch to Haydren. Another scrape, and fire bloomed on the second torch. The light surged, met the glow from Haydren's torch, and shrank back. The four companions were now well-lit, though the forest off the path remained in shadow. With the light from the final two torches, the growth of vines and trees assaulting the west wall of Quaran could be seen faintly at the edge of the glow.

Haydren turned to survey the rest of the Forest. The stories he had heard growing up led him to envision a tangled, choked wood that must be hacked through with a blade. What lay before him instead was quite the opposite.

If there existed a cathedral of earth and wood, it was here. The sanctuary floor of loose dirt spread beyond the torchlight, swept clean of undergrowth. Columns grew as spear-like tree-trunks, a measured four paces between each, supporting a formless ceiling too far overhead to see. Though he knew it was early morning outside, there was not so much as a pinpoint of light in the canopy above to prove it. Before him, the aisle of packed dirt ran as straight as any road carved by man.

"We'll have to walk close together," Geoffrey said, raising his torch.

"At least we came out on a trail," Pladt said as he stood.

"The beasts probably formed it," Haydren replied. "When they came to assault the castle."

Pladt swallowed, forcing a grin. "They're not still in here, right?"

Geoffrey turned from surveying the path and eyeballed Pladt. "Maybe not them: probably others. We should be on our way."

Haydren nodded, and shouldered his pack. "I'll take the lead. Geoffrey, take the rear since Pladt will not be as effective in close quarters."

Geoffrey's eyes glistened as he flicked them toward Sarah. She watched Haydren, a silent question in her cocked eyebrow.

"Right," Haydren said, twisting his mouth. "Um..."

"By all means, take the lead," she said, gesturing forward. "I'll walk in front of Pladt: fewer people to get in his way when creatures come from behind us."

"Do you think—?"

"That they'll see our torches before we see them?" she asked with an honest smile. "I would be certain of it. And these beasts are smart enough to attack from behind."

"Can't you make magical light or something for us?" Pladt asked, frowning into the gloom.

"I control air," she replied. "Is light, air?"

"It's in the air," Pladt replied with a shrug.

She smiled. "It's not air."

"What about blowing the leaves off the top?" Pladt asked.

Geoffrey growled. "Stop playing with what you don't know, Pladt. Our torches burn precious fuel."

With a deep breath, Haydren turned. The light spread only a few steps before him, and glistened darkly off the tree-trunks barely further than that. Grasping his sword firmly with his left hand, Haydren struck off.

They had made it only a few hundred steps when Haydren encountered a path intersecting theirs. He paused at it, waiting for the others to come up beside him. He thrust his torch down each way. They ran, as near as he could tell, straight to either side. The intersection was a perfect cross. Haydren turned.

"Straight through?" he asked. He received non-committal shrugs in return.

As they walked, Haydren glanced side to side, peering into the depths of the blackness in an attempt to see something, anything, that might give him some information. What information he sought, he did not know. But he was already growing weary of the unending darkness.

At the edge of his torchlight, another intersection came into view. He paused once again, and Sarah came up beside him.

"Perhaps we should start marking these," Haydren said, looking up and down the intersecting path. It was identical, and in fact could have been the exact same intersection they had passed before.

"It can't have curved so quickly, though." The question was clear even in her statement.

"A sharp curve, we may see," Geoffrey replied. "But without walking further apart, a gradual curve will certainly go unnoticed."

Haydren pulled out the dagger, the red pitted metal catching the torchlight and reflecting it in shards across the ground. His eyes hesitated on it, then he strode to the other side of the intersection and peeled two strips of bark from the tree, and laid them at its base in the shape of an arrow pointing down the path they picked.

The further they went, the deeper they sank into timelessness. Their feet found a rhythm, and the path circled below them. Intersections rose, passed, and disappeared. When they were hungry, they ate. They grew tired, and slept. But they could not track the sun or moon, and they could not keep count of the paths that crossed their route: those seemed to come more slowly, or the company grew tired more swiftly—whichever it was, eventually an entire cycle would go by with no path but the one they trod.

"There's no life here," Pladt said wearily one evening as they ate sausage and cheese, their chewing the only noise to be heard.

"There are trees," Haydren replied, though he knew what the archer meant. The trees did not have branches, and no breeze stirred their tops. There was no undergrowth, anywhere. No animals had been seen or heard since they entered the woods.

"It's not even that," Pladt said, pausing in his meal to gaze into the depths around them. "There's something else not here, but I can't place it."

Everyone else grew silent, final bites forgotten as they tried to sense what Pladt did. The rush of torches grew in their ears. Haydren rubbed his chin with a knuckle.

"There's no insects," Sarah said quietly, and everyone blinked. She was looking at the torches, where no moths flitted. The tree trunks' smooth bark showed no signs of borers, and no spiderweb had pulled against their faces as they had walked.

Pladt was the first to resume eating. "Good riddance," he said, but his tone bespoke the unease they all felt.

Their packs grew lighter, though the bulk of what diminished was precious water and fuel. Using Kirrin's trick, the fuel dissipated slowly, but their water skins drained at an alarming rate.

"If we slip through this entire forest without issue," Haydren said, one night as they prepared to sleep, "I wonder if we could have made it through the lines around Fūnik, too."

Sarah shook her head. "More likely the Forest emptied of beasts, and went south after Quaran. I believe that risk was still greater."

"Is that what you do for the Earl of Frecksshire?" Haydren asked. "Assess risks?"

Sarah considered him out of the corner of her eye. "Not exactly," she said, finally. "Or, not entirely. I was sent east to try to determine if the Woods were magical."

Haydren looked impressed. "Are they?"

Sarah shrugged, then glanced around them. "Standing outside of them? I would say no. There are many, completely natural reasons why a forest grows and expands, lies dormant for a time, and continues to grow at some later point." She hugged her knees as her gaze continued to rove. "Inside? I don't see how they aren't. The life and light that exist in every other forest...well, it exists in every other forest. It's part of it, somehow. The deeper the dark the less growth. Sure, there's no life here, as we've noticed. But with this little life there should be *no* life, not even the woods themselves."

"Do you study such things a lot?" Geoffrey asked.

"I have lived a lot," Sarah replied, a grin creeping onto her face. "And I've traveled a lot, and observed a lot. I only *study* magic. But enough observation is like study, just not as condensed."

"Seems like you would need a lot of time," Pladt said. "My father taught me a lot, but even he didn't know that much about the woods."

"Given a few more years, I'm sure he would have," Sarah replied.

Her words hung for a little while as Pladt and Haydren exchanged glances. Geoffrey's eyes remained on hers. Finally Pladt blurted out: "How old are you?"

"You shouldn't ask a woman her age, Pladt," she chided, smiling.

"Okay," he said. "If you were a tree, and we cut you down and counted your rings, how many rings would you have?"

Sarah laughed outright. Haydren chuckled, and even Geoffrey smiled.

"It's a legitimate question!"

"I was born in 1255," she replied.

The forest grew silent, and the men's faces went slack. Sarah arched an eyebrow at Geoffrey as they calculated.

"You're sixty-four?" Pladt exclaimed.

"You look thirty, at best," Haydren said.

"Well, I'm only sixty-three just yet; but thank you," Sarah replied, ducking her head with a smile.

"Magic," Geoffrey said, a slight growl to his voice.

Sarah sighed. "Geoffrey..." she said, then shook her head. "Affinity with an element gives life to the user," she said in normal tones. "But, use it too much, it takes the vitality back. Many magic-users—overly greedy ones, that is—end up with very average lifespans: sixty to eighty years. Others who only use it when necessary can live...some have lived upwards of three hundred years."

"And where do you fall?" Geoffrey asked.

"Oh, I should have died at twenty," she said, a spark in her eye. "Death won't touch me for how evil I am."

"Pladt, take the first watch, please," Haydren interjected, as Geoffrey's mouth opened to retort. "Let's get some rest, shall we?" he asked, glaring at the old soldier. "All of us," he added with a swift glance as Sarah's mouth opened as well.

⸺◦⸺

The first sign of life in the forest came the next day. As they walked, and Pladt's eyes roved—almost mechanically by now for lack of anything to truly grasp his attention—something to their right nudged his vision. But it took two more glances that way for him to realize it was indeed a pair of dots that were a glossier black than the rest of the blackness.

He nearly dropped his torch as he hissed an intake of breath, pulling everyone up short. A low snarl, almost contemplative, and he did drop it as his fingers scrabbled for his bow and arrows.

"Beast!" he managed, bringing the bow up but not loosing the arrow. His constant practice on the Shores took over: he had no real target yet.

"Where?" Haydren said as swords glided from sheaths.

"Where I'm looking," Pladt grated. Another pair of glossy specks appeared next to the first, the inky blackness swirling in them. Whatever it was, it was tall. Even with Pladt's rangy figure, he was nearly looking straight into...whatever it was.

"Behind!" Geoffrey whispered. Pladt turned, and at the very edge of the light a wolf froze in mid-step.

He had seen wolves before, but that had been in moonlight, and they had been only half the size of the creature which breathed at him now. He drew his arrow to his cheek. The wolf turned out of the light and bounded away. Pladt followed as best he could, waiting for a moment to loose his arrow. The wolf turned again and leapt. He let fly the shaft, but reacted too slowly and the arrow was swallowed by the night. The wolf closed, jaws snapping. Pladt stepped back, kicking the torch into the dirt with a thump and extinguishing it. The light from the other torches reflected off the gleaming teeth of the wolf as it bore down on Pladt.

He tripped as he took another step, his hand grasping wildly for another arrow. Moments before the wolf would have been atop him, it was viciously punched into the ground. Geoffrey put a foot against the wolf's side and thrust downward. Sarah's torch cast the old knight's face in half-light, and his features turned into that of a specter.

"Watch your shafts, archer," Geoffrey rasped. "You must be able to retrieve them."

Pladt gulped, and nodded. He rose shakily to his feet and retrieved his torch. "You reminded me of my father just then, Geoffrey," he said wryly. "See if you can *not* do that again, okay?"

Now in different light, Geoffrey's face returned with the easy smile Pladt knew best. "What do you mean?" Geoffrey asked.

"It was my first battle against a hydra," Pladt said. "We were in a room, and the fire from a burning building outside cast my father's face in a similar light. Some of my shots had missed, and he warned me much like you did."

"How old were you?" Sarah asked.

"Eleven."

"A little young, weren't you?" Haydren muttered, scanning the forest around them.

"Werine couldn't wait for me to grow up," Pladt replied quietly.

Haydren's gaze returned to his companions as he frowned.

"I never saw the other creature, Pladt," he said. "Would it not have attacked while we were distracted?"

Pladt lit his torch, and held it outward: he could see no sign of the swirling eyes. He looked at Haydren. "It's gone," he said.

Haydren sheathed his sword and gazed at his companions. "They will know we're here, now. We must be more vigilant from now on."

⸺◆⸺

Though there were no immediate attacks, his words remained true as shadows of shapes began to collect around them like moths not yet entering the lamplight. First two, then a third, then five. By the time they were preparing to rest, a dozen creatures accompanied them, just out of reach of the light, and just out of Pladt's ability to discourage them. They did not attack. They rarely made noise, except small welcoming howls and yips as more joined the bizarre parade.

Through their watches, the wolves remained. A few left, but came back shortly with dragging sounds—hunting. What they hunted, no one guessed, for whatever life they found came nowhere near the torches.

Hours seemed to drag by, broken only by the sounds of bones breaking and sinews tearing as the wolves enjoyed their meals. It was probably not a full night they spent, as each member of the party woke the next in line to watch when they could bear the noises no longer.

"Can't you do anything?" Haydren grated at Sarah as they prepared to leave: more wolves had arrived in the last watch, and he had woken to a pack of at least two dozen surrounding them.

"I should really be able to see them, to do something, but..." She trailed off as her eyes narrowed, then suddenly went wide and she gaped.

Haydren frowned. "What?"

"I can't..." She took a breath. "I can't feel anything."

Haydren cocked his head. Everyone was looking at her, now. "What?"

"I can't feel air," she said in a whisper. "My affinity. How did I miss it? But it's not there." Her eyes rolled in their sockets, the whites flashing in the torchlight.

"Well, isn't that just—"

"Haydren! I can't feel the air!" she said, turning on him. Her eyes held not condemnation, but terror. "I have no weapon, and I have no magic, and there are almost thirty wolves out there!"

Something in Haydren broke, a little bit. "Okay," he said, more gently, placing his hands on her shoulders. "Okay. They're not attacking anyway. Here." He held out his dagger, but she did not take it—she seemed not to even notice it. "Sarah, take this at least. Has anything like this happened before?"

She shook her head, accepting the dagger without looking at it. Her eyes glistened as her lips trembled.

"Sarah, we need to keep going, okay?" Haydren continued. "Keep a torch for Pladt. He may need to draw quickly. And let us know if anything changes."

"Okay," she whispered, taking a firmer grip on the dagger.

Haydren turned toward Geoffrey, widening his eyes incredulously. Geoffrey cocked his head slightly in agreement, though his eyes on Sarah mirrored only compassion.

They set off, their lethal entourage quickly falling into step, still silent and out of reach.

By the time the first attack came, the number of wolves surrounding them could not be counted for how much they darted around one another. Pladt drew quickly, and though Sarah dropped one of the torches and the already-unsteady light around them wavered even more, his shaft flew true and into the lead wolf. Two more came on from different quarters, meeting Follus and flame, and death. The companions turned in place, waiting for more attack, but none came. It seemed the wolves watched them—silent and still, considering the effects of their swift assault.

Finally, as their breathing slowed, the companions cleaned and sheathed weapons. Sarah's white knuckles pinked, and she put away the dagger with a tremulous exhale.

"Do you think we should just extinguish one of the torches, save the fuel by only burning three?" Pladt asked. "I think I can walk close enough to Sarah to see, but she won't be in the way if this happens again."

"We were trying to spread out to see if the trail turned," Haydren replied.

"And I haven't noticed a thing," Pladt said flatly. "So why continue to waste fuel?"

Geoffrey glanced at Haydren with an eyebrow cocked in agreement. Sarah only gazed outward. Haydren nodded. "You're probably right. Go ahead, Pladt."

Pladt dropped the oil-soaked ball into the dirt, rolling it with his boot to extinguish it. The lessening of light was nearly unnoticeable as they walked on.

Three more quick attacks came before they stopped to rest, each a little more successful than the previous.

"They're learning," Haydren noted as they finished another cold meal, eyeing the blinking, glowing lights that surrounded them. "That last one nearly got to me." He drew a long breath, glancing over his companions. His gaze lingered a little longer and a little more sourly on Sarah. It could not be her fault that she was almost entirely defenseless, but she had swayed their decision to go through the woods.

He sighed. Perhaps not, he allowed generously: on the map, it did appear to be the shortest route to Frecksshire, and he did desperately want to get there.

But at least if they had gone south, they would have been through the lines in a matter of miles. Now, he had no idea where in the Forest they were, or what day it was, or how far they had traveled, or—most importantly—how far they had left to go. If the trail indeed ran straight, and they did not turn off it, surely they had to be close.

The next raid came early, before they had finished packing. This time it let up only briefly, allowing them to scramble together the rest of their packs before forcing them down the trail.

Haydren struck down another wolf, his torch faltering in his hand. He glanced up in time to see Sarah make a feeble backhand, turning the wolf a little aside, but not killing it. Geoffrey came to her rescue as more wolves broke away from the outer circle.

"We have to run!" Haydren called. "Sarah and Pladt: in front. Our swords are better, and we may need Pladt's arrows in the days to come." Even as he said it, he recognized the staggering optimism in the words. He brushed that aside as his companions obeyed.

Haydren handed off his torch to Pladt. "Don't go too far ahead," he said as they ran on. "But I want both hands for my blade."

There were too soon nips at their heels, and the swordsmen turned to fend off the attack. Pladt and Sarah watched, Sarah's hand flexing on the dagger as she shifted her weight.

Three wolves were killed, and they ran forward until again forced to turn.

"They're really trying, today," Haydren grunted, his sword in an arc that barely kept jaws away from his shoulder. Geoffrey said nothing, his attention on his task.

"Haydren," Pladt said, trembling.

Haydren glanced at him: both he and Sarah were now almost beside them, though they were not looking at the wolves bearing down on them from the pack. Haydren had only time to notice they were gazing further ahead in horror before he brought his sword up to halt a flying leap aimed straight for his throat.

The force knocked him backward a few steps, past his companions. He swung downward, and the wolf yelped and was silent. A second leapt at him, and he staggered further back, into a tree.

His right foot shifted for balance, but it struck the same tree. His weight carried him backward and he pressed harder against the trunk.

Except the trees in the Forest were thin: this one was broad, and was not as hard as wood. Haydren stepped hurriedly forward, spearing the wolf before turning around to see what he had found—what Sarah and Pladt had been staring at.

He first noticed they were at another intersection, and wondered if they could somehow mark this before moving on. The next thing he saw was a pair of swirling black eyes regarding him with stone solemnity. Haydren blinked, realizing a massive shape blocked their path: a canine of absurd proportions, almost pony-sized, with short-cropped ash-gray fur. It growled deep in its throat, though its jaws remained shut.

Another head and pair of glossy eyes appeared to the right and a little above the first, gazing at his companions. A third, to the left, turned too and looked at Haydren. Thick necks almost entirely of rippling muscle held them, all three looming from the same great body.

"Geoffrey," Haydren said, shockingly calm. "We should go."

The thrum of swinging Follus ceased, and Haydren registered no further sound of running wolf's paws. The creature in front of Haydren remained still, its gazes locked on them even as they edged sideways, taking the path to the left.

The companions backed down the trail, step by quiet, careful step, until the beast was swallowed by the darkness of the Forest.

The companions stopped, watching the spot where the thing had been, having the awareness finally to gasp for breath. The Forest was gone completely silent; the wolves had disappeared.

The darkness behind them shifted, and the great beast charged. With a cry, swords came up. It leapt over them all with a great bark and bound, then sprinted into the dark of the Forest on the other side.

When Haydren turned back, a host of glistening eyes held their places in a line. There would be no going back to that crossroad.

They had been forced to turn, and their water and food were running low.

II

STRAITS

"I do not know how you do this."
"Years of practice; ages, even."
"Without knowing the future."
"Correct."

1319 — Spring

"I feel like Sir Cullins should have told me about something like that," Haydren murmured.

They were catching their breath, wondering if moving on would mean coming across that beast again.

Geoffrey snorted. "He probably told you to stay out of these woods at all costs."

Haydren was silent. Sir Cullins had said that. "I still don't know how we stumbled across it. How deep in the Forest are we, you know? And for it to be right there?" Haydren asked.

"We didn't find it," Pladt mumbled. "It's been following us."

Haydren rounded on him. "What?"

"I had been seeing something," Pladt said, swallowing. "Something that preceded every attack."

"Why haven't you said anything, then?" Haydren asked, sheathing his sword.

"Because I didn't know what it was!" Pladt replied. He sighed, glancing into the woods where the eyes had disappeared. "Before the very first attack, do you remember?"

Haydren nodded. "You said there was a beast, but I didn't see it."

"I saw what I thought was a bit of shiny darkness in the middle of the rest of this wretched, light-consuming darkness," Pladt said bitterly. "Not like the way the wolves' eyes shine; this was as though the eyeball was black: 'liquid, shiny black, like obsidian, reflecting the light in six points.' I only ever saw one pair. But that isn't the legend." He glanced around the forest. Haydren could only imagine what it was like for the archer, who was used to shooting at hydras out in the open. Not waiting for a creature to appear suddenly, and perhaps too close for a bow to be effective.

"Pladt, what legend?" Geoffrey asked.

"I heard it when I lived in Quaran," he replied. "Back then, patrols went into the Forest a lot. But if a hundred went in, they found nothing; if ten went in..." He shook his head. "They wouldn't come out."

"Except one time," Sarah murmured, glancing between Haydren and Pladt.

"Except one time," Pladt confirmed, "one man did. He was almost out of his mind with terror, and babbling nonsense. We finally pieced together something of a story, about the Cerberus of Kalen."

"I have heard of the creature, though not his association with the Kalen," Geoffrey replied. "There are some in remote regions of Andelen—far from men, though, after Sheppar, Kinnig of Andelen, cleared most of the man-hunting beasts away from their cities."

"Well, this one protects this city," Pladt replied. "It's said he guards the forest, allowing none to escape once they are inside."

"This would have been good information two weeks ago," Haydren said bitterly. "You, too, knew what he was talking about," he threw at the sorceress.

"As Pladt said, it was a legend, nothing more," Sarah said.

"Apparently those in Quaran were not convinced of its truth, either," Geoffrey responded.

"Who would be?" Pladt asked. "Who would believe the rantings of a lunatic about a three-headed creature that roams the entire breadth of the forest and kills those who enter in? You've seen the maps: the forest is enormous. According to the legend, it doesn't matter where you enter. How could such a creature know, and find you?"

"You did not believe it either," Haydren said.

Pladt shook his head. "I'd forgotten about it. But I also haven't lived in the shadow of the forest for almost fifteen years. It came back to me just now."

"Those in Quaran probably hoped we wouldn't come across it," Geoffrey added.

"So," Haydren said, planting his feet. "Not only must we be assaulted by wolves at every hour, but we are to be stalked by a three-headed beast that will ensure, should we find the exit, that we will not escape." He pursed his lips and nodded. "This was a really good idea."

He turned without another word, held out his torch, and strode off.

"We'll turn right at the next crossroads, if we can," he called back. "Then hopefully right again, and left—and hope it works that easily."

But they found no crossroads the rest of that day. No beasts had harried them, at least; but perhaps they no longer needed to.

"Their entire purpose may have been to keep us moving to the Cerberus," Haydren agreed at Geoffrey's suggestion.

"But if he's been following us," Pladt began.

Haydren shook his head. "There's no way to know, and no use in thinking about it."

Everyone stared at him until he noticed. "What?"

"That never stopped you before," Pladt said, his lips quirking with suppressed laughter.

Haydren gave him a withering look, though he grinned in spite of himself. "Maybe these woods are making me mad," he said. He pulled out a water-skin and shook it. "Uh oh." He glanced around the circle.

"I *might* have run out a while ago," Pladt said.

Sarah shrugged. "I have one or two left, I think."

Geoffrey shook his head grimly.

"Well," Haydren said after a moment. "I guess there's nothing for that, either. We find water soon, or we don't."

Sarah redistributed hers—she had nearly two full skins—and they arranged their beds, thankful it was cool in the forest.

But for two more cycles, they had found neither water nor a crossroad. The skins were empty and wrung, and even with cool air their throats itched and their tongues stuck in their mouths.

Finally, ahead of them, they saw a crossroad. Haydren jogged up to it, prepared to cut another arrow, when suddenly he glanced down. Undisturbed at the base of the tree were two strips of bark in the shape of an arrow, pointing down the path to the left of their line of travel.

"It curved," Haydren said, his head bowed. His shoulders shook in silent laughter. "But to where? This could be any one of the crossroads we passed since entering."

A dread silence fell. Haydren chewed his lip, his mind racing a hundred different directions. He had to lead. He had to choose. They could not stay where they were, that much was certain. If they went backward—it might be another week or more before they returned to Quaran. Forward on their current heading might take them northward into the very heart of the forest, and they did not have the torch-fuel for such a journey, and they could not last much longer without water.

Sarah approached and knelt beside him. "You're not alone, here," she said. "Don't take all the blame for every wrong turn."

"Oh, I definitely don't blame myself for forgetting the Cerberus," Haydren shot back.

Sarah gazed at him the way Mickel would have for such a statement, but her voice remained gentle. "Because Pladt and I are sure to survive even if the rest of you die?" she asked. "Our slip could cost us exactly as much as you. But I've seen you work, Haydren. I know you're thinking something right now: act on it."

Haydren scrubbed his forehead with the back of his hand and sighed. "How much fuel do we have left?" he asked as he stood.

"We should have something like two weeks' worth," Pladt replied.

Sarah rose, smiling.

Haydren picked up his torch. "We're going to turn left here," he said. "We'll judge about how far the next intersection is. Remember they were closer together at first? At some point, hopefully near the apex of the curve, we'll make a right turn. That would point us toward the western edge of the forest. And hopefully water appears somewhere along the way, that we didn't notice before." He shook his head. This wasn't going to work, but what other choices did they have?

No one spoke. It was as close to agreement as seemed likely for now, so he turned left onto the path they had already trod. He cut off another strip of bark, laying it beside the arrow.

"First intersection," he said. "If we somehow circle back again, we'll know which intersection it is."

They passed no more crosses before they stopped for the night. Wherever the loop had brought them, they were still deep in the forest. Studying his maps during his watch, Haydren felt confident he knew the general size of the loop in the trail, and determined to make the right turn at the third intersection.

The next morning, while rummaging through his fuel tins, Geoffrey found a water-skin that had somehow slipped to the bottom of his pack. They managed to ration it, despite parched mouths, and went on for two more days. At the appropriate intersection, with only a brief sigh, Haydren moved the arrow to mark their turn westward. His companions said nothing as they struck off down the new path.

Ten cycles after meeting the Cerberus, above the rushing of the torches, a new sound rose almost to a roar. Swords were drawn as the sound of a thousand wings echoed through the woods, though not a speck of dirt moved as by a wind, and all was stillness around them. The darkness of the canopy thickened and spread down the trunks, swallowing the trees and the torchlight.

"Sarah?" Haydren asked, instinctively ducking, fearing the void would swallow them by time it reached the ground.

"Well this is new," she replied, her casual tone wavering with the terror they shared.

"Is it magic?"

She remained silent as the forest descended. But it did not snuff the torches as it gleamed against the tree trunks and finally soaked into the earth.

Haydren reached out a finger, touched the trunk, then touched his finger to his tongue. "Grab the taps!" he said quickly.

Pladt swung his pack from his shoulder and searched for the metal spouts. "What is it?" he asked.

Haydren laughed. "It's raining; the water is funneling down the trunks. We have water!"

With broad grins they tapped the trees, driving the taps in just far enough to funnel rain and not sap, and watched as life-giving water dribbled into the waiting skins. When the roar above stopped, they had collected enough for another tightly-rationed week.

As they capped the last skin and put it into their packs, Geoffrey cautioned: "we must be on our way quickly. We're not out of these woods yet."

But as the journey wore on and their fuel tins emptied, their spirits sank from their former high. The attacks had suddenly resumed, heralded as Pladt double-glanced at the familiar swirling obsidian points from the woods beside them.

There was not a circling entourage as before. These wolves would appear straight out of the forest, leaping and snapping—and they were soon joined by kobolds. Pladt had never battled the strange humanoids with dog-like heads. Haydren had only learned of them. Sarah and Geoffrey had not fought ones such as these, who managed with silvery eyes to see as well in the dark as they did in torchlight. The four companions were on constant, wearying vigilance. At any moment, once Pladt spotted the eyes of the Cerberus, their foes could appear. Now, the kobolds would sometimes launch spears at them from beyond the reach of their torches before rushing in with yips and growls and short swords raised. The companions walked with swords drawn, and Pladt kept an arrow nocked, changing strings when he could feel one loosening. If there was any good from these events, it was the implication they had entered a different section of the Forest.

Eight cycles after the rain, they were settled down for another "night." They had discovered through desperation that a taste for—or at least a tolerance of—wolf meat could be gained, though they worried it might only incite further attacks as they sat around their evening meal. The wolves seemed inclined to attack regardless.

Haydren sat by his torch. Geoffrey, Pladt, and Sarah were lying on their blankets, though not under them: if they needed to rise quickly, they did not want to be tangled in bedclothes.

Pladt drew a long sigh. "We're not getting out of here, are we?" he asked, though he kept his eyes closed.

Haydren did not look up. The thought had long been with him since turning. They had been unable to replenish their water. The forest stretched endlessly around them, it seemed. They could not travel a thousand paces without being attacked. And they did not even know if they were going in the right direction. Haydren opened his mouth to reply, could think of nothing to say, and slowly closed it.

"Once, when I was a soldier," Geoffrey began, lying too with his eyes still closed, "we were dispatched to put down a band of rebels calling themselves *Uv Fehn*. They said it translated as 'The End;' I imagine they meant the end of the current ruler, though they might have meant the end of sanity. Either way, winter was well upon us when we left. Upon nearing their stronghold, a blizzard struck, and we could not move through the deep snow. They attacked us in short, fast raids in the night. They had strange devices on their feet, like webbing, which allowed them to walk on the snow; we floundered in it in our iron boots."

Everyone had turned to look at Geoffrey as he spoke. Sarah had a strange, reserved look on her face.

"For weeks they harried us. They killed as little as possible, instead stealing our supplies. The blizzard so blinded us, eventually we had no idea where we were. We thought we were all going to die, too."

"Obviously you didn't," Pladt said, yawning.

Geoffrey chuckled. "You always were astute, Pladt."

"So what happened?"

"After three weeks, they led us out," Geoffrey replied. He paused a moment. "They retreated, or so we thought. Our captain was so blinded by his orders, he followed them, still hoping to kill them or bring them to justice. We argued with him, saying we needed to return to the castle for resupply: fortunately he did not listen to us, and their tracks led us back."

"Why did they do that?" Sarah asked quietly.

"To show us they could do as they pleased, and we could not stop them," Geoffrey replied. "Or, at least, that is what the lord of the manor concluded. A week later, he handed rulership over to one of his counts, a man to whom the rebellion was agreeable. The *Uv Fehn* were never heard from again."

"So these beasts are going to lead us out?" Pladt mumbled, beginning to fall asleep.

"The God knows," Geoffrey replied quietly.

After several moments, the torches' rush and Pladt's snoring were the only sounds in the woods.

"Geoffrey?" Haydren asked quietly.

"Hmm?"

"There never was *Uv Fehn*, was there; you made it up to make us feel better."

Geoffrey was silent. Sarah watched him, her eyes glittering in the torchlight. "Keep watch, Haydren," he said finally, and turned over.

Haydren sighed, gazing into the darkness. Keep watch of what? A Kobold's spear could pin him to a tree before he could see it. He shook his head, and continued watching.

⋯◆⋯

Later in the night, as Sarah was preparing to watch and Geoffrey preparing for sleep, the sorceress glanced a few times at Haydren and Pladt, ensuring they were asleep.

"Geoffrey," she said quietly, "from Haydren's and Pladt's response to your story, I assume that was the first time you've talked about such things to either of them."

Geoffrey continued settling himself and his blankets, but said nothing.

"I seem to recall some stories coming out of Helgsciow about such a band, around that time."

Silence, and stillness.

"It wasn't as clean as you made it sound, though."

More silence. And then: "No."

"Is that why you hate magic so much, and those who use it?"

Geoffrey let out a long sigh. "I do not *hate* those who use it. But the words of the God of All should not be used by those who have so little understanding of it."

"We understand a lot more now than we used to," she replied.

Geoffrey's head twisted to look at her. "How many words?"

Sarah shrugged. "More than several hundred, across all elements."

"And how many words do you know in Rinc Nain? And how much damage do we still do to one another with those words, as well as we know them?"

Sarah did not roll her eyes as much as she was tempted to. "That's not the same, and you know it."

"*You* know it," Geoffrey corrected, and he settled in again. "I do not."

Sarah's mouth twisted, but she made no reply. As Geoffrey's breathing deepened, she wondered whether light *was* air, and could be manipulated. It would be fascinating, if so.

⸺◆⸺

The next morning they were hoisting their packs and trying to prepare themselves for another day, when a shrill cry echoed faintly down the path ahead of them. Everyone but Geoffrey straightened immediately, looking at one another to see if they had heard it, too.

"What is it?" Geoffrey asked. "I've not heard—"

He was cut off by another cry. It was high-pitched, yet muffled, and warbled like someone screaming underwater.

"Macao?" Sarah asked.

"What's that?" Geoffrey asked.

"It's a bird," Pladt replied. "But it lives only on the fringes of forests. Never deep within them."

"Let's go!" Haydren urged. They moved at a fast walk down the path. Haydren, in the lead, noticed the light around them grow suddenly dimmer. He glanced back. Pladt's torch had gone out.

"Relight it!" he said.

Pladt looked at him somberly. "There's no more fuel," he said, casting the used-up fire-ball onto the path.

Haydren pressed his lips together. "Let's continue anyway;. Sarah, since Pladt seems to be able to see the advance warning of...attack"—he did not want to say 'the Cerberus'—"give him your torch: will you be all right without it?"

Sarah handed her torch to Pladt, her mouth set in a grim line. They set off, but the bird had gone silent. By lunch, their spirits were once again at low tide.

As they ate, they watched in numb horror as Geoffrey's torch faded and went out. No sooner had it winked out than Sarah's too began to fade. By the time they set out again, they had only Haydren's torch to guide them.

After walking what seemed a few hours, they came upon another crossroad. Beside it, pointing to their left, was a bark arrow and a number denoting an intersection they had passed three days ago.

As they looked at it, Haydren's torch began to wane. Haydren gazed at the flame befuddled, as if he had forgotten what torches were. He bent down and pressed the shaft into the ground, then sat crosslegged beside it. The single blue flame hovered at the top, held impossibly long upon the horizon as Haydren waited with bated breath. Finally, when he thought it just might defy reality forever, it snuffed out and sank them into total darkness.

Sitting there, Haydren recalled Sir Cullins' mastiff of so many years ago. Despite what seemed impossible at the time, he recognized now how easily he could fight flesh and blood. Even with a simple gardening implement, he had been able to defend himself against a beast well over his size. But this enemy was intangible, insurmountable; there was nothing for him to attack with his sword, nothing against which to defend with a shield. The creatures hidden by the darkness were not hindered by it. It would not be the creatures, ultimately, that would kill them. But this impossible blindness, unassailable, unfathomable, would be their demise.

"Haydren," Sarah said, nearby. Her fingers found his arm, then to his shoulder, and squeezed gently.

You must lead them out. Look up.

Blinking, Haydren looked up. Unlike ever before, the whisper this time rang from the silence like a tolling bell, the echo overpowering and erasing from remembrance the stroke of its inception. It was as if the words sprang into existence from nothing, beginning before time and existing always as fact—and it spoke to him now beyond a whisper and almost like a voice: a voice with authority and knowledge outside of himself.

"Did you say that?" he asked.

"I said your name," she replied uncertainly.

He glanced around. He could sense Pladt and Geoffrey near him, and could hear their breathing. Were they looking around as well? He could not see.

Then, in the corner of his eye, he saw a light. He turned his head toward it, but it dimmed and went out. As his eyes cast downward, it reappeared.

"Is that...?" he muttered. "Pladt, to the right!"

He heard Pladt shift, then gasp. "It's a light!" he whispered hoarsely. "Light, coming through the trees!"

Haydren stood, knocking over his torch. He reached out and grasped Pladt's shoulder. "I cannot see it well," he said. "You must lead the way Pladt. Geoffrey, grab onto Sarah!"

Pladt started off, Haydren shuffling awkwardly behind him. His boots scuffed loose dirt as they left the path. He continued to swivel his head, watching the light brighten as they neared, but also when he viewed it in his peripheral vision. He was familiar with the phenomenon, and had used it to great advantage as a child in Hewolucs playing Seek the Traitor. Now, it just might save their lives.

As the utter darkness became a gloom, he saw to their left an inky bulk dotted with six obsidian points. He froze, gripping Pladt's shoulder tightly. "Cerberus!" he whispered hoarsely. Then, "run!"

Pladt bolted forward, his shoulder wrenching from Haydren's grasp. Taking hold of Sarah's wrist off his shoulder, Haydren pursued. When he was sure she was following, he released her and made for the light. Through the rush of air in his ears, the tramp of his feet on the earth, and the pounding of his heart, Haydren could hear the Cerberus' growl growing louder, and nearer.

Pladt tore through underbrush, spilling blinding light into the forest. Shielding his eyes, Haydren was close behind. A branch clawed at his pack, refusing to let him escape. It pulled. His feet carried forward, and he was on his back. Geoffrey leapt as Haydren struggled to rise and slipped in a dank pool of muddy water. Sarah glanced back as she waited for Haydren to rise and go on.

They were on the Low Moors, free from the forest. But the Cerberus of Kalen was swiftly closing in.

12

MAGICS

"You could not have foreseen that."
"I only needed to know the one who could."
"Your judgment was not so keen the first time."
"Wasn't it?"

Spring

Haydren turned, facing the dark hole now broken and ragged with vines and branches. He whipped free his sword. Geoffrey was beside him, Follus blade dully gray. Pladt was several paces back, arrow drawn, and Sarah stood with fists clenched and chest heaving. A low growl sounded from the void.

With an animal shout the Cerberus emerged, teeth and fur charging at Haydren. He braced with his sword; three hundred pounds of muscle and hate slammed into him, and he crashed into another mucky puddle.

Pladt's bow twanged, and one head of the beast recoiled with a roar. The second head lashed at Haydren, jaws slavering against his sword, pinned flat side up against his chest. A gust of wind blinded him with dank Moorish water, and as he cried out the Cerberus ducked further out of the gale just as it ceased.

"Get him off of you!" Sarah shouted.

Haydren heard a familiar hum as Geoffrey's sword sliced the air. With a deafening howl the Cerberus leapt away. Haydren made a desperate swipe as the beast slid backward away from Geoffrey's wrath.

Another gust of wind blasted the beast in one of its faces. It growled contempt as it bit Pladt's arrow free from its head. Haydren pushed himself upright, legs shaking as blood pounded through his veins. Another growl from the Cerberus: its eyes flashed and the darkness within them began to swirl.

"Cover your eyes!" Sarah warned. "And don't open them till the shadow passes!"

Haydren reversed his blade along his forearm and buried his eyes in the crook of his elbow just as the Cerberus jutted his heads forward. Immediately, Haydren felt as if he were sinking into thick mud. He struggled to move his legs, but they refused. Over his body the shadow and muck crept. It reached his mouth and tried to force its way in. When it reached his arm, an unseen strength tugged it downward.

"I'm drowning!" Pladt shouted suddenly. "Geoffrey, Hayd—" He cut off, and Haydren heard him splashing through the standing water.

"Pladt, it's not water!" he shouted.

There was a thump, a pause, a splash.

"Strike him with lightning or something!" Haydren shouted to Sarah.

"I have to see him!" she replied, sounding far away and above him. Haydren gritted his teeth and waited for the mud to go away.

It did, in a flash, as if someone had yanked him instantly from the puddle in which he'd been floundering. He lowered his arm. Pladt lay near the edge of the forest, unmoving. Haydren whispered quickly that the archer was still alive.

The Cerberus charged. Lightning pounded behind the charging beast. Haydren stepped back, and gasped in surprise as his leg gave way beneath him, betraying him. He kept his sword up, timing a vicious slash perfectly as the beast reached him. The blow turned the Cerberus' head, sapping some of the force and keeping the iron jaws from Haydren's throat as they crashed into his chest.

Geoffrey leapt in again, his blade quivering through space. The beast howled with each stroke. Haydren, flat on his back once more, worked his dagger free and struck over and over.

Then it was off him, limping back to the forest. Haydren leapt up, and with Geoffrey swift behind him, closed with the retreating beast. All the days of hopeless wandering, of incessant attacks and nauseating mortal fear, swept over Haydren and found release in his sword. With one final howl the beast gasped and collapsed. Geoffrey ensured its death with three powerful, severing strokes, and both men stepped back, panting.

"So passes the Cerberus of Kalen," Geoffrey said, glancing down at his sword now covered in thick blood. He knelt beside the carcass, whispering some kind of chant that Haydren did not recognize.

Haydren left him and approached Pladt, his sword tip dragging through the puddles. He paused, afraid to go forward for fear of what he might find. As he looked, he saw Pladt's chest rise and fall. He sighed and knelt down.

"Pladt," he called quietly.

Pladt's eyes fluttered open. He winced and held a hand to his forehead where a welt was forming. "What happened?" he asked.

"You tell me, I just heeded Sarah's warning," Haydren replied.

Pladt squinted and relaxed. "Oh yeah," he said. "The Cerberus can mesmerize its foes with its eyes." He sighed, and with Haydren's help sat up. "My bow?"

Haydren spotted one end of it sticking up from a puddle. It did not appear broken. Haydren returned it for the archer and helped him stand.

"Is he all right?" Sarah asked as they walked back. Haydren failed to hide his glower.

"I see you have your magic back," he said.

"I believe it was the Cerberus," Sarah replied. "As soon as Pladt hit him with the arrow, my connection with the element returned."

"Too bad your aim is not as good as Pladt's," he couldn't help but mutter.

"It's difficult..." She pressed her lips together. "I'm sorry. I had hoped to blind him with the water, so he couldn't launch his mesmerizing attack."

"Yet more information that would have been handy earlier." Haydren shut his jaw with a click, and decided not to pursue the topic.

"I'll be fine," Pladt replied, rubbing his forehead with a smile.

Geoffrey stood, produced a rag, and swiped the muck from his sword. "We should be going," he said. "It's growing late, and creatures are sure to roam from the woods at night."

"Let them," Haydren replied. "One look at that Cerberus should make them think again about attacking." Even so, he turned and led them west as he too cleaned his sword. He glanced once at Sarah, trying not to feel how useless she was. Pladt's weapon was limited, too. Yet she had not once used magic effectively since joining them, and he couldn't stop a pang of worry that she was not a true sorceress.

Further now from the shadow of the Forest, they walked through tall shocks of moorgrass—a soft, blue grass well fed by water that hid just below the ground's surface. As this water rose to the surface during spring and autumn, sinking the land below a freshwater sea, the name "Low Moors" was given to it. Their route took them between standing water and spongy dirt, the tread of their footsteps releasing an earthy smell like rich mushrooms. Low clouds dimmed the world, and soon opened themselves up with a steady rain. Drawing his hood over his head, Pladt cursed quietly.

"Do we know what day it is?" he asked presently.

"If these clouds pass, I can give us a good guess tonight," Haydren replied. "We will at least know what month it is, and which half of the month."

"I wonder if the year has turned," Pladt mused to himself. He squinted up at the sky and blinked. "Still feels like spring."

As the land darkened, the company managed a makeshift shelter using Geoffrey's and Haydren's scabbards and their nearly-empty packs. The rain slackened, and the clouds to the south broke.

"It's late Elfumon," Haydren said, and pointed. "Zedar still rises early."

"Zedar?" Geoffrey asked.

"The star-pattern that watches over Deewan," Sarah murmured.

"I remember that story!" Pladt said, brightening.

"So we were in the forest nearly a month?" Geoffrey asked.

"The Deewanians were under siege and in fear of imminent destruction," Pladt continued. "The Burieng Army was reported to be marching through the mountains with a force ten times what the Deewanians could hope to withstand."

"They were Keste at that time, Pladt," Sarah corrected with a smile. "It wasn't Deewan for several hundred years yet."

"To answer your question, Geoffrey," Haydren said, "probably. We had ten days' worth of pure fuel when we left, right? We certainly used all of it up."

"Right!" Pladt replied. Then he scowled. "My father always told it to me as Deewanians though."

Geoffrey shook his head. "Perhaps you should tell this story so we can have it done with?" he said to Sarah.

"Oh, he has everything else right," Sarah admitted. "The Keste were an ancient people, skilled in smithing, poetry—and song, especially. The King, Burieng, feared their sword-making skills. So he sent his army to destroy them. They used to be spread through most of the Endolin Mountains. Eventually, they lived only in a hidden village deep in the mountains—the village of Deewan, that Pladt is getting confused by.

"When Burieng found them, he sent his whole army to destroy them. They had nowhere left to go, so they waited and whispered. Then, a day before the army reached the village, a legendary Kesten commander appeared and led the villagers to a sweeping victory. He was supposed to have died long before, and according to the legend, it seemed during that battle that no sword or spear could touch him. As soon as the fight was over and the Endolins retreated, he disappeared again. That night, as they sang their victory songs around their fires, a new star-pattern appeared in the sky over Deewan."

"Zedar?" Geoffrey said.

Sarah nodded. "If you follow Zedar, you will find the village. If you come against it to destroy it, so the legend goes, Zedar will protect it. It no longer needs to remain hidden."

"And," Haydren concluded, "the pattern rises early in winter and spring. In summer, it is nearer the horizon and rises late. If I had the proper instrument, I could tell us what day it was in Elfumon, within a day or two."

"Quite a handy skill," Geoffrey noted.

Haydren's gaze diverted to the horizon, to the distant past. "One of many that Sir Cullins gave me," he said.

After a quick meal of cold meat, they drifted to sleep leaving Pladt to keep watch. Despite the promising break to the south, the clouds remained next morning. In time, their boots became perpetually soggy. Rain descended in waves, and the hidden sun gave them little guidance. Then, above the rain, they heard the rushing of heavy water. Cocking his head, Haydren glanced backward.

"The Tundee," Sarah said. Pladt and Geoffrey looked blankly at her. "It's a river that flows south, from the Seven Headwaters in the Kalen Woods to the Shadowmere," she explained. "If we are so near it, it means we came out of the woods as close to Frecksshire as we possibly could."

"So does that mean we'll be out of these rotten puddles soon?" Pladt asked, grimacing as he sank ankle-deep yet again.

Sarah paused, then nodded. "By tonight, actually," she replied.

From under their feet rose something of a path, ancient and worn and running westward. Broken in many places, it nevertheless offered them dry ground to walk on.

"This is more like it," Pladt said to no one in particular. "I mean, it rains all the time in Werine. Puddles, though... But look, it almost looks like the moors are strewn with jewels, doesn't it?"

Haydren cocked an eyebrow at Geoffrey, who grinned. Just then Pladt missed a step and splashed in a puddle with a groan. "Adventures are always better beside a fire," he muttered. He cleared his throat. "So how about these Inns?"

Haydren laughed. Geoffrey growled. "Well they're not going to be so near the forest are they?" Geoffrey asked irritably.

Pladt shrugged. "You got my hopes up is all I'm saying."

"A fool's hope, maybe," Geoffrey replied.

"Those disappeared fifteen years ago," Sarah said from the head of the party. "They were not as defensible as we hoped, and after a few attacks quickly went away."

"They couldn't build up their defenses?" Geoffrey asked.

"It didn't matter," Sarah replied. "Once your patrons have all been slaughtered by goblins, your promise of hospitality and protection rings...hollow."

"So what does that say for travelers without walls of any kind?" Pladt muttered.

"They had better keep a sharp eye," Geoffrey said, placing a hand on his sword-hilt.

The rushing water grew louder, and the land split before them. A rotting wooden bridge hung over the Tundee as it roared a few feet below.

"This is an illusion, right?" Haydren asked, staring dumbly at the crossing. "There's no chance our torches went out just in time to see a peephole in the forest wall, which happens to let out abreast of what must be the only bridge to cross the river for miles."

"I didn't even know this was here," Sarah replied.

"Perhaps someone is watching out for us," Geoffrey said.

Haydren looked scornfully at Geoffrey. "Zedar, perhaps?"

"The God of All sees all, Haydren."

"And he controls all, too?"

"As he wishes."

"Sounds like a fickle deity," Haydren replied.

Sarah glanced between them as Geoffrey turned to face him more squarely. "The God's will is perfect, Haydren. We cannot question it."

Haydren peered at the rushing waters beneath the bridge. "I can," he murmured.

Pladt looked skeptically at the rotting wood and gaping planks. "Hopefully his will is holding up this bridge," he said.

"Hopefully deceptively strong wood and nails are holding up this bridge," Haydren retorted, echoing Pladt's fears. When he stepped one foot on its deck it shifted, but only a little. "One at a time," he said, stepping onto it fully. Haydren crossed quickly. Sarah followed next, then Geoffrey. Pladt, slowly and more gingerly, came last. When he jumped the last few paces to the bank, the bridge collapsed into the river with a groan. Pladt retreated, swallowing hard as he watched the timber spin away in the flood.

"Apparently there was neither strong wood nor nails," Geoffrey said quietly.

Haydren glared at him. "Why is there a path leading apparently nowhere?" Haydren asked suddenly. "Running east just to die out in the...what, the Low Moors, and ending at the Woods?"

Sarah shrugged. "I would assume it used to be a road going from Frecksshire to Quaran, before the Forest got there," she said.

"Hey!" Pladt said brightly, playfully backhanding Haydren's shoulder. "We did go straight through!"

Geoffrey laughed. Haydren shook his head with a grin, and looked at Sarah with begrudging acceptance. "I guess that makes sense," he said.

Sarah kept her own smile low as they turned and continued walking.

The path continued westward, and the companions followed. The puddles thinned, and by supper the land had risen and become dry, and the path unbroken. The grass was shorter and scrubbier, too, and capable of cutting un-booted flesh. The wind rose out of the north, bringing wispy scents of sage along their itinerant streams. By night, the sky had been swept clean, and the company fell asleep on firm, dry ground under a brilliant canopy of stars.

Geoffrey had the morning watch, and when Haydren woke he was squatting beside an iron bowl as it sat over a crackling fire. Steam rose from it, and a scent of roasted meat filled Haydren's nostrils.

"Pladt, see if you can get us some water, would you?" Geoffrey asked, seemingly unaware Haydren was awake. "I saw a fold of ground not too far to the south. There might be a stream at its bottom."

There was a pause. "Geoffrey, remember last time...?"

"Gremlins are plains' creatures," Sarah replied. "You should be fine out here."

"Okay." Pladt rose to his feet and pointed. "That way?" he asked.

Geoffrey blinked at him. "The sun rises in the east, Pladt."

Pladt turned and looked at the sun and squinted. He turned a little dizzily and nodded. "Right," he said, striking off southward.

"Sarah, can you go with him?"

"As you wish," she replied, rising smoothly.

Geoffrey watched them go, shaking his head. He stirred the bowl a few times, tapped the contents off the spoon and then rang it against the side.

Geoffrey called out as he turned. "Hayd—! Oh, you are already awake. Soup is about ready."

"Is it?" he asked rhetorically, pushing himself to a sitting position. "What's in it?"

"Meat, spices, herbs," Geoffrey replied with a shrug.

"All of which you found where?"

Geoffrey shrugged again, glancing out over the moors. "Around."

"Around my pack?" Haydren pressed. "You made sure you knew what was what, right?"

Geoffrey thrust the spoon back into the bowl and gazed at Haydren. "You understand I have cooked my own meals for thirty years before you came to me, yes?"

Haydren looked at the pot, then glanced back up at Geoffrey. "Good ones?" he asked.

Geoffrey retrieved the spoon and pulled back as if to throw it at Haydren, who ducked, laughing.

"Don't let me interrupt you boys," Sarah said, smiling as she came up behind Haydren.

"I thought you were supposed to be watching over Pladt?" Haydren asked, his laughter ending abruptly as his head snapped around to look at her.

She chuckled. "I didn't mean to startle you," she said, coming over and sitting on her bedroll by the fire. Despite the bright sun rising, a spring chill clung to the moors. "There's nothing out here, not close and not dangerous."

"You know that, how?"

"The wind knows to what it gives breath," she replied. "A good breeze can help in many ways."

"Is that why you haven't been able to cast much magic?" Haydren asked, his tone tinged at the edges with disgust.

"I've told you why—"

"And against the Cerberus?" Haydren pressed. "You nearly blinded me with water. Was the best you could do was summon a breeze?" The tinge had spread, and hardened his gaze at the sorceress.

Sarah pulled a tough blade of grass from the earth and picked at its fibers. "I'm sorry I can't seem to do more," she replied. "Maybe if

Hyrdenark had let me in Tamecal—"

Geoffrey muttered. "That den of witches..."

"Oh say something different, would you?" she said, casting the knight a withering look. "Hyrdenark, maybe; but the rest are good magic-users."

Geoffrey smirked, but remained silent.

"Who's Hyrdenark?" Haydren asked.

"Headmaster," Sarah replied. "He decides who learns there and who doesn't. But that kin of witches wouldn't let his own daughter into Tamecal, even if she were to be the next Maerlyn of Gunda."

"Got water," Pladt said, walking up with his arms barely containing the bulging water-skins. Geoffrey took one, drank, and began ladling out the soup.

"Who were you talking about?" Pladt asked, receiving his bowl from Geoffrey and seating himself.

"A few people," she said with a smile.

"Marrylinn?"

"Maerlyn," Sarah said. "A sorceress from Gunda in the Clanaso Islands and one of the most powerful magic-users ever."

"I saw a statue of her, in Irii on Gunda, when I came through the Clanasoes," Geoffrey said, settling back with his own stew. "Did I pick the right spices, Haydren?"

Haydren grinned and nodded.

"I envy you that," Sarah said, sitting forward with sparkling eyes. "I came through Mayta, though."

Geoffrey looked at her with a baffled smile. "It's a gondola-ride away!"

"Well I didn't know it was there, did I?"

"Had she gone to Tamecal?" Haydren asked.

"No, I said she was a sorceress," Sarah replied slowly, then smiled. "Right: sorceresses and sorcerers are magic-users who haven't gone to Tamecal. If you complete the training there, then you become a wizard. Mages, because they don't focus on one element, don't go to the school at all."

"And witches?" Haydren asked.

"Are usually old women in cheap tents who know how to mix plants together to make smoke." Sarah shook herself, then smiled. "Sorry. Some people compare the two, when anyone can learn witches' potions. You can't teach an affinity to an element."

Geoffrey cleared his throat. "Is everyone done eating yet?" he asked, scrubbing his bowl with some moorgrass. "We may as well get moving. There are days left to reach Frecksshire and beds."

The others fell silent, hurriedly scooping the soup—now quite cool—into their mouths.

Their surroundings changed little, and they walked through the day with only one pause for lunch—a peccary strangely alone that Pladt managed to shoot with his bow as they walked. After days of wolf meat, it was heartily welcomed into their stomachs. That night, Geoffrey had taken the middle watch, and sat beside the fire as his companions slept. He gazed into the flames, remembering a similar fire many years ago, in a different country, surrounded by far different companions. He fingered the hilt of his sword—what had been a gift so long ago.

He had been traveling with Haydren for over two months now, and he was far too old a hare for the things which they had gone through already. He had no idea what might come in the future. If he could find asylum in this land, free from the Cariste side of the country forever, he did not see how he could do anything but bid Haydren fare well on the remainder of his journey. A journey which, Geoffrey realized, was probably unclear even in Haydren's mind.

He looked up as an old man stepped into the firelight. Geoffrey gripped his sword. Without looking, the old man held up a hand to stop him. Geoffrey settled back, baffled.

"Good evening, Geoffrey," the man said.

"You know my name?"

The man smiled as his hand dropped back into the folds of his red robe. "Of course." He stepped forward, leaning on a tall, gnarled staff, his gaze still bent on the fire.

"I do not know yours," Geoffrey said.

"You may call me Godfrind," the man replied.

Geoffrey nodded. "Welcome to my fire, Godfrind. I am sorry I have no food to offer you."

"Is it your fire, Geoffrey?" Godfrind asked, looking at him sharply. "I thought you said this was Haydren's journey?"

"How do you know these things?" Geoffrey asked, leaning forward. He had meant to stand up, but something kept him seated.

"I have been watching Haydren for many years, now," Godfrind replied, glancing at Haydren's sleeping form. "Long before he arrived here, in Burieng."

"You know who his parents are, then?" Geoffrey asked.

"Of course," Godfrind replied. "But he cannot get that information from me. He must discover it on his own."

"Tell me why I should not kill you right now!" Geoffrey thundered, still seated.

Godfrind looked at him calmly. "Tell me why you should," he said.

"You have information this boy desperately seeks, yet you will not give it to him?" Geoffrey said. "Do you know what we have gone through? How important this is to him that he would risk himself entirely for it? And you tell me you could let him know right now?"

"I just told you I could not tell him," Godfrind replied. "You have great concern for him, then?"

"No one should be tormented as he is," Geoffrey growled. "I have seen it in his eyes too many times. Oh, men need to be driven, but not by things such as that."

"Yet you will not see that urgent need gone from his eyes?"

Geoffrey sat back. How *did* this man know these things? "I have not decided," he said sullenly. "I hoped he would find whom he sought in Frecksshire."

Godfrind nodded slowly, returning his gaze to the fire. "He will not," he said quietly. "He has other choices yet to make." Godfrind was silent for long moments. He turned from the fire, glancing at Geoffrey. "So long, old knight," he said.

"If I see you again, I may yet kill you," Geoffrey growled.

Godfrind stopped short, inspecting Geoffrey critically. "If you see me again, Geoffrey, I think you will not even remember me."

"What?"

"As soon as I leave this fire, you will forget me."

"Then why tell me these things?" Geoffrey asked.

"Oh, you will remember your own words," Godfrind replied. "Though you will only think of them as your thoughts. Without my name, you will not remember me or anything I say."

"You gave me your name."

Godfrind chuckled warmly. "Geoffrey, Geoffrey," he chided. "You of all people should recognize: words are not always what they seem."

Geoffrey's mind raced as the strange man neared the edge of the night. In sudden realization, he leapt to his feet. "You said only I *may call you* Godfrind!" he shouted.

Godfrind chuckled as he reached the edge of the firelight. The darkness swallowed him and his laughter.

Geoffrey stood, sword in hand. Had he heard something? He could see nothing in the night. He turned and looked at the fire, and something tugged at his mind. What had he been thinking about? He sensed, somehow, that Frecksshire would not be the end of their journey.

"The God of All," he whispered, lowering himself back to the ground. "Give me strength for what must be done."

◆

The days that followed were blessedly warm and free. No creatures attacked them, and they ate their meals and walked the miles in relative ease. A slight breeze most days carried them toward Frecksshire. Between Pladt's bow and Geoffrey's cooking, they ate well, though they still longed for a bed made of something besides earth.

On the eighth day since exiting the forest, the clouds massed overhead once more. By evening the rains began, and after dinner it was falling in blinding sheets. They set up their makeshift shelter and settled in for the night, hoping the storm would break before morning.

Night came on, and they were lost in darkness. Geoffrey managed a small fire, setting it close enough to the tent that the wind carried the rain beyond the toddling flames. Geoffrey and Haydren took the opportunity to oil their swords against the damp as they discussed the night's plans.

To the north, a large pillar of white light thrust skyward and the sky blazed brilliant orange. From the pillar strode forth the silhouette of a massive dragon.

Gripping his sword tightly, Haydren sucked in his breath. Pladt yelped and dove further into the tent. Sarah watched him go, then turned her eyes back to the black form. Geoffrey rose and faced the pillar of light. The rain slackened, then stopped.

"Will we never be free?" Haydren said, rising to his feet.

"Perhaps not this night," Geoffrey replied.

The pillar extinguished as suddenly as it appeared, and darkness descended. The clouds scudded from before the moon, giving them enough light to see the land around them: the dragon could not be seen.

"Pladt, come out. We're not staying here," Haydren said. "We're going to make for Frecksshire castle. It shouldn't be far."

"I thought Paolound had died," Pladt muttered, coming out from under the tent. "Didn't Ell kill him a long time ago?"

"How do you know it's him?" Geoffrey asked.

"How many dragons live in Frecksshire?" Pladt responded derisively, handing Haydren his scabbard. "One," he answered his own question, handing Geoffrey his scabbard. "One in Frecksshire, one in the Endolin Mountains." He separated the packs and began stuffing them with their meager supplies. "That's if Ell hasn't killed Kaoleyn as well."

"He doesn't seem to have killed Paolound," Sarah replied.

Pladt stopped packing for a moment to glower at her.

"I've seen this before, usually closer to Jyunta," she continued, taking her pack from Pladt. "Durdamon was going to look into it soon, but couldn't find anyone able to."

"So exactly how many epithetic creatures are on this continent?" Geoffrey asked. "We have already defeated the Cerberus of Kalen; now we must fight the dragon of Frecksshire? I should have stayed in Andelen."

"Why didn't you?" Haydren asked, shouldering his pack.

Geoffrey ignored the question, taking his pack from the archer as well. "Let's be off."

Haydren kicked out the fire, and they set out westward, walking swiftly and quietly. They did not make it very far.

Flames shot out of the darkness, cutting off the path before them with a sheet of fire. They turned swiftly, Geoffrey and Haydren drawing their swords as Pladt nocked an arrow. Sarah gazed at the dragon, her lips ready but no spell coming. Up-lighted by the fire, Paolound's crimson head loomed on his long neck above the reach of the flames. With a cry, he reared back, preparing another blast of his fatal breath.

With a shout, Geoffrey shoved Pladt aside as he, Sarah, and Haydren ran the opposite direction. Fire spewed behind them, setting the grass ablaze. Pladt rolled to his feet, aimed, and shot. The arrow barely penetrated the dragon's thick hide, and fell to the ground when Paolound turned to glare at the archer. Distracted by his piercing gaze, Pladt didn't see the tail swinging out of the night. It caught him at chest-height, leveling him and knocking the breath from his lungs.

Sarah muttered under her breath, and a keening wind blasted the dragon in the face. As he recoiled with a muffled cry, Geoffrey rushed forward with blade upraised. A blast of fire coughed from the dragon's mouth, and the wind ceased with a moan. Paolound regarded Geoffrey contemptuously, swiping at him with his left forepaw. Geoffrey swung angrily. Settling back on his haunches, Paolound's left hand swept harmlessly over Geoffrey's head, and his right came from behind the knight and snatched him up into the air, gripping him tightly.

"No!" Haydren shouted. Paolound gazed at him, and squeezed. Geoffrey cried out and went limp. Paolound casually tossed him aside, and he thudded lifelessly to the ground.

A blast of lightning arced from the skies, and Paolound writhed out of the way. His tail lashed again, and the sorceress went sprawling with a cry that cut off abruptly as she hit the ground, her head cracking off a small stone.

Fighting tears, Haydren's knuckles went white on his sword. The flames near the hilt budded and fluttered with light, and he felt an energy pulsing through it. Gritting his teeth, Haydren approached the dragon, sword before him, trying to watch the dragon's every shift.

Paolound reared back and spewed flame, sending Haydren scurrying. The tail swept in again. Haydren leapt over it, but landed awkwardly. In that instant, Paolound backhanded him. His sword flew from his grasp as he sprawled. Paolound slithered overtop him, a paw clamping down on his chest, the dragon's terrible jaws hanging over him.

Haydren squirmed for breath as the dragon pressed downward. He grasped and pried at the dragon's fingers, immovable as iron. Haydren's chest-plate gave way, and his lungs refused to expand. Blackness crept into his vision as his thoughts rippled.

Geoffrey. The mysterious knight from Hodp, from nowhere. Whatever his journey through life had been, it was over now. Had the God of All seen to this, as well? Could Haydren fault the man for the source of his courage? The dragon's hot breath washed over Haydren, invading his nostrils.

Pladt. The famed archer, whose father had not wanted him to come on this journey anyway, would now die, if he had not already. Would he have chosen this? Or was it enough for him to pick his route one day at a time? The stench of the dragon's breath forced its way into his mind, choking his thoughts as the veil of blackness drew tighter.

Sarah. The sorceress seemed at peace with who she was, though lately something stilled her features in internal scrutiny. Her features would be interminably still, now. Haydren managed a small gasp, and the veil stayed its progress.

Maerie; Mickel. The kindly parents who had raised him would have no idea what had become of him—if Guntsen had not already killed them for whatever malicious reasons the spoiled Earl thought best. They had given him love at every turn, as much as any two parents could.

A tear of frustration rolled down Haydren's cheek. *Kitrel.* His only friend for so many years, killed by beasts. Perhaps Haydren's own father and mother had been killed by bandits. Quaran was destroyed. So much destruction and death plagued the country, and no one seemed able to quell it.

The veil slid onward. Haydren's head rolled sideways, and he saw his sword lying nearby, pulsing with a dim red glow. He released Paolound's foot and flopped his hand outward. His fingers brushed the metal, but came up short. A word leapt unbidden to his mind, impressing itself firmly upon his lips. Squeezing his eyes shut, he strained. His fingers fell onto the handle, and he spoke the word: the metal felt cold, then burning hot.

Paolound screamed in what could only be called terror, deafening Haydren as the veil nearly closed in entirety. The weight lifted from his chest, and air swirled into his lungs as he gasped.

Haydren's eyes flew open. His sword burned a brilliant red, brighter and purer than the dragon's flames surrounding them. Paolound was fleeing to the north, still howling in animal fright. Haydren's head fell backward, and the word he had spoken drifted from his thoughts. Pladt was running up to him; the darkness closed in, shutting him out from the world.

<hr>

Guntsen entered the cold room where Lasserain and his Earl, Hsroang Jgei, were conferring. If he had known he would have to encounter Jgei, Guntsen might never have agreed to Lasserain's plan. There was something horrendously wrong with the southern Earl. What it was, Guntsen couldn't place. But there was a constant stillness to Jgei that was entirely unnatural. Perhaps it was the fact that Jgei was only ever seen encased in armor.

"What do you want?" Guntsen asked, keeping his eyes warily off Jgei.

Lasserain straightened slowly—and painfully? Guntsen wondered.

When he spoke, his voice was strained. "The time has come. I cannot delay any longer, or much might be lost."

Guntsen eyed him, a smile playing at the corner of his lips. "Haydren is a tricky one, isn't he," he said.

Lasserain's eyes hardened, and Guntsen's mouth split open as something invisible forced its way in, straining the hinges of his jaw. A cry was forced immediately back into his throat.

"Your land is mine," Lasserain said, the strain in his voice suddenly gone. "You will stay here from now on, and you will daily give me reasons not to kill you." The mage turned to Jgei. "Send your troops, with this letter signed by the Earl of Kelian."

I never signed a letter! Guntsen tried to shout, but only tears came out of his eyes as his jaw creaked impossibly wider.

"Oh, he hasn't signed it yet," Lasserain muttered, glancing over the parchment before him. He gazed at Guntsen for several long moments. "Well come over here and sign it," he said, twisting the parchment toward him. He slid forward an ink bottle, and Jgei held out a quill.

Guntsen took several teetering steps forward. Gingerly he took the quill, dipped, and signed crudely. He dropped the quill. Lasserain inspected the letter, cocking his head.

"I suppose that should work," he said, and Guntsen's mouth was finally able to close.

"Anything else?" the young Earl whimpered, keeping his jaw as still as possible.

Lasserain sat back heavily, grasping his temples. Guntsen felt a heavy, gauntleted hand on his shoulder. Jgei's obsidian eyes met his from the deeps of a thick helm.

Guntsen could not suppress his shudder, and he left the room as quickly as possible. His reign had lasted a few months, anyway.

13

BURDENS

"Be careful you do not stoke your fire too high."

"That was nothing."
"He almost died. Again."
"He has greater obstacles than death to surmount."

Elfumon 1319 — Spring

Haydren awoke still on his back. Pladt hovered over him. His chest was tight, pained him when he gasped. His armor pressed in odd places around his torso. Pladt leaned over, fumbling with something on Haydren's side.

The laces of his armor popped loose, and his chest expanded fully. Haydren gulped, closing his eyes as cool air refreshed his lungs.

"Geoffrey," he said.

"I'll live," came the reply.

Haydren's eyes snapped open, and with Pladt's help he sat up. Geoffrey was propped up a few paces away, lips twisted between a grimace and a smile. Sarah's forehead was wrapped in a cloth, and she smiled reassuringly. "We both will, thanks to Sage Pladt, here," she said.

"'Sage'?" Haydren repeated.

"Well, I was working on it, before you two came along," Pladt replied, gently probing under Haydren's shirt. "Does that hurt?"

Haydren grunted. "Not terribly."

"Hmm," Pladt murmured. "Then you're better off than Geoffrey. Paolound cracked four of his ribs."

"His claws had the advantage of puncturing my armor," Geoffrey muttered.

"And you, Sarah?"

"I'll be all right," she said with a slight nod and a smile. "It bled a lot, which Pladt says is better, somehow."

"I thought you had died, Geoffrey," Haydren replied. "The force that he squeezed you, and threw you aside... And when you hit the ground, Sarah..."

"I wished, when he threw me, that I had," Geoffrey said with a wry grin. "How close are we to Frecksshire?"

"A few hours," Sarah replied.

Haydren winced as Pladt prodded again. He shook his head to Pladt's inquiring gaze.

"I'll need something for these ribs," Geoffrey said.

"I have spices still in my pack," Pladt replied, inadequately hiding a smile. Haydren grinned. Geoffrey remained silent. "Can't you mix something up, Haydren?" Pladt asked, clearing his throat. "Like you did for my ears?"

"Not here," Haydren replied.

"The Sage in Frecksshire will," Geoffrey said with a grunt.

"I imagine ten Sages in Frecksshire will have what you need," Haydren replied drily. "It is the largest castle in the breadth of Burieng. They say eagles leave their aeries in the Endolins to nest in its spires."

Sarah laughed aloud, but quickly covered her mouth. "Sorry," she said, grinning. "It's different when you've lived here as long as I have. It doesn't seem worth such eloquence."

Pladt glanced at her. "I would think we would have seen some farmhouses by now," he said.

She shook her head. "Not many places in the moors can support a farm. There are more around Frecksshire itself." She smiled. "Don't worry, Pladt. You'll see plenty of farmland tomorrow morning."

"Should we be safe enough to sleep here tonight?" he asked, rising finally.

Sarah shrugged. "Ask Haydren; it was his sword that frightened off the dragon."

Pladt shuddered. "I have never heard such a noise in my life. The first instant I thought it was you, Haydren." He paused, gazing inward. "I almost threw up. Then I realized it was Paolound, and I almost had a different accident." He fought off a grin. "What kind of sword is that?"

"I told you before, I don't know," Haydren replied. "I don't even know what kind of metal this is." He picked the sword up off the ground and glanced down its length. The fire was extinguished now, and it looked as it had before. The handle was still a little warm, but only as warm as if he had been holding it for some time.

"The flames look, I don't know..." Pladt cocked his head to the side. "Did you notice Mount Thoret to the east whenever you came to Werine? Did you see it in the morning when the top is lit by the sun?" Haydren nodded. "Those flames remind me of that," Pladt concluded with a nod. "I mean, up close, they look like what Thoret looks like far away. I've never actually been to the mountain itself."

"Interesting," Haydren murmured.

—◆—

Pladt awoke them all the next morning. Between Geoffrey's fidgeting and Haydren rolling every now and again off his injured side with a gasp, he had not slept. He checked their bandages quickly during breakfast. It felt good to be useful again, more useful than trying to shoot animals zipping in and out of torchlight. He wished now that he could have spent more time learning Sage-craft—surely the moors held something that could be helpful with Geoffrey and Sarah's scars.

They all shrugged him off though. The company set out, Pladt trailing behind again. He tried to keep his head up—they were on a grand adventure, after all—but no one seemed interested in conversation or remarking on the weather or countryside. Adventures were to be shared, he thought. It was no fun being awestruck alone.

True to Sarah's word, just as the towers of Frecksshire rose into view, gently rolling swells covered in just-sprouting wheat and corn stretched out before them. The path they were on met with the broad cut that was King's Highway, which stretched from the northern port of Estwind, down the length of Coberan Province, then east of the Shadowmere to the castle of Fūnik. The four descended the short dike that lined both sides of the road, and turned north. They had come upon the road at the top of a large swell that gave them enough of a vantage point to see several miles ahead of them. On the horizon, just now becoming visible, were the walls of Frecksshire.

Pladt's head came back up, his gloominess evaporating with such a view. Even from this distance, it seemed Haydren's rumors were not exaggerated. Great towers loomed over the walls, with banners impossibly high and snapping in the wind. Normally, a castle's inner keep was the highest structure. But though a flag could be made out at this distance, the building itself did not rise over the outer parapet.

Dotting the landscape, a number of small homes could be seen living in the shadow of the great castle. Farmers like ants were crawling across the deep brown fields, and smoke from cooking fires spiraled above several chimneys. Far ahead, just below the horizon, a detachment of soldiers on horses could be seen riding down the road toward them.

Pladt's steps faltered. Surely such a troop was not on their way to welcome them. Four armed people entering the Earl's domain unannounced? Junei would not have been pleased. Pladt continued to follow Haydren and the others, walking just to one side in case he needed room to shoot.

The horsemen galloped on, throwing clods of mud behind them. At the bottom of the depression between the swells they met, and the lead soldier held up a hand to halt his detachment in front of the companions. Though Pladt couldn't see the man's face between the bars of the helmet, his posture did not seem happy.

"Tho kegen kernet Kalen held?" the man demanded in a language Pladt didn't recognize—likely Rinc Nain. His voice was muffled behind the great, impenetrable helm. The other guards in phalanx blocked the road.

"Do," Sarah retorted, stepping forward. *"Hodl akna et'Quaran dafa Fūnik avod ruus: Ih av Sarah Lasgadt."*

Pladt glanced quickly between the two. Surely Sarah didn't mean to pick a fight with these men. They were, after all, on *their* ground. Not to mention Haydren and Geoffrey were wounded!

"Woathod," the soldier replied, lifting his visor. *"Ih riddi tun gurtho tho. Ih av Ketteran, Hagta it'Kinnligurleth Abta. Jet thol kilfeiti?"*

Pladt wiggled his fingers, itching for his feathers, but he dared not move until Sarah gave some kind of signal. Unless she'd forgotten again that he couldn't speak Rinc Nain.

"Haydren Loren, it'ruusligur Hewolucs; Geoffrey, it'Hodp; jet Pladt Grecce it'Werine," Sarah replied.

The man turned and glanced at his troops. *Now?* Pladt wondered, surreptitious glances at Sarah still yielding no signal. He held his breath, waiting.

When the soldier turned back, his eyes were wide in wonderment. "We did not know it was the archer Grecce who traveled with you," he said—in Cariste—with a hint of awe in his voice. "I am Ketteran, and pleased to meet you," he said.

Pladt was dazed, and a little proud. They had heard of him all the way out here? He was sure his father wouldn't believe him. Did this mean they weren't going to kill him?

Ketteran's gaze shifted. "Geoffrey is an Andelian name, is it not?"

"Just something my parents gave me," Geoffrey replied indifferently.

Ketteran smiled. "You need not be worried around Coberan Province, Geoffrey, as I can imagine you were in Kelian. We are not quite so ill disposed toward Andelen on this half of the continent."

Geoffrey remained silent, but nodded once.

Ketteran returned his gaze to Haydren. "Most of your movements have been observed since entering our lands, young swordsman," he said, his voice a strange mixture of authority and respect. "You have incredible luck, incredible friends, or incredible skill."

"I would like to think I have all three," Haydren replied with a small grin that quickly disappeared. "Especially the first two."

If Ketteran wondered at Geoffrey's glance toward Haydren, he did not show it as he bowed his head in acquiescence. "Perhaps. The Earl would be pleased to see you in any event. *Tatsalch,"* he said, turning slightly to face Sarah, and he continued on in Rinc Nain. Sarah did not respond except to nod once.

"His Grace honors us," Haydren replied. "However, Geoffrey is in need of urgent care. Our fight with the dragon was not without injury."

"His Grace is aware," Ketteran replied. "He will see you in a week, after you have had sufficient time to mend. I am to take you to our best Sage at once."

"We are in his Grace's debt," Haydren said with a short bow.

"You are indeed," Ketteran replied. He lowered his visor once more, and gestured for four un-laden horses to be brought forward. The companions mounted—Geoffrey a little more stiffly than the others—and rode to the castle. Geoffrey's mount was sure-footed and fluid, able to carry him without too much jostling.

Impressive as they seemed at a distance, the walls of Frecksshire were overwhelming up close. Fully thirty feet thick at their base, the walls soared impassively and impossibly upward, and Pladt had to catch himself from falling backward, craning his head as they passed under the gate.

Dwarfed in comparison, though still five or six stories high, the buildings inside the walls choked downward, preventing any good view of the blue sky overhead. The wide streets were clogged with merchants, sellers, farmers, travelers, horses, vendors' stalls, butchers' blood, and slop water. The sea of bodies parted before the gleaming armor of the troops, and closed just as instantly behind with barely a curious glance backward. This was the kind of press Haydren was accustomed to, and he longed to be on his feet among the mass, feeling the bump of the bodies while keeping one firm hand on his coin-purse.

Up the twisting road the procession went until, after several turns, Ketteran stopped before a shop with bundled herbs on the wooden sign above the door. He gestured for the three men to dismount.

"If you go back to the main street," he said, lifting his visor once more to be clearly heard, "you'll find the Dancing Piper, one of the best Inns in Frecksshire. His Grace requested I inform you that if you are searching for anyone, you may find news of them there."

Haydren's breath caught, but if Ketteran understood the message, he hid his knowledge well.

"The keeper knows you are coming," Ketteran continued. "Use your names. In eight days I will come back for you."

"Thank you, Captain," Haydren said. "May I ask one thing?"

"It is the first day of Haschina," Ketteran replied. "You spent five full weeks in the Woods."

"The Earl knows much," Haydren commented.

Ketteran searched Haydren's face a moment, then said simply: "He does." He touched the brim of his visor. "Fare well." The troop turned and clopped slowly away.

Sarah paused and glanced back. "Thank you for seeing me safely back," she said. "Fare well to you, whatever happens next."

"I think you suspect what happens next," Haydren replied.

Sarah cocked her head, then smiled and followed Ketteran without responding.

Haydren turned to his companions. "Shall we?"

The Sage had been forewarned, it seemed, and had the poultice already prepared with instructions written in Cariste and Rinc Nain.

"Do you suppose he knows we're Rinc Nain?" Haydren asked as they left the shop.

Geoffrey smirked. "He does now. But, more likely there are the two major languages in Burieng, and in such a cosmopolitan setting he writes in both, just in case."

They soon reached the Dancing Piper and found the common room packed with guests, and uproariously loud. The walls were lined with benches and long tables, and smaller tables and chairs dotted the main floor. Chandeliers of deer-antler hung by chains from the ceiling, with smaller antlers acting like sconces on black wooden posts.

"Happy New Year!" a stranger shouted as they entered. Three mugs of ale were thrust upon them, with shouts to drink up. Haydren rolled his eyes.

"Our timing is impeccable," he said.

Pladt hoisted his mug. "Absolutely!" he said with a smile. "What other day could we come and get free drinks?"

"You don't think we have more important things to attend to?" Haydren asked in as low a shout as he could muster while still being heard by the jovial archer.

"Bah!" Pladt returned, pausing to take a long swallow, to the cheers of many of the patrons. "Save it for Haschina second." He gave Haydren a meaningful glance. "It will quiet down a lot by then," he muttered in Haydren's ear. "What can you possibly hope to discover now?"

Haydren glanced at him with a new respect. He shrugged helplessly and downed a quarter of the mug with one draught. The patrons nearest him cheered loudly and thumped him on the back.

By evening the crowd had thinned, and the three companions found a moment to speak to the innkeeper. A tall, barrel-chested man named Terak (who at turns beamed ear to ear, and gruffly shouted orders to his hirelings), he did not quite fit the model of innkeeper Haydren expected.

"Probably puts the unruly patrons out on their ears himself," Pladt commented after they were shown to their room.

Thoroughly exhausted, the trio fell asleep in their beds while the sun's last rays still spilled over the western battlements. The long journey from Hewolucs was nearly complete. Tomorrow, Haydren decided as his eyes fluttered, he would find Lintasur Guinad and discover the meaning of the letter. If all went well, that was.

The days passed in fruitless searching. One After-Noon near the end of the week, Haydren came into the room and collapsed onto the bed, his head falling against one of their packs. Something fell with a ringing clatter, and Haydren twisted to look at the floor. His red dagger sat accusing him of its displacement. Haydren picked it up and regarded it.

It was almost funny. Its red surface and damaged appearance always made it seem like it had been used and put away dirty. Sir Cullins would have had several things to say about keeping a dirty weapon, especially: "run, student! Run faster, and cleaning it next time will not seem such a bother."

Sir Cullins might have much to say, if he were here and could tell what Haydren was thinking. But he was not here. It was possible that he was not even in Hewolucs, not even alive.

The pits of the red blade drew Haydren in. For seven years he had trained to protect the Earl, and the Province. And there was only one way he was meant to do that—by the blade. Haydren had been fine with that, had acted on it several times. What had changed? Was it the fear in the eyes of the men? No; the bandits had shown fear when Haydren was not as easy a mark as they had thought. When he made death more real to them than perhaps they had previously known, of course they were afraid. But still their swords came out.

No. It was the soldier in the grove, the one who last held this dagger. It was the look in his eyes.

Remorse. Fear had been there, too, but behind that was sadness, and a realization that his choices had caught up with him. Haydren had recognized a little of it at the grove, and was not triumphant over the taking of the dagger as he knew Geoffrey thought he should be. But Haydren did not fully understand the remorse until Paolound, for then he felt it for himself. The fear of death had invaded Haydren like Paolound's heavy breath. Paolound's weight had crushed his armor; realizing it was his decisions that brought his friends to the brink of death had crushed his soul. As far as the soldier in the grove had been concerned, Haydren had been Paolound; except, Haydren had succeeded where the dragon had failed.

Haydren blinked, and the dagger blurred a little in front of him, becoming even more fluid—even more like blood flowing from a hilt. Was that its point? Did it hide the blood of its victim, seem more harmless and innocent? To soften for the wielder the blow of the work he had just done, to make the taking of life less of a strain? Once one became used to its appearance, the stain of blood would be almost entirely unnoticeable. More liquid, perhaps, as it seemed now: but no more red or gleaming.

Geoffrey came in just then and looked at Haydren. "You have not found him?" he asked.

Haydren put the dagger quickly in the pack and returned his gaze to the ceiling. "He has not made himself easy to find, which I would expect if he had truly sent for me," he said, swiping at his eyes as if tired. He cleared his throat. "I inquired at a number of the largest inns, according to what Terak told me. I've even begun asking random merchants. No one even recognizes the first or the last name." He sighed and closed his eyes. The floorboards creaked as Geoffrey moved across the room, saying nothing. After a time, Haydren drew a breath. "Where's Pladt?" he asked.

"Stocking up on arrows."

Haydren turned to frown at Geoffrey. "Why?"

"We're not staying here forever, are we?"

"Aren't you?" Haydren said. "I thought this was as far as *you* were going, at least."

"Are you going further?"

Haydren looked at him several moments longer, and returned his gaze to the ceiling. "Geoffrey, I..." He shook his head and sighed. "I'm just so tired."

"I know."

"And...I'm sorry." He glanced over. Geoffrey only gazed at him. He turned back to the ceiling. "I've turned away from everyone, except those who cannot help me anymore. I've tried to ignore your advice, and Pladt's too, all the while wishing for parents and friends that weren't there. I don't want to do this alone, and yet I've done everything to make sure that I am."

"Do you think I would not have opposed you if I thought you were doing something utterly wrong?" Geoffrey asked.

"I suppose I might have taken that from your silence, but it felt more like you were just laying all responsibility on me. And I know I've been making the decisions all along the way, and I may have even seemed like I knew what I was doing, but..." He paused. "I really have no idea."

"Haydren, you got us across Kelian Province, through the Kalen Woods, and all the way to Frecksshire," Geoffrey said.

"Nearly getting us killed in the process," Haydren interjected.

"Well this country is teeming with dangerous beasts a little more than most, as I've already noted," Geoffrey said with a grin. "If you want to take us somewhere with less danger, then we'd better start looking for a boat. What exactly are you expecting of yourself?"

"Well, I wouldn't mind making at least one informed decision," Haydren replied. "All along the way, what choices have I had? I've felt just as I did in the forest: I had just enough light for the next, what, ten steps? Beyond that was darkness. And now," he said, gesturing in frustration toward the ceiling, "now, I have no idea what to do next. Without Guinad, I have no idea where to begin looking for my parents—if I even should! I should probably just accept Mickel and Maerie as my parents. But if I don't, the best place to begin looking for my true parents is probably on the other side of the continent, back on the Eastern Shores. And how much time have I spent running away from there? And the only thing that might possibly suggest we're on the right track is this..."

Haydren stopped mid-gesture and trailed off, pressing his lips together.

Geoffrey cocked his head. "'This' what, Haydren?"

Haydren took a deep breath. "I've been...there have been these times..." He stopped, sighed, and spread his hands. "Let's call it ideas—thoughts that come to me every now and then. It started simply enough, when I decided to come to you for help. But even then, it was *kind* of like a thought, but still different. Then, when we were approaching Devil's Thumb, it came again, warning me to stop—and, almost like a whisper, prodding me to go into the camp." He paused again, wary of Geoffrey's knowing glance and nod. But, quickly, his gaze turned inward again. "There was a man, when I was twelve I think, who attacked the Inner Tower with just a dagger. I think it might have been the day Guntsen had locked me... Anyway. The man claimed he heard voices that wouldn't go away until he had nearly run himself onto a guard's halberd. My father's friend left for here—for Frecksshire—mostly because of that incident."

Now Geoffrey's gaze was quizzical. "Haydren, why—?"

"When we were in the Forest, after my torch went out, I heard a voice telling me to look up. It was in much the same manner as the other times, except it sounded like someone speaking, clearly and loudly, right next to me—I thought it was Sarah at first, but..." Haydren paused, piercing Geoffrey with his gaze. "It seems like this—whatever we want to call it—is looking out for me. But what if it isn't, suddenly?"

"I think he is, Haydren," Geoffrey said quietly. "I think he has been for a long time."

Haydren rubbed his forehead, ran his fingers into his hair, pressed his eye. This was not the answer he sought, and he knew it would come from Geoffrey. Why had he even started talking about it? He wanted Geoffrey's advice, his companionship, but not this: not losing his ability to choose before a God who already knew what he would do.

"Have you whispered to the God of All?"

"Geoffrey, not right now," Haydren said wearily.

"Is there a better time?"

"Yes."

"When?" Geoffrey murmured.

"Not right now!" Haydren sighed, and rubbed his forehead. "The last thing I want to think about right now is that I'm somehow bound to some quest that some all-powerful God has in store for me."

"I would find it most comforting," Geoffrey said. "Would his plan end in your death, do you suppose?"

"I wonder how many martyrs asked that question," Haydren said with a snort.

"Everybody dies, Haydren."

Haydren turned and looked at him coldly. "Do you suppose I am less likely, or more likely to be aware of that, Geoffrey?"

Geoffrey bowed his head. "I'm sorry, Haydren."

Haydren's gaze returned to the ceiling. "I still have some hope," he said quietly. He turned and regarded Geoffrey with a tired grin. "Not much, but some."

⚬

Two days later, after taking early baths and changing into clothing that Pladt had purchased them, they were as prepared as they could be when Ketteran returned to the Dancing Piper. On horse-back—by now, Geoffrey's ribs only pained him occasionally as they rode—they threaded their way through streets marginally less-cluttered than what had greeted them at New Years'.

The keep was no less impressive though it barely peered over the parapets. Surrounded by a second moat and outer gatehouse, it had only a few windows near the base, and those barely more than arrow slits. In its upper reaches, larger windows let much daylight into what Haydren supposed—correctly—to be the throne room. But if there were any catapult able to make it this deep within the fortress, he knew it would not be sufficient to loft anything more than a pebble to such a height as the windows above.

Just inside the gate, there was a small courtyard with stables. Here they dismounted, and a stable-boy took their horses to feed and water. The captain led them in through massive double doors set on great black hinges. The Earl's aide met them inside, thanked Ketteran, and led them up the many flights of stairs to the throne room with barely a word of comment.

They reached another set of double doors, these guarded by soldiers in full armor polished to reflect the torchlight like mirrors. Without a word, the soldiers opened the doors. The aide stepped forward and announced his charges.

Haydren led, with Geoffrey and Pladt a pace behind and to his left and right. Sarah stood off to one side, resplendent in a cerulean dress with silver scrollwork around the bodice. Freshly scrubbed and with her hair pulled back into a half-braid, she showed her strange mixture of youth and maturity more clearly than ever before.

But Haydren's eyes were quickly drawn to Earl Forion Durdamon, who rose from his throne to stand atop the short dais. He towered over the three companions at a height Haydren judged to be well over six feet. He was older than Earl Junei, as Haydren best remembered, though his hair was not as gray. His garb was far simpler than his eastern counterpart: dark brown, supple leather encased him, and a rich mantle of red velvet almost like a day-journey traveling cloak he kept thrown behind him, that flowed down to his waist. He was obviously powerfully built, and Haydren imagined the sword at his side was not simply for duels of honor.

Reaching the foot of the dais, the three bowed deeply. The Earl inclined his head only marginally.

"So, you are the few who have done, what?" he boomed, in Cariste, gesturing them to rise as he returned to his throne. He tapped his chin for a moment as he glanced at Sarah, then began counting off on his fingers. "You traveled safely through the Kalen Woods, killing the Cerberus of Kalen after escaping its depths; and upon journeying across my moors, met and fended off the dragon Paolound; and this after several, minor skirmishes in the east."

Haydren, flabbergasted still at the extent of the Earl's knowledge, could only nod. "Though," he said, finally finding his wits. "Our journey through the forest did not feel entirely safe to us, Excellency."

"Nor will much of your journey outside it feel so," he said, straightening a little. "There are many grave threats upon my lands, and a band as hardy as yourselves should not be wasted. I wonder if you might help me."

"Are you offering us a choice, Excellency?" Haydren said cautiously.

"You have a great deal of choice," Forion replied flatly. "You may serve me, a Rinc Nain like yourself; or you may return to your Cariste master, Guntsen, who is very eager for your return. Though," he added bitterly. "I should warn you he has formed an alliance with Lasserain."

Haydren gaped, and he could not bring himself to breathe. The Earl regarded him wordlessly for several moments, and then nodded.

"Any doubts we had about the King of Burieng allying himself with the mage has been erased. It seems many lords are pledging allegiance to him, for any number of causes. Three-quarters of the continent now lie under his command, and the beast army we have been trying to repulse now guards Kelian's border. Whatever may be your Earl's reasoning, it is far beyond the guess of any of my spies.

"Geoffrey, you have a similar choice," he continued, moving on quickly and maliciously. "I'm sure the King of Rinc Na would be most pleased to discover you still alive. If you wish, I may deliver you to him. I owe him a certain amount of allegiance, and paying him such an enormous favor will undoubtedly work in my benefit."

It took all of Haydren's willpower not to look back at the old swordsman. "And Pladt, Excellency?" he asked instead, his words whispering across a dried tongue.

The Earl laughed. "Actually, Grecce would put me in his debt. He seems to be the only pure soul among you."

"My father would have it no other way, Excellency," Pladt replied with a bow.

"I am certain," Forion replied. "So, gentlemen, what will it be?"

"What are your Excellency's wishes?" Haydren asked without pause.

Forion Durdamon did not smile victoriously as Haydren imagined he would. Instead, his brows drew down in thoughtful concern. "You carry a letter," he said. "Two letters, actually, that when read together become very troubling. And I may have concern for the first, as it contains knowledge that I could have used months ago," he added with a glance at the sorceress. "But that is a matter for another time. And even though we have not found any hints similar to your second letter, aimed at Coberan, the breadth of it by itself cannot be ignored."

"Excellency, I cannot help but be amazed that you know that," Haydren said, unable to contain himself.

Durdamon gazed at him coolly. "Many things can be learned from the wind," he said simply, with a glance that lingered briefly on Sarah. He turned back to Haydren. "But not everything. Some things must be seen first-hand. Which is why Sarah first went to Quaran, and why you now are going to the mage's home in the Kalen Woods."

Haydren's brows shot up. "Haschina?" he blurted.

Forion's fist clenched spasmodically, and he extended a finger in warning. "I would not speak the name so lightly, Loren. Not when the Woods are growing once more." He sighed, and his hand dropped. "But yes, in his village."

"I had thought the village was burned twenty years ago, Excellency," Haydren said.

"But some reports say Lasserain preserved it," Forion replied. "In fact, it is more likely that the burning was invented. I believe Lasserain himself began that story to justify his rampage into the Endolin Mountains. He had long been practicing his arts, too far secluded from the rest of the world, unchecked by reason. What purpose could he have for such power except to use it?"

"What would you have us do, Excellency?" Haydren asked.

"First, go to Jyunta," Forion replied. "There is a man there, Corith: a most excellent guide into the woods. Sarah knows him well," he said with a gesture toward the silent sorceress. "Travel to the mage's village and see what you can find, and report back to me. But beware as you travel to Jyunta: it has been under assault a number of times, though Lord Garoun assures me he defends it well. I trust you to decide how best to proceed."

Haydren kept his reaction to a few swift blinks. "Is that all, Excellency?"

"That depends on what you find, Haydren Loren," Forion said testily.

"Of course, Excellency; I apologize for my tone," Haydren said, bowing deeply.

The Earl nodded. "Now, for the one who is not in my debt," he said, looking at Pladt. "Is there anything you would ask in return for fulfilling this task for me, archer?"

Pladt shrugged, then glanced at Haydren's back. "You knew we were looking for someone when we arrived, Excellency," he said.

Forion's eyebrows rose in surprise. Haydren, too, glanced quickly back. "What else am I supposed to ask for?" Pladt whispered to Haydren.

"What precisely would you ask of me, archer?" Forion pressed further.

"Your knowledge is most extensive, Excellency," Pladt said. "And your spy network is large; Haydren is trying to find out who his parents are, and we came to your castle with the impression that a man named Lintasur Guinad might know something about it."

"That is barely a favor to you: I wish to find this man myself. You have nothing else to ask?" Forion said. Pladt shook his head once. Forion smiled. "It will be done," he said. "Regardless of what information you bring me, I will give you what you ask.

"Ketteran will continue to be your...guide, as it were," the Earl said by way of dismissal. "He will give you supplies. I understand Geoffrey may be too weak to travel yet, but remember the timing of the bandit raids in the east. Leave when you are ready, return as fast as you can. I do not believe you will let Frecksshire rest on the brink of annihilation. Fare well," he finished with a wave of his hand.

The three bowed, and with one last, swift glance at Sarah, Haydren led the way out of the throne room. They met Ketteran at the stables, and during the entire ride back to the Inn, Haydren said nothing to address Geoffrey. Once they reached their room, Haydren checked the hallways, closed the door, and turned to his companions.

"Now, Geoffrey," he said calmly, but firmly. "Perhaps there is something about you we should know?"

Geoffrey sighed, and gestured toward the bed. "Best sit down," he said; "this story may take some time."

Haydren and Pladt arranged themselves soberly as Geoffrey clasped his hands behind his back and watched. Once they both were attentive, he began.

"The story I told in the Forest," he said.

"*Uv Fehn?*" Pladt asked.

"I should have thought that Sarah might remember such a story," Geoffrey replied. "She told me as much in the Forest, after you two had gone to sleep. I can only guess she told the Earl."

"We're here now," Haydren said.

"Right. Well, the story I told was true, up to the point of them leading us back home and disappearing. In truth, when our captain began pursuing them again, in what we thought was sheer lunacy, many of us defected. It took some time to prove ourselves to our new allies, but we did it. I did a better job than the others, and was soon a leader among the *Uv Fehn*. A very good leader."

"Did you receive your sword from them?" Haydren asked, hoping now the door was open, a few more unanswered questions might pass through.

Geoffrey's gaze fell, and he nodded. "As far as I know, it was the only one in all of Rinc Na. We acquired it in a raid—a very dangerous mission, that our General believed would not have succeeded except for some of my actions, so he awarded it to me. King Ulgar Furth likely would want me dead for that mission alone." He paused, his gaze drifting to a different, distant time. "I have made terrible choices, against men I called at different times my friends—"

The door was opening too wide. "You don't need to share that with me, Geoffrey," Haydren said. "Whatever you have done is your own. Some wounds do not heal when re-opened," Haydren continued swiftly to Geoffrey's sharp glance. "And I'll not force you to reopen this one."

"But I have done despicable things, Haydren," Geoffrey said, his gaze dropping again. "Things that friends now should know."

"That's as may be," Haydren said quietly. "But as long as you promise not to do those things again," he continued with a gentle smile. "I will trust you. It was another country, at a different time of your life. You have done nothing but aid me for the past two months, far beyond what I could have expected when I first knocked on your door." He paused, considering the expression that had appeared on Geoffrey's face. "Or is that *why* you did it?" he asked. "To balance what you had done in Rinc Na?"

Geoffrey regarded him somberly, and nodded. "I recognized you as a Rinc Nain the first time I saw you, as I said—saw in you the same sort of young man I had been. I had hoped by helping you possibly avoid choices I had made when ostracized by my community, I might make right the myriad wrongs I had committed."

"And I thank you for it," Haydren replied, rising to his feet. "But you need not continue with me if that is your only motivation."

"That may have been my first motivation, Haydren," Geoffrey replied. "But it is no longer. I will see you find the information you seek, or die in the attempt."

Haydren glanced at him sideways, and grinned. "Let's hope it doesn't come to that," he said gently. "For now, we need to supply ourselves for the journey ahead."

Geoffrey smiled, finally relaxing fully. "Very well," he said.

14

FRIENDS

"I'm beginning to see what you mean."
"Oh?"
"This started long ago; before Haydren."
"It began when time began. This is but a scene in a play."

24 Haschina 1320 — Summer

One evening two weeks later, Haydren found Geoffrey in the stable yard behind the Inn practicing his swordplay. He watched the quivering thrusts and parries of the Follus blade concert with Geoffrey's grunts and breathing.

"Getting better?" Haydren asked as Geoffrey paused with his sword raised.

Geoffrey tested his ribs with a few windmills of the blade. He winced a little.

"Well enough to travel, I think," Geoffrey replied. "Hopefully Paolound can leave us alone for another week or two."

"Do you mind?" Haydren asked, gesturing to his own sword. Geoffrey waved him in. Haydren vaulted into the enclosure and drew his blade. "First blood?" he asked with a grin.

"First decapitation," Geoffrey replied with a smile. "Makes it more serious."

They began, and Haydren concentrated on Geoffrey's body, fighting to keep his eyes undistracted by the humming blade. With each parry, the Follus' sharp pinging rang in his head and shook his focus. He held his ground, relying on his foot-speed to keep the ringing blows to a minimum as he danced out of the way of the blade more than he deflected it. He caught, quickly, Geoffrey's approving smile. His eyes shifted a moment and suddenly Geoffrey's blade rested on his shoulder.

"Seems like you're ready," Haydren said.

"I think you are, too," Geoffrey replied. "I've had more time with this sword than many knights you're likely to meet."

"Pladt did say you were old," Haydren returned with a smile.

"Where is he, in the room?" Geoffrey asked, his voice mirroring the sudden concern in his eyes.

Haydren nodded. "He has been quiet of late, hasn't he?"

"Since New Year's, I think," Geoffrey agreed. "Probably just the strange country. For now we need to get word to Sarah that we're ready to leave."

"I'll take care of it," Haydren said.

Two days later, Haydren was in the stable making preparations to leave when he heard hooves outside, and a voice speaking in Cariste. He could only see the back of the stable-boy, who was trying to understand the different language.

"Well find me someone who can speak the language, would you?" the voice said, rising in authority and frustration.

But the boy still misunderstood, trying to grasp the reins and do his duty as the rider continued to protest. Rolling his eyes, Haydren moved to the door to try to help. As soon as he exited the stable, he froze.

It was Semmelle, lieutenant of Guntsen's Mages.

"Are you the farrier?" Semmelle demanded. Whether he was distracted by anger, or Haydren had changed since leaving Hewolucs, he didn't seem to recognize who stood in front of him.

"Just someone trying to help," Haydren said.

"You speak his language?"

"Yes."

"Would you please tell him to use the brush in my saddlebags, and not handfuls of dung-filled straw when he brushes down my horse?" he asked. "The idiot at Fūnik made him smell like all the wrong parts of a stall when I passed through."

Haydren quickly relayed the message. The boy grimaced. "I don't want horse-dung on my hands either," he muttered.

"He understands perfectly," Haydren said to Semmelle.

"Good." Semmelle turned to his saddlebags and retrieved a small book. As Haydren made to duck back into the stable, Semmelle turned to him again. "What was your name?" he asked.

"Uh, Ketteran," Haydren replied.

Semmelle nodded, moving off toward the inn as he paged through the small book in his hand. Haydren returned to the stall to quickly finish saddling his horse.

Geoffrey and Pladt arrived shortly, noticing Haydren's hurried movements. "Something wrong?" Geoffrey asked.

"Semmelle is here," Haydren said, pointing to the horse that the stable-boy was rubbing down with straw.

"Wasn't he the—"

"Yes."

"I hope Sarah is on her way," Geoffrey said, throwing a saddle-blanket over his mare. He hefted the saddle and placed it gently on her back, then settled it firmly into the blanket. "He didn't recognize you?"

"It didn't seem like it," Haydren replied, sliding the bridle over his gelding's head. He patted his horse's neck, watching as Geoffrey cinched the saddle tight. "How did he follow me all the way out here?" he muttered.

"You say it like Frecksshire is deep in the back-country," Geoffrey replied with a grin. "The better question might be how he expects to find you in such a large castle."

"Well now he has," Haydren replied. "Let's not get started on the odds of that."

Sarah entered the stable leading her own horse just as the others were finished preparing theirs. "Ready to go?" she asked.

"Very," Haydren replied, hoping his glance and his silence about Semmelle would warn Geoffrey not to bring it up. Whether it worked or not, Geoffrey said nothing.

The morning was chilly for summer, but the fog burned off quickly as the four companions exited the farmland surrounding the castle and entered the Moors proper. Between broad planes of stunted mute-green grass were equally broad but shallow vales marked by breaching rock, and moss where shadows and small springs clung. Groves of trees sprang up, much like the land around Werine. The trees here were short and scrubby, with bare trunks and high branches that twisted and knuckled and ended in thick pine-like needles that offered little shade as they passed underneath.

"You're silent today, archer," Sarah observed as they rode toward Noon.

"So is everyone," Pladt replied. Sarah grinned.

"I expect it from them," she replied; "unless I ask Haydren about history or geography, or Geoffrey about magic." She winked quickly as they each glanced at her. But Pladt only shrugged, and kept his silence.

After-Noon passed, and it seemed to Haydren that the sun dragged through its long path toward the flat horizon. At dusk, a squat stone building arose to the north, just off the road.

"See, Pladt?" Geoffrey said, pointing. "I told you they would have Inns a day's ride apart in this country."

Pladt smiled, but Sarah glanced quickly at them. "Umm..."

"What?" Geoffrey asked.

She smiled grimly. "You'll see."

As they neared, they could see the ragged remains of the collapsed roof. Riding closer revealed scorch-marks streaking the stone walls, and what was left of the door hung awkwardly on its hinges. They stopped and dismounted. Pladt approached first and ran his fingers along a set of deep grooves, barely worn by time, clearly made by thick claws.

"I told you there were not many inns left that withstood the beasts' uprising," Sarah said as they stood in glum horror.

Geoffrey glanced around. "We could still stay here," he said. "The floor is intact, and the walls will keep off the wind."

Pladt let his hand drop from the claw-marks. "That's okay," he said, in the closest he had been to his usual humor in several weeks. "I don't care how wet or windy, as long as it's far from here."

The rest agreed, and they rode quickly up the road to make camp before dark.

The next day dawned bright, and they rode with spirits unlimited by a high clear sky. A light breeze picked up from the northwest, stirring the grasses and horses' manes. They rode more leisurely, lulled by cicadas buzzing in the summer sun. As their shadows lengthened they stopped early, hoping to set up camp and cook another good meal.

But as they prepared to strike the fire, the wind paused, eddied, then blew steadily from the east.

Sarah stiffened. "Storm," she said, pointing. As the party glanced at the towering midnight-dark clouds engulfing the horizon, Sarah took a step toward her horse. "A big one!"

They lashed down bags quickly and leapt on their horses.

"Why didn't we set up camp?" Pladt yelled as they rode.

"It's too big for that," Sarah replied. "We need walls, stone ones. A roof would be nice, but I don't know if we're close enough..."

The clouds raced onward and erased the landscape below it. Lightning fell like rain across the horizon, narrowly at first. The companions galloped onward as the wind rose evermore. The lightning spread like drawn curtains as the storm neared, closer and closer. Fat drops fell randomly: one hit Haydren squarely in the eye and stung his vision. The lightning had nearly encircled them when the edge of the blackness like a tide appeared on the grasses and swept over them. Thunder crashed and rain pelted them like pebbles as the wind threatened to blow them off their skittering horses.

They slowed, then stopped and dismounted, circling their horses and huddling near each other.

"We should walk!" Sarah said, her hair already matted to her face in soggy clumps.

"To where?" Haydren shouted back, blinking away the rain.

"There should be a farm soon. He took over an old inn."

"Who did?" Geoffrey asked.

"His name's Dasillion," she replied. "He's..." She shrugged and her voice dropped a little. "He's Dasillion. Let's see if we can get there."

They walked, keeping their horses windward. The lightning flashes slowed, then stopped, sinking them into a soaking darkness like they had not seen since the Kalen Woods.

They trudged on, every twenty steps sinking further into a deepening ooze. A trickle down the western side of the road became a stream, then a torrent. Haydren, behind Sarah, glanced back to Geoffrey, who glanced back to Pladt, who walked with head bowed, never glancing up to curse the rain and the wind.

They would slip, get back up, and stumble on. Haydren's horse, who had kept his head turned toward his owner as they plodded, suddenly swung his head around to look eastward. The rain, no longer shielded, blasted Haydren in the face. Grumbling, Haydren yanked on the reins to bring the horse's head back around, and he stopped. Haydren shouldered him to get his attention, but he whickered.

Sarah, glancing back, stopped. "What's wrong?" she shouted.

Haydren shook his head, glanced at his horse, then down at the ground. "What side of the road is Dasillion's farm on?" he shouted.

Sarah set her jaw, then came around from behind her horse to look east. Haydren peered over his own horse's back, sweeping his gaze across the darkness. A flutter of light caught his attention: it looked like a fire—one that could not exist outside in this weather.

He patted his horse's muzzle. "Good boy," he said, leading him off the road. Haydren pointed ahead after Geoffrey's inquiring gaze. Geoffrey turned and waved to Pladt, who had come up directly behind him before noticing everyone had stopped.

The tough moorgrass made for firm footing as they moved toward where Haydren had seen the flame. When Haydren stepped and suddenly sank to his ankle, he knew they had found cultivated land. A providential bolt of lightning lit up the farmstead, showing a split-rail fence circling a low stone house. Beyond was another stone building a little smaller, and what had to be stables near that.

They circled the fence quickly and went to the porch that surrounded three sides of the house. As soon as his boots hit the boards a terrific baying came from within the home. Haydren paused, handed his horse's reins to Sarah, and walked up to the door.

When he knocked, the door cracked open almost immediately. Haydren bent backward with a yelp as a sword thrust through the crack and nearly speared his head. At the other end of the sword, eyes wide, stood a man well advanced in years, yet possessing a virility nearly equaling Geoffrey, Haydren judged.

"I-I'm so sorry!" said the man, lowering the sword and nearly casting it away behind him. "Goblins have been bothering me of late. I thought perhaps you were one. Or four of one, seeing as there are four of you. Though they don't typically ride on horses—but I didn't see them until just now! Please, come in and get warm. The fire'll do nicely to dry out your things. Oh, the horses: Dwereth can get them into the stables. Quiet, Vesta, they're guests! Come in, come in!"

Bewildered, but too soaked to bother with questions, the four handed their horses to Dwereth, who had just appeared wearing a thick, shimmering cloak and didn't look at them. They stepped into the man's house. As soon as the door was shut, and the wind and driving rain were securely outside, the group felt a little warmer. The farmer went to the fire and stoked it high, and bid them lay out their cloaks to dry. Vesta, a bloodhound, curled up on a blanket in the corner. Dasillion pulled some chairs up close to the flames and told them to sit while he finished preparing a stew.

"Dasillion is my name, though few speak it anymore—only Dwereth and he's a silent one," he said, stirring a pot of steaming golden liquid. "I've lived out here on the moors for too many years to have many frequent guests, I suppose. Most people stay at the inns along the road, though I hear more have been closing down like this one, recently. Those goblins are a mighty problem. Don't seem to bother me as much as the waysides. Oh, I have a few now and then: smaller ones, usually, who can't take on anything else. Look at me! There's not enough meat on me to bother anyway. Stick 'em with my sword a few times, and they run howling away. What's your names again?"

Haydren fought off a grin; they had never once had the chance to tell him. He gave introductions quickly.

"Pleasure, pleasure," Dasillion responded. "I think I remember you," he said to Sarah with a nod. "But then you folks rarely stay long enough to remember properly. A sort of strange bunch you are, though it's not a bad thing. Different abilities make for broader capabilities, I always say. One can't do it all. Though neither can four, if you think about it. But four can do a lot more than one, unless all four are the same, you see? I can farm, but I can't hunt. How often do you think I eat meat? Except the rabbits which fall into my snares, of course."

Pladt, unable to understand a word, sat silent and detached as he gazed into the fire and warmed himself. Dasillion, pausing for breath, glanced at him.

"He seems distracted," he noted to Haydren and Geoffrey, "though it's not necessarily a bad thing. Looking inside is the best way to get to know yourself I suppose."

"He doesn't understand Rinc Nain," Haydren explained. "Only Cariste."

"And here I am rattling on!" Dasillion said. "I'm sorry, I don't speak Cariste either. But tell him he's very welcome in my home. Ah! Soup's ready!"

Haydren relayed the message while Dasillion prepared four bowls of the stew. Pladt startled, smiled, and asked Haydren to thank the farmer. Dasillion nodded with a large smile, saying "Tho've kanem!" loudly and slowly.

"I don't think he'll understand any better, no matter how slowly you say it Dasillion," Haydren remarked with a smile. Geoffrey concentrated on spooning out a mouthful of the spiced broth.

"He gets like that, from time to time," a new, unmuffling voice said behind them. Pladt jumped again, and all four turned to see a dwarf emerging from a pile of blankets against the wall. "Like a penitent thief to the gallows, Dasillion, prattling on and on."

"Runacron!" Sarah exclaimed, surprising all. "Why are you down here?"

"I would ask the same, but we expect you to wander," the dwarf said, not unkindly.

"He's another one who stayed," Dasillion said with a nod. "Helps out with the farming, a little, like Dwereth. And shoeing horses for plowing. He never said why."

"You entertain me, farmer," Runacron allowed with a gracious bow. "Else I'd be with Dwereth, hiding in the stables no doubt, braver in the face of wind and rain than in front of your hospitality."

Dasillion roared laughter. "Too true," he said. "Dwereth has a habit of leaving every time guests arrive. It took me two weeks to coax him back inside after Runacron showed up. I suppose it gets all bottled up while no one's here and gushes out when they arrive. But my friend dwarf, you'd be back in the mines as you'd left Jyunta planning, not cowering in some drafty stable."

"Trading my battle-axe for a pick-axe," Runacron said, aside to the travelers. "My father was right, rest his bones in the deep earth's slumber: war's no place for me, as I've no place for war."

"Sometimes war isn't so accommodating," Haydren replied, a little testily.

"And neither are warriors," Runacron said, seating himself before the fire and pulling a deep-red blanket tight around his shoulders. A finger left his clenching hand and waved over the group. "You lot look like what I mean. And you'll be needed," he added with a nod. "'They are sieged nightly, they will not fall; armies massing nightly to an unheard call: who will come to their aid? No one answers, and they will fall; no one answers the wailing call: where is the dead king laid?'" Runacron shook his head and sniffed loudly.

"Does it go badly for Jyunta?" Sarah asked. "The Earl was told Garoun defends it."

Runacron gazed at her for several moments, then readjusted his blanket, wrapping it tighter. "I expect he did say that," the dwarf muttered. "They've not been overrun yet, so he's not lying, I suppose. He probably also said he would defend it to the death, defend it till the bleeding castle lay in ruins. Well it will!" The dwarf's eyes blazed. "And Frecksshire will be next, and what'll be left but thousands of people who defended the country to the death!"

"And so you retreat to the mines?" Haydren asked.

"As an ailing man retreats to his bed when sickness strikes," the dwarf replied. "And no one thinks him a coward then, do they? But ask a Lord to spend men's energy on building walls and gates and you've abandoned courage. No! It's sharpened steel that wins the day! Standing and fighting! Faugh. They create fictitious enemies that fight according to their strategies while their young men are slaughtered by the real thing and called heroes."

"But winds change, and herald the coming of a storm," Sarah said with resolve.

"Jyunta needs a hurricane," Runacron replied.

"Is that some sort of prophecy?" Haydren asked quietly, rubbing his eyes.

"Prophecy," Runacron grumbled, settling himself more. "It's a proverb, lad. Ever notice the winds changing just before a storm strikes?"

A sudden crash of thunder brought their startled gazes to the windows, and chuckles from their mouths.

"Yes it did," Haydren said with a nod. He turned back to the dwarf. "And we're supposed to be the changing wind?"

Runacron shrugged. "Hopefully. They need it."

Pladt's face split into a yawn, and he stood to retrieve his bedroll. Haydren took note of it. He gestured to the archer. "Pladt has a good idea," he said. He turned to the farmer. "May we use your floor, Dasillion?" he asked.

"Certainly!" Dasillion replied, seeming insulted that Haydren would presume he might kick them out of his house. "He can move closer to the fire, too, if he wants."

The next several moments were a bustle of blankets unrolling and dishes being gathered and cleaned. The fire was stoked once more, and fuel added. All other lights were extinguished, and the travelers and their hosts eventually laid down to sleep. Gazing into the flames, Haydren heard Runacron whispering to himself the lines of an unfamiliar poem.

"What is that?" he asked in wonder.

Runacron said nothing, his eyes fixed on the fire.

Dasillion shifted a little upright. "I think you should, master dwarf," he said. "The night is dark enough even without the talk we've just had, and that poem might do the trick."

Runacron turned onto his back and gazed at the ceiling. "It wouldn't sound the same," he replied gruffly.

"The same as what?" Haydren asked.

Runacron paused. "As hearing it in Deewan," he said hesitantly. "Safety and a communal fire are better accompaniment than raging winds."

"We have a communal fire," Haydren said, his gaze returning to the blazing hearth.

Runacron looked at each in turn, and they each waited. Pladt alone lay with his eyes closed.

Runacron nodded finally, and Dasillion smiled. After another moment's pause, the dwarf began:

"From a land across the sea,

a merry dwarf came happily.
And so we tell the joyful tale,
of our friend named Bowin-Dale.

Bowin-Dale, short and red-haired,
wondered how other lands fared.
And so he bought the biggest boat,
so big it almost didn't float.

He sailed here and there in search,
of the biggest, bestest church.
And when he found that holy shrine,
he sallied back into the brine.

Next he looked both far and wide,
for the smallest place to hide.
And when he found that little nook,
he wrote for it a little book.

Soon he was in search again,
this time for the biggest men.
He found them on a tiny isle,
and stayed with them for a while.

But Bowin-Dale could not rest,
and so he wagered who was best.
Dwarves or giants, who could say?
So Bowin-Dale won, that day.

Satisfied he sallied forth,
this time turning to the north.
Looking for the deepest snow,
also for the blackest crow.

These he found in one location,
on a northern island nation.
Snow so deep he couldn't walk,
crows so black he couldn't talk.

Leaving there he soon moved on,
wondering where the wind had gone.
Though he longed for other sights,
the wind was still all through the nights.

Then one day the wind did blow,
bringing with it heavy snow.

Bowin-Dale cursed his luck,
the water froze and he was stuck.

Biding time and playing sports,
building little toothpick forts.
Wandering the snowy streets,
accosting everyone he meets.

Winter passed and spring was sprung,
freshest air filled every lung.
So entranced by this was he,
he wrote a little poetry.

But off he went into the west,
searching still for all that's -est.
Oldest wizards, strongest mages,
humblest monks and wisest sages.

East and west and north and south,
smallest shoe-size, biggest mouth.
Up and down and in and out,
smallest whisper, loudest shout.

And so he circled 'round the globe,
clad in finest silken robe.
Sailing on the many seas,
drinking wine and eating cheese.

His thirst for '-est' would never end,
dull-est knife and sharp-est bend.
So he loved the very '-est,'
he changed his name to Bowin-Dest.

His family knew not his name,
in vain attempt to hide their shame.
And Bowin-Dest went so insane,
he grew a beard and called it 'mane.'

Of all the manes, his was best,
according to old Bowin-Dest.
He steered his ship, hunched lazily,
his searching eye roved crazily.

All who saw him ran and hid,
acting as a rabbit did.
Bowin-Dest paid them no mind,

still looking for the '-est'est kind.

Finally as he grew old,
his wine and cheese turned into mold.
His sails torn, his ship was leaking,
his clothes were tattered, he was reeking.

So the traveled Bowin-Dest,
laid his weary head to rest.
Still he dreamed of all that's '-est,'
north and south and east and west."

The companions lay for some time in bittersweet silence.

"Why would they call that a happy tale?" Haydren said finally. "It doesn't end very happily."

"It ends as does any other life," Runacron replied. "It's happy because of the way he lived his life."

"He went crazy!" Haydren protested.

"He saw the world as no one else did," Runacron countered. "And that's what made him crazy. But it doesn't mean he didn't grasp true reality, does it?"

"And what reality is that?"

"That something exists that we might never grasp," Runacron replied. "And those who seem insane are just the one who see it and continually reach for it. Bowin-Dale sought the best, the absolute highest that existed in life, and died without seeing it. But he died still in the hope that it existed. How can we know without searching that nothing exists to fulfill our dreams? And just because *he* didn't find it doesn't mean *you* won't."

"What dreams do you have, Runacron?" Haydren asked. The silence stretched so long he began to wonder if the dwarf had fallen asleep, and grinned at the irony.

Finally, the dwarf whispered: "The deep earth. I used to hate workin' in the mines, and dreamed for adventure like most. And I found it, sure enough. Some people can have their open air and broad mountain-top views. There's so much beauty just below your feet that you'll never know."

"And for that you would leave Jyunta to its fate?"

"I'm not a warrior any more than you're a miner, lad," Runacron replied. "If you have it in you, do it. The world certainly needs you. We can't all be everything, can we?"

A sudden thought struck Haydren. "Runacron, you're familiar with a lot of metals, aren't you? As a miner?"

Runacron suppressed a chuckle. "I wouldn't be much good to my father or my family if I wasn't."

Haydren reached out and pulled his sword quietly from the sheath. Runacron gasped.

"Where did you get that?" the dwarf whispered, flames dancing in fireplace, sword, and eyes.

"My father gave it to me when I was very young. Do you know it?"

"Not the sword itself, though it stirs a Deewanian poem to me." He held out his hand cautiously. "May I look closer?" Haydren handed it over, and Runacron held it toward the ceiling. "The edge is Bultum," he said, brushing it gently with a finger. "The flames," he continued, tapping those with a knuckle, "are from a very rare ore called Cretal. This—this sword has magic, lad; that I know from the metals, but also from the poem. Four of them were made and scattered abroad, not all alike, but similar. If this isn't one of those four, I'd go back to Jyunta."

"Scattered?" Haydren said, propping up his head. "Where?"

Runacron shook his head. "The poem doesn't say. It only speaks of their history and purpose. Ah, my mind's a blank. But those that made it will know, if you ever make it to Deewan. And if I'm right about that sword, you need to," he concluded, handing the sword back.

Haydren took it and sheathed it slowly, and the glow that had lit their mattresses went out. They spoke at length about the sword and the metals, and Deewan. When they finished, Runacron turned over, but Haydren gazed at the ceiling with hands behind his head, glancing occasionally at the weapon beside him.

When Haydren eventually fell asleep, his dreams were filled with an inexpressible joy, brought to him by the final possession of something indefinable. He would run, and search, and seek, until he had found that thing, and he was filled with a warmth that was complete.

Once, as he attained the thing, a word came to him written in pale metal like liquid silver, etched into his vision yet tenuous as a whisper. It was a word familiar yet forgotten, and seemed always on the edge of his vision. His joy faltered as a yearning distracted him from what he possessed. He tried to turn, but couldn't: his eyes were fastened in their sockets, his neck fused and immobile. He concentrated, trying to trace the spectral lines of the strange script, but they curved and looped so intricately that his mind was lost upon it. He stopped struggling, and the word edged into view. It was the word that had come upon him as death encroached and Paolound pressed upon him:

Aerithion.

As soon as he apprehended the word, his sword was in his hand, rust-like flames blazing brightly enough to illuminate the world yet somehow without blinding him.

He awoke suddenly to a slate-gray world that was cold and uninviting, and a day devoid of joy of any kind. The tempest had passed, but the heavy clouds lingered. Dasillion was awake, stoking the fire and preparing a hot breakfast.

"There you are," said the farmer as he caught sight of Haydren. "I'm not sure what you two talked about last night, but Runacron left an hour ago. Said he needed to get to the mines; he'd had enough of nightmares and day-dreams, and wanted to get back to what he'd been made for. Can't blame him or call him crazy. Most folks think I am for living out here. But we all get by, don't we? Breakfast?"

As Dasillion bustled about, Haydren blinked and sat up, and glanced at his sword. He knew without knowing how he knew that the name was true. It was just another sense, along with the song from his harp and the man in his dream, that he knew came from his former life. But how could he explain that to his friends? Those who now woke, and lethargically re-packed their bags as Haydren went about in reserved silence. Geoffrey checked the horses, who had weathered the storm as well as could be expected. Dwereth accepted their thanks for tending the horses so carefully, but ducked back into the stables as Dasillion came out to announce breakfast. The low moors were on the horizon, their marshes flooded and sparkling in sunlight that lurked far away from the farm.

They ate in silence. As they finished, Dasillion spoke up. "There is another farm, belonging to a man named Faschek," he informed them. "It is just a days' ride north; he should let you stay the night there."

"Is he a friend of yours?" Haydren asked absently.

Dasillion paused, squinting. "I might call him so; he would probably not call me so," he replied. "Faschek is...well, Faschek."

"Sarah said the same about you," Geoffrey said with a grin. The sorceress squinted at him, and smiled.

"He's not an enemy?" Dasillion replied hopefully.

Haydren glanced up. "Sounds wonderful," he muttered. "Very reassuring."

"His is the only rest between here and Jyunta," Dasillion said, bristling. "Camps are hard to strike on the low moors. Once you leave Faschek's, you should easily reach the hill country around Jyunta in another days' ride. Be kind to him, and he may grant you some sort of rest, is all I'm saying. You will certainly be in a better position than not asking at all."

"Very well," Haydren replied, suddenly attending Dasillion with a calming smile. "We will; and thank you, Dasillion, for your hospitality and advice."

Dasillion smiled in return. "If you make it back this way, stop in and see me."

"We will," Haydren promised.

They rode off with Dasillion's well-wishes, striking the low moors before the sun reached Half-Noon. The land here was no different than the low moors they walked through upon escaping the Northern Forest: puddles and streams laced the plain, and shocks of grass sometimes hid boggy ground. Their horses seemed better able to pick the firmest lines, and so they continued much of the day with slack reins.

By Noon, the high moors had disappeared behind them, and the glittering moors stretched everlastingly around them. They lunched on an island that rose abruptly before them, and continued under a cloudless sky until evening.

"How did you know Runacron?" Haydren asked, trying to keep his mind off his rumbling stomach.

"We were together in Jyunta, before Durdamon called me south to advise him," Sarah replied. "I was surprised to see him there—and now a little troubled, after talking to him. Lucky that storm hit before we made camp. We might have missed him if we'd stayed out."

"Right," Haydren said, biting a corner of his lip. "Lucky."

Lagging behind, and gazing despondently around the moors, Pladt suddenly sat up. He picked up his reins, and trotted his horse to the right. Sarah, turning in her saddle, watched the archer.

"What are you doing, Pladt?" she asked.

"There's a strange puddle over here," Pladt replied. "It looks kind of purple, all of the sudden."

Sarah bolted upright, snatching the reins. "No, Pladt, get away from there!"

As the others turned confused looks at her, the puddle in front of Pladt exploded in a fine mist. A dark creature, streaked with green, wrapped him in thick arms and carried him off his horse into the water on the other side. The horse screamed and bolted. Haydren and Sarah both spurred their mounts forward as the goblin rose from the mucky waters with Pladt spluttering in his grasp.

Human-shaped, but with a neck as thick as its head, the goblin writhed with musculature under thick, serpent-like scaly skin. One arm wrapped around Pladt's throat, the other hand splayed on Pladt's chest, ready to plunge vicious talons into his heart. The thundering hooves of Haydren's horse distracted it. Haydren leapt off mid-stride, Aerithion drawn, and dealt the goblin a blow to his shoulder. It would have done as much good as striking him with a club, for how little effect the blade had on the goblin's thick hide. With a deep-throated bellow, the goblin retreated a few steps as Geoffrey approached with sword drawn.

"Remember Dasillion mentioned sticking them with his sword?" Geoffrey said, keeping his eyes on the goblin, who in turn eyed the new threats warily. "I think they respond to thrusts better than slices."

"Sir Cullins neglected to mention that," Haydren muttered.

A deep rumble grew in the goblin's chest. Sarah began to mutter something, and a piercing whistle sounded near the goblin's head near Pladt's ear.

The goblin screamed and fell backward, wagging his head. But before he released Pladt the hand on the archer's right side convulsed, and his talons pierced quickly.

Pladt cried out and fell sideways. Haydren ran to him and inspected the archer's side where deep punctures marred the flesh beneath his ribs. In the silence there was a hissing squish as Geoffrey stabbed downward with his blade. The goblin twitched, the water discolored, and it was still.

"Is he all right?" Sarah called, still atop her horse, which danced nervously beneath her.

Haydren wiped a bit of purple liquid from Pladt's wound and smelled it. His horrified expression met Sarah's.

"We must find Faschek's house, immediately," Haydren said, lip quivering. "Or he's going to die."

15

ENEMIES

"You are watching closely?"
"Very."
"What of Andelen?"
"After they've reached Jyunta."

28 Haschina 1320 — Summer

Fountains of water sprayed into the wind as Haydren, Geoffrey, and Sarah thundered across the moors. Haydren let the horse guide itself, as it seemed capable of doing, as he held onto Pladt. Pladt's horse trailed dutifully behind, empty stirrups swinging.

The foam that began to gather on the horses' necks was washed quickly by the spray of Moorish water. As the horses began to slow, a house rose on the horizon.

Haydren reined to a stop before a porch similar to Dasillion's, though not as broad. Geoffrey leapt down and ran to the door, pounding for admittance as Haydren slid Pladt's still-limp body from the saddle. Sarah came beside Geoffrey just as a gaunt man of about thirty years of age answered the door. His hair was greasy and ragged and beginning to thin on top.

"Faschek?" Geoffrey asked.

"Faschek Belfrind," Faschek replied in a thin, gravelly voice. He cleared his throat and coughed. "What do you want?" he asked, his voice stronger now as he spat.

"Our friend is injured," Haydren replied, walking up the steps with Pladt in his arms. "We need hilsop and thielem; I know it's popular on the moors. Do you have any?"

Faschek paused to look Pladt up and down. "Goblin?" he asked, noting the pallor of Pladt's face and the ragged cuts in his shirt.

"Yes," Haydren replied hurriedly. "Do you have what I need?"

Faschek paused to spit again. "You know his chances aren't good," he said.

"They're nothing if we don't give him the herbs!" Haydren replied with eyes blazing. "Do you have them?"

Faschek turned and went back into the house. The door remained open, so Haydren carried Pladt inside. Sarah came last, a curious hesitance in her glance.

"Take the horses and stable them," Geoffrey said, turning on Sarah. "We're going to be here for a while."

"Geoffrey—"

"Just go!" he said, turning her and pushing her toward the door.

Sarah marched out with one quick glance behind her. A breeze nudged her as she exited the house, but she ignored it, snatching the reins of two of the nearest horses and yanking them toward the barn. Itinerant eddies threw her hair in her face, and she clamped her teeth.

When she reached the barn, she let out a frustrated growl. "Idiot! We're in a place he doesn't know with someone who does, and he wants to ignore counsel." She threw her shoulder against the first horse's rump, and turned him into the nearest stall. "If Pladt dies from this, I'll strike him with so many bolts of lightning he'll be a thunderhead all his own."

The second horse stabled, Sarah strode back out to get the last two. Haydren and Geoffrey were on the porch discussing something in low tones; as Haydren went back inside, Geoffrey turned and glanced at her, but stayed where he was.

Don't want to help? She grabbed the last two pairs of reins and hauled their cargo to the barn. She got the first horse in, but the second refused to back up to his place. She tugged the reins, but he just tossed his head and snorted, his eyes rolling white.

"And what's your problem?" she asked, pushing him with her shoulder. He took two steps forward, and she stared up at him. Would magic do anything?

She glanced at the stall, then again. A socked foot stuck up from the hay.

"Thiol, thiol. Mol eo diler li valime re dol kohthaka verit alon tife!"

A gust of wind rustled the hay, blowing bits into the air and uncovering the body.

It was Faschek.

As Sarah ran from the barn, she heard Haydren inside the house shout: "Geoffrey, get in here!"

Geoffrey turned from the porch without looking at Sarah, yanking free his sword as he plunged into the house. She came in behind him. The house was empty except for Haydren and Pladt, and Haydren's sword was thrust into the wall.

"Where's Faschek?" Geoffrey asked.

Haydren looked at Geoffrey without blinking. "I don't know," he replied evenly. "I was about to stick him through, and just before the sword reached him, he vanished."

Geoffrey's sword drooped. "He vanished?" he repeated.

"Faschek is in the barn," Sarah replied, glaring at Geoffrey. "Dead and buried in straw."

Geoffrey glanced quickly at her, then back to Haydren. "How did you know?" Geoffrey asked Haydren, sheathing his sword.

"He claimed we needed to let some of Pladt's blood," Haydren replied. "But I saw where he was about to make an incision. I struck a man in that same spot once," he said, touching the spot on his inner thigh, "and he died—with only a finger-width incision."

"I know that spot," Geoffrey replied. He gestured to the wall. "Take your sword down before it falls on Pladt."

Haydren did so, and sheathed it. "What are we going to do about Faschek?" he asked. "Who *was* he?"

"A sorcerer, no doubt," Geoffrey replied. "It's rumored they can perform such tricks. We must keep a good watch, tonight, should he return."

"'It's rumored?'" Sarah echoed. "To answer the question you two don't seem to want to ask *me*: no, that shouldn't have been possible. Not for...years..."

Haydren gazed at her. "You don't think..."

Sarah's mouth twisted sideways. "What do you think?"

Haydren sighed, moved to a chair, and sat down. He sat in silence for several moments. "I don't know," he said. He chewed his lip. "I want to get Pladt back to Werine."

"Why?" Geoffrey asked.

"Something Runacron mentioned," Haydren replied. "'We're not all warriors,' he said. Pladt knows hydras, and should be home fighting them; that's where he does the most good."

"And how would you intend on getting him home?"

"Maybe before we go to Haschina," Haydren replied in thought.

"I think, after today, we need to get to Haschina as quickly as possible," Sarah interjected.

Haydren glared at her for a few moments. "I could take him to Estwind and put him on a boat," he said.

"You should not decide for him, though," Geoffrey replied. He held up a hand to silence the protest in Haydren's open mouth. "You get some rest. I'll take the first watch."

As Haydren laid out his bedroll, Sarah moved beside Geoffrey. "I know you don't like what I do," she said quietly, but firmly. "And for some reason you and Haydren go on like I'm not here. But both of you risked Pladt's life even more by ignoring me today. I could sense Faschek wasn't right, and I tried to warn you."

Geoffrey's head ducked, then turned toward Pladt.

"Why do you both act like I'm not here, sometimes?"

Geoffrey turned to her, then nodded his head toward the door. They stood.

"Haydren, I'm going to check on the horses, and do something with Faschek's body," Geoffrey said. "I'll leave the door open. Shout if anything happens."

Haydren nodded, and watched them go.

"Sarah, I know what answer would make sense," Geoffrey said as they walked toward the barn. "But we did not get to know you that well in Quaran. You weren't able to help much through the Forest—I am not blaming you," Geoffrey said quickly as Sarah took a breath. "But that was how it was. Then Earl Durdamon knew things about us that no one should know, and you were standing apart from us while he set us up for this mission. Haydren, Pladt, and I have been nothing but honest with one another—sometimes painfully so." They reached the barn, and stood in the doorway. "So far, we have seen little of that honesty on your part."

Sarah folded her arms and leaned against the doorframe. "Earl Durdamon knows *everything* that no one should know," she said. "I've only met one other person who was like that, and he was the strongest wind-wizard I've known. Durdamon has never let on that he has magical affinity, but... I did not tell him anything about you. You can disbelieve me," she continued, and Geoffrey flashed a grin as his eyes fell: he had failed to keep his eyes from rolling. "But this is me trying to be honest with you. I came to Kelian with no weapons, as I had escorts. I know my abilities with wind, and how they might be limited, but it was not safer for me to bring anything else. I think, instead, you all knew each other by the time you met me. And you, Geoffrey, didn't care to get to know me because I'm a Rinc Nain who uses magic."

"For which you still haven't explained yourself," Geoffrey cut in.

"I don't need to," she replied. "You have made your feelings quite clear, and for now I reject them. And if I do, that is between the God and myself, not you. Tell me, did you join *Uv Fehn* before or after you came to believe the Histories?"

She hadn't meant to deflate Geoffrey so completely, and she instinctively reached out and grasped his arm. "I'm sorry," she said. "I could have opened that door more gently. But I'm sure you chose as wisely as you could, at that point, and have since asked forgiveness. I, too, may have to ask for forgiveness. But I have to act as wisely as I see now."

"I wish I could save you from having to ask the forgiveness I've had to," Geoffrey replied.

Sarah released his arm, and pushed some hair out of her face that the wind had pulled free. "Don't be quite so sure of yourself," she said, folding her arms. "I meant that generally, not about magic specifically.

Either way, you two need to start letting me in. I know this land. I've lived here for twenty years. I've met Faschek before, and Dasillion, and others. I know the land around Jyunta, and I know the Jyuntans—including Lord Garoun."

Geoffrey caught her emphasis. "You sound like we might have trouble with him."

"I know you're going to have to put *Uv Fehn* behind you," she said, fixing Geoffrey in her gaze. "And you're going to have to learn to be able to take my advice, and accept that just because you might know one thing that I don't, that doesn't mean you know everything."

—◦—

Later that night, Geoffrey sat beside Pladt with his sword across his lap and Sarah's words across his mind. Surely it had been more than pride that changed her mood so quickly, and made her release his arm. He glanced at his sleeve, the cloth no longer wrinkled where her fingers had held him, there no longer the proof of her touch.

Pladt's eyes fluttered open. He glanced across the ceiling, down to the bed, then at Geoffrey.

"Good morning," Geoffrey said with a small grin.

Pladt glanced at the window. "It's pitch dark," he replied. "How long have I been laying here?"

"Since late Evening," Geoffrey replied. "Though, you went unconscious at Evening."

"Great."

Pladt fell silent, studying the ceiling. Geoffrey watched him. Finally, he said: "Pladt, you have been silent a lot these past few days. Ever since we arrived in Frecksshire, even."

"What would you like me to say?" Pladt replied. "I don't speak Rinc Nain."

Geoffrey glanced sharply at him. "What does that matter?"

Pladt sighed. "It's just like back home. No one wants to hear me speak, hear what I have to say. Just keep killing those hydras, Pladt, we'll take care of the important things." He closed his eyes. "Finally that had changed, when I came along with you and Haydren. Now we're in Coberan Province, where I don't speak the language everyone else does. And you and Haydren are perfectly fine to go on in Rinc Nain with everyone else. Now look at me," he said, glancing down at his bandages. "I can't even use my bow effectively to help protect Haydren."

"Pladt, are you upset that you can't speak Rinc Nain, or that you have had a string of ill fortunes?" Geoffrey asked.

"I'm upset that people don't take me seriously," Pladt said, turning and looking at Geoffrey. "Back in Werine, I was old enough to save them week after week from hydras. But let me try to enter one conversation, and suddenly I'm too young to know anything. Now you guys don't bother to translate for me, or speak in a language I can understand: why? Is it not worth your time? Can't I help with anything?"

Geoffrey laid a hand on Pladt's shoulder. "I'm sorry, Pladt," he said. "I guess you were so quiet, we never thought about it. You are still an important part of Haydren's company, I promise you that. Your skills with a bow will not go unused. I get the feeling Haydren's journey is far from over, and he's going to need all of our help to finish it."

Pladt laid his head back. "Okay," he replied. "Just don't leave me out of you guys' plan-making, okay? I do know a little bit about protecting people."

"You and Sarah should talk to one another," Geoffrey muttered. When Pladt glanced at him, he smiled. "We won't, Pladt. And I know you do, just as well if not better than anyone else."

Pladt smiled too, only a little hesitant. "Thanks, Geoffrey. So what's next?"

"You need to rest. In a few days, the poison should pass, and we'll be on our way to Jyunta."

Pladt craned his head. "How is Haydren doing, anyway?"

Geoffrey glanced at Haydren's sleeping form and sighed. "He's surviving," he replied. "Still confused and struggling, but surviving. It seems like we should have died many times over by now. But still he keeps going. And despite the obstacles, he continues succeeding. Whatever I may have said back in Frecksshire," he said, glancing at Pladt—but the archer had fallen asleep. Geoffrey smiled, and finished, whispering to himself: "I would follow Haydren only to see what he can accomplish, if nothing else."

⚬

Storm clouds slid back in the next day, drenching the low moors ever more. Pladt gained strength with each hour as Haydren tended him.

That night, Haydren had the watch. He took a position beside the archer, sword on his lap. He gazed into the fire, alone with his thoughts. A quick yawn cracked Haydren's face, and he shook his head trying to clear cobwebs from his mind. Why was he suddenly so tired? He glanced down at his sword, and the flames along the blade were pulsating with faint light. Another yawn, and his eyes fluttered closed. Though his mind shouted warning, he could not seem to keep his eyes open. He got out a muffled "Sar—" before a final yawn devastated him. The last thing he saw was his sword blazing a little brighter, and then darkness closed around him.

When he awoke, Aerithion was still in his lap, and Pladt still rested comfortably in the bed beside him. Geoffrey and Sarah were stretched out on the floor near the fireplace, where they had been last night.

But their packs, which had been arranged by the door and ready for departure, were gone. Haydren sighed, stood, and sheathed his sword.

"Wake up, you two," he called.

Geoffrey stirred, and looked up at him. "I dreamed Faschek—or who-ever—came back and took our things," he said, his voice thick. "I was trying to go after him, but he turned into a rat and crawled away."

"Then next time go to sleep with a net, so maybe you can catch him," Haydren replied. "Because he did come and take our stuff." He gestured angrily to the blank wall where their packs had been. "He must have cast some kind of sleeping spell on me, because in three breaths I went from wide awake to fast asleep." He glanced down at his sword. "Aerithion tried to warn me, but..."

Sarah sat up and rubbed her eyes. "Aerithion?" she asked.

Haydren swallowed. "My sword," he said. "I don't—the name came to me, at Dasillion's house, in a dream. I can't say for certain—I mean, it may not be—"

Geoffrey waved him to silence. "I'm certain it is, Haydren. Memories come from strange places. Well, the sword must have done something, or else why didn't he kill us all? He didn't hesitate to try and kill Pladt the first time, even with you standing right there." He yawned and threw the covers off. "Do you think Pladt can travel today? We shouldn't stay here too long."

"I think so," Pladt called from the bed, where he now sat up with his feet resting on the floor. "It would have been better if what's-his-name had given us another day, but I'd rather be dead tired than just dead. Ha!" His bark of laughter ended with a cough, but his three companions smiled.

"I'll gather the horses," Sarah offered, standing and heading outside.

"Glad to see you're back, Pladt," Haydren said after she had gone.

Pladt waved him off and stood shakily. "Any more of the yummy pond water you've been feeding me?" he asked. "I usually feel a little stronger just after taking it."

"Sure," Haydren replied, retrieving the bottle for him.

"Are you sure that's what's in there?" Pladt asked, peering into the bottle's mouth. "I can't understand what's-his-name only taking our packs and nothing else."

"I think we can call him Semmelle," Haydren said, taking the bottle back and sniffing it. After touching his finger to the rim, he gingerly tasted the liquid. He raised his eyebrows and shrugged. "Tastes like it's supposed to," he replied. "Perhaps Geoffrey's right: our packs were right next to the door."

Sarah returned, empty-handed. "So, it seems he took our horses," she said.

Haydren handed the bottle back to Pladt. There was not much left, and the archer drained it quickly.

"Well that makes leaving that much quicker," Geoffrey said, strapping on his sword. "We'll leave the bedrolls here and get new ones in Jyunta."

Pladt stood and picked up his bow and quiver, and with nothing else to carry they set off northward.

Pladt's energy flagged quickly, and by Noon they had barely traveled ten miles. The pond-dotted horizon firmed into the higher lands leading them to Jyunta. They reached dry land after a last moorish lunch provided by Pladt's bow. Exhausted but exuberant, Pladt fell to his knees, then onto his side upon reaching firm ground again, and rolled onto his back.

"Land!" he exclaimed as the others watched curiously. They smiled, following Pladt's gaze skyward to a pale blue expanse marred only by a few tall white clouds that drifted lazily on high breezes. A shadow raced over the plains, enveloping them as a cloud blocked the sun. But behind the shadow, the sun ran toward them once again as the cloud drifted away.

Pladt sat up, shaking a fist at the moors. "If I never see them again, I'll still die a little upset for having trekked through them to begin with," he said, flashing a smile.

"Well if you don't get up, we'll leave you here to keep staring at them," Haydren joked. Pladt stood, and the four continued their march northward.

They camped early, for Pladt's strength had not yet fully returned. By the time the eastern stars began appearing, they had made beds of cut grass and wrapped themselves in their cloaks to ward off the early summer-night's chill. Their progress the next two days was slower than typical, but better than Haydren anticipated. Though he did not have his maps—yet another thing for which to promise revenge upon Semmelle—he felt sure they would reach Jyunta the next day.

That day was, by Pladt's estimation, a perfect summer day. The sun was warm, but a fresh breeze blowing from the south cooled them as they walked. And though he missed the horses, Pladt was back into walking shape, and the company made good time as the land continued to rise, along with their spirits. Anticipation at reaching Jyunta propelled them past dinner and into the night. A Progenitor Moon—the first full-moon of the year—had risen, casting the grass in spectral silver, but still Jyunta did not mar the horizon.

Here, the land was no longer flat, and hidden valleys—shallow, twenty or thirty paces deep in the center—began carving themselves out of the terrain. The grasses were dry, and only knee-height. Few trees broke the horizon, flourishing instead in the valleys. As they continued, a deep scar appeared. Into that scar they descended, and trees loomed out of the shadows. A small rock-pool fed by a spring was at the valley's center. After refreshing themselves, they mounted the other side of the valley.

As the surrounding plains came into view, a light flared up ahead. Dark against the sky was the squat silhouette of a large fortification. The torch which had been lit upon the ramparts was thrust into a sconce on the outer wall. Soon, another torch was lit, and another, and those too were pinned in sconces, until the entire castle wore a ring of torches like a glistening crown.

"I suppose we're there," Pladt remarked as the four stood abreast upon the edge of the valley.

"I don't see much of a gate," Geoffrey said.

Pladt gazed ahead, whistled low, and shook his head. "No, there isn't one," he concurred.

"Strange," Sarah said. "We should be very careful—"

She was cut off by a sudden and familiar flash of orange, and bright white light to the north-east. Paolound had reappeared. Haydren and Geoffrey drew their swords, Pladt nocked an arrow, and a tuft of wind swirled Sarah's cloak.

From the white pillar strode the dragon. He did not make for the city, which was nearer, but rather for the four companions. The fire from his mouth began in his eyes. He had come to finish what he had started a month ago.

"Stay far apart," Haydren said in a low voice. "And watch for his tail."

Pladt sprinted right; Geoffrey, left; Sarah and Haydren held their ground. Paolound paused, watching them. He was too far away yet to spew his fatal flame. But the man in front of him held The Sword, so his measured steps moved forward once again.

An arrow hissed through the darkness, piercing Paolound's eye, and he bellowed rage as flame burst from his mouth. Pladt, finding more strength than he knew he had, jumped and tumbled out of the way. Geoffrey charged in from the left. Paolound began to swipe at him with a paw. Haydren could see the dragon's tail beginning to twitch.

"Watch his tail!" he shouted. Geoffrey ducked the slashing talons, hurdled the tail, and Follus hummed as it bit into the dragon's flank. Not pausing in his dash as Paolound roared greater anger, Geoffrey ran past the dragon and back into the night, flame chasing him in vain.

When Geoffrey was well clear, a great fist of lightning cracked against Paolound's back, punching him to the ground. He moaned anger and staggered to his feet again.

Haydren sprinted forward. Aerithion pulsed in his grasp, its red light shimmering down the blade. Haydren whispered its name, and the Bultum surged. Pure red light shone forth and the flames danced as if alive.

Paolound turned, eyeing the madly dashing swordsman who bore his doom. He cried out in anguish, in fear. He did not want this, but the whisper in his head compelled him. Razor talons grasped; Bultum cut them. Fire shot forth, and was met by Cretal defense. Paolound screamed; Haydren shouted. Another arrow from the darkness completed the dragon's blindness, and searing, stabbing fire erupted in the dragon's heart.

The whisper vanished with a hollow shriek. The dragon's veins collapsed. Muscles gave way, and the great Paolound crumpled to the ground.

Haydren, gasping, barely leapt clear of Paolound's lifeless head as it crashed to the plains.

Geoffrey entered the light, sheathing his sword. "Do you know what you have done?" he breathed.

Haydren's chest heaved as the fire in Aerithion reduced to bare embers. A shout echoed from the top of the walls, and a cheer swelled from within them—leaked out, Haydren noticed, through gaping holes and derelict stone. Runacron's tale of war had not been limited to Paolound, and the dragon's death would not win it.

"It wasn't just me," he said, quenching Aerithion in its sheath. Sarah and Pladt came forward, chests heaving from exertion and awe as they all gazed at the still form of the dragon.

From the gap in the wall where the gate should have been, a procession poured out, enveloped them, and carried them forward into the castle with deafening cheers and resounding thumps on their backs.

It seemed the entire city was alive, though there were barely as many people as Haydren had seen at one time in Hodp.

The impromptu parade dropped them in front of a large stone building near the center of town where a large man dressed in rich clothing stood at the top of a short flight of stairs. Torches held high lit the square to daylight proportions, and cheers and chants of "Dragonsbane!" echoed up and down the street, in defiance of the large man's raised hands of protest.

The townsfolk up front finally noticed, and silence flowed down the street until it seemed the entire town waited on his words with bated breath. He lowered his hands and gazed at the four in front of him.

"We welcome you heartily to Jyunta tonight, friends and dragon slayers!" he said. A cry of "Dragon slayers!" echoed up and down the streets.

"I am Lord Garoun," the large man continued as silence was restored. "Our city cannot thank you enough for your salvation this night. Though we had seen the Pillar of the Dragon many nights to our south, we dreaded the day he might approach our walls. But on this fateful night, when it seemed the dragon would finally devour us, saviors have appeared!"

Haydren glanced around as the people cheered. Paolound had never approached the walls, and it seemed clearer to him that Paolound had arrived to attack him and his friends than the city of Jyunta.

Suddenly, above the cheers, a scream sounded from down the street. Haydren craned his neck, as did his companions. The people, oblivious, renewed their cheering. But more screams echoed through the night, and the cheering scattered and broke off.

"Goblins!" came the first coherent word, quickly repeated in fear. The parade became a mob as women, children, and old men scrambled to empty the square. Lord Garoun disappeared into the building behind him. Haydren drew his sword. So, lords were the same no matter where you went.

Sarah had already gone, her instinct for protecting the city returning instantly. With Geoffrey and Pladt by his side, Haydren ran toward the sounds of a mounting battle. Geoffrey pointed to a ladder beside a low building, and Pladt scrambled up to the roofs. Geoffrey and Haydren continued together until they reached the fighting.

Two soldiers waved halberds at three goblins, desperate to keep them at bay in the narrow street. As Haydren and Geoffrey neared, two other goblins stepped into the road behind the soldiers. With a shout, Bultum and Follus thrust forward, ending the threat. Now, with help behind them, the Jyuntan soldiers wielded their halberds with greater confidence, dispatching two of the goblins before them. The third broke and ran. Moments later a sharp twang from overhead sent it twitching to the cobblestones.

A sharp crack of lightning thundered throughout the city. More shouts erupted down the blocks. All four men moved at once, with the archer scampering nimbly across tiled roofs. They reached a group of five men encircled by eight kobolds; arrows rained, Bultum sang, and Follus hummed—but not before two of the embattled Jyuntans fell slain. The others paused, hovering quietly over their fallen friends, until Geoffrey gripped them by the shoulders.

"There are others still alive," he said gently. "Come with us."

⚬

They moved through the city all that night, following the shouts, until the stars in the east began to fade. By Geoffrey's estimation, nearly half of what remained in Jyunta's defense would not see the next sunset.

"Is this every night?" Geoffrey asked the band of fifteen who followed them.

"Nearly," replied several at once.

"You do no better than wait for them to come in, and try desperately to keep in groups large enough to not be picked apart?" he asked.

Haydren glanced up quickly, notching his head sideways.

"Our commander was killed weeks ago," said the oldest of the group. "We had no one to replace him."

"So you..." Geoffrey trailed off, gazing hard at Haydren first, then the men, then around at the city. So they waited. Maybe in hope of a miracle—for Earl Durdamon to send someone. More likely they waited for their destruction. The image of Quaran fastened itself in Geoffrey's mind. He could see the charred scape of Jyunta, the lord's stone building the only thing left, and these men before him piled in a heap—if their bodies even remained.

Had he not done much the same? Would he not lead these men, if they repelled the beasts, in total annihilation of—something? Anything?

He had before: a leader with nowhere to go will make any excuse to go everywhere.

He sighed, looking back at Haydren: he promised to help this young man, wherever he was going. Geoffrey knew he couldn't stay here if he wanted to. Besides, he was getting too old to go campaigning.

The men still stood staring at him: maybe he wasn't too old quite yet—at least not for a few days.

"Haydren, I've been with you for a while, now," Geoffrey said in a low voice. Haydren cocked his head. "Now, I need you to do something for me."

"What is it?"

Geoffrey grinned. "Trust me."

As day dawned, they found Lord Garoun wandering his city. The wails of mothers, fathers, children, and wives echoed through streets that had once resounded with jubilation. Lord Garoun's eyes were swollen. They waited on him in solemn respect.

"You seemed perhaps in consternation of our celebration last night, young swordsman," Garoun said, addressing Haydren. "Now you see why. We have little cause for celebration these days. The death of Paolound is the best news we have had in many months."

"We were told, Lordship, that your reports say you are defending Jyunta," Haydren said.

"Of course they do," Garoun scoffed. "The reports that used to say we needed help were ignored, or replied that he was counting on us to defend his northern lands. He was sure we had it in hand." Garoun wiped his lower lip. "So that is what I told him; what he demanded to hear. He says he is determined not to be as overbearing as the east. Each town under his rule is granted far more autonomy than those of Kelian Province. He claims it is more Rinc Nain that way. It is far beyond my ken, though, where he assumes the bestial army will go once they have done for Jyunta."

"My lord," Geoffrey said, clasping his hands behind his back. "I cannot say what may be on the Earl's mind, but I wish to offer my services in your defense."

"What is it you wish to do?" Garoun asked, facing him squarely.

"I would have Haydren take Paolound's body to Estwind, and trade for it whatever he can. In the meantime I would stay here with Pladt and Sarah to aid in your defenses. And, in three days, I would hope Haydren would return with a mercenary army."

Garoun glanced at the three of them. Then, with a crooked finger, said: "Come with me, and let us talk."

They followed him back to his hall, leaving the soldiers of Jyunta to finish burying the dead.

16

PLANS

"You leave now for Andelen?"
"I think it should be yours, Teresh."
"Are you certain?"
"You will do well. I stay with Haydren."

34 Haschina 1320 — Summer

"My lord, a fog is coming in," Geoffrey said with as much patience as he could muster. "If Haydren rides out under it, any spies that might be out there won't see him leave."

Lord Garoun shifted. "Perhaps, but I still do not like losing such a valuable sword now, when that bestial army still threatens our city."

Haydren cut in. "My lord, my companions and I cannot hold back this army, no matter how valuable our swords. Or bows. You need an army. With Paolound's hide, I can buy you one. Geoffrey, Pladt, and Sarah would still be here, and I trust them with my life. I would certainly trust Geoffrey with your soldiers."

"I did not have the opportunity to see him fight," Garoun admitted. "Though, his sword seems interesting enough. Can it transfigure into fire, as yours can?"

Sarah moved forward. "Geoffrey can organize your troops. After what I saw last night, and have heard this morning, they need that more than one or two new swords. Tactics can be employed by all."

Garoun rubbed his chin. "Yes. Yes, I see what you mean. I suppose there is really no other way, then. Well," he said, clapping his hands once. "You will need a fast horse, and a small number of supplies. Estwind is a single hard-days' ride north. There is an inn, the Mercenary Inn, where I hear mercenary captains often find work. We have not been able to spare anyone to go," Garoun explained. "Even though we knew where to find them, we do not have the assets to hire the army we need. Now, perhaps, and with the luck you seem to possess. But!" he said suddenly. "The fog will burn off while I sit here and speak on. And whatever you may think, someone is watching this castle, and it will be far better for you to leave without being noticed. See Thessar, he will equip you quickly with a horse." Garoun gestured to his aide, who ushered the three companions from the hall. Sarah remained behind with Lord Garoun.

At the stables, Thessar quickly saddled a large black stallion while Geoffrey and Pladt stood aside with Haydren.

"I hope you're right about this," Haydren said. "If they come before I get back, the Earl's mission is forfeit."

"It may as well be forfeit if we leave the Jyuntans to themselves," Geoffrey replied. "And I am only as sure about this as any other decision I've made."

"I thought you were a pillar of confidence, Geoffrey."

"You wished I was."

Haydren glanced over the stallion as Thessar fitted the bit in his mouth. "I did."

"I'm sorry I was not the leader you hoped I would be," Geoffrey said. "But you have helped me find that ability again."

Haydren grinned. "I think you should thank Sarah for that one."

Geoffrey cleared his throat; this boy had a tendency of speaking words with greater weight than he realized. "You don't intend to take Pladt to Estwind, then?"

Pladt glanced quizzically at Geoffrey, then at Haydren. "Should he?"

"He's aided in the defense of a city far longer than either of us, Geoffrey."

"You told him to say that, didn't you?" Pladt asked, barely getting the question formed around his broad smile.

Haydren raised a brow; Geoffrey waved him off. "Garoun thinks we are a great boon, coming to him now," he said. "If he's right, if someone is watching this city at all times, they're going to come expecting a dragon slayer. They're going to come in great force. I could sense it last night: whoever is coordinating these attacks is growing weary of the game. The next assault will be to finish Jyunta completely, if it can be done."

"You think someone is coordinating these?" Thessar asked as he approached.

"We walked across much of this country," Haydren replied. "Never have beasts come in diverse numbers, organized enough to attack when the people are distracted by celebration. Yes, we think someone is coordinating these. The horse is ready?"

Thessar nodded. "It should get you to Estwind in one stretch," he said. "Water it at the Vilde River and slow up some. But it can run all day if you pace it well."

"Thank you," Haydren said. He turned to Geoffrey and Pladt. "You must hold for two days," he said.

"It will take them a while to get organized, or even gathered, if they're going to come in as large a size as you think," Pladt said.

Geoffrey nodded. "There's a lot of good men left here. We'll hold. The God speed you on your mission, Haydren."

Haydren paused a moment. "I hope he will. And may he be with you as well, Geoffrey."

Pladt rolled his eyes. "You would think you guys had just met!" he said. "You and your formalities. Good bye Haydren! And if you don't come back in time, I'm going to stay right here as a ghost and harass you for the rest of your life." With that, he wrapped Haydren in a bear-hug and lifted him off the ground. When he released him, Haydren stepped back as a grin crept onto his face.

"Good to see your strength returning, Pladt," he muttered, glancing at Geoffrey.

"Oh, don't expect him to pick you up," Pladt said. "Far, far too old."

Geoffrey nodded toward the horse. "The fog's lifting," he said.

"Right," Haydren said. He turned and climbed onto the shifting stallion. "Two days!" he said, then spurred toward the front gate.

Geoffrey and Pladt watched him turn north onto the road and disappear. Already, several men were wrestling the better parts of the dragon into three large carts, each with a team of six draft horses to pull them. They would not chance a slow journey following Haydren's heels.

<hr>

"The young one rides north," Jgei said, straightening from the map table.

It always bothered Guntsen when Jgei did that, but this time the news tickled him too much to worry about its presentation.

"To Estwind?" he asked gleefully. "Haydren's fleeing? I always knew he was a coward. Do you think he makes for Andelen?"

Lasserain slid his gaze from the behemoth of an Earl to fix Guntsen in one of his most uncomfortable glances. "You really do pay no attention to him whatsoever, do you?" he asked.

Guntsen sat back, sullen. "How's your headache?" he asked.

"Still sitting before me," Lasserain hissed, a chill wind blasting Guntsen's cloak.

"I don't know why you have me here," Guntsen said as he stood and wrestled his clothing straight. "Why couldn't you leave me in Hewolucs to govern my province?"

"Because even here you think it is your province," Lasserain replied, twitching a finger toward the door. "I might be afraid of someone supplanting your gelatinous bulk and posing a threat."

As the door slammed behind Guntsen, he tugged his tunic straight. "It may not take some *one* to take over," he muttered, striding down the stark corridors. "Some mage might already have overthrown me." He returned to his chambers, passing a tray of still-steaming ham as he made for his sword.

———◆———

"Do you think he'll come back in time?" Pladt asked.

Geoffrey nodded. "This siege has been going on a long time, Pladt. I would not be surprised if fifteen mercenary armies were in Estwind, waiting for someone to come and pay them to fight."

"Why wouldn't they just come here?" Pladt asked.

"And risk arriving in the middle of a battle, and fighting for free?" Geoffrey replied with a grin. "They'll be there. And Haydren will be back the day after tomorrow. Which means," he continued, growing serious, "we need to prepare. I need to speak to Lord Garoun. You wait outside. If he tells me what I need him to, I'm going to need you immediately."

"Of course," Pladt replied.

Geoffrey returned to the hall just as Sarah exited.

"He's expecting you," she said, laying a hand on the doorknob. "Geoffrey, he's been lord of Jyunta for a long time. Make sure he sees you as a general, not another lord."

"That should not be difficult," he replied. "I'm sure I don't want to be a lord."

"Not wanting it, and not *sounding* like you want it are two very different things," Sarah said with a smile. "Consider his position—not how you feel his position is—one of desperate need—but how he sees it: as sole leader of an embattled people. And address him as you would want to be addressed in his situation."

"Thank you," Geoffrey said, and he meant it. He *had* been considering Garoun in the former position. Sarah stepped back, and Geoffrey entered to find Lord Garoun still gazing into the fire.

"My lord?" he asked as he approached.

"You call me 'lord' because that is what I am supposed to be," Garoun replied quietly. "Your coming here has cast me in rather a poor light, though, has it not? My subjects, so close to death and destruction, were quite certain I was doing everything that could be done." He smiled, and glanced at Geoffrey quickly. "And then you four arrive, full of hope and promise."

"Perhaps we are just what you need to save your city, my lord," Geoffrey replied. "Until now, perhaps you have been doing everything possible. I have not been here, and I cannot judge. What is important, my lord, is what you have us do now when circumstances have changed."

"I have given the order already, Geoffrey," Garoun replied. "You are the city captain: an order from you, especially concerning the defenses, is an order from me. The leader of the troops should be on his way. He doesn't think of himself that way, so the men tend not to, either. But he knows the city, and will be able to get you anyone or anything you need. Will that serve you?"

Geoffrey's eyebrows shot up in unfeigned surprise. "It is far more than I hoped, my lord."

"Is there anything else?"

Geoffrey paused. "Your city will be saved, my lord."

Garoun said nothing, but gestured his dismissal with a finger. As Geoffrey turned, Garoun's quiet voice made him pause. "We're a country trying to figure out who we are," he said, his gaze still bent on the flames.

"My lord?" Geoffrey asked.

Garoun glanced up. "Burieng. We're half Rinc Nain, half Cariste—other parts Endolin, Keste..." he paused and nodded toward the door, where Pladt presumably waited. "Werine: I recognized Pladt, who he was. Even the Ancient Kalen, long since gone from these lands, still hold sway over it within the Forest. If both Earls could come together, imagine what might be accomplished against Lasserain? Instead, here we are: divided, unable to make a decision for fear it's the wrong one—about to fall."

"That is indeed true, my lord," Geoffrey said, though his thoughts were not on Jyunta alone. "And I would that all Burieng will one day be united. But if we wait too long, it may be united under Lasserain."

"Yes, I know," Garoun said, returning to the fire. "Good luck, Geoffrey."

Turning on his heel, Geoffrey departed. Pladt was conversing with another man several years younger than Geoffrey, but not many. Sarah had apparently disappeared. As much as she wanted to be part of the company, she could not seem to stay around when he might need her.

Pladt looked up. "Geoffrey, this is Corith. He says Lord Garoun sent for him. He even speaks Cariste!" he added with a broad grin.

Corith, Geoffrey recalled, was to be their guide through the Northern Forest. He wondered—doubted—if Corith knew. Short and lithe, Corith did look the part of guide—a man who could get himself into and out of just about anywhere. It was no small wonder that Corith had gotten the attention of Earl Durdamon.

"Many in Jyunta speak the language," Corith explained. "We're not quite as cosmopolitan as Estwind, true. But if that port sees it, so do we, at least in some small measure. For traders, there's no other route overland."

"True enough," Geoffrey replied, descending the stairs with hand outstretched. Corith took it and gripped it firmly. His spirit, at least, was yet unbroken. "What does the city have as far as builders?"

"We have three masons and five carpenters, all with apprentices," Corith replied. "At least, we had before the battle last night. We may have lost some. I have been tending to the troops since then."

"Yes, troops: what soldiers are under your command?"

"I don't command them, really—"

"I asked how many."

Corith shifted. "About thirty men—"

"About?"

Pladt's eyes widened.

"Sir," Corith replied, straightening as he recognized the tone in Geoffrey's voice as well. "I have twenty-eight men without scratches. Another five are wounded, but should be able to fight if pressed. Another three will take a few days to heal. The city has other men of fighting age. I cannot say how many for certain, but less than we would like. I have not had time to train any as yet."

"Weapons?"

"Five men with halberds, the rest with swords."

"Don't you have any bows?" Pladt muttered. Corith glanced at the archer, then at Geoffrey.

"For the next few days, Corith, think of me as your Captain and Pladt as my lieutenant."

"Sir. Our armory has in excess of a hundred bows," Corith replied, addressing Pladt. "But the men who had been trained to use them were among the first to die. The beasts came in close quarters too quickly."

"Very well," Geoffrey replied. "Get me two men who can lead the carpenters and the masons and bring them to me. Then prepare your troops, only those most able. Do you have horns for sounding alarms?" He paused until Corith nodded. "Good. Get them, and prepare them to move out with the carpenters. There is a thickly wooded valley just to the south-east where we will be drawing wood. Your men will guard the workers. Spread them out as thin as possible. Their job, Corith, is to sound the alarm and get back to the castle, nothing else. I will not leave them without swords, though I would prefer it, do you understand?" Once again, Corith nodded quickly. "Go. Just send the builders to me, and prepare your men.

"Pladt," he continued without break as Corith turned and hurried away. "Go through the city. Corith said most should speak Cariste. If you need an interpreter, employ whomever you must. But find those who can handle a bow and set up a range outside the walls. By the time you find them, I will get you access to the weapons so you can begin training. They will not have to be experts," he said, noting the look on Pladt's face. "I believe the same as Haydren: the army that will be coming will be thick enough that targets will not be sparse. As long as they can shoot a bow and not injure themselves or others, it will be better than we have now. Have you seen Sarah?"

"She was leaving as I walked up," Pladt replied.

Just then, a young man of about seventeen walked up. "Geoffrey?" he inquired.

"You are?"

"Perry, sir," the young man responded. "Corith sent me. I can go between you and the masons."

"You are a mason?"

"Yes sir. Perry the Mason, that's me. Well, not yet. I have to some years of training left," he said with a nervous chuckle.

"Very well. We need to fortify the walls, Perry," Geoffrey said. "The masons will need to do what they can to repair the existing sections, as well as prepare the broken sections to receive wooden fortifications."

"You don't want that, sir," Perry interjected. "Stone is much stronger, and joining wood to stone is barely strong at all."

Geoffrey smiled and nodded. "I understand, Perry," he said. "If I could, I would build up these walls as high as Frecksshire, but we haven't the time. Can the masons do as I ask, though?"

"Yes sir," Perry replied. "It can be done."

"Then go do it. Whoever is your senior mason, let him know I would like to see him outside the main gate by Mid-Morning."

"Yes sir," Perry replied.

Geoffrey turned to Pladt, who stood watching the retreating apprentice. "Why are you still here?"

Pladt glanced over and shrugged. "Because I'm lazy," he said evenly.

Geoffrey shook his head, but grinned. "Get out of here. Get those archers and start practicing."

As Pladt left, another man approached, in his late thirties. He had the unmistakable red hair and black brows of a pure Rinc Nain. When he spoke, his voice was deep and his accent thick and pure.

"Corith sent me," he said.

"Your name?"

"Peyden," he replied. "Carpenter."

"Peyden, you and the other carpenters are tasked with, first, building new gates for the city. There is a valley to the south-east. Do you know it?" Peyden nodded once, slowly. "We need to get lumber from there."

"I know the woodcutters. They will do it."

"Perfect. Once gates are fashioned and hung, we're going to need to fortify the most damaged sections of the wall, and then build something nearing ramparts on those sections."

"That is much labor," Peyden said.

"What doesn't get done before the next attack may determine whether we survive," Geoffrey replied. "If you can arrange the woodcutters, I would appreciate it. I will be outside the main gate all day. If anyone has questions, send them to me."

"Very well," Peyden replied, and departed.

Geoffrey turned and saw Garoun's face disappear from a window. The lord's pride would need rebuilt, but later. Much, much later.

Pladt was lost. Well, not entirely lost: he had managed to find thirty men, and a few strong women—ten, for Geoffrey would want to know numbers—and sent some to the main gate with instructions on how to begin setting up a range. The rest he sent around the city to recruit whomever they might know. And he could find his way back to the last two men, if he had to.

But he needed to find the main gate. Or a person who could tell him. He was not particular.

So he wandered the unusually straight, but narrow alleys. The several-story buildings leaned together, leaving one jagged crack of thin blue sky above him. The walls were near enough for him to reach out and touch both sides simultaneously. He enjoyed the feel of rough walls beneath his fingertips. In Werine, he would often find himself wandering random streets, feeling the brush of stone warmed by the sun, or cooled by shade. He knew every quarter of his town—he called it his because he defended it.

He paused, glancing up and down the alley. Was there a place just like this in Werine? It almost looked familiar. He smirked. After spending so much time in Werine, wishing to be somewhere else, here he was thinking he was still back home. He had thought a lot of home, about his father and mother, especially since his encounter with the goblin. He was a complete stranger in Frecksshire, unable to even speak the common language, and unaware of the dangers. Few of them were as terrifying as hydras, but he knew hydras—could tell when one was about to spit fire.

Maybe his father was right, trying to keep him in Werine. Pladt always assumed it was for selfish reasons, and maybe there still were. Perhaps, while. the bird that is free is content to sit on its perch, the caged bird can think of nothing but spreading its wings.

He continued down the alley.

The road opened into a square, with three other alleys threading away to the quarters of the wind. In the center, rudely formed where the cobblestones had worn away and dislodged, was a small garden of flowers. A floral mirror of the sun that peered through crowding rooftops, marigolds and lilies and chrysanthemums of orange and yellow shone in the midst of dull gray and brown. Pladt stopped short, transfixed by the beauty struggling in the midst of colorless oppression.

The wind, gusting around the rooftops, sounded nearly like waves breaking against a quay. The voices of men—the foresters, he presumed, hitching up teams to wagons—could be bent, just a little, into the cries of gulls. And just like that, he was back in Werine. In a small square not too far from his house there was a similar garden, though less of an accident than this one appeared. And yet it spoke just as surely that those who could not wield sword or bow still wielded beauty.

Pladt moved closer, the fragrance soon overpowering the smell of the gutters. The sticky sweet stamens of the lilies pulled toward his nostrils, dancing through his head and rolling around his tongue as he drank them in. This was defiance stronger than the flight of an arrow, resiliency of spirit more solid than a shield. How many times had kobold or hell-hound charged through this square? He could see the trampled lilies on the verge. But day after day, told by the absence of weeds, the gardener returned to fix what had been broken.

Jyunta, the garden of Qalat County, had been ravaged for sure, and more than the verge was mauled by tooth and claw. But now it would be weeded and tended, and on its borders the best of defenses.

If not the best, then with Pladt's help the most fletched.

Pladt turned and walked toward the eastern alley, which he thought might take him back to the main gate. He stopped at the edge of the square and turned back for one more look, to remember it as long as he lived.

Then he turned quickly and strode away.

Finally down a side alley, he saw two men who were having a quiet conversation. Scimitars hung at their hips, and they looked to Pladt to be quite capable with them. As he walked over, the one leaning against the wall noticed him, and nodded to his partner. They straightened.

"We need archers," Pladt said as he approached. "I don't suppose you two already know how to use bows?"

"Filly does," said the first, gesturing. "At least, better than me."

"And your name?" Pladt asked.

"Arik."

"Very well. Go over to the main gate, there's a range being set up," Pladt said, pointing vaguely to where he thought the main gate might be. "When I get there, I'll equip you with bows and train you. Okay?"

Arik glanced at Filly, then nodded once. "Sure thing."

"Thanks," Pladt said. He turned away, paused, and then turned back. "Say," he said quietly, "do you guys know which direction the main gate is from here?"

———◆———

Sarah paced her old room—sparse with only a bed, a maple chest and nightstand, and a table that leaned when she wrote—running through words in her mind. Of course she had left all her best parchments in Frecksshire. She'd intentionally abandoned many of the ones here in Jyunta, and with good reason: they were gibberish, or stained too badly with too many words blotted out, or too powerful for her to attempt just yet.

Hethikto kohthaka. Maybe simply because of its impossibility, those words kept coming back to her mind. Unless *hethikto* was not a compound word, but one single word she had never learned—which she doubted—the two together meant five thousand horse-speed. Fast enough to travel the width of Burieng in a blink.

Too powerful! It could not happen. But there it was. It was one of the clearest spells on one of the most blotted-out parchments—all the words legible, except the size of the spell. And no indication of what it might be useful for.

She had used *five* horse-speed against Paolound, so the spell was not entirely foreign: but how and why five *thousand?* This was the trick, and one that sent her pacing the pale line in her old room. Someone had done something that seemed impossible, but maybe only impossible because of one blotted-out word. No matter how small she could think to make the spell, five thousand horse-speed would kill her—should kill anyone. But it was written down, and nothing around it said "never do this, for you will die."

It should say that, but it didn't. Jyunta could fall, and she could be killed with everyone else, and all Coberan go with it. Still her first question of the God would be: *Five thousand? How is that possible?*

Perhaps she should be thinking about Jyunta. But no, she had those spells decided: a few to convince Geoffrey that magic was helpful, and a few comfortable others—basic spells that were always effective.

At the size of a tailor's pin, five thousand horse-speed would be a minor drain, but not very useful. At least, no more useful than an arrow. And magic should always be more useful than man-made implements.

Hethikto kohthaka. She turned and paced back.

⚬

The work progressed quickly the rest of the day. Geoffrey saw little of Sarah, and he put her out of his mind. By noon, Pladt had gathered fifteen more men and equipped them with bows, and kept the entire contingent—fifty-five was far more than Geoffrey dared hope the young archer would find—on the range until sunset.

Geoffrey halted the work. The gates had been hung, and the east wall was as strong as it would ever be without stonework. The south wall, Geoffrey's next project, had been readied for wooden supports. But, despite the tireless efforts of the laborers, it would not be finished that day.

A red western sky found Geoffrey on the east ramparts, looking over the work. Only the mightiest catapult would make easy work of the defenses here, and from information given to him by Corith, the beasts would not have catapults.

Pladt stood beside Geoffrey. He had halted training when the troop's fingers were too raw to hold the string. He gave them each a salve to cool the blisters and prepare them for the forthcoming battle, then joined Geoffrey on the ramparts.

"Do you think they'll come tonight?" Pladt asked.

Geoffrey folded his arms as he surveyed the plains. "They would be here by now," he said.

Pladt grinned. Geoffrey raised an eyebrow. "What?" he asked.

"I think that's the shortest statement you've made today," Pladt replied. He sobered as Geoffrey returned his gaze to the plains without responding. "Why the change?" Pladt asked gently. "I've never seen you take charge like that before, even just before you went in to see lord Garoun."

"I've never needed to," he replied simply.

"I didn't know you were *able* to," Pladt said with a snort.

"I was captain of the *Uv Fehn*. Do you remember them?" He sighed. "If you must know, Pladt, I was afraid of taking charge again. I led those men so far astray, distracted by what I thought was right. They loved me too much to argue with me, and they paid dearly for it." Geoffrey leaned on the battlement, and closed his eyes. In his mind, he saw campfires surrounded by men who had loved him, whom he had loved, and who were now dead. He saw them surrounded by friends, and then dying alone, and then looking at him with somber and distressed eyes.

He looked up again, trying to chase the visions from his mind. Pladt was looking at him with eyebrows furrowed in concern. He drew a deep breath, and forced a grin. "But after Sarah prepared me days in advance—however she knew to do that—I knew what I would have to do," he continued. "It came back much easier than I thought it would."

Pladt grinned compassionately. "It took me some time to convince Corith that you wouldn't kill him if he made a mistake," he said.

"Does he know our mission from the Earl yet?" Geoffrey asked.

Pladt shook his head. "I didn't tell him. Haydren wouldn't have had the chance to." He paused. "I haven't even seen Sarah."

Geoffrey caught the undertone. "I'm sure she knows what she's doing," he said. "At least in part."

⸻◦⸻

They resumed early. Satisfied with their ability to shoot their bows, Pladt took the day to instruct them in measuring distances and reloading arrows as fast as they could. With barely a day of training, the display seemed more a comedy but for the tragedy of what might come by tomorrow. By After-Noon, the south wall was finished, and work was done to the stone to reinforce it along the other walls. Though there were only three Master Masons, their apprentices worked quickly with the help of able-bodied Jyuntans. And the north and west walls showed less wear.

By Evening, though there was daylight left, Geoffrey let the men rest. He anticipated an imminent arrival by the bestial army. They had taken too long to arrive already, and the walls were as durable as they could be made with wood. Corith and his men remained out away from the castle, to sound an alarm when the army approached.

As daylight faded, Geoffrey and Pladt met again on the battlements. Wearied, they sat with their backs against the wall. As they discussed the several accomplishments of the day, and marveled at how swiftly the work had progressed, Sarah strode up the stairs and sat beside them.

"Glad you could join us," Geoffrey said.

"Good evening," she returned, as she tilted her head back against the wall and closed her eyes.

"Long day?" Pladt asked.

"Several," she replied. "It feels almost as if I've gone across the width of Burieng and back in two blinks of an eye."

"I feel like that would kill you, not weary you," Pladt replied.

Sarah laughed long. Rubbing a hand across her forehead, she looked at him appreciatively. "One day, Pladt," she said, "remind me to tell you why that was the most appropriate thing you could have said."

"Thank you," Pladt said with an amused glance at Geoffrey.

"The walls look strong," she said. "And a gate? You spoil us, Geoffrey."

"Hopefully so the enemy does not," Geoffrey returned.

"I'm serious. I wasn't sure you could do it, to be honest."

"Oh?"

"It's always harder when you command people who don't know you. It shows something that they listened to you as they did."

"It was not without missteps," Geoffrey replied.

"Even so, we have walls and a gate where there had been none for weeks. And you got it done in two days." She shook her head.

"I enjoy accomplishing things of material use," he replied simply. Sarah said nothing, though there was a tension in the silence.

Geoffrey leaned his head forward. Something was wrong, he could feel it. The winds were eddying uncertainly. He glanced at Sarah, whose expression mirrored his.

"What is it?" Pladt asked.

"I hope they don't have a wind-user," Sarah muttered. She glanced worriedly at Geoffrey. "I'm not as young as you might think I am, and I have more skill in magic than many I've met." She paused, and her eyes hardened. "But remember I also haven't had the training of many others I've met." She stood, and gazed out over the wall. She drew a deep breath. "There's something to be said for high vantage points," she said, glancing at Geoffrey and Pladt as they remained seated. "And for clear eyes."

"Why—?" Pladt began.

Suddenly, a horn winded long and it wailed over the drifting breeze. Then another horn sounded, and a third. As Geoffrey and Pladt leapt to their feet, the thundering of hooves echoed against the wall as Corith and his guards retreated to the castle. In the distance, a long column of darkly moving shapes cut a line through the plains.

Corith and his men entered the streets below as the gates boomed shut behind them. Corith mounted the stairs to the wall and stood beside

Geoffrey. "They came right where you thought they would," he said. "I could have left half the men here to rest for tonight."

Geoffrey glanced between the evening sun and the advancing army. "I doubt the battle will be joined until the morning. Haydren should have his army by now. Pray that they may move quickly back here." He glanced quickly at Pladt. "We're going to need them."

17

EXECUTIONS

"How is your young soldier?"
"Delayed. And yours?"
"On their way. They were not so difficult as Haydren."
"Hopefully."

36 Haschina 1320 — Summer

As night fell, and the army advanced on Jyunta, torches were lit along the column—carried, Geoffrey assumed, by kobolds. In the hierarchies of beasts, it seemed the humanoid dogs occupied the lowest rank. As the column neared, Geoffrey could see wolves, kobolds, hellhounds, Moorish goblins, and even the occasional Plains goblin with short, tan fur and not the poisonous secretions of their watery cousins.

In the darkness, the army began to array itself against the city. Those on the battlements could do little else but watch.

As more beasts poured into the broad plain before them, Geoffrey caught sight of a thing near the middle of the column that chilled his heart.

"Pladt," he said. "Your eyes are better. Is that—?"

"It's a golem," Pladt affirmed quietly. "So much for the gates."

"Keep your eyes open for the manipulator," Geoffrey said. "He should stand out in a field of beasts."

"I have never seen one of these," Sarah said.

"Golems can rarely be found living wild," Geoffrey replied. "They may be only a little larger than a human, but there is great strength hiding in their compressed bulk. Manipulators control a golem to do their bidding. They are able to forge some sort of link between their minds and see through the golem's eyes to control it. But if the manipulator can be killed—"

"He won't let himself get close enough to be shot at," Pladt interjected. "Why would he?"

"Because if he doesn't, we're going to die tomorrow," Geoffrey replied matter-of-factly. He glanced at Pladt and grinned. "Besides, he doesn't know we have a world-famous archer with us, does he?"

"Your optimism is inspiring, Geoffrey, it really is," Pladt said. "However misplaced it may be."

"Don't forget you have a sorceress with you as well," Sarah murmured.

Geoffrey glanced at her. Sarah kept her eyes on the field below with the barest shake of her head.

Far afield, they could see the end of the column. Thousands of beasts were massed before the castle under hundreds of glittering torches. The golem had seated himself in the middle of the congregation. The manipulator was nowhere to be seen.

"You don't suppose they brought a golem without a manipulator, do you?" Geoffrey asked.

Pladt gazed at him for several long moments, then shook his head and looked away. "So, so misplaced," he muttered.

Geoffrey shrugged. "Perhaps. This army will take until morning to get organized. We may as well sleep while we can. Pladt, would you take the first watch? Corith can go second, and I'll take the last."

"I can watch too," Sarah said with a sharp glance.

"Indeed you can," Geoffrey replied mildly. "I thought you might want to reserve your strength for the battle."

"I'm sure you did," she muttered. Nonetheless, she sat and leaned against the wall.

"What's gotten into you all of the sudden?" Pladt whispered. "Be nice. She is capable of saving lives."

"But at what cost?" Geoffrey whispered in reply. "Magic is not something to trifle with."

Pladt sighed. "I've got the watch, Geoffrey. Sleep well."

After several hours, Sarah stirred and rose, moving to the stairs and descending. Geoffrey watched her go, then settled a little deeper into his slouch. Corith glanced at Pladt and shrugged. Pladt set his jaw.

"Would you mind taking over for a spell?" Pladt asked, glancing as Sarah retreated further into the town.

"Go ahead," Corith said. "I'm awake anyway."

Pladt hurried after Sarah as he tried to recall her last turn in his mind. He didn't want to get lost again.

He caught up just as she reached a door. She startled as he approached, and was muttering something.

"Wait! I just want to talk," Pladt said hurriedly, flinching aside in case the spell was already on its way.

Sarah smirked. "Ducking wouldn't necessarily help," she said.

"That's what I want to talk to you about."

She gave her shoulders a slight shake. "Well come inside," she said. "It's a little too chill out here."

He followed her inside to what was evidently her study. Books were scattered across a long table, with corresponding gaps on a shelf on the far wall where even more and dusty volumes sat on bowed wooden boards. He seated himself on a thickly padded chair while she took up a place on a worn yellow chair behind the table.

"You want to learn magic?" she asked.

Pladt froze. "Can I?"

Sarah cocked her head. "You tell me."

Pladt frowned. "How would I know? Is there some sort of test?"

Sarah smiled. "What did you want to talk about?"

"Oh, right. Well, Geoffrey really doesn't like you using magic." He shrugged. "I just wanted to learn more about it, to see if he might be right."

"Did he send you?"

Pladt shook his head vigorously. "N-no, I'm really, honestly curious."

Sarah drew a deep breath, and let it out. "Do you know anything about it?"

"You can apparently kill a bunch of gremlins at once with it," Pladt said. "And aggravate a goblin." He gave a tentative smile.

"And knock down a dragon," Sarah added with a raised forefinger. "Let's not forget that one."

"Oh no, of course not," he said, smiling broader. After a moment, it faded slightly. "But you can't destroy this army?"

Sarah grimaced, and shook her head. "Magic, most basically, is using the language that the God of All used to create the universe. Except we manipulate. We cannot create, like he did. I can't create air; but I can tell the existing air to do certain things."

"I would think a strong enough gale could blow the whole army away," Pladt offered.

"It could. But I can't." Sarah hummed. "That doesn't help you. Okay, it has to do with energy—a person's energy. The element will take energy from the caster in order to perform the command."

"Do you mean, you can tell the wind to pick up a rock, but only as big a rock as you can lift on your own?"

"Hmm, not quite. Because then why don't I just pick up the rock on my own? See, how big a rock I can lift deals with my strength. But if I pick up a small rock and move it from one pile to a different pile ten feet away, then go back to the first pile and pick up a second rock, I can do that for a good portion of the day and end up moving a pile of rocks much larger than the pile I could pick up all at once."

"Oh. That makes sense."

"The danger is, we don't always know what a spell will do, or how much energy it will take, because sometimes no one has used that spell in centuries."

"What happens if you cast a spell that you don't have the energy for?"

"You die," Sarah replied flatly. "It takes so much energy from you that your heart can't beat."

"That sounds like fun."

Sarah barked a short laugh. "To drive that point home, there are spells in Cariste that have been left going, because its size was just enough to cast, but also killed the caster. Sort of a fool magician's memorial: always know what your spell will do before you cast it."

"They left it going?" Pladt asked. "So they're able to cease it, if they wanted?"

"Oh, yes, ceasing a spell is easy," Sarah said, nodding. "Anyone with an affinity to the element can cease any spell—we're not sure why, whether the God put it in as a safety measure. Some have speculated, and Geoffrey would probably be one, that the elements don't want to do our bidding so they'll take any excuse to stop. That's helped more than one caster, because sometimes the energy is enough that you only become unconscious, and whenever a spell is ceased a small portion of energy returns to the caster—so casters rendered unconscious came back when someone ceased the spell."

"What's the command to cease the spell?"

"*Kiet fiol thoi.* And make sure you're focusing on the spell that you want to cease."

"Can you cast a small spell, to see if I can cease it?"

Sarah laughed. "No, there's no need. If you have an affinity for an element, you know. It effects your mood, usually, or it will tell you things when it's present."

"Oh." Pladt paused. "Is controlling an element hard? Does it ever not listen? I mean, if you thought you had an affinity, but your spells never worked..."

"Pladt, when you have an affinity, you know it," Sarah reiterated, a little wearily. "It would be like telling me..." she trailed off with a gesture, searching for an appropriate simile. "I don't know, the sky wasn't blue, or Rinc Na was a southern continent—there we go. I can't tell you why it's in the direction it is, but I know it's north of Cariste, and there's no continents further north of it." She paused as Pladt nodded understanding. "But no, it's not always easy to command the elements. If you pronounce the word wrong, or—especially early on—if your affinity isn't that close, sometimes it will ignore you."

"You can get closer?"

"Sure, it's like a friend," she said. "If someone knows you very well, cares about you, and you ask them to do something they don't already want to do, they're more likely to do it than someone who doesn't know you, maybe doesn't even like you. That has gotten some casters into trouble, too, trying to command the wrong element."

"What do you mean?"

"Well, imagine asking someone who hates you to do something to help you. Aren't they likely to do the exact opposite, just to harm you?"

"You make the elements sound, I don't know...like people."

"In a lot of ways, they act like people—sentient, is the word you're looking for. No, I can't explain that. It's just the way things are."

"Is there one element thats harder to get along with than any others?"

"Do you mean is there one that's harder to control?" She asked. Pladt nodded. "Fire," she answered promptly.

"You didn't have to think very hard about that," Pladt noted with a grin.

"Remember I said we can't create anything, only manipulate what's there? Fire needs fuel, it needs something to burn. Have you ever rubbed your hands together to create heat? And how much energy that took? And you certainly couldn't start a fire with it, much less keep one going. But if you blow air on an existing fire, that doesn't take nearly as much energy, and you can get a blaze going by doing that. Very much the same—but that's the difficult part, from what I've heard: you don't always know exactly what's going to be needed to get the fire that you want. It *might* equate to blowing on an existing flame. Or it might be trying to rub your hands together with enough force and speed to start a flame."

"And you'd burn your hands in the process anyway."

Sarah chuckled. "Right."

Pladt took a breath. "It does sound really dangerous. Aside from using the words of the God, which I think is Geoffrey's biggest problem, it sounds like it could be dangerous to you and the people around you—if elements are sentient, able to oppose you or do more than what you imagine or want..." He trailed off with a shrug.

Sarah considered him for a long moment. "I've been doing this a while," she said finally. "And I'm very careful." Her eyes glittered. "It will only be dangerous for the army attacking us. Which I assume you *don't* have a problem with?"

"I might, if it ends up killing you," Pladt said. "I think Geoffrey would, too."

"I doubt that."

"You shouldn't," Pladt said, standing up. "I know him better than you. I think his primary concern most of the time is people not dying." He shrugged. "But that's up to you, I guess."

"Thanks," Sarah said, her gaze drifting.

"Get some rest," Pladt suggested, turning to leave. Sarah said nothing, and he closed the door behind him.

As dawn broke under Geoffrey's watch, kobolds were running to and fro within the enemy camp. The torches had died out in the night with no one to relight them, and for a brief span Geoffrey could almost forget they were there. But soon their ghostly, huddled masses rose from the plains under dim light.

Geoffrey nudged Pladt with his foot. "Better wake up," he said. "It will begin soon."

"I dreamed they got tired and went home," Pladt said, his eyes still closed. They opened groggily. "Maybe that was me, actually." He peered over the battlements, and yawned. "No, it wasn't them or me. Rotten dreams."

Geoffrey shook his head with a grin. "Pladt, I swear," he said.

Corith stood, as did Sarah. Soon the entire wall was awake and gazing out over the sleeping horde before them. The sun spilled into the sky, chasing the shadows from the plains. A lone, thin trumpet sounded, and as one body the beasts rolled onto their haunches or their knees and stood, all in perfect formation. It was enough to snatch the breath from every soldier atop Jyunta's wall.

"Nicely executed," Geoffrey muttered. "Could you tell where the horn came from? It wasn't blown by the lips of a beast."

Pladt's eyes swept the field, but he shrugged helplessly.

A lone kobold carrying a white flag broke from the lines and lurched forward with many a backward glance. One of the hellhounds snarled at him, and he jumped forward, approaching the walls at a faster walk.

Geoffrey set his jaw. "Pladt," he said. "Give them our answer."

Pladt cocked his head for a moment, and in one fluid motion drew an arrow, nocked it, and loosed it in a smooth arc that terminated in the kobold's chest. With a strangled cry, it pitched to the ground, the flag crumpling over top of it.

A snarling bark rose from the bestial army. Muscles strained, and an occasional hellhound would sprint out, stop, and slide back into formation. Kobolds beat spear against shield, and the goblins squealed and barked in slimy voices that mirrored the muck and mud of their native terrain.

"This is not it," Geoffrey said, his voice low and meant for his companions only. "This is not the end," he said again, louder, for the ears of all nearby. His voice rang from the battlements. "This is not the day for the end of Jyunta! When songs are sung of this day, they will be triumphs sung around the fires of men, not of beasts. Let no dirge be sung by men. This is our city, and our land. They came expecting a broken city of shattered walls and spirits. But we will give them the might of mankind! Let us give them a shout that will be heard from Estwind to Fūnik. Let them hear our cry all the way to Galessern. This is our day: for Jyunta!" Geoffrey cried. With bows raised, the soldiers atop the wall took up the cry, chanting it until it reverberated across the plains. If their thunder did not make it to Fūnik, Geoffrey thought, it made it to the Northern

Forest at least.

With a roar in return, the bestial army advanced. The hellhounds were in the lead, with kobolds behind them. The golem, for the moment, remained where he was. The chant of the humans continued.

Then Geoffrey saw Sarah narrow her eyes, and her lips moved as if talking to herself. Slowly, a mist began to form on each side of the front line of beasts. It thickened until it was opaque, and the beasts, sensing it was magic, pressed together to try to avoid it.

"Pladt, now!" Geoffrey said in an excited whisper.

Pladt was already gauging it, then shouted a command to the archers upon the battlements. Arrows were drawn, and nocked. Geoffrey glanced at Sarah, who gazed at him without smiling. Several tense moments later, beasts were compressed at the narrowest part of the mist.

"Pull!" Pladt cried. One hundred bowstrings creaked as they were drawn. Below, the beasts in the second and third rows were piling up behind the first. "Loose!" Pladt shouted, releasing his own bowstring with a sharp twang. "Volley of four!" As the beasts attempted to regain formation, four hundred arrows fell among them, and scores yelped and fell.

The line of hellhounds finally broke through and were spreading out. The kobolds had been forced to go through it by unseen commands, and were forming a long, thin line. Muttering to herself, Sarah leaned forward and stared hard at them. With a suddenness that even made Geoffrey jump, a line of jagged lightning stabbed into their lines, and abrupt, strangled cries came from within.

The goblins, advancing behind the kobolds, hesitated at the edge of the mist. Another shower of lightning in their ranks pushed them into the funnel with a start, but not before hundreds fell dead.

The kobolds finally stumbled past the front edge of the fog in great disarray, and as a group were entirely disoriented.

"Hold your arrows!" Sarah shouted as Pladt raised his hand. Glancing at her quickly, he held steady. She gripped the edge of the ramparts and shouted into the wind. Her face was red, and Geoffrey could see the veins standing out on her neck. When the last word came out, she collapsed suddenly.

A howling shriek yanked his attention back to the army below. Under the din, he could hear the frantic yipping of the kobolds. As he watched, their shields led them on a stumbling charge to the north.

"It's wind!" Pladt shouted, pointing with glee. "She's blowing them away!" Exactly what he had suggested to her, he thought exultantly. He glanced down, saw her almost unnaturally still. "Oh no." He knelt. Had she killed herself too, as he had suggested she might? As he rolled her over, he heard Geoffrey mutter something. He glanced up, but Geoffrey was looking over the wall at the army. When Pladt looked down again, Sarah suddenly gasped, and her eyes opened a fraction and she sighed. She did not come fully alert, but she was breathing.

"That's why he waited!" Geoffrey seethed.

Pladt glanced back up. "Did you...?"

"Get up," Geoffrey said. "She'll be fine. You need to be ready, now."

Pladt stood warily, not taking his eyes off the sorceress until Geoffrey gripped his arm hard and pointed.

The golem had stood.

The hellhounds hurled themselves at the gate. But it had been built solidly and did not even sway inward. Above, men with buckets of stones dumped their loads onto the beasts.

Yet, Pladt still felt the tremors of the golem's strides vibrate through the ramparts.

Some of the goblins assaulted the wooden fortifications where they extended closest to the ground. It was toward this threat that Pladt's archers directed their attentions now. Some of the goblins made valiant efforts to scale the walls, but those were singled out and quickly shot down.

The golem stalked onward. Geoffrey's eyes darted across the bulk of the army still massed, waiting to move forward. "Pladt!" Geoffrey cried, pointing. "The circle of kobolds! The manipulator is within them!"

Pladt's head snapped up to where Geoffrey pointed. He held up his fingers, measuring the distance. So close to range! He cast a frustrated glance at the golem, then turned back to the manipulator. He drew an arrow and nocked it. With a deep breath, he pulled the string back as far as he dared, aimed upward, and let loose.

The arrow sang through the air, burying itself into the kobold directly in front of the golem master. His head bent in concentration, viewing the battle through the eyes of the golem, the manipulator did not react to the kobold's death. The other kobolds, terrified, shrank back.

"Again, Pladt!" Geoffrey cried.

The golem thudded closer, the tremors of his footfalls reaching the walls. Pladt drew another arrow. The old man twitched his fingers as the golem approached the gate. Pulling back once more as far as he dared, and knowing the string would be weaker from the first pull, Pladt let loose the arrow. It arched through the air, its course true.

The old man's eyes snapped open as the arrow embedded itself. At the city, the golem's clenched fists crashed into the gate, splintering it like kindling as it exploded inward. The old man reached down and pulled the arrow from the ground, thumbing the dirt off the head as he inspected it.

At Jyunta's gate, the beasts which had been pent up outside now strained to get in. The golem stood to one side, its job finished and the manipulator distracted by the arrow. Hellhounds, goblins, and wolves poured through the gate.

Geoffrey's fist clenched around his sword, and he drew it swiftly.

"Corith!" he cried. "Bring your men below!"

A terrific crack of thunder just then jolted him, and he turned to see

Sarah clinging to the wall. In the field below, the bearded old man now lie huddled, his cloak a bonfire. She looked at Geoffrey, her eyes weary and rimmed in red.

"I'm sorry," she whispered.

Geoffrey left her there and turned to the fighting within the city.

The beasts had broken off into detachments and angled down every street. This part of their battle plan had been perfected over months of attacks. But in addition to building ramparts, Geoffrey had overseen the construction of narrow walkways, where needed, for the archers on the walls to go from rooftop to rooftop to support Corith and his men as they now ran for the castle hall. Outside its door, the men formed a large circle. There was no other way into the hall, and here they would defend the remaining townsfolk until help arrived or they were killed to the last man.

The detachments of beasts, which had worked so excellently in times past, worked against them now as they approached the hall in small groups which the soldiers could handle with relative ease. Soon the beasts knew the city was empty, and they converged on the last stand of Jyuntans.

Pladt stood with his archers above the houses, and could see the beasts approaching. He shouted the warning to Geoffrey, and directed his men to begin shooting at the beasts whenever a good opportunity arose.

Like a tidal wave, the hellhounds and goblins swept into the small square that had seen so much celebration only two nights ago. Instead of cheers, animal yells and valiant shouts echoed across the cobblestone. Instead of fists pumped in joy, swords and halberds thrust in defense. Arrows from above entered the melee with deadly accuracy. Pladt had trained his archers well, and for a time, the circle of men was well defended.

Then, Pladt heard a scream from one of his men. He glanced over, at the two men with scimitars that he had recruited. Arik and Filly cut their way through the archers with bared scimitars. In two swift movements, snarling anger, Pladt shot the traitors, emptying his quiver.

Below, the arrows had suddenly ceased, and the tide of beasts rolled toward the encircled soldiers. Steel flashed, and a wave was broken, but another was on top of it. Faltering under the sudden lack of support, the circle of men drew tighter against the door of the hall. Geoffrey stood back to back with Corith and a young boy wielding a mace that was nearly as tall as he was. A hellhound leapt, jaws agape, and the mace clattered to the street. Follus hummed. Another beast came on, and was struck down by Corith's blade. A goblin split the human ranks and advanced on the door, crashing against it with all his weight and might. The door shivered, but held, and four swords thrust inward. Two more goblins charged, and another human weapon fell uselessly to the ground. The oaken door to the hall was struck again, and forced inward a few finger-breadths, but held. Steel and Follus returned the blow, and for an instant the wave of beasts receded. The men at the door were barely able to draw a breath before the beasts surged forward once more.

A horn sounded down at the gate, and the wave faltered. The horn winded again, stronger this time, and hooves could be heard thundering against the pavement. The cry arose from the rooftops: the dragon-slayer had returned.

Haydren led his army with Aerithion drawn, urging his horse to more speed as they rounded the corner and saw the plight of the Jyuntan army.

"To our brothers!" he shouted. The goblins and hellhounds turned too late, and were swept away by the charging horsemen. Haydren whirled his sword, felling foe after foe with vicious strokes. The haggard men at the door could only stand and watch as the bestial army was swept aside in a current of mercenaries and horses.

When the square had been cleared, the mercenaries broke off into detachments to clear the city. Haydren trotted his horse over to Geoffrey and saluted with his sword.

"I thought I told you to hold them," he said with a grin. Before Geoffrey could retort, Haydren wheeled his horse and rode after the mercenaries, to rid Jyunta of beasts once and for all.

Geoffrey stood with Corith and his men, surveying the corpses piled in the square as their chests heaved. It had been a good fight, but many men and women had lost their lives. Geoffrey looked up to the rooftops, but saw no one. Probably they had gone to support the mercenaries with what arrows they had left.

By Evening the work was finished. Jyunta had been cleared of beasts, living and dead. They were piled far outside the city to be burned, while the human dead were carried to a nearby field for burial. Old men, women, children—even lord Garoun helped to dig the graves for the fallen soldiers. Not one unarmed citizen of Jyunta had fallen.

Haydren found Geoffrey, Corith, and Sarah standing by, watching solemnly as the graves were being dug. The young man with the mace who had fallen behind Geoffrey was being lowered gently into the ground. An elderly woman sat by the grave, weeping. Haydren dismounted and stood beside the other three. After watching for several moments, Haydren turned to Geoffrey.

"Where's Pladt?" he asked quietly.

"He went to help support the mercenaries," Geoffrey replied.

Corith turned to them, his expression grave. "Geoffrey," he said quietly, hesitantly.

Both knew immediately by Corith's expression. He blinked a few times and swallowed. "Just as Haydren arrived," he said. "I saw the young archer surrounded by kobolds. But Pladt had no arrows left..."

Sarah bowed her head as silence fell over the four of them. "I saw it too, from the battlements," she confirmed. She gazed at Geoffrey and

Haydren, her eyes shimmering. "I was too weak to do anything—"

"No," Haydren muttered, shaking his head forcefully. "No, he couldn't have. Not Pladt too! He's stood up to hydras his whole life. A Cerberus, a dragon, and a goblin couldn't take him, a yapping kobold can't either!"

It was Kitrel, again while Haydren was off somewhere else, unable to be near, and unable to help. That same darkness that opened beneath him in his room in Hewolucs opened now in the plains near Jyunta. Haydren fell to his knees, pounding his thigh with a fist. "It can't be," he said, his head wagging as tears dripped to the ground. "Not again."

Geoffrey knelt beside him, pulling Haydren's head to his shoulder as he continued to weep. Geoffrey, too, swallowed hard and blinked as the sun steadily set.

Later that night, Haydren, Sarah, Geoffrey and Corith were gathered around a mound of earth. The tomb was empty except for a bow and a quiver. The building upon which Sarah and Corith saw the archer's last stand had burned, and few of the bodies that had stood on its roof were found. The bow had been retrieved a little way down the street, and was easily recognized as Pladt's. The quiver was taken from the armory.

The sky was purple, silhouetting a small stone with Pladt's name engraved upon it. As they sat, Corith pulled an object from his cloak, a flute of many reeds, which he began to play. Haydren started, as it was the same song remembered on his harp the night after Kitrel died. He fought back tears once more, as he still could not remember words to go with the tune. Just as he was about to ask Corith to stop playing, Geoffrey began singing. Sarah soon joined in, and together they sang:

"Do you know where robins go?
Or the color from the leaves?
Can you see the winds that blow?
Or the wounds of hearts that grieve?
But this we know,
The seasons come and go.

"Why do children cry and scream?
Why is there no rest at night?
What is it that's in our dreams?
That draws our young men out to fight?
For this we know,
The seasons come and go.

"Why is hoisted flag and shield?
Why are swords and halberds drawn?
Why do conquered never yield?
Till all men are dead and gone?
But this we know,

The seasons come and go.

"Why do mothers stand alone?
Why are none seen at the plow?
Why do seeds remain unsown?
Why are there no young men now?
Because this we know,
That life will come and go."

As the last of the notes floated on the wind, the sun disappeared below the horizon. Torches again ringed the castle in fiery halo, casting flickering shadows across the graveyard.

"I felt good when I was leaving Estwind," Haydren said. "I thought we would make it back in time."

"You did, Haydren," Geoffrey replied. "If that last wave had come at us, you would have returned to a castle run by goblins."

"I suppose," he said. "Interesting, sometimes, how things just barely work out for us. One moment one way or another and events would have turned out far differently, wouldn't they?"

"We could all wish things had happened differently, Haydren," Sarah said, her eyes still on Pladt's grave. "If I had saved my energy, I could have killed the golem manipulator before he had the chance to breach the gate."

"If I had taken the time to train more men, we might have had some to post behind the gate," Corith added.

"That's my point," Haydren said, glancing at all three. "What had to conspire for Pladt to die?"

"Look around you, Haydren," Corith said angrily. "Are you the only one who lost friends? Look at where you sit. Good men die, Haydren, all the time. They are not to be missed more greatly because you knew them, or missed less so because you didn't know them. We sang a dirge for your friend, the greatest honor that can be bestowed by a Rinc Nain. I know you must grieve, but don't think you grieve alone."

Haydren bowed his head. What could he say? When he looked up, Corith and Sarah were gone, and Geoffrey alone gazed at him.

"You missed a tremendous battle, Haydren," he said quietly. "And your return was sorely needed. But now we must look ahead to the Earl's mission. Sleep tonight. We will approach Corith in the morning."

18

RETURNS

"I suppose you expect me not to worry this time?"
"You should only worry when they choose wrongly."
"And what makes this time different?"
"Their lights will not go out."

37 Haschina 1320 — Summer

A pearl sun rose the next day, finding Haydren, Geoffrey, Sarah, and Corith—along with the mercenary leader, Hrothgar, and his lieutenant Logdthar—in the hall. Haydren produced the letter from the Earl and handed it to Garoun. The lord read it quickly, set it down, and glanced at Geoffrey and Haydren with a sigh.

"Well, I suppose we should be thankful that you brought us the army to defend our city first," he said.

"What is it?" Corith asked.

"Orders, for you to lead this company into the Kalen Woods in search of the mage's village," Garoun replied.

Corith set his jaw, and nodded at Haydren.

"Very well," Corith said. "I've been hoping for a chance to search the Woods again. It would honor me to guide the dragon-slayer and the city captain on such a search."

"The city captain title was honorary, and temporary," Garoun replied with a glance at Geoffrey. "When you return, Corith, the title will be yours." He turned to Hrothgar. "I am uncertain what terms Haydren offered when he purchased your services, captain."

"I am paid until they return from the woods," he said.

"Good, excellent," Garoun replied. "Well, Haydren, I will supply you with horses to get you to the Woods, and a man to return them after. Gather what supplies you need. The merchants will undoubtedly recognize you, you may tell them I will compensate them for their wares. The God go with you all, and may you find what it is you seek."

Upon exiting the hall, Hrothgar and Logdthar returned to their men. Instead of risking any chances, Lord Garoun had ordered repairs on the walls to resume, and the mercenaries currently manned them. Corith turned to the other three.

"As I told Lord Garoun, I have been hoping for this chance," he said. "I have most of the supplies we'll need, minus food."

"You won't need torches," Sarah interjected, stepping forward. "I have a substitute."

"It would be nice to not have to carry fuel," Haydren said.

Geoffrey opened his mouth to retort, but then closed it. "What about water?"

Corith grinned at him knowingly. "Despite what I assume your experience was, there are places to get water when it isn't raining. Lord Garoun will have his man at the stables. You two may gather him and our horses, and meet us at the front gate. I will be there shortly."

"As will I," Sarah promised, and both turned and departed.

They found Lord Garoun's man, Rifkar, waiting with the horses loaded and ready. "I will never understand how that man gets orders out so quickly," Geoffrey muttered. They rode to the gate where Corith and Sarah shortly arrived, each with packs on their backs. Corith led a donkey laden with food.

"He'll carry it to the Kalen Woods," he said. "Then we'll worry about carrying it the rest of the way. Everyone ready?"

"Sarah what is on your hip?" Geoffrey asked.

"I told you I know the limitations of my magic," she said. "This will help me be more effective this time through the woods. It's actually quite light."

She pulled the mace from her belt: an arm's-length shaft of white ash was pommelled with an iron knob, with a black leather grip, and capped by a thick gold-hued disk. Around the edge of the disk, eleven spikes a finger-length each gleamed in red. A strange blue symbol was in the center of the disk. She swung it a few times as if to show how light it was, then returned it to her belt.

"It looks very nice," Haydren said patronizingly.

"And very deadly," Corith added.

Haydren gazed at him. "Mount up," he said.

Rifkar led them east, followed by Haydren, Geoffrey, Sarah, then Corith. The sorceress and their guide conversed in low tones; the others rode in silence. The same hidden valleys and cuts marked their trek across the plains of Qalat County. With Rifkar's guidance, they reached the banks of the Vilde River on the second day, following it south as it curved near the Northern Forest.

When they reached the edge of the plains, where the terrain dropped into the low moors, a bridge took them across the Vilde. They set up camp on the far side, falling asleep to the river's gentle gurgling.

The next morning, as the horizon darkened with the tops of the Kalen Woods, Sarah spurred her horse forward to speak to Haydren.

"Do you know how Corith is getting us through there?" she asked.

Haydren kept his eyes ahead. "I assume I'll find out shortly after entering," he replied.

"You mean you're not curious?" she pressed.

"Not really."

She paused her horse until Geoffrey came alongside. "Something is wrong."

Geoffrey nodded gravely.

By Half-Noon, they stopped at the forest's doorstep and dismounted. Corith quickly divided up the packs, then looked expectantly at Sarah. "You mentioned torches?"

She reached into her pack and retrieved a wooden rod with a head of intricately woven branches. She cupped her hand around the basket and whispered a few words. When she swept her hand away, she presented it triumphantly to Corith: within the basket burned a brilliant white flame that did not consume the wood. Corith held his hand near it, and grunted when it did not burn him.

"A gift from a friend," she said. "Enchanted with fire. I speak the words, it lights. Also, it will burn orange at sunset, blue at night, and red in the morning. So we can keep track of the days, as well." She produced three more, lit them, and handed them to the others.

"Also, these," she said, reaching into her bag and producing three small pouches. "Small vials of liquid that I'm told grant a measure of strength to the weak."

"Cerebrine?" Haydren asked, inspecting one of the bottles of orange fluid.

"I didn't bother to ask. As long as it works, the witch can call it whatever she wants."

Haydren replaced the vial and grinned at her playfully. "You don't approve of potions."

"Why should I? It takes no skill, just learning. Any dolt with time on her hands can learn to make a potion."

"It also takes very little energy," Haydren returned. "I doubt many battles were nearly lost because a potion could not be made."

"Haydren!" Geoffrey barked.

Sarah ducked her head. "Perhaps," she admitted. A breeze stirred her hair, and she glanced up. "But I doubt many were won because a potion *could* be made."

Rifkar gathered their horses and bid them all fare well. As Rifkar rode away, Haydren turned his back on the sorceress, drew his sword, and cut a hole in the growth at the perimeter of the forest. One by one, they all stepped in. Corith held his light forward, showing their way deeper into the woods.

"No path," Haydren noted.

"Perfect," Corith replied. He glanced at Haydren and smiled. "Little known fact about the Kalen Woods," he explained. "The rows of trees are straight. It's the paths that twist and turn. If we stay off them, we won't get lost."

"If that's not irony," Geoffrey said with a grunt. "I don't know what is."

Haydren sheathed his sword and gestured ahead. "Lead the way, Corith," he said.

As they walked that day, they came across only one path. Corith glanced up and down it, motioned to the others, and sprinted across. "The beasts often watch the paths," he said when they had regrouped. "It's best to be across them as quickly as possible."

"I would think they could see our torches long before we could see them," Geoffrey noted.

"I'm sure they can," he said with a nod. "But I've never had one attack me when I'm off the path. I can't explain it, but it works."

Soon their torch-flames sprouted thin tongues of orange fire which grew to consume the baskets. Just behind it, traces of blue rose, signaling night. Haydren called a halt to set up camp. After a brief dinner, guard times were set, and everyone rolled out their blankets for bed.

"We should reach the first of the headwaters of the Tundee early tomorrow," Corith informed them. "We'll cross seven over the next three days, ranging from springs to little rivers. And there are no bridges." He rolled over and closed his eyes.

Geoffrey volunteered the first watch, but soon he roused Haydren. "May we talk?" he whispered.

Haydren nodded. "Always."

"I thought you might not want to earlier, with so many listening ears." Haydren cocked his head. "Why is that?"

"I wanted to talk to you about Pladt, and what you think about it," Geoffrey said slowly.

"I told you what I think about it, the night he died," Haydren replied. "Corith didn't sway you?"

"Corith doesn't know the entire story," Haydren said. He sighed, looking off into the darkness. "Geoffrey, from the very beginning, I feel like I haven't had a lot of control over things. I would make decisions completely blind, hate it, and yet somehow it was the best possible decision I could make. I've talked to you about this before," he said, glancing quickly at Geoffrey. "But especially with Pladt. I mean, someone—we can only assume Semmelle—knew we were coming, posed as Faschek, and tried to kill him. Why? Why go to that trouble? Surely he wasn't just randomly trying to kill passers-by, and by all accounts we should assume he was coming after me. And for that matter, almost every creature we faced nearly killed Pladt. They have been trying to kill him for a long time."

He paused, and his gaze bored into Geoffrey. "When I arrived at the end of the battle, I didn't see any kobolds. Not one."

Geoffrey paused. "Sarah summoned a wind," he said, recalling. "It tore through their ranks and blew them away."

Haydren raised his eyebrows. "That must have been something to see," he said, unable to hide a grin. Geoffrey nodded, also grinning at the memory of all those beasts tumbling away like leaves. "But," Haydren continued, drawing their attention back to the problem at hand, "where did the kobolds come from who killed Pladt? After being blown away, did they come back and happen upon the roofs where he was?"

Geoffrey paused. "The manipulator," he said, quickly relating that part of the tale. "He had some kobolds left around him after Sarah struck him down. Do you think they came in specifically for him? That it was fated for him to die?"

"I'm saying too much happens around me that I can't explain or control," Haydren replied. He went on, quiet again. "I had a memory, in Estwind. I saw my parents. We were in a wagon traveling somewhere. In the memory, I fell asleep, and when I woke up, the carriage was on fire and my mother was pushing something long, thin, and hard into my arms and pushing me outside. I think she was giving me Aerithion, and I think we were in Burieng. The memory ended just as I left the carriage." Haydren paused, and Geoffrey let him sit without questioning him. Finally, Haydren continued: "The memory was sparked by something one of the mercenaries said. He said 'sit down, child' to one of the other soldiers. It was the same phrase my mother used at the start of the memory, when I was gazing out of the window of the carriage." He looked at Geoffrey. "If I had not gone to Estwind, to that tavern, at that time, I would not have heard that phrase. But it's not just that; we wouldn't be here at all if we had not fought and defeated the Cerberus, which would not have happened if we had not gone into the forest in the first place. And then there are those strange thoughts coming into my head, that we talked about in Frecksshire." Haydren shook his head. "I'm just waiting for some old man to tell me everything has been foretold, and that there is some great quest that I am the prophesied hero of."

"That would be strange, to say the least Haydren," Geoffrey said with a grin.

"It's not even that," Haydren replied. "Even if that doesn't happen, I just want to be in control of my own life."

"You want freedom in a land of serfs?"

"Yes, just a little. I want freedom from the will of another. Even if," he added with a meaningful look at Geoffrey, "that will is some supposedly benevolent other-thing which, you say, always wants the best for me. I want to make my own choices and live with them, and I want to be confident in doing it."

"We all have to serve someone, Haydren," Geoffrey said. "Right now we have to serve the Earl. When we have completed this mission, what did you plan to do?"

"I don't know," Haydren replied, settling into his blanket. "I suppose it will depend on what we find out."

Geoffrey's eyebrows shot up. "What do you expect to find?"

"Proof that Lasserain was behind what happened to me, and to my parents, to Kitrel, and to Pladt," Haydren replied.

"In which case you will serve a thirst for revenge?"

"What would you have me do?"

"Whatever the God of All willed you to do," Geoffrey replied.

"So you would have me serve him instead, when you haven't even proven to me that he exists," Haydren said in disbelief.

"He does exist, Haydren," Geoffrey said. "And I would rather serve him than anything else in this world. This world is selfish, Haydren, and corrupt; is there anything of good influence in it?"

"I didn't need the God of All to defend Jyunta," Haydren replied hotly. "Was that also because of evil influence?"

"You say you didn't need the God of All," Geoffrey replied. "The fool says he moves the branches by shaking the trunk, when it is the wind that's in the treetops."

"Proverbs according to Geoffrey," Haydren muttered. "May I go to sleep sometime before I have the watch?"

Geoffrey gazed at him a few moments. "Of course," he replied quietly. "Sleep well, Haydren."

⸺⸺◆⸺⸺

The next day, after crossing the first headwater, Sarah stopped short as a pair of green eyes winked on in the darkness.

"Wait!" she cried as all reached for their swords. They hesitated, glancing at her quizzically. She mouthed a few words, stopped, and bit her lip with quick glances at the others. She had already told them to wait: could she say 'never mind; go ahead'? The eyes drew nearer. A growl rumbled through the trees, and the beast bounded toward them.

Focusing intently on the ground in front of the charging animal, Sarah whispered a quick spell—but nothing changed. Haydren quickly drew his sword. Sarah gazed at him unconcernedly.

Suddenly, just as it entered the torchlight, the wolf collided with something none of the party could see. He bounced back a little and collapsed, then quickly scrambled to his feet and leaped back into the shadows.

"It worked!" Sarah said exultantly.

"What was it?" Geoffrey demanded as Haydren sheathed his sword.

"That spell I found, that I told you about on the walls of Jyunta," she replied. "It thickens the air—well, it's more of a small section of air, about the size of a parchment, that blows with incredible force, making it feel solid from one direction. Of course," she added with a laugh, "if you come at it from the other side, it'll suddenly blow you over."

"Very effective," Haydren granted.

"I think that spell has been lost for centuries," Sarah went on as they continued. "I may be the first person to have used that spell since the end of The War, even. The piece from where I learned it seemed old enough." She glanced at Geoffrey, surprised that he said nothing, did not even grimace.

The days passed without further event. After they had crossed yet another headwater—this one approaching the width of a river, though it was still shallow and slow-moving—Corith said: "Fill up your skins. This water is quite pure, and it's the last we will come across for many days."

Five days later, after they had been walking long past lunch with no conversation, Haydren suddenly exclaimed: "How long do we have to travel east? I feel like we've been walking a straight line for months."

"In that case, we'll be walking a straight line for another two or three months," Corith replied with a grin that no one else shared. "Listen," he continued, sobering. He turned to face the other travelers. "This is the longest part of our trip. We're walking from the farthest western edge of the Kalen Woods to a point directly south of Iridescent Bay." He raised an eyebrow and nodded for meaning.

Haydren sighed. "That is a long way," he admitted.

"After that," Corith continued as he turned and resumed walking, "The most we'll spend walking in one direction will be five or six days at the most. Besides," he continued in a lighter tone, "you get to see all the major sights of the Kalen Woods: Iridescent Bay, which you hope we get to see at night. Monte-Ir, the great fallen fortress of the ancient Kalen. And the mage's village, if it hasn't been burned to a crisp. And you've already seen the Seven Headwaters of the Tundee: not many get to see even that!"

So they continued walking for days upon days, until Haydren lost count. "Nine," Corith informed him flatly.

"Since we came into the woods?" Haydren asked.

Corith grinned. "No, since you first complained about how long we had been walking. We've been in the woods for two weeks, now."

Finally, twenty days after entering the forest, after a brief lunch, they crossed another path—this one ran obliquely to their line of travel—and Corith suddenly turned left and began walking up another hall of tree trunks. "Going north," he said. "Four days to Iridescent Bay!"

"Why do you hope we get there at night?" Haydren asked. When learning geography, he had of course learned of the location of the bay, but he had never heard anything special about it.

"I said *you* hope we get there at night. And, you'll see," Corith replied with an enigmatic smile.

Four days later, they did see. While the torches still burned white, they came upon a wall of vines and brush. At Corith's cue, Geoffrey and Haydren drew their swords and cut a hole. Stepping through, they found themselves on a white-sand beach with turquoise waves gently lapping against the shore. They were at the apex of a cove of the bay, with the walls of the Northern Forest bounding it in. The sun was setting behind the trees, sinking the cove in cool shadow. Various bits of driftwood had collected in spots, and near the mouth of the bay fronds of palm and fern hedged in.

Corith glanced at the sky. "It's worth waiting until the sun sets," he said. "We won't lose that much time on our way to Monte-Ir."

So they waited, relishing the cool ocean breeze that wafted into the bay. The bay proper was large enough that they could not see the peninsula that bordered it to the east, but only saw the Forest's shadow stretching toward an aqua horizon.

Then, as the cove darkened, the water in the bay turned an iridescent green. Crickets took up a rhythmic chirping. Bullfrogs, hidden in the driftwood, added their deep-throated bass, which echoed from within the hollow logs. A pair of birds, resembling herons, swooped over the bay. Their wings of red and orange shone as their feathers burned in the evening sun that lay hidden over the tops of the forest. Their songs blended with the crickets and bullfrogs in a swelling symphony of nature. The ocean waves, still lapping against the shore, throbbed with green light that stretched to the treetops, then receded, then stretched again in pulsating beat to the song.

As Sarah watched what laypeople might call a magical scene, she took a hesitant breath. The air spilled into her, calling her with its familiar song. This time there was a menacing undertone that seeped into her with every breath until it became unnoticeable. Had that undertone been there all the time? Or did it exist only here, in the Woods that had swallowed Monte-Ir, birthed Lasserain, and threatened to consume Quaran?

She thought back to Jyunta, the last time the sentience of the element had flowed through her the strongest. She had desired to show off the power of magic on those now-distant walls, and had risked their destruction. Every spell she cast destroyed, as if that were its only purpose. But had not the God of All used it to create? Geoffrey thought so. And it made sense. And here was a moment that seemed magic in every way, and it was beautiful and soothing, something to revive the soul, not rend it.

So she stood, afraid to breathe deeply for fear of a tainting element, yet desperately desiring it for its regenerative balm not only as it calmed those around her, but also as it would calm her as its ambassador. Her eyes drank in the glow, her ears thrilled to the symphony, but her heart trembled in fear.

As the sun lowered, and the company watched in rapture, the birds ceased their circling and retreated behind the towering trees. Lower the sun went, and the bullfrogs too trailed off. As the shadow descended fully, the green light of the bay winked out, leaving the crickets to finish the melody in hiding.

Corith turned silently to his companions. Their gaze said all that needed to be said. They set up camp on the shore that night, sleeping restfully at Corith's assurance that no creatures of the woods ventured into the sacred harbor.

19

LEGENDS

"He nears."
"He is beginning to be afraid."
"But not you?"
"When your enemy is afraid, Teresh, you're doing something right."

29 Mantaver 1320 — Summer

As the sun rose above the clouded horizon, they looked across a bay that was as ocean-green as any other body of water. With hesitating backward glances, the party returned to the gloom of the woods, torches outstretched.

"One day heading west, then it's north to Monte-Ir," Corith informed them as cheerily as he could.

For two days, they had only their memories of the bay to hold back the too-familiar pitch darkness of the Woods. Then, that afternoon, the first Haydren had ever seen in the woods, a dim, natural light shone in the forest, raising the blackness to a gloom. Further on, a brilliant shaft of light thrust through the canopy overhead. Where it struck the ground, a crumbled stone building, bleached white, stuck out from the dark dirt like an ancient bone. In its center, a wand of sassafras poked through with green leaves as still as forgotten dust.

As they passed the building, stones worn by time peeped through the forest floor, but quickly disappeared. Then, ahead of them, another group of broken buildings, some with intact roofs but many with sassafras, maple, elm, and sycamore growing from their floors rose in a bath of pure light. Here, the flagstone road came to the surface and remained, and the ancient city of the Kalen rang again with footsteps.

"Can you imagine what this might have looked like, when it was in full-bloom?" Corith said as they passed another set of tall, broken structures. "Even though I've been here before, I can't help but think again what it would be like to clear the Woods, and to rebuild this city."

Further ahead, the city center came into view. Buildings clustered and towered overhead, some two or three stories tall—or, they would have been when they were still standing. Now, only small columns and rare bits of unbroken wall rose up to their once-glorious height. The road wound around the buildings as if an after-thought, until it brought them to the town square. They found a dried fountain, its basin filled with leaves from the pin oaks that grew around the square.

Even after the respite at Iridescent Bay, the company hesitated to move on, and decided to spend the night in the city. They sat in the square, or walked among the ancient ruins, marveling at the craftsmanship of ages now gone.

"Who were the Kalen?" Geoffrey asked. They had all gathered back at the fountain to enjoy a lunch as they admired the buildings around them.

"I don't think anyone knows," Haydren replied.

"Hmm," Corith mumbled noncommittally.

Haydren raised an eyebrow. "Do you?"

Corith took a deep breath, twisting a ring on his left forefinger. "I have an idea," he said. When everyone looked at him expectantly, he sighed. "I think they were elves."

Haydren barked a laugh. "Elves? Seriously?"

"Well it fits the legends," Corith replied. "I mean, look around you. Anywhere there is a building, the Woods don't tread. The elves respected nature, so why shouldn't nature respect them in return? The buildings are just like the ones in the old manuscripts."

"Which the authors probably got from visiting Monte-Ir," Haydren said. "First, there are trees growing up through some of the ruins. And the Northern Forest isn't natural," he added soberly.

"They say the Kalen Woods is revenge, a curse from the Kalen in return for destroying their civilization," Corith replied. "They say it is growing again because it wants to reclaim the old kingdom, and the elves will return when it has finished that task."

"How big is the old kingdom?" Geoffrey asked.

"All of Burieng north of the Endolin Mountains," Haydren replied.

Geoffrey whistled. "That's not good news for most of the country, then," he said.

"If it were true, it wouldn't be," Haydren replied.

"It would be good news for the Kalen though," Corith retorted, a spark in his eyes that died quickly. "I'm not saying I have irrefutable proof. But I have some documents from my father, and what it says leads me to believe the legends of elves are true, and that they are who the

Burieng call Kalen, and this was their capital."

"Could you imagine the festivals they probably held at Iridescent Bay?" Sarah said. "It's certainly close enough to travel to for special occasions."

Corith shifted again. "One document my father gave me indicates they held wedding ceremonies there. That they taught the crickets and frogs and birds to do that in celebration of the union." He glanced furtively at Haydren, who held his peace.

It was not that Haydren wanted to disbelieve the legends of elves. It was just so commonly held that they were simply legends. In many places, they did not even carry the weight of legends, but were mere children's stories to try to instill ethics in little boys and girls.

They spent most of that day investigating the city, wandering with trepidation into old cellars and overgrown buildings. One reminded Haydren closely of the large church in Hewolucs, with massive columns that arched near the top before breaking off. Much of the architecture was not impressive by modern standards. But the fact that it was built so long ago and had withstood the downfall of an empire was what caught the travelers' breath and would not let it go. It certainly seemed as if nothing living had come to that city in ages, and nothing more would come to it for ages more.

But, later that night during Haydren's watch, he heard a strange scuffling down the road south. He sat back into the shadow of a column, looking out to see if the creature would come into a light where he could see it. As it drew nearer, however, the sound became the distinguished tap of measured footfalls. Haydren went to Geoffrey and shook him, holding a finger to his lips as Geoffrey's eyes snapped open. Geoffrey pulled his blanket aside and stood. Together, they moved to a pair of columns near the entrance to the square. Slowly, cringing at every scrape, they drew their swords and waited as the footfalls neared. Geoffrey peered around the column. He glanced at Haydren, and then down at Haydren's sword. The light within the Cretal flames was flickering, just as it had the night at Faschek's house. Geoffrey's brows knit, but Haydren shrugged helplessly.

Geoffrey glanced out again, then at Haydren and nodded quickly. They both stepped out, swords raised. An elderly man stopped short, dropping his bundle of sticks and his torch with a gasp. Haydren's sword-point was at his throat, and the light of the flames had surged to the tip and flickered hungrily at him.

"Who are you?" Haydren demanded while the man was still distracted by the flames.

"Tagnier Belfrind, of Salme, in Salmea," he rattled off.

"Belfrind?" Haydren repeated with a glance at Geoffrey.

Tagnier lifted his eyes from Haydren's blade and glanced between them. "Something wrong with the name?"

"We've run into a Belfrind before," Geoffrey said, raising his blade higher. "With less than happy results."

"It's quite a common name in Salme. Very large family from there. Relations all over the place. As a rule, quite nice. But there's always rotten fish in the crate, isn't there?" Tagnier said, glancing furtively at the swords.

"Why are you here?" Haydren asked.

"Seapot, the King of Salmea, is interested in Lasserain's village," Tagnier replied. "He sent me to find out what I could."

"Seapot?" Haydren repeated, lowering his sword. "Why is he interested in anything on Burieng?"

"He's not," Tagnier replied, a little more comfortable with half the amount of sharpened metal at his throat. "But Lasserain's stench does not stop at Lune's Inlet. After Kelian's Earl allied with the mage, the threat to our nation is even greater. But one does not rush into the teeth of the Cerberus without learning its weaknesses, no? At least, I assume that's why you all are here too. Judging by your Rinc Nain accents, you are from Coberan."

"Quite right," Haydren said with a quick glance at Geoffrey, who now lowered his sword. "Earl Durdamon has sent us on a similar mission. Though he thought wise to send four of us, while you are alone."

"As you say," Tagnier said wearily, "Seapot cares little for Burieng. Little enough that he does not learn *all* the dangers of certain areas before sending his men to them. I came with three others, who perished before we even reached the Forest. Though I am alone, I thought better to attempt to complete my mission than return to the King empty handed."

"Some kings prefer that," Haydren said with a wry grin that quickly faded. "We lost a friend as well, on our journey. You may join us for now. Your return to Salmea will be upon your shoulders, though."

"I thank you," Tagnier said. Haydren gestured toward their sleeping companions. As Tagnier moved off, Haydren whispered to Geoffrey: "Our guard shifts remain the same. We don't have Coberan accents, and we both know that. Don't think because I'm congenial that I trust him. But he hasn't tried to kill us yet, and I don't want to kill him unnecessarily. If it is Semmelle in disguise, somehow, he would make a move on us soon. Keep an eye on him, and let Corith know when it's his turn."

Geoffrey nodded quickly. "I'll take my shift over for now. Just get some sleep."

The next morning, Corith told them of a stream some days to the west they could simply follow north until they reached the village.

They walked in silence that day. For most of them, their minds turned frequently to Monte-Ir, and Iridescent Bay, and the possibility of an ancient race of elves which inhabited both. Haydren's mind, however, was going over everything that had happened at Faschek's house, comparing it to Tagnier's interaction upon first meeting them. He didn't like that his sword had reacted the same way as that night, or that it had done so with Paolound. That Faschek's and Tagnier's last name were identical could be a coincidence. But a dragon? And if it simply reacted to evil, why not any of the other beasts they had fought, or bandits? There was no answer Haydren could come up with that satisfied him.

Sarah halted suddenly. "Are we ever going to eat?" she exclaimed.

Haydren glanced back and sighed. "Stop complaining, sorceress. We've barely begun walking today."

Sarah eyed him closely. "No, Haydren, we've been walking for hours," she said slowly.

Haydren stared at her. "Do you think I can't track the passage of time?" he said. "We set out from Monte-Ir just a little bit ago. Geoffrey, how long have we been walking?"

Geoffrey shifted his weight a little. "It's been a while, Haydren."

"See?" Sarah said loudly, her hands on her hips.

"I was waiting for you to tell us to stop," Corith said when Haydren looked at him. "I was wondering what you were waiting for."

"I'm sure it hasn't been that long," Haydren said.

"It has, you idiot," Sarah fumed. "Here I am starving, thinking it's only me. But no! Our supposed leader has gone out of his head."

Haydren sucked in his upper lip, trying to calm himself. "Don't question me right now, sorceress," he warned.

"When should I?" she demanded. "I can't do it after we all die from starvation. 'Hey, whitened bones, am I doing okay?'"

"Don't press me!" Haydren said, stepping forward and jabbing a finger at her.

"What are you going to do, deprive me of food? Oh! Wait!"

Haydren gaped at her. "Did your women's custom start today?" he asked.

Sarah's mouth dropped open, and her eyes bulged. "Did my...are you...?" she gasped. Her mouth clamped shut, and her tongue clicked against her teeth.

Suddenly, the air around Haydren's head thickened, almost solid, and he could not breathe. When his mouth opened, the air sucked from his lungs and he felt as if his chest would collapse. His eyes bulged. Geoffrey was gesturing frantically and shouting at Sarah, though it came through muffled as if he were a hundred paces away. Haydren shut his mouth, and his lungs burned for breath.

Sarah, for her part, looked terrified. Her mouth moved soundlessly, and suddenly Haydren could breathe again. He gulped air, bending over as his chest heaved.

"I-I'm sorry," Sarah said timidly.

After several moments catching his breath, Haydren straightened. He opened his mouth to say something, then stopped and laughed bitterly.

"What is it?" Geoffrey asked, still beside Sarah.

Haydren only pointed. The torches were beginning to turn orange. The day was nearly over.

Later that night, when everyone else had dropped off to sleep, Haydren stayed awake with Geoffrey.

"I know what I felt, Geoffrey," he said. "I know now that the day had passed, obviously. But it still feels like it was cut in half. And I was only in my thoughts. This isn't like I was ten and playing in the fields."

"What do you think happened, then?"

Haydren shrugged. "I don't know. But I know Tagnier was watching most intently while Sarah and I were having it out. And he seemed, I don't know, almost unhappy when Sarah released me. Not unhappy like you were, that she had put a spell on me in the first place. Unhappy that she had taken it away. Guntsen would get the same way when a student's punishment was over, like he didn't feel they got everything they deserved."

"I was afraid of that happening, too. Magic is too powerful and too easy to use to be coupled with anger," Geoffrey said. The gaze he cast toward the sleeping sorceress was not of wrath, but of remorse, Haydren felt. "Nothing good comes from using magic."

"I'm not worried about Sarah, but Tagnier," Haydren said gently. "Could he have affected our torches, do you think?"

"If he is a magic-user, he might have. That's a question for Sarah. It doesn't explain the rest of our perceptions of time, though."

"True enough."

"What do you want to do about it?"

Haydren sighed. "I don't know. Maybe we should just kill him before he has a chance to do anything." He paused, looking at Tagnier's sleeping form. "Everything inside me says he can't be trusted, that he's dangerous and means us harm. But for some reason I can't bring myself to do it, or to have anyone else do it."

"Get some sleep, Haydren," Geoffrey murmured. "We'll keep an eye on him. It's not a bad thing to be hesitant to end someone's life."

Their journey continued without incident. Six days later, as the torches began to turn to the orange of nightfall, the rippling sound of running water echoed beneath the canopy. With smiles that belied their weariness, they quickened their pace until they stood at the banks of a swiftly-moving stream cascading down a series of rock slabs.

"It's been a long journey for all of us," Haydren said. "I think a dip in the stream would be refreshing for everyone. We can spend the evening here, and be on our way in the morning." He glanced at Sarah. "One of us should be close by to keep watch, whoever you trust the most."

"Probably Geoffrey," she replied with a smile. "I don't see him as the kind to steal unwanted glances, especially at a heathen like me."

"Nor would I if you were a saint," Geoffrey replied.

Sarah's smile barely faltered, but her eyes glittered with poorly-hidden curiosity in the torchlight.

That evening, Haydren noticed that Corith sat quietly apart, and didn't join in any of the conversation. At the end of the meal, as everyone laid out their blankets, Haydren squatted beside him.

"You've been quiet," he murmured. "Anything on your mind?"

"I don't know if I should tell you," he said with a nervous laugh.

"You can try."

"Well, I've never actually been to Haschina. And its location is as much a fact of mine as the Kalen are elves, to you," he said.

Haydren froze, still looking down at the blanket folded in his pack. He drew a deep breath, and glanced at Corith with a reassuring smile. "I had no idea what I was doing when I first entered the forest," he said. "Not even a notion. I believe we'll find the mage's village, though."

But by the end of the next day, they had not. According to Corith's rough estimate, they should have. Haydren said nothing to the others, and Corith, too, held his peace, finding comfort in Haydren's trust. But as the third day dragged on, even Corith's hope began to fade.

Then, as night approached, an orange glow grew to the north. It was arch-shaped, as if a hill blocked their way. They continued forward, and scrambled up the rise. They burst out of the woods—there was no wall of brush as they had encountered everywhere else—and found themselves on a tall hill looking down into the village of Haschina.

Every building, as much as they could see, was engulfed by towering flames.

20

FIRES

"One word from you and this is over."
"It is not that simple."
"This close, it isn't simple yet?"
"A scene in a play, Teresh; yet still a play."

5 Thriman 1320 — Summer

The party stood atop the hill, gazing speechlessly at the village below. As the fires continued to burn, and yet the buildings did not, their shock turned to confusion.

Corith moved first, approaching the nearest flames his sword drawn. Though the noise of the fire beat their ears, there was no crackling of wood, and even up close, no heat struck them. Corith poked at the flames, but his blade stopped short. He pressed his palm against something solid, but invisible.

"I think someone else discovered your wind-trick, Sarah," he said, still pushing. Sarah stepped forward, gingerly reaching out with a finger. When it struck the same invisible wall Corith encountered, she pulled it back.

"So it would seem," she agreed. She stepped back, her face growing pale.

"What is it?" Haydren asked.

"This is...far too much magic," she said.

"'Too much'?" Haydren echoed.

"It had to have been cast almost all at once, to stop the flames," she said. She wiped her mouth, her hand trembling. "But to cast a spell around an entire village... To cast it on one home would have killed me."

Haydren snorted, but Geoffrey laid a hand on his arm. "She knows what she's talking about, Haydren," he muttered. Haydren startled, then realized Geoffrey's hand was trembling too.

"I was telling Pladt this before," Sarah continued. "Fire needs fuel, even if its magical fire. But nothing is burning, which means all the fire, all the wind keeping the fire in, is feeding only off the energy of the one who cast it. Have you ever tried to start a fire just by rubbing your hands together? Because that's what he's doing. And whoever cast it—and we can guess who did—is still alive. I don't know if you've ever had an entire mountain crash down on you with the speed of a thunderbolt, but Lasserain could do it. Because he's a *mage:* if he can do something like this with one element, he can do it with them all."

"Well, let's see what we can find, if anything," Haydren said, drawing his sword. "Spread out, but be wary."

Sarah snorted. "Wariness for what?" she muttered. "If he can do this, he could rain lightning down on us while he's safely tucked in Galessern and not feel a drain. Close by, he could uproot Haschina and throw it into the sea. We don't need to be wary, we need to run away." Yet Sarah went forward, scanning the buildings.

The party spread out through the village. Most of the structures were hidden behind the flickering shield of fire. When they regrouped on the other side, Haydren turned back and sighed. Suddenly he noticed a spot where the flames were much lower than anywhere else, at the back of one of the buildings. Still with sword drawn, he strode over to it. As he neared, he felt the heat.

"Here!" he cried to the others. He took off his cloak and beat the fire, but it sprang up undiminished.

"Let me try," Sarah said, stepping forward. "Hopefully he hasn't completely broken the rules. *Loth, Loth; kiet fiol thoi!*"

The flames winked out. Sarah glanced at Geoffrey with a large smile. He gazed back without expression. Haydren pushed on the door; it was locked. He jammed his sword near the handle and pried. With a groan of splintering wood, the door popped open.

Inside was a small room about five paces across, furnished only by a table and chair of knotted pine, a bed with faded quilt, and a reed carpet in the center. There were a few utensils hanging, and some bowls. Corith inspected them. "Clean," he said. "Recently. And if this is the mage's house, we must be cautious."

"It also means there must be more to it," Haydren replied in equally low tones, as though Lasserain himself might hear them from Galessern and come to kill them. "He would keep his things somewhere, surely."

"Why wouldn't he have them in Galessern?" Sarah asked.

"Because then he would have no reason whatsoever to come back," Haydren replied, pointing at the bowls. "Yet he has."

Geoffrey reached down and flipped over the rug. The floorboards beneath were uncut. "It was worth a try," he whispered, putting the rug back in its place. When he stood, he and Haydren both looked at the bed, then at one another. They moved—Haydren to the headboard, Geoffrey to the footboard—and lifted the bed, then shifted it over several paces. Underneath was a small trapdoor, with a large iron ring embedded at one side.

"Do you think he sealed it somehow?" Haydren asked.

Geoffrey grasped the ring and pulled. Nothing. He exhaled and opened the door wide. Dimly lit stairs ran downward from the dark mouth.

"We won't get down with our packs," he said as he slipped off his own. "Stack them by the door for now, but bring your torches."

After a brief flurry of cloth rustling over the sound of the fires outside, they descended the stairs into a dry cave. A narrow hall led back, with only small rooms to one side or the other. A torch thrust through the opening was enough to ensure the rooms had been emptied, and they continued down the hallway.

Suddenly Geoffrey glanced to his right, then peered closer. He reached out and grasped a handle-shaped bit of rock and pushed. The crack of a door appeared suddenly, and with a creak the door swung open. Geoffrey paused, but Haydren pushed forward and peered into the room.

Inside, a large desk faced the door. Bookshelves lined the walls all around a room which was at least as large as the house above. Lamps and candles stood scattered in sconces and on flat surfaces, unlit. Haydren approached the desk and opened some of its drawers. He found a taper, and blew gently on it. A flame sprang upward, and he lit some of the lanterns on the desk.

"If the taper is still hot, he must have been here very recently," Haydren whispered. "Corith, keep watch at the door. Sarah, you as well. Geoffrey and I will search the room."

Geoffrey went to the bookshelves and glanced over the spines. "He has an enormous collection of books translating languages into Rinc Nain and Cariste. I haven't even heard of some of these languages! These are for you Sarah: he must have ten spell-books here."

"He has others on the desk," Haydren said from where he stood. "Some other papers concerning moving of goods."

"By river?" Geoffrey asked, recalling the raft materials they had found in the bandit camp south of Werine. Haydren glanced up at him and nodded. "So he's responsible for the bandits, at least," Geoffrey concluded.

"He must be supplying Galessern for a war," Haydren agreed. He pulled out a small chest from one of the bookshelves near the desk. He found a key in one of the drawers and tried it on the lock. With a click and a snap, the chest opened, and he began flipping through the loose parchments inside. "He has a lot of articles in here," he muttered, glancing over the titles. "*The Colonization of Burieng; On Dragons; The*

Discovery of the World; On Magic—the list goes on, but there's not much useful to us."

"Over here!" Geoffrey called. He was wrestling with a large chest of ornate design. Haydren helped him pull it to the middle of the room. There was no keyhole, and there was only a faint crack discernible where a lid should have been. Geoffrey pulled a small knife from his belt, but he could not force it into the crack.

They sat back, studying the chest. Haydren reached forward to reposition it in the dim lamplight. When he grasped it they heard a faint click from within the chest. Haydren glanced at the side where his hand had fallen, at a carving of a map of the world. The rest of the continents and islands were in myriad colors against a blue ocean. When Haydren pushed on a continent, the wood gave way a little, and a click sounded within the chest. But no matter how he pressed them, nothing happened except the noise. He sat back again.

"Who settled which continents?" he asked, something tickling the back of his mind.

"Rinc Na settled North Pal Isan, the Clanaso Islands, Andelen, and West Burieng," Geoffrey replied. "Carist settled South Pal Isan, Gintanos, and East Burieng."

Haydren pushed the continents in order of their settling countries, but still nothing happened. Suddenly, he leapt to his feet and returned to the desk. He grabbed a parchment from its top, then returned and sat down with it next to the chest. Scanning the paper on the settling of the world, he pushed each continent in the order it was settled chronologically. This time, a deeper *thunk* sounded from within the chest, and the lid popped open.

"You also forgot the Abandoned Isles," he said.

Inside were more stacks of papers, all in Rinc Nain. Geoffrey and Haydren each took out a stack, and began reading. As they read, their hearts fell.

"He has been responsible for everything," Haydren breathed. "The beasts, the attacks against Quaran, the bandits. He's coordinated everything. By the God!" he gasped. "He even made the Forest grow! But how—?"

He trailed off, continuing to read, but the parchment did not answer his question. Sarah came over from where she had moved to the desk and stood beside them. "And Jyunta?"

Geoffrey looked up somberly and nodded. "According to this," he said, turning the parchment briefly toward her, "each species of beast has something like a king over them. Lasserain captured all of the beast-kings, and subjected them. Through the beast-kings, he was able to coordinate attacks against the cities."

"*On the Triumvirate,* this one is called," Haydren said, his brows knit as he read. "There is a group of three men, former wizards, who allege to be in communion with the God of All. Their job, it seems, is to attempt to maintain peace and order in the world. They are able to travel throughout the world and manipulate men, including putting thoughts into their heads." He glanced up at Geoffrey briefly. "Their true names are Melnor Firelien, Kanala Withewon, and Teresh Gretsblood. Apparently they don't give their names out—not sure how Lasserain learned them, then. Most often they manipulate men only through thoughts. But when they must appear to them they often use the name *Godfrind*."

Geoffrey's head snapped up. "Godfrind?" he declared. "Godfrind came to me just after we left the Northern Forest!"

"Why didn't you say so before?" Haydren demanded.

"Because I didn't remember until you said the name," Geoffrey replied. "He told me I wouldn't be able to, that I would only remember my thoughts as if they were my own. It's all coming back to me now! Whoever this Godfrind is, he knows all about you Haydren. He said he had been watching you long before you came to Burieng."

"What did he look like?" Haydren asked, scanning the parchment. Geoffrey gave him the description as Haydren read. "He was Melnor, a former wizard of Fire," Haydren said. "Their appearance is determined mostly by what element they were."

"You keep saying 'former,'" Sarah said. "What *are* they?"

"I don't know," Haydren said, shaking his head. "But they aren't as living people anymore. Something more spirit, I assume. Lasserain isn't clear."

"Haydren," Geoffrey said quietly, glancing up from the parchment he was reading.

Haydren looked at him, and recognizing the expression said: "Read it."

"'I have just received splendid news of a caravan leaving Westide for Hewolucs with a very precious cargo aboard: a sword of Bultum and Cretal fire. How fortunate that I had the bandits already in place! I have sent word to them to be extra violent, and to bring me this kingly gift.' Then, a little lower, it says: 'So much for the bandits! They cannot obtain a simple sword when I ask them. No matter: the people of the envoy are dead. Perhaps they will find the sword eventually.' I'm sorry, Haydren."

"So, there it is," Haydren said, nodding slowly. "When we couldn't find Lintasur in Frecksshire, I had begun to suspect. That letter probably was created by Guntsen to try to get me away from him, and it probably was Dillion who came to me telling me of Guntsen's plan to kill me." He paused, looking down at the parchment in front of him. Sarah laid a hand gently on his shoulder, but he paid it little attention. "But what if it was this Melnor?" Haydren asked suddenly, looking up. "If he has been watching me since before I arrived in Burieng, maybe he sent the letter, and warned me at night, and has been 'watching' me ever since, trying to get me to do his will. Just like we talked about before, Geoffrey."

"What are you going to do?" Geoffrey asked.

Haydren snorted bitterly. "What can I do? Lasserain killed my parents, he destroyed Quaran and tried to destroy Jyunta, and he's swallowed up all but Coberan Province. And every step I've taken has brought me here. Do I actually have a choice? Apparently I have to try to kill him."

But behind his sarcasm, another idea bit deep: if the Triumvirate were true—and with Geoffrey's vision it seemed certain they were—then the God of All had to be real, as well. Or was he? Haydren glanced across the parchment again. Whether the God was real or not, Haydren's choices were being manipulated as if he were. Confidence: the side of the coin he must accept. If the parchment told the truth, there was much that Haydren must accept—with no choice. His eyes fell, and his hands sagged toward the floor.

"Killing Lasserain is not going to be easy," Sarah said. "If he's powerful enough to do everything you say he did, what can one person do?"

"Wait a moment," Geoffrey said, glancing down a new parchment. "Unbelievable," he said. "There's one more thing he did."

"Geoffrey, I would find nothing unbelievable now," Haydren muttered.

"What did he do?" Sarah asked.

"He killed Paolound," Geoffrey said, holding out the parchment. "Fifteen years ago, when he was trying to convince the dragon to ally itself with him."

"But if he killed it..." Haydren said, eyes up again, alert.

"He reanimated it," Geoffrey replied. "He learned how to cast spells of Life. But it puts him in control of the dragon. Paolound's spirit would no longer have been in it, but Lasserain's would have."

"But, wait..." Haydren began. Something was itching the back of his mind again.

"He's not allowed to do that!" Sarah said. "Life, Time, and Shape are dead magics. Tamecal outlawed them centuries ago."

"Shape?" Haydren asked. He glanced at his sword, and his mouth dropped open. "Corith!" he shouted, leaping to his feet. "Where's Tagnier?"

Corith turned from the doorway, his eyes wide. "I don't think he came down here with us."

Just then, they recognized that the sound of the flames echoing down the hall of the cave had changed: wood now cracked and popped as it burned. Dropping everything, the party dashed for the stairway. When they came out into the house, the roof was burning above them and smoke filled their lungs. They scrambled for the door. When Haydren burst through, the flames seared his face. He collapsed onto the cool grass beyond as the others tumbled out behind him. Corith came last, screaming as his cloak caught fire. Haydren leapt over to him, quickly putting out the flames with his own cloak. Grabbing Corith by the arms, Haydren pulled him upright and the four companions scrambled to the top of the hill. Coughing and catching their breath, they turned and watched as Haschina finally and truly burned.

"Our packs?" Haydren asked.

Corith shook his head, coughing. "They weren't there. I looked for them."

"Is that the best thing he can think of?" Haydren muttered.

"Who?" Geoffrey asked.

"Remember the flames of my sword flickered when Faschek came back and cast a spell on me, and again when Tagnier first came to us in Monte-Ir?" he asked. Geoffrey nodded. "Well, it did the same thing when Paolound approached. But Paolound wasn't Paolound then; his spirit was Lasserain. Which means Faschek and Tagnier were Lasserain too, just in different forms. Not Semmelle." Haydren sighed as he gazed at Haschina. "That's why he was in the Forest. He had been here. Either of those times, I could have killed him."

"Who's Semmelle?" Sarah asked.

"Magic-user, a wizard I guess," Haydren replied. "I saw him at the junction outside Quaran, and again in Frecksshire. He was at the inn just before you arrived."

"How do you know him?"

"He's in Guntsen's Mages."

Sarah's eyebrows shot up. "A magic user from Hewolucs shows up in Frecksshire and you don't tell me?"

"I thought he was only coming after me," Haydren replied. "I didn't want to be delayed. I hoped we could simply escape him by leaving. I don't think he recognized me."

"He saw you?"

"I kind of talked to him, a little bit," Haydren admitted.

"And somehow didn't recognize you, even though he was sent to get you," Sarah said, folding her arms.

"Well, I guess he *wasn't* sent to get me," Haydren said with a shrug. "Since it was Lasserain and not him this whole time. I guess he must have come to Frecksshire for some other reason."

"You think? Haydren, Coberan is under assault from every side. Is it possible this Semmelle was in Frecksshire as a spy?"

"I thought he was just coming after me," Haydren muttered.

Sarah took a deep breath. "Haydren, you really aren't *that* important," she said, gazing out over the village. "Hopefully I can get word to Durdamon in time—hopefully he already knows."

By now the sun was setting, though the raging fires cast an orange glow nearly as bright. Berating himself for letting Tagnier live, Haydren tended to Corith, who had minor burns on his back. Geoffrey managed to bring down a large bird that had come to investigate the new happenings in the old village. He fashioned a crude spit and began roasting it as the last light of the sun disappeared from the sky.

"Should we really stay here tonight?" Sarah asked. "What if Tagnier—Lasserain—comes back?"

"He hasn't before," Haydren said. "Besides, I don't think this village has given up all its secrets just yet." He glanced at Geoffrey meaningfully. "*Something* just tells me."

After they had eaten, Haydren wandered alone nearer to the village, where some of the taller buildings still burned. He paused beside one of them, the acrid smoke filling his nostrils as the heat of the fire warmed him. He glanced sideways at the building. His eyes unfocused as the smell and the heat awoke something in him. He blinked, then closed his eyes and breathed deeply.

It began near the end of the last memory: *he was waking, disoriented by shouting and screaming. There was fire around him; he could feel the heat. His mother was pushing something into his arms, and thrusting him out of the burning carriage. Smoke filled his lungs and made him choke, and the heat of the fire was unbearable. He ran from the caravan. Something hit him from behind and knocked him over. He fell atop the sword his mother gave him as a bandit crouched over top of him. Haydren could smell sweat, and flies. He didn't even know you could smell flies, but he smelled them. His hand flailed to his belt and he pulled free a red dagger, whose metal seemed pitted like it was coated with heavy rust. He began swinging wildly at the bandit. His eyes closed as blood poured over him. He kept screaming, and swinging, until the bandit collapsed on top of him. Struggling free, Haydren grabbed the sword and yanked it from underneath the bandit's limp body. The blood-covered dagger dropped to the ground, and he began running.*

Haydren's eyes snapped open, and he retreated from the village. At the top of the hill he said nothing to his companions. Removing his cloak and wrapping it like a blanket around himself, he shivered though the heat from the fire reached even to their camp. Was it Melnor too, he wondered, bringing memories to him? Were any actions or thoughts his own?

He attempted in vain to retreat into sleep.

The next morning, a warm sun streamed over the treetops. As they finished a short breakfast of leftover bird, Corith's eyes roved across the charred and smoking landscape. "Why does this have to happen? Do you know how long Haschina has been hidden? And just as we find it, the hatred of Lasserain destroys it completely. Nothing left but a blackened crater, a wound and a scab in the middle of the Woods." He let out a sharp burst of air. "So help me, it sickens me."

There was no answer. Haydren stood and went back down to the village, among the charred skeletons of houses. Tendrils of smoke rose hissing from the few hot spots that remained. Sarah followed him, but Corith and Geoffrey stayed near the fire.

Avoiding the hill where they had arrived in the village, Haydren and Sarah walked to the west side of the village. There, an enormous tree like an oak, though nearly as big around as a house, towered skyward. Distracted by the burning village, they had not seen it until now. It rose straight and tall, with a limbless trunk. At the top the branches sprang outward like a fountain. Turning slowly as he traced their line, Haydren saw that the branches encircled the entire village in an arboreal embrace. At regular intervals, several paces apart, stalks like thin tree trunks sprang from the underside of the branches and thrust downward until they reached the ground. Peering beyond the massive tree, deeper into the forest, Haydren could see that the branches with their stalk-like supports continued into the woods as far as the light reached.

In fact, the branches and their stalks *were* the forest as far as the light reached.

"The Kalen Woods is...a tree?" Sarah gasped in wonder.

"Geoffrey! Corith! Come here!" Haydren shouted.

Both men leapt to their feet and came running, freeing their swords as they drew near. Haydren pointed wordlessly to the tree. They studied it with knit brows.

"What is it?" Geoffrey asked.

"The Kalen Woods is a tree!" Sarah exclaimed.

Geoffrey and Corith looked more closely, following the branches as they circled the village, their eyes wide.

"I'll be..." Corith muttered.

"Can we bring it down?" Geoffrey asked, craning his neck upward at the branches.

"Look at the size of this thing!" Haydren said, standing beside the trunk. Geoffrey couldn't help but snort a chuckle. It made for a comical image. But Haydren was right.

"I can try a spell," Sarah said quickly. "You should probably stand back, though."

The three men retreated deep into the burned-out village. Sarah regarded them with a withering look. "Not that far back!" she said. She turned and glanced at the tree. "On the other hand..." she muttered to herself, taking a few steps backward. Focusing on her target, she spoke a few words. From the clear sky a thunderbolt struck, knocking Sarah onto her back as it exploded against the trunk. When she shook herself and looked up, the tree had a massive burn-scar down its center, but still it stood. Sarah pushed herself to her feet and dusted herself off.

"One more time, I guess," she said. Haydren approached and laid a hand on her arm, restraining her. When she looked up, she saw the bark had begun to heal. By the time her mouth dropped completely open, it was as if nothing had happened to it.

"Let me try," he said. Sarah set her teeth, but motioned him forward. He walked over and drew his sword.

"I do not know how dangerous it is to use your magic," he whispered, looking over the blade. The flames did not flicker, but the sword warmed in his hand. "Just enough to rid Burieng of this festering wound is all I ask." He closed his eyes, and whispered the name of the sword. Instantly the metal cooled in his hand. He opened his eyes, and Aerithion burned with white fire. With a shout, he thrust the sword into the tree. It cut like butter, and the blade buried nearly to the hilt. Haydren released the sword and took a few steps backward, waiting to see what would happen. He could see the flames near the hilt, and saw that the light from them suddenly ceased. He sighed, and glanced at his companions. Apparently it was not strong enough. When he looked back, a blinding flash of light seared his eyes, its source at the hilt of Aerithion. The light compressed near the guard, then suddenly punched into the trunk of the tree and lit it from within like a shuttered lamp. With a shattering shockwave that knocked Haydren over and battered against his companions further into the village, the tree splintered into a thousand shards that were caught on the wind and blown across the sky, scattering across the Northern Forest.

21

FORTUNES

"You did that."
"What makes you say so?"
"That sword was not made for that."
"It is a channel. Sometimes channels flood."

6 Thriman 1320 — Summer

When Haydren finally stood, Aerithion was thrust point-first at the center of the blackened circle where the tree had been. Far above, the broken ends of the branches hung limply, tattered ends waving in the breeze. Haydren retrieved his sword and sheathed it as he approached his companions.

"I feel like, if Pladt were here, he would mention we promised the lord of Quaran we would do something about the Forest, if we were able," he said with a smile. "Didn't realize it would be in such a fashion." He glanced back to the gaping hole where the mighty tree had once stood. "Some life surely comes from the stalks, but with the trunk gone the forest will die off as well." He took a breath. "I think it is time to leave. West, Corith?"

He nodded. "A fire on the shore might attract the attention of a ship on its way to Estwind."

"And for food?" Sarah asked.

Haydren shrugged. "If it is Melnor's intention that I should kill Lasserain, then he'll just have to provide us with food to keep us alive," he said. Geoffrey glanced at him sharply, but said nothing.

As they journeyed, still avoiding the paths, gaps appeared in the canopy. Here and there across the forest, thin shafts of white sunlight appeared, and flowers sprang up where they touched the ground, their seeds apparently rendered dormant while the tree had lived. By the morning of the third day, they were able to douse their torches and walk in the glow from hundreds of such beams.

Sarah kept her eyes down much of the time, squinting as they walked through sudden patches of light. It should have been her magic, not the sword's. It could have been, if she hadn't relinquished the opportunity. Another glow of sunlight blinded her: that was why her eyes burned suddenly.

Each day, morning and evening, creatures crept near enough—disoriented by the new sunlight in their realms—for Geoffrey to take down with his small bow. Then, in the After-Noon of the third day since departing Haschina, they strode out of the forest onto a beach. The shoreline curved northward, far out to a cape. They ran to this point, and as the sun lowered they gathered wood and built a raging bonfire.

The sun set, and stars speckled the night sky. Soon after the moon rose, a small light appeared on the horizon and drew nearer. They could hear the creak of rigging, and sails billowing in the wind.

"What-ho there!" came a cry from the ship. "Who's out there?"

"Four travelers on a mission from the Earl of Frecksshire!" Haydren shouted back. "We need passage to Estwind!"

There was a splash, and the clunk of oars turning in their locks. A lamp near the prow of the dinghy lit four men pulling for shore. When they landed, a burly man jumped out.

"I don't suppose you have any proof of this?" he rumbled.

Haydren pulled out their orders, though the parchment was now badly tattered. The man read it, squinting in the low light of the lamp on his boat. Straightening, he handed the parchment back to Haydren.

"Good enough!" he said. "I am Pelman, first mate of the *Night Sky;* Bomor, Captain. We trade from Andelen, but a good wind carried us some off course as we passed Mage's Finger earlier tonight. We might not have seen your fire, otherwise."

As he climbed back aboard, the companions followed him as silently as he led. Pulling swiftly, the seamen soon had them aboard the trading vessel. The winds rose and pushed them steadily toward Estwind.

"I've never seen anything like it!" Bomor roared at Haydren the next morning. "You've some luck, boy; can I pay you to stay aboard my ship for a few runs? At this rate, we'll raise Croden Island in four days, and Estwind in five."

Geoffrey glanced at Sarah, who reclined in some rigging near the stern.

She took his glance, smiled, and gazed into the sails and the sun.

When Geoffrey shook his head and turned away, Sarah's smile faltered. Why could he not see it? Speed was important, and she lent them speed. The man would never be satisfied.

"You look right comfortable," said a voice, the first kind—and feminine—voice Sarah had heard since Jyunta, and she looked up with a start. Wrinkled but ample cheeks made small caves out of which merry eyes shone like sparkling gems, but gems that faded with concern as the old woman looked at Sarah. "Oh, but you don't look too happy though," she said.

Sarah tried to smile. "It's a pleasant day," she said, gazing up.

"And a good wind guides us," said the old woman as she looked at the sails stretched taut against the spars.

The sails began to sag. Sarah glanced at them. She whispered a few words, and they bloomed anew. But again, just before they were fully grown the wind ceased and the canvas flagged. Sarah cocked her head, her eyes wide.

A soft chuckle brought her gaze around. The woman had her face turned to the sails, but her eyes were on Sarah. Her lips moved quickly, and the sails strained. Bomor, near the helm, shook his head and returned to his charts.

"I am Chlo," said the woman, easing herself onto a nearby stool. "It is a pleasant day, you look comfortable, and your fair wind guides us. But you are unhappy."

Sarah gazed across the deck to the waters past the bow, where in a few days Estwind would rise, and, later, Jyunta, and then Frecksshire, and then—where? Galessern, eventually? Where then? To some other desk in some other place, poring over ancient texts with barely legible spells, waiting for the day she cast the one that killed her?

Her hand went to her tunic, where an ancient book lay tucked in a pocket. She caught herself fingering the closed pages. So did Chlo.

"Something you've found?" she murmured.

"We needed speed on our way back to Frecksshire," Sarah said, and gestured to the creaking spars. "Isn't this giving us speed?"

"I've seen a fleet destroyed when too much wind caught its sails," Chlo said. "It came too fast to take them in, and every mast broke in half, stranding hundreds of sailors hundreds of miles out to sea."

"A sorceress could have stopped it, if she'd been there," Sarah said.

Chlo laughed. "It was a sorceress who started it," she said.

"Were they coming to attack?"

Chlo shrugged. "No, it didn't seem so. But they were unwanted."

"Was it..." Sarah paused, swallowing. "Was it you?"

"My mother."

"Why?"

"Probably because she could," Chlo said simply. "And because the people who admired her asked her to. Clansmen are so typically wary of foreigners."

"You are from the Clanasoes?" Sarah said, surprised.

"Gunda."

Sarah gazed at her in wonder. "Was—was your mother..."

Chlo nodded solemnly. "She was Maerlyn. A great sorceress, and eventually wizard—I'm sorry, habits die hard: she *was* a powerful wizard. How great she might have been..."

"Geoffrey told me there is a statue of her in Irii."

"Was that the man who seemed to disapprove of your magic?" Chlo asked.

Sarah nodded. "Is it there?"

"It is. Looks nothing like her, of course: in her youth she was gluttonous. In her age, shriveled and hollow. But to the one who sculpted, she was a god."

"Even though she had destroyed so many ships?"

"But they asked her to," Chlo said, piercing Sarah with her gaze. "The thing matters not to those who beg for it. Once you have what you want, it is difficult to say it is no good thing."

"Then how are we to know?"

"That is a good question. Many have sought that answer, with no results."

"Thank you," Sarah said, gazing across the waters once more. "I definitely feel happier now."

"Just remember this, young one: desire, born of rightful motivations, takes us to good things. Desires born of selfish motivations take us blindly to destruction. Oftentimes, those who don't share our selfish desires show us most easily how selfish they are."

"So you think I should listen to Geoffrey?" Sarah asked with a sigh.

"I think you should listen to your heart," Chlo said. Her keen glance went to Sarah's tunic. "Or whatever that is, that's in your pocket," she added with a smile.

As Chlo leaned back, closing her eyes to the sun, Sarah's hand went back to the book she had found in Haschina—the book that was Lasserain's diary. She frowned as she picked habitually at the pages. *Surely...I mean, not all magic-users went this way?*

◆

True to Bomor's word the companions walked onto the docks in Estwind five days after the *Night Sky* had picked them up. Haydren turned to the captain and offered his hand.

"Thank you very much for the rescue, Captain," he said. "I don't know what we would have done if you had not picked us up. If you can find us again in a few hours, I can repay you..."

"Don't even think about it," Bomor replied. "Bringing your fortunes aboard my ship, and getting us to Estwind two days ahead of schedule, is payment enough."

After they had left the docks, Geoffrey leaned toward Haydren. "Are we to walk all the way back to Jyunta then?" he asked. Haydren glanced at him with a smile, but said nothing. Instead he only led his friends to the Mercenary Inn. The bartender looked at him in surprise when he sat down.

"Haydren!" he said. "I didn't know you would be returning."

Haydren laughed. "You hoped I would not be returning, Losch," he said. "But I need some money, for horses for myself and my companions. Would you be so kind as to get it for us? And something to eat, as well."

"Of course," Losch replied, bowing low.

When he had gone, Geoffrey looked at Haydren quizzically. "He owes you money?" he asked.

"I didn't need all the money from Paolound to buy the mercenaries," Haydren explained. "I had Losch keep it for me. We'll be well supplied on our journey south."

"What do you intend to do when we reach Frecksshire?" Sarah asked.

"Given what we have accomplished for the Earl," Haydren said, sitting back in his chair, "I intend to ask his permission to leave his service for a time. Then I will go to Galessern."

"I may come with you," Sarah said. "After what he has done already, I intend to see him—see what he has to say."

"I'm sure he will say nothing interesting," Haydren said with a glance at Geoffrey.

"Of course I am with you," Geoffrey said.

"I may stay in Jyunta," Corith said quietly. "My soldiers will need me. Lord Garoun will need me as well. Jyunta will still need to be rebuilt."

"As you wish, Corith," Haydren replied.

Just then, Losch arrived with a sack of jingling coins, and four mugs of ale that he set before the companions. Sarah sniffed it, then held it out to him.

"I will just have water, thank you," she said, shaking her head.

When Losch returned, he brought their food as well. After they had eaten their fill, and paid for rooms for the night, they went into Estwind and supplied themselves for the journey to Frecksshire, securing four of the fastest horses they could find for sale. They went to sleep that night warm and full, and slept until the sun rose the next morning.

They did not push their horses hard that day, and made camp halfway between Jyunta and the Vilde River. The next day, however, they spurred their mounts to a gallop as they approached Jyunta. No one hailed them from the walls, and there was no sound from inside. The gates were torn from their great hinges and sat askew upon the walls. Their hearts in their throats, they rode into the city.

Their horses stopped as the companions gazed in despair, for inside Jyunta was the same landscape that they had found inside Quaran. The ground was charred, and all had been razed but a few buildings and blackened spars. The hall still stood near the center of the city, but the doors were gaping wide. They rode to the square, dismounted, and climbed the stairs, entering the destitute structure slowly. Bodies lay strewn everywhere. Deep in the corner, Hrothgar sat against the wall, his lieutenant Logdthar beside him on his left, closer to the door. To Hrothgar's right, furthest from the door and sheltered by the two mercenaries' bodies, was the body of Lord Garoun.

Haydren went to them and knelt down. "This was recent," he said quietly. "Within a few days." He pivoted on his heel and looked at his companions with watering eyes.

"Then I am going with you to Galessern," Corith said quietly. "After we bury these dead."

"I must report to the Earl," Haydren said, rising and wiping his eyes. "Geoffrey will come with me. You two may join us when you have finished. If all goes well, we will be on our way south before autumn arrives. And if whatever has guided us to this point continues with us, Lasserain will not see another winter."

22

LESSONS

"You're not going down?"
"Not yet."
"But what if she—?"
"I think she will not."

17 Thriman 1320 — Summer

Corith entered the hall out of breath to find Sarah gazing at the bodies, chin on her fist.

"What are you doing?" he asked.

"Trying to think of a spell, to..." Her voice trailed off.

He gazed at her for several long moments, then moved to another body. "If you spent as much time thinking of spells as helping me, we'd be done by now." He grunted as he positioned the mercenary leader across his shoulders.

Sarah's hand dropped. "I'm sorry Corith," she said quietly. "I can't move them like you, not fully armored. But I can't..." She trailed off, looking at him pleadingly.

"I know," he said, staggering toward the door. "I hope these mercenaries don't expect a certain ritual of burial."

"I'm sure they won't know," Sarah replied as the door slowly swung to. With a sigh, she went to Lord Garoun's body, now clear of the two mercenaries guarding him. It seemed strange, to her, the way they were positioned. She squatted, trying to pull the former lord's body forward though she barely wanted to touch it. She strained and grunted, but his bulk wouldn't budge. She let out a frustrated grunt and stood back.

She couldn't do this. She'd made her life out of making the elements aide her, and now when she needed them perhaps the most personally, there was nothing to be done. Surely there was something! If she could make them carry themselves out, somehow: a bed of solid air? But how to make it travel...

She folded her arms, and felt the press of Lasserain's diary. Now, Paolound—*there* was a corpse that could move on its own. Furrowing her brow, Sarah pulled the diary out. Did Lasserain ever discuss how he'd accomplished that? If she could have this room cleared within a few sentences...

The script on the pages she read became more frenzied, and showed a mix of swift scratches and hesitant blots. She paused where a dense page had one Rinc Nain word—*Bultum?* was scratched near the middle. The rest was in magic language. She scanned till she recognized the word for *shield*, and moved on. Lasserain was approaching something profound, she could tell. Another page—and there it was.

Sarah bit her lip. She wouldn't need the spell to last long. She wasn't trying to bring them back to life, just get them to move on their own. She took a deep breath, reading over his words. Lasserain had even put accent and stress marks, so she knew the pronunciation would be accurate—but would she have the affinity to Life? She didn't even know if she needed it.

She glanced backward at the door. Corith would be another several moments—it was something of a walk to the impromptu pyre they had constructed. She took a deep breath to calm herself, but the shaky exhale that followed bolstered her doubt more than her faith.

She focused on Garoun, and spoke the words.

For a moment, nothing happened. Then, just as his eyelids began to flutter, the energy fled from her body. *I shouldn't have done this,* she realized as she sagged to her knees, even her gasps fading. Her eyes drifted down to the page, managed to focus and find what looked like the ceasing spell. As her eyeballs dragged back upward, Garoun was staring at his hands, at her, leveraging himself to his feet. She spoke the few words—again an agony as nothing happened.

Then, as Garoun collapsed as if suddenly struck, Sarah's breath gave out and blackness overtook her.

⸻◦⸻

She came to, coughing, and Corith was hovering over her. He settled back on his heels and gazed at her in relief.

"What happened?" she asked, pressing a hand to her chest.

"You tell me," Corith replied. "I came in and you were passed out on the floor. Did you try to pick up Lord Garoun?"

Sarah sat up, rubbing her head. "I was trying to drag him," she said.

"But then...something..."

She had tried to cast Life magic, something forbidden in Carist and in her own mind for as long as she was alive and trying to become a wizard. And it had nearly killed her. But the details were still fuzzy.

She looked up slowly, her eyes resting unfocused at the floor near Garoun's feet.

Not all magic-users have to go this way, do they? She closed her eyes. *Does that matter? I'm going this way. Again. Trying to extend my power beyond where it should go.*

She blinked, and saw the diary on the floor near her. She picked it up, noticing as if for the first time the feverish scrawl of a mage losing control. Corith nodded at it. "What is that?" he asked.

She stood, with Corith's help, and cast the diary aside. "It doesn't matter," she said. "I'm okay now. Thanks, for whatever part you played in reviving me. Would you mind helping me with this?"

She grasped a hold of her former lord and tugged, gasping and grunting. Finally Garoun's corpulent body toppled sideways and his head thumped sickeningly onto the wooden boards.

There was a muffled cry, and something shifting.

Sarah stood, her body turning for her mace, but nothing moved. She stepped closer, and suddenly noticed the square cut around the boards where Garoun had once sat. "There's a trapdoor under Garoun!" she said.

Corith was quickly by her side, wrestling the body aside. As Corith drew his sword, Sarah yanked open the trapdoor. A woman's terrified face below turned quickly to surprise and joy.

"It's you! Are we safe then?" she cried.

"Come out, mother," Corith said to the woman he didn't know, lowering his sword and extending his hand. As she came out, others swiftly followed. The women shielded their children's eyes from the carnage around them. The men, most old, had seen as much before and looked about grimly.

"What happened? Why is Lord Garoun out here?" Corith asked one of the men.

"Was his idea," came the reply. "He thought if the enemy found him out here, they would take it to mean everyone was here. Surely the lord would be best protected, aye?" The man shook his head slowly. "Saved over fifty of us, sitting right on top of us."

"How is the city?" someone else asked.

Corith shook his head. "There's little left but the walls," he said. There were gasps, and a sob.

The first man straightened his back. "It matters little," he said. "We've got strong men here. We can rebuild."

"You're a fool Tornir," someone said. "You heard Corith. Rebuild from what?"

"There's still lumber outside the walls, isn't there?" Tornir replied.

"Are the crops damaged?"

"Little," Corith replied. "It will be ample, though, for—" he faltered, glancing around what few folk remained of his once-proud city.

"And who'll lead us then, aye? Garoun is dead."

"I will," Corith said quietly.

Tornir's eyes gleamed as he smiled. "I'll follow ye," he said firmly. There was silence for a breath, then others began pledging their allegiance until the room resounded with oaths. Corith finally raised his hands to silence them.

"Then," he said, eyes glistening. "Let's set straight what we can for tonight, beginning by making this hall proper to sleep in. We will have a hard road ahead of us."

⸺◆⸺

The next morning, Corith arose and went outside to find Sarah saddling her horse.

"You're going, then?" he asked.

Sarah glanced at him briefly, then returned to tightening the girth. "Yes," she replied. "Haydren is going to need help, and I need to see that Lasserain pays for what he's done here, and everywhere."

Corith folded his arms and gazed out over the scarred landscape. "His magic has caused much destruction," he said quietly. "I wonder what makes men thirst for such power?"

Sarah's fingers faltered, and she swallowed. "It's easier to get what you want, I suppose."

"Perhaps," Corith allowed. He gazed compassionately at the sorceress. "The God go with you, Sarah," he said.

She squinted at him, and managed a small smile. "Thank you. You as well."

With that she mounted and was soon through the gate and on her way to Frecksshire. As she rode, she still pondered the events of the previous day. She had remembered more, as she lay awake. She remembered trying to cease the spell before she fainted. Always—always, when a caster ceases a spell some energy returns. Except yesterday, when the Life spell ceased, it had taken even more energy from her. She remembered feeling the energy leave her.

Was that why it was an outlawed magic? Did Time, Life, and Shape take energy when it was cast, and again when it stopped? A caster would then have to know the energy to cast the spell, and have enough in reserve for when the spell stopped operating.

Sarah sat upright suddenly. That was why Lasserain—as Tagnier—didn't do anything to them in the Forest: they had just killed Paolound, and forced him to cease being Faschek. That was why he could do no more than appear in slightly different form, and alter Time in

Haydren's mind.

And then they destroyed an entire Forest grown from what must have been a Life spell.

Sarah shouted to her horse, galloping hard for Frecksshire. Haydren had to know. Lasserain would be weakened from what they had done.

This changed everything. But it had to last until they made it to Galessern.

<hr>

"Did you mean what you said back at Jyunta?" Geoffrey asked. "About the one who guides us?"

They sat in their room at the Dancing Piper, having arrived at Frecksshire that morning, and were waiting to have an audience with the Earl that evening. As they waited, and after much thought, Geoffrey decided to broach the topic that had been nagging at him since they had left Jyunta five days earlier.

Haydren looked at him and sighed. "Whether I like it or not," he replied. "It seems to be the case."

"So do you believe in the God of All now?"

"That document seems to prove it."

"A lot of documents speak about the God, Haydren," Geoffrey said. "That has never meant anything to you before."

"Then perhaps I just hope he does," Haydren exclaimed in exasperation. "Lasserain has destroyed two cities, and killed a dragon. Now I go to try to kill him. I'm not prideful enough to think I can do it alone. But hopefully, as you say Geoffrey, the wind will be in the treetops."

"I believe it will, Haydren," Geoffrey murmured. "I believe you have been called to this purpose."

"So it would seem," Haydren said. He smiled tiredly, and repeated: "whether I like it or not."

Later that evening, they stood before the Earl. "What did you discover?" he asked when the doors had shut behind the guards.

Darkness descended outside the windows of the keep long before Haydren finished, and even longer before Durdamon was done questioning him further. Water and food were brought, and they sat at table.

"This is such mixed news, Haydren," Durdamon said wearily, leaning back in his chair. "Though you have accomplished much, I cannot gauge how effective it might be."

"There was one more thing," Haydren said. "Before we left, I recognized a man from Hewolucs here, a magic-user."

"Semmelle?" Durdamon asked.

Haydren's head notched a little sideways. "Yes, Excellency."

"That was another victory, whose effects are not yet fully realized," Durdamon said. "Semmelle was sent to Quaran by your Earl to see what might be done about the Forest. Apparently, Junei did not yet know what Lasserain was planning to do with his province after he'd handed it over. But even after Semmelle reported back, Junei did nothing. So Semmelle made his way here. He defected."

Haydren nodded once, remembering Sarah's rebuke on the hill in Haschina. "May I ask your Excellency a question?"

"Of course—Lintasur Guinad?"

Haydren nodded.

"I have found little to help you, except perhaps the letter did not originate with a man by that name," the Earl said. "It was commissioned and sent by a man named Jeyetna, who claimed to be working on the orders of a man named Godfrind." The Earl shook his head. "My men could find out nothing more."

"They did not hurt him?" Haydren asked in alarm.

"Of course not," Durdamon said scornfully. "The information meant little to me. Do you know him?"

"My father knew him; Jeyetna that is, Excellency. It does help to clear up some of the mystery for me, Excellency. I beg leave for one more request." The Earl gestured for him to continue. "I would ask, Excellency, to be released from your services for a period of time which I cannot define, but it should not be more than a few months."

Durdamon sat forward. "You have already accomplished far more than I could have hoped, Haydren. Jyunta's destruction was hardly your fault. I release you from my services completely." He sat back once more. "Sarah is on her way down from Jyunta, I have been told. She is released as well. That is all, Haydren. The guard will escort you back to your rooms. And Haydren," he called as the doors opened and they stood to leave. "The God of All be with you," he said. They bowed deeply, and Geoffrey followed Haydren out of the Earl's chambers. As they passed the guard, Geoffrey noticed the man's mouth suddenly tighten in a line. He glanced back, noticing Durdamon's hands clasped strangely, with one finger tucked into the arch of his palm as he talked aside to one of his advisors. Durdamon glanced up, and his hands disappeared below the table as the doors boomed shut.

◆

Sarah arrived the next evening, and found Geoffrey and Haydren at the Dancing Piper.

"You come alone," Haydren said.

"There was a remnant," Sarah replied. "They hid beneath the hall, and came out when we were burying the dead. Corith remained behind to lead them. He intends to rebuild Jyunta."

"I would trust no one else to such an undertaking," Geoffrey said solemnly. "Corith has a great leader inside him, if he will only let it out."

"That's not all. Haydren, the outlawed magics Lasserain is using—Time, Life, and Shape: they take energy away when they are stopped," she said, her eyes shining.

Haydren only gazed at her. "I'm not sure..."

"It means, forcing Lasserain to stop being Faschek...killing Paolound...killing the Forest..." she paused, and made continuing motions with her hands. "They weakened him, Haydren," she finished when he remained silent. "It took even more energy away from him, rather than giving him some back. That's why he didn't do much to us in the Forest—he wasn't able to."

"You're sure about this?" Haydren asked.

"As sure as I can be."

"How long will he be weak?"

Sarah hesitated. "I can't be sure of that," she replied. She felt fine now, after her failed attempt with Lord Garoun. But that was far less than the staggering forces Lasserain was attempting to balance. "But it definitely means we might find ways to weaken him before we meet him. He might not be able to use magic at all, if we attack the right spots first."

Haydren drew a breath. "Well, it's something," he said hopefully. "I'd feel better if I could come at him with a blade as equals," he added with a grin.

"Oh, speaking of which," Sarah remarked, suddenly turning grave. "We found this, Haydren," she said, holding out a red dagger. Haydren gazed at it quietly for a few moments, then reached out and took it.

"Why did we find it there, Haydren?" Sarah pressed.

Haydren chewed the corner of his mouth, then sighed, shrugged, and grinned. "I never really used it," he replied. Sarah and Geoffrey both only looked at him. "I traded it to the mercenaries, as part of the deal to bring them to Jyunta."

"Haydren, I think this dagger is very powerful, and very important," Sarah said.

"Why?" he asked quickly.

"Because I know magic," she replied just as swiftly. "Please don't give that away again."

Haydren shrugged and tucked the dagger away, then informed Sarah of the Earl's release. Sarah looked at him dubiously.

"The Earl is not one to release those who help him so greatly, but to keep using them," she said. "More than likely he knows what you plan, and hopes you can do it without his sacrificing his own soldiers."

"Then he will get his wish," Haydren replied, his gaze firm.

"Of course he will," she said, her eyes perfectly matching his.

23

GUIDES

"You would not before, but now...?"
"He already knows."
"That seems to happen a lot, to you."
"At some point, continued secrecy becomes tyrannical."

23 Thriman 1320 — Summer

They departed the next morning under slate skies and with a chill breeze toward them. The road ran south-east toward Thuden; here, the inns along the way were still open, and the company grew spoiled on soft, warm beds and hot meals that did not have to be hunted first. They resupplied at Thuden and were quickly on their way to Crevane, where the Tundee and Coberan Rivers met on their way to the Shadowmere.

As they rode to Crevane, Haydren glanced back as thunder slowly rolled. A storm was on the horizon and from under its shadow another horseman approached: an old man with a flowing red robe and a gnarled staff in his hand. Haydren recognized the description Geoffrey had given him, and turned to face the road ahead.

The old man drew alongside Haydren. "Good afternoon, Haydren," he said.

"Good afternoon, Melnor," Haydren replied.

He didn't flinch. "Do you think as one who can live in your head that I should be surprised that you know my name?" he asked.

"Do you speak with the God of All?" Haydren asked in reply.

"Do you want me to?"

"Or we can continue to converse in questions, which you seem to prefer," Haydren said.

Melnor laughed. "Sometimes there are many more questions than answers, are there not? I suppose all questions must eventually come in a row."

"I did not think you could come when others were around," Haydren said, glancing at his companions.

"If you're wondering why they ride without looking at you, it is because you are looking ahead the same way they are," Melnor responded. "The same as if you were dreaming. You only think you are looking in my direction."

"A neat trick," Haydren said.

"We all have abilities according to our calling," Melnor responded. "You have been given skill with a blade. Pladt had skill with a bow. Geoffrey can lead. Corith can guide, and has been given wisdom. Sarah is compassionate beyond what she knows she can be, and that gives her the strength to defend those she cares for, and to make peace."

"And what was Pladt's calling?"

"He defended Werine," Melnor said. He turned, and pierced Haydren with his gaze. "And he defended you. Do not think you survived Jyunta by your own blade, Haydren. The actions of Pladt Grecce on that day have yet to cease echoing through history."

Tears welled in Haydren's eyes. "Will I see Pladt again, then?"

"It is not yet known to me," Melnor replied. "I cannot tell all things."

Haydren blinked away the tears. "Why do I feel like you're lying to me?" he asked.

"I haven't a clue," Melnor replied frankly. "I cannot say anything that is a lie, Haydren. In my realm, lies do not exist."

Haydren gazed at him for several moments. "Yet you call me 'Haydren'..."

Melnor returned the gaze, and smiled. He led his horse off the road, and faded away.

"Is my name, truly, then...?" Haydren began to wonder.

Last one there is dead flowers!

He was running down a street, tiny legs pumping to keep up with the children in front of him. But they were all older than he, and they quickly pulled away.

"Not fair!" he called at their backs. They only laughed at him.

Stop. The voice came to him then just as it would in Burieng. He stopped, gazing down a dark alleyway. He had been near it before, but his friends told him a crazy old woman lived down that alley who liked to eat young children. But something was calling him, something glinting in the late evening sun, buried under a pile of trash near a wall.

"What are you looking at, Haydren?" a girl asked. The rest of his friends crowded around him, peering down the alley.

"Let's keep going," one boy said, hugging himself though the day was warm. "Haydren's just dead flowers anyway."

And yet, Haydren's tiny legs took him down the alley. "Wait, stop!" the girl cried. "Mother will kill me if you get captured and eaten by the crazy witch-lady!"

But Haydren did not stop. A wind shrieked down the alley, ripping at his shirt. One of his friends screamed. Haydren ran, plunging his hand under the pile of trash and grasping the glittering thing and running as fast as he could back to the main street.

"What is it?" his friends asked, crowding around him once more. He unwrapped the heavy cloth from the object: a black leather scabbard with silver stitching in the form of scales. When he drew the sword, he saw the blade was a pale liquid-red, with ruby red flames down the center. Tied to the hilt was a scrap of paper with Rinc Nain writing. But in his memory, Haydren could not recall what it said.

He returned to the road to Crevane, blinking more tears from his eyes. Surely they had come to Burieng to go to Deewan where the sword was forged. They came because of him.

And he'd had a sister. One that was *not* with them in the caravan. He was sure. But why would they have left her in Rinc Na?

They passed through Crevane, keeping on the King's Highway to the east of the Tundee River. They entered the low moors once more, but where the Tundee began widening into the Shadowmere, the ground hardened into the Endolin foothills. The road hugged the shoreline of the Shadowmere, while great hills rose to the east and across the lake to the west.

"Why is it called 'Shadowmere'?" Geoffrey asked as they rode. "It mirrors the sky brilliantly, right now."

"Things are often named after what makes them unique, not what makes them the same," Sarah replied. "At unpredictable times, the Shadowmere doesn't mirror the daylight sky, but the night sky. When it does, strange things happen."

"Strange things?"

"Some have washed in its black waters and been healed. Other times, a tide of war changes abruptly and without explanation. Always when the waters turn black, something strange happens—sometimes good, sometimes bad."

"So you wouldn't wish for the shadow to come," Geoffrey mused.

Sarah grinned. "Not in good conscience," she replied. "You can only accept the good that comes, and deal with the misfortune."

They arrived at Suthet at the first of the month, fifteen days after leaving Frecksshire. "We'll need to find a guide into the mountains," Haydren said. "Perhaps one of the innkeepers will know where to find one."

They found an inn called the Light of the Shadowmere, and inquired within. The bartender glanced at them while furiously wiping a mug, then turned to a man further down the bar who had entered just after the four companions.

"Julian!" he growled. "These be needing you."

The man turned to them. "What is it?" he asked.

Haydren approached. "We need a guide through the mountains," he said.

"Wilcer Creek feeds the Shadowmere south. Follow that past the sentinels at night and when you come to it, take the left fork through the pass. The Bawelen takes you north-east or south-west. Kaoleyn Creek takes you where you don't want to go."

"It is not so much where we need to go," Haydren said quietly. "It's what we wish to avoid."

Julian gazed at him, inspecting his eyes. "Five thousand," he said. He took a sip of his drink as Haydren watched him.

"Three thousand is all we have," Haydren replied.

"Then you'll need to find another guide. Unless you can find fifteen hundred more, and nothing less."

Haydren studied him. "I think we'll only pay two thousand."

Julian coughed into his drink and *thunked* the mug onto the counter. "Do you understand how bartering works?" he said with a laugh.

Haydren's eyes grew hard. "Should I go down to fifteen hundred?"

Geoffrey's eyebrows knit as he glanced between Haydren and Julian, curious. Julian stared at him for several moments, and then glanced around the room.

"Two thousand is fine," he said, barely loud enough to hear.

Haydren smiled. "I'm sure the Earl will reward you handsomely, Julian," he said reassuringly. "Make sure supplies are ready for us to leave tomorrow morning. We'll be here for the night."

Julian pushed himself away from the bar, glowering at Haydren. He threw a coin down beside the mug and stomped off.

"How did you know he worked for the Earl?" Geoffrey asked with a smile as Haydren turned to him.

"I didn't," Haydren admitted with a grin. "He didn't call my bluff, that's all."

Geoffrey grunted, and took a drink. "Well played," he said.

Julian was waiting for them in the common room of the inn the next morning, and they rode out of the gates of Suthet soon after. Julian knew his craft, and their bags were well stocked for the journey south. They followed Gorges Road south-west as it wrapped around the bottom of the Shadowmere until they reached Wilcer Creek. Here, Julian led them south along the river. As the hills grew and began to turn to rock, a narrow path formed along the bank of the river.

"We'll follow this as it winds through the mountains," Julian said. "But be careful. Keep a tight rein on your horse, or you may end up riding the rapids right back to the Shadowmere."

They soon took the left fork, and for several days they followed the creek as it diminished in size and velocity. Each night, they would find a small cove carved out of the rock large enough to build a camp, and the pines that carpeted the sides of the mountains hid their fire from any prying eyes.

"Scouts have used this path for decades," Julian explained. "Some of these coves are natural. The others were built as needed."

"It seems like someone could roll a boulder down the mountain and kill us all," Sarah said, glancing warily at the crags overhead.

"They could," Julian agreed. "So keep a good watch, yes?"

As evening approached the next day, they rode along a widened path, and the forest had thinned upon slopes that were not quite so steep as they had been.

"How near are we to Deewan?" Haydren asked Julian, who rode just ahead of him.

"We may make it tonight, if we ride into the night," Julian said.

Just then, there was a loud screech from the valley upstream. Julian looked through the trees up the slope beside them, and stood in his stirrups to try to look ahead.

"This way!" he shouted, turning his horse up the mountain and spurring it onward. Knowing the maneuver was too foolish to try on a whim, Haydren turned his horse after him without question, and the others quickly followed suit. The horses' shoes slid on the rock, but slowly they climbed toward a crevasse halfway up the slope.

"What is it?" Haydren asked as they finally made it to a rock overhang tall enough for the horses and deep enough that they could hide in the shadows. Julian ignored him, quickly taking out feedbags and putting them around each of the horses' muzzles.

"They must keep silent," he whispered as another screech echoed along the valley. The horses pricked their ears and swished their tails, but seemed content to munch their oats. "This is exactly why I brought these," Julian said, gesturing to the feedbags.

"But what's out there?" Sarah whispered, peering out of their shelter.

Just then, an enormous bird like an eagle—but with a wingspan that stretched the length of four horses standing muzzle-to-tail—soared along the valley floor. Its feathers were deep purple, and its beak and eyes glistened yellow.

"It's a Roc," Julian whispered. "It can turn you to stone by looking at you."

"I thought those were just myths," Haydren said breathlessly as the Roc turned at the head of the valley and swooped back along the river toward them. Sarah shrank back into the depths of the crevasse.

"In the north, they are," Julian replied, watching the bird as it flew. "Even in the south, there are maybe two. One patrols along Wilcer Creek, the other along the Durimas River south of Chalon. It might be the same bird, though it should have died long ago if there was only one left."

"Can't you do anything about it?" Haydren asked, turning to Sarah. "Hit it with a gust of wind or something?"

Sarah hesitated, then dropped her head and shook it once.

"Why not?" he asked.

"I just...I cannot," she said. "If I get too close to the edge, it could see me. Besides, just as with bow and arrow, a moving target is very hard to hit."

"If the legends I have heard are true," Geoffrey chimed in, "that Roc will sense any magic done with air, and we will still possibly die."

Julian glanced at Geoffrey dubiously, but said nothing about it. "We have a good spot here," he said instead. "We can spend the night. It will leave eventually, continuing its patrol north. We just have to wait for it to pass."

So they took out their blankets and spread them in the depths of the cave, though they could not risk a fire while the Roc was still below.

Geoffrey took the first watch, and waited till he heard Haydren's breath deepen in sleep before moving quietly over to Sarah.

"Sorceress," he whispered.

"Yes?" she responded immediately.

"Why won't you cast a spell, suddenly?"

There was silence for many moments. Finally, she replied: "I have seen what magic can do. I managed to hide some of Lasserain's documents, from his journal. And, back in Jyunta the night before I left, I read how it corrupted him." She drew a deep breath. "I had hoped to use magic for good, and thought I was doing so. But I saw in me the same hunger for more spells and more power that overthrew Lasserain. You were right, Geoffrey: just because we can use it, does not mean we should. I have seen Lasserain's hunger for power in every spell-search I've made for the past forty years. The only thing that stands between him and me is the limit that I can attain. Either I would die first, or become crippled. But I would not stop growing as long as I could help it. Lasserain just managed to possess more skill and more lifetime than most."

"Even though just one more spell would keep us from sitting up in this crevasse for another night, you would not use it?"

"We humans are funny creatures, Geoffrey," Sarah replied. "The lessons that eventually stick with us are the ones hardest to learn at first. Too often we look for the easy way out, and spend our lives in luxury and relative ease. But then when unavoidable hardship does arise, it nearly kills us. Perhaps if we had not rushed out of the difficulties of life, we would be better people. Don't you think?"

Geoffrey smiled in the darkness. "With all my heart, Sarah," he replied.

"Can I go to sleep now?" she asked.

Geoffrey chuckled quietly. "Of course."

"Geoffrey?" Sarah whispered.

"Yes?"

There was a pause. "Don't tell Haydren yet," she said finally. "If he knows we go to fight Lasserain without a magic user, he may despair more than is necessary."

"As you wish," Geoffrey replied.

He returned to his seat nearer the edge of the crevasse. Below, the Roc still patrolled on rustling wings. As the moon rose and glittered on the rapids below, the Roc turned once more and sped northward, leaving the valley in peace.

The next day, they led their horses back to the path and continued south. By After-Noon, Julian once again led them off the road and up a ridge. When they crested the top, in a broad bowl below them, surrounded by the jagged rock rim of the mountain's peak, lay Deewan.

24

TEACHERS

"So, after eleven years..."
"He took the long way around."
"Will you tell him?"
"He must survive the next weeks, first."

8 Halmfurtung 1320 — Autumn

Julian led them down a path through a patch of trees and into the village. A group of children gathered, curious at the new visitors.

"Hey, that looks like Aver's," one of the children said through Julian's interpreting, gesturing to Haydren's scabbarded sword. "Only a little different."

He glanced sharply at them. "Whose? Is he here?"

"He is," rumbled a deep voice ahead of them. Haydren looked up to see a large man in leather and fur standing before them.

"You speak Rinc Nain?" Haydren asked.

"Killik Ik Tal, this is Haydren, Geoffrey, and Sarah," Julian said, pointing to each in turn. "All, this is Killik, head of the village of Deewan. He and I trade, sometimes, and so learned each other's languages."

"Come with me," Killik said. "Your coming to us now is not a coincidence, and we must see and hear what your designs are."

They dismounted and followed Killik into the center of the village, to a three-story log building with two chimneys rising from its slate-tiled roof. Inside, the lower floor was one large room, with fires raging in hearths at either end. In the center of the room was a long table surrounded by high-backed chairs. Already, a group of men filled many of the chairs near one end. One of them, his back to the door, had a sword belted at his waist that was nearly identical to Haydren's.

Killik gestured to some of the seats before taking his own at the head of the table. "We have little time for introductions," he boomed as the three companions and their guide took their seats. "But it is important to know who the newcomers are, and for them to know Aver, a trader from Gintanos, who possesses Skyalfamold, the Sword of Earth. Haydren possesses Aerithion, the Sword of Fire. That two swords have come so near one another cannot be an accident, when the other two remain hidden. Tell this council, Haydren, what your designs are."

"We are on a route through the mountains to face Lasserain, and to kill him," Haydren said simply.

The other men glanced at one another and whispered in Deewanian—or was it still Kesten, Haydren wondered.

"That is a difficult task," Killik said finally, when their conversation had ceased. "Why have you undertaken this mission?"

"Lasserain has caused the death of my parents, and the destruction of Sarah's city," Haydren replied. "As well as untold destruction all throughout the northern provinces. Thus far no one has been able to stop him. With Aerithion, I hope that I shall."

"You cannot simply approach Galessern and sneak in and kill him," said one of the men at the table. "What exactly do you intend to do?"

"I do not claim the wisdom of those at this table," Haydren said, bowing his head. "But without intent I have slain both the Cerberus of Kalen and the dragon Paolound, and have destroyed the Northern Forest. My only help was my companions, all but two of whom you see here, and my sword."

"And the two we do not see?" Killik asked.

"One was slain in Jyunta, defending against an army of thousands sent by Lasserain for the attempted destruction of the city," Haydren replied. "The other stays now to lead in rebuilding the ruined town."

"Your victories thus far are no less than impressive," said one of the men respectfully.

Killik turned to Aver. "And will the trader from Gintanos go with them?" he asked.

Aver shifted uncomfortably. "My fortunes are somewhat less than Haydren's," he replied in a thin, high voice. "I was nearly killed innumerable times upon reaching Burieng. My wagons were lost, and all supplies stolen. I have no such reasons to go after Lasserain as this man does, and far less motivation. My only goal was to find out about this sword, while I was in the area, as it were."

"But they will need much help!" one of the older councilors said in a wispy voice. "Skyalfamold would be most useful!"

"Even so, I am of little use dead," Aver said in a whining voice.

"Good gentlemen," Haydren spoke up, "I would ask no one to come with me who fears death, for I see little hope of life."

"Then why do you go?"

"Someone must do it," Haydren replied. "And it may be that while we wait for someone to step forward who is more capable, Lasserain will strike against the north again. I cannot have seen Jyunta and Quaran destroyed, and allow another to face the same fate while I may have the power to stop it."

"I had seen Quaran," Aver said quietly, shaking his head. "I foolishly went there to seek trade—I found it just as you had, Haydren."

Haydren's eyes burned at Aver. "And yet you do nothing?" he asked.

"But we may raise an army," Aver responded. "Can we not send an army after him, instead of just a few men?"

"And how many mothers must lose sons to this man?" Haydren returned. "No. If it can be done with a few, it must be done with a few. I and my companions have a better chance of slipping in than an entire army, which Lasserain would surely simply destroy."

"Very well," Killik said, rising. "You have shown that you will not be easily turned from your mission. I will have a man take you to Tikiko, whose family smithed your sword. He will teach you its magic. Then you may stay at the Huckleberry Inn, and we will supply you in the morning with food and counsel. And may the gods speed you on your way."

The friends departed, not remaining to see what the elders would say to Aver. Outside, a man named Grithwier instructed Haydren's companions to wait at the Inn, while Haydren went alone to meet Tikiko. He led Haydren to the forge where a thick-armed man in a singed leather apron was hammering furiously.

"Tikiko!" Grithwier shouted over the ringing. "Aerithion has returned!"

Tikiko ceased his hammering, and came over to Haydren. He gripped Haydren's hand with iron fingers. "Come this way," he said. "Away from hearing."

He took him outside the village, deep within a crack in the mountain. "This is powerful secret," he said. "Most dangerous for anyone to learn. Take off your sword-belt."

Haydren did as instructed, and handed it to him. Holding it reverently with both hands, he held it up to the light. "When the blade is pulled little, the crystal reveals the lettering," he said, holding it so Haydren could see. Indeed, within the etchings on the crystal mouth, lined up now with marks on the blade still inside the sheath, there formed an angular script that Haydren could not read.

"It is Kesten," Tikiko said solemnly. "And worn badly; but let's try." He turned back to the blade and gazed at the lettering. "The song for painful magic is: 'Dragonsbane, strike the foe, help my urgent need. Dragonsbane, light the way, and lend me all your speed.'"

He flipped the sword and sheath over and squinted at the other side. "The song for healing magic: 'Dragonsbane, healing flame, a grievous wound I bear. Dim your fire, calm your ire, give me healing care.'"

"You must be careful," he continued, handing the sword back to Haydren. "The song will weaken the edge for a small time, and the sword can't sing more than some times a day. One song will not break it, but two, too soon, may. Use it wisely."

"I thought Bultum was made to be magical?" Haydren asked. "Why would using it weaken it?"

Tikiko gazed at him quietly a few moments. "I sense you are on a great mission. There is something none but the Keste have known for many grandfathers, Haydren. You understand this secret?"

The entire forest seemed to grow quiet, and Haydren swallowed. He did not want to break the silence, and only nodded.

"The words of magic are not written on the Bultum," Tikiko said.

Haydren blinked, and somewhere a bird called once. "Well I know it's not, you just..." Tikiko's gaze finally caught his attention, and Haydren's breath caught. He glanced down at the sword, at the Cretal flames running its length. "Tikiko," he said. "If I had a dagger that was also not made of Bultum..."

"I would not lose that dagger for ten lives," the smith replied.

Haydren glanced up. "You said I must speak those verses to summon the magic," he asked suddenly. "How is it that, before, I needed only to call its name and the magic came?"

"How did you learn its name?" Tikiko asked sharply.

"It's a long story," Haydren muttered. "But it came to me in a dream."

"And you used it?"

"Twice."

"So it is worn," Tikiko said, shaking his head. "Too many more times, the writing would have been gone. But it should not have been. Speaking its name alone does nothing."

"The magic in it is of fire?" Haydren asked, thinking of an old man in red robes.

"Of course."

Haydren buckled the sword around his waist slowly. "Thank you, Tikiko," he said. "It will help me greatly on the last part of my quest."

Haydren returned to the village with the blacksmith, bidding him farewell at the forge before returning to the inn to find his friends. The inn, true to its name, was surrounded by huckleberry bushes, and a bush speckled by blue dots was carved onto the sign that swung over the doorway. As Haydren entered the common room, a familiar form turned to look at him.

"Runacron!" Haydren said with a grin. "You left without saying good-bye."

"And now you meet me again without saying hello," the dwarf growled, though a grin crept onto his face. "Do you blame me for leaving quickly? You stayed one night, after all. That dratted Dasillion wouldn't keep his mouth shut for anything."

Haydren laughed as he sat next to the dwarf. "We were in such a hurry to get back to Frecksshire, we didn't stop in to say hello to him."

"It wouldn't have done any good," Runacron replied. "He followed me here! Said after you three were gone there was nothing left for him, and he decided to take my lead. I can't keep away from that yammering mouth of his!"

"Dasillion's here? In Deewan?" Haydren asked incredulously.

"I'm surprised you didn't hear him talking while you were still down by the river!" Runacron said. "But I'm sure you'll see him tonight, at the fire."

"Are they singing tonight?" Haydren asked. "I had hoped to see that."

"They sing almost every night. Now, especially with Skyalfamold and Aerithion in their village at the same time," Runacron said, "you're sure to hear many songs about the swords."

Haydren leaned back, remembering their last conversation together. "Did you find your dreams?" he asked quietly.

Runacron's grin blossomed to a full smile. "Aye, lad; I did," he replied. "I've been made Scout Major, recently. I seem able to look at a rock and see what's behind it. Like it speaks to me." He paused for a glance at Haydren, then pulled himself a little more upright. "But look at you, now! Finished the Earl's mission with valor, I hear. And you've made your way here to learn about your father's sword."

Haydren grinned distantly. "It seems I have. I'm not sure I would have called those my dreams, though."

Later that night, they were indeed treated to many ballads concerning the magical weapons. The three companions sat with their guide to translate the songs, and with Runacron. About halfway through the night, Dasillion finally spotted them across the fire and came to speak with them. They talked much, in between the songs, of events after they had parted ways. Dasillion was greatly intrigued to hear of their exploits after leaving his house, and was especially distressed when he heard about their ordeal at Faschek's.

"He seemed like a decent enough man, when I used to talk to him," he said. "Strange, very strange. But he would help out, if it was completely necessary. He didn't seem to appreciate company the way I did, certainly. But he never denied me anything when I asked for it. And he tried to kill your friend? I can't believe that."

"Well, it was not actually Faschek," Haydren said, suppressing a grin. "But someone else, claiming to be Faschek."

"Yes! That's right," Dasillion replied, bobbing his head. "Faschek would never do such a thing, not to anyone he had accepted into his home. He was a bit odd, sometimes, but he never denied me anything when I truly asked for it. I haven't seen your friend, the archer! I've learned some bits of Cariste I was hoping to try out on him."

Haydren's lips pressed into a tight grin. "He fell. In Jyunta."

"Oh, I'm so sorry Haydren. I didn't know," Dasillion said, laying a hand on Haydren's arm. "Was it the war Runacron had spoken of?"

"It was," Haydren replied. "I was so concerned with helping them, I didn't even think of Pladt." Dasillion gave him a quizzical glance, so he continued: "I thought briefly of getting Pladt back to Werine, where he belonged. He was better equipped for helping with their problems than my selfish ones."

"Oh, we don't get to decide that," Dasillion said. "If Pladt stuck with you in a countryside that didn't often speak his language, he probably wouldn't have left you when things got rough either. Sometimes the best we can do is take from such things what we can."

"It's given me a lot to think about," Haydren agreed. "And in its own way, it's part of what has brought me here. What that might mean…" He trailed off, still uncomfortable thinking about what lay ahead. Many hoped he would succeed, but few would say his plan was a good one.

"Well, what we think a thing will mean and what it ends up meaning are rarely the same," Dasillion replied. "Too many people try to force understanding and knowledge. That's something that has to come to you, not be given by you. Now you take this one day, when I was still out on the Moors…"

Haydren grinned and shook his head as Dasillion kept talking until the villagers near him shushed him as the next singer began.

The night wore on, and just as the sun began to sink, Killik rose and stood beside the fire. He began a song in his deep voice, the words rolling across the village and into the mountains. Women began gathering their children for bed as he sang:

"The sun is resting on the peaks. The sky is fiery red.
Sleep is all the weary seeks upon a feather bed.
Dwarves are working in their halls,
and in the mountains, night falls.

"Daylight's fading on our fire. The east is starry black.
Overhead the birds soar higher; their young ones call them back.
Air is filled with owl calls,
and in the forest, night falls.

"Clouds are wisping on the ridge. Shadows are far-reaching.
Fish are dancing under bridge, to their young ones teaching.
Gurgles sound on waterfalls,
and on the river, night falls.

"Sparks are flying in the sky. The moon is shining white.
Wind caresses with a sigh, and drifts toward the light.
Horses whicker in their stalls,
and in the farmyards, night falls."

By ones and twos the women were returning. Killik continued to sing:

"Lamps in windows burning low. The fire is waning too.
Streets are laden thick with snow, the world is faded blue.
Children safe within our walls,
and in our village, night falls.

"Nighttime creatures start to wake. Crickets start their singing.
Water's tranquil on the lake, waiting for day's bringing.
On the floor the baby crawls,
and in our houses, night falls."

The entire village rose to its feet, and joined Killik in singing the last stanza:

"All is silent in our land. No creature is a-creeping.
Children grasp their mother's hand, and soon they are a-sleeping.
So they dream of cornhusk dolls,
and in their rooms, night falls."

"And a good night," Runacron whispered, dropping his head to his chest.

As the villagers dispersed from the fire, Sarah turned to Haydren. "I need to ask Killik about something," she said. "I'll meet you back at the inn."

Haydren shrugged. "Sure." He and the other three got up and walked back toward the inn as Sarah made her way over to the head of the village.

"What did she want?" Geoffrey asked. Haydren shook his head and shrugged.

By the time they had gotten back to the Huckleberry and prepared for bed, Sarah had returned. She said nothing about her discussion with Killik, but went directly to her room.

25

QUESTIONS

"Do you ever think sometimes they do very well without us?"
"No. Perhaps sometimes."
"I've run into some trouble in Andelen."
"The world reeks of trouble. You will be fine."

9 Halmfurtung 1320 — Autumn

The next morning they prepared quickly, knowing the Deewanians wanted to see them off. They were not quite ready for what was in store.

The entire village had gathered at the start of the path south out of Deewan. Banners in the reds and yellows and oranges of the different clans were snapping in the breeze, and somewhere in the crowd a mother was trying to hush her baby. Killik stood surrounded by the elders at the head of the path.

"We wish to bid the gods go with you," Killik said. Haydren's horse stamped nervously, and he put a hand on its muzzle to quiet it. "You undertake this mission for yourself, and for the entirety of Burieng, but also for us. As our protectors, you are our brothers; these are your clansmen, your mothers and fathers, sisters and brothers, and children. When you go, you go to defend them and the thousands of others throughout Burieng. Defend them as if your family were behind you—because they are."

Killik stepped back, sweeping his hand to the valley with a slight bow. As the companions made their way through the throng, the villagers carpeted their steps with flowers and heads of wheat. As they neared the end, one of the children handed Haydren a flower of red petals. Haydren accepted it and held it near his heart as the child gazed at him with eyes wide.

As they made their way down the hillside, Julian said: "The heads of grain were to signify that you were in authority over their livelihood. That by your step or misstep, you might crush their food, or allow them to gather it up again."

"Good thing I stepped over them, then," Haydren muttered.

Julian shook his head. "It's more symbolic than anything. If you had stepped on them, it would not have caused offense."

During the night, the villagers had restocked their saddlebags. More than once Haydren wished they had not bothered, as the bulging sacks threatened to push the horses over the side of the path and into the raging waters of the Bawelen River that flowed north toward Kelian.

"We keep to this road for a few days," Julian informed them. "In less than a week, we'll take a narrower path through the mountains to try to pass Dubril to the north. It will be a treacherous path, and difficult to cross the Koniero Highway. But it will be much swifter than swinging south of Earl Jgei's fortress. There is not a pass through the mountains for several days south of his castle."

"They say the Earl is immortal, you know," Sarah spoke up.

"As are the Knights of Galessern," Julian replied. "But that is difficult to prove, since they wear identical armor, and do not carry coats of arms."

"The Earl does not distinguish himself in battle?" Geoffrey asked.

"The Earl is rarely seen in battle," Haydren replied for Julian. "Most often, it is a small raid conducted by ten to fifteen knights, and then only near the borders."

"Even so," Julian said, "part of the deal of giving Lasserain a stronghold from which to strike was that the King's best men would not die."

"And how exactly did that information get out?" Haydren asked with a grin. "From what I heard, it was not even confirmed except by sheer coincidence that Lasserain's stronghold was in Galessern."

"So our direction right now is based on hearsay?" Geoffrey asked.

"It's a little stronger that hearsay, now," Haydren replied. "But yes, there is a perfectly good chance of us arriving at Galessern and not finding Lasserain. Two things make me think he is there, however: first, he's found us twice before, so I believe he's looking for us. So if we go there, he will follow if he isn't already there. Second, everything started after he'd arrived in the Mountains twenty years ago. That's where everything has come from since, if not from the Woods. We know Haschina was one stronghold, Galessern makes an obvious second. He's just finished an attack against Jyunta, and probably needs to rest. We know he can't be in Haschina, so Galessern it is."

"Didn't your Earl ally with Lasserain as well?" Julian asked Haydren.

"Guntsen, yes he did," Haydren replied, shaking his head with a grin.

"You find that humorous?" Sarah asked.

"I grew up with Guntsen," Haydren replied. "I suppose I'm not surprised he did what he did. I would just be amused to hear his reason for why he did it."

"What makes you say that?" she asked.

"He was never particularly strong, nor did he think much of anything else outside of himself," Haydren replied. "So I don't know if he did it out of fear, or some sort of benefit for himself." Haydren's expression sobered and he continued quietly: "I know his father was very concerned for the threat to all of his borders, while he was alive. He did everything he could to prevent even one of the villages under his rule to fall to Lasserain. Now, within months of Guntsen ascending to the throne, there goes the entire province. I'm almost afraid to return home, to see what has become of it. I hope Mickel and Maerie are all right."

Over the next few days, they conversed little: sound carried well in the valleys of rock, and even the clopping of their horses' hooves seemed to echo forever. They left the headwaters of the Bawelen, striking now directly south through a broad valley cut through the mountains.

On the third morning since leaving Deewan, shortly after setting out from their camp, the quiet of the valley faded into a dull, pounding roar that grew in volume. Julian paused and glanced back at the rest of the company.

"We're at the falls," he said. "You see that peak ahead? That's where Kaoleyn Creek plunges off the cliffs where it forms. But this valley to our left will take us to barely a goat-path, and it will hopefully lead us safely past Dubril. Then the most dangerous part of this journey will be over, at least until we reach Galessern."

They turned, and guided their horses up the narrow, rock-strewn valley. At the top, it immediately pitched downward into a forest of evergreens. Here, the horses' hooves were muffled by a carpet of pine needles. Birds, perched in the branches, sang sweetly as they passed. The valley was long, and it was not until nearly evening that the floor sloped up once more and took them out of the forest and back onto rocky paths. This was the goat-path to which Julian had referred, and before long they stopped to lighten their packs to make them small enough to fit in the narrow clefts.

They camped that night in the rocky pass, at a small plateau that was wide enough to accommodate them. The sky was clear, and the stars brilliant in the cool air.

The following days were much like the first. They rode through broad, long, yet shallow valleys of young forest, capped at each end by tall and narrow passes. On the fourth day, as they climbed another narrow pass, the mountains suddenly opened before them, and a body of water shimmered far below. Their path took a sharp right, and switch-backed down the face of the mountain to a valley of older-growth forest: oaks, and maples, interspersed with older and taller firs than those growing in the valleys they had traveled thus far.

"That's Dubril Bay," Julian said, pointing. "Cutting through the forest below, and tracking the coastline all the way to Naaseb, though you can't see it yet, is Koniero Highway."

He led them silently down the face of the mountain. After days of quiet seclusion among hidden valleys, Haydren felt they were exposed for the entire world to see. Though spies could have lurked in the mountains anywhere along their route, this path would not have even needed spies. Anyone in the forest below could look up and see four travelers riding their horses down the mountain. It was no small wonder in Haydren's mind that Julian called this the most dangerous part of their journey.

As the sun passed its zenith, the company finally reached the forested valley. Unlike the softly carpeted valleys above, this floor was strewn with dried leaves and dead branches, which crackled and snapped loudly under the horses' hooves.

"If we make it through here without bringing down the entire Galessern army, it will be a miracle," Geoffrey muttered.

"And this is not the place for miracles!" a voice shouted, thickly accented. In an instant, the forest was filled with the thundering of horses' hooves as armored knights appeared all around them. Haydren reached for his sword, but was stopped short as ten bowstrings creaked, arrows pointed at his heart.

"We'll have none of that, now," the voice said. "In fact, take all your weapons off slowly and throw them onto the ground."

Haydren glanced at his companions. Sarah's lips muttered, but suddenly her eyes widened as her mouth gaped.

"If you're wondering why your sorceress suddenly looks amazed," their leader said. "It's because she has a mouth full of air. It's really the best way to make sure she casts no spells. Now: your weapons?"

With shoulders drooping, the companions slowly unbuckled their sword belts and let them fall to the ground. Geoffrey took the bow and quiver from his back and dropped it as well. Sarah continued to look around in wonderment as she pulled the mace from her belt and dropped it to the ground.

"She'll be fine for now," their leader said. "Now, dismount slowly. Gatson! Michalak! Bind them, please. And someone tell Rivas to bring up the carts!"

"Yes, Sir Cooley!" rang a chorus of voices. One of the knights pulled Sarah roughly from her horse. Though her chest heaved as if she grunted, no sound came from her mouth. The knight quickly tied her hands behind her back.

The others were similarly bound as a cart rattled through the woods toward them. At sword-point, they were herded into the back and thrown roughly to the floor. Their weapons were bundled together and thrown into the seat beside the driver.

"There are no stops on this carriage ride!" the driver cackled. "Straight on to the finest accommodations of Dubril's dungeons—heh ha!"

"Rivas!" barked Sir Cooley. "Just flay those horses before I flay you!"

"Yessir!" Rivas said, snapping the reins upon the horses' backs. The wagon started forward with a jolt, and bumped over every rock and root the entire way to Dubril Castle.

The southern Earl's castle was perhaps the most impressive fortification Haydren could recall. Nestled between two massive peaks, which would be far too steep to climb with ballistae, Dubril appeared every bit as massive as Frecksshire, even with mountains to dwarf it. As they neared, Haydren saw that its eastern and western walls were not even built of stone, but rather cut from it. Massive iron doors were tucked into the granite front, and boomed and roared open as they approached.

After the doors crashed shut behind them, fifteen men with halberds surrounded the cart, weapons leveled at the company. Under this escort, they were taken through a small door cut into the wall and down five flights of stairs. At the bottom, a few dim torches sent black smoke swirling to the ceiling where it remained, perhaps since the dawn of time. Haydren could only guess. Hallways ran in four directions, and they were taken down the left passage. Cell doors lined the walls. There were prisoners in some, who did not even look up as the company passed. Most striking to Haydren, they were all powerfully built men, though now a little lean from malnutrition. To the last man, they were scarred or maimed in some way. Some were missing entire limbs. Shuddering, Haydren kept his eyes on the floor.

"Products of The Duke," Sir Cooley chuckled, noticing Haydren's averted eyes. "Knights of the Earl's who performed less than satisfactorily during a raid."

At the end of the hall, a door to a large cell hung open, the key-bearer standing nervously by. To Haydren's relief, they were all herded into the same cell. The door slammed behind them. The key was thrust in the lock and turned several times before being returned to the bearer's pocket.

"Stay near them, Wilkins," Sir Cooley ordered. "The Earl will want to see them—or, at least," he added with a grin, "one or two of them at a time."

"Y-yes sir, I'll keep a good watch, sir," the guard mumbled, his smile making it sound like "keemp a good wat." Haydren could almost see the wagging tail of a dog patted on the head by its master.

Sarah glanced around the cell: the hard stone floor had a thin layer of straw which might have been five years old, and reeked of mold. Water coursed down one corner of the cell and puddled on the floor.

"So, what now?" Julian asked.

Haydren knew this was not what the guide signed on for, and guessed that no amount Earl Durdamon could pay him would make him withstand what some other prisoners in the dungeon had endured. Haydren worried that Julian would tell everything he knew, and maybe one or two things he didn't know but had guessed. "I don't know," Haydren replied, sitting down on the floor far away from the pool of rank water. "There might be a way to get out of here."

"We need to get Sarah back to normal," Geoffrey whispered, watching as she paced around the cell and squinted at the walls.

"That'll be easier than you think," she muttered under her breath, keeping her mouth as gaping as possible. She glared at them in warning as they stared at her, dumbfounded.

"I don't know a magic user alive who isn't able to avoid being gagged with air—especially an air-user! Jgei's user must be the barest acolyte. I felt him beginning to cast and ceased it, but put on the act so they would leave me alone."

"So can you do anything to get us out of here?" Haydren whispered.

She tilted her head, glanced at Geoffrey, and shook it. "Something is hindering me from accessing the elements," she said. "I haven't tried, but I can feel it."

"Hey, shut up, the Earl's coming," Wilkins rasped to them. He stood up straight, keeping a firm grip on his keys as footsteps echoed down the hall toward them.

"Do you think he's dumb, or dumbly loyal?" Haydren whispered to Geoffrey.

"Dumbly loyal," Geoffrey replied with a nod.

Just then, Earl Jgei stepped into view at the door of their cell. He wore his full armor, as well as a great sweeping cape of blood red that flowed from his shoulders to the floor. Though his helmet covered his eyes, his mouth could be seen through the bars of his visor.

"May I ask why you are here?" he asked with deadly calm. Whether it was some trick of the helmet or not, it sounded as if his voice came from the walls around them rather than the man in front of them.

But the company held their silence. Perhaps Julian was not ready to betray them yet.

"It makes no difference," the Earl said. "I thought you may want the easier way out, though it's far less entertaining. Bring the old knight, and their guide."

Wilkins opened the door, and four men came and grasped Geoffrey and Julian firmly by their arms and took them from the cell. As the door clanged shut, Earl Jgei said: "Perhaps, if their tongues are not loosened, yours will be when they come back."

Haydren closed his eyes and sighed as the Earl left. He looked at Sarah, who gazed back with sickness in her eyes.

"Should we tell them anyway?" Haydren asked quietly. "Does it really matter, now?"

"Say nothing," Sarah replied, her fists balled at her sides. "One way or another, we'll get free of this place."

Just then, a scream echoed down the hallway. Haydren started, then turned to the sorceress, swallowing hard. "That was Geoffrey," he said.

For what seemed hours, the interminable silence was broken intermittently with cries of anguish. Sometimes they were abrupt screams, ripped from between gritted teeth. Other times they were moaning howls that started low, rose, and slowly tapered off.

Haydren paced back and forth. With each scream he pounded his thigh with a fist. As each echo faded he reconsidered once more their vow of silence. Sarah sat motionless against the wall, a tear quivering perpetually on her eyelashes.

There was one final scream that cut off abruptly, and then all was silent.

———◄O►———

Guntsen grunted in effort, trying to blink the sweat from his eyes that blurred the post in front of him. It was no swiveling mannequin, but it resisted his sword strokes that struck like hail against the cracked oak. He moved his feet, dancing around the post as he would dance around Lasserain when the time came—how dare the mage, taking his province away from him like it was never his father's, and his father's before him.

He growled, striking left, right, left, thrust—a feint! Now from the right!

"You move like a chick-less hen," Lasserain growled, suddenly in the doorway.

Guntsen lowered his sword and stood as if he had been doing nothing.

"I've not seen a fighter move the way you did," the mage continued, striding forward. Guntsen backed up a step and jostled a table with a pitcher of water on it. He turned to steady it, but a whisper from Lasserain and it smashed against the opposite wall. "Who is the post today, Guntsen? Do you still cling to the imp you refuse to see as a god?"

"I've quite forgotten Haydren, thank you very much!" Guntsen snapped, casting his sword against the thin mattress upon the floor that served as his cot. In the silence that followed, he tried to catch his breath and hoped he hadn't spoken out loud.

"Have you indeed?" Lasserain asked quietly. "And who might you want to kill so badly, then, that you bother to sweat?"

Guntsen wiped his forehead on his sleeve, but did not look at the mage. "You didn't treat King Burieng this way," he muttered.

"I killed the King of Burieng."

Guntsen's eyes lowered, and he sniffed.

"You know exactly what I can do to you," Lasserain said, turning and walking away. "Why do you bother?"

The heavy door slammed, and Guntsen's shoulders hiccuped. If he ever had the chance, he would not only take his province back, but take Lasserain's from him as well! That would show him, if he could be alive to witness it.

A dragging sound came from the hallway, approaching the cell. Two guards appeared, carrying Geoffrey between them. Wilkins opened the door, and they cast Geoffrey to the floor inside. He hit the straw with a dull thud, clearly unconscious. Below his left shoulder, mid-bicep, his arm had been cut off and blood soaked into the stone.

"You fatherless children!" Sarah screamed, leaping up from her sitting position and hurling herself against the cell door. Wilkins had not closed it firmly, and did not expect the viciousness of the sorceress' attack. She forced it open, crashing into the hallway and pummeling the guards with her fists.

"Get her back inside!" the walls boomed. The guards grasped her by the wrists and struck her face and stomach until she sagged. They wrestled her back inside as she still bucked against their grip, finally disengaging from her and hurling her against the wall.

"Get that door shut this time!" the walls echoed. Wilkins, stammering and bobbing his head, clanged the door shut and locked it.

Sarah, sobbing fully now and scrubbing her face with her sleeve, knelt beside Geoffrey. She turned him over gently. A bag sailed through the bars of the door and struck the floor beside her.

"You'll find what you need in there to tend to his wounds," the walls spoke as the Earl stood in the doorway. Haydren felt a chill run through him. There was something not right about the Earl and the manner in which he appeared before them.

"Your guide told us everything we wanted to know," Earl Jgei said. "You will find permanent residence within these walls until my master's plans are complete. And I may find need of entertainment before then."

Jgei turned and left. Haydren turned back to Geoffrey as Sarah snatched the bag from the floor and rummaged through it.

"Killik gave you that bag," Haydren noted. "Is that what you spoke to him about the night before we left?"

"It's simple healing herbs," Sarah said, her voice cracking. "And some bandages. I thought we might need them," she added through gritted teeth.

She took a mortar and pestle from the bag, as well as several pouches of dried leaves. She took a strip of cloth and bound it tightly on Geoffrey's arm, cutting off the blood flow. She ground together a few different herbs and mixed them together with water from a small skin that was also in the bag. When it was finished, she smeared it on a clean cloth and pressed it against the stump of Geoffrey's arm. He groaned. Sarah bowed her head and blinked away tears as she tied the cloth around his arm, securing the bandage. She blended a few uncrushed leaves in with the rest of the water, and slowly dripped it into Geoffrey's mouth.

When she had finished, she sat back, pressing her clasped hands against her lips as the moments slipped past. Haydren watched in silent anticipation as well, hardly daring to breathe.

Finally, Geoffrey groaned again, and turned his head as his eyes fluttered open. Haydren let out his breath. Sarah smiled, but still wiped away tears. She reached forward and touched his cheek. He blinked, and looked at her.

"I'm glad that's you," he said in a raspy voice. "If Haydren touched me like that, I might have to kill him."

His right arm shifted a little, and the stump of his left arm smacked the floor. He groaned, and his head fell back.

"Careful!" Sarah whispered hoarsely. She moved beside him, placing an arm under his head and helping him to sit up. Geoffrey glanced down at his left arm, and closed his eyes briefly.

"Oh, right," he muttered.

"Geoffrey," Haydren said quietly, and swallowed. "Julian told the Earl everything. You shouldn't have—"

"You can't blame Julian," Geoffrey whispered. "This was not his mission, except the Earl gave it to him. Would you stand up to torture for money? I wouldn't."

"Don't talk too much," Sarah said. "You've lost a lot of blood."

"Perhaps, but that poultice you made is incredible," Geoffrey replied. "I can hardly feel my arm at all, right now."

"Something I knew grew in the mountains," she said.

"We have to think of a way to get out of here. Surely Lasserain is going to move quickly to finish his plan for Burieng." Haydren turned away and moved to the door.

Sarah glanced at Haydren, who stood apart and ignored them, then turned back to Geoffrey. Fresh tears flowed as she looked at his arm, and into his pained eyes. He could feel the pain, and she knew it. "Geoffrey," she whispered, low enough that Haydren could not hear her. "I could have cast a spell down here. I could have done something to get us out before this happened to you."

Geoffrey shook his head and smiled. "No, Sarah; no cost is too great. Evil can never be used to combat evil. Do not forget your vow when the Roc threatened us. We do not know what betterment might come from this suffering."

"What good might come from the pain you suffered?" Sarah gasped, a fresh course of tears flowing.

"Sarah," Geoffrey breathed, shaking his head. He gazed at her with a smile. "Beautiful Sarah. If you never use magic again, I would pay any cost."

Her smile was confused as she looked at him. "Two months ago, I thought you didn't want me to use magic because you didn't want me to be the strong woman I could be. And I know that, right now, I need to be able to not use it. But so many men have just wanted me to sit quietly in a corner and do nothing, letting them do what they thought best..."

"But strength—or power—and independence are not the same thing," Geoffrey replied; "nor are they linked. I tried to understand you from the beginning. Sometimes you were the perfect diplomat—kind, wise, gentle. Other times you were a petulant child who brooked no offense."

"I don't know why I do that," she said, keeping her attention close on him.

"I thought it was a tick of your frustration, at first," Geoffrey said. "But every time your attitude changed, you pushed your hair out of your face."

"It falls, sometimes," she said, running a finger behind her ear, though her hair now was still in place.

"Falls?" Geoffrey asked. "Or is blown out of place?"

She was silent, only blinking.

"Sarah, it's when you open yourself to the wind. It tells you not to be treated in some way or another, or not to take correction—especially someone telling you not to use it, doesn't it?"

More silence.

"I told Haydren once that we all serve someone," Geoffrey continued, glancing quickly at the young swordsman. "I don't want you to serve me, or put me in any kind of position of authority unless you completely trust me to be in that kind of a position. Because you know I would never ask you to do something you shouldn't do. I don't want you to serve anyone, or any*thing* that you can't trust in that same position. And I think you're realizing that you shouldn't trust the wind with that position, aren't you."

Sarah smiled, and sighed. "I am." She cocked her head. "How did you know that? About the wind talking to me?"

Geoffrey looked past her again, to Haydren. "How do you think you came back to consciousness, on Jyunta's walls?" he asked, his eyes coming back to hers.

"I...I thought..."

"I ceased your spell, Sarah."

She gazed at him, her eyes getting steadily wider. "You can use magic?" she asked, forgetting to keep her voice low.

"You what?" Haydren said, coming over from the door. "Since when?"

Geoffrey rolled his eyes, chiding Sarah with a smile. "Since I was young. But I haven't for many years now."

"Wait," Haydren said, holding up a hand. "So you could have used it at Jyunta?"

"You could have killed the golem master and kept that entire army out of Jyunta until Haydren got back," Sarah added.

"So could have Pladt. He almost did it."

"Don't you—" Haydren jerked a finger at him. "Pladt could still be alive if you had used your abilities!"

"Sure!" Geoffrey said, struggling to sit upright. "I could have saved him—could have saved everybody. Maybe could have saved my own arm, just now!"

Haydren swallowed, and cast his gaze downward as Geoffrey continued. "No one needed to die. Just use magic, use something you can't control but loves controlling you. Do you know how many people I have killed with magic? All of my friends, all at once! Remember the *Uv Fehn?*" he asked, looking at Sarah. "You know the stories. How were they finally defeated?"

"The King employed a powerful wizard..." she trailed off, suspecting she had heard the story utterly wrong as Geoffrey laughed bitterly.

"Oh, yes, a powerful wizard indeed," he said, shaking his head as his eyes began to glisten. "He didn't need to employ a wizard. It was me. I was preparing as powerful a spell as I thought I could manage—and just when I needed to project the image of the target to the element, I suddenly thought of all my friends around me, and how I wanted to protect them. And instead of victory, a row of thunderbolts tore through them and killed them all." He leaned back against his good arm with a gasp, unable to hide the tears coursing down his cheeks. Haydren and Sarah only watched in silence for a time. "I saw it coming down the line," he continued quietly. "One bolt after another, into one body after another, drawing closer. Each scream drawing closer. One struck the man next to me—he had been with us for four years. I had eaten dinner with his wife and two children anytime we were in his village. I wanted the next bolt to strike me, waited for it. But the spell passed over me and struck the man to my right. We had been in the Guard together, had known each other... And then it continued down the line, one after another. I tried to stop it, but it had torn my heart so completely from me that I couldn't muster the authority. I could only mutter the words, and the element ignored me."

He fell silent again, still shaking with tears. Finally Sarah laid a hand on his arm and shushed him. "It's okay, Geoffrey," she said. "It's okay. It's done. You did—" She paused to glance up at Haydren, then back at Geoffrey. "You did the right thing, abandoning your ability. We didn't know. I'm so sorry."

Geoffrey groaned, and sat forward. He rubbed his face with his hand, now free, and sighed. "I see them in my dreams all the time," he went on, his voice a little steadier now. "Every time I do, I renew my vow to never meddle with the elements again—they are not for us to try to control."

"So can you actually use magic down here, Sarah?" Haydren asked.

Sarah nodded slowly.

"But you've made a similar vow?"

Sarah looked down at Geoffrey, smiled, and nodded again more certainly.

Haydren took a deep breath. "Well, I suppose we'll have to make do somehow," he said, and sighed. "Nothing more assuring than approaching a magic-user with two magic-users who refuse to use magic."

"We've made it farther than should be expected without much magical help," Geoffrey said.

"Unless we count Melnor." Haydren shook his head. "Perhaps the next time someone comes to that door. After your last attempt at freedom, I believe Wilkins could be easily overpowered."

"I wasn't trying to escape," Sarah replied, glancing up. "I wouldn't have left Geoffrey here. I just wanted to kill them."

Haydren smiled. "That can still be useful."

A loud, thundering roar broke the silence, sounding like it echoed into the dungeon from outside. There was a great crash, as of a suit of armor falling down a set of stairs. Or, Haydren mused as he glanced toward the door, down five flights of stairs.

"Hey!" Wilkins shouted, stepping away from the wall and down the hallway. His shouts, echoing, were suddenly in Endolin—then: "Hey! You shouldn't be down here! Who are you?" Wilkins broke off with a cry, then there was silence.

Haydren turned to his companions, who stared back at him, equally confused. Haydren turned back as keys rattled down the hall, and footsteps approached. Whatever he might have been expecting, it did not prepare him for the one who stepped in front of their cell door, keys in hand, and a broad grin that lit up eyes the color of a forest canopy with a strong summer sun behind it.

26

CHOICES

17 Halmfurtung 1320 — Autumn

"Pladt!" Haydren shouted, not believing he was actually saying the name. "What are you—we thought you were dead!"

"There's no time now," Pladt said, thrusting the key into the lock. In his surprise, Haydren barely noticed a strange quality to Pladt's voice, similar to Earl Jgei's though less ominous. The door sprang open. Sarah and Haydren helped Geoffrey to his feet, and the three exited the cell as another thundering boom echoed from outside.

"What's going on out there?" Haydren asked.

Pladt's lip trembled. "I'm sorry I couldn't get you guys out earlier," he said, "but perhaps I can still help." He reached out and touched Geoffrey's arm just above the amputation. Geoffrey closed his eyes and breathed deeply. When he opened his eyes again, he stood free from Sarah and Haydren.

"That does feel better," he said, looking at his arm in awe. "When did you—?"

"I'm so glad to see you," Haydren said, reaching out to touch his friend's arm. It may have been a trick of speed as Pladt ducked out of the way, but he would swear his hand passed right through.

"Not now!" Pladt pleaded. "We have to leave before the castle crashes down around us."

Amazed and curious, but hurried along by Pladt, the company ran down the hall and bounded up the stairs. When they entered the stone courtyard, there arose a piercing cry overhead, and the roof of one of the massive towers crashed to the pavement in front of them.

"Wow, is she angry!" Pladt exclaimed. "Let's go this way!"

He led them around the outside of the courtyard. As a military castle, Dubril had few houses or shops—mostly barracks, smithies, stables, and kitchens. Soldiers were shouting frantically to one another, and archers high in the towers were shooting arrows as fast as they could draw them, but the company could not yet see their target.

Another shriek grabbed their attention and drew their eyes upward to the streaking form of a blue dragon as it crashed into another tower, sending rock and archers plummeting to the ground.

"Is that—?"

"It's Kaoleyn," Pladt affirmed. "I didn't think a few missing eggs would make her so angry. Hopefully I can get you guys out of here alive. The door's just up ahead. Come on!"

After dashing ahead another several hundred paces, Pladt stopped before a small postern. He drew a key from his pocket and punched it into the lock, then shouldered open the door. He led them down a narrow tunnel to another locked and heavily barred iron door. Opening this, he led them outside into a narrow canyon.

"What about our weapons?" Haydren asked as he hurried after Pladt.

"I've taken care of that," Pladt said, not slowing. "They're well hidden. We just need to get away from the castle."

Distracted by the dragon, none of the soldiers who should have been guarding the path were to be seen, though Haydren recognized well-hidden perches all along the route. After another several hundred paces, they finally exited into a thick wood. Their path continued down the hill, and they could hear the sound of rushing water below.

Pladt turned suddenly aside. "Wait out here," he said, crouching down and creeping into the hollow trunk of a large oak tree. Once inside, he began handing out weapons. Aerithion came first, then Geoffrey's sword and bow, which Haydren took, and Sarah's mace. He handed out several bags, which had been their supplies. Finally, he backed out of the trunk and stood.

"Below, you'll find a dock with some boats tied up," he said. "There are three guards. Take the boats down river, and after two miles you'll see a small gravel beach. I'll be there waiting for you, and we can talk." He glanced back toward the castle. "I have to make sure Kaoleyn doesn't kill herself taking down Dubril." He turned and pointed down the hill. "Now go!"

Before they could protest, he ran back up to the rocky file and disappeared around a bend. Haydren turned to his companions as Sarah finished helping Geoffrey belt on his sword. Haydren drew a deep breath.

"Let's go," he said.

"Haydren," Geoffrey said, and his voice stopped Haydren in his tracks. "I will not be able to fight with only one arm. You know that, as a swordsman. But I have an idea..."

After relating his plan, they made their way quietly down the hill. Near the bottom the trees thinned, and they could see the dock. Though the soldiers below glanced frequently up the hill as the crashes of rock against rock echoed down, they remained seated near the boats.

"A distraction may be out," Geoffrey said, watching the actions of the guards. "We might just attack..."

"Uh huh," Haydren agreed with a nod. "Well, let's get as close as we can. I'm sure the three of us can take three guards. Actually, Geoffrey," he added suddenly. "Let's try our best to just frighten them off, okay? Stick to your first plan."

Geoffrey glanced between Sarah and Haydren and shrugged.

As Geoffrey strode boldly down the path, making sure his sword and scabbard were clearly visible, Haydren and Sarah swung wide off the path and trod quietly toward the river whose rapids drowned out their own footfalls.

The guards looked up as he approached. The one nearest to him stood and studied him.

"Tu therek til kamapa ta?" he asked.

Haydren froze for an instant. Of course they wouldn't speak Cariste or Rinc Nain—the others were probably veteran raiders and used those languages easily, and to make sure Haydren and his companions knew who was in control. As he stole forward, taking advantage of the guards' distraction, he vowed that after defeating Lasserain he would move to a country where only one language was spoken.

Geoffrey said nothing, keeping his head bowed. The guard took another step forward as Geoffrey approached the dock. "Ke!" he said louder. His gaze raked Geoffrey. "Duwa tan til kiaka teik...?"

Just then, Geoffrey drew his sword and stabbed forward in one swift motion. The other guards shouted in surprise, rising to their feet and grasping at their belts. Haydren charged out of the woods, Aerithion gleaming overhead. The guards turned as their scrabbling hands found and finally freed their swords. But as they took a step toward this new threat, Sarah stepped out from the woods in the other direction with her mace upraised.

Turning back to Geoffrey, whose Follus sword was already dancing through the air—not smoothly, but an edge was an edge—both guards dropped their weapons and dove headlong into the rushing Kaoleyn River. Watching them go, Geoffrey solemnly sheathed his sword.

"See? Just because it's Follus. Though," he added, "I would have thought they would be more accustomed to it."

"Apparently not," Haydren muttered as Geoffrey went to one of the boats and loosed its moorings. All three clambered into the boat as

Geoffrey cast the rope into the bottom of it. Sarah and Haydren grabbed the oars and pushed it into the current, allowing the river to take them swiftly downstream.

As they rushed along, the mountains rose beside them and they were soon floating along a deep canyon with sheer granite faces on either side. Rounding a bend, they could see the gravel landing Pladt had told them about. Indeed, Pladt himself was on the shore, standing beside a crackling fire with fish already on a spit suspended over the flames. He looked toward them and waved them over. Grasping the oars, they guided the boat across the river and ground it against the shore.

"Welcome to my fire," Pladt said with a smile. "Have a seat, and let me tell you how I came to free you."

"And how you got onto this shore without passing us on the river," Haydren said, looking at the high granite walls. "There's no other access except by river."

"All will be explained," Pladt said reassuringly. "Enjoy some fish while I tell you my story."

After they had seated themselves, he began: "When the kobolds surrounded me, back there in Jyunta, they didn't kill me, only knocked me out," he said as he began to serve his friends. "When I woke up, I was tied in a cart, surrounded by goblins, hellhounds, kobolds—all yapping, snarling, growling...they had surrounded me before, but I could defend myself then. Now I was at their mercy. I had never known terror like I did then. At any time they could have killed me." He paused for a moment, then said quietly: "Better if they had."

The companions sat quietly, and not one had touched the meat on their plate. Pladt continued: "They carried me in the cart to Dubril. Occasionally a kobold fed me. What it was, I shudder to think, but as starved as I was..." He drew a breath. "When I arrived, soldiers carried me to the dungeons. One took a hammer and smashed my legs and arms. Each night he came back and re-broke them, to keep me from escaping. I could hear his footsteps coming down the corridor toward my cell each night. He would tap the hammer against the cell doors as he approached, to make sure I knew it was him. I couldn't move, couldn't try to crawl away, but there was nowhere to go anyway. I lay on my back and waited for him to come, and for it to be over with."

A tear from Sarah's eye dropped onto her plate, and the men's eyes glistened too. "Eventually, they started taking me to see The Duke; they would drag me through the halls, ignoring my—I thought my skin would rip and tear my arms off at any moment. When they let me go, I could feel bone cutting into my flesh. Then the Duke would begin to work with his tools. He poked and sliced and bent—always Earl Jgei was there asking me about you: how you killed Paolound, why you were in Jyunta in the first place, what Earl Durdamon had planned—"

"You should have told him," Haydren interjected in a whisper, unable to look up into Pladt's eyes.

Pladt smiled and shook his head. "Your mission was too important, Haydren. My suffering was minimal compared to what Burieng has endured. And honestly Haydren? I wasn't sure what to tell him, because I wasn't sure what you had chosen."

"As if I had a choice." Haydren's whisper turned bitter.

Pladt let the comment pass as he continued: "But one day, The Duke slipped. It was a comparatively small pain, but I lost control of my body. My muscles went entirely limp, and I couldn't even draw a breath. Darkness closed in, and I felt almost as if I was falling.

"But when I landed!" he said, his smile broadening. "I woke up in a fragrant field, in a soft bed of grasses. All the pain was gone, though I still couldn't move. A man came up to me and extended his hand, but I couldn't reach up and grab it. He said: 'Your time is not yet finished. Arise, be well.' Instantly, I reached up and grasped his hand, and rose to my feet."

"Who was it?" Sarah asked breathlessly.

"I don't know," Pladt said, his eyes clouding over. "But he gave me the ability to return to you, and to help you." He shrugged, and his eyes cleared as he smiled. "Sounds a bit like Zedar, doesn't it? Maybe the Deewanians were on to something."

Sarah shook her head with a grin. "They were Kesten, Pladt."

"I keep forgetting. Anyway, I seem to be able to appear where and when I wished. I learned the hidden pathways of Dubril, knowing, somehow, you would be coming that way. When you were captured, I stole Kaoleyn's eggs and told her the Knights in Dubril had done it. She reacted as I suspected, though certainly with more violence than I anticipated."

"And our weapons?" Haydren asked.

"I had them with me—sort of. Inside me. I knew healing Geoffrey had raised too many questions already, and I didn't want to start pulling weapons from my body to give to you. That would have just been...weird," he finished with a grin.

A smile flashed across Haydren's face, but quickly disappeared. "So now I have lost a friend twice," he said quietly.

"But if you had not lost me the first time," Pladt replied; "you wouldn't have lost me the second time, and you would be still in Dubril—if you would not be dead too."

"Is that how it is justified?" Haydren asked. "Does that make your sacrifice worth it?"

"Does it?" Pladt asked, his gaze lowering as if considering the thought for the first time. "It doesn't feel like it. But I was too close to it, I suppose." He looked into Haydren's eyes. "I simply became caught up in the consequences of other people's choices, as have countless others across Burieng—and that only after I chose to leave Werine. The world is too complex to blame one thing, or to simply look for balancing scales."

"Perhaps," Haydren agreed. "But the scales must be balanced for the loss of my parents."

"You have done much to complete that already," Pladt said. When Haydren glanced quizzically at him, he smiled. "Remember the man in Werine, who reacted so strangely to your sword? It was because he had seen it before. He was the one specifically tasked to retrieve it in the first place. He killed your parents looking for it, but by then you had already escaped. And the bandit in Devil's Thumb, the one who had your dagger? He was the captain, all those years ago; didn't you recognize the dagger in your memory? He found it on the field when all was finished. Both of them were killed by you—or, at least because of you."

"Was all that the manipulations of the Triumvirate?" Haydren asked, letting slip a sneer.

"I know what you want, Haydren," Pladt said, his smile faltering a little. "You have choices. You always do. But confidence comes only from trust. You could have trusted Geoffrey. You could have trusted me, or Sarah. You could have trusted the God of All, even. By choosing not to, *you* gave up the confidence offered to you. The Triumvirate aided you in dispensing justice against those two men."

"Is that the only choice? To kill? Is that the only justice?"

"Asks the man on his way to kill another," Pladt said, regarding Haydren closely. When Haydren remained silent, Pladt glanced away. "They all chose a dangerous life. Death did not surprise them, and only death would have stopped them."

"It surprised one of them," Haydren said, still vividly recalling the regret in the soldier's eyes in the grove.

"The timing surprised him," Pladt said. "He had not reached the position he aspired to, and he had been offered the choice to stay back in the grove or go to the road. That was his regret, not the death you brought."

"How do you know this?" Haydren asked breathlessly.

"I don't know," Pladt replied quietly. "Have you never forgotten how you learned something? But you did not choose their death, Haydren. By continuing until death stopped them, *they* did. Do you think any of them did not accept that they just might end up that way?"

"No one thinks they're going to die."

"You do."

Haydren glanced up sharply. Pladt's eyes were deep, fathomless green as they gazed back at him. "That is your choice, Haydren: to do what you believe you must, even if it means death by doing it. Those bandits did the same, and Lasserain does the same. The only difference is that you don't believe Lasserain does what is *right*."

"He can't be doing what's right, can he?" Haydren asked, suddenly confused.

"He believes he *must*, and so he believes it is *right*."

"How could you possibly think such things *must* be done?"

"Maybe that's what you should ask him," Pladt said with a smile. "Still, that choice is yet to come. The time is growing late, and you must be on your way. The river will take you to Galessern. Lasserain is reeling from the loss of Earl Jgei. The Earl was Lasserain's first real test of Life magic, and the Earl's spirit was tied to his castle. With Dubril gone, Jgei died as well. His Knights will be in disarray, and Lasserain must be concerned for his northern border. Your journey to Mount Travistone should be unhindered."

Though the companions had never touched their fish, they felt refreshed. They remained a little while, talking to Pladt and saying their final good-byes. Sarah was first in the boat. After several moments, Geoffrey joined her.

Haydren remained on the beach, gazing at Pladt, seemingly unable to make himself leave.

"Your friends are waiting, Haydren," Pladt said gently.

"Yet I cannot seem to go," Haydren replied, trying unsuccessfully to smile. "You were the best friend and traveling companion I could have had. The first time, you left without giving me a choice. Must I choose to leave you now, knowing this time I will not see you again?"

"I'm afraid so," Pladt said.

"How can I do that?" Haydren gasped, suddenly at a loss for breath. "I wanted so desperately to get you back to your father, back to lands you knew. I could have done it. Can you not come with us now?"

"Haydren, you speak as if my life was in your hands," Pladt said with a smile. "It is not now, nor was it ever. You cling only to the emotion in your heart. However you may have perceived it, I have only ever been under the care of the God of All—regardless of whether He allowed you, or Geoffrey, or even Sarah to accomplish that. The world, and my fate, is not in your hands. Don't complicate life by thinking otherwise."

Haydren swallowed and took a calming breath. His smile came this time, though still with difficulty. Pladt glanced again at the boat and said: "Your friends are waiting."

Haydren nodded, and turned to the boat. He climbed in, pushing it off the beach and into the current. The companions gave a few powerful strokes to start them downstream, then turned and watched as the beach—and Pladt—slid away behind them. Pladt held his hand out in farewell until they rounded a bend, and he was lost to their sight forever.

The river sped them swiftly along, and the cliffs lowered. By nightfall, they were able to find a suitable landing where they set up camp and slept. By Noon the next day, the river was winding its way through wooded foothills, and gradually onto a broad plain with the mountains towering behind them. On the fourth day since escaping from Dubril, Mount Travistone rose before them, with Galessern like a granite crown near its peak. Below, the river turned right around the mountain, flowing toward the Salmean Sea to the south. The Kaoleyn River Road ran to their right and up the mountain, and it was toward this bank they now steered their boat.

They were able to tuck the boat under a bank of rushes, and stole quickly to the road. There was no traffic either way as far distant as they could see.

"Do we have any idea how we're getting into that fortress?" Sarah asked as they watched the road.

"Potentially," Haydren answered. "Though I hoped to see more wagons traveling toward it by now. The bandits have been sending supplies for a long time. Surely one will come along soon enough."

"And then what?" Sarah asked.

"I was thinking we'd do something like what Geoffrey did at the dock," Haydren said. "We'll dress him in the wagon driver's clothing, with his sword and everything, and we would hide in the back."

"And what if they search the wagon?"

Haydren shrugged. "Then we'll think of something else," he said.

"Listen!" Geoffrey hissed. Faintly on the wind, they could hear the clattering of wooden wheels. After a few moments, a wagon appeared through the woods. It was alone, and its cargo bulged against a tarp.

As it drew near, Haydren and Geoffrey crept near the road, swords drawn. Just as it passed, Haydren leapt out and quickly struck the driver with the pommel of his sword, knocking him unconscious.

Geoffrey grabbed the reins and stopped the horses before they entered the broad plain, where they might be seen from the castle. "What's in it?" he asked as Haydren peered under the tarp.

"You've got to be kidding me," Haydren said, holding his nose. "Why would they be bringing bodies to Galessern?" He pulled back the tarp and allowed Geoffrey to see the corpses stacked like cordwood before pulling it snug again.

"I don't imagine they'll be inspecting this cargo too closely," Geoffrey muttered waving his hand in front of his nose. "That question is answered, at least."

"Sarah's going to love this," Haydren said with a grin as she approached.

"I am not riding in the back of that," she said resolutely as soon as Haydren told her.

"Sarah, if you were worried about them inspecting the back of this thing, you don't have to be now," he replied.

"Instead, I have to worry about smelling like a dead body for a month," she retorted. "Why are they bringing bodies to Galessern anyway? Who are they?"

Haydren shrugged. "Can't ask them," he replied with a grin. "Now can we go? We need to get inside the castle."

"You owe me the means to get about fifteen baths, after this," Sarah said before leaping up into the back of the wagon. "Oh, they're cold," she complained.

Geoffrey quickly threw the driver's cloak over his own. "You know," he said. "I can't speak their language, if they should ask me anything."

Haydren drew a deep breath. "I know."

Geoffrey adjusted the cloak with a shrug of one shoulder. "Get in," he said.

Haydren leapt in and nestled down among the bodies as Geoffrey snapped the reins on the horses' backs. They lurched forward, and were soon climbing the long road to the top of Mount Travistone.

27

DECISIONS

"Actors in a play follow a script."
"These actors do not know the script."
"Then successful completion of the play?"
"Knowing what the playwright seeks to say."

21 Halmfurtung 1320 — Autumn

Unable to see out, the two held their breath as the wagon crept to a stop. A great wooden boom sounded as the doors to Galessern swung open. To Haydren's surprise there were no questions, no footfalls sounding of a guard even walking around the wagon. A few words were spoken in Endolin, a leather slap of reins, and the wagon jolted forward.

After a time they stopped again. Geoffrey's boots slapped to the ground. "Get out!" he whispered hoarsely.

Sarah and Haydren squirmed free of the corpses. Adjusting the weapons at their belts, they continued on foot up the road toward the keep.

The death they had ridden with much of the morning lay in a pallor over the city sprawled around them. No hawkers cried their wares, and those on the street went about furtively as though prepared at any moment to be caught. The mutilation they observed in Dubril continued here, and Haydren saw more than one former soldier sitting in a gutter or weaving slowly down the road maimed as Geoffrey was.

What was not there, Haydren noticed as they drew closer to the keep, were living and active soldiers—not even a roaming guard. It was as though anyone able to bear arms had already abandoned the castle. Even the walls were unmanned.

"Has he already begun the attack?" Haydren said quietly, knowing his Rinc Nain speech would draw attention.

"Pladt said the soldiers would be in disarray," Geoffrey suggested. The double-doors of the stronghold were abandoned, one leaf hanging ajar. They ducked inside, and found themselves in a large antechamber, with a broad staircase leading to a second floor before them.

"Why do I feel like this is a trap?" Haydren said, looking around the room. But nothing crashed down, no pits opened, and no soldiers appeared.

"We've seen Quaran, Jyunta, and Haschina," Sarah offered soberly. "Does Lasserain really need soldiers to defend his keep?"

"Upstairs?" Haydren said, pointing. His companions nodded, and they went up the flight of stairs. A broad hallway ran both directions, and the stairs continued up to the next floor. Still no soldiers were in sight, though many doors lined the hall. Silence reigned.

A servant appeared with a tray, skidding to a halt when she caught sight of them. Haydren held a finger to his lips, too late as the tray crashed to the floor. Tea service and sweetmeats scattered, and the servant pelted away, though she rose no cry of alarm.

Haydren looked at the food, smelled a sharp scent of spiced wine, then smirked. "Guntsen," he said.

"Most throne-rooms are at the uppermost level," Geoffrey said in a whisper that still echoed. Agreeing, the companions continued up the winding staircases until they had made their way to a fifth floor. There they came to a smaller antechamber with one set of double doors, ornately carved of mahogany with black iron bands. With a deep breath, the companions drew their weapons.

"I don't think we're going to catch him by surprise," Haydren whispered. "So it actually might be to our advantage to enter slowly, so he does not catch us by surprise."

"Haydren, if he is in there," Geoffrey began. Haydren turned to him. "Let me go first, okay?" Geoffrey asked. "I have the least to lose..."

Haydren nodded slowly. Sarah gripped Geoffrey's arm, but he turned and gently shook his head. He moved to the door, opening it just a little and peering in. He swung the door wide and stepped in.

Inside, Guntsen sat at a little chair near the throne, a young page by his side. Guntsen smiled as the three companions entered, their weapons drawn.

"You may go, now," Guntsen said to the boy, tousling his hair. The boy obeyed, exiting through a side door, and Guntsen rose.

"So, we come to it at last," he said smugly. "I've waited a long time for this day."

"Why?" Haydren asked, his sword held low as he stepped ahead of his friends.

Guntsen blinked several times, confused. "Because I finally get to kill you," he said.

"Why should you want to kill me?"

Guntsen blinked several more times. "Are you serious? After all your arrogance, after you stole my father's affection, you expect me to let you live?"

"Guntsen, I didn't do that intentionally," Haydren said.

"I don't care what you intended," Guntsen spat, swiftly pulling free his sword. "You should have known your place, and accepted it. Not try to use my father's weakness to assert yourself above your station."

Guntsen advanced, and their swords rang in the halls. It was clear to Haydren that Guntsen had not gotten better over the last year.

"How do you know what my station is?" Haydren asked, advancing on Guntsen this time and driving him back. "My father might have been a king, for all you know."

"Ha! As if," Guntsen shot back as Haydren slowed his attack. "King's sons are not so easily lost. If you were a prince, if you were *anybody* of importance, they would have come looking for you long ago."

Haydren paused briefly. Guntsen pressed an attack, and Haydren allowed himself to be driven back slowly.

"But I am likely from Rinc Na, Guntsen. They might not have known what happened to me."

"Oh I know! Even worse," Guntsen said. "As if an orphan could be of any lower status, yet you have achieved it. And what did you do with your status? Poison my father against me! You would have taken my inheritance, if you could have."

"Do you think Lasserain is Cariste?" Haydren said, circling to his right as Guntsen pressed on. "Yet you serve the one who destroys your own country and your own people! Why?"

"Because I knew he could help me to kill you," Guntsen replied, following him. "I knew enough about the Earl of Frecksshire that if you ran to him, he would not give you back to me but use you for his own purposes. The only way to make sure I killed you was to join with Lasserain."

Haydren stopped circling as he stared at Guntsen. "You endangered thousands of people for the sake of killing me?"

Guntsen growled, and lunged forward. Haydren quickly parried and punched Guntsen in the nose. Guntsen backed up quickly, covering his face with his hand. "That's not how you duel, you rotten orphan!" he cried. When he lowered his hand, his nose was bleeding profusely. "Use your sword, if you know how."

"Why should I?" Haydren said. "This sword has slain a dragon. Why should I sully it wounding someone like you?"

Guntsen lowered his sword-point to the floor. "I'll make you a deal," he said. "If you can defeat me with only your blade, I'll tell you where Lasserain is. If not, I let him find you and kill you. Fair? And they can't help you," he warned, pointing toward Haydren's companions.

Haydren shrugged and raised his sword. With a smile, Guntsen struck at the wall near him. Three ropes were cut, and three chandeliers crashed to the floor. The candles snuffed out and sank the room in darkness. As Geoffrey and Sarah shouted their disapproval and contempt, Haydren took a large step to his right, trying to adjust his eyes to the gloom. His heart launched into his throat as a flash glittered briefly in the dark, and he heard steel cutting the air near him. His sword-arm fluttered out: Aerithion found nothing but space. His eyes darting wildly, Haydren took another several steps away. His foot caught on something, and he stumbled. As he regained his footing, he saw a stitch of motion. Aerithion swept upward. Steel met Bultum in a cacophony of ringing. Disengaging, Haydren backed diagonally away, catching his breath.

"How do you like the darkness, Haydren?" came Guntsen's voice, sliding through the shadows. "Do you still hide under your blankets?"

Remember the Forest.

Haydren crouched low, glancing toward the windows whose darkened panes glowed purple in the dark. Guntsen's silhouette moved cautiously in front of one and waited, his head cocked, trying to listen. Haydren watched, drawing a long, quiet breath as his heart slid back down into his chest. He dug into a pocket, pulling free a small coin. He tossed it so Guntsen would cross to another window. As the Earl moved quickly, so did Haydren, coming up behind him with silent footfalls. Guntsen turned, trying to listen. Haydren rose from his crouch, Aerithion swinging. With a crash shattering the silence, Guntsen's sword was ripped from his grasp and clattered with a sound of thunder against the stone floor.

"Haydren?" Geoffrey bellowed.

Haydren summoned Aerithion, and the fire relit the room as Guntsen fell with a shout and crabbed backward against the throne. Haydren kicked Guntsen's sword over to Geoffrey, and took a few steps toward the Earl.

"Where is Lasserain?" he asked.

"That wasn't fair!" Guntsen said. "You used magic!"

"After you already fell on your backside," Sarah retorted.

"You don't speak to me like that, woman!"

Sarah shook her head. "Can we leave this pitiful being here, and go?"

Geoffrey moved to one of the chandeliers and relit a few of the candles. As the glow spread, Haydren gazed back at the dethroned Earl.

"Lasserain, Guntsen," he said. "I beat you fairly."

Guntsen sagged against the dais. "He has a garden, at the foot of the mountain. He's down there."

The fire drained from Aerithion, and Haydren sheathed the sword. "Thank you." He turned to leave.

"Aren't you going to kill me?" Guntsen called after him. "I would have killed you."

Haydren paused at the door. "Guntsen, you are an Earl. There are a great many things you can do in such a position. Killing me is the very least of them. After I deal with Lasserain, go back to Kelian and make it a better place."

Guntsen got up slowly. "They won't take me back after I went over to Lasserain," he said. He wiped his nose of blood, looking at his hand for a moment. "Do me a favor, Haydren, and leave me my sword."

Haydren faced him. "Of all the bad decisions that have brought you here, Guntsen, that would be the worst. Stay here. Earl Jgei is dead, and the Endolin mountains will need a ruler. If Hewolucs will not take you back, perhaps the strongholds of the south will."

Guntsen nodded slowly. "We shall see. Good luck. On the fourth floor, take the third door down the left hallway. You'll find a passage that will take you straight to Lasserain's garden. Be careful. He is weakened from the death of Jgei, but he's still very powerful."

"Thank you, Guntsen," Haydren said, bowing. "And the God be with you."

They followed Guntsen's instructions, and descended a spiral staircase deep into the mountain. At its base ran a long gray-stone hallway lined with torches. At the end of this was a small oaken door that opened with effort into a deep, narrow ravine with sheer rock sides that would only allow two men abreast. When they had stepped through, the door slammed shut behind them, and they could hear a bolt being thrown.

Sarah turned and pulled on the door, but it did not move. They heard laughter echoing from within. Sarah turned on Haydren with mild disapproval.

"You have got to be more willing to kill people, Haydren," she said, though her tone was not condemning.

Haydren paused. "Do I?" he said. His eyes came up to meet the sorceress', then turned and glanced over the rock walls as they moved down the canyon. "Trying to flee Hewolucs, I killed two men. I killed another five running north when I could have passed them by. More died in a grove of trees I could have avoided. Was my life worth more than theirs?"

"They were all bad men, Haydren," Sarah replied.

"They were," he said, "and now none of them have the chance of doing anything good. They're beyond redemption—in the grave or whatever lies beyond it. I'm still here, and I want to make sure I make the right choices. I don't think that means permanently canceling the choices of others around me unless absolutely necessary. Even if it means my death."

"And what about preventing the deaths of others?"

"Preventing death with death," Haydren said with a sigh. "I hope there are better answers than that. For now, let's just find a way out of here."

As they walked down the narrow file, streaks of orange and red spread in the sky as the sun set out of sight, and the shadow within the crevasse deepened. They came suddenly upon another wall at the end of the ravine. There was no way out except to climb.

"Sarah and I will climb up," Haydren said to Geoffrey. "And then we'll pull you up."

"I hope Lasserain doesn't suddenly appear," Sarah said quietly as they began searching for hand- and foot-holds in the sheer rock. Slowly they climbed as the sun continued lowering overhead, and deep purple stained the clouds.

But Haydren knew that the mage would be waiting well outside the crevasse. Lasserain had too many opportunities before to kill him, and had not. No, everything that had come before in Haydren's life had brought him to this point. All of his trials and battles were not ends in and of themselves, but guides toward this final climb, this final battle. All his achievements had their own consequences, outside of him, and were perhaps beginnings or ends for others. But he understood now that completion did not come early in life—that perfection is never attained, only striven for. The man he had been in Quaran was the man he needed to be then. It was a far different man who fought the Cerberus upon the other side of the Kalen Woods. And he was yet a far different man now—who gripped and strained and pulled at hidden clefts of rock in growing darkness—than the one who had faced and slain the three-headed monster. Even in this upcoming battle with Lasserain, he would not be complete or perfect. It was likely that this final battle would be just another stepping stone in his life, just one more event between who he was and who he could eventually become. One choice would not be an end, until his death—and death was not up to him to choose. A choice, instead, was bound by the moment; once it passed, it only made him who he was tomorrow. He might not be able to reverse or negate it, but he was always capable of changing the trajectory of his life by a choice the next day, and the day after, and the day after. It was why he hesitated to kill, even someone like Lasserain. If there was any way to leave this battle without the mage's death, he had to look for it. He had to at least offer Lasserain the choice.

With one final heave, Haydren came over the side of the crevasse. His purpose was clear in his mind, and he waited only to help Sarah over, and to lower a rope to Geoffrey and pull him out of the crack as well.

The garden Guntsen had spoken of was true. They descended a short slope into a forest. Gently rolling hills stretched as far as the trees allowed them to see. Firs stood with their lower reaches limbless, their blackened trunks like pillars rising from a floor of verdant green fern. Here and there thin shafts of sunlight pierced through the trees and glowed in the forest floor.

The company walked warily along a path deeper into the woods. It did not seem possible that they would meet a man of such destruction in such a peaceful place as this. Somewhere nearby, they could hear a tinkling trickle of a stream running over rocks, and gradually it seemed the path was taking them toward it.

The path bent, and ahead of them was a small wooden bridge seemingly fashioned out of the boughs of two trees. The stream they had heard flowed clear and pure underneath, and a pair of birds sat warbling in the branches just overhead. On the far side, sitting with his feet dangling in the stream, was the young boy whom Guntsen dismissed.

Haydren crossed the bridge slowly. The boy's attention wandered, sometimes to him, usually to the surrounding forest.

"What's your name?" Haydren asked as he approached, waving a hand to keep Sarah and Geoffrey on the other side of the stream. His glance at Geoffrey said: *Yes, I remember Tagnier.*

"Westin," the boy replied.

"You speak Rinc Nain?"

The boy nodded.

"Where are you from?"

"A village up north." Westin bent down, inspecting something near the bank. He reached down, and a water skeeter shot out into the stream.

"Why are you here?" Haydren asked, moving and sitting down beside the young boy.

"My family was all killed," Westin replied, going still. "Family, friends... Soldiers came one day and destroyed everything. I had to watch from hiding as they did it. My mother wasn't the first to be killed, you know? But I saw her, with my sister. Jolet..." He trailed off, tears coursing down his face as he yet smiled. "Jolet would do anything for me. She did, too. She helped me hide, and went back for my brother Arthrin. She didn't make it back before they came to our house. They had all the people gathered at the edge of the village, and started going through one by one. I saw them approaching my mother, and Jolet, a countdown of death." As he spoke, Westin's voice grew deeper. "One by one, making their way toward my family, death by death. I thought they might wait a moment, appreciate the significance of my family because I watched. They didn't. Two breaths: thrust, thrust, and then the next in line."

"Why do you tell me this?" Haydren asked.

"You asked why I was here." The boy's voice had returned, no longer deep and mature, and Westin glanced around the forest. "I'm here for the same reason you are. Because my family was killed."

"But the one who lives here killed my family," Haydren replied. "You serve him."

"And you serve the ones who killed my family," Westin said, his eyes piercing Haydren as he focused for the first time. "The ones who sent the soldiers. The ones calling themselves Godfrind."

"I don't serve them," Haydren said, with a slight shake of his head. "And I would guess those soldiers didn't, either. Not truly. They may have come with their name, but not with their instructions."

"Because you know them so well?"

"I have met one," Haydren said. "And I have spoken with them on occasions."

"Did they tell you to come here?"

"No," Haydren said emphatically. "I came on my own."

"For revenge?"

"At first. Now, to understand."

"They've tricked you," Westin said, a smile curling his lips into a sneer. "As they do everybody, manipulating them to their own ends."

"If that were true, I would be trying to kill you right now." Haydren spread his hands. "Do you see me doing that?"

"Weakened resolve," Westin replied. "A month ago you wouldn't have hesitated."

"I hesitated in the Forest."

Westin went still again, except for a quick glance at Haydren, and his boyish voice returned. "Why did you do that?"

Haydren shrugged. "I think so I could end up here," he said. "Talking to you."

"Why?"

"To tell you that you don't have to finish whatever you've started," Haydren replied. "You can walk away right now, start doing something else—rebuild what you can, give restitution as you can."

"I don't think Quaran or Jyunta will let me do that. I don't think *you* will actually let me do that," Westin said, gazing first at Sarah, then Haydren.

"But you don't have to go forward with what you're doing," Haydren said—pleaded. "You can stop. You have the choice."

"Perhaps I can," Westin said, swirling his feet in the stream. He shrugged. "But I just don't want to."

He muttered something, and a wall of flame exploded between the two of them and the bridge. Haydren leapt to his feet as the flames raced, encircling them in a broad ring. Without having to touch it, Haydren knew there would be a pillow of air containing the flames. He turned back to Westin. The boy rose slowly, becoming Lasserain as he stood.

"Welcome, Haydren. Do you like my little trick?" the mage asked, gesturing to the wall of flames with a smile. "I quite like it, personally. Fire has always been tricky to tame, even as a magic. Of course, the Keste did quite well with your sword," he continued, looking at scabbarded Aerithion hungrily. "I would so enjoy getting to know your sword."

"I think most would be happy for me to acquaint you with its edge, for all the damage you've caused."

"The damage I have caused?" Lasserain said with a laugh. "You should have died twelve years ago, but you refused, didn't you? And what have you done since?" He paced slowly to his right, and Haydren followed with his gaze. "There is not a step you have taken that is unmarred by the blood of my armies." He held up a fist and began counting on slender fingers, his voice rising with each extended digit. "You killed my bandits; you slew the Cerberus that has defended my home for centuries; you destroyed Paolound almost as an afterthought, who took me weeks to revive; you forced me to burn down my own village, which I had sustained for twenty years; and you made me waste untold energy destroying Jyunta as retribution." He stopped and waggled his hand. "I've run out of fingers! And we haven't even gotten to the destruction of the Forest, and the Earl who was like a right hand to me."

"I didn't ask for any of that," Haydren said. "You stood them in my way, when I only wanted to escape Guntsen. You began it twenty years ago. I responded to your choices."

"Oh, but you've made some of your own," Lasserain said, shaking a finger at him. "Because you're here, now, instead of on your way to Rinc Na or somewhere you belong. By your actions, you asked for all of it and more."

"I did not ask for my mother and father to be killed," Haydren said quietly. "Nor did I ask for your Cerberus or your dragon to attack me and my companions. And if Haschina meant that much to you, you would have saved it instead of destroying Jyunta. But it means nothing to you anymore."

"Stop!" Lasserain shouted, thrusting a finger at Haydren. Suddenly, the air around Haydren's body grew thick, and he found himself only able to move his head. "'Nothing'? Haschina was everything! It was mine, but Melnor couldn't stand having a corner of the world that he could not control. He sent the soldiers that slaughtered my people, and that after they had already subdued me. They could perhaps not be as responsible if I had only been hiding. But I was helpless as the soldiers went through my village, burning and killing. They made me watch, and I could do nothing!" Lasserain's eyes blazed, and his voice echoed in the confines of the fire as a rushing wind ripped through the trees. Lasserain drew a breath, and the winds calmed. His voice, as he continued, lowered to a mournful pitch. "If you want stories of power and destruction, Haydren, read the histories of the Triumvirate. Rife with power grabs and manipulation—as they manipulate you now to fight me. Is that justice? Pure justice?"

Haydren blinked a few times, his head throbbing from the echoes. "It wasn't your mother and sister, was it?" he said. "Because you kept forgetting to mention your brother again."

Lasserain gazed at him silently.

"It was your wife and daughter."

"Your attention is wandering, Haydren," Lasserain said, but he made no move.

"Did they do more than kill them?"

Lasserain drew a breath. "Yes."

"Between you, your bandits, and your soldiers, you've done far, far more than kill my parents," Haydren said. "But you will not see death by my blade."

"Why not?"

"Because you need to know you can do the same."

Lasserain looked at him intently. "Can I?" he mused. "Let's see what your friends think of the idea." He looked toward the wall of flames. He gestured with his fingers, and Haydren heard exclamations of surprise. First Geoffrey, then Sarah floated over the wall and came to rest facing Haydren.

"Welcome, welcome," Lasserain said to them. "I am the mage, Lasserain, who has destroyed Quaran and Jyunta, and sent bandits and beasts all across Burieng. Haydren came here to fight me, yet now claims he does not want to."

"Release me and I'll fight you!" Sarah seethed, struggling against her air-formed bonds.

Lasserain laughed. "No, it will not do for me to die by a woman's hand," he said. "Nor by one who is short an arm. Only Haydren is worthy to fight me. But for some reason, he will not."

"Haydren, what is the matter with you?" Sarah demanded.

"You haven't heard what has happened to him," Haydren replied. "You don't know what he needs."

"What he needs is someone to stop him from killing more people," Sarah said.

"See?" Lasserain asked. "Why can't you be more like them? But she's right, so let's make this more immediate." He drew his sword as he stood behind Haydren's friends, and tapped each in turn on the head with the flat of the blade. "Which one will it be?" he asked. "Sarah? Geoffrey? Or will you fight me?"

"Very well," Haydren said with a sigh. "If it means that, I will."

Haydren felt his bonds fall away. He stood and drew his sword, cursing himself for summoning Aerithion in his fight with Guntsen. He could sense it was too soon now to call upon its flames.

Lasserain stepped forward, his sword cutting through the air with the sound of a mother's switch—an airy hiss that terminated in an explosion of clanging metal. The force of the blow sent Haydren reeling backward, and he tripped and landed heavily on his back. He scrambled to his feet as Lasserain marched toward him. Another powerful swing sent Haydren stumbling. He turned, slashing at the mage. Lasserain parried the blow and dealt Haydren another strike that sent him crashing back into a tree.

"Oh, Haydren," Lasserain said mildly, pausing with his head canted a little. "Have you completely forgotten everything you've learned in the past year? I had truly hoped our fight would go a little better than this."

Haydren flexed his muscles, keeping his sword before him, and was silent.

"How many creatures have you fought, hmm?" Lasserain asked, his sword held low by his side. "I counted off a few of them just a moment ago, but there were many more, I believe. Did all those victories teach you nothing? Did Sir Cullins teach you nothing? Have you forgotten EVERYTHING?!"

His sword came up swiftly. Haydren parried it right, stepping behind Lasserain's and turning his wrist to bring the sword across the mage's back. Lasserain, for being off-balance, managed somehow to evade it, and laughed.

"Finally!" he exulted, turning blazing eyes upon his quarry. "That was actually a good move—well executed! But clearly still not good enough. I have a plan, would you like to hear it?" His finger flicked, and Haydren was again wrapped with invisible cords. Lasserain paced left, his sword dangling from his grip. "I'll give you a refresher," he said, his eyes downward as if in thought. "I'll let you fight every creature across Burieng that you have already fought, just to make sure you're really ready to fight me. Okay?"

"Do I have a choice?" Haydren asked.

Lasserain stopped and pivoted toward him, his eyes glimmering. "Now," he replied, holding up a finger. "Now I think you are beginning to understand."

The mage disappeared, and so did Haydren's cords. Free, Haydren briefly considered going back to his companions. But a rustling of the undergrowth caught his attention, and his sword came up reflexively.

Glip? chirped a small voice. Haydren flexed his fingers as a gremlin crept out from the ferns, glistening eyes observing him.

Haydren stood erect, and his sword drooped. "I never fought a gremlin, Lasserain," he said wearily. "Pladt did. If you're going to do this, get the facts right."

The gremlin paused, also straightening as it looked at him. A tiny blue tongue stuck out of its mouth before it turned and went back into the underbrush.

In an instant, a wolf bounded toward him, jaws snapping. Haydren brought his sword up just in time to avoid the sickle teeth, but did no harm to the wolf. It turned, circling him. But now he was ready, and as it leapt Aerithion snapped downward: just before it would have been cleft in two the wolf disappeared and a fly pelted Haydren in the nose and slid buzzing into his eye. Haydren backed away, swatting at it, and managed to catch it. Before he could squeeze he had a kobold's left arm clenched in his fist—but the right arm waved free and was bringing a spear to bear.

With a shout Haydren leapt backward, his sword coming up in a wavering arc. The kobold launched his spear. Haydren managed to deflect it from his heart, but the sharp stone tip tore through the flesh of his upper arm.

Haydren grunted, his knuckles going white for a moment before he advanced on the now-weaponless kobold. It hissed at him, balling hands into fists. Two steps before he was within sword-reach it leapt, wiry muscles propelling it with surprising speed. Haydren dipped his sword-tip to try to spear it, but was too slow—the sword fell along its neck, but did not cut. Bony fingers grasped as Haydren tried to duck out of the way. It had him by the shirt, drawing him close. Haydren reversed his grip, punching out with the dragon's-wing cross-guard and pulping the kobold's nose and jaws. It snarled as its grip weakened. Haydren dragged the blade downward, but before he could cut too deep into the flesh the kobold disappeared and a chipmunk scurried away.

Haydren gasped air, glancing down at the cut on his arm: it was bleeding, but not too badly. He wondered if he had time to bind it, until he heard a great snuffling and roaring.

From around a great tree a Moorish goblin stomped, arms wide and swinging. It dropped briefly to its knuckles as it glared at Haydren.

He wondered again about the cut on his arm, and if the poison secretions of the goblin were real, or as much a figment as the rest of the goblin. Its eyes observed him, then dropped to his wound, and the goblin seemed to smile. Haydren swallowed. It probably would be real, somehow.

It leapt, arms wide to bear-hug him. He ducked out of the way: even if he managed to stick it in mid-flight, its weight might carry forward and he still might get poison on him. It seemed to know that as it turned and leapt again, as if it cared not for his sword.

With a grunt, Haydren again leapt to the side. He caught his balance, and took two more steps to his left as nonchalantly as he could. It might not have mattered. The goblin caught himself, turned, and leapt again almost instantly.

This time, when Haydren ducked aside, the goblin went head-first into the tree Haydren had positioned himself in front of. It shook its head, a little dazed, but somehow managed to duck aside and avoid Haydren's thrust. It turned on him, backing away a bit with one hand on its head and a look of wrathful appreciation in its eyes. Haydren wondered briefly how much of Lasserain was in there: he seemed constrained, still, to each creatures' ability for speech and movement.

One final shake and it was advancing again, this time more slowly. Haydren adopted a different stance—one he had not trained as much with, but it kept his injured arm to the rear. If Lasserain the goblin could tell he was less practiced, he did not show it.

A taloned hand shot out. Haydren twisted his arm, parrying easily. Another swipe. He did not like how intently the goblin watched his reactions. He advanced this time—two quick thrusts, then he kicked out to try to put the goblin off-balance.

But Lasserain did have the musculature of the goblin, and grabbed Haydren's boot and threw him to the ground. Haydren rolled swiftly, clenching his teeth as his arm struck the ground two, three, four times as he rolled away. When he made to stand, the goblin stepped on his sword, trying to pin it to the ground. With a mighty twist and heave, Haydren pulled it free: the skin on the underside of the foot was not, somehow, as tough as the top side and the goblin howled as mucus-like blood stained the ground. It limped away a few steps as Haydren advanced ruthlessly, then disappeared just as Haydren's sword-point pricked its flesh.

"See?" Lasserain's voice came from nowhere—strained, it seemed to Haydren. "You're remembering, and you're getting better. We've still got one or two left to go, though," he crooned. "Remember?"

Haydren froze, and swallowed. The pain in his arm was subsiding, and though the skin pulled tight when he flexed, it did not seem to hinder his movement. But the thing Lasserain appeared as next would test him much, much further than a goblin or kobold. He glanced down at his sword: no light flickered in the Cretal flames. He took another deep breath, and waited.

When the Cerberus appeared, it did not move swiftly as the other creatures had—Lasserain probably knew he didn't have to. Haydren watched closely, but there was no limp evident as the massive creature stepped out from the underbrush to face him. He probably healed himself, Haydren thought with a grim set to his jaw. Must be nice.

The Cerberus' lips curled as the eyes began to glow and swirl. Haydren reversed the grip on his sword, preparing to shield his eyes.

Attack!

The voice startled him to the point he almost didn't listen. It had been weeks since he'd last heard it, it seemed. But as soon as the shock passed, he lunged forward, bringing down Aerithion with both hands.

The Cerberus screamed as its left-most head came free, backing away and shaking the other heads as though assaulted by a thousand hornets. Haydren pursued, Aerithion singing. The Cerberus dodged sideways, roared, and clubbed Haydren with its center head. Teeth snapped as he stumbled, taking a chunk of his right triceps.

With a gasp, he dropped Aerithion, barely managing to catch it with his left hand as he hurried away from the beast. It still seemed preoccupied with accepting two-headedness. Haydren flexed his fingers, but nearly all the strength was gone from his last two fingers. He could not hope to bear his sword with only three working fingers. Still no flames flickered between the Bultum. Why was it not responding to Lasserain now?

Well, he was left-handed for the rest of this fight, and probably unable to sever another head. He swung his sword a few times. He didn't need to kill the Cerberus as he had before, did he? Perhaps just enough damage...

The beast was panting, heads held low. Was it trying to entice him forward? Abruptly the tongues went back in their mouths, and the panting stopped. Two heads snapped up to stare at Haydren, teeth bared and snarling. This time it moved swiftly, its legs propelling it toward him with incredible speed. He managed to step sideways, twisting the point of his sword just so as the Cerberus passed and drilling a long, trailing piece of flesh from the stump of its left head. Another quick flip, and though it did not cut deep, a red gash appeared on its hindquarters.

It was unbalanced, accustomed to running and pivoting with the weight of all three heads. Lasserain nearly fell as he rounded on Haydren again, his faces pulled tight in pain and fury. This time when he lunged he made Haydren go right, where his outboard head remained. Seeing he wouldn't dodge in time, Haydren turned the flat of his blade.

Lasserain struck it, knocking Haydren backward, but low enough that he landed on his feet. He swept his right foot back and planted it, bringing Aerithion around in a cracking windmill. His aim was true enough, and the right-most head was rendered as useless as if it weren't there.

This time as Lasserain backed away, Haydren pursued violently, knowing this could mean his life. Aerithion darted forward, now bringing the pain to the image of the hornets. Amid snarls, snaps, and barks, the Cerberus finally disappeared, and after a few moments Haydren could hear Lasserain coughing and groaning.

Not that Haydren was in much better shape. If Paolound emerged, Haydren would die. If only Aerithion—!

And suddenly, it did. A red glow danced along the flames, and the sword fairly vibrated in Haydren's grasp. He gazed at it for a few moments, not so lost in thought that he missed Lasserain's sudden silence: the mage was healed again, and a dragon was sure to soon emerge. Did he simply use the destructive magic, as he had before? Would it remain in the sword until he used it, or could Paolound/Lasserain avoid him until it dissipated? Or he could heal himself. But there was no guarantee he would win without magic.

Haydren pursed his lips, and blinked. It might be interesting to see what it did...

The words barely left his mind when the dancing flames became a diffuse glow across the surface of the Cretal. He glanced at his right arm, eyes widening as muscle rebuilt and skin wove itself back over the wound. The laceration on his left arm sealed, the cut pinking and then quickly fading to normal flesh-color.

But it did not stop there. Weariness left him. His breathing slowed. He felt as if he had just finished a bath in a cold stream and had let the sun dry him. As he gazed toward where he knew Lasserain would soon emerge, even his mind hardened; there was no despair, no worry, barely a thought to distract him from his purpose. Aerithion became comfortable again in his grip, and he waited patiently—though not joyfully—for the opportunity to finish what Lasserain, in his pride, propelled him toward.

When Lasserain as Paolound emerged, he paused. Haydren was whole, and there was not a trace of fear in his eyes.

Paolound grinned.

He advanced with a bellow to shake the forest. Haydren spun lightly to one side, sword lashing out. Without waiting, he danced again, and two more streaks of red appeared on the dragon's flanks. Paolound's tail swept forward as he snarled. Haydren leapt nimbly, coming forward again with furious and painfully-accurate strokes the instant his feet touched the ground.

Paolound kicked. One toe caught Haydren's arm and spun him. He caught himself against a tree, gasping but not knocking the wind from him. Paolound turned swiftly now, razor talons skimming near Haydren's head as he ducked away. Fire followed him as he sped behind a tree, slapping at his back as his tunic caught.

He wrenched his shirt off, baring his arms and the armor that still showed a little wear from Paolound's crush on the Frecksshire Moors. He cast it aside, still burning, and turned, Aerithion light in his hands. But he misjudged how quickly Lasserain had come after him. A great paw grasped the blade while the other struck Haydren in a fist in nearly the same spot where he had dented the armor so long ago.

Miraculously, Haydren managed to keep a grip on Aerithion as he tumbled backward. His head smacked against a tree, and his vision swam.

Lasserain approached, back in the form of a mage with his sword held low. Haydren blinked quickly and took a calming breath. As Lasserain neared he continued to stagger. The mage stopped, so close yet just too far, and gazed at Haydren in sadness.

"You can't do it, can you?" he asked quietly. Haydren put a hand to his head, but his eyes were alert. "I truly believed, after watching you so long, you would be better than this." Lasserain took a step forward, and Haydren's sword flashed upward.

But the blade stopped a finger's-breadth from Lasserain's chest and quivered as an axe in a thick tree. The mage sighed, blasting Aerithion from Haydren's grip with a blow from his sword. "I learned that one only recently," Lasserain said, a smile curling his lips. "I needed something to keep magic attacks from piercing me. I thought I had found it, but it seemed to reference Bultum. Once I discovered the properties of the metal, though, I realized it was indeed what I was searching for."

Lasserain's fist smashed into Haydren's mouth, and Haydren fell to the ground. Something cool and round pressed into his palm beneath the ferns. His fingers closed, and he wiped his mouth with his other hand.

Lasserain gripped him around the throat and lifted him to his feet. "Now, Haydren," Lasserain said. "I see what Guntsen saw in you." He grinned. "The weakness, and worthlessness. Before you die, I want you to know I will not stop. When you're dead, I will kill your friends, and my armies will unleash upon the breadth of Burieng, and I will continue to kill and destroy until Melnor himself must come and try to kill me. Then the world will finally be rid of his meddling."

Haydren coughed, and blinked. "I hoped you wouldn't say that," he rasped. With a jerk, Haydren thrust his Cretal dagger into Lasserain's chest and twisted it. Lasserain's eyes opened wide as he stepped backward, grasping the dagger by the hilt and pulling it free. The red, pitted blade seemed to glow. Lasserain dropped the dagger and gazed at Haydren in confusion.

"I think you have that spell wrong, Lasserain," Haydren said. "The Bultum is not magic, the Cretal is. But since, in my sword it is almost fully encased in Bultum, your spell stopped *that* from piercing you."

Lasserain looked at him with a strange expression, almost of gratitude; yet also, it seemed, of triumph. "Thank you," he whispered.

Just then, Sarah stepped from a tree behind Lasserain. She whispered something, and struck him in the back with her mace. He stumbled forward, but instead of hitting the wall of air around the circle of fire, he plunged directly into it. The flames surged higher as he shrieked. When his scream faded, the fires fell, and the forest was silent once more.

"He's not the only one who can cease a spell," she said, resting the head of the mace on the ground, and crossing her hands on the pommel. Geoffrey stepped into view, grinning and shaking his head at her.

"How did you do it?" Geoffrey asked Haydren. "We couldn't see. It sounded like he was beating you pretty thoroughly."

Haydren bent over and picked up the dagger. "My father's dagger," he said, holding it up for them to see.

"I didn't see Pladt give that to you back at Dubril," Geoffrey said.

"He didn't," Haydren said, looking upward. "I think he kept it to give it to me now—so Lasserain wouldn't know I had it."

Just then, a loud groaning sounded through the forest. The trees wilted, collapsing around them. The ferns curled up and retreated into the dirt. The company huddled together in a sudden whirlwind, watching as Lasserain's garden shriveled, dried, collapsed, and was blown toward the sea. When nothing was left but bare rock, the winds ceased. Night had fallen during the battle, and when he looked up, Haydren saw a crescent moon just rising over the horizon.

An anguished cry echoed from the castle. In the light of an upper window of the keep, Guntsen stood staring in horror over the ruined landscape. Silhouettes appeared in the room behind him. The company watched helplessly as blows were struck. Guntsen cried out again, and plummeted from the window, disappearing behind ramparts that shielded the companions' view of his final demise.

Haydren closed his eyes and shook his head. "How many chances does one get? Why, in the face of every choice, do so many choose death?" He glanced sideways at Sarah.

Sarah bowed her head. "Everyone dies," she said. "I guess we're used to the idea that it's supposed to be that way." When she looked up, she sighed. "Like this forest," she continued. "It might have gone this way eventually. Should we mourn its passing less when it dies over the normal course of time?"

"It was a beautiful wood," Haydren agreed.

"No matter how beautiful it seemed," Geoffrey said, "it was still the product of evil. Now that Lasserain is gone, I suppose it must go too."

"It is good for it to go," Haydren said, nodding. "As must we. It is a long journey home."

28

TRAVELS

22 Halmfurtung 1320 — Autumn

Though there was death outside Galessern, the pallor inside had lifted. The companions moved through streets among people walking as though woken from a dream. Near the keep, they met those who had killed Guntsen. There was no cheering as there had been in Jyunta, but a quiet acknowledgment that impossible, heavy chains had been struck from their wrists. When they fumbled with the language, one finally brought them to a merchant who traveled, and had learned enough Rinc Nain to convey the story.

When word had come of Haydren's approach, the soldiers that remained in the castle were hidden ready to spring out on the command. But something like a soft whisper had come to them all that Lasserain's end was nearing, and so the alarm was not raised. Of those who hid, many had died when Lasserain fell, for their spirits had been tied to his as Paolound's had been. The soldiers that were still alive in the castle were more than happy to disown the mage and the former King, who had been killed and revived by Lasserain over fifteen years ago. For fear of their lives they had served the undead King; for gratitude of their lives, they agreed to serve the new Earl, Filrin, who had slain Guntsen. Though Burieng had once been united, many years ago, it had not been for a long while.

Haydren suspected, even with Filrin in power, it might remain separated still. But the tensions along the borders would be gone, the raids would cease. With his province so crippled, Filrin would never risk angering his northern counterparts. The company departed in good faith that the war was indeed over.

Dubril was shattered, and not a man challenged them as they took the Koniero Highway north along the gulf. The road was long and treacherous, and it was over two weeks before they reached Naaseb, the castle which maintained a line of forts along the Aonan province's border with both Coberan and Kelian provinces. Haydren informed the soldiers there of Filrin's ascension to power, with a letter the new Earl had signed and sealed. They had already known Lasserain was dead, for many of their soldiers had also fallen the day of the mage's death.

Six days later they passed through Endol, the border-castle facing Kelian Province and their road north toward Hewolucs. Their time there was shorter than at Naaseb, and the next day they crossed the border to Balath in Tarthip County. They continued north to Raka, where Haydren paused at the gravestone of Kitrel and mourned.

After passing Kontar and turning east, forty-two days after defeating the mage and beginning their journey home, they entered lands Haydren began to recognize. The sun shined brightly in a crisp blue sky as the broad plains waved in the breeze. A group of merchants passed them on their way to Kontar, waving cheerily, no longer needing to fear for beasts. Bandits, too, seemed in disarray. As the sun crested on its path through the sky, Hewolucs rose before them.

The bustle in the castle was exactly how Haydren remembered it. A contingent of guards walking by looked just as they had. Hewolucs, then, was not under enemy control. As he neared the house in which he had spent his first years in Burieng, a lump rose in his throat. Would they still be there? Guntsen had not said anything about what he might have done to them. Would they have moved? But where?

Then he turned onto the street, and Maerie was sweeping in front of the house. Haydren pulled his horse to a stop and gazed at her, his vision clouding. She paused, looked up, and the broom clattered to the pavement.

Time stopped for a long moment. Those watching saw Haydren dismount and run to Maerie, and Maerie run to him, and for them to collide in a long embrace. Haydren remembered nothing except the tears running down his face as he saw his adoptive mother once more, and feeling her kiss his neck and hold him tightly just as she used to when he was young.

Finally they separated, and Maerie glanced at his companions. "Oh, of course," Haydren said, turning. "This is Geoffrey. It was his house in Hodp I had told you about. He helped me after I first left the castle and has kept me alive ever since. Sarah is from Jyunta, and has been with me for some months now."

"You are all very welcome in this household," Maerie said. "Much has happened here since you left, Haydren," she said, turning to him.

"A lot has happened to me since I left too, Maerie," he replied with a smile.

"Did you know?" she asked, placing a palm on his chest as her eyes lit up brightly. "The bandits are gone, and the beasts too. They even say Lasserain has been killed."

Haydren smiled broadly and laughed, along with his companions. "I had heard something like that," he replied, his eyes twinkling. "But where is Mickel? Is he still in the towers?"

"Of course," Maerie replied. "Sir Cullins would have it no other—you don't know, do you? How could you? Oh, Haydren, so much has happened. Sir Cullins is the Earl of Kelian, now!"

Haydren gripped her arm in surprise. "He is?" he said. "The other lords approved of it?"

"Not at first—especially the Count of Ives. You know how he is. But those ways were dying anyway."

"I was worried....I didn't know if Guntsen might execute Sir Cullins—and you two—or maybe he had died during my escape..."

"No, he was fine," she replied. "He was advisor to Guntsen for a while, until Guntsen left. A new batch of soldiers came, saying they were under orders from him, from Earl Guntsen. We tried to resist, but they took over. After a few months, Sir Cullins led the rebellion against the soldiers and took back the castle. Of course everyone told him to take over, since he had done so well taking the castle back. I'm sure he will want to see you, now that you're here."

"Perhaps I will," Haydren said. "But that can wait until tomorrow. There's so much we need to catch up on."

The company spent the night at Mickel and Maerie's house, enjoying the celebration when Mickel returned for the night to find his adopted son and companions. Beer and ale were brought out, and they talked late into the night.

The next morning, before his companions awakened, Haydren slipped out and went to the keep. The guard there recognized him, and let him in to see Sir Cullins. When the aide announced Haydren, Sir Cullins almost didn't remember the name, thinking his pupil would be long gone.

"Haydren? Haydren!" Sir Cullins shouted as Haydren entered. "Why are you still here? Why did you come back? Did you hear?"

"I hadn't heard," Haydren said, smiling as he approached. "But I hoped after killing Lasserain, things might be different up here."

Sir Cullins gripped Haydren's arm as his eyes widened. "You did that?" he asked in wonder. Haydren nodded humbly, and Sir Cullins laughed. "Did you happen to come across that coward Guntsen while you were down there?"

"I did, actually," Haydren replied. "He was killed by one of the south's soldiers, Filrin—he's the Earl of Aonan Province now."

"I don't know him," Cullins asked. "Does he seem peaceful?"

"He seemed tired of the destruction to his homeland," Haydren said soberly. "If he does anything with his Earlship, it will be to rebuild his Province. You don't have to worry about him, Sir Cullins. Those whom we told—all tired of war—approved of his coming to power."

"I suppose you're right," Cullins mused. "Speaking of coming to power, Haydren, Guntsen's betrayal has left a lot of castles without lords. As Earl, I have the power to give you one of them. Surely killing Lasserain has earned you that?"

"'Lord Loren'?" Haydren mused. "I don't think I like the sound of that."

"Something closer to home, then?" Cullins said. "How about captain of my guard? You would have the respect so long denied to you. No one would call you 'orphan' after that."

Haydren smiled. "A year ago, your Excellency, I would have taken that from you without thinking."

"But now?"

"I would be honored if you would give it to Mickel," Haydren said. "I have unfinished business elsewhere."

"I see," Cullins said, seating himself slowly. "If you wish, Haydren; the job is his. He conducted himself most appropriately during the Knights' occupancy; I'm sure the people of Hewolucs would not object to his appointment."

"Thank you, Excellency," Haydren said.

Later that day, after Haydren had returned home, Mickel came to him. "I just received word from Earl Cullins," Mickel said. "He has appointed me captain of the guard."

Haydren smiled. "That's great news, Mickel," he said.

Mickel sat down. "You already knew," he said. "Which means you must have asked the Earl for it. That's two promotions I owe you now."

Haydren's smile faltered, and he shook his head. "Not really," he said. "When I asked for you to be reinstated the first time, I didn't do it for you. I had hoped that, with you as a guard-lieutenant of the towers again, some of the boys at the school wouldn't look down on me so much."

"I see," Mickel said quietly with a nod. "And this time?"

"You and Maerie did so much for me, taking me in and risking your well-being for my sake," Haydren said, gazing into Mickel's eyes. "And I know the two of you want me to think of you as father and mother. But things have begun coming back to me—memories of before Burieng." He paused and drew a deep sigh. "I know my true parents are dead, and I wish to return to Rinc Na to see if anyone else of my family still live—I believe I had a sister, back there, that didn't come with us to Burieng. But I didn't want to leave you and Maerie without thanking you. I had hoped a position as Captain of the Guard might convey that."

"Just saying 'thank you' would convey that," Mickel said with a smile. "When you survived the attack on your caravan and made it all the way to Hewolucs, we knew you meant to make your own way. We just hoped we could make the journey a little easier."

At that, Haydren and Mickel embraced. Haydren spent the night, and in the morning packed to leave. He paused as he held the Cretal dagger, wavering upon putting it in the bag with all the rest of his things. It had been passed down, clearly, to him. Should he save it to pass down to his future son? Could he?

He pulled the blade from its sheath, gazing at it. Lasserain's blood had been cleaned from it long ago, but it still looked as if it had not. Haydren had thought, once, that the red, pitted metal made the stain of blood blend in, made the death disappear. But as he looked on it now he saw that the stain had not gone. Rather, the blade was permanently stained by every drop of blood it had ever spilled. It did not make Haydren feel the death less, but so much more so that he loathed to even keep the weapon. Suddenly he wished every weapon did not clean so easily, that every weapon made the wielder loathe to keep it, for fear they should have to use it again.

That, he could pass down to a future son.

When next he saw Sarah and Geoffrey, they glanced at one another, then at Haydren, and smiled.

"What is it?" Haydren asked.

"A letter came from Earl Durdamon," Sarah said, holding it up.

"For who?"

"For me." Sarah opened it and glanced at it, then looked up again. "Sheppar, Kinnig of Andelen, is a friend of Durdamon's."

"Geoffrey mentioned him before," Haydren said with a nod, then laughed. "I didn't understand the 'Kinnig' part then, either."

"'Little King,'" Sarah replied with a grin. "It's a new honorific. He's not king the way we think of kings, wielding all the power. More like what Durdamon is to the west."

"So what does the letter say?"

"He wants me to go to Andelen and see if I can help him," she replied.

"You're not going with me to Rinc Na?"

"I do want to return there, and soon," Sarah said with a nod. She shrugged. "Just not yet."

"And you?" Haydren asked, turning to Geoffrey.

"I need to see Kerrik, Pladt's father, to tell him what happened," Geoffrey said.

Haydren nodded once. "Tell him I'm sorry, would you?"

"I will."

"And after?"

Geoffrey drew a deep breath. "I want to stay with Sarah," he said with a tight smile. She grinned as well. "We'll both make it to Rinc Na after we see what can be done in Andelen. We'll find you there."

"It's a big country," Haydren said.

"We'll find you somehow."

"I wouldn't have made it along without you two," Haydren said with a quick nod.

"None of us would have, without each other," Sarah replied.

"You sure we'll be able to now?"

Sarah and Geoffrey chuckled. "You'll do well," Geoffrey said.

Haydren shook Geoffrey's hand, and Sarah gave him a warm hug. "Get to Rinc Na quickly," Haydren said as he stepped away.

"You too," Sarah said with twinkling eyes.

So Haydren rode out of Hewolucs alone, and two days later was aboard a ship, the *Sword Dancer,* departing from Westide and bound for the Clanaso Islands. As the great ship left the harbor, the sailors running up and down the rigging and across the deck with shouts and calls to one another, Haydren stood by the railing watching Burieng fall slowly astern. He glanced up, once, and was sure he had never seen a sky so blue.

THE END
of
By Ways Unseen

THE FIRST TO FORGIVE

Book 2 of The Triumvirs

Daniel Dydek

BEORN

BEORN PUBLISHING, LLC

CONTENTS

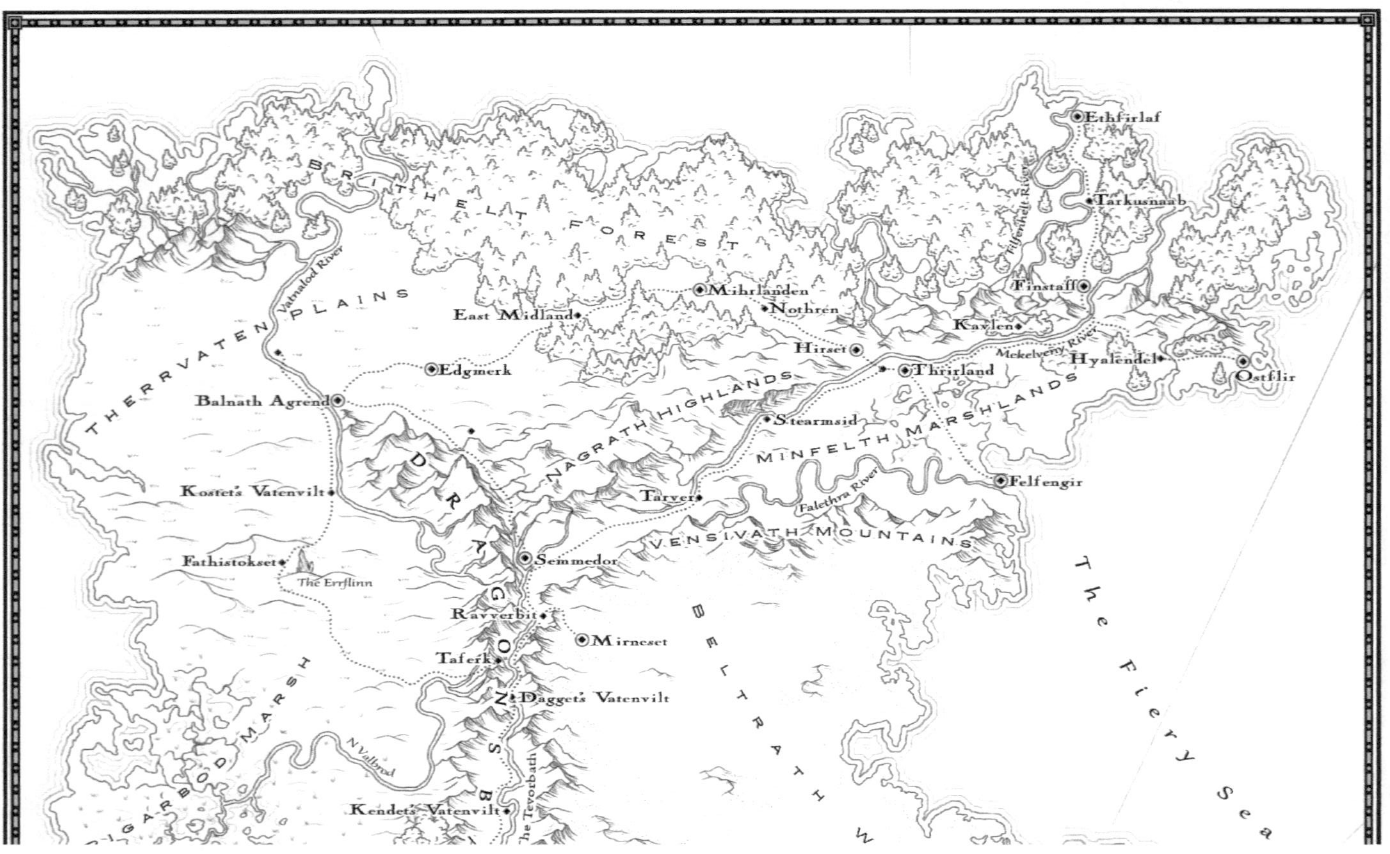

BRITHELAT FOREST
Ethfirlaf
Tarkusnaab
Tilfenhelt River
Finstaff
Mihrlanden
Nothren
East Midland
Kavlen
Mekelveny River
Hirset
Hyalendel
Edgmerk
Thrirland
Ostflir
THERRVATEN PLAINS
Vatmalod River
NAGRATH HIGHLANDS
Balnath Agrend
Stearmsid
MINFELTH MARSHLANDS
Kosteri Vatenvilt
Tarver
Falethra River
Felfengir
VENSIVATH MOUNTAINS
Fathistokset
The Errflinn
Semmedor
DRAGONS B
Ravverbit
Mirneset
BELTRATH W
Taferk
Daggeti Vatenvilt
GARBOD MARSH
N. Vallbrod
The Tevorbath
Kendeti Vatenvilt
The Fiery Sea

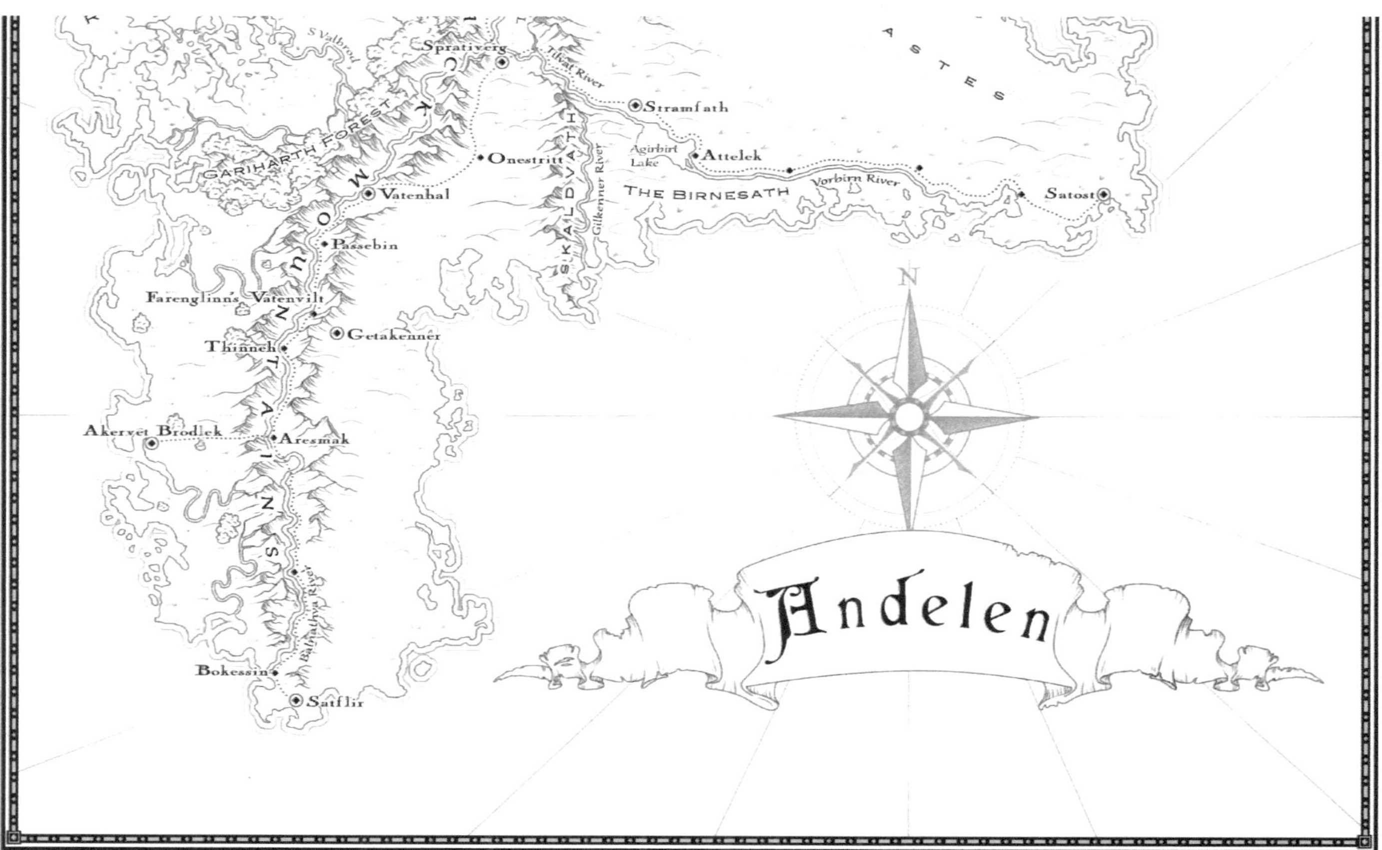

Andelen
N
ASTES
GARIHARTH FOREST
S Valbrod
Sprativerg
Tikat River
Stramfath
Onestritt
Agirbirt Lake
Attelek
Vorbirn River
Satost
Vatenhal
SKAILDVATH
Gilkenner River
THE BIRNESATH
Passebin
Farenglinn's Vatenvilt
Getakenner
Thinneh
MOUNTAINS
Akervet Brodlek
Aresmak
Balriathva River
Bokessin
Satflir

I

Night Visions

"They are making good time."
"It is not necessary for us both to be here."
"I have nothing to do."
"Let us correct that."

33 Haschina 1320[1] — Winter

"Would you tell Roth Kamdellan I need to speak with him?" Catie asked the young guard, trying to sound as though she saw Roth all the time.

But the boy never blinked. "No," he said.

She crossed her arms and shrugged. "It's your fault if this information doesn't come to him."

"What information?"

Catie's mouth twisted. "I can't tell you that," she said. "It's for Roth only."

"I'm sure it is. See, the thing is, we've already asked Roth about you, and he has no idea who you are." His eyebrows flared. "So you can keep coming here day after day, and trying your same ploy with all different guards, but we've already all been told about you."

Catie's arms drooped. "I've only come here three times."

"Five, and I can give you the names of all the guards. Now go away."

---

1. See Author's Note on Calendar for explanation of dates

Catie turned and moved away. She wiped her face, then paused. "How did you all know about me?" she asked quietly.

"Because we all talk about what happens when we're on duty," the boy replied. "In case anything seems important."

"Is that part of your training?" She sniffled in the cold.

The boy shifted. "No, we just talk about things," he said. "In the barracks."

"Oh, that makes sense," she replied. "I didn't realize you all had barracks here."

"Well, they're not proper barracks. We put up in the west wing of the inn."

"Thanks!" Catie called as she strode off toward the building the boy had indicated.

"Wait, where are you going?" he said, taking a step toward her.

"You're not leaving your post, are you?" she asked in a clear, strong voice, her stride quickening.

"You can't—oh, no... Would you stop and come back—Why are you—would you stop?"

But Catie continued down the street. Five guards knew about her, did they? They obviously didn't know about her resolve.

She stopped by a small bakery—Akervet Brodlek was littered with them—and purchased a few fresh rolls. She didn't have much coin, but if this worked, she would need very little more. She smiled to the baker, wound the rolls tight to keep them warm as a light snow began to fall, and continued on her way.

Though she had only been in Akervet for a week, she knew the town well enough, knew which inn would have a wing, and be comfortable enough for Roth to keep his soldiers. They did like to stay warm, and they didn't only rely on beds and blankets to do so. Catie slid one side of her cloak off her shoulder, and undid a lace from her buckskin jacket—but just one: it was still cold, and she valued herself too highly to give *too* much away.

She approached the inn, glimpsing a soldier as he exited the west wing. She smiled as she passed, saw his eyes drop below her chin and linger. She resisted the urge to close the jacket until he had passed, then gave heed to a chill that was not only from the air. Resolve. That's what she needed.

She could almost feel the heat of the roaring hearths inside as she knocked on the door. It cracked open, and a balding head with squirrelly eyes peered out at her. "Who are you?" he asked.

"I thought you might like some warm bread," she said sweetly.

The door opened wider, and three more pairs of eyes squinted in the sudden sunlight. "That would be very nice," the squirrel-eyed one said, not yet taking the offered gift. He didn't seem to want to risk her leaving as soon as her errand was done. "Would you like to come inside and get warm?"

"Oh, thank you," Catie replied, stepping quickly through the door.

It was *very* nice and warm. Once the door was shut, she handed them the loaves, and stood beside the fire as they remained awkwardly quiet behind her. She almost wanted to laugh as she could sense the men working up some sort of courage. But they were taking too long. She swept her cloak behind her, and sighed.

"Truly, I don't know how you stay in so warm a room," she said, taking the cloak off completely. "It seems so uncomfortable." She shook out her hair—which actually made her feel warmer, but men always seemed to like the loose curls. Dannid had.

"Well, there are ways to keep cool," said one—not the squirrel. "And other ways to keep warm besides fire."

She rolled her eyes before fixing her smile and half-turning toward the speaker. "Oh?" she asked. "Could you show me?"

"Well, first, you need to be further from the fire," the same speaker said quickly, trying to be faster than his friends in coming toward her without making it seem like a competition.

She took a step backward. Toward him. "Like, here?"

He managed to laugh. "No, a little further than that. Here, come with me."

Looking sideways at his friends, the tall, broad-shouldered guard led her into a side room, and shut the door. "See how much nicer it is in here?" he asked as he gently slid the bolt closed.

"It isn't so hot, in here," she agreed, glancing around the room. It looked to be a more private quarter, and she wondered whether he had rank, or poor judgment. The latter would serve her nicely. Or both.

"It isn't hot—yet," the guard said, maintaining his cryptic tone. "But you can change that, too, and make it warmer." He pulled a chair up in front of her and sat down. His hands reached out and gripped her hips.

Catie quickly held up a finger. "Not yet," she said, her eyes still casting about for—there it was. She pulled away from him, amazed he let her go, and picked up a chamber pot near the bed. She quickly checked to see that it was empty.

"What—?" was all he said before she struck the pot off the floor, then stomped her feet a few times. He stared at her as a scuffling could be heard outside the room.

"Is everything all right in there?" asked a voice.

Catie looked at him, drawing her arms behind her and pushing her chest forward as she batted her eyelashes and smiled.

"Uh, yes, everything's fine! Go away!" he snapped. His voice lowered. "What in the name of the gods did you do that for?"

Catie smiled, then smashed the pot over his head, stomping her feet a few times as he fell to the floor, unconscious. She darted to the door, pressing her ear against it to listen for anyone approaching.

"What in the bloody Marfey is going on in there?" muttered what sounded like the squirrel-eyed one.

"Marfey's got nothing to do with it, Steth," said another. "Sergeant's up for it, anyway. Did you see her face? I don't think there's a woman made better than brown hair and matching eyes, like that. I'd be up for it too, if it was me."

"You always were for the faces, Korgan," said the third. "I go for the part what strains the laces, if you know what I mean."

"It was chestnut hair," Steth said quietly. "But I think I prefer the part that doesn't matter what clothes they have on."

Korgan glared at him. "What's that, their wits? Gods know you don't know what to do with anything else."

Steth, for his part, put up a loud argument. Catie, still amazed her plan was going better than she hoped, slipped out through a window with a new set of armor, complete with a helmet that would hide a fair portion of her face. As the fight continued inside the inn, she checked her boot for her hunting knife. She took a deep breath and, pulling the helmet over her head, struck off back for the building occupied by Roth Kamdellan, leader of the rebellion against Sheppar, Kinnig of Andelen.

⸻◦⸻

"'Kinnig,'" Roth scoffed. "Do not call him that in front of me. I refuse to call him by that title. Who would think of saying 'no, don't call me king; call me *little* king'?"

"I'm sorry, sir," Rodigger said. "I *am* sorry. I had called him that for a long time."

"Your whole life, I know," Roth said, gently now. "I am so glad I could save you from that. I know it seems disrespectful to only call him 'Sheppar', but what he has titled himself is even more disrespectful. And if he cannot respect himself, how does he expect the rest of the country to do so?"

"Right, sir," Rodigger said. "But, back to the original point..."

"Oh, yes, of course," Roth said, shaking his head. "Please—"

He was interrupted as the sweat-smell from the helmet finally made Catie sneeze. The force of it echoed back in her helmet, and rang in her ears.

"Ow," she said, then squeezed her eyes shut at how plainly feminine her voice was.

Roth straightened, his eyes going hard. "Seize..." He gestured. "...that." The guard on the other side of the door did himself credit, grasping her swiftly despite his shock. Rodigger was in front of her in two steps and yanked the helmet from her head.

"I have some information for Roth alone?" Catie said hopefully.

"Then by all means, give it," Roth said.

"Your guard is holding down the arm I was going to deliver it with," she replied.

"Sir?" the guard asked.

Roth regarded her for several moments. "Rodigger, check her right boot, would you?"

Rodigger glanced down, and his shoulders stiffened. He bent over and yanked the knife from her boot, then turned and handed it to Roth. "We should throw her deep into a hole somewhere," he whispered.

Roth's gaze never left Catie's face as he took the knife. "She may have a very good reason for what she attempted," he replied. "And considering how far she made it *this* time, I am almost curious to see how far she might make it the next time."

"Sir?" Rodigger said, his brow furrowing.

Roth addressed the guard. "Put her outside the walls, and don't let her back inside," he said, turning away with a backward wave. "If she makes it to the next inn, she deserves to live."

"I need my horse," she said quietly, already knowing the answer. But today had been a day of foolhardy hope.

"I suspect you do," Roth returned lightly. "Rodigger, once she's gone, please show in my other guests."

"Sir, you're not giving her the, um..." Rodigger paused as Roth glared at him, then turned to the guard who still held Catie. "You heard him, get her out! And make sure the guards know her so they won't let her back in."

She went willingly back into the cold, through the streets as people gazed curiously at the strange parade. The snow by now had gathered in corners and on ledges, shading everything else a little whiter as it came down in lazy flakes. Catie stumbled along a little from numbness, a little because the guard who restrained her took his charge very seriously.

Once outside the walls, the doors did not boom shut as she thought they should. But the guards' crossed spears were as unyielding as anything made of oak, and she turned her face resolutely down the road and began to walk. The snow, for spite, fell thicker.

———◆———

Roth looked up as the doors shut behind the two men he had summoned from Balnath Agrend several weeks ago. He had truly been uncertain that Gabriel would come. The fact that the mercenary would visit the enemy of his friend spoke volumes of his situation. And of course if Gabriel came, Deuel did too. They were a package deal in the mercenary world—and an expensive deal, but worth the coin.

But if they had been two sides of a coin, one side had apparently fared far worse than the other.

"Please, sit," Roth said, gesturing to a couch opposite his own chair. Rodigger stood inconspicuously to one side, observing but not too alert. He was a good lad. He would do fine.

Deuel remained standing, his posture exuding an ability for sudden and decisive movement even as his muscles relaxed. His cloak was thick, and Roth thought briefly that he seemed to wear it a little too carefully. But then, the man was strange entire. From his face, one might think he was twenty to thirty years Gabriel's junior. But a glance in his eyes told a story of ages, older it seemed than the mountains far to the east. It was rumored a glance was usually all one could withstand before looking away. Roth tried quickly, and confirmed the tale. What was it, in those depths?

It did not matter. Gabriel sat down, very nearly slouching, and seemed prepared only to move if buttered biscuits were set before him. But, according to other stories Roth had heard...

"We're here," Gabriel said. "What do you want?"

Roth settled back, his eyes narrowing. "I want to hire you," he said.

Gabriel blinked at him. "No kidding? I thought I was coming down here for tea."

Roth glanced at Deuel, who regarded him with unnatural stillness. Roth's eyes went back to Gabriel as he hurried to regain control of the meeting. "Very well," he said. "No pleasantries, then. Do you know of the Berkarfor?"

"Hidden goblets of legend..." Gabriel trailed off, gazing at him for several moments, then burst suddenly into loud laughter. "That's what you propose?" he asked between gasps. "Pay me now, and I'll give you cups," he said, snapping his fingers.

Roth waited until Gabriel's mirth subsided. "The Berkarfor are real," he said quietly, his gaze level. "The first can be found near Agirbirt Lake."

The humor in Gabriel's eyes was gone but for a faint spark. "How did you find this out?"

"Careful study," Roth replied. He raised a small glass from a nearby table and took a slow drink. "When you find the first, it should lead you to the second—and so on."

"Why us? I'm old," Gabriel said. "I might die before I find them all."

"That is my risk to take," Roth replied. "Besides, I believe your partner will be most helpful to you."

Gabriel betrayed his surprise only by the slightest glance at Deuel. Deuel did not react at all. "He does seem to know things no one else does," the mercenary replied. "But he never mentioned to me knowing where the goblets are."

"I am sure he doesn't. But the riddles to be solved to learn the location of the next one should be less difficult to one with his...experience."

"This gets better and better. And what is the recompense for a mission such as this?"

"Five thousand nerist," Roth replied. Gabriel hid his surprise better, this time. "To start," Roth continued. "Another five when you return successful."

Gabriel slid his palms against his knees, and Roth knew he had him. Normally one would haggle at this point, but one was not normally offered ten thousand nerist for search-and-find. "This is very important to you," Gabriel said.

"It is important for Andelen," Roth corrected smoothly, setting down his cup. "Without the Berkarfor, my work for my country will never be finished."

"And without your pay, my work for myself will never be finished," Gabriel said dryly. "We'll set out tomorrow morning. I assume we have rooms, somewhere?" The mercenary rocked to his feet. Deuel barely shifted, but one glance told Roth his muscles were alert again.

"Would you like to look over what I have concerning the first hiding place?" Roth asked, rising as well.

"Have it put in my saddlebags. It'll be a long journey to Agirbirt."

"Very well, my aide will place them for you. The Rustling Ivy has a room prepared for you, and stall-space," Roth said, extending his hand.

"Are stalls something hard to find?" Gabriel asked, grasping the proffered hand and releasing it quickly.

"I have many horses," Roth replied with a thin smile that held, barely, until the mercenary and his partner exited the room. Then he snatched up the glass and drained the contents. "Rodigger, you are going with them," he snapped. He glanced up just as the young man shut his mouth decisively. "I don't like this man, and I somehow don't trust my offer to keep him faithful. If you must, take over the mission. And bring me those Berkarfor!" he finished, managing to refrain from hurling his empty cup to his protégé.

He made it to the door, hand on the latch, before he stopped. His gaze was down, focused on nothing. Then his eyes slid sideways. "Actually," he said, "I think your missions will be two-fold." His hand left the latch, and he turned. He drew close to Rodigger. "Or perhaps three. Word of our cause needs to spread outside the Fallonvall, and you will be in a unique position to do that. But there's something else—or, some*one* else. I need you to keep alert for a man." Roth's smile grew. "A very particular man. And here's how you will know him..."

⁂

If Catie reached the inn by moonset, it would be a miracle. And as far as she was concerned, she had used a lifetime of miracles getting that close to Roth in the first place.

But she still had her cloak, and wrapped it tightly around her. It would serve for now. Roth risked little by letting her keep it. The sun—a vague bright spot on the clouds—was past noon. The day would be long, as the plains here were utterly flat. But there would be little dusk, and the temperature would fall as swiftly as night. And she had small way of making fire: there was precious little fuel adequate to burn, not until she reached the Dragonsback Mountains almost two hundred miles away.

Or the inn that was a tempting, but futile, thirty miles away.

As she considered it, she wasn't sure why she walked. It kept her warmer, which was something. But it could not do so forever, not this time of year. Perhaps because she had rarely stopped moving for the last two months—not until she found out Roth was garrisoned in Akervet. She should have been on her way home. She *had* been, and was passing through Aresmak in the 'Back. She should have continued up the mountains, then east to Agirbirt Lake and home.

When she made the decision to turn west, she hadn't had a plan. She simply went, hoping everything else would fall into place. Some decisions were made that way, it seemed: one step led to an entirely different road, and she walked down it. Her Grandmother had told her that, more than once.

And so she did, without thinking. Even when she'd gotten to Akervet, no real plan had formed. Each step followed another until she sneezed and gave herself away.

She would have died in that room, if she had succeeded. She knew that, and had accepted it. But to die now, in the cold, while Roth lived on in the warmth? It had not seemed like utterly the wrong road until that moment. She had strode confidently along, reaching Akervet, petitioning the guards for entrance, figuring a way to slip inside on her own, and actually standing in the same room as that man while he talked on, oblivious to her presence and the death she had intended to bring. The whole time, it had seemed the right road. But in two moments...could it happen that quick? Had there been no warning signs that she was making a bad decision all the way back in Aresmak?

Sure, there had been small obstacles, but barely more than briars overreaching the verge. Now she was locked in a thicket, no way out, and night and cold were descending like stooping falcons. It did not seem like the same road, at all. More like she had been plucked from one path that was free, and clear, and led precisely where she wanted to go, and set instantly down on a path she had not meant to trod.

Yet here she was, still walking. Why? She glanced backward, and was surprised to see how small the village had gotten behind her. When the snow flurried just right, she almost couldn't see it. She turned forward again, wrapped her fingers around her collar, and twisted her face in frustration, anger, sadness. She wanted to cry, knew it would be a release. But nothing came. Walking was pointless, but she had to do it, knowing it served no purpose. She had made a stupid decision, which got her only this walking sentence, and no justice. Roth, that smug, arrogant, witless catfish didn't have the decency to kill her outright, when Catie had very little will to live, anyway.

Her steps faltered just once, and then resumed their normal cadence. She didn't mind the dying—that was supposed to have happened. But why must she go on with this worthless living for so long before it came? And what did it serve to have so much time to think, when she would meet no one before night, and would die before dawn?

This time tears did come, and froze against the collar of her cloak.

By the time the glow of the sun behind the clouds reached the horizon, her pace had slackened. The snow, blessedly, had stopped. But Catie was already chilled to the marrow. And the waning full moon wouldn't rise for some time yet, so it was about to get very dark as well as very cold. Certainly no conditions in which to walk.

With what little daylight remained, Catie wandered off the road until she found a low area with thick shocks of knee-high grass. Pausing occasionally to blow into her cupped hands, she pulled up the blades and piled them. Perhaps, if she could gather enough, she might make something of a nest. Such things served the birds that stayed for winter.

By the time she had anything of a bed, daylight had gone. She laid down, tried to burrow deep without going so deep as to reach the frozen ground, failed because she hadn't been able to get quite enough of a nest built, and turned over on her back to look up into the sky. She would have liked to see the stars, one more time. But as weariness from cold and shivering clouded her brain to match the sky, she knew she wouldn't. The wind rustling through the grasses, though chill, calmed her.

Sleep came, but she would not stop living yet. In a dream she went far to the south, to Bokessin near the coast, to the square she knew well, that would be emblazoned in her mind eternally. The pool in the middle of the square already ran red. The resistance had failed, and Roth's blades were sharp as his vengeance. A crowd had gathered at spear-point, and Catie was among them. Those terrible swords, flashing in the sunlight. It had been a remarkably beautiful day, and the bloodshed in that square was not enough to dim it. Every detail was captured perfectly: every prisoner, every sword-stroke, every death. One by one, and Dannid in line, working his way toward death step by shuffling step. He was saved for last, and Roth himself performed the act, because Dannid had started it, and led it to what it had become.

Dannid stepped forward, that last step, with the same confidence as he had stepped toward Catie only three days before. Roth did not know she was in the crowd, wouldn't have cared if he did. Because he still wouldn't know that Dannid and Catie had just been married.

She tried to turn away, but this was a demonstration for the people of Bokessin, and a guard was close enough to prick her with a spear until she turned forward again. Dannid's head was at the edge of the pool. Roth's sword—perfectly clean and brilliant in the sun—came down swiftly.

Catie's eyes snapped open. The dream left her, as did the weariness from the cold. There was a sound on the air, like a kitten trying to mew, except the note held and seemed to echo across a vast distance. She looked to the horizon, and her brow furrowed as she slowly sat upright.

Far to the south, beyond the horizon, an orange light—thin as a blade of grass held sideways but immovable as the Dragonsback Mountains—pierced through the night sky. Where it originated, and where it went, was impossible to determine. She sensed somehow that it did not even originate in Andelen.

All at once the light disappeared and the sound ceased, and Catie's breath was ripped from her lungs. She sat gasping, not sure of what she had just seen. And yet she felt at once a terrible anguish and an incomparable joy—and a will to live as she had never known. She felt at that moment as though the Dragonsback Mountains could bury her, and the Fiery Sea could drown her, and she would dig and swim until she found daylight again.

And yet she did not know where to go. There was only a sense of flight, and a vague direction northward. But like a bee drumming against a window, her thoughts knew only *go! go! go!* while her destination was blocked firmly from her mind. Somehow that didn't matter. She knew that nothing would stop her, ever, until she reached wherever it was she was supposed to go.

That was, until she heard hoofbeats rumbling in the distance along the road from Akervet.

——◆——

In the hotel room, a sudden movement woke Gabriel from his slumber. The darkness was nearly complete, save what washed in from a fading moon. He searched for what had woken him, and saw Deuel sitting upright in his bed.

"*Skald?*" Gabriel asked, rising to his elbows.

Deuel's head drooped, then turned to gaze at Gabriel. "Paolound is dead," he murmured.

Gabriel levered himself up. "You thought that before."

Deuel shook his head. "He had died then too, but someone revived him. I do not think he will be revived again. He is dead, Gabriel. The Call is strong."

Gabriel sighed quietly. "This is not good timing, *Skalderon*. I will need you now—"

"I know." Deuel lay back down slowly. "I cannot help the call, Gabriel. I felt it, and it woke you, and now you know. I will see how long it will last this time. Good night."

To all appearances, Deuel resumed his slumber. Gabriel knew both their thoughts ran swiftly behind closed eyelids, and mostly together. He did not whisper to the God of All much, at least not formally. But to whom else could his thoughts go as they floated through his mind: *let us find these goblets quickly. Don't make him miss this opportunity again.*

2

STRANGE RESPITES

"I thought you hid those long ago?"
"It seems they seek to find them again."
"You leave now for Andelen?"
"I think it should be yours, Teresh."

34 Haschina 1320 — Winter

Catie turned onto her stomach, eyes searching the thin gloom. The moon had risen, and with snow-shine gave shadows to the landscape. She could see the thin line of the road. And there, not one but two horses, one empty-saddled, coming toward her.

She shuffled on her elbows, craning her neck. It was odd that someone traveled so late at night, and odder that they led a riderless horse. It was still too close to Akervet for something to have gone amiss, so the rider had to have brought the horse riderless from the town. And if they were simply heading for Aresmak, they would have waited and left in the morning, wouldn't they?

As both horses neared, she stood, knowing her brown leather would show up starkly against the snow—which reminded her how cold the night was. Her arms came up reflexively and crossed, her shoulders stooped as she felt the light breeze.

Horses and rider stopped, their breath squirting into the air. The riderless mount squealed and turned toward her. Catie straightened as she recognized the voice: it was Kelsie, her mare.

Leaving her cloak and nest, Catie trotted to Kelsie's head, forgetting the rider for the moment. Her mare ducked as Catie pressed in and curled her fingers in her mane.

Catie backed away, still scratching Kelsie's muzzle as she finally looked up at the rider. Her fingers stopped as she noticed his squirrelly eyes, and could imagine the balding head under his warm cap.

"My name is Steth," he said. "And yours is Catie?"

"It is," she replied, suddenly feeling the gap in her boot where her knife had been.

"You tried to kill Roth, which is why you came to the barracks."

"Yes."

Steth tossed her the reins. "And he didn't kill you outright?"

Catie resumed her scratching, rocking a little as Kelsie pushed into her. "He felt if I could make it to the next inn, I deserved to live."

"Did he say exactly that?"

"Yes."

Steth looked eastward, and adjusted his seat with a creak of leather. "Then I don't feel wrong for helping you. Who deserves life more than one who can win the hearts of her enemies?"

"And how did I do that, exactly?"

Steth turned back to look at her. "By coming closer than anyone else to killing Roth Kamdellan."

Catie's fingers moved up behind an ear. "You're one of his soldiers," she said.

"Who better to know the failings of a leader than one who serves him?"

Catie shrugged. "I've known a few people who knew his failings well enough, who would never serve him."

"Some have that luxury," Steth said. "Others have families."

"Some have that luxury, too," Catie murmured, tracing the star between Kelsie's eyes with her thumb.

"I'm sorry?"

Catie shook her head. "I can't repay you for bringing me my horse," she said with a smile.

"Yes, you can," Steth said, turning his horse toward Akervet. Catie looked up, squinting. Steth smiled. "Come visit Roth again, sometime. If you can. Hopefully better prepared, next time."

"Are you that certain he's wrong?"

Steth cocked his head. "I cannot say about his ideas. But certainly his methods."

Catie watched Steth as he rode off, slower now that his mission was complete. She could agree with that: whether or not Roth was right about Sheppar and how he was handling his rule, Roth's way of fixing it had to be stopped. But how? As Steth said, she needed to be better prepared. Simply going to Akervet and 'seeing what happened' would not work again.

Again. Catie glanced at her nest where her cloak still lay: clearly it hadn't worked the first time. And why should it have? Her father might have taught her much about survival before he left, but that was survival in the absence of others—not survival in dealing with others. As much as Dannid might have influenced her, too, they had only known each other for two years. And little of that time had been spent training in assassination.

Catie sighed, and retrieved her cloak. Part of her just wanted to be home again. Another part wasn't sure how she would tell her story to Grandmother. In the three years since she had run away, she had joined a resistance, gotten married, seen her husband executed, and was herself nearly executed for trying to assassinate someone. What every Grandmother wanted, surely.

She shook the snow from her cloak before wrapping it around her shoulders. Another part of her remembered the light that pierced the sky. That part was still trying to understand what happened, and why she felt an enormous pressure to go home, while also knowing that same pressure would not keep her there. That it would pause for a time, but only a temporary stop before going on to something else. How could she possibly know that? And how did an orange light and a faint keening make her know that? Or did she just dream it?

She glanced toward her departing savior. She should have asked Steth, but he was far down the road now, and the night was cold.

She turned. Kelsie was staring at her. And why *was* she still standing in the cold when a horse waited to take her to a warm fire? Kelsie whinnied and tossed her head as if reading Catie's thoughts, and Catie smiled. They had been through a lot, they two. Maybe the mare *could* read her thoughts, by now. She mounted, and Kelsie turned for the inn without prompting.

Despite the cold, she fairly slept in the saddle as Kelsie made her unerring way. Catie blinked when Kelsie stopped and huffed: the inn was before them. Still in a weary haze, Catie stabled her mare, fed some hay into the trough, and circled to the front of the building. Her hand rose and yanked the rope to ring the bell inside, then stood in front of the door, waiting to be recognized and allowed in.

But no one came. The breeze picked up again, and she shook with chill. Fear crept back, waking her a little. Had it closed? She had never heard of that. The scrapes on the stone near the door from goblins and hellhounds trying to get in were all old. Surely...

She returned and rang the bell again. Something brief and likely colorful was muttered inside, and the rope suddenly sped through the hole and disappeared.

"Hey!" she cried, her hand leaping out in reflex alone, as the rope was long gone before she moved. "Let me in!" she shouted, kicking the door.

Miraculously, it opened. It was mostly dark inside, the fire having died to coals, but she could see well enough the spindly old man in thin red cotton night clothes and heavy boots. His white hair grew long to make up for what was no longer there, and still kept in the filthy manner that had probably led to his balding in the first place.

"Why didn't you come in daylight?" he demanded.

"I wasn't here in daylight," Catie responded, twisting sideways past him and into the warmer interior. She went straight to the fire and began tending it.

The old man shut the door, but remained near it as he watched her work. "You're supposed to come in the day," he said. "You could have been a hellhound or something."

"Ringing the bell?" Catie asked, leaning three logs together, and throwing some bits of bark underneath to help them catch.

"Goblin."

"They don't exist anymore." She blew on the coals. They glared, then stuck thin tongues out at her. She continued blowing until the bark caught. Kindly flames greeted her, then, and went to meet the logs.

The keeper harrumphed. "Of course they exist. Why else am I here?"

Catie waited to answer until the logs caught. She sighed, steadying herself as her head lightened. Weariness crept in again. She sat on the hearth, shedding her cloak so the heat would soak into her skin faster, and turned to the old man.

"My name is Catie," she said. "And I'm frozen and hungry."

"I'm Lothan, and I don't much care," he said, remaining steadfast by the door.

"You don't remember me?" Catie asked. "I was through here a few days ago."

"I don't remember people, they die too much. Dinner was hours ago, as was bed time. My inn keeps you safe from big nasties, and that's all I owe you."

"Big nasties are all gone, Lothan," Catie said. "Remember? Sheppar killed them all thirty years ago."

"All by himself?" Lothan asked, crossing his arms.

Catie stared, then turned to make sure the fire was still growing. "I'm sorry I had to wake you in the middle of the night," she said gently. "But I was sent out from Akervet in the middle of the day, on foot."

"You could have been killed!"

"So many different ways," Catie muttered.

"Exactly," Lothan said. "Goblins, hounds, vipers...not vipers, it's too cold, I suppose."

"Lothan, there aren't vipers on the roads anymore," Catie said, rubbing her eyes. She was beginning to warm, and realized she hadn't slept much since—well, for several months now, if she really thought about it. "Sheppar and his soldiers cleared all the wilds. It was a massive campaign."

"Rumors and myths," Lothan replied with a grunt.

"Have you had many attacks, lately?" Catie asked, then yawned.

"Just because I haven't doesn't mean I won't," he said. "Why would I be here if travelers didn't still need my protection? The reason these inns were built was to protect travelers, and that's still what we do."

"Do you please have anything to eat?" Catie asked. "Even something cold."

"Breakfast is at Morning," Lothan said, leaving his post by the door and heading toward his personal chambers, near the kitchen.

"Fine," Catie replied. After the door banged shut behind the keeper, she stared at it for several moments, hoping he was only angry at being disturbed so late. She glanced at the fire and shook with one final chill. The heat had reached most of her bones, by now, and she had to ignore her hunger. That left only her exhaustion. Her upper body pitched forward as that need washed over her. She caught herself, pushed herself upright, and after one brief moment to collect her shambled resolve she got to her feet.

After that was another haze of moving toward the back where the communal sleeping quarters were, to the first of the row of cots. And she woke up *underneath* the blankets, so that happened at some point, too.

Thin, vertical slits in the walls near the ceiling allowed the morning sun to shine through and wake the occupants, alerting them that they would need to be on their way soon to make the next inn. These slits were well-designed, and piercing sunlight fell precisely on Catie's eyelids, waking her instantly despite her every desire not to. The smell of frying bacon hit her nostrils an instant before she understood the sound, and she smiled. He was already making up for his surliness the night before.

After a good breakfast—though a silent one: Lothan served her, then sat behind a game of *feth* and glared at the scattered pairs on the board till she finished—Catie was off properly, whispering to Kelsie of a better night's rest at the next inn. It was a sunny, clear morning, promising more of spring to come than remembering winter past. She had inexplicably survived death yet again, and her soaring spirits dragged the sun into the sky with them.

⸺◆⸺

Before the sun brightened the mercenaries' room, two soldiers came and shook them roughly. Gabriel slapped away the hand of the soldier standing over top of him.

"Roth said to wake you," said the man as he folded his arms.

"Even for five thousand, he does not own me," Gabriel retorted. "And you may awaken me more gently, lest you lose your hands."

"I will be sure to kiss you next time," the soldier replied. "And Roth does own you, on pain of death, not promise of money. Get up. Your companion and your horses await."

"Companion?" Deuel said.

"Roth will not leave you to your own devices," the other soldier replied. "He is sending one of his own, whom he trusts, to go with you."

"Oh, splendid," Gabriel replied. "The help will be appreciated."

They rose and gathered their gear, then followed the men into the crisp morning. A thin blanket of snow covered the grass, and the horse's nostrils steamed.

Standing by the horses was a vaguely familiar young man in his early twenties. His red hair scraggled just above his shoulders, and a thin beard covered his chin. He slouched just a little, though his eyes scanned constantly. When Gabriel approached, the young man straightened a little and extended his hand.

"Rodigger Kytes," he said pleasantly, though without smiling. "Aide to Roth Kamdellan, and companion to you."

"You were in the room last night," Gabriel remembered aloud, shaking the proffered hand in passing. He stopped suddenly as he looked at Rodigger's horse. "Is that what you're riding?" he asked.

"Why? Shouldn't I?"

"It's a Therian," Gabriel said. When Rodigger only blinked, he continued: "We're likely spending a lot of time in the mountains, you know."

"Gared and I have been through them before," Rodigger replied. He glanced at the others. "Your horses don't look like that much."

Gabriel glared. "You named him 'Gared'?" he said, his voice rumbling. "Is that supposed to be funny?"

"Roth said it was a good name," Rodigger said, his voice faltering.

"I'm sure he did," Gabriel muttered. He mounted his horse. "Berok and Rodan are Midlands," he said, indicating his and Deuel's geldings. "They'll beat you up the 'Backs, and I don't like waiting for anyone."

"Not even a companion?" Rodigger asked, extended his hand to Deuel. Deuel ignored it and climbed onto his horse.

"Accomplice, perhaps," Gabriel replied, swinging Berok around. "Acquaintance, maybe. But Deuel and I choose our companions. Mount up, if you're going to follow."

The two friends cantered down the road and out into the countryside. Rodigger leapt onto his own horse and spurred after them, setting his chin grimly.

When he caught up to them, he stayed a a few lengths behind. Gabriel noted it: he could be called on if necessary, but they could still speak in private. He begrudgingly admired the tact. He called Rodigger forward.

"Sir?" Rodigger asked when his mount had approached nearer.

"Why does Roth fight this revolution?" Gabriel asked.

"To help the people," Rodigger answered promptly.

Gabriel and Deuel blinked at one another, and Deuel turned his head to the fields. "I assumed that much, Kytes," Gabriel answered with a thin smile. "I was not aware the people needed help."

"They do, sir," Rodigger replied. "I have heard Roth talk about it many times."

Gabriel sighed loudly. "Rodigger, before I allow you to return to your trailing position, would you mind telling me exactly what the problem is that Roth hopes to correct?"

Deuel turned to glance at Rodigger as his back straightened a little. "Sheppar does not want to protect the people," he said. "He does not want to be King, and takes on a debasing diminutive. He wants to hand his power over to city magistrates, and turn control of the countryside over to them."

"Sounds like good news to the city magistrates," Gabriel commented.

"But bad for the farmers," Rodigger countered. "The magistrates will be more concerned with city-folk than the farmers who also rely on the community to sustain their way of life. Their needs will be overlooked, and the heart of Andelen will suffer because of it."

"So why does Sheppar want to give over control?"

"Because he doesn't want to be King."

"Leave us alone, Rodigger," Gabriel said.

The young soldier opened his mouth in hurt retort, but closed it quickly and allowed his mount to drop back.

"He is trained well," Deuel commented when he was out of earshot.

"I doubt he resisted the training," Gabriel replied. "If he was trained well, he would have better answers, not the same answers repeated three times."

"Do you think he lies?"

"Not intentionally," Gabriel said, glancing back at Rodigger and pausing. "And most likely not entirely," he added. "Sheppar's reasons may be a mystery, but his actions are probably not. And we'll probably get the same answers as our young friend's until we are out of Kamdel-lan-controlled territory."

"Sprativerg, then?"

Gabriel nodded. "More than likely."

The night's snow did not stick, and diminished through the day. As the lowering sun set the grass afire, the travelers' shadows stretched for the fortified inn. The two mercenaries reached it first, Rodigger still trailing behind. By the time he caught up they had dismounted and were unlading their horses.

"You still carry those? Even here?" Rodigger asked as Deuel and Gabriel belted on sheathed daggers.

Gabriel gave him a swift glance, then nodded. "Oh, old habit. I forgot the paradise your benevolent Roth brought to the Fallonvall."

"I'm sorry," Rodigger said, smiling. "I just meant..."

"Forget it," Gabriel said. But he did not take the weapon off as he entered the inn with Deuel close behind him.

Rodigger shook his head, rubbing his Therian's muzzle. "I'll keep going if you do," he whispered. Gared tossed his head and shook it. Rodigger smiled. "Me neither."

Though it was a squat, unadorned building of thick round stone, the sun that washed its face invited Rodigger through the heavy wooden door and into the well-lit and primarily oak interior. With hundreds of these inns scattered across Andelen, they were not much different from one another. Rodigger enjoyed the game of trying to notice the little touches each keeper inevitably brought. In this one, stone columns rose from a wooden floor to support a wooden roof, though Rodigger knew more heavy stone lay above that. Broad antlers decorated the walls and columns, serving as sconces and candleholders. That was not rare, but not standard either. The common room was small, as there were never that many travelers this deep in the Fallonvall. A small archway led back to the cot-room. Across from the bar a fire roared beneath a leering goblin's head. As small as the skull was, it probably came from after Sheppar's almost entirely successful campaign.

Behind the bar was another door that would lead to the kitchens, and next to which sat the inn's keeper. He glanced up from a *feth*board as Rodigger entered, and before the young soldier could ask he jerked his head toward the back, and returned his attention to the game.

Rodigger carried his gear into the cot-room. Gabriel and Deuel had claimed two of the cots, and the great mound of another traveler had clearly claimed a third as he lay with his back to them at the far end of the room. Iron-banded chests sat at the foot of each bed, a key protruding from their locks—definitely standard. Rodigger moved to one across from his companions, checking the lock before opening the chest and placing his tack and bags inside. He pocketed the key and turned to Deuel and Gabriel.

"Who's he?" he whispered with a nod toward the sleeping figure.

Gabriel shook his head and shrugged. "He was like that when we came in. I'm sure he'll be joining us for dinner."

"Dinner?" called a voice, deep and rumbling as the figure turned over and picked up his shaggy head. "Already?"

Rodigger glanced at the face mostly of black hair, then back at his companions.

Gabriel spoke up. "Soon, I imagine. Sun's set."

The man blinked a few times, then smiled. "Of course: no windows. And those slits are little help, after dawn." He pushed himself upright, settling his stocking feet on the floor. "I kept thinking it was no darker in here than when I went to sleep." He rose to an enormous height. His brown rough-spun tunic and trousers must have cost two long-wool sheep apiece to make. He crossed the length of the room in four strides, a meaty hand swallowing Rodigger's whole, but gently, as Rodigger introduced himself.

"Keltan," he replied. He turned to the mercenary.

"I'd say you are. Gabriel."

Keltan laughed as he shook Deuel's hand last, though his mirth faltered a little as he looked the thin man up and down. "Mam tells everyone I was born this big, and she could think of nothing better to call me. Said I came out with this thing, too," he added, burying his hands in his beard with another chuckle.

"What brings you out here?" Gabriel asked.

"Lothan," Keltan said, nodding toward the main common room. "He's the best challenge I can find south of Sprativerg. I always stop in if I'm coming down this way."

"*Feth?*" Rodigger asked, trying to wipe the surprise from his face.

Keltan nodded, then gazed toward the archway. "Wonder if he's made a move yet."

"It looked like he was still studying when I came through," Rodigger said.

Keltan's eyes twinkled. "I left him in quite a bind. I suppose I should check on him."

The big man left. Gabriel shrugged and led them back to the common room. Keltan was looming over the bar, grinning in good-natured malevolence as Lothan's forehead still puckered over the board.

"Your guests want food, Lothan. Make your move."

"You're always in my light, Keltan," Lothan replied with a sharp glance.

Keltan gave a slow nod and a wink at the three companions. "Excuse me, Lothan. Curse of my birth." Long arms and fingers grasped four mugs and filled them from a small cask against the wall. Keltan nodded toward a table, gesturing with the mugs of ale.

Gabriel led the way, and the four sat down while Lothan pondered his next move.

"And what brings you three out this way?" Keltan asked.

"A job," Gabriel replied.

Rodigger coughed and spluttered into his mug. Keltan's hand came down against his back a few times, nearly bashing his teeth into the rim. "I'm alright," he said, holding up a hand to stop the blows. "Took a little too much foam, is all. Gabriel, do you think—?"

"I had you pegged as a soldier as soon as I rolled over," Keltan said. "And these two are not soldiers, but they can handle themselves: mercenaries?" Gabriel gazed hard at Rodigger, who returned to his mug. "You haven't been on the road long, which means you came from Akervet," Keltan continued. "Which means Roth and the rebellion."

"Revolution," Rodigger corrected automatically. "So why did you ask?"

Keltan laughed. "Because if you lied, the job was important. It's the moves that the player tries to make subtly that you have to pay the most attention to. Right Lothan?"

"Aha!" the keeper exulted. "Take that, you wily, elusive, unnoticeable Keltan."

The big man roared laughter and rose. "First I'm always in your light, then I'm unnoticeable. Next you'll tell me I'm only good in the kitchen."

"You are, at that," Lothan replied as he stood. "So I can count on your help, since your deviousness cost these travelers a timely dinner?"

Keltan glanced at the board, grinned, and gestured to door behind the bar. They exited, leaving the other three with only the sound of the rushing fire.

"Probably shouldn't question my methods again," Gabriel said, taking a drink.

"You told him the truth, but completely diverted him from more questions," Rodigger replied, shaking his head.

"Almost like I've done this before."

"I thought maybe you would think we were safe enough in the Fallon-vall, or that you didn't care much for the revolution..."

"Me?" Gabriel said with arched eyebrows. "Who still carries a dagger into a fortified inn? Feel safe?"

Rodigger shrugged and smiled.

"But as for your rebellion, you still haven't answered my question," Gabriel continued in lower tones. "Why should the Berkarfor, which were scattered ages ago, be gathered again?"

"Revolution. They were scattered for a reason," Rodigger replied in equally hushed tones, with frequent glances toward the kitchen. "What if that reason is past? What if the reason they were made in the first place has risen again? I actually like the symbolism: Andelians are scattered as well, and must be re-gathered. By gathering on this smaller scale, Roth will be given the power to gather on the larger scale."

"And if Roth's power should harden? If the goblets should need to be scattered again?" Gabriel asked.

"I know him," Rodigger replied. "His rule will be just, because he cares for the people of Andelen."

"I wonder if everyone would agree with you," Gabriel said softly.

"Why shouldn't they?"

"Because many people have died opposing the *revolution*, Rodigger. Those who survive them might not understand why."

If Rodigger caught the understatement, he did not show it.

⸺◆⸺

The road ran straight across the plains, giving the town toward which Catie rode its name: Arrow's Mark. Of course, time and use had eventually made it 'Aresmak'. Only older towns and cities kept their Old Rinc Nain names, like Akervet Brodlek—which, she had probably heard in Stramfath, translated literally to 'Field at Road's End'.

As the sun reached its height that afternoon, the horizon was jagged with the Dragonsback Mountains, but it was three more days before she reached their feet. There had been some travelers at the inns, heading to Akervet. But she mingled little, and they did not seem bothered by it. Roth had not taken her coin, blessedly. But every time she pulled out her purse she double-checked it, hoping for more coins lost in the folds.

There never was. She knew what was left would last her a little while, yet, but certainly not all the way home.

The road zig-zagged upward, peeping out here and there where the mountain leaned back, before finally crossing a low saddle. Kelsie plodded slowly, but steadily and predictably—she was a Midland, and had probably been born on a mountainside.

They crossed the first range by After-Noon. On the other side, Aresmak could be seen next to the Balnathva River below. Great fir trees marched up the mountain to greet travelers, sending out advance riders of juniper and sage. Calling out orders faintly behind them was the river itself, swollen here from its long journey through the length of the 'Back and now tripping headlong over a granite cascade. It seemed the noisiest place to put a village. But here the roads met, and where roads meet so do travelers. Travelers here just spoke a little louder.

She lay awake that night, listening to the sound of the river through her pillow and a few layers of blanket. She had asked for a room away from the river, but of course those were already full. With a deep breath she closed her eyes, and now saw again the strange orange light and the distant mewling sound. As she also thought of the feeling afterward, it seemed to stir up inside of her, though not as strong this time. She lay motionless, barely breathing, as something in her spirit willed her to leave Aresmak. But she could not discern what. It was not a feeling of danger, exactly. At least not mortal danger. But through her exhaustion, ideas of travel surfaced more readily and stayed with her longer than they should have. Her eyelids were shut like a portcullis, but her mind ran like a carnival.

Suddenly the feeling disappeared, and she knew nothing until the morning sun spilled into the room.

3

THINGS GAINED

"She will not run?"
"She may."
"But then...?"
"You look too far ahead, Teresh."

2 Mantaver 1320 — Winter

The Dragonsback Mountains loomed ahead of the three riders, the inn on the fourth night lost in their shadow as the sun rose the next morning. Before the sun could clear the peaks, they were on the road up through the first pass. Here Rodigger's Therian became a rockcrab, his hooves skittering and clattering against the stones. Rodigger fell into the motion more easily than his first several trips into the 'Back, but now his jaw set as his companions' horses plodded sure-footedly ahead of him, just as Gabriel said they would. Despite Gabriel's threat, they did wait at switchbacks and curves for him to catch up. Though all three labored in the sudden steeps, Rodigger's was the only one flecked with foam when they stopped at a natural plateau.

The road ran through a low saddle. On the other side it plunged straight into the valley—the mountain walls here were just gentle enough—and Aresmak could be seen slightly brown against the gray rock below. They descended, their path of rock fading below first sand, then into good earth where junipers took root, their winter skeletons rattling and whispering in the wind.

Rodigger knew Aresmak well. The revolution had spent a summer here last year before Roth decided to move west to Akervet, disliking how swiftly the river might bring boats of soldiers to his doorstep. The valley allowed some sheep-farming, and attendant textile production, but a lack of dyeing meant most of the village relied on the traders making their way up and down the peninsula. Small and secluded as it was, there was still much to be had in Aresmak, and Rodigger knew exactly where to find it.

Larens was busy with a customer when Rodigger walked in, so he made his way to another corner and glanced over some of the goods there. A collection of carpenter's tools caught his eye, their iron shafts and wooden handles polished and gleaming. He picked up a hammer, feeling the ash press into the heel of his thumb as his little finger balanced the other end, then swinging forward, the weight pitching against his index finger and catching against the outside of his palm. It was his weight, a hammer he could wield with precision.

"Can I help you—Rodigger!" Larens broke into a wide smile as Rodigger put the hammer down and faced him. The shopkeeper caught him in an embrace, then held him at arm's length. "Are you still growing?" he asked, gazing at the top of his head.

"I think you're shrinking, Larens," Rodigger replied, returning the glance with a smile.

"Hah." Larens waved a dismissing hand, and moved to a chair near the counter. "What brings you back here?" he asked as he eased himself into the chair with a short sigh.

"A job," Rodigger replied.

"And how is Roth? I wish he would come back here. He always has a home in Aresmak."

"He is well, and he knows that. But the river..."

Larens waved him off again. "Too swift," he said. "Any army would be dashed to pieces before they made it halfway from Thinneh. What's the job?"

"Do you remember the legend of the Goblets?"

A smile spread across Larens' face. "My Oldmother told me that story every time I asked. Twice a night, sometimes." The smile disappeared. "Why?"

"Roth thinks they were not just legends, and he sends me with two mercenaries to try and find them."

Larens shifted uncomfortably. "Rodigger, how is the revolution? Really? We haven't heard much lately, and the merchants from up north are certainly believers in Sheppar. Costs have never been so high. And if Roth is turning to this legend for some faint hope..."

"We'll find out in a few weeks, Larens," Rodigger said gently. "The first is supposed to be around Agirbirt. If we can't find it, then the stories he found are just taking the legend too seriously. That's not what I worry about."

"Oh? What do you worry about?"

Rodigger scrubbed his scalp. "A lot of things: some big, and some small ones. The mercenary I'm traveling with, he mentioned something about not everyone understanding why so many have died during the revolution. And, since then...I don't know. I can't help but think he might have agreed to this job just to make sure it fails."

Larens scratched his chin as he studied Rodigger. "What's his name?"

"Gabriel," Rodigger replied. "Gabriel Owens."

Larens' head bobbed. "I know of Gabriel. He served under Sheppar in the last part of the Beast Campaign."

"And that's supposed to make me feel better?" Rodigger exclaimed. "I didn't realize he was that old."

"He served him young. And he's done much since then, for anyone who would hire him. Mercenaries are the same everywhere. They work for money, not anyone or anything else."

"I hope so," Rodigger said. He put his hands on his hips. "It figures Sheppar would allow someone young to serve his ends."

Larens shrugged. "We know that. The trick is getting the rest of the country to see it."

"Don't remind me," Rodigger muttered with a grin.

Larens cocked his head. "Remind you?"

Rodigger took a deep breath. "The other reason I'm going along is to try to get people to believe in the mission of the revolution, so when we finally do break out of the Fallonvall, we'll have some support already." He sighed. "But now, with what I've seen of Gabriel and what you've told me, I think I'm going to have to work for his and Deuel's support first."

Larens' fingers twitched, but he smiled. "Well, you still have some time to work on them while you're in the Fallonvall," he said, then cleared his throat. "You might also start with some of these traders. They've convinced too many of Aresmak to abandon their Andelian traditions and buy from them this Starfall."

Rodigger cast him a condescending glance. "Larens, Starfall is not Andelian, you know that. It's left over from our Rinc Nain oppression, and should have been cast off after we won our freedom centuries ago."

"Oh, you're right, you're right," Larens said, his head bobbing in time. "Perhaps these old bones just wish for some rest."

Rodigger smiled, too, though he thought sadly that rest would not come till he ruled the *feth*board over his companions.

⊰◈⊱

Gabriel also knew Aresmak well, though the goods he sought were not traded for money. At least, not usually.

"Good morning, Eidemon," he said, sitting next to a man whose Rinc Nain eyebrows were beginning to whiten. His hair similarly carried a few struggling braids, though the rest was better kept than Gabriel's. Thick wolf pelts padded a thin frame, and mittens hung from strings to allow gnarled fingers to strip chunks of meat from the goat leg in front of him.

Eidemon took a drink, then glanced sideways at Gabriel. "Hello," he said in a deep, quiet voice. His eyes continued toward the door, then around the room. "No *skalderon?*" he asked.

"He's enjoying the wilderness."

Eidemon grunted. "I bet." He chewed through a few more chunks as Gabriel retrieved a mug of ale for himself. "What brings you here?" he asked.

"What always brings me here?"

Eidemon shook his head, drank, then gazed directly at Gabriel. "Remember when this made a difference, what we said to each other?"

"The world has grown safer, Eid."

"Tell that to the wolves," he replied. "Sheppar forgot to tell everyone what was a dangerous beast and what was natural predators."

"You seem to have figured it out," Gabriel replied, raising an eyebrow at his friend's attire.

"All from wolves I found killed and left to rot," he replied, returning to his plate. "So who is it this time?"

"Roth."

Eidemon's teeth stopped halfway through tearing another morsel as his eyes leapt to Gabriel's. He bit down slowly, and chewed even slower. "Is it that bad?" he asked.

Gabriel took a drink, gazing at nothing behind the bar. He saw the fires of Bokessin, the ruined houses, his wife inside to whom he swore he would never leave... Then he saw the cold winter in Balnath Agrend, the apple he was so tempted to steal, the ghost he followed to Balnath's cemetery, Deuel waiting for him when he returned home, and a messenger from Akervet. He took another drink, and pulled on his lower lip. "Yep."

Eidemon sat back and finished his mug in four long pulls. When it *thunked* back to the table, he looked at Gabriel. "Someone was speaking against Roth, last night," he said. "Badly drunk, I heard. They're maybe a day ahead of you, and not happy about it. So be careful."

"Who?"

"I saw a hood, and heard a voice. I came in late, and he left quickly."

"What kind of hood?"

"A green one, from underneath well-fitting brown deerskin. He looked quick, and quiet." He cast a sideways glance at Gabriel. "Like you, thirty years ago."

"Thanks," Gabriel replied drily. He finished his own drink and dropped a coin next to the empty mug. "See you around."

She rode through fields littered with herds of sheep that morning, giving way to three separate convoys headed deeper into the continent. She had not been this far north since she was going the opposite way two and a half years ago.

After Sprativerg. After meeting Dannid.

Sprativerg was a city full of ideas, so it had surprised her when Dannid wanted to leave. He had said something angrily about being a man of action as well, didn't she know? And he had almost left her there. Now she was not too sure of returning, even to pass through on her way home.

But that was some time away. Her next full stop was Thinneh, high up on a cliff overlooking the valley. As she counted out her coins that night to the innkeeper, she knew it would be more than her usual stop: she would not be continuing past Thinneh until she had some money to get the rest of the way home. The inns between here and there would not charge much—during Sheppar's campaign, he had forbidden it, and came down hard on any keeper who disobeyed. It became a habit they now found hard to break. But lodging was never free.

Eight long days later, she arrived—hungry, for she had not the coin to eat at the last inn, and no food grew in the wilds. As she walked through streets that had changed little from the past, she began to remember bits of what she and Dannid had spoken of on the way south. It seemed he knew a lot about villages and towns, at least in some abstract ways.

In Thinneh, there were vendors stalls everywhere. It was the first town that was both large enough to accommodate longer stays of merchants bringing goods from Burieng, and was not so near a thundering river that every traveler wanted to be on their way as soon as possible. And it was high up on a ridge, so there was little fishing to be done, and no pastures. So the only way Thinneh survived was by convincing those merchants to stay, and offer their goods there to sell. The sale was everything. And Catie had no means to purchase anything.

She stopped in front of an inn. Dusk was settling, and a general clamor inside the inn punctuated as someone went through the door before her. The door closed as she tied up Kelsie, and she followed the patron into the storm.

The tables were nearly all full. Four serving girls were kept busy among patrons ranging from warmly-dressed tradesmen to men whose bulk owed to a life cutting trees, to others—men, mostly, but also a few women—with oiled boots and lower garments spun thicker than upper garments: fishers, if they dressed anything like fishers from Catie's hometown. A few she thought she recognized from the last inn, closer to the water.

Along the wall to Catie's left was a bar, equally full, and one bartender who—at the moment—was not busy. Catie approached, wedging herself between two men whose eyes darted to her, then down and back up. She ignored their grins and got the bartender's attention.

"What can I get you?"

"Is the owner here?" Catie asked.

The two men beside her chuckled as the bartender gazed at her. "No," he said finally. "I left a while ago, and haven't come back yet."

The two men laughed, which she also ignored. "Do you have anyone to sing or play music tonight?" she asked.

"They seem to be staying for the beer," he replied. "And it couldn't get much fuller in here."

Catie turned to glance at the room just as three younger men, tradesmen by the look of them, shuffled past and went out into the night. She watched them go, then turned back. "I guess they didn't get any beer," she said.

"What's your name?" he asked, now the center of attention instead of her.

"Catie."

"I'm Farris," he said. "You do what you want. And if people are staying, you can too."

She paused. "Do you have a Tamis flute?" she asked. Farris stared at her, and she waved him off. "I'll figure it out." She picked her way across the room to the corner the tradesmen had just emptied. She sat down on the table, her feet on the bench, her hands on her legs. She glanced at Farris, who was still watching, then down as she tried to think of an appropriate song.

Her hands started tapping on her legs. The nearest patrons glanced over, their eyes narrowing as they saw she was not sitting like the rest of them. The beat that her fingers found on their own finally reminded her of a song, and as she drummed with greater purpose she began to sing.

It had the lyrical simplicity of a child's song, but that was why she liked it. Her voice did not travel far in the din, but enough that those who heard stopped talking. The silence spread, and more eyes turned from their food and drink to her.

As she finished the first song, another came immediately to mind. Pausing only to swallow, she launched into it. A livelier song, and the people near her began to drum their hands against the table. The lyrics to this one were also simple, and soon they sang along with her.

When she came to the line: "And for all, my lads, drink up!" someone actually handed her a glass. She paused quickly to drink, then hoisted the cup with a smile as the room laughed. She got up onto the table and began a simple dance as she sang. That line repeated often in the shanty, and each time she sang it the room lifted their mugs and drank. By the time the song was over, everyone needed their mugs refilled, and when Catie caught Farris's eye he nodded.

After three more songs, Catie paused and looked around the room with a finger on her lips in thought. "Long ago, deep in the Brithelt Forest," she began. She eyed the patrons as they sat up, curious. "There lived a master craftsman—a blacksmith and whittler named Karan Tamis. Many of the days he worked in an open forge amid the trees, and shafts of sunlight filled the woods. And keeping almost a protective ring around Karan were birds of every sort and color, and they used to sing to him as he worked the bellows, or when he rested.

"But one day a terrible storm tore through the forest where he worked, stripping trees of their boughs and leaving no loft from which the birds could sing. Karan carried on his work as best he could, but soon he could no longer, so much he missed the warbles and wheeps that sang to soften the strike of his hammer. He wept long, and hard he wished for a way to honor his lost friends, and to draw them back, to fill the forest again with their song.

"So Karan laid down his hammer and quenched his forge, and picked up instead his carving knife. And from the shattered remnants of the boughs he began to fashion a peculiar flute—one which played not only quiet notes, or shrill notes, but both equally, as the piper willed.

"When I was a child, my Grandmother taught me to play this Tamis flute. I would like to play it for you now, that the Brithelt Forest full of birds may enter this distant inn."

When she finished, she inclined her head to their applause. She looked up, and smiled hesitantly. "Um, does anyone have a Tamis flute?" She laughed at the absurdity. The room laughed too, and all the harder as a young boy stood up and held one triumphantly aloft. She thanked the boy as she sat back down onto the table, taking a few drinks as she allowed her pulse to slow. When everyone was settled from their latest rounds ordered, she began to play.

Her voice had been enough to keep patrons seated. As she played the flute, it brought them in from outside. Farris' smile—wide already at the evening his inn was having—grew wider as more and more beer flowed from his barrels.

By the end of the evening, though she was still starving, she was warm and full of joy as the patrons enjoyed her singing and playing. They had been a good crowd, humming and drumming and singing along and laughing. When Farris showed her the room for the night he handed her a bag of coin.

"They left this for you," he said. "At least, this is what's left of what they left for you—I gave you the opportunity, after all. I'll have Mareth bring you some food." He turned to go, then paused. "Will you stay long, here?" he asked, innocently enough.

Catie hefted the bag and smiled. "Maybe just one more night. Although you'll have to ask that young man if I can borrow his flute again."

"Oh, I forgot." Farris smiled and reached inside his shirt to pull out the flute she had played. "He left it for you. Said he hated learning it, but loved hearing you play."

"Oh," Catie said, taking the Tamis from him. "I loved playing it," was all she could think to say—but it was true.

Word had apparently spread, and the room was full next evening when she finally came down to begin. She did much as she had the first night, with a few newer songs that she had remembered. She told the same story, this time being able to pull the flute out straight away when the story was over.

By the end of the evening, she had earned almost double what she had made the night before—more than enough to make it home.

"Well," Farris said when she told him, "I'm sorry to see you go. If you wanted to, you could certainly stay on here."

"I know," Catie said. "And I might be fine with that, if things were different. But I need to go back home."

"You wouldn't have to work as hard as you have," Farris said quickly as she turned away. He snatched at her arm to keep her from leaving. "We would make a good partnership, you and me," he continued, his grip softening until only his fingers rested against the back of her arm. "You could make a good life here."

"Farris," she said gently, "you were kind to give me the chance to earn my way. That has not earned you the right to touch me like that." As she said it, and without thinking too hard, the feeling in her heart...*pushed.*

Had he not been gazing into her eyes, he might not have dropped his hand so quickly. "I'm sorry," he said, flexing his fingers. "You're right; I..." He trailed off, then turned quickly and left.

As she shut the door, Catie drew a long sigh. What was it she did? It had not been her words—it never was. And it was a conscious thing, though she sometimes did it without thinking. Whatever 'it' was. It felt as though she projected her emotions tangibly, making them into something physical. Something a person *had* to react to, the same as stepping around an obstacle in their path. It wasn't just rejection, as it had just been with Farris. She could make people love her, pity her, even fear her. If she felt the emotion strongly enough and pushed it outward—that was the only way she could think to describe it—and the person was looking in her eyes, it seemed they felt it too, as if it were their own.

She shook her head, and pulled off her outer garments. She didn't like the ability in the abstract. But when it was useful, she was glad to have it.

She blew out two candles that sat on the desk, then turned to the lantern beside her bed. She gazed at it, blinking as strange dread came to her mind. Was she afraid of the dark now? And yet, her hand shook as she trimmed the wick. She blew out the flame, sinking the room into complete darkness.

Fear slammed into her gut, and she nearly knocked over the lantern in her haste to relight it. But she stopped, the taper near the wick as her mind revolted at the idea of striking too bright a light. She blinked in the darkness. What was *this,* now? It shrank a little as she considered it, but did not go away. A worry? It felt almost familiar, like when she had heard the rebellion was nearing Bokessin.

She blinked a few more times. It was *very* much like that. So, not worry: dread. But not, she thought, like when Roth's soldiers came and took

Dannid. It was not that immediate.

She lowered the trembling taper, put it back in its stand. Why ever she felt this, it was not immediate. But it was approaching, and may be immediate by morning.

Faint moonlight streamed through the clouds and into her room, enough to see her clothes, and she dressed again purposefully. Did this terror approach from the north, where she needed to go? Or did it come from where she had been? It was impossible to tell. Perhaps the night would be dark enough that it wouldn't matter.

Her father—and her own curiosity, after he had died—taught her to survive without soft beds and sturdy roofs. She only needed to get outside Thinneh. Nothing should follow her. Everyone traveled during the day.

Unless this was some strange return of the creatures Sheppar had wiped out. Many people thought they would. A few even thought that they should.

Catie exited the room. The inn was dark, and no light from the common room warmed the wooden staircase. If such a thing occurred as all the creatures returning—what, from the dead?—it made sense it would begin with some strange orange light in the night sky and a faint keening sound.

So much was possible, but very little was practical. She blunted the fear by focusing on her escape.

Kelsie was already looking toward the door when Catie entered the stables, tossing her head without vocalizing her impatience. Catie cocked an eyebrow at her mare's prescience.

As silently as possible, she saddled Kelsie and led her outside. Catie had not yet decided to turn north, though it was the way she needed to go anyway, but as soon as her right foot was in the stirrup Kelsie was off without being prompted.

The fear drained from Catie's gut as they reached the edge of town and began down the long path to the valley below. The sky had cleared, and Kelsie was in her element. With nothing else to do, Catie rested in the saddle, letting the road pass beneath her.

4

LOSING FAITH

"I feel like I'm doing nothing."
"You are."
"And I feel like I should be doing something."
"When she arrives at the inn..."

11 Mantaver 1320 — Winter

As the mercenaries approached Thinneh the road climbed away from the river as the valley ahead became a narrow canyon. Countless switchbacks carried them across the face of the mountains and up. At each turn, Gabriel and Deuel waited while Rodigger's Therian struggled again on the rocky slopes. Dusk came and went before the road crested the pass, where a dozen of the lonely huts they had passed on their way up gathered for the warmth, if not the fellowship, of Thinneh.

At the sparsely filled inn, though it doubled as the village tavern, groups of two or three sat silently apart, and many of the tables nearest the fires were empty. As they drank their own ales, Rodigger considered the various patrons. Those men with bits of sawdust still trapped in the hair of their forearms were carpenters. A little further away, they all had oiled boots—fishermen. Still another group, further from the fire, had heavy traveling coats and thick fur hats—traders.

He had been as far north as Thinneh once, delivering a message when this was the front of the revolution. He still recognized some of the men, but despite how small the village was, most were unfamiliar.

As he thought about it, he still could not understand why Thinneh did not support the mission of the revolution. If Roth's vision were mirrored here, these men would all be around the same table, sharing stories, food, and drink. The inn would be alive with music and laughter. There would not be cringing and glancing around with deep frowns when a mug hit the table a little harder. No, this—this was what Sheppar wanted: islands, self-sufficient and selfish. Perhaps the revolution should revisit some of the towns and villages.

But here he was: he *was* the revolution, wasn't he? He was certainly supposed to be, once they went north of Vatenhal. Could he practice here? Should he?

One of the fishermen was glaring at him. Before he could think he smiled and raised his mug in salute. The man's frown deepened, and he returned to his mug. Rodigger's fist tightened on the handle of his ale.

"Are we not both Andelian?" he muttered.

Gabriel and Deuel glanced up, then turned to follow Rodigger's gaze.

"Do you know him?" Gabriel asked, his voice low but clear.

"Your answer lies in the answer to my first question," Rodigger replied.

"I don't understand," Gabriel said. Deuel's eyes glittered as his gaze pried into Rodigger's mind.

"This is exactly what the revolution is about, Gabriel," Rodigger said, gesturing around the room. "Look at these men. Feel this silence. A far cry from Keltan, isn't it? That inn was noisier than this with a third of the patrons. And why are they separated and quiet?" He gestured around again. "Carpenters, fishermen, traders—they see themselves separately, instead of all Andelian."

"People come and go in Thinneh," Gabriel said. "It's a lot easier when you have time to get to know someone."

"But that's why we need to build that commonality, and spread it across all Andelen," Rodigger said, pointing hard at Gabriel. "Then it won't matter where you come from. Everyone you meet will share at least one thing, or even ten things, regardless of their daily life."

"And how do you do that?" Gabriel asked, his hands spread. Deuel sat back, his interest seemingly lost. Rodigger tried to ignore it.

"Traditions," he said.

Gabriel scoffed. "Now you sound like a Cariste, celebrating every full moon."

Rodigger scoffed too. "What does that celebrate? Full moons? All the world has full moons. We need celebrations that honor Andelians, and the work they do. Celebrate fishermen," he said with a nod at their table. "The carpenters, the traders." His gaze lingered on Gabriel a few moments. "The mercenaries. We should honor and remember one another. And we should look to Andelen's history for those traditions, *after* we won our freedom from Rinc Na."

"So which traditions should we practice?" Gabriel asked. "You tell me which ones."

Those words went in Rodigger's ears and swelled in his throat. He swallowed, but it stuck. Roth had never talked about which particular

Andelian traditions. He had denounced many, but as Rodigger's mind buzzed with the silence in his ears, he could not remember Roth advocating any.

"Look to your history books," he said, with as best he could muster of Roth's mix of authority and derision. But his voice began to fall away. "Ask your...father, and mother." Something Rodigger had vowed never to do again. "We are all Andelian," he muttered again. His gaze fell to his mug of ale.

"Well my mother and father aren't here," Gabriel said. "Or my history books." Deuel gave the mercenary a glance, and Gabriel gave a short sigh. "Fine. Maybe when we get to Stramfath. You can look it up and let me know." Gabriel gazed at Rodigger for a few moments from underneath his eyebrows, then returned to his drink.

Silence remained the most present guest. Rodigger glanced sideways. A few tables away a young man sat with a group of men who appeared to be his father and father's friends. The young man drew a deep sigh and spoke something. The men around him glanced at him, and their mood seemed to darken. Rodigger returned his gaze to his drink. What had the young man said? *I miss the Tamis flute.* Rodigger wondered if Gabriel would know what that meant. But a swift glance that only made it halfway to the mercenary's face was all he allowed himself.

⸺◆⸺

Though it was cold, the nights were also shorter. Now she should have time to reach the next inn at least a Shift before daybreak—enough time, with a horse that could guide itself, to nap before striking out again at daylight. Whatever was behind her, if it took only one day in Thinneh, would still be a day behind her.

She did not think about how to escape it completely, because she did not know enough about it. It might not even be after her. "It," she muttered. Kelsie's head continued to bob ahead of her. "Talking about my feelings like they're something real." Her mare tossed her head once and squealed. Catie cocked her head, considering. "Don't even pretend you can understand me," she said. "Then I'll really think I've gone..." She cut off as her mare turned a considering eye upon her for several moments. "Fine. Shall we give my fear a name? Pob? How about Pob? Or Vorbet? I never did like Vorbet, he always looked at me...well, too long for a man his age—back to ignoring me, then?"

A waxing moon allowed her to see more clearly, and let her remember the steep road as it switched back and forth. Far below, near the river, the moon gleamed off block walls. It seemed close enough she should reach it by Mid-Night. But then the road crooked, and for the next leg the inn moved further and further away behind her. When they turned again, it felt even further away.

Somehow they reached the door as the sky above the eastern slopes turned indigo, and the weakest of stars began to fade. Smoke curled from the chimney in streams too thick for a fire banked for the night. The keeper was awake.

The stable in back was empty. She loosened the saddle's girth only a little. They wouldn't be staying long, and she could ease Kelsie of the tack once they were further down the road. She left her with soft apologies and oats, and went inside. The keeper—a man barely older than she in shirt and breeches that shined in the firelight—looked up with a confused smile when she entered.

"You're not here the normal time," he said, though he rose in preparation for her request.

"Um, you're right," she said. She hadn't thought of a way to explain that. She was still deep in the peninsula, wasn't she? "Message from Roth for the front lines, and he wants it there quickly. I'll only be here a few hours. Do you have anything prepared?"

"Some fish," was the reply. "Trout, actually, pulled from the Balnathva yestereve."

Trout was all she had in Thinneh, just about. "Perhaps just a few rolls?" she asked hopefully.

The young man was looking at her intently, while trying to seem like he wasn't. "It's really good fish," he said.

Be careful.

Catie smiled. "Why not?" she said. "As fresh as that—and I'm sure you can prepare it just right. Living this close to the river you probably make fish all the time."

His smile was broad. "Oh, all the time," he echoed. "I'll run to the back and fetch some for you."

He exited into the kitchens. Catie paused only briefly to look at the fire: it would have been nice to warm herself for a few minutes, at least.

Instead she tiptoed out, then ran to Kelsie. She knew she should be angry or at least shocked, but maybe she was too tired. Maybe she was over-reacting. But when she saw her mare again she knew she wasn't. If only he hadn't been so keen on feeding her fish. And trout, no less! He could probably put ten thimbles of sleeping draught in that dish and she wouldn't taste it until she woke up half a day later, at best with a lighter purse, at worst... And with the aftertaste stuck in her teeth for days.

"What a twerp," she said to Kelsie, who only blinked at her. "We won't go far," she promised. "There's sure to be some secluded spot along the river to sleep. After that we'll talk about having strange thoughts pop suddenly into my head." *What next?*

Yet, when Catie mounted, her usually-spirited mount only plodded away from the inn into a light snow that was drifting through the valley.

The weather continued against them. The wind soon howled between the mountains and swirled in among the only rocky nook they could find to build camp, icy off the waters that cascaded through there. Catie managed a small fire, and shared as much of her blanket as she could with the mare lying dutifully beside her. But it was small comfort.

Catie wondered if the—Vorbet—coming behind her would stay at that inn. Of course he would. But she wondered if he might fall prey to a trap she only avoided because of Dannid. Whatever people might say about those who think the world is after them, sometimes fear kept you safe if tempered a little.

The sky brightened as Catie's eyelids grew heavy despite the wind and the cold. "At some point, I'm going to have to try to see what's following me," she said to Kelsie, who nickered shortly. "I can't keep thinking of it as Vorbet. And what if he's more than one?"

Then, her fear might be warranted. She would not stand against two or three. At least, not in a fair fight.

Despite the cold, she finally fell asleep, waking again as the sun reached its zenith and shone over her sheltering rock and into her eyes. She laded Kelsie quickly, with only a few glances up the mountain to see if she could spot anyone following her. She thought maybe she saw a flash of green behind her. Surely Vorbet—she rolled her eyes—was not that close? Closer than when she was in Thinneh, but without the sense of dread?

After several moments of wind and rushing river, but no further glimpse of movement, she shook her head. Early sign of spring, perhaps, but now lost among the rocks. She turned body and horse northward, and rode.

<hr />

As they rounded a switchback, Deuel suddenly pointed below. "There," he said to Gabriel. "A rider with a green hood."

"What about him?" Rodigger asked, his voice still shattered of confidence.

"He was speaking against the revolution, some time ago," Gabriel replied with a sideways glance. "How far ahead, Deuel?"

"Too far. We might catch up to him in Getakenner, but not find him."

"Outside it though? Still in the 'Back?"

Deuel glanced at Rodigger, then Rodigger's horse. "Probably not."

Gabriel frowned. "Oh, right. Well, hopefully north of Getakenner then, at one of the inns."

They rode without speaking, though Rodigger's thoughts whirled. Gabriel had reminded him of some hope last night: Stramfath, one of the towns Roth wanted most to reach. At the head of Lake Agirbirt, it had managed to collect more books and schools of learning than anywhere else in Andelen. If Stramfath could be turned to the revolution, there would be no stopping Roth's march. His ideas and beliefs would spread to every corner of the country with the power of the scholars of

Stramfath.

But Sprativerg still lay between them and the Agirbirt, and Roth would also desperately want that city, for its trade if nothing else. The loss of Sprativerg would be staggering to Sheppar, forcing trade from Burieng north to Ostflir, and clogging the road west of Ostflir to Balnath Agrend.

But Sprativerg was massive, a tree centuries old and broad as a house that would tempt Rodigger to carve a palace for Roth. But to attempt the carving would take his entire life and remain forever unfinished, while hundreds of Andelians would suffer in the cold because he distracted himself from the simpler homes he could build instead. No, Sprativerg would be for the older, wiser, and swifter wood-smiths. But perhaps Rodigger could still make some initial markings. Until he could study in Stramfath, they would be the merest of scratches, and might be mistaken later for woodgrains—

Oh, what was the use. Gabriel and Deuel rode ahead, again, horses close and voices low. Rodigger let Gared drop a little further back. In two weeks of traveling, he could not even convince his companions of Roth's way of thinking. What could he hope to accomplish when they spent only one night at any one place? What could Roth have hoped for him to achieve?

"So, Rodigger," Gabriel said as they tied their horses at the inn on the valley floor that night. "These inns are a Rinc Nain tradition as well. Should we get rid of them?"

"They are not tools of oppression," Rodigger replied absently, his gaze on the light spilling over the far mountain and sparkling in the waters. A shadow was growing from the foot of the mountains, darkening the turbid river and creeping ever nearer as the sun sank.

"Isn't any tradition forced on a nation oppressive?" They entered the inn as a cluster, Gabriel trying to watch Rodigger as he spoke, Rodigger with his eyes on the ground and only trying to move forward, and Deuel trapped somewhere in the middle.

"Only when that tradition has nothing to do with the nation."

"I think people are more individual than you think," Gabriel said as they continued into the cot-room. They each put their effects in the chests. "I don't think you can make everyone—what did you say? Honor everyone else? Why should the farmers around Akervet honor the fishers of Thinneh? They'll never deal with them."

"We've traveled," Rodigger replied. "Why shouldn't they?"

"Maybe they should. But they don't."

"Then it will be good for them not to forget they aren't the only ones in the world. Can we eat? I'm hungry."

"They're going to forget why they follow the traditions," Gabriel said, leading them back out into the common room. "Two or three generations, and they'll be following an Andelian tradition with the same attitude they follow Rinc Nain traditions."

"What's wrong with Rinc Nain traditions?" the keeper asked, approaching as they sat down.

Rodigger's shoulders drooped, but he kept quiet.

Gabriel glanced at the keeper and smiled. "They're oppressive. Your best dinner, please."

"I remember that rebellion leader coming through here," the keeper said, taking Gabriel's proffered coin. "He thought the entertainment he provided should have covered his stay."

Rodigger's head sank lower as Gabriel cocked an eyebrow.

"Entertainment?" he asked.

"All my guests that night thought he was hilarious. They stayed eating and drinking for hours listening to him."

Gabriel grinned broadly as Rodigger's head finally came to rest on his crossed arms.

"I had never heard that story," Gabriel said. Another coin appeared in his fingers. "We're also looking for a friend, in deerskin and a green hood."

The keeper took the coin. "No one has been through here in two days," he said.

Gabriel's smile disappeared. "Then give that back!" he said. Rodigger's head came up as the keeper glanced over the three of them.

"That's still information, isn't it?" he asked, turning swiftly toward the kitchens.

Gabriel's mouth gaped until Deuel shrugged. Gabriel shrugged too. "I guess it is. Why would he avoid the inn though? We saw him this morning too far ahead to not have stopped around here for the night."

"I don't like this," Rodigger said, crossing his arms a little tighter. "He acts like a spy, or worse."

"Perhaps his coin was low," Gabriel said, casting a glare toward the kitchen door. "Or perhaps he knew something about this inn that we don't."

"Like what?" Rodigger asked.

"Like why no one has been through here in two days," Deuel said. "This might not have been his first time down this road."

"Well, didn't you stop here before?" Rodigger asked.

Gabriel shook his head quickly. "We did, but it was packed that night, at least ten other guests. Probably too full to try anything."

"Should we move on?" Rodigger whispered. "Find somewhere else to stay?"

Gabriel shook his head again, slower. "Too late now, probably."

"He might also be pursuing something else," Deuel murmured.

"Well, as long as it's not us," Rodigger said.

The windows were black, candlelight glaring off the obsidian panes. The door to the kitchens opened and the keeper approached, three plates steaming with fish and assorted boiled vegetables.

"Here we are," the keeper announced, setting the plates before them.

"And let me refill your mugs, as well." He quickly retrieved a jug, topping off the mugs with foaming ale. "Let me know if you need anything else."

Deuel raised his mug and sniffed it, then tasted it gently. His eyes took on a faraway look, then he shook his head. "It's fine."

Rodigger breathed a sigh of relief, and started on his food. He was not lying when he had said he was hungry. It had been a short day, true, but they had eaten while riding, and just a few rinds of cheese and crusts of bread. This fish was cooked to perfection, and the vegetables seasoned expertly. It was the best meal Rodigger remembered since leaving Akervet.

"Don't eat the fish," Deuel said, scraping the piece off his fork and moving on to the vegetables.

Rodigger choked on a chunk of filet already crawling down his throat, trying in vain to cough it back up.

"Is it poison?" he whispered hoarsely. Gabriel and Deuel regarded him solemnly.

"Why didn't you wait till Deuel had tried all of it?"

"How was I supposed to know?" Rodigger said. "He had tried the ale, that's the easiest thing to poison. How do you know it's in the fish?"

"Deuel has been eating foods for a long time, Rodigger. He knows when something is wrong."

"Well I've been eating all my life, too. But what's in it? Am I going to die?"

Gabriel smiled. "Rod, you're, what, nineteen? Deuel's been eating for hu-aaa—a lot longer than that."

"What's in it!" Rodigger grated, pounding a fist against the table.

"Is everything all right, gentlemen?" the keeper asked, looking over in concern.

"Fine," Gabriel replied as Rodigger's eyes bulged. "Our friend just cut his tongue on his knife."

"It's a sleeping agent," Deuel whispered.

Rodigger glared at them, then pinched his tongue with thumb and forefinger and managed a rueful shake of his head for the keeper's benefit.

"I hate the boaf of you, wight now," he muttered, then glared at his fingers and wiped them on his pants. "What do we do with the fish? He'll know if we don't eat it, and he might try something more drastic."

Gabriel snorted. "I'm not sure it's his style. There's probably only enough to make you sleep through the night, and soundly enough for him to take your key and some of your gold."

"When we're the only ones here?"

Gabriel shrugged. "How often have we checked our bags after staying at an inn? No one does, because everyone keeps their things locked safely at the foot of their bed."

"Surely someone would have noticed eventually."

"When? After a day? Two days? They'll have traveled through two other inns by then, if they even suspect a..." Gabriel cast a quick glance at their keeper, who occupied himself with a book.

"Deuel," Gabriel said, flicking his eyes toward the man. Deuel's eyes slid to him a moment, then back.

"His eyes aren't moving. He's not reading."

"Finish your fish, Rodigger," Gabriel said. "You've already started, and he probably noticed how quickly you went after it. You can't say you're just not hungry anymore."

"And what if there's more than Deuel suspects in here?"

As one, they replied: "There isn't."

"Oh," Rodigger said, brightening sarcastically. Hesitantly, but finally, he began picking at the fish again. "What about you two?" he asked around the mouthful suddenly too dry but to chew it a hundred times.

"Oh, I'm not that hungry," Gabriel replied. "Neither is Deuel. We'll probably just pick at it, really."

Rodigger glared, helpless, bolting the fish down with two slugs of ale. True to his word, Gabriel and Deuel did eat some of their fish. The keeper showed no surprise as he cleared their plates, only smiled and asked if they enjoyed it and if Rodigger's tongue was not cut too badly. They went to their cots assuring Rodigger that Deuel would be able to keep watch.

Even as he smiled hollowly at them, he plunged headfirst into darkness.

⸺◈⸺

He awoke as someone cried out. His eyes opened sluggishly, and the blear was hesitant to follow. There came a slap, another cry, and faint light flickering against the wooden ceiling. Voices muttered, one calm, the other under duress. Rodigger blinked and stretched his jaw. The voices became clearer.

"This is no way to run a respectable inn, Lindo," Gabriel's voice said. "So tell us the truth: you've seen the green-hooded traveler at some point, haven't you?"

Another slap, and cry, and some babbling. Rodigger turned his head, but the bunks beside him were empty. Finally, with effort, he raised his head.

Gabriel and Deuel had the keeper—Lindo, apparently—tied in a chair against the wall. His face was red, but his eyes were still defiant and his lips were pressed into a thin line. Rodigger tried to lever himself into a sitting position, and it was not until Deuel glanced sharply at him that he realized he was groaning.

Gabriel glanced at him, too, then came and helped him sit up while Lindo glared on. "Are you okay?" the mercenary asked.

Rodigger blinked, then felt his head going up and down. He sensed the wool blanket against his feet and hands. They had taken off his boots but he had still slept otherwise fully clothed. The glow from a nearby torch warmed him a little—at least he could feel the bloom of heat against his cheek. His tongue rolled in his mouth like his mother's ball of dough in a mixing bowl when it needed flouring. And the room smelled wretched, as if someone sicked up and let it harden.

"Did we catch him?" Rodigger mumbled.

"No!" the keeper shot out. "I came in to check and make sure my guests were sleeping soundly when this panther leapt upon me." He drew in a long sniffle, glancing warily at Deuel, who folded his arms. "S'not natural," he muttered, then turned his hard gaze back upon Gabriel.

Nothing about him is natural, Rodigger thought. *He even wears that silly thick cloak in the middle of the night.*

"And do you commonly drug your guests?" Gabriel asked quietly.

Lindo looked truly hurt. "My duty is to give my guests a quiet night's rest. I try to aid them in that, and they assault me in the darkness."

"A quiet night's rest," Gabriel repeated slowly. "And a lighter load for the next day's journey?"

"Did I?" he asked, looking at Gabriel a little too keenly. Gabriel's glance and Deuel's sigh answered enough: they had not caught him in the act of thievery. His gaze lowered. "Exactly. Now untie me before I complain to Roth's soldiers. He'll do you up right."

"Oh, he already did," Rodigger muttered, rubbing his eyes and nearly falling backward in the process. "He sent me with these two."

Lindo swallowed, but said nothing. With a sigh, Gabriel rose and untied the man. "We require your attention no longer," he said lightly. "No need to check on us further."

"I wouldn't think of it," Lindo replied, glaring at Deuel. The thin man uncrossed his arms, and the keeper scuttled out of the cot room.

"Sorry you woke for that, Rodigger," Gabriel said, capping the torch to extinguish it. "Good night."

Rodigger fell backward, knocking his head a little against the stone wall, and slept till the sun shone against the western mountains.

———◆———

"I still want to report him in Getakenner," Rodigger said the next morning. "He's a menace, and destroys the very foundation of the inns."

"Do as you like," Gabriel replied, swinging onto his Midland. "Though I doubt the lord of Getakenner cares much for an inn three days to his south. Deuel?"

Deuel gazed ahead—though what he expected to see escaped Rodigger. The road wound around giant boulders thrown from the river, or carved from the banks, keeping beside the Balnathva for another day.

Yet, miraculously, the strange, impossible man pointed ahead. "Climbing that rise," he said, then shook his head. "If he doesn't stay two nights in Getakenner, we won't catch him there."

"Ah well," Gabriel said, and they rode out.

Rodigger kicked Gared, and the Therian moved out at a reasonable pace, flicking its ears in irritation. Rodigger's mouth twisted, accepting the rebuke. But that innkeeper! Roth was trying—Rodigger too—to bring Andelian together, building compassion for one another no matter if one hailed from Satflir and the other from Ethfirlaf. And the inns were the earliest realization of that, even if they were a Rinc Nain idea, older than Roth by almost a century. Yet that man insulted not only Roth's ideas, but the very idea of what he ran, with such tactics. The sun grew warmer, and with it Rodigger's ire as he stewed over the insult.

Before Noon the road sloped upward, climbing the rise upon which Deuel had spotted the stranger in the green hood as it briefly left the river.

It took everything Rodigger had not to turn his horse around and go back—if going to the innkeeper would be in vain, at least back to Thinneh and report him there. But he knew their mission was too pressing.

Roth! As they crested the climb, Rodigger knew Roth would want to hear of this rogue innkeeper who destroyed the revolution's core beliefs in their territory. "I'll send a message to Roth when we get to Getakenner," Rodigger said aloud with a smile.

Gabriel glanced back briefly. "Okay."

Rodigger nodded his head. That would take care of it. He glanced off the side of the road to where the Balnathva coursed below.

The next three inns had seen no one in a green hood, though Deuel managed to pick him out almost every morning, climbing this rise or that rise, or appearing past a switchback when the road climbed out of the 'Back again. This time the road did not stop till it dropped into the pampas of East Fallonvall.

⸻◆⸻

East Fallonvall was a geographical oddity: despite the mild rains that fell east of the mountains and the lush farmland it generated, waterways never seemed to coalesce, leaving no ready supply of water except what could be dug from the earth. After Getakenner had been established, along with the farms that supplied it, settlement of the rest of the East Fallonvall halted. Getakenner grew large enough that it was no bother for the road to divert out of the 'Back, and it remained a renowned center of grapes, especially fermented ones.

Catie looked behind her, back toward the river that now raged silently below, and it was then that she saw them: three men on horseback making their way along the road behind her. She may have paid them little mind—the Fallonvall, and Getakenner lying just inside it, was a common destination—except that one of the three men seemed to be regarding her. It was less that she could see his eyes—they were too far back to tell that—but his face was definitely upward, and she *felt* something inspecting her. Her Grandmother had given her the same feeling as a child when she told a story that may or may not have been true. It was impossible that she should feel that way from the gaze of someone so far behind her. And yet...

The road wound down the slope below her, then flowed across the gently undulating plain between the mountains and Getakenner. Kelsie was winded from the long climb up, but Catie knew there was more in her. And she wouldn't need to push too hard. Those behind her still faced the same ascent, and were probably not pursuing her. Despite that chance, Catie wanted to come to them on her own terms. All the better if, when they crested the ridge, she was nowhere in sight.

Her height above the town played tricks, seeming further away and less attainable than it was—or Kelsie had more energy reserved than even Catie hoped. Either way, Catie rode through the great doors of the west wall before Evening, and a quick but casual glance to the far ridge gave away no hint of movement. It had been enough time for a new suspicion to be recalled, a memory even more distant than her Grandmother, but far more vivid.

—◦—

As they crested the pass, Rodigger sat a little forward in his saddle, and his horse mimicked his excitement. Getakenner sprawled below, encircled by well-tended earth that reminded Rodigger of the combed and oiled hair of the vintners who tended it. The lines were bare now, the vines pruned back to start afresh in the spring. The dearth outside was balanced, Rodigger knew, by the plenty in the cellars inside. There was always more food and drink than citizens, though they tried hard to reverse it. Roth had found great support here, Rodigger remembered, and he looked forward to returning.

But great dark clouds were building on the horizon and sliding swiftly on a steady east wind. His eye measured the road before them, and he hunched his shoulders.

The snow hit a mile from town, covering roads and fields quicker than even Rodigger had anticipated. He followed Gabriel and Deuel, who seemed to be picking their way along well enough. Their descent out of the mountains would have been impossible in these conditions, Rodigger knew. He also knew, embarrassingly, that difficulty would have been mostly with Gared.

They pressed on in timelessness, as the sun only lent a hazy gray glow to the world. Soon enough, the great doors to the city gaped wide before them. A few hardy merchants in thick furs and grim smiles were only now pulling in their meats, cloths, leathers, tools, ornaments, services, and supplies. A few spared glances at the passing riders, but none asked to trade.

"What are we looking for?" Rodigger asked after they turned right, heading back in the direction they had come.

"A good inn," Gabriel replied.

"It's Getakenner," Rodigger scoffed as he wrapped one arm tight around himself. "We could stop at any home and receive just as warm a welcome as any inn."

"Perhaps," Gabriel replied. Deuel's head was swiveling up and to each side, then twisting back at the way they had come. They had crept to a stop in front of The Therian's Stall as Deuel glanced around, down the street, craning his neck as if to see around a faraway corner. He glanced at Gabriel and nodded.

"Perfect," Gabriel said, dismounting from his horse in front of the inn. Rodigger glanced at the sign of a tall horse pawing the earth, then back at his companions.

"It is?" he asked. "We want to stay at an inn which indicates sleeping on loose hay and horse manure?"

"We've stayed here before," Gabriel replied as if deciding the truth of the statement on the spot. Deuel only gazed at him, and Gabriel shrugged a shoulder.

Rodigger sighed and swung down from his horse. There was no point in arguing. He was, still and regrettably, only there as an aide if needed. Surely there would be patrons enough to talk to, for practice.

⚬

Though Catie had not been to Getakenner in years, she had spent enough time there to remember it well. If she was right, she knew to which tavern the three riders would come. She had made her way there, stabled Kelsie quickly, but went into a store down the street and began an interest in the herbs collected in the window.

"Is it a healer?" an old woman crooned as she came out of a light doze, her face bearing a line for every memory of her life.

"No, not today," Catie replied with a smile. She flared an eyebrow. "A spy."

The old woman chuckled. "And who does she hope to catch, then, ay?"

"I don't know," Catie said, a little distantly. "Three, perhaps."

"Those are the best catches: unknown and many." She chuckled again. "Such an adventure! But why does she seek that, ay?"

"Sometimes they come whether you seek them or not."

"Ah." The old woman clicked her tongue. "And to one so young?"

Catie's eyes dropped from the herbs to the floor. "Sometimes."

"Is there a war going on, then, ay?"

Catie's eyes came up to meet the old woman's, then went distant again as she thought back over her journey from Bokessin. She shook her head, and met the woman's gaze. "It's hard to say, sometimes," she answered frankly.

A hesitant smile added a hundred creases to the woman's face. "It sounds wrong," she said, her tone rising in hopeful question.

"Yes, it does," Catie replied simply, looking through the window in time to see the three men who had been pursuing her arrive in front of the inn.

"Will you catch them?" the old woman asked, back in their game, her voice a conspiratorial whisper.

Just then, the strange man whose gaze pierced her from almost three miles away fixed her through the window, through bunches of hanging herbs. Catie's mouth opened, but her voice stuck. Finally the men went inside, and she breathed out a sigh. "I don't think so," she said, glancing at the old woman with troubled eyes.

The old woman only chuckled one last time, and drifted back to sleep. Catie shook her head with a wistful grin: she hoped to be that old one day, and spend her life just so. First, she had to make it through this meeting.

—◆—

The cold of the streets was quickly rebuffed by the warmth of the inn. Roaring hearths battled each other from across the common-room, and nearly every table was full. Serving girls strode to tables, barely pausing to unlade their trays before scampering to another table, or to the back. One flashed them a smile as she passed, but said nothing as a patron's bawl recalled her attention.

They caught the eye of the keeper, who gestured absently towards the tables before turning and attending some other business. Gabriel nodded.

"Help ourselves," he muttered, turning to his companions and indicating a table against the wall beside the fire.

"Why did you pick this particular inn?" Rodigger asked as they sat.

"Because," Gabriel replied, pausing as a server dropped off three mugs of ale. "Because it wasn't full."

"You didn't know that outside," Rodigger said with a grin.

"Deuel did."

Rodigger's grin slipped. "Deuel did."

"Yeah." Gabriel glanced around as he took a drink, then back at Rodigger's level stare and shrugged.

"How could he know that?" Rodigger asked, screwing up his face.

"He's..." Gabriel shrugged, meeting his friend's emotionless gaze. "He's very good."

"Oh, whatever." Rodigger returned to his drink with a sigh.

⸻ ◆○◆ ⸻

She exited the shop silently, then paused briefly before the inn door to take a quick, calming breath. She was more sure about the stranger's identity now. Normally, that would have comforted her, but she still knew nothing about the other two with whom he traveled. Straightening, she pushed through the door and entered the inn.

5

MYSTERIOUS
CONVERSATIONS

"Now?"
"Yes."
"And say what?"
"Teresh…"

16 Mantaver 1320 — Winter

"There he is," Deuel muttered, gesturing toward the door. Rodigger turned, catching sight of the green-hooded man as he stepped into the common room. Surely it was no coincidence that Deuel led them straight here, but how could he have possibly done that? Rodigger glanced at Deuel, and when he turned back, suddenly the man was no longer there. In his place was a woman with a fire in her hair that was surely lit by the spark in her eyes, fueled by her grace as she moved unerringly toward them. Rodigger felt himself stand barely more than he heard his companions do the same.

"I'm Catie," she said, extending a hand to no one in particular. "You've been following me."

Rodigger grinned and stepped forward, but Gabriel had been closer and got to her hand first. "Gabriel," he said. "And you came in after us."

"Deuel." He did not shake her hand, but his gaze was ever-piercing.

Rodigger's hand was still outstretched. She turned and glanced him over, and her smile widened just a little as she shook his hand. "Rodigger," he managed, then left his mouth open for something else to come out, something witty and charming. Nothing did, and it shut.

"I hid across the way," she said, turning back to Gabriel. "I wanted to see who I would be walking in on."

Gabriel arched an eyebrow. "Well done," he said. "I thought Deuel might mention something if he had seen you," he added, casting the same eyebrow upon his friend.

"How would he have known?" finally tumbled from Rodigger's mouth as his gaze tore from Catie.

Catie gestured at Deuel. "Because, he's—"

"He's very good," Gabriel finished. Catie's own sharp gaze searched Gabriel's face, then Deuel's, and turned quickly back to Rodigger.

"Just look at the way he carries himself, and how quiet he is," she said, with further gestures. "It's the quiet, poised ones who always know everything that's going on."

Rodigger nodded once, and his mouth formed a voiceless "oh."

"Shall we sit?" Gabriel asked, glancing around the room. He smiled and placed a hand on Catie's shoulder as if they were old friends. Rodigger swallowed hard as his gaze flailed from Catie, to Gabriel, to Gabriel's hand—though his smile stayed desperately in place.

Catie smiled and nodded, and the four sat down with scraping chairs and rustling clothing. "So why are you following me?" she asked, quietly in the general din of the common room.

"We're just traveling," Gabriel replied, raising his hand for more drinks. "You happened to be in front of us—though, avoiding the inns." He paused and smiled at the barmaid as she refilled their mugs and left. "So one might ask, instead, why you were following us from the front."

Catie's smile faltered, and she gazed at Deuel as though deciding something. "I had a close call with one of the innkeepers," she said finally.

Rodigger's fist came down hard on the table, causing more than just those who sat around it to jump. "I told you I need to report him," Rodigger fumed with a jabbing finger. "It wasn't just us, and it's not going to be just us. We should go back and give him steel—one foot of it for every ounce of draught he put in his patrons' fish!"

"How will you know how much that is?" Catie asked. "I knew better, so don't count me in your tally."

Gabriel's arms folded and his eyebrows raised expectantly at Rodigger.

"Well...at least a foot of it, then," Rodigger said. "That'll still do enough damage for me."

"It only takes a few drops to put someone out," Catie continued. "Who took it?" she asked, her gaze only including Gabriel and Rodigger.

To his credit, Rodigger noticed. "Oh, of course Deuel didn't get any, because he's very good, right?"

"I was being diplomatic," Catie confessed, looking directly at Rodigger. "I knew Gabriel wouldn't have, either. I am sorry. Did you have a headache?"

He did *now*, he thought, his peripheral vision locking onto Gabriel's quivering lips as the mercenary barely contained his laughter. It was a quivering that Rodigger knew from childhood—but one that he did not see in Catie. As his mind refocused on her, he realized she seemed genuinely concerned, and he smiled a little.

"No, not really," he replied, noting how her eyes drifted down to his mouth as he spoke. Again he found himself trying to think of more to say, to keep her gaze on him, but his mind failed once more. She turned back to Gabriel, her departing eyes taking a little of Rodigger's spirit with them. He lifted his mug to drink.

"You're not traveling anywhere near Agirbirt, are you?" she asked.

Rodigger coughed up his beer. Gabriel and Deuel both gave him withering looks. Catie only blinked.

"Would you like to travel together?" she asked, as if the answer had been given to her plainly.

"I fear that would be a bad idea," Gabriel said. "Our purposes otherwise might not mingle."

Catie glanced around the table. "I only said I was going to Agirbirt," she replied. "Is your purpose somehow for me to not go home?"

"You were overheard," Deuel said.

She rubbed her lip. "If I had been serious about that, would I be going north, or south?" she asked.

"It doesn't matter where you're going," Rodigger said heavily, his chest feeling like it had dropped entirely to his waist. She couldn't have denied it? "You oppose the revolution, and you tried to kill Roth once already, and we can't trust you."

She glanced at him, then back around the table. All their countenances were set. Her eyes narrowed and she stood. "I might find you again in Sprativerg," she said. "I think by then you'll find great masses of people who oppose the revolution, who might have even thought about killing Roth if they had the opportunity, that you can trust now." Her gaze lingered on Deuel for a moment. "Good day."

As she turned and left, Rodigger's foot came from behind the table before he stopped himself—or rather, Gabriel's stare stopped him.

"Don't you dare go after her," the mercenary growled. "You started it."

Rodigger's mouth gaped. "You said our purposes might not mingle, as I recall."

"'Might' being the key point, *hetan*," he replied. "But she was absolutely right. If she had been serious, what does she have to gain in Agirbirt, where she is undoubtedly from?"

Rodigger paused, then his eyes widened. "Maybe she knows about the Berkarfor!"

Gabriel drew a long breath. "You know Rod, one day Deuel, myself, and Roth won't be here. Who exactly do you expect to do your thinking for you then?"

Catie exited the inn, stopping just outside the door despite the swirling snow. Across the way, the herb shop was dark, the old lady returned to her home. A voice in Catie's head sighed: she missed her Grandmother. She missed warm beds, and familiar surroundings. She missed Dannid. Her throat hardened as she swallowed, and the winter sting in the wind did not help the water in her eyes. The door behind her opened, and the boisterous noise inside pushed her as firmly aside as the drunken tradesmen who exited. She caught her balance, but stayed, her eyes still upon the frosting panes of the shop where she had taken refuge for only a few moments—but long enough to remember times not so long past when the world was right. She wanted it all back, all that time spent traveling, meeting people, doing things that seemed to make a difference at the time—she would trade all of that, everything she had become, would do over again all the years at her mother's side learning. If only for the opportunity to choose the right fork instead of the left.

She turned away. She liked this inn: the beds were soft, and gentle on her shoulder blades where a terrible ache had grown a few years ago and never left. Dannid had used to massage there, but stopped when it made the ache worse. And the muscles there never seemed to relax, anyway. It's how she knew the three men would stop here—not that Deuel had aches in his back, but with what did rest upon his back, it made sense.

And Rodigger didn't know. A feeble grin came to her lips, then strengthened at the thought of the moment when he learned. And they would have to travel together for presumably some time longer after that.

Her grin faded as she walked to find another inn. What could their mission be? Agirbirt had little more than historical significance. It was on the road toward the port of Satost, but they did not say they were headed for the port. It was not as though the lake held mystical properties. And her village of Attelek was just that: a village. A fishing village, with perhaps a few more inns than fishing villages normally had as it was on the way inland from Satost. But it didn't attract visitors for itself. At best, the lake was part of a legend of...

Catie stopped, her head bowed. Her grin returned, and her shoulders shook in silent laughter. She traced an eyebrow with her finger: the Berkarfor. This pathetic little man who had killed her husband so ruthlessly was so desperate as to seek such a legend. And he sent a twit of a soldier, an aging mercenary who only by miracle stayed in his saddle on steep pitches in the mountains, and so great a being as Deuel to find them.

Oh, they probably existed. Her feet continued carrying her through drifting snow. Almost assuredly, they did. But, knowing the people of Andelen, those three would probably stop for a few days in Stramfath. A fine place for learning, to be sure, but only about the things that people already agreed were mostly true. Almost no one believed in the Berkarfor.

No, she would see them again. They would need to come to Attelek. They would need to see Catie's Grandmother. And they would probably need Catie to find the rest.

⸺◆⸺

The sun was muted the next morning by a frosty fog, though the rumor of it dazzled against the Dragonsbacks as Rodigger, Gabriel, and Deuel continued on the road northward. After a few moments of straining his eyes forward, hoping to see a rider somewhere up ahead, Rodigger sat back with a sigh. Gabriel shook his head with a grin that Rodigger ignored. He glanced at Deuel. Though the man's eyes pierced toward the mountains as well, nothing in his face betrayed what he might have seen. *Nothing in his face ever betrays anything,* Rodigger thought as he sneered silently. A good illusion of wisdom.

Deuel's eyes turned and fixed upon Rodigger, who swallowed his sneer thickly and watched the back of his horse's head bobbing. Why did he have to *do* that? What kind of man had such abysses for eyes that to look in them seemed instantly as if you had been plopped into a cave with no way out except five thousand passages leading into darkness?

Rodigger glanced again, barely, out of the corner of his eye in time to see Deuel's gaze shift forward. *This is going to be the longest ride, ever. Why did that beautiful woman have to leave without us?* Rodigger's eyes darted to Deuel again, in case the man could read thoughts. But, of course, his expression revealed nothing.

⸺◆⸺

"Why aren't we at the inn?" Rodigger asked, glancing around the docks at Farenglinn's Vatenvilt—another of Andelen's oddities, for those who traveled elsewhere.

"Because I like the smell of the river," Gabriel replied, watching the rushing waters go by down the middle of the course. Here at the docks was a natural eddy, and the reason for the Vatenvilt: boats laden with supplies could slow, and dock.

When Rodigger was silent for too long, Gabriel looked at him, then rolled his eyes. "It's a 'vilt, Rodigger: I'm having something delivered."

"We have everything we need," Rodigger said.

Gabriel glared at him. "Perhaps *you* think you do. I, having stayed alive much longer and under much more pressing circumstances, know I do not." He turned back to the river and crossed his arms.

"So we stand here and wait? For how long?"

"Probably a week."

"Gabriel..." Deuel rumbled, but somehow in a way Rodigger knew was not threatening. That was another thing about Deuel that unseated him.

"Rodigger, find us comfortable lodgings, please?" Gabriel said, not taking his eyes off the river. "It won't be long."

Before Rodigger could open his mouth, Deuel's gaze locked onto him and he scuttled off as if he had never intended to sit there and wait with them.

"You should be nicer to him," Deuel said when Rodigger had gone. "This does not promise to be a short journey."

"I'm cold and I'm tired, *skald*," Gabriel replied, his voice sounding as thin as the air around them. "Do you think they only hid the Berkarfor?"

"No, they are guarded."

Gabriel cocked an eye on his friend, reading in Deuel's tone precisely what the man had put there. "You would have stopped me from having these sent, otherwise," Gabriel confirmed. Deuel did not have to nod, and they both watched the river.

———◆———

Rodigger trudged along the road into the vatenvilt, paying no attention to the hawkers on either side. At least they were calmer than those normally found in cities, because they knew travelers stopped in the 'vilt for specific wares. What Rodigger could not fathom—a feeling he was tired of being accustomed to—was how Gabriel already had something on the way. He hadn't even looked in any of the shops to see if what he wanted was there. He had gone straight to the dock, spoke to the magiss for all of five breaths, then waited, looking upriver. No hawk had flown upstream with an order, and that's how things were brought into the 'vilt.

He continued, his eyes on the road as the noises of the 'vilt moved around him. Inns were always at the edge of the vatenvilt, and farms beyond that—all according to some law of the 'vilt that permitted only shops within the jurisdiction of the magiss. No telling where that had come from, but probably was not Andelian.

Rodigger reached the crossroad, and gazed at the three identical inns. The one on the far left seemed the quietest. He went in, secured a room for the three of them and a mug of ale for himself, and sat by the fire as he waited to learn what was going on. Hope, it seemed—however malnourished—had not left him yet.

———◆———

"Why do you carry these?"

The question, asked by one of the guards at Vatenhal, was the spoken echo of Rodigger's silent question that had rang in his head since they left Farenglinn's two weeks ago. Gabriel had never unsheathed them in Rodigger's presence, but they were clearly not normal swords.

"We are heading out of Roth's domain," Gabriel replied smoothly. "We don't know what we might find in the wilds of Sheppar's kingdom."

You mean his kinnigdom, thought Rodigger snidely. *Whatever that even is.*

The guard handed back Gabriel's sheathed weapons, and glanced over the staff Deuel still held. Rodigger had been impressed. The guard had made a valiant effort at almost taking the staff for examination, stopping just short of asking aloud. Rodigger had never even made it that far, and could barely imagine it. And as much as Rodigger had wished it, the guard had not bothered to unsheathe Gabriel's weapons, either. All he knew, still, was what stuck out of the sheath: it almost resembled a sword, except the two-handed grip was bare, the half-guard was wrapped in leather like a grip, and a cuff-like half-moon of metal was attached perpendicularly where a pommel would be. He could also tell by the sheath that the blade was off-center, as if it sat on the opposite side from the cross-guard and cuff. It looked, on the whole, completely lopsided and entirely unusable—and Gabriel had two of them. But given the pitted and rusted appearance of the cuff, it would seem he took care of neither of them.

The dubious expression on the guard's face mirrored Rodigger's thoughts. Weapons had not been used on either side of the front lines in many years. The guard glanced at his companion, who shrugged. "Very well," said the first. "But I don't want to see them drawn within the city. There's no use for them." He made the last sound like a general statement, one which Gabriel clearly ignored as he rode through the gates.

Of all the times of the year to visit Roth's crowning conquest, Rodigger thought, winter was the worst. Vatenhal rested high in the mountains. There were no nearby peaks to disturb the wind that blew almost constantly, and it was near enough the edge of the Dragonsback mountains that storm clouds from the west would not have dropped their snow before arriving at Vatenhal's doorstep.

What had made it such a crowning achievement were some of the same reasons it was detestable to visit in winter: those distant peaks were also too far away from which to launch ballistae, and the single wind-swept road on which they had approached switched up from the valley below twelve times, too exposed and within reach of Vatenhal's own defenses before it arrived at the double-gated entrance. How exactly the castle had been attained was something of a mystery to Rodigger, but he knew it had involved months of building up sympathy within the walls. Despite some contrary comments, Roth's power—Rodigger felt—was always in his ability to persuade others. Rodigger knew, bitterly, that it had not been an army that had taken this castle.

They stopped at the first inn on the thoroughfare, and tied their horses to the post outside. When they entered, the common room was perhaps half-full, though it was the middle of dinner time. Gabriel approached the bar.

"Two Midlands and a Therian outside, for one night," he said.

The keeper looked at him, astonished. "You brought a Therian up here?" he asked.

"He did just fine," Rodigger lied hotly.

The keeper glanced at him, then briefly past him, then back at Gabriel. "I'm afraid we're full tonight, but have a couple ales for whatever ails you," he said with the barest of grins.

Gabriel cocked an eyebrow at the keeper, but Rodigger looked around quickly and spotted two men with black cloaks and hoods pulled back. "Over there," he said quietly, nudging Gabriel. "Three, please," he said, hoping to savor this moment when he finally knew more than his companions. But with one look at Deuel, he knew there was no mystery, and he nearly snarled as he looked away.

They sat, not with the two men, but nearby, drinking for several moments in silence until a bard returned to the small side-stage and began to strum.

"Is it watched?" Rodigger asked quietly, looking sideways at the bard. He turned back to the two men in time to see one rub his nose. Rodigger blinked, and felt his heart teeter on the precipice. "How long?" he asked, looking at his companions. There was motion again as the second man scratched where a ring might have been on his third finger.

Rodigger's heart fell. *Three weeks.* Too long for Catie to have gotten through—at least, not on her own. "Have you helped anyone else through, recently?" he asked.

There was a pause as both men's eyes darted around: that hadn't been part of the script, and in the end the first man simply shook his head.

I bet Gabriel and Deuel are loving this, Rodigger thought, rubbing his forehead. When he glanced up, he saw the amused smirk he had expected to see on Gabriel's face, but for once Deuel wasn't even looking at him.

"What time," he asked flatly, his enjoyment in the secretive conversation now completely gone.

The first man stood, and began walking away. The second spilled a few coins on the table, then picked up four of them: after Mid-Night. Both men paused at the door and pulled up their hoods, then exited.

Gabriel was watching him with a cocked eyebrow. "Do we still stay here, after the keeper said it was full?" he asked.

Rodigger swallowed. "No," he replied. "There's another inn two streets up where we'll have a room already ready."

"I guess you thought of everything," Gabriel said, draining his mug and standing. He tossed a coin on the table and turned, then twisted his head back to look at Rodigger. "Is it okay that I did that? That's not code for anything, is it?"

Without waiting for a response, Gabriel headed for the door. Deuel was looking at Rodigger again, whose knuckles were white around the handle of his mug.

"What?" Rodigger snapped, his eyes boring into Deuel's chest.

"I apologize for my friend," Deuel murmured. As if those words broke something free, Rodigger's gaze came up to meet Deuel's eyes and—for once—he was able to keep from looking away.

But Deuel said nothing else before standing and following the mercenary to the door. Rodigger, after figuring out how to close his mouth, stood and went with them.

⸺◆⸺

Rodigger, Deuel, and Gabriel sat at the edges of their beds, saddlebags packed and tied. Rodigger glanced out the window. It was a new moon tonight, and he had always had trouble telling time of night when that happened. He knew vaguely it had something to do with the stars, but usually he was asleep by this time, or someone told him what time it was. He would not ask, now. He could not even bring himself to look at Deuel, again. Whatever barrier had fallen earlier in the evening was re-erected.

Deuel glanced at Gabriel, and Gabriel at Rodigger. "It's time," the mercenary said, rising with a sigh and a hearty push with his hands against his knees. Deuel rose beside him. Rodigger followed them out, sparing one final glance around the room before closing the door quietly.

They made their way downstairs, and into the dark. No one seemed to be about, though with no moon anything could have been hiding in the dark. Snow sat in thin drifts in the corners of streets and buildings, and the rest of the streets looked wet and dull. It was a perfect night, despite the cold, for moving without being seen.

"How do we get outside the walls?" Gabriel whispered. There was not even a taunt in his voice.

Rodigger said nothing, but took the lead, heading toward the main gate. "The guards are most definitely on our side," Rodigger said finally, whispering only because in such darkness it seemed appropriate. "It's okay if they see us."

For a time as they left the castle and began the descent down into the valley, the only sounds of the night were their horses' hooves. Soon enough the river rushed steadily ahead of them. Here it did not cascade but was a wide, flat ribbon in a broad valley.

The road turned north, and so did they. Rodigger slowed, his eyes darting around the gloom for some sign of their guides. How foolish it would be to pass them by and stumble directly into Sheppar's troops! His blood thrummed in his ears, mocking his attempts to listen. The clouds overhead slid in front of the stars. He tried to slow his breathing, but his intermittent gasps made it worse.

Suddenly they were before him. A short cry left his lips, and the hand he clapped over his mouth echoed even louder. He could almost feel the cold glares coming from the utterly black hoods.

But they said nothing, moving quietly off the side of the road and down a series of boulders arranged nearly into steps. Rodigger, Gabriel, and Deuel followed. The narrow ledge led downward, never switching, till the river flowed hard beside them.

"We will be in the river a few times," whispered the first guide, pointing at the waters. "Try to slide your feet through the water instead of splashing, yes?"

Rodigger nodded as the second man relayed the instructions. They pressed on. The man in the lead glanced upward frequently. Rodigger followed his gaze once, seeing a lip in the rock above where the road had to be. If anyone came to the edge and looked down, surely they would be dark shapes against the river. Rodigger shuddered once, then focused on putting silent feet upon the narrow track.

He was four sliding steps through the water before the iciness hit his feet. He gritted his teeth with a small groan, fighting desperately against the urge to pick them up out of the water. He could feel them growing numb, but could not see where the path rose above the water again—where, hopefully, was some relief.

But when they reached it, that relief did not come. He could feel almost nothing by that point, which was *some* relief. But at the next ford, the water came even higher, numbing him halfway up his calves before the track rose above the river once more.

Twice more they forded. He wondered briefly—since she was rarely far from his mind anyway—if Catie had found this route, and if she had turned back when she hit the water. Or if, by some miracle, she made it through and might still find them on their way to Agirbirt. The warmth of those thoughts did not quite make it to his feet, and after slipping and nearly falling completely into the freezing waters his mind returned fully to the task at hand.

Finally the track went upward. The guides paused near the top, peering backward along the road. The second man hissed quietly, holding up a hand for a few moments. After several breaths he beckoned urgently, and both guides moved at a crouch down the road. The three companions followed, leading their horses in long strides to keep them from picking up a canter.

A few hundred steps down the road the guides ducked behind three large boulders. Rodigger came upon them, his breath hard and thick in the frosty air.

"I'll be glad for spring," he whispered as Gabriel and Deuel squeezed in behind him, and coughed quietly as he placed a hand against his throat.

"You should be fine after this," said the first guide. "You might not want to be seen on the road, or as little as possible, until reaching an inn, or until Onesstritt, so it's less obvious that you came from the south."

"Tradesmen don't move from the south to the north?" Gabriel asked.

"Few enough," Rodigger said, glancing at the mercenary.

"And you aren't tradesmen," the first guide said flatly. "You don't even look like ones."

Gabriel shrugged and grinned. "Thank you," he said.

The two guides glanced at Rodigger. "Good luck," they said.

As they watched the two men slink back down the road, Gabriel took a breath. "Fortunate, isn't it, that small path skirting right where the kinnig's forces put their outpost."

"I don't question good fortune when it smiles on me," Rodigger replied.

Deuel took a shorter grasp on his horse's reins and moved away from the shelter of the boulders.

Gabriel smiled at Rodigger. "Yeah, I—"

"We should head further in," Deuel said, cutting Gabriel off. "And build a fire to dry our boots. Riding now will turn them to ice."

Being reminded of how cold his legs were distracted Rodigger from the shock on Gabriel's face. Rodigger followed Deuel, not even paying attention to the fact that he now walked in between the two friends.

Deuel took them off the road and deep along a canyon for some time, past several turns, before stopping in a small bowl where—almost miraculously—a small pool and shocks of matted grass were surviving the winter.

Later, after Rodigger had dropped to sleep, Gabriel turned and faced Deuel. "Choosing him over me, now?" he whispered. "You know what he's going to say when he finds out what you are."

"And he will still have to travel with us," Deuel replied. "Making him a worse enemy now will not make him a better companion later."

"He's a terrible companion right now," Gabriel grunted. "You know *ked* well there were no soldiers back there. This rebellion is only in Roth's mind—and Rodigger's, because he has no mind except what Roth gave him."

"Then we have little to fear on the road northward," Deuel replied. "And one terrible companion is often made by two people."

Gabriel glared at Deuel's back as the man turned away from him. "You're the worst *skalderon* there is, right now."

"I am the best *right hand* there is, right now," Deuel murmured, "because I will not allow the body to which I am attached become corrupt and evil."

Gabriel's mouth gaped for a few moments, then muttered several grumbling curses as he turned away and tried to get comfortable against the thin earth.

Rodigger lay with his eyes closed, keeping his breathing deep, feigning sleep. *He has no mind except what Roth gave him.* Was that so terrible? He would have thought it a wonderful thing to mimic so great a mind. But the way Gabriel said it... He managed to avoid sighing. At least Deuel seemed to be on his side. *"When he finds out what you are."* What, 'very good'? *He already knew that.*

As he began drifting toward sleep, his thoughts drifted back to Vatenhal, to the code. It excited him, being given that by Roth before he left Akervet, made him feel even more a part of the revolution than he had. Of course, he could not remember that without remembering the other code: one who looked for the man with wings. Was that what it was? Something like that. And no explanation of who would say it, or where, or why he would be looking for a man with wings, or how the man had wings. Nothing but that it was critical that Rodigger help that person however he needed—maybe to the extent of abandoning the Berkarfor.

Rodigger shifted fitfully. That made him worry. How would he know? He thought the Berkarfor were everything. What if he hadn't found them? What if the mercenaries were threatening to stop looking for them? Who would the code-giver be? How...?

6

SEARCHES BEGIN

"Everyone seems to be doing fine on their own..."
"They should be together, right now."
"How do you know?"
"That's the way the God of All would always have it, Teresh."

20 Thriman 1320 — Winter

Two and a half weeks later, they passed through the Skaldvath Mountains—a slender arm coming down from the Dragonsbacks and splitting the Fallonvall from the Birnesath. This broad plain was bordered on the north by the Beltrath Wastes, and the south by the Fiery Sea. Agirbirt Lake glimmered in the distance, a sapphire plume spilling from Stramfath and over the horizon.

Rodigger paused when they first caught glimpse of the lake. He had never seen anything like it. As they rode, Gabriel told him it would take more than seven days to ride around the perimeter of Agirbirt—something they might have to do to find where the hidden Berkarfor lay.

"How much do you know about these goblets?" Gabriel asked as they plodded toward Stramfath.

Rodigger shrugged. "Not more than Roth told me," he said, hiccuping when Gabriel snorted. "There are only four, but they're scattered all over Andelen. They were made during the Age of War, used by the kings of Andelen to gain their freedom from Rinc Na, then hidden for fear that their power would be misused. Now, though, Roth says..."

Rodigger trailed off as Gabriel suddenly turned off the road toward a clump of trees. Stramfath was at least an hour away, and the sun was descending. Rodigger followed silently, knowing any questions were pointless. Gabriel and Deuel dismounted and tied their horses to some branches. Rodigger climbed down hesitantly.

"Check out the lake," Gabriel told Deuel. "See if there's any spot likely for something to be hidden. Don't go swimming just yet." Deuel nodded and stepped away from the grove.

"But I thought you said it would take days...to..."

Rodigger stiffened as Deuel threw back the thick cloak that had been perpetually wound around him. Great, leathery wings reached out from his back and stretched, having been folded for so long. His gaze locked onto Rodigger for a few moments before he leapt, and with three great bursts from his wings he shot into the sky.

Rodigger took a step back as his gaze snapped up to follow the swiftly-receding silhouette of Deuel. "He's—He's..."

"Behamian," Gabriel grunted with a nod. "A dragon-son." His gaze, too, went to the sky where Deuel was now a thin dot gliding over the lake.

"But that's—that's an abomination!"

"You say so," Gabriel said darkly, staring hard at Rodigger before returning upward. "I don't think he can help it, though."

⬥

"Catie!" a young man shouted in surprise.

She actually startled, looking around for the source. To her right, standing in mid-step, was Teyor, his smile wide in disbelief. She smiled hesitantly in return, seeing that others in the square were noticing. She had walked almost to the middle of her hometown without being recognized, which was why Teyor's outburst caught her quite by surprise.

"Hi," she said, with a little wave.

And just like that, everyone nearby suddenly streamed toward her with smiles and welcomes, while others near the edges of the square shouted to people unseen and waved them over. She had almost expected this—well, it would either have been this, or everyone running over to throw her out of town. She had not been sure. She had gone back and forth between the possibilities ever more frequently the closer to Attelek she came.

But as they pressed around her, it was all friendly smiles. Names she could not recall on the road sprang to mind as their faces bobbed before her, and hands outstretched to touch her as if to make sure she was real.

"Jayna; Dejor; Friela, hi again. Peyt, how are you? Catie Two!" she said, beaming wide and hugging a girl her own age who had come to Attelek from Satost fifteen years ago and was the only person in the village to share a name with someone else. "Oh, it's so good to see you all again. Velta! I've missed your *piraltas* in the mornings. Oh, they're the best fresh; I'll be by in the morning tomorrow. I know, Dath," she said with a quick laugh, her hand on his bony shoulder—it was bonier now than she remembered. At his well-concealed wince she slid her hand to his shoulder blade and rubbed gently. "I—probably, Sar. Definitely for a while." Her head swiveled around the small crowd. "I'll need to talk to—hi, Tyafor! Do you even realize how big you've gotten? Is Gandreth putting you to work or something?" Those nearest chuckled as she winked at the blacksmith, who stood with arms folded but smiling at the edge of the press.

Heads suddenly turned and the questions went silent. Catie, still smiling, glanced behind her then turned fully. The crowd parted as Grandmother made her way forward, her hand gently on the shoulder of a small girl that Catie didn't recognize. Of course, when Catie had left, the girl would probably have been two or three.

This meeting was still one Catie had feared, for she had defied Grandmother in leaving—at least a little bit. Catie knelt, her head bowed, her heart hammering. Surely if the others had welcomed her back so completely...

A withered but surprisingly still-strong hand cupped her chin and lifted till she was looking in Grandmother's sparkling eyes, and her heart soared.

"It is so good to see you healthy," Grandmother said. "Please stand up and let me look at you, Caytaleane."

Catie stood. Grandmother always used the full old names, and now Catie knew she was home.

⸺◆⸺

Rodigger stood resolutely facing his horse as Deuel returned. His stomach convulsed as he heard leathery appendages flapping and folding—couldn't help but see them in his mind wrinkling and tucking behind a cloak that would no longer hide the truth. He rubbed Gared's forehead.

"You probably have questions," Deuel said quietly, not far enough behind Rodigger.

Rodigger frowned and shook his head. "Surprisingly? No."

Teeth clicked, then clothing ruffled. Gabriel spoke next. "Let's head into town," he said. "We'll look into the libraries tomorrow morning, first thing. Get the goblet from here and move on."

Rodigger took his time getting into the saddle, letting the others mount and move ahead of him. Maybe he could drop far enough back that he wouldn't instantly be associated with them, riding into town.

But the roads were empty, the day drawing late. He sighed, looking forward without trying to look at anything. But Deuel's back still was in view, the cloak draped so carefully.

The man with wings.

Rodigger spurred his Therian. He needed to be in front. Then maybe he could forget about it. Gabriel and Deuel watched him go by without comment. They knew. He knew they knew. That was why Deuel had been nice to him, to try to seem less of a disgusting creature than he was. And Rodigger was far from done with them. How in all of Oren was he supposed to continue this journey, knowing what he knew? His heels dug deeper, as if a swifter wind might clean the filth that seemed to coat his body.

***

"Why do you come back to us now, Caytaleane?" Grandmother asked, her tone merely happy curiosity.

Catie stood quietly, glancing around Grandmother's kitchen—a place she could not recall before, but now could not remember leaving. Was it the same bread baking in the oven as when she had left? The towels had definitely been folded just so, and even the chair Grandmother gestured to was where she had left it when she had gotten up to leave. Surely she had only walked outside, then turned around and came back in. She sat down, the seat still warm from her body.

There was one difference, and now it seemed to gather all her attention: the little girl. She stood in the same corner, but now grown by some years—or perhaps some magic? Luceldar. That was her name. Brought here to replace Catie as Newmother. Lucie's parents, too, were gone. But hers were most definitely dead, drowned. An accident: not her fault, and not their choice. For a moment Catie couldn't smell warm yeast, didn't really feel the familiar seat beneath her, and didn't notice Grandmother arranging herself in a chair on the opposite side of the table. The whole room was only Luceldar's presence: the smell was her sunburnt hair, the sound was her breathing, the feel was her cotton dress. Catie's mind was Luceldar's mind. Bereft, still, but not guilty, not uncertain. Sorrowful, but not wondering what it was about *her* that made thus, so.

Luceldar's presence shifted, and Grandmother was smiling, welcoming, not caring why thus was so but only glad. Catie blinked into an uncertain smile, a small sigh.

"Because everyone keeps leaving me," Catie said, still smiling through the gasping sob that escaped quite without her permission. Suddenly, months of tears unshed rushed forward, not waiting behind her eyes for their turn. Almost maniacally she tried to hold her smile, until Grandmother's stricken face allowed her to drop that, as well, and she knew only weeping.

***

"...get up. Rodigger, wake up. Rodigger!"

Rodigger swiped the hand from his shoulder frantically and squirmed away. It was Gabriel, though—but still Rodigger had to catch his breath.

"Bad dream?" Gabriel asked without sympathy.

Rodigger stared at him for a few moments. "Yeah, yes, it was." *I thought you were Deuel.*

"We're going to the libraries. Let's go."

"What about breakfast?" Rodigger asked as he swung his legs off the bed and grabbed his boots.

"Grab something from a vendor on the way there."

"You're in a hurry," Rodigger mumbled as he pulled on his shirt.

"You would rather this job take longer than necessary?" Gabriel asked coldly as he headed out of the room, clearly already knowing, and not wanting to hear, Rodigger's response.

Rodigger shrugged. Fair enough.

Most large towns in Andelen—Rodigger had heard—had, as a remnant of their past, the large center spike that was the keep. It was the building that could be seen from nearly every quarter of the rest of the town, unless one was hard up against a taller building. In Stramfath, however, what dominated the view from nearly every direction, was the libraries.

Though the word was plural, the building was singular in every sense: seven stories tall, and long enough to block five through-ways, it was the largest collection of books in Andelen, and probably points across the oceans as well. The keepers of the libraries were known everywhere. Many said that the entire place could go up in flames, but find the keepers and they could recite to you its contents in detail.

Oddly enough, it had not been here that Roth had found his stories of the Berkarfor—but perhaps those who hid them so many centuries ago planned that. Stramfath was known even then as a center for knowledge, and the Berkarfor were supposed to fall outside of knowledge.

But those who hid them had not planned on Roth, Rodigger thought with a boyish grin. Of any man to replace Rodigger's father, he could not have picked better than Roth.

So, even though he could not see Gabriel or Deuel when he exited the inn, he could see where they had likely headed. He wasn't quite ready to face Deuel anyway. He knew he would have to, and would have to continue for perhaps months to come. Before falling asleep last night he had almost settled that within himself. But a few extra hours of preparing to face that reality was fine by him.

He did not dawdle, but he did not rush either. He stopped at a few vendors and looked at what foods they had before finally parting with a few coin for a piping hot *tetan* and chilled goats-milk. He slowed his pace now, if only to keep from slopping his breakfast as he continued toward the libraries.

As he approached the main doors, he licked the last of the cinnamon from his fingers and wiped them on the squirrel-skin now drained of milk. He tossed the empty skin to the gutter, and entered.

There were great windows set to allow in rivers of sunlight, and the stacks glowed where sunbeams struck gold- and silver-embossed books. Thick trunks supported an alarmingly thin lattice of iron, it appeared, that were the floors of the six levels, so that—when Rodigger craned his neck in surprise—he could see all the way to the cedar roof almost one hundred feet overhead. Row upon row of shelves soared upward till it seemed they would have to fall over. In front of him, as he brought his head down dizzily, the shelves ranged to the far wall in an impossible-to-fathom number. He swallowed hard. How were they to find what would surely only be a few books on the Berkarfor among this labyrinth?

"Can I help you find a particular book?" asked a gentle voice beside him.

Rodigger turned swiftly, and again dizzily. A small man, perhaps five feet tall, draped in a thick maroon robe, smiled up at him. The man was nearly bald, and his forehead folded tightly into a few wrinkles as his soft eyebrows arched in polite inquiry.

"Um, I'm looking for something on..." he trailed off. He probably should not talk about their mission specifically. "Actually, I'm meeting two friends here."

"Ah! You seek the Berkarfor as well?" the man asked in rapture. "A most interesting subject. I had not read on them for years, but I soon shall. Follow me, please!"

Rodigger waited to glower until the man had turned away. Those two had no sense of discretion! Rodigger's mouth twisted sideways: truthfully, Gabriel had no sense of discretion. Deuel had probably said nothing. Maybe that was just as bad.

Rodigger quickly set off after the keeper as the swirling maroon robe disappeared up a staircase.

⸺◦⸺

Catie awoke, blinking. A white oak chest of drawers she did not recognize glowed in the slanting morning sunlight, nearly blinding her. She nestled into the pillow a little, stretching her back, and sniffed. The lavender-scented sheets she knew, and some of her clothes hanging behind the chest she knew. After a few more wonderfully thought-free blinks, she raised her head and looked around.

She was in Grandmother's spare room.

No.

It was her room. Hers after her parents had gone, when her home had been too empty for her to stay. But it had never been *hers*. She would not have put the things in there that were there, and certainly not where in the room they were: they made no sense where they were. She had been fitted into the room, loose around the edges and uncomfortable in some places. She utilized it as best she could, but did not have it hemmed. It was not hers. In that sense, it mirrored her life in just about every way.

She glanced again at the white oak, angled her gaze to try to look out the window but could not. Still, if the sun was up, so was Grandmother. Another blink and the scent of maple syrup sprang to life in her nostrils. Memories of last night's exhaustion slipped away as she inhaled deeply, and smiled. After generous helpings of what Grandmother was making, she would be ready to talk, memories buffered now by sugar and love borne by sharing a good meal.

Catie rose and dressed quickly, then made her way to the kitchen. Grandmother was turning from the oven, wooden paddle laded with cakes fresh from the fire. A jar with canted lid sat near the flames, and she knew the source of the warm syrup smell was there. Catie smiled and sat before she noticed Luceldar in the same corner as last night, silent and watching, and Catie's smile wavered.

"Fetch us a few mugs," said Grandmother, to almost no one in particular. Luceldar moved silently and immediately. Grandmother seemed to think that was right, so Catie settled more firmly into her seat.

When all was arranged Grandmother looked to the ceiling. "May we accept this bread from your hands," she said, "and give back at the end of this day the bread of our labor."

Catie bit into her cake quietly. It had been years since she had offered that simple supplication, though she very much liked it. She only hoped—if the God of All took her—she would not go until she had given back equal to what she had taken that day. It seemed only fair.

They ate without speaking. Grandmother's house sat near the edge of the village, and behind it were a dozen large trees. So the birds did not permit the silence to hang heavy. Luceldar cleared the dishes when they had finished, and returned to her corner.

"I met a man in Sprativerg," Catie said. "Named Dannid. He was...bursting with ideas," she said, smiling a little.

Grandmother smiled too. "You always liked the quiet, thoughtful ones."

"Oh, he was not quiet," Catie replied. "The quiet ones still ponder. Dannid had finished pondering and was past ready to speak. I think that's why I liked him more..." Catie's voice lowered. "That's why I loved him."

"But he has gone?"

"He was taken," Catie murmured resolutely. She could no longer be timid about her thoughts, and how she expressed them. "By Roth, personally. In Bokessin."

"That sounds far away."

"Almost on the tip of the Fallonvall, in the Dragonsback," Catie affirmed with a nod.

"You were deep in Roth's territory."

"A week or so from his headquarters," Catie said, with another nod. "Or, where he was supposed to be headquartered. Dannid achieved too much, and Roth came down to put a stop to it. He was very successful."

"You were close to this man?"

"We were married," Catie said, her lower lip quivering a moment before she pressed her lips together. She paused to collect herself with a deep sigh that she released audibly. "For three days, before Roth arrived."

"You're a widow?" Luceldar exclaimed from her corner. When both sets of eyes swung on her, she looked appropriately mortified at speaking those thoughts aloud, though her eyes were still wide with incredulity.

"At twenty-three years old," Catie responded. It was not as if that were the first time the realization crossed her mind. When widowhood in a child's mind is always associated with *old* women, the two are hard to separate. It was only slightly easier for Catie.

"So you came back here," Grandmother said.

"I tried to get revenge on Roth," Catie admitted. "He had a moment of luck, though. I sneezed, and he could hear my voice. It's a longer story," Catie said with a wave of her hand. "But he also had a moment of mercy and only sent me out of the town without my horse, and with only a few hours until sunset." She proceeded to tell the rest of the tale, including meeting Gabriel, Deuel, and Rodigger—but she left out the strange light that pierced the sky that first night. She wanted to contemplate that on her own, for at least a little while longer. She did not normally keep things from Grandmother—why would you, when wisdom sat right in front of you?—but until she could bring her thoughts closer to bear on those events, she would wait.

"I know I could feel him. Deuel," Catie said. "Which was strange. But I know—well, I wondered if he might be a dragon-son. You remember telling me about those..." Her posture affected a question if her inflection did not.

"I would like to see him," Grandmother replied carefully. "You found him in the right spot. And your description of his eyes seems to fit. But they are so hard to find." She wagged her head and smiled. "I haven't seen one since..." Her eyes flashed, and she shook her head again. "What will you do now?" she asked.

Catie ran her finger up and down the side of her empty mug. "I don't know," she murmured. "I'm not sure if I'll stay here, or..." She shrugged, but did not look up. "I don't know."

"You want to try to travel with these men?"

Catie drew a deep sigh. "I don't know," she answered more firmly. "Not yet."

⚬

"Thorgiar got it wrong, Jahsonn, I read it in Kuelgar's *Treatise on mid-Ancient Rinc Nain.*"

"You are the only one to have read that ridiculous work, Perator," Jahsonn replied wearily. "Not a single one of Kuelgar's contemporaries agreed with him—and few enough even recognize such a dialect! It simply doesn't exist in any accredited work."

"But it is worth recognizing that, in the absence of practical proof, this explanation is certainly better than none as to why that verse sounds the way it does."

"There isn't enough research!" Jahsonn's voice was rising in strain if not as much volume. "Just because no one has *found* it, does not mean the evidence is wrong. Almost no one is looking for it!"

A third figure in maroon robes walked up. "What is this arguing?" he asked in a deep rumble.

Gabriel rolled his eyes. "I guarantee they could not begin to tell you," he muttered. Rodigger looked on as well, though his eyes were glazed over. Deuel was still among the books.

"Jahsonn is trying to say that *Berkarfor Hidden* is translated absolutely properly, when anyone who has read anything on the work can tell it was shoddily done. Just reading the text in translation, there is so much that doesn't make sense!"

"The translation is the best we have," Jahsonn replied. "Perator is arguing for argument's sake because he fears he isn't valued here."

"These men seek a perfect translation of *Berkarfor Hidden*?"

"Oh," Jahsonn replied as Gabriel fairly growled. "No, Kreath, they seek the Berkarfor."

Kreath's gaze went to Gabriel, then to Rodigger, who still was not paying much attention. Without taking his eyes off the two men, he plucked the book from Perator and tucked it under his arm. "The Berkarfor do not exist," he said quietly, but firmly.

Rodigger's eyes snapped to, then. "Yes they do," he said, just as firmly though much louder.

Kreath ignored him, proceeding to the shelves where he put the thin book back in the thin hole where it had been. "You are not the first to look for them, and you will probably not be the last. Anyone whose dreams rest on such a preposterous idea are made to let them die by chasing a non-existent breeze. As it should be. If you want power and influence, then earn it the same way as everyone else."

Kreath turned on his heel and disappeared among the shelves. Perator and Jahsonn looked everywhere but at Rodigger and Gabriel for a few moments, then with swift glances turned and left as well.

"What—what now?" Rodigger asked, too stupefied to be angry. Gabriel turned to look at the shelves, then down the line at the thousands upon thousands of books in the libraries.

Deuel walked past, his cloak rustling slightly as he moved. "We chase the breeze," he said without hint of concern.

Gabriel squinted, then followed. Rodigger, his mouth propped open, came last.

7

WORDS MISTAKEN

"How is yours doing?"
"He seems to be accepting it. Yours?"
"I think he is accepting it, as well."
"So you do not choose the one I suggested…"

21 Thriman 1320 — Winter

The three men rode through a crisp, clear day. The air was still, and they plodded slowly enough to almost enjoy the day. Perhaps Gabriel and Deuel did. Rodigger did not. That…*behamian*…rode in front, leading them the God only knew where. The lake lay flat and sapphire to their left, broad tan fields lay to their right. In between the heavy hoof-falls of their mounts was the crunch of the short grasses still awaiting spring's birthing—there was no road on this side of the Agirbirt.

Deuel's eyes roved far out across the lake. How far or what he was looking for, Rodigger did not care to guess. The dragon-spawn had not said what he had found in the books, if anything. Rodigger shifted to his right to relieve a twinge in his knee, and sighed as quietly as possible.

He wondered, not for the first time, if Catie would have been able to help them find the Berkarfor. There was no reason she should have, any better than they themselves, but at least they could have passed the time in her company. He sighed again, not worried about muffling it this time. He sensed more than saw Gabriel shift to look at him, and kept his eyes everywhere but on their guide.

Deuel had stopped, completely and unnaturally still. Rodigger scoffed at himself: the entire man was unnatural, anything he did would be unnatural. But this time he exuded as much life as a bit of timber. It made Rodigger shiver, though that might have just been the brief, chill breeze that sprang up from across the lake.

Deuel's eyes returned forward, and their horses resumed their plodding.

"What did you see?" Rodigger asked. "Or think you saw?" he added, not realizing it was going to come out of his mouth until it was entirely too late.

"The breeze," Deuel replied.

"You saw the breeze?" That wasn't too scornful, was it?

"I saw it ruffling the lake," Deuel replied. "I hoped it was something else."

"If I knew what we were looking for, I might be able to help," Rodigger muttered.

Gabriel's disdainful snort carried. Deuel made no such noise. "The first Berkarfor is in the middle of the lake," the dragon-son replied simply.

Rodigger's Therian felt him go still and mimicked, while Gabriel and Deuel rode ahead. "It's *in* the lake?" he asked faintly.

Gabriel twisted to look at him, and reined in his horse. "Well, hopefully it's more *on* it, than in it. Like an island might be in the middle of it."

This made enough sense for Rodigger to continue riding. "But why didn't he see an island when he scouted it, earlier?"

"The most obvious answer would be that it wasn't there to be seen," Gabriel replied patiently.

"It might be sunk," Deuel replied, up ahead. "I could not come too low for fear of being seen, so it may hide well under the waters."

"We won't have to row all over this lake, will we?" Rodigger asked, then wished he hadn't. He might not want the answer.

"Someone probably already has," Gabriel replied. When Rodigger gazed at him silently, he pointed.

It took Rodigger a few moments, against the white horizon, to spot the slowly-moving masts of small fishing boats that had no wind to propel them. He pursed his lips. Villagers from Attelek, of course, would range all over the lake for fish.

"Why didn't we just go straight to the village?" he asked, managing to keep mention of Catie to himself.

"We are," Gabriel replied, his gaze still sweeping the lake.

A few heartbeats passed. "On the road," Rodigger added.

"Because everyone takes the road," Gabriel replied. "It would be a terrible place to hide something like an island."

"We will stop and rest ahead," Deuel said, gesturing forward to where Rodigger could just make out a small hill on the horizon. "I may try to scout again, there."

Rodigger shuddered, and wished he were in Attelek.

Catie walked the familiar streets filled with unfamiliar people.

That wasn't entirely true: everyone over the age of fifteen looked the same, or nearly. Lederor apparently thought he looked better with a full beard, but he changed himself more than Eltsabech changed her dresses, so that was not surprising. What unnerved her were the children, who would stare at her until she finally recognized them, or realized she was supposed to. She almost never remembered them properly, taking them for their older siblings. By lunchtime, she figured she had distanced herself from at least half the village's young people because of it.

The buildings and streets, thankfully, were exactly the same. Wannaker's dress shop was next to Kalador's candles was next to Jutes and Peteyda's stone and iron cookware was next to Hadera's pottery. Geezer Matteuer, for a wonder, still stood griping to Canatheta, who looked just as weary of hearing it as he did every day. Yet somehow they met in front of the forge every morning between errands.

Catie's head tilted as she walked, remembering the day long ago when she suddenly thought that calling Matteuer "Geezer" sounded absurdly disrespectful. Then, as now, she had found him near the forge. The setting was so similar, she found herself reliving the memory.

She walked boldly up to him, barefoot in a linen dress.

Matteuer's scowl softened only a little as she approached. Canatheta looked completely relieved.

"Caytaleane," Matteuer growled.

Catie smiled. She also knew, for Matteuer, this was him at his friendliest, and it pleased her.

"Why," *clang!* "do you let," *clang!* "us call you th—" *clang!* Catie glanced at the forge; so close. "That?"

"Call me what?" he replied, with the appropriate pauses.

"Geezer!" Canatheta said loudly.

"What? One at a time, now."

"And why do you try to hold a conversation right next to the forge?" Catie asked, almost losing the end of her question for how long it took to ask.

"I don't usually have to answer so many—oh for—what was the question? Not supposed to ask so many questions!"

"Why do you let us call you 'Geezer'? It's not very nice, really."

"It's my name," he replied.

"No it isn't."

"It's not, Geezer," Canatheta agreed.

"Then why do you keep calling me that?"

"Well, because..." Catie paused, glancing at Canatheta and flushing a little.

One of Matteuer's great, white, bushy eyebrows rose in anticipation as his gleaming eyes flicked back and forth between the two, but neither was able to answer him. "Because I'm an old geezer?" he asked.

Catie cocked her head a little, and nodded.

"Or because that's what you keep calling me?"

Catie's head straightened, and her brow furrowed. Matteuer bent and placed both his hands on her head, and glared at her. She blinked for several moments. His hands gripped a little tighter—except the skin was soft, not calloused, and held her still rather gently. The eyes that gazed into hers were a crystal blue, shining as the Agirbirt on a clear day. His scowl—no, that was his mustache. Now that she looked this closely, she could see the line of his lips curving upward, slightly, behind it. His eyebrows were thicker at the center, but the tops rose from outside to inside, they were not drawn down in anger.

"You call me that because you have always called me that," Matteuer said quietly. "And you see me that way because you have called me that and did not bother to look closer. When what you see agrees with what you believe, Caytaleane, then you must ask the harder questions."

He released her, and as she stepped back his scowl returned. She blinked a few times, trying to focus. He was still smiling ever so slightly. She shook her head. "You could make a better effort," she said, grinning.

He did, smiling widely, and he looked so absolutely comical that she burst out laughing. "Okay, fine," she said. "You know yourself best, I suppose."

"That is something almost no one believes," Canatheta said, jabbing his finger at her.

"Do you believe it's true?" she asked.

"Not in the least," Matteuer replied. "But it's a better starting point than the opposite. But don't you have better things to do than stand around talking to a couple of old geezers?"

"A couple?" Canatheta said, sounding hurt.

"Yeah, I only see one," Catie said.

Geezer squinted at her, putting on his best, actual scowl. "Be off, with you both!" he said, forgetting to pause for the strike of the hammer.

She smiled and waved as she passed. Geezer's face split into his comical grin, and she laughed. It was good to be home. But almost as quickly as she thought it, her heart stirred northward.

※

Deuel flew, skimming across the water with his wings flat and wide. Rodigger watched him grow larger and fidgeted. He was going to be able to stop, right?

The wings suddenly showed their broad sides, vein and bone in sharp relief. Deuel hit the ground running, quickly folding them away and steadying to a walk.

"I do not believe there is anything out there," he said. Was it exertion, or did he sound disappointed? Rodigger blinked and looked at Gabriel.

"They wouldn't drop it just into the lake, would they?" the mercenary asked.

"That would hide it," Deuel suggested.

"They were not hidden so that they could never be re-found," Rodigger said firmly. "There has to be a way. Or it's somewhere else."

Deuel said nothing, but returned to the horses. They had hobbled them at the base of the hill. The side facing the lake had fallen away, leaving a short cliff perhaps ten paces high, and would make good shelter in a storm.

"We'll continue around the whole lake, seeing what we see," Gabriel said. "Surely something will stand out."

⸻◆⸻

She had been back in the village for over a week and still had no idea what to do with herself. She had revisited all the old friends, all the old shops, and even a few of the old shores of Agirbirt. Her mind knew she needed to restart her life, find something to do around the village. She would not live with Grandmother forever. But her heart was not attuned. Something told her she would not be staying in the village, though nothing told her why. She recalled a vague sense from so long ago that she would return home, but not stay long. None of the urgency was there. One day, as a test, she tried to fake the urgency, but it refused. And yet neither could she force herself to think of staying at home.

And so she walked, enjoying the sunshine today. It was spring, finally, and winter had the urgency to leave that she lacked. Already tulips raised bright green buds skyward, and the robins dotting the fields wreaked havoc on the earthworm population. The lake was a calm blue, the river running out of its south-eastern end frothing over the rocks. Attelek's full complement of fishers were out, already preparing to stock for next winter. The Agirbirt never quite froze over, but if they could fish on a day like today, and not those of two weeks ago, why wouldn't they?

As a breeze tickled her hair, Catie's smile faded. Before she looked up the road toward Stramfath, she knew what she would see: three riders, one whose eyes could pierce her before she could even make them out. Without fully knowing why, she turned and went back into the village.

"They're here," she said, standing in Grandmother's kitchen doorway.

Grandmother paused only a few moments. "I've just put a pot on," she said gently. "But if you want to bring them by, they would be most welcome."

"I—" *was hoping you would come with me, so I could hide behind your skirts,* Catie didn't say. "I'll see why they're here. They may just be passing through."

Rodigger came in the lead, glancing around the small collection of houses. It was surprisingly well-established. He had expected huts ready to be blown away by the first storm off the lake—but perhaps that had occurred already in the village's history, and they had learned better.

"We'll see if anyone around the village knows anything," Gabriel said behind him. The silence at the end of his sentence caught Rodigger's attention strangely, and he turned to look at the mercenary. Even Deuel was gazing at his friend as Gabriel's eyes roved unhurriedly around the scene before them.

That man was getting too old, Rodigger decided. He was enjoying things too much. Rodigger had fidgeted every moment as they wasted six days circling the lake, another back in the libraries in fruitless search, and three more riding back to Attelek. What could a village like this possibly know that Stramfath didn't?

Stramfath said the Berkarfor didn't exist at all, said a small voice inside Rodigger. It was a good point, and the part that criticized himself the most was surprised he had thought of it. But who to ask?

Catie.

Someone young, perhaps. They were the most learned, usually. Maybe one of them had studied at Stramfath but had returned for any number of reasons. Someone who had traveled.

"I wonder how hard it would be to find Catie?" Rodigger mused aloud.

Deuel and Gabriel reined up short, and he turned. They were staring at him.

"I just thought—she did say to find her if we came out this way, didn't she?"

Gabriel's mouth twitched. "No," he said.

"I thought she did. Either way, we probably want someone traveled, learned, someone who may have actually heard about these things. So I figured..." he trailed off as he suddenly realized they both were looking past him. He turned forward.

And there she was. In a light dress, though what of her legs showed beneath the hem were protected by thick wool leggings and leather shoes. She was striding toward them confidently, her slender arm giving a slight wave, her smile filling Rodigger's vision. Her hair waved and bounced almost joyfully as she walked, though her pert—

Rodigger's Therian shifted, and he gripped the saddle horn tightly, pretending to ease himself in the saddle as he shoved desperately at the thoughts in his mind.

"So, did you find what you were looking for?" she asked, innocently enough.

"Afraid not," was Gabriel's easy reply.

She cast a raised eyebrow around the trio. "What about what I said you would find?"

It must take an angel to say 'I told you so' and make you feel better about yourself for it—and the angels must have come to Catie to learn, Rodigger decided. He grinned with genuine happiness. "I suppose we did," he said. No one outside the Fallonvall thought what Roth did was right, and yet Rodigger had not once felt in danger because of it. He felt in danger for other reasons, but not that one. "Actually, I was thinking you might be able to help us find what we're looking for, or at least get started," Rodigger said. Her smile seemed easy enough, Rodigger thought, and yet...

"And what is that?" she asked.

There it was: the tone Roth took with him when his mentor already knew the answer, and just wanted to hear Rodigger say it. Rodigger glanced at his companions, who looked back at him and made no sign of reply.

So he didn't bother to explain. "The Berkarfor," he replied simply.

Catie's gaze locked onto him. Why couldn't it always be that easy? But then her smile faded as she nodded. "Then you'll need to see Grandmother," she replied. With a final glance at the others, she turned and walked back into the village. The men dismounted and followed.

Catie said nothing, did not even look at them again as they reached a house and tied up their horses outside and then followed her inside.

"Grandmother," she called out as they entered. "I have brought three who need to speak to you."

They entered the kitchen, and there sat an old woman—Catie's grandmother, apparently—and a young girl of about seven or eight, Rodigger thought. Catie's sister? She seemed too young for that, but too old to be her daughter, surely. Hopefully.

The woman rose, and assessed them all in a glance that would have made Deuel proud. "Welcome," she said. "I'll have fresh bread in a few moments. You must stay."

"That would be wonderful," said Gabriel, bowing his head. "I am Gabriel Owens. This is Rodigger Kytes. And behind him is Deuel."

Rodigger stepped quickly out of the way with a grimace. How had that happened?

"From Burieng?" she asked. Rodigger glanced up, then over at Deuel as the dragon-son gazed at her.

"I am," he said.

"Your name," the old woman said, with a brief wave of her hand and a small smile. "It is not Andelian." Deuel inclined his head briefly.

"And what is your name?" Rodigger asked as politely as he could.

Her smile strengthened as she looked at him. "Grandmother," she replied, as though it settled the matter. Glancing at the others, it seemed she was right. "Do you not have a Grandmother where you are from?" she asked, her gaze directed at Rodigger.

"Well, of course," he said. "Or, I did. Two, but they both—what?"

"An Elder Woman?" she asked gently.

"Oh," Rodigger said flatly. "Yeah, not anymore. No need."

"Ah yes," Grandmother said, lowering herself back into her seat. "Everything is in books, and in the minds of the young, educated people."

It was almost as if she had read his thoughts, so why deny it? He nodded once, gently.

"Yet here you are," Grandmother continued with a sharp glance. "What aren't they teaching you, anymore?"

This time Rodigger did not reply as he steamed under her rebuke, and squirmed for looking the fool in front of Catie.

"The Berkarfor," Gabriel replied for him.

Grandmother sat back, her expression cooling. "Why do you look for those?" she asked.

"Because I am paid to," Gabriel replied.

"It is a sad motivation."

Gabriel snorted. "Then it is because I am hungry," he said.

"Interesting how our ways of life are worn like our skin," Grandmother said, rubbing gently over the backs of her hands. "You do not feel it until someone pokes or prods. For most of us in Attelek, the need for food does not so instantly equal the need for money. Just a bit of work. Those who spend most of their time in Balnath Agrend, I imagine, could not grow and harvest their own food if they wanted to. Can I say to them 'scorn your coin and do a bit of work'?"

Gabriel bowed a little at the waist. "No, Grandmother, you could not."

"What do you know of the first goblet?"

"Beqart el laken zeum finten qa Berkarfor peya on de traschen," Deuel replied. "The first was hidden in Agirbirt Lake."

Grandmother stood, turned to the oven behind her, and pulled out a loaf of black bread that rested near the edge. She cut off a few slices and lay them on a bit of cloth. "These will need to cool a moment, but they should not be too cool, to be enjoyed most."

"Is that to help us, somehow?" Rodigger asked, thinking she still spoke in riddles.

But the corner of her mouth quirked upward. "This will only help Gabriel's hunger a little," she replied. "It would do very little in answering the larger question."

"Can you help us?"

Grandmother seated herself again, her gaze bent upon the table as she sat silently for a long while. Catie stepped forward first to claim a slice of bread. On her cue, the three men did the same, and they ate in silence. Rodigger could feel his shoulders relax as he ate. The warmth of the bread and the silent camaraderie in sharing a simple meal was not lost on him. He was pleased to see Catie did not snap at her bread, or chew unevenly—he could not stand it when a girl ate noisily, or bit down too swiftly. He could see the muscles of her jaw working, the thin, small lines that flashed at the hinge of her jaw as it worked.

He took another bite, then noticed Grandmother was watching him. He blushed, then scratched at his forehead to obscure his face.

As they dusted off their hands of crumbs, Grandmother finally spoke. "The answer lies in your translation. Or, rather, your interpretation. Deuel's translation is perfect, as I would expect," she continued with a respectful nod. She paused, then took a crust of the bread and set it on the table before her. She wadded up a towel, and placed it over the crust.

"Where is the piece of bread?" she asked, glancing around those gathered.

"Under the towel," Rodigger replied first.

"Very good." She grasped the towel and lifted it. The crust was gone. She overturned her hand, showing the bread in the folds of the cloth. "Now where is it?"

"In the towel..."

"It's under the lake," Gabriel said with a nod. "In a cave, under the lake?"

"For your sake, hopefully," Grandmother replied with a smile.

⎯⎯⎯◦⎯⎯⎯

"How exactly will you help us find it?"

Gabriel knew the answer, but enjoyed the animated gestures Rodigger was making behind Catie's back, trying to convince him to let her come along.

"I know this area, and I know the lake certainly better than you do," she replied.

"We've been around it once, already," Gabriel said, though Catie had not quite finished speaking.

"And the fishers will probably talk to me, before you," she finished.

Gabriel considered this for several long moments before slowly nodding. He thought Rodigger might just turn into a puddle of relief. Catie smiled as she turned away, but it was almost a smile that shared in his joke, rather than eased in relief. She knew she was going. This girl was bright, and would probably prove immensely useful.

As Catie fetched and saddled her horse, Gabriel stood physically with his companions while his mind wandered around Attelek. It reminded him of Bokessin. Not because of the surrounding landscape: Bokessin was deep in the mountains, and Attelek, well, Attelek was not. That far south, the mountains around Bokessin had begun their descent toward the sea. But here one could stand at the edge of the village and see, flat outward, to the horizon. The fields nearby offered just enough grains for breads, and probably beer, with a little extra for Sheppar's collectors when that time of year came. Most of the rest of their needs came from Agirbirt's fish or Satost's traders.

But it was more than that, more than the smallness of the village or the simplicity of life: it was the people. It was the culture he knew lived here. He could see it as he glanced around, saw people on paths oblique or at right angles stop, and wave, and talk. It took a lifetime to get to know someone, and that's what they had, here and at Bokessin and dozens of other villages around Andelen: a lifetime. Gabriel was rarely in one place long enough to find all the best spots to eat, let alone get to know anyone. It's what they had at the inns, most times: common-rooms and shared quarters meant that no one meeting at night on the road were strangers for very long. A shared meal was more than just sustenance, it was commonality.

It was, he had to admit, what Roth wanted—commonality on such a grand scale that a villager from deep in the Brithelt could travel to south-eastern Fallonvall and still find it. It was a grand, beautiful, impossible idea. Grandmother had said it best: she could not tell a citizen of Balnath Agrend to grow their own food. She could, perhaps, persuade them to drink Attelek beer. It amused and surprised Gabriel, sometimes, how the slightest of commonalities made for the fastest of friends. But never would one get to know another beyond those little details unless they put down some roots, became part of the forest. Or plain, as the case may be.

He sighed as Catie rode up. Perhaps it *was* the simplicity of life here. He pulled himself into the saddle. Perhaps it was the camaraderie. He had Deuel, sure, but he no longer wondered what commonality they had. There was none. Circumstance, at one time, perhaps. But Gabriel was past getting old. Deuel had a few centuries, hopefully, before he would start to think he might be approaching old age. Of course, by that time, Gabriel would still be a human, and Deuel, hopefully, would not.

"Why did Grandmother look at you like that?" Gabriel asked Deuel as they began their route out of the village.

Deuel's eyes glittered. "I do not know."

"What did she do?" Rodigger asked, riding up beside them and scattering a few villagers in his wake.

Gabriel looked straight ahead for a few moments, then shook his head and looked at Rodigger. "Didn't know you missed that. When she asked if he was from Burieng, it wasn't just because his name isn't Andelian."

"Grandmother knows about *behamien,* or at least a little," Catie said from behind them.

"Everyone knows a little about them," Rodigger muttered, though his gaze was carefully away from Deuel.

"Well, a little more than most," Catie responded. "She knew at least one before, personally."

Deuel's posture shifted. "Did she say his name?" he asked.

"Who said it was a he?"

Gabriel and Rodigger both took a quick glance. Deuel's silence felt like he acceded the point.

"She never told me, actually," Catie said. "It might be a he. She doesn't *say* much. But you can tell she knows."

"This was a common topic?" Deuel asked.

"Sometimes," Catie said slowly. "I find them—you—or whatever...fascinating."

"That's a word for it," Rodigger said. All eyes shifted to him, but his gaze remained resolutely toward the lake now coming into view.

"When did you find out what he was?" Catie asked.

Rodigger kept his silence, but a glance showed Gabriel his jaw muscles writhing.

"I had Deuel scout the lake," Gabriel replied. "About a week ago."

"You just up and flew, in front of him?" Catie asked. "Whew. I bet that was rough."

"Can you talk about me like I'm here?" Rodigger demanded, swiveling his gaze hard upon her.

"I was talking *to* you, silly," she replied. To his credit, he deflated a little. "You need to keep looking at people, even if you don't like what they're saying."

Gabriel smirked as he saw Rodigger's eyes go puppy-dog again. "It was definitely a surprise," Rod said.

Catie nodded with big eyes. "I can imagine. You probably haven't met—"

"Any," Rodigger interjected. "Any *behamien*. I had heard quite a bit, though."

"Like you said, everyone has," she agreed.

"Don't tell me you think what he believes is right?" Gabriel asked, turning his own fierce gaze upon her.

"Oh, what I think probably doesn't matter," Catie replied quickly. "We all create our world out of our thoughts, and you didn't give him much of a chance to think before smashing your fist into his world."

Rodigger's grin was silly as he looked at her. Gabriel frowned, stung, though she was right. He was too grumpy just now to admit it though.

"Of course, you should probably take some time to get to know Deuel for who he is," Catie continued easily. "Just in case you're wrong. Ho there!" she called, raising her hand toward a boat just landing itself on the shore.

There: his jaw muscles writhed again. Gabriel rolled his eyes and watched Catie approach the fishers.

"If you were a cave under the lake," she said as they neared the fishers, "where would you let people in?"

Grins split all their faces, but it seemed they were accustomed to Catie's methods. "How do you know I'd let you in?" the man at midships asked.

"Because I'm the sunniest girl in the Birnesath, Maf," she replied. "Also, you let people in before."

"If I existed."

"If you existed."

The men in the boat glanced at one another. "Whale fin?" one asked eventually.

"Yeah, or chopped grouper top," Maf said.

"Why those?" Gabriel asked. "Why not anywhere along the shore?"

"Because we assume you want to find it," said Maf. "And as you've already ridden all the way around the lake, you know a hole in the ground anywhere might be hard to spot."

"Where are these places?" Gabriel asked.

"There," chorused several of the men, pointing in opposite directions. Maf raised his hand playfully as if to strike them.

"Whale fin," he said, pointing one way. "Chopped top," the other direction.

"So, another week of searching," Gabriel said with a grunt.

"Unless you guess right the first time. Then it's only a few days."

"Whale fin is the cliff?" Deuel asked. Catie and the men in the boat nodded. Deuel glanced at Gabriel. "There."

Without word or waiting, Gabriel turned his horse toward the first direction. Deuel followed, then Rodigger. "Thanks, guys," Catie said with a wave, coming last.

"So long, sunrise," Maf replied with a sparkle in his eye.

8

TROUBLING WATERS

"I don't know why you make this sound so hard."
"Let us go speak with the God of All."
"Do we have to?"
"You do."

32 Thriman 1320 — Spring

It took them two days to reach the small cliff where they had rested while Deuel flew over the lake, and they spent that afternoon searching.

"It does almost seem like this would be a place to hide an entrance," Catie said.

"They hid the Berkarfor," Rodigger said sourly. "I'm sure they couldn't control where the entrance was. It's probably not even under the lake."

"*Passet dem halta hinter laken, diese shulte cararven paken,*" Deuel said. "It is near this hill."

"Are you sure you interpreted all that correctly?" Gabriel asked with a grin.

"Wait, the hill?" Rodigger said, straightening. "It's not a hill, it's a cliff."

"It's half a hill," Gabriel offered.

"Does the verse say it's half a hill? And where did you find this, anyway?"

"A small book I recognized," Deuel replied. "In Stramfath. But when the Berkarfor were hidden, this was a hill. This side was washed away."

"By what? There's no river here." He saw Catie turning her head. "That lake is all the way over there," he said, cutting off what he knew she was going to point out. "There's no way it took out this hill, or made this cliff."

"Well, wait," Catie said, catching Deuel's attention. "If it didn't pull the soil all the way into the lake, wouldn't that mean we're standing on it, still?"

Deuel, Gabriel, and Catie all looked at one another. "So the entrance might have been buried," Gabriel said.

"And the lake wouldn't always have been over there," Catie added.

Rodigger stared at the dirt. "We could dig for days, and turn out to be wrong."

"Did anyone bring a shovel?" Catie asked.

There was silence as Rodigger's shoulders slumped even lower. "Cheer up, Rodigger," Gabriel said finally. "Turns out we can't dig for days."

A breeze arose, and Catie and Deuel both straightened, looking southward. "Oh, no," said Catie.

"Now what?" Rodigger asked, turning. Behind them, on the horizon but fast approaching, were piles of black clouds.

"Let's see how this cliff holds," Gabriel said, already leading his horse over to its base.

"If I know these types of storms," Catie said as they followed, "we might want to get comfortable."

"All day?" Rodigger asked, patting Gared's muzzle.

"If we're lucky," Catie replied. She reached into a saddle bag and pulled out six metal spikes, each as long as her forearm, a thick roll of canvas, and a wooden hammer. "The wind should blow most of the rain over us, but just in case," she said, handing a corner of the tarp to Deuel.

By the time the clouds rolled overhead they had a makeshift lean-to stretching over their heads from the side of the cliff. The rain pounded down around them, but as Catie predicted most of it fell beyond their shelter. Between their own body heat and the horses' it stayed warm, but the clouds brought night early.

The wind did not slack overhead, and they could hear it roaring over the top of the cliff. They were able to make a small fire with some fuel Catie had brought and heat a decent meal.

"Did you expect this?" Rodigger shouted over the storm. Catie shook her head, but smiled.

"I've been away some time," she said. "But I remembered. These are common in the spring, and you always want to be prepared when you go out."

"I didn't even think about the fact we wouldn't be near an inn," Rodigger said.

Catie shrugged. "I didn't travel much when I was little. Papa kept me close. But we did have our own little adventures not too far out of sight of Attelek."

"We didn't meet him," Rodigger said.

Catie's smile softened. "He's been gone a while."

"How did he—I mean, where did he..."

Catie's mouth said "I don't know" but Rodigger couldn't hear the words for the storm. She looked up. "He left when I was eight. Went out fishing one morning and didn't come back."

"Lost on the lake?" Rodigger asked.

"He didn't take his boat, and it was a calm day," Catie replied, her tone a little harsher on those points. "He was a fisher. No. He left, and no one told me why."

Some piece of Rodigger's mind knew he was on dangerous ground, that he shouldn't push his luck. That piece did not convince him. "And your mother?" he asked.

Catie glanced sharply at him. He hadn't meant for it to come out that way, and he was at least as surprised as she was at his almost accusatory tone. Miraculously, she let it pass. "She left four years later," she said simply.

Now Rodigger didn't regret his tone. "Why?" he demanded.

Catie's eyes squinted a little, and she looked down at their small fire. Again she spoke below the storm, but Rodigger could not read her lips. "What was that?" he asked.

She straightened and approached near him. She was his height, just a little shorter. With her shoulders square and her body erect, she was tameless as the cliff under which they huddled. Her eyes glinted, and Rodigger could barely meet her gaze. Just before he dropped his eyes, hers softened—but only slightly. "I said: 'you don't get to know that, yet.'" Then she was moving past him deeper into their shelter. As Rodigger turned to watch her, he noticed Deuel looking at her with an expression nearing curiosity. Rodigger wondered, too, why she felt the need to confront him in such a way, in front of the other two. Something to work on, perhaps.

"Come look at this," Gabriel said, standing just outside the entrance to the lean-to. Rodigger and Deuel both approached. Catie remained near her horse, stroking its neck.

"Look at the lake," Gabriel said with a brief gesture.

Rodigger watched. Rain pelted it. The wind made the rain fall unevenly, sweeping great braids of ripples across the surface, pebbling it. But nothing extraordinary, except that Gabriel and Deuel both watched it as if some great secret were being revealed.

"I don't see it," Rodigger said.

"Shocking," Gabriel muttered. Then, louder: "Look at the shoreline. Does it look higher to you?"

"I guess it does," Rodigger said vaguely. "Except right there..." he trailed off, gazing at it. Nothing in the contour indicated the shoreline would extend at a point directly in front of the cliff, and yet it did, almost thirty paces out into the lake and another twenty or thirty paces wide.

"Why is it doing that?"

"The water is draining," Deuel replied.

Rodigger's shoulders slumped. "So it *is* buried?"

"Somewhere along that line, it would seem," Gabriel replied.

"We're going to have to dig *all that* out?" Rodigger gaped.

"Well hopefully not," Gabriel said brightly. He turned on Rodigger with a nearly evil grin. "But maybe."

"Good thing someone thought to bring spades," Catie said, startling Rodigger.

"I thought you said we didn't?"

Catie shook her head. "You need to start paying attention to what people say—what they *actually* say."

"You asked if anyone brought a shovel!" Rodigger said. "What am I supposed to think that means? Even Gabriel thought you meant that."

Catie shrugged. "And you were both wrong," she replied. "Notice how quiet Deuel is? He didn't assume what I meant."

Rodigger's eyes shot skyward briefly, and he glowered at nothing in particular. "Deuel's always quiet," he muttered.

"As soon as this storm lets up..." Gabriel cast his glance cloud-ward. "Hopefully in the morning, we'll see what we can dig up."

⊰◦⊱

The first thing Rodigger noticed when he awoke was a great damp spot beneath his bedroll, and soaking into his pants. He blinked a few times, worriedly, then confirmed a small amount of rain had made its way down the cliff-face and through the seam at the top of the lean-to.

The second thing he noticed was a great chorus of birdsong that some recess of his mind knew occurred only on bright, sunny mornings. He picked his head up, gazing out of the shelter at dirt and grass aglow with yellow light.

He sat up, noticing he was alone in the tent. Had they really started without him? He didn't mind the sleep—and certainly couldn't be blamed if no one woke him—but he was surprised.

"About time," Gabriel said from behind him. He startled and turned. The fire was going, and everyone gathered around a skillet someone had rigged to suspend over the flames with a large stick. "You almost got breakfast for free," Gabriel continued, holding out a small kettle.

Rodigger shuffled out of his blankets, and out of the tent, then took the kettle from Gabriel. He stood for several moments in silence.

Gabriel squinted up at him. "Water," he said.

"Oh," Rodigger said, glancing down at the kettle. "Right." He stood for several more moments, glancing around for a spring of some sort.

"Rodigger," Gabriel said slowly.

"Hmm?"

Gabriel pointed without looking, and Rodigger followed his finger. He blinked, slow and hard, then moved toward the lake amid intentional silence from the others.

They breakfasted on sausages and small eggs, and Gabriel made tea. When the sun was a hand-span above the horizon they began digging test-pits. By the time the sun reached its zenith they had found a large rock beneath the sand and dirt that was a dark, almost satin black like faded coal. It took them another shift to find the crack that, when levered against, opened the rock like a door. Steps carved in the hole led down into blackness, though some small, faint sheen came from below as from a distant light.

"Torches, and weapons," Gabriel said after they had gazed into the cavern for some moments.

"Weapons?" Rodigger echoed. "To fight what, the darkness?"

"You *hope* that's all that's down there," Gabriel replied, already moving back to the lean-to. "But for something that's been hidden for centuries, it sure was easy to find."

"So we've been lucky," Rodigger said, following Gabriel only to continue to be heard, not to retrieve a weapon—in truth, he had none.

"Then it's about time for our luck to run out, eh?" Gabriel asked as he ducked inside. Catie was close behind him.

"No verse denied defenses," Deuel said quietly. "But none mentioned it. I would not worry."

"I'm worried he's going to hurt one of us," Rodigger lied. He didn't know why he did that, even with normal people. Lying to Deuel was as useless as a whittling knife on stone, and he knew it.

He heard a thin rustling noise, and looked up as Deuel snatched his staff out of the air. Gabriel was striding toward them, strange swords at his hips, still sheathed. But he had armbands on, now, of some sort—another rusted red band similar to the ones on the cuffs of the weapons, but one had a thin yellow stripe around its center like amber, the other a bright red stripe like ruby.

"Jewelry?" Rodigger asked, gesturing to the armbands.

"Don't worry about it," Gabriel said with vast indifference. "If we do find something down there, though, don't stand in front of me."

Catie emerged next with torches and handed out one apiece. With a brand from the cook-fire she lit them, then glanced at the three men. "I don't really have a weapon," she said finally. "So I'm not too hung up on ladies going first."

Gabriel turned and led the way. Deuel came next, then Rodigger and Catie. Rodigger gave one quick glance around the sunlit skies as he descended, hoping he would see them again soon.

It was a short flight of stairs till a hall opened before them. Though the path continued downward, it was a gentle slope, and a gutter of sorts ran along the left wall. Gravel lay strewn across the floor, washed and carried as far as it could be. Their footsteps crunched and squished as they walked, and the still air was filled with the mineral smell of cold, wet rock. Somewhere in the distance, droplets *plonked* as from a great height into a deep lake.

"A lake beneath a lake?" Gabriel asked as the sound grew louder.

"That verse would make even more sense," Catie offered, her voice hushed though she wasn't sure why.

Gradually as they descended, the tunnel began to curve this way and that, and the gleam from their torches was overtaken by some other light, a bluer light. Another sound rose as well. It took longer to notice it, because it sounded like their own breathing, except thicker and louder.

When the tunnel finally leveled off, the light was bright enough they could have extinguished their torches. They did not, unsure of what the light-source was. And the breathing, almost snuffling sound echoed up and down the hall. Rodigger scratched at his hip, wishing now that he had a knife of some sort—or perhaps a full-on broadsword.

They approached a sharp turn, and Gabriel had no sooner stepped around it than a piercing shriek sent him scrambling backward, suddenly out of breath. Rodigger winced as the echoes reverberated, pummeling his ears.

The shriek ceased. Gabriel stood braced against the wall, his eyes nearly wider than his mouth.

"What was that?" Rodigger demanded, a little too loudly. Another shriek came, not as piercing, but still alarming. Gabriel's eyes rolled, but he was silent.

"Snehr-byor," Deuel said. He leaned his torch against the wall, and peered out from behind the corner. Rodigger gritted his teeth, but no shriek came. "He is walking away."

"Could we sneak up behind him?" Gabriel asked.

Deuel shrugged, and stepped out from behind the wall. He had no sooner disappeared around the bend when another shriek, louder this time, sent him sprinting back.

"By the God!" Rodigger shouted, pressing his hands hard against his ears. "What did you say it was?"

"It is *snehr...* Yeti," Deuel replied.

"It's no *kend* yeti," Gabriel snarled. "Yeti are myths. Myths that can be defeated in books. No one has ever written a story about killing a *snehr-byor,* because no one would believe it. The tale would never tell."

Rodigger twisted his mouth sideways, gazing at Gabriel out of the corner of his eyes. That sounded a bit extravagant. If the man didn't want to hunt down the Berkarfor, he could just say so. Rodigger moved to the corner, raising his eyebrows to ask permission from Deuel. The dragon-son gave him a glance, approval mixed with...mirth?

Rodigger rolled his eyes, then peered slowly around the corner. His body froze in place as his eyes grew steadily wider, and traveled upward. And upward, until massive yellow eyes glared back at him from hairy sockets, like snow-covered caverns in their own right. With a small, choked yelp Rodigger ducked behind the corner again.

"That thing is a house!" he whispered hoarsely. "It's a mountain! It's a chain of mountains with spires for teeth!"

"It must be something," Catie said from the rear. "That's the most descriptive I've ever heard you be."

"What are we going to do with this thing? This has to be the hiding place, so it has to be beyond him."

"Well," Gabriel said slowly, then drew a long sigh. "You're standing in front of me."

"What?"

"He said if we found anything to not stand in front of him," Catie said quietly, with a small smile.

Rodigger swallowed, then moved away from the corner. Gabriel approached, drawing his weapons from their sheaths. Rodigger's assessment had been correct: the blades were fixed to the underside of the wooden poles. Gabriel gripped the crossbar, and the cuffs fit around the bracelets he had put on his arms, snapping into place as he held them. The blades were the same rusty-looking metal as the other points of metal Rodigger had noticed. It was now that he also noticed it seemed too proper to actually be rust—its appearance was not an accident or a force of neglect, but as though the metal was supposed to look like that.

"Cretal," Deuel said quietly behind him, probably catching Rodigger's gaze as he caught everything else in life. "It channels the elements."

"He's using magic?" Rodigger hissed, grasping Deuel's arm as he forgot his distaste for the briefest of moments.

"No, not yet," Deuel replied in such a serious tone that Rodigger had no chance of finding it funny. Catie did not have that problem, and a smile briefly split her face.

"It's walking away again," Gabriel muttered. "Why does it keep doing that? It could fit back here to attack us. Might even be better for it if it did."

"Not better for us," Rodigger replied, aghast.

"My point is it's not acting the way it should be."

"So, it's easier to kill," Rodigger replied. "It probably hasn't fought anything in centuries. Lucky for us."

"Lucky for *us*," Gabriel emphasized, tossing an elbow toward Deuel. "You all don't have weapons, remember? Because danger doesn't exist anymore."

Rodigger said nothing, and Gabriel's gaze returned to his friend. "You ready?" he asked. Deuel's gaze answered him. Gabriel rolled his head once. "Then let's go."

He peered out, hesitated, then ran forward. The *snehr-byor* bellowed again bare moments after the two left, but they did not come scrambling back immediately. As the cry ceased, Catie's head came up. She darted forward to the corner and peered around it.

The *byor* stood staring at the two mercenaries, who were likewise motionless. It took a few deep breaths, then another wavering cry echoed through the chamber as it strode forward a few steps. Still the two held their ground. Again when the roar ceased, there was almost a hiccup as the *byor* drew a breath.

Gabriel's weapon came up, pointing at the beast. "Gabriel, wait!" Catie shouted, striding forward. Rodigger's eyes gaped as he watched her go.

Gabriel's weapon-point faltered, but he did not take his eyes of the *byor*. "Why am I waiting?" he asked as it stood, lips pulled back in a snarl as it panted at them.

"Look at it," she said, standing just behind the two men.

"I'm not looking at my fingernails, lass," he replied.

"No, I mean, look at *it*, not the *snehr-byor*."

"You make no sense! What do you think—"

"It's not roaring anymore," she said. "It's not advancing. It's just looking at you. Look at it as if it were not a dangerous beast."

"Catie," Gabriel rumbled in warning.

"It's crying," Deuel said suddenly and quietly.

"It's trying to," Catie replied. "But I don't think it can."

The creature panted a few more times, staring at them with eyes that, in any other socket, would appear rimmed in red. Its chest and shoulders bristled at them, but every other muscle was limp, barely holding the creature upright.

"So what do we do, then?" Gabriel asked, his weapon already lowering.

"Let's back up a few steps and sit down," Catie said, leading the way. They all kept their eyes on the creature, but backed up a few paces and sat. Its snarl subsided, its upper body deflated, suddenly rendering it frail and weary. It turned and shuffled away across the cavern, glancing back at them only occasionally.

Rodigger approached quietly. "What by Oren happened there?" he hissed, keeping his eyes firmly on the far end of the cave as the *snehr-byor* disappeared down another passageway.

"Let's find out," Catie said as she rose. She entered the cave proper and looked up, her pace instantly slowing. "Oh, wow," she breathed.

"What is it?" Deuel asked, coming forward. Catie only pointed upward. Then they saw where the light was coming from.

They were underneath the lake, and the cavern ceiling was probably not far from the surface. Somehow the roof was clear, as though comprised of thin and remarkably pure quartz. Sunlight streaming through blue waters entered and rippled against the walls, bouncing off sparkling rock and lighting the way as far as it could. A school of fish went by above, their shadows slithering across the cavern floor.

A moaning wail from the passageway pulled their attention back. Catie led. The two mercenaries followed, weapons still drawn but held low. Rodigger remained gaping at the quartz roof and refracted light until he heard his companions' murmurs wafting from the hall.

"...wait here," Catie was whispering as he approached.

"Always 'wait'," Rodigger said in normal tones. "Glory waits for no one." He made to continue down the passage, but suddenly Catie was in front of him, her glittering eyes on his, her hand splayed on his chest and making its supple presence felt. He backed away a step before she could feel his heart's thrill. "Why?" he managed to demand, wanting desperately to show her he had worth without weapons.

"Respect," she said. He cocked an eyebrow, and she stepped aside so he could see down the passage to dimly lit cavern, where the *byor* hunched over another *byor* that lay utterly still on the ground.

"Is it dead?" he asked stupidly.

"Probably its mate," Catie said, her voice again in a whisper. "It doesn't want to kill us, it wants to grieve."

"It's a *snehr-byor*," Rodigger enunciated. He glanced at the mercenaries, but could tell instantly he did not have their support. "Oh, wow," he muttered. "The only one without weapons is the only one not afraid to use them."

With a snap, Gabriel disengaged his strange swords from his arms and held them out toward Rodigger. "Okay, then," he said, eyebrows up.

Rodigger's heart squeezed once. "No no," he said, holding up his hands in mock defense; "wouldn't want to interrupt the *byor's* grieving."

Gabriel snorted, but before he could reply, Catie hissed at them. Ahead, the *byor* had lifted its partner and had turned to face them. They stood gazing at one another for several long moments.

"Let's go back into the cave," Catie suggested, keeping her eyes on the *byor* as she retreated. The others followed—Rodigger wagging his head slowly—and as they moved the *byor* took cautious steps forward, keeping the same distance.

When they reached the cavern again, Catie gestured toward the back wall. The *byor* entered after them, pausing to glance sideways at where they stood motionless. It inclined its head toward Catie before moving to the center of the room and laying its partner on the ground. It knelt, back to them, and did not move. A low thrum echoed through the chamber. It took Rodigger several moments to realize it came from the *byor*. The thrum built and grew. Above the quartz, schools of fish paused. The thrum slid into notes, then split into many. Soon a chant grew that was also a song, and the *byor* weaved back and forth as it sang. Its hands danced and pressed upon the fur of its fallen partner in some pattern he could only half-see.

The *byor* went still as the song ended without fade or echo. Rodigger's eyes felt suddenly as if they had not blinked for long moments as his gaze locked onto the back of the *byor*. "Catie?" he whispered from the side of his mouth. When she didn't respond, his eyes darted sideways. She was no longer with them.

Before he could wonder, Gabriel gasped and Rodigger's eyes snapped forward. The *byor* had stood and turned to face them, gazing at them impassively. Rodigger registered that the dead *byor* was suddenly gone, and knew he should wonder about that. But all his attention was on the one still living.

It placed its fists on the ground and bent double as if to sniff the dirt at its feet—but it was bowing. It touched its forehead to the ground, then straightened and drew a deep sigh. As it exhaled, it evaporated suddenly as if into dust and drifted away.

"Ummm..."

"Oh, it wasn't real," Catie said, suddenly beside them again. "Here." She held up something wrapped in burlap, something in the shape of a goblet, but just out of anyone's reach. "And if you want to find the next one, you'll take me with you."

9

CONCERNING DEUEL

"See? That worked itself out."
"Teresh, there is more to do."
"I don't know what will convince him."
"That is why you must actually speak to him."

33 Thriman 1320 — Spring

"When did you know it wasn't real?" Rodigger asked, ignoring for the moment that Gabriel had taken the burlap bundle and began to unravel it.

"Whenever we arrived here just in time to see it mourn its dead," Catie replied. "Convenient, wasn't it?"

"I don't understand," Rodigger said.

"Shocking," Gabriel said. "Here. Is this it?" He held out the cup, finally diverting Rodigger's attention.

It was primarily silver, undimmed by centuries underground, with gold piping running a geometric pattern between gems of ruby and sapphire. It was not deep, or broad, but it was not meant for casual drinking, either. Rodigger paused as the refracted light from above ran across it, and a vision floated across his eyes of lifting the Berkarfor himself, accepting the draft.

Light and vision disappeared at once, and he nodded. "It is," he said. "Does it say where to find the next one?"

Catie held up a folded parchment, then quickly held it out of reach. "Were you listening, earlier? I found the first one, and I know how to find the second, and third, and fourth. But I'm not doing it from here."

"And how do you know we can't find the third and fourth without you?" Rodigger asked.

Catie's hand dropped, and she gazed at Gabriel. "Is he serious?" she asked.

"His jokes aren't as funny," Gabriel muttered.

"Just give us the note, okay?" Rodigger said, holding out his hand.

Catie looked at him several long moments, her smile widening. She shrugged, and put the parchment in his hand.

"See?" he said, glancing at the mercenaries as he unfolded the parchment. "Sometimes you just need to be forthright." He smiled, and read the words on the page. As Catie's smile peaked, his faded. "What the *houl* does this mean?" he asked finally.

"I can guarantee only Deuel will know," Catie replied. "Oh, and me."

"Oh, and you?" Rodigger asked scornfully. "And how does that work?"

"Because I'm very good, too," she replied.

As Gabriel took the parchment from Rodigger and read, Rodigger caught, briefly, Deuel looking at Catie with an odd expression on his face—if it was more fully developed, Rodigger might have called it curiosity. But he doubted the dragon-son lacked enough knowledge to even be curious anymore.

Gabriel was reading aloud:

"Cliffs squarely squat and mutter at the sky,
Angled angrily aground and never gaining high
Wanderers wend and waggle here, send and haggle here.

"Rainbows reach and ruin, dashed slap-dash at doors,
Wars wage and blare far beneath the floors,
Wendol ward the pass, guard the glass here."

"I may know where that is," Deuel said, the closest thing to uncertainty in his voice Rodigger had ever heard.

"So we don't need Catie?" Rodigger asked lightly, his mind buzzing with consternation for suggesting such a thing.

"We still want her," Deuel replied, his look again as if reading Rodigger's mind. "She sounds more confident than I am."

Gabriel looked at him. "Hnnn," he said. He re-folded the parchment and gave it to her. "Let's get back to Attelek. Then Catie will tell us where to go next."

⚬

But Attelek had not had a cliff or tarp to shelter it from the storm the previous day. As they neared, they could see every fifth building had a crew of townsfolk atop it, repairing roofs. Many homes in between had no crew though they still showed need of repair. Catie dodged between a few friends, speaking rapidly. It seemed no one was hurt, though Velta would not be making breakfast for a while: the roof above her stores had been hit early and everything inside drenched.

Forgetting about the three men for a while, though still keeping possession of the note, Catie ran to Grandmother's. Her house seemed undamaged. It was old, and had not survived so long by being frail. Catie went inside. Two other tired-looking men were in the kitchen, standing patiently by as Grandmother wrapped still-steaming bread in linen and placed the loaves in a basket.

"Welcome back, Caytaleane," Grandmother said, her voice clear though her eyes and hands were busy elsewhere.

"I'm going with the men to find the others," Catie said, knowing it was almost silly saying it in such a way, but knowing Tiamen and Arul would find it sillier if she said it plainly.

"I thought you might," Grandmother replied, glancing up with a smile. "It will be good for you, too. I think you will find much of what you're looking for."

"Are you sure you don't need help here?" Catie asked.

Grandmother glanced out the window, and straightened a little. "No, I think we will do fine," she said distantly.

Catie followed her gaze. Her brow furrowed at the scene unfolding outside. "I'll try to come back," she said absently, then left the building.

Rodigger and Deuel stood on the street, gazing upward as Gabriel positioned himself on a roof peak, helping a few of the men secure the topmost row of shingles. Catie approached, her gaze also on the mercenary.

"What's he doing up there?" she asked.

"Shingling," Gabriel called down. "You may have noticed a few houses around here need it."

"We need to go find..." Rodigger glanced around the street. "You know."

"Go ahead," Gabriel replied, leaning backward and handing a hammer to one behind him. "Throw me that rope before you leave?" he asked, pointing to a rope and bucket filled with more shingles and another hammer that was at their feet.

"Deuel, would you...?" Rodigger said, looking at the behamian.

But Deuel only gazed intently upward. "I think it will not help," he said finally.

"Try."

"*Aloik,*" Deuel called softly.

Gabriel's jaw clenched, and he gazed downward. "Halm and Ro Thull are yours, again," he said quietly. He made a gesture with his left hand near his right shoulder. "Halm and Ro Thull are yours," he repeated.

Deuel surprised them all by gasping. He stood, his mouth open for several long moments. "You cannot..."

"Catie, would you throw me that rope, please?" Gabriel said angrily. "Staring at me while I'm trying to work. It's senseless for me to come all the way back down there..."

Catie bent over, grasped the end of the rope, and tossed it to the mercenary—or was he simply an old man, now? Gabriel pulled hand over hand till the bucket was close, then quickly tied it off at his waist.

"Thank you," he said. He turned his gaze back to Deuel for several moments, then up and across the plain toward the lake. "I'm tired," he said quietly. "A good day of honest work will do wonders, I can feel it. Maybe many days. It used to, before I started this, before I found and lost Tormina." His gaze lowered to nothing at his hip, then into the bucket. Without another word he pulled out a shingle and a few nails, and began hammering.

"Deuel," Rodigger said, almost pleading. "What is he doing?"

Deuel's mouth had closed, and his customary impassivity returned. "Shingling," he said, quickly fixing Rodigger with a stare that froze the young man's mouth open. "We will be on our way, where Catie leads us," he continued, turning to look at her, the question unformed but present.

"The other side of the Tevorbath," she replied.

"Very well."

"But what happened?" Rodigger said, trying to keep in the behamian's view as they moved toward their horses. "What is Halm and Ro Thull? What was this?" he mimicked the gesture, poorly, that Gabriel had made toward his right shoulder.

Deuel paused by his horse before mounting. "His weapons," he replied. "He is no longer my *aloik;* I am no longer his *skalderon.*"

"Oh," Catie said softly.

Deuel looked at Rodigger. "I am free."

⚬

Catie stopped one final time inside Grandmother's kitchen. The two men were gone out to distribute the warm loaves, and even Lucie was out helping in any ways she could. Catie felt a slight twinge of betrayal, leaving her home and friends when she had only just returned, when they needed all the help they could get. Even if Gabriel was staying behind.

But one look at Grandmother and she knew it would be okay. How many times had her presence engendered such peace? Catie hoped she could do the same for others, one day.

"We're leaving," she said.

Grandmother smiled, but there was still something in her eyes. A guarding, it seemed.

"What is it?" Catie asked, sitting down.

"Where do you go?" she asked.

"North of the Tevorbath to start," Catie replied. "From there...?" she trailed off with a shrug. "But I'll come back as soon as I can. I prom—"

Grandmother cut her off with a wave. "Make no such promise," she said quickly, her insistence surprising Catie, and hurting her.

"You don't want me to come back?"

"I want you to be who you were born to be, whom the God made you to be," Grandmother replied.

"I don't know what that is."

Grandmother's smile was pleasant, full of hope. "You will. This journey will teach you. Catie..." Her smile lessened.

Catie's was gone. "You never call me that," she said. Why was she talking so differently?

"Caytaleane," Grandmother said; "there is something you must know, before you leave. Your father did not die by drowning."

Catie sat quietly. She had all but known.

"Some men came from the northeast, came looking for your mother, to do her harm. Jular led them away, and died keeping them from her. We knew she would not be safe here, knew that you would not be safe with her. That is why she gave you to be Newmother, and left. It was not your fault. Nor, truly, hers."

The edges of Catie's vision swam in tears. "Do you know where she went?"

Grandmother took a deep breath, and blew an unsteady sigh. "North of the Tevorbath," she said. Her eyes fixed on Catie. "So many years ago, there is no knowing where she might have ended up, how she might have..." Grandmother twisted her hands together. "But there is more. I'm sorry I haven't told you yet, my Caytaleane, but your mother made me promise on oath to keep this secret until a day I deemed it absolutely necessary. Now, I believe you are leaving to never return and so I must. Please forgive us both, if you must. We did what we thought best."

"I always trust you, Grandmother," Catie said honestly. "You have wisdom far beyond my years."

Grandmother smiled genuinely. "Then I will not try to defend our decision to you. But you must know now: Kerlyn your mother came to us from the north when you were small, and Julan she met here."

Catie sat silently and still, comprehending. "So..."

"Julan helped raise you, and loved your mother," Grandmother continued. "But he did not give you birth."

Her breath left her for several moments. When she spoke, it came out a near-whisper. "Who did?"

"Kerlyn never told me, and as far as I knew she did not tell Julan either. But, as you journey north, perhaps you will find out. Perhaps, too, you will find healing for the hurt Roth has dealt you."

Catie pressed her lips together. "That is part of why I go..."

Grandmother's eyes cast down, and she shook her head. "Not that way. What has broken inside you is your trust—trust that you can love again."

Catie sat back. No, she definitely could not see herself loving someone else. "No one will ever compare to Dannid," she said. "You never met him, but he was..." She trailed off, seeing him in her mind's eye as they rode through the Dragonsbacks, wind through his hair as he laughed and told her his plans. She blinked away the memory before it was too late.

Grandmother was looking at her with a guarded smile. "You felt joined to this man, Dannid?"

"We were married," Catie replied.

"That is not what I asked—Bolgad and Hathar are married, aren't they?"

Catie chuckled. "Yeah, well, Bolgad and Hathar—"

"Did you feel joined to Dannid? Did you feel almost as though you were one—not one single person, single-minded in everything—but as though you moved together?"

"We spent so much time together, in Sprativerg, through the mountains south, in Bokessin..." Catie paused. "I don't know how much closer we could have been."

Grandmother watched her closely. "I think, too, that one day you will know. True marriage is this: that the two are close-knit as one, united in purpose and heart."

"It sounds like I would have to give up who I am."

"Some, as he will have to give up some of who he is. Remember when Radolf painted his house?"

Catie wrinkled her nose. "That looked horrible," she said. "That's what marriage is?"

Grandmother laughed. "No, at least it is not meant to be. Do you remember how he made the color?"

"He mixed red and yellow dyes together."

"That is what marriage is: the red dye does not stop being red, nor the yellow, yellow; but together they add another hue to the myriad in the world. No orange will ever be like the orange Radolf made."

"Let's hope not," Catie replied with a smile.

⸺◆⸺

They rode in silence much of that first day. It may have been a normal silence, if Gabriel had been present, but his absence made it awkward. Too awkward to break or pay much attention to.

The storm, though some days past, had made the road thick with mud, and travelers were scarce. Merchant trains did not exist. Rodigger paid for their beds, and they fell asleep to the sound of one another's breathing.

As the sun neared Noon the next day, the dragon-son cantered up to ride beside Catie, who led.

"You knew what it meant for Gabriel to give me my swords," he said, though his eyes stayed on the road ahead.

"Grandmother has told me some things about the behamien," she replied, her voice no louder than necessary.

"Why did she do that?"

Catie blinked, and frowned. "She has told me many things," she said finally, though creases appeared on her forehead as well.

"And your father left fourteen years ago?"

"Fifteen," she corrected automatically. She would untangle that situation later.

"That is a long time."

"For me, perhaps," she replied, and some of her creases disappeared.

Deuel glanced at her, now, and she felt his enjoyment of her joke. It reminded her, suddenly, that she didn't feel fear of him. Almost absurdly, she searched for it, tried to conjure it, but it did not come. And yet every other sense turned as if he were laughing openly, and she wanted to laugh with him, to smile, to recognize the outward signs that they had bonded, in some small way.

But her eyes told her he only looked at her. She tried to see the twinkling in his eyes, even, but they were the same cavernous yet not-empty pools they always were.

But then something else turned in her, as if the joke had recalled a painful memory or knowledge, and she felt a deep but slow-moving sadness—whether of the past or for the future, she could not tell. Before she could study it further Deuel looked away, and the feeling passed.

Like a thunderclap, she was back on the road, felt the warm spring day, heard the heavy hoofbeats, smelled the breeze carrying scents of horse-sweat, leather, and something like last winter's chill still oozing from the deep parts of the ground.

And Rodigger still maintaining his awkward silence.

"Have you ever been through the Tevorbath?" she called back.

Silence for several breaths, almost enough for her to think of repeating the question. "No," came the small reply.

"I haven't either, but I've heard the stories," she said. "Beautiful and bountiful beyond compare. And we should have pleasant weather by then."

Another silence, shorter this time. "It's a valley," he said. "How could it be beautiful?"

"Do you prefer standing on mountains?" she asked.

"No, I mean, it's land, it's just—space between two hills."

"Today is a beautiful day, isn't it?"

"It's not cold," he said.

"Rodigger, come on," she said, turning finally to look back and see if he was joking. His face was serious, and she gave a short sigh. "The weather is fantastic, it is not cold, it's even mildly warm, the sky is blue..."

"Okay, fine, yes! Compared with the days when it's cold and cloudy, today is beautiful. So compared with land that's flat and rocky, a valley is probably beautiful."

"Has he always been this pleasant to travel with?" she asked Deuel quietly.

Without looking at her, the dragon-son shook his head. "Well," he amended. "He is always this way toward me. I do not know why he would be this way toward you."

Catie chuckled. "Thank you for that," she said, smiling though she noticed he was not looking at her. She raised her voice a little. "It's an interesting point, though," she said. "That beauty only exists in comparison."

"Okay."

"Isn't that what you were saying?" she asked. She edged her voice with indignance. "You know, you could ride up here so I can talk to you instead of at you."

More silence. Catie shifted, letting a wrinkle work itself out of her pants that was chafing something awful. "That's okay," Rodigger said finally. "And I wasn't really thinking about it like that." A pause. "Here's where Gabriel would snort and say something about not being surprised."

"I don't snort very much," Catie replied, "or make assumptions. You're allowed to think about it however you want to."

"And that's where Gabriel would say he's surprised if I think at all."

Catie reined her horse up hard, so that Deuel was several strides ahead before he stopped. She turned to Rodigger. "Gabriel is not here," she said firmly, staring into Rodigger's eyes. "Not himself, or his attitude, or his thoughts. It's us. And quite frankly I'd appreciate losing the idea that I might think or feel the way he does."

Rodigger glanced quickly at Deuel, between blinks, but the dragon-son saw it.

"I am of the same mind," he said. "He is no longer my *aloik*. He has no say over my words or actions."

Rodigger managed to gaze at Deuel, this time. "Well, when he did, he must not have wanted you to speak very much."

As soon as he said it, Rodigger looked horrified, but Catie could feel Deuel's wry chuckle. "He did not hold as much sway over me as when he was younger," Deuel replied calmly. "As he grew older, I grew more silent, rather than say something he did not wish me to say."

"Oh," Rodigger replied. "Was he that bad?"

"I do not know what you mean by 'bad'," Deuel said as they continued riding. "It is the nature of the bond, it is amoral."

"I don't understand," Rodigger said, riding closer, but still behind them.

"You may be thinking of the relationship of a slave," Deuel said. "Masters may be kind or cruel in the eyes of some—though in the eyes of others, that bond, too, is whatever the master wishes. Behamien bond with humans for the sake of the bond, not for the sake of the human. A slave master is benefited by the slave," Deuel continued when Rodigger made a still-confused grunt. "And so he is above, the slave is subservient. As *skalderon* I am more like a student."

"Studying what?" Rodigger spluttered. "You know more than any of us, and you look like you know more than everyone."

"But I do not know what it means to be a human," Deuel replied, simply and quietly.

"So what?" Rodigger asked.

"One day, I hope to no longer be behamian. If I succeed," he continued, turning to look plainly at Rodigger. "I must not desire to kill you."

Rodigger did not get a good night's sleep until they were through the Skaldvath Mountains and nearing Sprativerg. Not that he was more comfortable with Deuel even at that point. He was simply too exhausted to care. Catie had looked thoughtful for a day, after Deuel's bizarre words, but had returned to her smiling, care-free self by the next morning. She trusted people too much, too quickly, he decided. Not a good quality, when they were setting out for lands where none of them had traveled before. Maybe he would talk to her before too long, about that.

It was exciting to think about, he had to admit—spending a life with Catie, helping her become a better person. She possessed many good qualities already, to be sure, enough to be a wife. But she was far from perfect. It pleased him that her looks did not distract him from her shortcomings, though her looks were certainly distracting enough. More than once he had imagined her standing before him on their wedding night, patient as he enjoyed the moment before stepping toward her...but that thought was never more frequent than the long talks they would have as he shaped her into the woman he knew she could be.

But then he was caught up in Sprativerg. The city was ripe for Roth's influence. Rodigger was there for only a day, tragically, but could feel the people crying out for purpose, for community. How he would have loved to take even a month to begin speaking to the people!

Instead, they rode out of the north gate the next morning, the peaks on the horizon a dark silhouette like the teeth of a great maw into which they rode, growing larger and descending upon them with each passing mile. At least those were far away, still, and not truly maleficent. Deuel's ever-presence loomed directly in front of him, and apparently desired to kill him unless he learned enough about what it meant to be human. What did that even mean?

Some of the comfort Rodigger had found over the past several days ebbed as he glanced at Halm and Ro Thull, Deuel's strange weapons, wrapped behind the dragon-son's saddle. Rodigger had been around soldiers since he was small, and had never seen weapons like those. And what were the bracelets that Gabriel had worn? He hadn't really seen them since then. And what kind of names were those? Halm, and Ro Thull. They sounded—

"What about them?" Catie asked as she rode between them.

Rodigger gaped at her. Had she somehow read his thoughts?

She turned and glanced at him. "You said 'Halm and Ro Thull'."

"Did I?" Rodigger asked as Deuel glanced at him.

Catie nodded with a grin. "Well, you muttered it, so I guess you might not have meant to say it out loud."

"Oh. I guess I'm just wondering..." What was he wondering? Was Deuel going to kill him with them? His shoulders sagged as he looked at nothing, at Gared's ears swiveling to the wind. "Do you know how to use them?" he heard himself say.

"Yes," Deuel replied. A smile flashed across Catie's face, and Deuel turned further to look at her. "It has been many years."

"Why did Gabriel have them?" Rodigger asked, coming to himself.

"The bond," Deuel replied. "A behamian gives his weapons to the *aloik* until he is free."

"Well, how long did Gabriel have them?" Catie asked.

"They were his when he was born," Deuel replied.

"I thought they were yours," Rodigger said.

"They were given to Gabriel by his father, as his father had given it to him," Deuel explained. "I first gave them to Gabriel's grandfather. It is the nature of the bond."

"For three generations?" Catie asked.

"At least."

"So, how long ago...?"

"One hundred years."

They rode in silence for some moments, a light, warm wind shifting in from the south as Catie and Rodigger both looked at the two weapons rocking behind Deuel's saddle.

"How old *are* they?" Rodigger asked first.

"They were made for me by the Kesten, in Burieng, for my eighth year."

The Kesten? Rodigger wondered. The name sounded familiar. Was it something Roth had told him, once? He couldn't remember.

"Why do you give up your weapons?" Catie asked.

"We must know vulnerability," Deuel replied, shifting in his saddle.

"For a hundred years?"

"For as long as it takes to understand it," Deuel replied. He drew a small sigh. "Gabriel did not return my weapons because I had learned it, but because he no longer wanted the responsibility of me. I do not know what this might mean."

"There's always someone stronger than you," Rodigger said with a firm nod. Roth had told him that since he was fourteen. "With or without weapons."

"Perhaps," Deuel said. "If I have a knife, and you have your sword, am I not inherently more vulnerable than if I have a sword? Unless I am the best knife-fighter and you are the worst swordsman."

"I suppose," Rodigger said.

"Tactics," Catie spoke up. "You might be smarter than him."

"The analogy breaks down quickly," Deuel said. Catie smiled again as if they shared a joke. "But let us maintain it for a moment: similar tactics, similar strength, similar ability, different weapons, different standing. Yes?"

They both nodded.

"Same swordsman against a dragon?"

There was a pause before Catie spoke up. "He better have an impressive sword."

"That is most often the case," Deuel replied gravely. "And others to help him. But if a dragon finds a man alone, he must understand vulnerability. Thus a *skalderon* may only have a small knife, one that does little harm."

"In case you want to kill them?" Rodigger muttered.

"Do you not want to kill me?" Deuel asked, almost lightly.

Rodigger glanced quickly at Catie's sharp gaze. "No," he said, hoping he chose the right tone from the myriad his mind desperately presented.

"You do not think the behamien should exist," Deuel said. "We are...an abomination."

"That doesn't mean...I mean, killing someone..."

"I exist," Deuel said, cutting him off as he stopped and turned his horse to face him. "The only way for me to not exist is to die. This is your reality, which you must accept. If you cannot, then your reality is *skef*."

Catie rode her horse between them, staring hard at Deuel—and there it was again, something like curiosity showing itself on Deuel's face, more pronounced than back in the cave, but still nowhere near normal human expression. But, of course, that made sense...

Rodigger swallowed as Catie's gaze swung to him, and his eyes cast downward. "Exactly," she said through gritted teeth. Rodigger's horse snuffled as the wind rose and shushed through the grasses. "I don't want to be facing whatever is guarding the next goblet, and worry about facing it alone. Do you?"

Assuming she was still looking at him, Rodigger said: "No."

More silence until Deuel said: "You are right."

"Then let's go."

Rodigger finally looked up as hooves thumped against the road. Catie and Deuel were already moving, so he nudged Gared forward. He had answered Catie honestly, but he already believed he *would* be facing the next guardian alone.

———◆———

That night at the inn, at the top of a ridge in the Dragonsback Mountains, Catie watched Rodigger finally succumb to sleep two cots over. He had taken again to sleeping as far away from Deuel as possible without being completely rude, saying something about having a hard time falling asleep when he could hear people breathing. The wind roared outside, still from the south, but funneled up the passes from the broad Fallonvall.

Waiting a few more moments to verify his measured breathing, Catie finally turned over. "Deuel?" she whispered.

She felt him come alert before he answered, almost like turning and seeing someone looking at her. "Yes?" he said.

"Sometimes, when we're traveling—or, I guess, when we're talking, but not necessarily..." She wound to a stop, and gave a short sigh. "There are times when I feel like I know what you're feeling."

There was a pause, and the sense of his gaze became more acute. "Sometimes, a behamian will project his feelings, almost as if he were speaking them or showing them," he said.

Catie hesitated. It seemed like he didn't enjoy speaking about this. Something in his tone had changed, at least, and she wished she could see him in the darkness—not that being able to see him always did much good. "But do you control that?" she asked.

There was a much longer pause, and the sense now of intense scrutiny. "Not always," he said finally. "And once someone feels it, they are more keen to pick it up the next time."

Catie wavered for a few moments. "I used to be afraid of you," she said finally, not knowing where the topic would lead and being a little afraid of that, too. But she felt she must know, and so she took the first step.

"When?" he asked. He felt amused, now.

"Before I met you all," she said. "It was another reason I stayed ahead of you. I felt some sort of danger, from you. I mean, I didn't know it was you at first, until we were nearly at Getakenner. It's why I decided to finally face you, so I could try to see what I was afraid of."

"Are you afraid of me now?"

"No!" she said, her voice suddenly above a whisper. She brought it back down. "No, it stopped once we met."

"That is how it often happens," Deuel said. "I do not know if it is for our defense or yours that those feelings are foremost, until face to face with a behamian."

"It doesn't seem to have worn off Rodigger," Catie said wryly. She felt his sudden sadness, and her grin disappeared.

"His is a fear that nothing I do will erase," Deuel said, "because I did not create it. Only the one who planted the seed, or the one who continues to water it, can kill it."

"I'm sorry, Deuel," she said.

"He is many," he said simply, though still a little sadly.

Catie let out a small sigh. "And I'm sorry about that, too."

10

TURNING TABLES

"That was not as difficult as I supposed."
"That, Teresh, is a lesson everyone needs to remember."
"Do you ever think sometimes they do very well without us?"
"No. Perhaps sometimes."

9 Halmfurtung 1320 — Spring

Early the next morning, they came to the place where the Balnathva River plunged over a cliff above them, falling away from the road to straddle a knife-like ridge two hundred feet below them. The right side of the ridge gathered a few springs, and continued southeast as the Tilvat, and filled the Agirbirt Lake. The left continued as the Balnathva to the Turidian Sea south of Bokessin.

"Just around the next bend," Catie said as they passed the falls.

"We're almost there, already?" Rodigger asked.

"Ha! Ahem. No," Catie said, covering her mouth briefly. "No, we're not even halfway yet, sorry."

"How far away is this place?"

"Well, we have to cross the Tevorbath, first."

"I thought you said it was just on the other side of that?" Rodigger said, swiping at a fly that buzzed near his ear.

"Well, not 'just'," she said. "And there's a whole lot of Andelen on the other side of the Tevorbath."

Rodigger groaned, shifted in his saddle, then was silent.

Soon the breadth of the Tevorbath came into view: 'The God's Feast' it had been named. A broad valley stretching as far as could be seen northward, bright green grass flowing from the banks of the Balnathva up the slopes until it turned into forest. Sheep floated on the hillsides like shadowed clouds, fallen from a sky almost perpetually blue. What true clouds formed at the head of the valley sat trapped by its walls, drifting slowly along and watering the land as evenly as a gardener. Below the herds of sheep, nearer the river, were great brown strips of newly-planted fields, whose crops would ripen as surely as the seasons changed. Out of this one valley came almost half of Andelen's food. In sacks, dried, or pickled, it shipped to far corners by endless streams of merchants and wagoners. The only way into the valley was to be born or married into it. Every farmer and shepherd who knew about it wanted his or her own plot, but for most it was only a dream.

For travelers, it was a place to be savored. Fair weather most days and guaranteed fresh food made it a favorite corridor, if one needed to traverse its length. News and entertainment ran aplenty. Since Sheppar's campaign thirty years ago, entertainment was more common than news, though travelers from the south often brought word of Roth's campaign, now.

The inns were almost always near-full, and one evening they took the last three beds there were. For a time, they enjoyed themselves as they traveled: Rodigger kept from insulting Deuel, though he still rode at the back. But the warm spring air and constant flow of travelers worked to cheer their spirits.

One day, about After-Noon, just two days after leaving Kendet's Vatenvilt nearly a third of the way through the valley, they came upon a herd of sheep milling on the road. Deuel and Catie glanced about, while Rodigger cursed and nudged his Therian forward as best he could.

"Where in all Oren is the shepherd?" Rodigger fumed.

"That's a very good question," Catie replied, standing in her stirrups and peering around the valley. She paused gazing eastward, shading her eyes. "It looks like the herd is coming across a bridge of some sort."

"Wouldn't it make sense for the road to continue following the west bank?" Rodigger asked, finally managing to bring his horse closer to his companions.

"It does," Catie said, sitting down again. "But the herds have to access the east side of the Tevorbath somehow, and it looks like they do it over there," she finished, pointing. "I think we should check it out."

"We should do no such thing," Rodigger exclaimed, kicking out slightly at a sheep who was taking a little too much interest in his pants leg. "We should continue north, to whatever destination you've concocted."

Catie glanced coolly at him. "I've reconsidered the words of the poem," she said. "I think what we're looking for is over there, across this little bridge. Maybe they're guarding it?" Without waiting for reply she urged Kelsie eastward.

They finally broke free of the milling herd and across a bridge wide enough for all three horses to cross abreast. Once over the river, Catie stood again, glancing along the hill sweeping up toward the far peaks of the Dragonsback. She paused suddenly, staring. "Over there!" she cried, spurring her mount forward.

As she drew near, the lumps she had seen resolved themselves into clothed shapes huddled in the grass. Catie stopped, her hand going to her mouth. When Rodigger finally came near enough to see, she wondered if he was stifling a retch as much as she needed to.

"By the God," he mumbled, turning away.

Catie swallowed a few times as she looked closer. The heads of both men were nearly detached. Their clothes were torn, and exposed flesh was lacerated and bloody. One man's leg lay a little separate from the rest of him.

"The sheep did not trample them," Deuel said beside her, his eyes scanning the wood-line near the base of the mountain walls. "This was done by weapons."

"Why would someone do that, though?" Catie said quietly. "They're shepherds!"

"Land dispute?" Rodigger said, still turned away.

"I don't think they're prone to carrying swords as a rule," Catie said. "Land disputes that end like this would happen in the moment, wouldn't they? Like, someone found them trespassing and the argument went badly. They would use what was at hand."

"We keep going until we find a farmhouse," Deuel said. "They will know."

"What if it's on the hillside, or in the trees somewhere?" Rodigger asked as Deuel pointed his horse back toward the road.

Deuel paused, gazing northward. "Smoke," he said finally, turning a little up the valley and nudging Rodan to a walk. Catie and Rodigger fell in behind, also looking up the road till they spotted the thin curl of gray on the horizon near the river.

"I guess it wouldn't make sense to be so far from water and trade," Catie muttered as Rodigger continued to ride beside her. She flashed him a calming smile, which he mirrored with little more enthusiasm.

As they neared, she could see a few chickens scratching around the side of the house, and a milk cow grazing further up the valley. But the farm itself was silent. Catie called out as they approached, to no answer. Deuel made one circuit of the outside. They saw little amiss, but the house was plainly deserted.

Catie took a deep breath. "Let's see what's inside, then," she said, almost muttering it. A hundred scenes went through her head of what they might find, and none of them did she want to see in person. As she approached the door, Deuel suddenly cut in front of her.

"I will look first," he said quietly, glancing quickly at Rodigger, who had hung back.

Catie cocked her head. "Why."

For a brief moment, Deuel's eyes flashed. "Because these are not my people," he said, before his eyes returned to the deep, calm pools she was used to.

She bowed her head, and took a step back. Deuel put a hand on the door. It was not barred. He slipped into the darkness inside, and Catie held her breath, waiting for the slightest noise.

Light flared in one of the windows as Deuel lit a lamp. Catie glanced between window and door as the light grew, then faded, then cast shadows. One of the chickens had made its way around to the front of the house and gabbled quietly. Kelsie snorted, and Catie glanced back at her, then at Rodigger.

"Come in," came Deuel's quiet voice.

Catie made a quick gesture to Rodigger, heard leather creaking, and entered the house.

It was not in wild disarray, as she thought it might be, but neither was it tidy. One wooden chair sat back on two legs against the wall, next to the fireplace whose fire was banked low. A table took up most of the center of the main room, and Deuel stood beside three other chairs gathered around it. There were several rude furnishings, but clearly only what was needed between sunset and sunrise. The rest of the day would have been spent outside the house.

"No one else here, at all?" Catie asked. Rodigger entered just then, and Deuel shook his head.

"But what is here?" Deuel asked.

"Not much," Rodigger said, glancing around. "There's barely a second room."

Deuel pointed silently at two doorways leading off the main room. Peering through the one closest, Catie could see a bed spread with wool blankets and a small wood-stove tucked in the corner, with its pipe bending through the stone wall.

"Is that a bedroom too?" Catie asked, pointing at the far doorway. Deuel nodded.

"Okay, so, one for each," Rodigger said with a shrug. "Wouldn't it be more odd if there weren't?"

Catie glanced around again, then at Deuel. "Four chairs," she said.

Deuel cocked an eyebrow briefly. Rodigger folded his arms. "Huh," he said. "So where are the other two? Figure they killed the ones we found?"

"I do not think so," Deuel said. "The second bedroom is far...nicer, than the first."

Catie's heart solidified. "Women?" she asked. Deuel nodded gravely, and Catie's breath escaped her.

"Well, that doesn't mean much," Rodigger said. "They might have done it, for some reason."

"Do you think it's more likely whoever killed the men took the women?" Catie asked.

"Oh," Rodigger said, his face falling. "Yeah, I guess so."

They were silent for a few moments. Catie's eyes continued to dart around the room, hoping for some sign of what had happened there. When that failed, her mind went to work.

"Where could they have taken them?" she asked aloud, though mostly to herself. "They couldn't stay on the roads, there's too many travelers. They can't take them to an inn—could they?"

"What inn would let them in?" Deuel asked.

"What inn poisons its guests and steals from them while they sleep?" Catie asked.

"Yeah!" Rodigger said.

"One that does not see many guests," Deuel replied calmly. "None like what we have seen so far in the Tevorbath."

"Exactly!" Catie exclaimed. "Surely they don't live completely on their own up here. They must go somewhere to get supplies they can't get from sheep, chickens, or cows."

"Like what?" Rodigger asked, glancing pointedly around the sparse room.

"Axes," Deuel said. "For firewood."

Rodigger drew a sigh. "It's more likely they replace their own broken handles, and sharpen their own axe-heads," he said. "It's a poor crafts-man who can't fix his own tools."

"Clothes," Catie said. "I don't see much here for making textiles."

Deuel glanced down, then over at the second bedroom.

"Oh, come on," Catie said, her shoulders sagging. "Surely someone knew they were out here, or would know who they were, or would care that they're not here anymore! Besides me!" She could feel Deuel's gentle rebuke, but continued to stare at him unflinching.

In the silence, a whip cracked outside. Catie's eyes widened as she turned and bolted out the door. Deuel and Rodigger quickly followed.

"Hey!" she shouted as chickens scattered and Rodigger's Therian shied a little. There were two wagons, barely big enough to need their four wheels, hitched to a single horse apiece. The driver in the lead, his brown shirt pulled tight across his torso and collar hidden behind a great bushy beard, hauled back on the reins.

"What is it?" he asked as the second wagon came to a halt behind him, the similarly-dressed but thinner driver gazing at her with barely concealed annoyance.

"Do you come through here a lot?" she asked. "Do you know this area?"

"Sure, some," he replied. "We always do the run from Kendet's up the valley about halfway to Dagget's."

"Have the people here ever purchased anything from you?"

"Can't say they purchased it," the driver said with a broad grin. "S'there family owns Kendet's!"

"They do?"

"Sure! S'that strange to you?"

"No, but it complicates things," Catie said with a sigh. "We found the two men dead up the hill," she continued, gesturing away. "Killed. And we're guessing there are two women, who aren't here."

The bearded wagoner's face grew grave, and he turned and glanced at his partner, and a slow sigh turned into a rumble in his chest as he turned back to Catie. "And what were you all doing this way?" he asked in a low but meaningful tone.

Catie blinked. "We were heading northward," she said. "Sheep were blocking the road, and we wanted to see why."

"She wanted to see," Rodigger piped up. "I wanted to keep going."

"Where northward y'headed?"

"Tarver," Catie replied.

"Oh, is that where it is?" Rodigger asked.

As the bearded one turned to glance again at his partner, Catie turned slowly to Rodigger. "Do you have any idea how this looks?" she hissed. "Why would you try to make it worse?"

"Well we didn't do it!" Rodigger exclaimed.

"Why are you carrying weapons?" the younger one asked, his eyes finally finding their horses, and Deuel's weapons strapped to the back of the saddle. "Ain't been goblins and such for years."

Deuel took several strides forward, his gaze locking onto the young man's. "Those were given to me long before you were born," he said quietly. "Ask the eagle why its nest is still among the cliffs."

"Seems if you have 'em, you'd still use 'em," said the elder. But when Deuel's gaze shifted to him, he glanced quickly back to Catie.

"We didn't," she said evenly. "At least, not yet," she continued. The elder cocked an eyebrow. "Where could you hide four people around here?" she asked. "The women are missing, probably taken, and probably taken by more than one."

The elder paused a moment, rubbing his thumb on a rein. He glanced back at Deuel, then pointed ahead and to the east. "There's caves just inside the tree-line," he said. "Probably find a path. S'good storage places, keep things cool." He paused a moment, then looked Catie square in the eye. "You go find 'em. We'll head to the next inn. Bring 'em there. If we don't see you, believe we'll have everyone out looking for you. You try to go south, we'll send folks that way, too."

"You do not have to do that," Deuel said. "Stay here with them," he said to Catie and Rodigger. "I'll go alone."

"That might not be a good idea," said the elder. "If there's more'n you expect...ain't worth dying over."

"I will be fine," Deuel said. He strode over to his horse and pulled the sheathed weapons free, buckling them around his waist. He searched his saddlebags, pulling out two of the strange cuffs and sliding one each on his arms.

"Deuel," Catie said, watching him.

"What are your names?" he asked, ignoring her and looking at the wagoners.

"Eck," said the elder. He hooked a thumb toward the younger. "This is my son, Wallan."

"Eckuthan, do you believe in dragons?" Deuel asked.

Eck shifted a little. "How did you know the old name?" he asked.

"It is traditional," Deuel replied, gazing at him. "A dragon once flew the Tevorbath."

"Garedardan," Eck replied, almost a whisper.

"He ate what he wished, plundering herds, hopefully missing the shepherds as he flew—"

"No!" Eck cut in forcefully. "He kept those of the Tevorbath safe from raiding parties. We wouldn't have survived without 'im."

"I am glad you remember," Deuel said quietly. "I am Deuel." He threw back his cloak and leapt into the air.

The shock of their faces vanished as Deuel gained height. It always hurt, the first several thrusts after keeping his wings for so long immobile behind his cloak. It took some time for blood to fill the veins, for the muscles to remember they had movement. Maybe he was just getting old. Maybe he needed to fly more often.

As the land receded below him, he passed briefly above the peaks, saw outside the Tevorbath: to the east was brown and wide and desolate. The west was rimmed with trees around land that blurred the line to the sea. So much land to see, and this just one small portion of one small continent! Imaginings leapt briefly, unbidden, through his mind of the vastness of Rinc Na, or Cariste. Or Gintanos.

But he did not have time to enjoy the view. And he would fly north first, if he were free, to where the tip of the Dragonsback Mountains could not yet be seen. But that was not why he flew today.

He dropped, wings spread wide as cool air rushed over him. Between the conifers he could see a thin track, broken but extant, until it disappeared into rubble. He circled once. Nothing moved below. He carried himself to a point above the rocks, folded his wings, and dropped feet first. As he passed the tops of the trees, he flared his wings. With a great rustle his descent slowed, and he landed lightly on the rocks above the trail's end in a crouch. His wings returned beneath his cloak with a shiver.

Deuel sat for several moments, until a bird warbled nearby. He heard nothing else, saw no movement. He strode quietly to the edge of the rocks and peered down. It was indeed a cave. He continued to watch and listen. Then, as the wind dropped, he heard the careless metal ring of someone trying to be quiet and failing, followed by a sniffle.

Deuel calmly drew out Halm and Ro Thull, watching the cuffs snap over top the bracelets. He felt it almost instantly, that old connection. His right arm warmed slightly, the left felt suddenly unbreakable. Deuel took a steadying breath: he had not used these in decades. For a brief moment he tumbled around inside his head, recalling things he had not had to recall for three of Gabriel's generations. Then, as old friends, the names came back—smiling, hands outstretched in greeting, pints on the table behind them and an empty chair still saved for him in their circle.

Deuel stepped off the rocks, twisting as he fell to land facing the cave.

Two men stood in loose brown clothing, faces wrapped except their eyes and foreheads. Their hands went quickly to swords sheathed at their waists but Deuel was faster, Halm and Ro Thull swinging outward and slicing throats. The men fell gurgling as Deuel strode by. His irises switched quickly to the gloom, seeing everything in light grays.

Movement ahead, this in deep black. Something warm, blood flowing through its veins. A brief cry of alarm. Deuel pointed with his left blade. *"Binten."*

Another cry, this one in fear, and rustling cloth as the man struggled against the stone that had swallowed his feet. Halm parried a frantic swing. Ro Thull thrust. Three.

A clack, and whizzing of feathered vanes. Deuel ducked right as the arrow sailed wide. A thrust with his wings carried him ten paces forward in an instant, both blades outstretched and sinking deeply into the fourth's torso.

The tunnel turned right, and Deuel paused at the corner. He could hear voices, quiet but frightened, giving orders. He recognized the syntax and cadence, but only some of the individual words. His veins chilled at the sound. *Why are* they *here?*

Footsteps, then, carefully edging closer. He glanced at Ro Thull, feeling the warmth pulsing in his arm, but he needed to know where the prisoners were before releasing such magic. Instead he bent his ears to the shuffling steps. There were three pairs, judging by the sounds. Two sounded closer to one another, but further back in the corridor, likely afraid. The third was closer.

He stepped out, wrapping one wing tightly around the first and pinning the man's arms to his side, useless. Three powerful strides brought him within reach of the other two, whose swords shook. He knocked them aside, razor edges of The Twins scoring and slicing. He unfurled his wing and thrust quickly, finishing the third.

Up ahead, light flared. His eyes adjusted again—greens this time for the cool rock, with lesser heat in yellow and great heat in red. Light or dark made no difference. Helpful in darkness lit by torches, it also helped him see someone in daylight at a far distance, when the need called for it.

He could see the two women huddled near a table, with only one left to guard them.

"Your men are all dead," Deuel said, his voice the deepest rumble he could make it. He spread his wings wide and fluttered them. That always seemed to unnerve men when he did that.

The yellow shape moved, roughly hauling one of the women to her feet. A thin line of green appeared at her throat—a knife, Deuel realized.

"I will kill her," the man said. She mewled, but Deuel was not sure of whom she was more afraid. He tucked his wings behind him again, looking at her and pushing compassion, and comfort.

"You will not die," he said, his voice calmer.

"That's not up to you," the man sneered. The knife, Deuel noticed, moved a shade further from the woman's throat.

It was a mistake. Ro Thull came up.

"Spearken."

The man shrieked, pushing the woman away as he swatted the air behind him. He danced, turning, the back of his cloak on fire. He faintly heard the rustle of leathery wings before one sharp pain bloomed in a kidney, a second in a lung.

—◦—

Eck and Wallan's horses stood utterly still and calm. Rodigger fidgeted in the silence, and his Therian mimicked him. Catie stood beside Kelsie, rubbing her muzzle gently. Eck cleared his throat and spat, and his horse tossed its head twice, then was still again.

Catie drew a breath. "Didn't you say your horse's name was Gared?" Catie asked Rodigger.

"Yes, well...Roth said it was a good name."

"You didn't realize you had named it after a dead dragon?"

Rodigger only gazed at her, waiting for her derisive follow-up.

"Yer father didn't teach you that?" Eck asked, leaning back and squinting at Rodigger.

Rodigger scoffed. "No, he wasn't much for teaching. Nothing useful, anyway."

"Your mother?" Catie offered. Rodigger's glare answered her. "Just Roth, eh?"

"Roth expects something of me—expects me to make something of myself, not sit by and make something for everyone else while my family falls apart around my ears."

"What did he make, your father?"

Rodigger grimaced and looked away without answering. Catie glanced up the mountainside, looking for Deuel. She thought he would be back by now.

"He was a carpenter," Rodigger said, drawing her attention back to him. "He expected me to be one as well, even as mother lost more and more of her mind while he ignored it."

"Were you any good?"

"What difference does it make? I don't want it. I want what Roth wants for me: to be someone that people listen to, that they respect."

"Nothin' wrong with honest work," Eck growled.

Silence fell again. Catie watched Rodigger for a while, then turned to Kelsie, checking the saddle and bridle.

"I did like it," Rodigger said finally, quietly. He was looking at his hand, rubbing his thumb across his fingers. The hand dropped and he looked up. "But it doesn't matter. No carpenter ever wrote history. You know, you could—" he cut off suddenly, glancing quickly at Eck and Wallan. He took a step toward Catie and lowered his voice. "You could be written into history too. I could make that happen."

Catie arched an eyebrow. "Oh, could you?"

"Well, sure," Rodigger said, his eyes lighting up. "I mean, there's a few things we need to work on, but it shouldn't be too hard for you."

"Things we need to work on?" Catie asked, turning toward him.

"I mean, no one's perfect, so don't take it too hard," he replied. "And we can do one thing at a time."

"Oh, so, you mean there are things *I* need to work on?"

"Well, I mean, little things I've noticed since we've been together, that's—"

He cut off as a whistle echoed down from the slope. Catie turned, looking north and east: three figures were on their way down. Catie leapt aboard Kelsie, then gave a low whistle to Rodan, Deuel's horse. He followed her obediently as she made her way up the slope toward them.

The two women, both just a little older than Catie, did not look too much worse for wear. One had a small bruise on her cheekbone, and their hair was disheveled. But a frightened look only haunted their eyes, warring with relief when they glanced at Deuel and at Catie.

"Thank you," said the bruised one, reaching a hand out for Deuel's horse. Rodan tossed his head once, but a shush from Deuel calmed him. Catie dismounted, offering her hand to the other. "I'm Catie," she said. "You two should ride. I can walk."

"Priska," said the one without a bruise. Her voice still trembled, but the fear was leaving her face.

"Disceya," said the other. She paused beside Deuel's horse, looking down at the road below where Rodigger and the wagoners waited. "That's not Kielar down there," she said.

Priska, preparing to mount, stopped. "Nor is it Pyera." She turned to look at Catie, too closely for Catie to lie. "Where are they?"

Catie blinked. *You didn't have to watch him die,* she thought, before she could stop herself. *Be glad of that.* But they wouldn't be. And did it matter, really? She shook her head. They didn't know how their husbands had died, and that was something.

Priska and Disceya were both looking at her. Disceya's expression hardened. "I suspected as much," she murmured. She looked down, then at Deuel. "You did well," she said.

Tears had begun tracks down Priska's face, but she looked at Deuel too, and nodded some sort of thanks. Catie could feel nothing from him, and he did not return her glance.

"Eck and Wallan are down there," Catie said quietly. "Do you know them? They can take care of you, wherever you want to go."

"Yes, thank you," Disceya said, then pulled herself into the saddle. Catie touched Priska's elbow as the woman hesitated. Priska sniffed, then pulled herself up as well.

Rodigger had found some of his calm, at least, when the four of them returned. Catie glanced at him. He stood behind his Therian, and his gaze was restless.

"Hello, Priska," Eck said gently. "Disceya. Are you—did they—?" The women each shook their head. Eck's glinting eyes fell on Deuel. "Thank ya," he said with a nod. "S'good you were here, then." He glanced down at Deuel's sheathed blades and drew a breath. "Thought we were done with those," he said heavily. The women were dismounting, looking at their farmhouse though neither seemed eager to move toward it. "Almost can't imagine it, traveling with weapons again, havin' t'defend yourself."

Rodigger made some small noise, but few paid him any attention.

"What are we going to do?" Priska asked quietly. Eck glanced at her.

"Might be best to take you down to Kendet's," he said. "T'yer family."

"I know it sounds silly, almost, but what about our farm?" Priska asked, turning toward him. "What about the chickens, and cows, and...and the sheep?"

"We can't abandon it," Disceya said, more firmly, as she turned to face Eck as well.

"Y'might be able to find someone to take it over for you," Eck said, casting a quick, helpless glance at Catie and Deuel. "Animals will be fine for a few days, won't they? D'you really want to stay here tonight, anyway?"

"The inn toward Kendet's is too far, Eck," Disceya said. "Would you two stay with us tonight?"

"We can't be delayed," Rodigger spoke up.

Disceya glanced around, then back at Rodigger. "I didn't ask you to," she said.

"Well...right."

Catie's eyes narrowed at him, and his gaze fell. She turned back as Eck shrugged with a glance back at Wallan.

"I suppose we can, at that," he said. "But y'will go back to Kendet's?"

Disceya sighed. "I suppose we must, even if only for a time." She turned to Deuel and Catie. "Thank you, both. Would the God had brought you a little earlier..." She went silent, and her jaw tightened. Priska's head bowed, and Disceya went quickly to her.

Rodigger approached, subdued, as Eck and Wallan brought their wagons up closer to the house. "You've done well," Eck murmured as he pulled alongside the three. "We'll take care of them."

"Thank you," Catie said.

With quick handshakes around, Deuel, Catie, and Rodigger mounted and continued up the road toward the next inn.

They reached the inn shortly after night fell, and it was another one packed wall to wall. They managed a table in a far corner, though for a time no one spoke. Finally, Catie took a breath and leaned forward.

"What Eck said was right," she said. "About carrying weapons. It's been unnecessary for so long..."

"It may be worse than you think," Deuel said. "The men were nomads."

Catie's eyes widened. "From *Beltrath?*" she hissed. "What could they be doing here?"

"Sheppar should know about it."

Rodigger snorted. "What makes you think he would care?"

"What makes you think he wouldn't?" Catie shot back.

"He'll say Kendet's or Dagget's should handle it," Rodigger said. "He wants the Magiss' to handle everything, remember?"

"The 'vilts aren't set up to handle something like this, and they're too far away anyway," Catie said.

"Exactly."

Catie sighed, and gazed at Deuel. "Do you think they were on their own?" she asked.

"I cannot imagine nomads crossing that deep into the Tevorbath just to kidnap two farmwives," Deuel replied.

"How many were in the cave?" Catie said.

"Eight."

Rodigger's eyes went wide. "You managed against...?"

"We said he was very good," Catie said with a wry chuckle. *Eight?* she thought to herself, though. *And not a scratch on him.* "But, seriously, that is more than a simple raiding party."

"The nomads have not been seen outside Beltrath since long before the Tevorbath became what it is," Deuel replied. "Nor has anyone been into Beltrath to see what is going on there. Something may be driving them out." He paused, then said again: "Sheppar should know about this."

Catie drew a deep breath, but Rodigger got there first. "We can't abandon the mission," he said firmly. "If a problem is growing, getting the Berkarfor to Roth will help more than getting a message to Sheppar."

"So you believe," Catie shot back.

"Did you notice the rule and order in the Fallonvall?" Rodigger asked.

Fire surged through Catie so fiercely her shoulders ached as she stared at Rodigger. Did he have any idea how Roth maintained that order? He had to have, so he simply didn't think about anyone who might have cared about who Roth killed. Her fingers tightened around the handle of her mug. One good bash, and maybe if she tore his eyes out, that smug look would leave his face.

As quickly as it came, the fire left. She blinked a few times, easing her cramped fingers. She glanced at Deuel, who was gazing intently at her. She took a few deep breaths, and a drink. She wished, briefly, that terror would come just so Rodigger could see he was wrong—but saving him from ignorance would not be worth the lives it would cost to accomplish it.

They would get a message to Sheppar somehow. They had to. The Tevorbath, the God's Feast, was no longer the haven it had been.

II

ANSWERS QUESTIONED

"I assume we cannot tell him."
"What they say about assumptions is not always true."
"So we wait?"
"Or you talk to the ones who have the knowledge."

16 Halmfurtung 1320 — Spring

A number of wagons lined the road by the time the three companions saddled their horses. The air was chill, but clear skies promised a warm day once the sun rose over the mountains.

"Wonder where they're headed," Rodigger muttered, glancing away from a heavily laden wagon pulled by only two donkeys.

"You should ask them," Catie replied. "They really shouldn't be driving those poor donkeys far."

"What difference does it make to me?" he asked, hunching a little and rubbing his left arm.

Catie shrugged. "You asked the question. I thought you actually wanted an answer. It's not like it's hard to ask someone a question, just because you've never met them before. I had more faith in you, Rodigger."

That straightened his back, and a considering eye fell upon the merchants. "Where are you taking those poor things?" he demanded suddenly.

Catie's eyes bulged momentarily as every eye in the caravan swung toward them, and she discovered a sudden itch on her nose that took her whole palm to scratch. *Say 'Balnath'* she thought to herself.

The sizable owners of the donkeys finally recognized Rodigger was looking at them. "What's it to you?" asked the slightly larger one, turning to face the companions more squarely.

"You've got a great big wagon and your great big selves, and only two donkeys to pull it all," Rodigger said, sitting even more upright in his saddle now. "If that cargo is any kind of important to whomever you're delivering it, I fear it will never reach them."

Oh, just say 'Balnath'. This plan was going quickly awry.

"This from a boy who brings a Therian into the mountains," snarled the smaller. "Or do you suppose this is the first time we've hauled a wagon?"

And Rodigger had no response. Catie could see it in his eyes. And she had led him into it.

"Many an animal can be treated cruelly for great lengths of time before it dies," Catie said. "And how do we know it isn't the first time those particular donkeys hauled that wagon?" *It's not like we'll be traveling with them anyway, if they end up hating us.*

It must have partially worked, because even the other wagoners were eyeing up these two, now, and they knew it. "How we run our business is our own!" said the fatter. "Who asked you to be inquisitors?"

"Roth Kamdellan cares for all of Andelen!" Rodigger announced loudly, and Catie could not stifle her groan. Rodigger didn't hear her. "As Andelian, you should care about doing a job well, not cheaply," he continued. "Would you like if another countryman sold you a product at the same cost when his own expense had been lessened? Would that not feel like being cheated? But on the backs of these pitiable creatures you cheat your fellow man!"

"We're going to Taferk!" the larger exploded. "You judgmental, self-righteous sheep-spawn! All three of you!"

Deuel glowered at him. "I said nothing."

"Well, two of you then," the man quailed. "What did you accost us for?"

The silence hung heavy, and Catie glanced up and down the line, keeping her head low. "Are any of you going to Balnath?" she asked only as loudly as she needed to be heard by the majority of them.

Rodigger turned quickly on her, the hurt flying out of his eyes. Catie tried to ignore him, looking instead at the row of wagoners who all gazed at her in varying amounts of dumbfound. She gave a small smile. "Anyone?"

But no one replied. A few eyebrows arched. All turned back to their wagons. Catie sighed, then spared a glance at Rodigger. His jaw shut, and he turned and rode away. Deuel followed him with his eyes, then looked back at Catie.

"I've had ideas that worked out a lot better," she said in a tiny voice.

"You would've had to," he rumbled.

She sighed. "Why doesn't Sheppar have patrols anymore?" she asked, nudging Kelsie after Rodigger.

"It's safe now," Deuel replied, following. "Rodigger would say it's because Sheppar does not care about the people."

"That can't be true," Catie said. "The man who rid the land of roaming beasts can't just suddenly not care."

Deuel shrugged. "It's safe now," he repeated, then glanced at her. "Does he need to care anymore?"

"He's still king, though."

"He's kinnig," Deuel corrected. "And what more does he owe this country, after such a campaign as he completed?"

"There's more to being king *or* kinnig than just solving one problem," Catie said.

"That was a very large problem," Deuel said. "Cannot the villages and cities solve the little problems?"

"And this new one?"

"This was unforeseen."

"Funny how so many of the big problems are unforeseen," Catie retorted. "You'd think, being that big, you could spot them a long way off."

"The problems become big because they are not handled when they are small," Deuel said. "A nomadic, non-allied collection of peoples on the other side of a great range of mountains is a small problem, but still a problem if they do not recognize your rule."

"So Sheppar's campaign should have included them?"

"Why do you think solving a problem means eradication?" Deuel asked, then shook his head. "I fear for Rodigger, then."

"Do you think they would have just recognized our rule if we asked them to? Do you think it would have kept those men still in the Wastes? Or would there be even more of them on this side of the 'Back?"

"Catie, we have no knowledge of why those men were here, we have no knowledge of what sent them out of Beltrath. That is what Sheppar will need to address first. They may need our aid."

Catie sighed. "So, first I need to understand Rodigger?"

"Rodigger is easy," Deuel replied. "He believes what Roth believes—and he likes you."

Catie stared at Deuel as he gazed levelly back at her.

"Do not look surprised," Deuel said. "That is why you got him to ask your question."

"That wasn't *why*," Catie said lamely. "I thought he would just cut me off if I tried to ask. And I thought men in general liked to please women."

"They do," Deuel replied. "But when you coax him, you make him think you like him as well."

Catie sighed. "Oh, no." She rode silently for several moments. "What happens when they find out they were wrong?"

"If you are very lucky, he thinks you hate him."

"If I'm lucky?" Catie repeated in an incredulous whisper. "What if I'm not lucky?"

"He believes you think he is a fool."

———◦———

They stopped for lunch on the banks of the Balnathva as it swung close to the road. Though Rodigger did not sit far away, neither did he appear willing to talk. His eyes seemed lost in thought, and he did not notice—or flat out ignored—Catie's gaze as she tried to figure out how to approach him.

Perhaps I should just let him think. It would be good for him.

Goodness, I do think he is a fool.

Well, isn't he?

I don't know what's going on in his mind!

He probably doesn't either. Stop that!

Maybe he doesn't need to question everything; maybe he's happy with what he believes.

That is no excuse; happiness in stupidity is still stupidity. Cease this line of thinking right now!

I'm trying! I don't want to think he is a fool; we have too far to go yet for us to be at odds with each other.

You need to get him—

The thought broke off suddenly, and Catie blinked as if awakened. She glanced at Rodigger, noting his deep frown as he gazed at the river. She opened her mouth, but couldn't think of anything to say and closed it. And yet, there was something she needed to convince him of—some aspect of their plan? She couldn't imagine why, suddenly. Trusting him with their next step might mollify him. She paused. Deuel would keep her around, though she wasn't sure why. The behamian was interested in her—not in that way, she could tell, but something intrigued him. After that many centuries of life, it was surprising and more than a little heartwarming—if only she knew what it was. But Deuel was not her concern this moment.

"Rodigger," she said, before she could change her mind.

The only indication that he heard was a deepening of his frown.

"The riddle takes us to Kavlen, in the Nagrath Highlands," she said.

Deuel's gaze swung to her. Rodigger barely moved, though he stiffened.

"I wanted you two to know, just in case." She paused for a moment. "Not that I think anything will happen, but... We need to trust one another. We should look for the Grandmother when we get there, as we did in Attelek. She will remember the old legends better than anyone else."

"Have you ever been to Kavlen?" Deuel asked. Rodigger shifted. He was listening closer.

Catie shook her head. "I remember a story though," she said. "I hesitate to tell it, just because it's a little thin to be hanging all of the riddle on." Rodigger's gaze snapped to her, now. "I mean, I can't imagine another place like it, so it most likely is, but..." She paused and shrugged.

"I believe you are correct, though I did not make the connection immediately," Deuel said. "I have been to Kavlen, many years ago. It fits."

"Do you want to explain it, then?" Rodigger asked.

"Oh, I think the riddle does it justice," Catie replied with a smile. "Beyond that, you'll have to see it for yourself."

"You don't think I'll understand your description?" he asked.

"No, Rodigger, that's not it," Catie said. "I'm sorry I did that this morning. It was thoughtless, mean, and selfish. I just thought you would stop me if I asked if anyone was going—"

"I would have," Rodigger cut in. "If Sheppar can't control his own lands—or won't!—he shouldn't be in control of them."

"So those two shepherds deserved to die to prove a point?" Catie asked quietly.

"You give them too much import," Rodigger replied. "The point is made no matter who proves it. The point is reality."

"But if we can avoid more deaths by delivering a message—"

"He'll ignore it. It's too easy!" Rodigger said, lifting a hand. "He mounted his first campaign after hundreds of deaths, if not thousands. And that after the fortified inns were already built. Sheppar is a man of least required effort. He conducted his campaign because it was necessary. As soon as it was successful, he ceded responsibility back to whomever he could. He'll wait for others to respond to this new threat, and only involve himself after another several thousand deaths."

Catie opened her mouth, then closed it. Rodigger's gaze on her sharpened. He had the makings of a point. "We should still try," she said quietly. "If he ignores it, that's his responsibility. Ours is to call attention to it."

Rodigger's jaw clenched, and his eyes flicked to Deuel. "How fast..." The muttered words trailed away.

"Not fast enough," Deuel replied. "Once we were in Semmedor—"

"But by then we can probably send a messenger to him from there," Rodigger finished. He glanced back at Catie. "Is that good enough?"

"Y-yes, that's fine," she said. The nomads might still gain a foothold while they delayed. Rodigger probably knew that, knew the risk and took it anyway. But it was an improvement on his attitude toward her. "Thank you, Rodigger," she said.

He was, she decided, trying a little too hard to still look grumpy. She had him back. She swallowed, then. Best not to encourage him too much, though. But as she saw the glint in his eye behind the frown, she worried.

No, she was almost terrified. Swallowing again, she glanced at Deuel. His face, always still, looked hewn from rock as his eyes fixed on her. "Deuel," she croaked, but couldn't think what to say next. He shook his head slightly, his gaze still locked. The fear gave way to a brief moment of relief, and then anger—no, fury. Catie's eyes widened. Deuel shifted, and the fury subsided. But why was it there in the first place? A trace of fear returned, more purely hers this time. Where were these emotions coming from? Deuel? Why would he be frightened, then angry? Her eyes darted to Rodigger. Nothing the soldier had said should evoke this.

Another wave of peace washed over her, and her eyes went back to Deuel. He too seemed more at ease, though still not fully.

"What. Was—"

But Deuel's shaking head cut her off again. He would talk to her about it later.

Rodigger was looking at them warily. Catie forced a grin. "I thought I heard something," she said.

Rodigger grunted. "I thought I heard you say we needed to trust each other."

"Well, now it's your turn," she replied gently. "I'm not going to tell you everything about me right now, am I?"

Rodigger shrugged one shoulder. "I guess not."

Catie glanced up at the sun. "We should be on our way."

They agreed, packed, and set out for the next inn.

◆◇◆

Catie was exhausted that night, and fell asleep quickly despite the questions racing through her head. It startled her, then, when she awoke in the darkness to a hand lying gently on her shoulder. Before she could draw a conscious breath the hand left, and she saw the dark shape of Deuel leaving the cot room. His profile lit briefly as he exited into the common room where the fire still glowed.

Catie turned her head. Rodigger had taken the next cot over, as the inn had been nearly as crowded as all the others. She managed to pick out his breathing among the myriad other snorts, rumbles, and snores: it was deep and even. She lifted her covers and slipped out, managing not to kick any of the chests on her way out.

Deuel had taken a table in the far corner, and sat facing the cot room door. Catie went to the hearth first and pushed the logs together, adding one more for good measure. It was not particularly cold, but neither was it comfortable. She went and sat at an angle to Deuel, so she too could keep an eye on the cot room.

"What was that?" she asked as soon as she sat.

"I told you those who can sense a behamian once, do so in increasing amounts."

"I figured that, because it felt like it was coming from you. At least," she amended, "the suppression of the initial feelings certainly came from you."

"The sense works both ways," Deuel said, placing his hands on the edge of the table, then rested his forearms. He looked like one who was uncomfortable trying to force a comfortable posture. "I can tell when you are sensing me, or sensing something that I also sense."

"Then what was that? Why did I feel fear and then anger?"

"Is that what you felt?" he asked, piercing her directly with his gaze this time.

Catie drew a breath. "I felt terror, and then fury. I felt utter emptiness, then I was suddenly filled beyond bursting. Why?" she asked, filling that single word with every bit of frustration, fear, and anger she could.

Deuel sat back. "I do not know," he said, then held up a hand as her eyes goggled. "That is a deeper question than you understand," he said quickly. "You felt something coming from Kaoleyn. Why you felt it, and why she felt it, is a mystery to me."

"Who is Kaoleyn?"

Deuel glanced at the cot room door, then away at nothing. Finally he drew a sigh and bowed his head. His arms left the table and went back to his side. Catie waited as he drew another deep breath and looked at her. "Kaoleyn is my mother," he said quietly. "In Burieng."

Catie could only stare at him for a few moments. "Kao—she—why did I feel something from—Burieng is so far away!" She glanced, along with Deuel, at the far door, then dropped her voice. "Well it is!"

"I know where it is," Deuel murmured, and she felt his amusement.

"Or did I just feel it through you?"

"Not at first," Deuel said, and she felt chagrin. "I only felt it after you did. But that sense is not limited by distance, only power."

Catie sat in silence for a moment. "That's why you're so reserved," she said finally. "If you were emotional, you would affect every behamian everywhere."

"Very good," Deuel said. "And I would affect everyone with the sense like you."

"Deuel, why do I have that sense? How does someone get it to begin with?"

"We do not know. Long ago only behamien and dragons had it. We suspect wyverns do as well, but that is difficult to prove."

"Why is it difficult to prove?"

"Because wyverns by nature are capricious, and do not have a language we understand," he replied. "Sometimes it seems they respond to our emotions, but it might be coincidence."

"Is it possible...I mean...am I..." She shrugged.

Deuel shook his head. "Do you remember when you were seven?" he asked.

"Of course."

"Did you live with a dragon?"

Catie smiled and shook her head.

"Behamien live with their dragon parent until they are eight, learning to speak and learning the ways of the people where they live before being sent into it."

"So why aren't you in Burieng? And how do you learn the language? I didn't think dragons could form words." She could feel his chuckle at her barrage of questions, and she smiled. "Sorry."

"Behamien are even less welcome in Burieng than in Rodigger's reality," Deuel said. "And we learn through our sense connection. You are right, dragons cannot speak human words. Everything we share with our parent is through that sense. But we can practice actual speech with our siblings."

"You've said a couple times about your 'parent'. Aren't there two?"

Deuel gazed at the cot room door for many long moments as if listening. Catie turned her head as well to listen, but she heard nothing. Finally Deuel turned back to her, and lowered his voice to just above a whisper. "Yes, there are two. But only two dragons may live on one continent. No one must know this!" His ferocity slammed into her and she could not breathe for a few moments. "I do not know why I trust you with this," he continued as she gaped at him, still breathless, still locked into his gaze as tightly as if bound by great chains. "Yet I do. Paolound—my father—is dead. One of his sons must replace him. I believe—" He cut off quickly, and as his gaze dropped Catie was released and took a deep breath. "I believe they are safe now," Deuel continued with less intensity. "But I believe someone tried to steal Kaoleyn's eggs today. That was her terror and her fury, for with Paolound gone and them stolen, our survival on Burieng, and perhaps the rest of Oren, was in great danger."

"I'm sorry, Deuel. When did he die?" Catie murmured.

He shook his head once, and she felt his turmoil. "I thought he died many years ago," he said. "But then suddenly he was not. He died again a few months ago, after we received our mission from Roth."

Catie's head snapped up. "What?"

Deuel gazed at her, and she knew he could feel her quivering. "This means something to you."

"It was late at night?" she pressed. "The night after you came to Akervet?"

"How did I know?" Rodigger mumbled from the doorway. Catie's wide gaze snapped from Deuel's intense look to Rodigger's groggy one. Rodigger shuffled in, moving toward the fire as Catie's thoughts railed against the injustice.

"Why are you awake?" she asked, unable to keep all of her frustration out of her voice.

Rodigger eyed her as he warmed himself in front of the fire. "Something woke me up," he said, his voice becoming clearer. "Having secret meetings now?"

"This has nothing to do with the mission," she replied, regaining control of her tone. *And everything to do with my life!* "We were almost done, anyway."

Rodigger waved her away. "I won't be able to get back to sleep now," he said. "It's amazing the racket sleeping people can make, when there's enough of them."

"I will try," Deuel said. Cate glared at him. *I won't!* she thought as loudly as she could. She could not tell if he sensed her as he stood. His glance as he began to leave said he did not—or he was very good at hiding that he had. As he moved past Rodigger, she sensed he wanted to put a hand on Rodigger's shoulder, but he made no motion.

After Deuel left, Rodigger turned and came to the table and sat. Catie only looked at him as his gaze stayed on the table. *This just gets better and better.*

"What do you think we'll face, in Kavlen?" he asked quietly.

He's frightened.

Catie took a deep breath, trying to wrench her thoughts from that night outside Akervet to the young man sitting in front of her. Had she witnessed, in some way, the death of Paolound? And why did that awaken something in her? Deuel said she could not be behamian, and yet he clearly showed surprise and interest in her ability to sense dragon-things.

Rodigger's eyes lifted from the table to hers, and she forced herself to look into them. His eyes did not look like ones who had seen death, or faced their own mortality—though perhaps they were, in some way, doing so now. But she also knew *fear* of pain or death was a far step removed from truly comprehending the *possibility* and nearness of death. He was still young. Or was she, perhaps, older than she should be? It felt like it.

"I do not know," she replied finally. "The riddle sounds as though there is some conflict going on. We might use that as a distraction."

"Conflict?" Rodigger asked. "I thought it just mentioned guards. You know..." He didn't speak it, but made some gesture.

"'Wars wage and blare far beneath the floors,'" Catie quoted. "The first goblet was underground. I assume the second will be, as well. Probably all of them will be."

"We three of us can't win a war," Rodigger said. "As good as Deuel supposedly is, so far we only know he faced eight men and lived." He paused under her appraisal. "Well, fine, eight is a lot. But he probably surprised them, and we don't know if he'll be able to again."

"We also don't know how many Wendol 'guard the glass' there," Catie offered. "It might only be two."

"That would be enough," Rodigger muttered. "They were the hardest for Sheppar's army to eradicate—and apparently they didn't even do a thorough job."

"Lucky for us, though, right?" Catie said. "If they had, we'd be short a goblet and wouldn't know where to look for the next one."

Rodigger shrugged. "Fair enough. But killing two Wen—It's not going to be easy."

"We didn't have the kill the *byor*, though, right?"

Rodigger blinked. "Right. But if they're guarding it..."

"The *byor* guarded, too, against those who would simply try to rush in and take the Berkarfor," Catie replied.

"So I guess I just have to trust you," Rodigger said with a wry grin.

"You need to trust yourself, as well," Catie said. "Take a moment to think—as small a moment as you want," she continued gently. "The world will probably not end because you take two breaths to consider something from a second angle. What you said earlier about Sheppar being a man of least effort—I like Sheppar, and I'm not convinced he is as bad as you say. But you gave me something to think about."

Rodigger's mouth twisted a little. "Roth told me that, first," he admitted. "So, Roth gave you something to think about."

Catie hoped her irritation didn't show on her face. How could he so willingly follow a man like Roth? After what he'd—

He probably wasn't there.

"Rodigger, were you at Bokessin with Roth last winter?"

Rodigger sighed, and a rueful grin flashed across his face. "No," he said. "I wanted to be. But Roth insisted it was better for me to stay in Akervet. Were you there?" he asked.

Catie nodded silently.

"Did you get to see him?" he asked, his tone as one who shared some awe-inspiring sight.

He had no idea what Roth had done there. She wished he had been there, to know who this man was he worshipped. Her heart cried out, and the words nearly left her mouth. But as she looked at the light in Rodigger's eyes, she wondered how dark they might go if that light left. Did disillusionment have to be so violent? Would it be better for knowledge to come swiftly? Or slowly? Would he even accept what she had to say? And if he did, would he allow her to continue, believing—rightfully—that she sought the goblets only for another opportunity at justice? If he still believed Roth was right, he would not. He seemed convinced, for whatever reason, that she had abandoned that hope. *Rodigger likes you* floated across her mind.

"Not really," she said, forcing her own rueful grin. "I had...other concerns that pulled me away after only seeing him briefly."

"That's a shame," Rodigger said, still smiling.

"It was," Catie agreed. She paused. Normally she didn't fear answers, and yet... "Rodigger, there was a time you thought I should be thrown deep into a hole, somewhere..." She trailed off with a quick glance.

"Oh." Rodigger shrugged. "Roth must have had his reasons for not doing that. And he never told me to stay away from you—just not to let you inside Akervet again."

They sat in silence for a few moments longer, Rodigger gazing at her, Catie looking toward the fire. She glanced back at him, finally.

"Okay," she said. "I think I'll try to get back to sleep, too. Good night, Rodigger." She stood, and his eyes followed her.

"Good night," he replied. "I'm going to stay out here for a little while

longer."
She smiled, and left him to it.

12

FINDING WOUNDS

"I suppose you think that went well."
"You are improving."
"Small comfort."
"You want too much, Teresh."

17 Halmfurtung 1320 — Spring

"You know, maybe it wouldn't be a bad idea to start telling people about what happened," Rodigger mused as the sun cleared the mountains and scattered glinting jewels across the Balnathva River.

"No?" Catie asked.

"People should know there may be dangerous men around, and take steps to defend themselves."

Catie cocked an eyebrow at Deuel. He remained emotionless. "Well, should we wait for everyone to catch up, then?" she asked, nodding her head back down the road where the merchant convoys could barely be seen. Unburdened as the three companions were, they made better time up the road and daily left the more laden travelers behind.

Rodigger twisted briefly, then shook his head. "Oh, it's not that important. We'll see them at dinner tonight."

"But it might be safer for us and them to travel together," Catie said. "Like you say, we're all going to the same place."

Rodigger squinted at her as if trying to see if she were making fun of him. He rolled his shoulders. "I mean...we're probably fine. To keep going, I mean. Anyway, we can protect them from up here, too. They'd be more likely to attack the three of us. We could end up flushing them out."

"Sounds pleasant," Catie said. "Why don't you want to wait for them?"

"I said we'd ride with them tomorrow."

"Rodigger."

"Because I don't want to travel with a big group of people, okay?" he said, setting his Therian's ears swiveling.

Catie grinned slowly. "But you said we'd ride with them tomorrow."

"Tomorrow is further away than—" He jerked his head backward.

Now Catie laughed, but gently. "I didn't know you didn't like people. What about when we're staying at the inn? They've been packed since we came into the valley."

"Yeah, and I've hardly said two words the whole time," Rodigger said, settling down into his saddle. "And it's not that I don't like them, I'm just not comfortable talking."

"I thought you were supposed to be talking to people? Convincing them of the glory of the revolution?"

"And look how well that's turned out so far," Rodigger muttered.

"Well, you have to keep trying! No one gets it right the first...you know..." Rodigger glared as she looked at her fingers. She cleared her throat. "Bunch of times. So I'll be telling them about the nomads then?" she asked.

"Well, I can do that part. I *should* do that part, probably. Well, they might believe me more easily than you," he said when she shot him a look. "I mean, guys like these probably won't think you're trustworthy."

"Probably true," Catie said. "But then, if Deuel gives them a look or two, they'll believe probably anything."

"I wonder if you can do the same," Deuel replied.

Catie swallowed. Also probably true.

Rodigger glowered. "I'll tell them, that way neither of you have to glare at them for anything."

"I was only teasing, Rodigger," Catie said, though her heart wasn't in it.

"But you do *do* that," Rodigger replied. "How?"

She glanced up, frustration piling the words behind her teeth, but Rodigger was looking at Deuel. The words came out as silent breath as she glanced at the dragon-son.

"It is nothing I do," Deuel replied. "It is who I am."

"But you said she can do it too," Rodigger said. Catie sat up a little in her saddle. Was Rodigger about to ask her question for her? "So how does she do it?"

She settled back. Too advanced a question, then. She cocked an eyebrow at Deuel after he was silent for too long.

"Perhaps it is a trick of those most open and honest," he said finally. Catie's eyes widened and she looked away.

"Great," Rodigger said. "So I'm just closed and a liar?" he asked.

Deuel gazed at him a few moments, and Rodigger looked quickly away with a curse. Rodigger took a tighter grip on his reins, and urged his Therian forward ahead of them.

"Am I part behamian?" Catie asked quietly when Rodigger was out of earshot.

It was like a wall suddenly towered before her where there had been an open forest: infinite denial instead of obscured improbability. "No," Deuel replied. "Behamien do not mingle with humans."

"What happens if they try?"

"We die," Deuel said. "That," he continued with a meaningful glance at the seething young man ahead of them, "is an abomination. We only mate as dragons. It cannot happen any other way."

Rodigger cried out ahead of them. Deuel was racing forward as Catie only tried to see what was happening. Her eyes started toward Rodigger, but Deuel caught her attention as he pulled his blades free. He was alongside Rodigger when Catie finally nudged Kelsie into an unwilling trot. Deuel's right arm extended, and some word she didn't recognize came to her quietly. She yelped as a sharp, bright flash of blue and a low scream came from a stand of trees to their left.

Rodigger was staring at his arm, and as she neared Catie could see the darkening of the shirt sleeve on his forearm. "I was just brushing a fly away," he said slowly. "It kept getting stuck in my hair."

"You're okay," Catie said, coming alongside. She heard Deuel's voice again, but still jumped when a sound like small thunder cracked from the trees again. She called out: *"Leih par dak* you didn't get them yet?" But no answer came from Deuel.

"Catie!" Rodigger said, eyes goggling. "Did you just say that?"

"Let me look at it," she said. She took his hand and pulled his arm toward her. "Can you get Gared to stand still? Kelsie, easy." Hoof-beats diminished as Deuel left them. "Well, it's through the outside, not the center of your arm, which is probably actually—yeah, see how it's shaped?" The arrowhead resembled half a spade. "Usually you do that for fishing, with a line tied to the end so you can haul the fish back in. That's for really big fish though, pike or something, that would chew through a net. Rodigger, you're not looking."

"I got shot through the arm!" he said, still staring resolutely ahead.

"You're still lucky it didn't go through the middle...or through your head."

He whimpered.

"Sorry, I guess we don't need to think about that. Do you want me to take it out?"

This time his eyes moved, to stare at her wider than she knew his eyes could go. "Leave it in, please," he said in a whisper. His eyes crossed, focusing on the arrow. He fought back a retch and turned his eyes forward again.

"I meant did you want *Deuel* to take it out," she said. She saw his jaw muscles writhe. "Okay." She let go of his hand and gripped the arrowhead. With a mighty twist she broke the shaft, and Rodigger cried out again. Before he could make it worse, she pulled on the back of the arrow and yanked the whole thing free from his arm. His cry this time was deeper in his chest, and he swooned forward.

"Don't do that," she said, grasping his shoulder and hauling him upright again. "This is the best part of the whole event. Now we just bandage it and you heal. You already missed the best time to faint."

She heard hoofbeats, and glanced up quickly. Deuel was returning. "How many?" she asked.

"Only two," Deuel replied. He gestured to Rodigger. "He's bleeding."

"Right." Catie dug her free hand into a saddlebag and pulled free a rolled strip of cloth. "I guess we should wait for the convoy, now," she said. "Do you think your sleeve will go up?"

Rodigger nodded, pale, and tugged half-heartedly with his other hand.

"I'll get it," Catie said, tucking the roll under her leg and gently pulling his sleeve back. "Okay, hold that. Just a pair this time? Only watching the road, do you think? For another crossing?"

"And in the least inhabited portion of the Tevorbath," Deuel agreed. "We do not know how many may actually be here. But if they are ambushing small groups already, they are probably here in force."

"I hope those two women are okay," Catie said. "We didn't really leave them in a stronger position than they had been."

"We didn't know how bad it was, then," Rodigger murmured. Catie had the wound covered, and he was gazing at the bandage as she finished tying it off. Blooms of red still grew.

"He will probably need more than that," Deuel said gently.

"I was hoping he wouldn't," Catie muttered, rummaging through her saddlebag again. "Do you have—oh, the arrow shaft. Can you grab it for me?" She pointed with one hand as she twirled another roll of bandage, unwrapping it. As Deuel dismounted, she cut off a section, tucking the remainder under her leg. She tied the piece she'd torn off around Rodigger's bicep, leaving it loose. Deuel handed her the shaft and she ran it through, then began twisting. She watched the bandaged forearm. Rodigger groaned, but she did not stop until the blooms stopped growing. She used more bandage to secure the tourniquet, then drew a deep sigh.

"It'll stop you from bleeding out," she said, daring a glance at his face. His eyes were squeezed shut.

"It's incredible to think about how much this hurts," he said, gasping.

"Then don't think about it," she said, resting a hand on his shoulder and giving a small squeeze. She glanced at the sun, then down the road where the convoy behind them could still be faintly seen. By the time they arrived, they should loosen the tourniquet for a little. Hopefully someone in the convoy had tools a little better for handling such a wound.

"Do you want to scout to see if there's a larger force nearby?" Catie asked Deuel. "They surely wouldn't be far from water."

"They are nomads," Deuel said. "They know how to find water besides in rivers. But yes, I will before the convoy arrives. Keep him in the shade, and give him water."

"Should you leave us alone?" Rodigger asked, licking his lips. "You're the only one set up to defend us, right now."

"I will scout nearby first, and thoroughly," Deuel replied.

"Can you help me get him down, first?" Catie asked. As she nudged Kelsie away and dismounted, Deuel caught Rodigger as he slid out of his saddle and set him on his feet. They tied all the horses in the nearby trees, and Catie and Rodigger set themselves up at the base of a spruce, still in sight of the road.

"I will return," Deuel said. He took two long strides out of the woods, then leapt into the air. Catie gave a little shiver, and rolled her neck.

"I love watching him do that," she said.

Rodigger coughed, then braced his wounded arm. "I could do without it."

"Close your eyes, then," she retorted, then sucked on her lips. "You should rest," she said, gentler. "You haven't lost a lot of blood, but you're not in a good way."

"Thanks," he said. "I had noticed."

"I'm sorry, Rodigger, I don't mean to—"

"Yeah, but you do," he cut in, giving a little sigh. "Which means you must really think it, since that's what comes out when you don't have time to think about what you're going to say." He paused as she remained silent. "Right?"

Amazing, his ability to be perceptive at the worst times. A thousand responses came into her head, ways to defend herself, try to appease him—mostly lies. A light breeze rose, shushing through the pines. She felt it at her back, let it embrace her as she took a breath. "How much of what you say comes from Roth?" she asked finally.

Rodigger shrugged his right shoulder. "He's been my mentor. Probably most of what I say, at least about the sorts of things he talks about, is from him."

"What about what you think?"

"Why should I do that? Roth is right! If I disagree with him, I'm wrong. It doesn't matter how long I think about it, or what feels right or wrong to me."

"But, everything he says?" Catie asked. "No one has that many right answers."

"You said yourself the ideas I told you about Sheppar gave you something to consider. That came from Roth."

"Exactly! I'm *considering* it. I'm not sold on it. Especially without being able to talk to Sheppar about it, or anyone who knows him. You're making assumptions just on a few of his actions, without finding out what motivates him to act that way."

"No, that's fair. He's clearly doing a great job in securing this country," Rodigger said, lifting his wounded arm slightly.

"If he's made a mistake, then we tell him about it," Catie replied. "If he doesn't do anything after that, then we'll know he's not fit to run the country anymore."

"And if he does do something about it?"

"Then I get to tell you 'you were wrong,' and laugh at you," Catie replied.

"What about the Berkarfor?" Rodigger pressed. "You know what Roth wants them for. If you think Sheppar's doing such a great job, why do you want to see Roth succeed?"

"There's a great difference between gaining the goblets and succeeding," Catie replied.

Rodigger blinked a few times, his brows knitting. "Why are you helping us find these?"

"I needed something to do," Catie replied.

"No," Rodigger said, shaking his head. "No, no. This isn't just a distraction. This is way too dangerous to just do because you're bored."

"Well I didn't know it was going to be this dangerous," she said, gesturing to his bandage. "Did I? Couldn't know that."

"You want to get back to Roth, don't you? I'm not taking you. Once we find the last goblet, you're on your own. No! There is no—no! There is no way I'm taking you to see him. Why, so you can kill him? Or try to, again?"

"Calm down, already," Catie said, resting a hand on his good arm. "He said he wanted to see me try again, anyway. But no, that's not why I came along."

"Yeah right."

"I came because of Deuel."

Rodigger looked at her a few moments. "You two are as close as a groove joint, aren't you?"

She took her hand away. "I'm not sure what that is. Close as eel-skin?" she offered.

He stared where her hand had been. "What is eel skin close to?"

Catie opened her mouth, then shut it and squinted. "Its body?"

"Everything's skin is close to its body."

"Not a wrinkled lizard."

He looked up. "Well, it's still right there, I mean—"

"Rodigger..."

"You two are always talking about stuff! Always a little ahead or a little behind, heads together, sharing these little looks and expressions like you can read each other's minds."

Catie pursed her lips. *Probably shouldn't tell him—no.* "You know, if you tried to ride with us, we would either be forced to stop or turn to a gallop if we truly didn't want you around. Which might actually be funny," she said with a grin, "you chasing us down the road. We'd probably cover two inns a day."

Rodigger did not smile. "What's that supposed to mean?"

Catie looked at him seriously. "You always ride ahead, or fall behind, Rodigger, because Deuel makes you uncomfortable—maybe I do too, I don't know. But that's your choice, not ours."

"But...you know what he is," Rodigger said, his voice dropping to a whisper.

"Okay, let's say he is what you say he is, morally," Catie said. "And so to show your displeasure or disapproval, you ignore him, and get as much distance from him as you can. And let's say everyone who thinks the way you do, reacts the same way. Now Deuel is only surrounded by people who don't have a problem with who or what he is. If you think he can change, or you want him to change, or you *expect* him to change, how is the situation you've put him in going to do that? Or do you think he values your company *so* much he'll do whatever it takes to reconcile you to him, even by trying to ignore who he is?"

"I guess that's up to him," Rodigger said, gripping his left arm with his right.

Catie drew a sigh, and shook her head. "I think you don't care about Deuel, at least not as much as you care about your own piety. Whatever else you may say or think or believe, your goal is not the betterment of those around you, only the ability to say 'at least I'm not like them'."

"It's not like I'm the only way Deuel knows what he's doing is wrong," Rodigger returned. "He's been around a long time. I'm sure he's heard it before."

"A thousand drops of rain fill the bucket, Rodigger, but one makes it overflow." She peered south through the trees. She could hear, faintly, wheels clattering as they made their way up the sunbaked road. "Deuel better get back soon, that convoy is almost here."

As if in answer, Catie heard a footstep behind her, and she turned—but it was not Deuel. She leapt to her feet, already drawing the dagger from her boot as she yelped: "Rodigger!"

And then, before she could do anything else, Rodigger had leapt to his feet, drawing his own short blade from his boot, and with a sweep and a lunge both nomads fell to the earth. She gazed at him as he stared mutely over his work, both of their chests heaving.

"How long have you had that?" she asked quietly.

He looked at the blade, then quickly away. "Um, a while now. Why are they up to their ankles in mud?"

Catie looked, then looked again. They had fallen backward, knees bent, feet buried in what had to be a hands-breadth of mud.

"Magic," Deuel replied, striding down the hill toward them.

"Oh, thank the God," Catie said.

"What?" Rodigger asked Deuel.

"It was only supposed to hold them till I could reach you," Deuel replied, putting his blades away as he neared. "But you did well."

"You can use magic?" Rodigger asked.

Catie rolled her eyes, barely suppressing a sigh. Now he would hate Deuel for that, too. What a waste of a conversation.

"Halm and Ro Thull can," Deuel said. "You should clean your blade, and let us meet the convoy."

Without seeing if Rodigger would comply, Deuel untied his horse and moved toward the road. The lead wagon was nearly abreast of them, and he called out loudly with a raised arm.

Catie glared at Rodigger as she moved to Kelsie and untied her as well. "You're trying too hard," she said.

"No, he's making it very easy," Rodigger replied. "You're trying too hard to accept him."

"Fine, keep ignoring him," Catie spat. "Let me know how it works out."

"You should ignore him, too," Rodigger replied. "If everyone pushed him away, he would change. The human need for companionship is one of the strongest motivators."

"I suppose that comes from Roth, too?"

"What if it does?"

"Deuel's not human," Catie replied. "So your plan is flawed. Not to mention you will never get everyone to do what you want. In lieu of that, you might try my suggestion of actually caring about Deuel, and not yourself."

Are you coming?

Catie looked sharply toward the road, where Deuel stood beside the lead wagoner staring at her. *Did you just talk to me in my head?*

It was probably too far to see if he reacted, but she saw nothing, and felt nothing either. But it had sounded like him, at least a little. Maybe she had just suddenly become aware of how much time had passed. Maybe she was just tired of speaking to Rodigger. She led Kelsie through the trees without another word to him.

The merchants did have medicinal items. Catie cleaned and properly bandaged Rodigger's arm, still without speaking. The right glare, and he seemed to know what she expected of him. Probably he was smart enough, just didn't care to think ahead. It was a shame, really. He had just somewhat heroically saved her life, without regard for his pain, had done it out of apparent reflex. As if coming to her rescue was the deepest seed in his heart. But it didn't much matter when she knew his reaction would be far, far slower—petrified, probably even—if it had been Deuel in her place. Maybe that wasn't fair. How like life.

Once the story of Rodigger's wound was told, the merchants were more than happy to have some fighters—well, one at least—with them on the road north. They set out as the sun began to dip, with assurances they would reach the inn with some daylight left.

"Can either of you use weapons?" Deuel asked as they rode, now in the midst of the clattering wagon wheels and merchants' banter.

"I have been taught to use a sword, by Roth," Rodigger replied.

"I've used a bow for hunting," Catie said. "And I know my way around a Nagrath Dagger, if we can find one."

Rodigger smirked. "You think that will be useful against a sword?"

"If we find one, I'll show you," she replied sweetly.

"Why do you know that dagger?" Deuel asked quietly.

Her gaze darted to him. "My...father taught me before he left," she said uneasily. *He loved me like one.* "He wanted me to be able to take care of myself."

"Wasn't a very trusting man, was he?" said Rodigger.

"And yet here I am, in need of it," Catie replied, lofting an eyebrow.

They continued in silence, until Catie turned back to Deuel. "Where did those other two nomads come from?" she asked. "I thought you checked the area closest to us first."

"I did," Deuel replied, radiating regret. Catie gave him a forgiving grin, and he went on. "They are camped in a valley not far to the west."

Catie's grin faded. "They?" she echoed. "How many?"

"Too many," Deuel replied. "I do not know how they crossed the Tevorbath without being seen."

"Were you able to...?" She glanced at the back of his saddle, where his blades were sheathed.

"Too many," Deuel repeated.

"We're in a pretty remote area," Rodigger suggested. "If they crossed at night, who would see them?"

"And how did they cross the Balnathva?" Catie asked. "They would need a bridge—oh, no." Her eyes widened as she thought of Priska and Disceya. A glance at Deuel said he thought the same thing. "Maybe another sheep farm in the area," she said aloud, probably for Rodigger's benefit. She drew a deep breath. They would have done to it what the others did to Priska and Disceya. "But why would they risk it?" she wondered aloud. "There's nothing over there, is there?"

"We do not know why they are leaving the Wastes in the first place," Deuel replied.

"All the larger settlements are on the west side of the river, aren't they?" Rodigger asked. "I mean, they have been so far."

Catie nodded, her brow furrowed. "Well, outside of Ravverbit and Merneset, I think it's called. But Merneset is in the Wastes, so they don't need access to it. I wonder if there's a way to get news from there."

"Probably in Ravverbit," Deuel said.

Catie shook her head and sighed. "Plenty of answers to be had," she said. "And they're all a month away."

They continued in silence as the sun fell. When an orange smudge still lingered to the west, they could see lights far ahead on the road, marking the inn. But they had seen no farms or bridges across the river.

Around dinner, they discovered one of the merchants was carrying hunting bows bound primarily for Dagget's Vatenvilt. After dinner Catie purchased one. With Gabriel gone, Rodigger's funds were stretching even further.

"I'd like to practice, some," Catie murmured to Deuel when Rodigger was distracted by two merchants who were especially proud of Sheppar's kinnigship. Deuel followed her silently out of the inn.

In the stables, she found an empty sack draped over a stall and stuffed it with hay. While Deuel watched by torchlight she practiced until she could cluster three arrows in a hands-breadth from twenty-five paces. He stood silently nearby as she emptied the sack again

"Why do you not still have your father's Nagrath Dagger?" he asked suddenly, quietly.

Catie busied herself with inspecting some of the arrowheads. "I, uh, threw it into the lake," she said absently. She sighed and lowered the arrows, looking at Deuel. His gaze showed nothing in return. "Actually, he wasn't my father. He helped raise me, but..." She told him the rest, as Grandmother had told her before they left Attelek. "My mother, when she said she was leaving, said I would be able to take care of myself since he had taught me the Dagger. I guess I hoped she would stay if I lost it." She looked away for several long moments, then briefly shook her head, turned, and muttered gentle nothings to Kelsie. Finally she cleared her throat.

"How do your blades work?" she asked.

"You do not despise magic?" Deuel returned.

She shrugged. "I guess I should," she said with a brief glance. "I'm sure you've heard of things going on in Burieng because of it, too."

Deuel gazed at her for a few long moments. "I am not sure how *you* have, though," he said.

She turned back to face him now. "Oh, in Bokessin. I met a merchant who had recently come back from a voyage there."

"And yet you are curious."

"That's generally true," Catie replied with a small grin. "But you know how magic is, running around and doing all this damage by itself, with no one to control it."

Deuel appreciated her sarcasm. "You know how magic works."

"Some, just from being told why it's so wicked."

"Do you know there is a metal that has affinity to the elements? That can conduct it, like riverbanks conduct a river?"

Catie shook her head.

"It is called 'cretal'," Deuel continued. He pulled up a fold on his sleeve, revealing the bracelet underneath. It looked like rusted steel, but softer and clearer like rubies. Around the bracelet in a thin circle was a band of blue. He lifted the other sleeve. That bracelet had a band of red. "Water and fire," he said. "I have two others for wind and earth, but they are less versatile. Cretal also runs through the cuffs of Halm and Ro Thull, and through the rods and into the blade. The bracelets draw the magic and send it through to the blade."

"Why don't the blades have the magic in them? Because you would need four blades," she answered herself quickly. "Can you only do one spell each?"

Deuel shook his head. "I can speak a number of spells, and channel them through the blades. Some can be shot forth like an arrow, some remain on the blade until it strikes its target."

"So, who would win," Catie began.

"A magic-user," Deuel said quickly. She felt him smile. "If I were limited to using magic."

"You are otherwise very good, though," she said with a genuine smile. Something like a chuckle from him fluttered against her chest.

"I have my uses," he said.

"Deuel, how old are you?" she asked before she could stop herself. She instinctively reached up and began scratching Kelsie's forehead, her eyes boring into the mare's white star as she fought down the warmth surging into her face. After a few moments of silence, she glanced sideways.

Deuel was gone.

13

CHANGING MINDS

"They're almost there."
"Okay."
"Would this be a good time?"
"Better than most, I imagine."

24 Halmfurtung 1320 — Spring

They passed the days in peace as they approached Dagget's Vatenvilt. They noted only one crossing, a dilapidated but secure bridge across the Balnathva. There, too, the ground was torn by countless hooves. Catie was able to breathe a sigh of relief when the merchants told her that farm had been abandoned years before—no one to be killed, then, to be kept silent. With this viable crossing in place, the question remained of why they had also crossed further south, risking exposure and requiring such brutal murders to make it happen.

"And whether those two women made it out of there before anyone else came along," Catie added, rubbing her eyebrow. "They were probably trying to maneuver another group of soldiers across there, right? And why? What could they want?"

But no one could answer. The merchants had no dealings with the nomads, or with Merneset in the Wastes.

As the Vatenvilt wound into view, Catie hoped someone there might have news. It was not a large 'vilt, so close to Taferk, but for those heading south it was the last stop on the long road to Kendet's and Sprativerg. Many merchants would come from the north and turn around there, just as these merchants would turn back south when they left in the next few days.

The three companions went first to the Magiss. Rodigger's sword was easily purchased, but he scratched his head a few times at Catie's dagger.

"I know what they are," he said sourly. "We don't get much call for 'em. I could send you a hawk to Kostet's, maybe. He usually has stuff like that."

Catie cocked her head. "Where's Kostet's?"

"Just south of Agrend, corner of the Aug," he said.

Catie's eyebrows rose. "Could you send a message, instead of an order?"

The Magiss chuckled. "I can send one with an order: just a message is a waste of hawk, unless you pay me what I could make from a whole shipment floated down."

"No," Rodigger said loudly.

"I wouldn't, obviously," Catie said, rolling her eyes.

"No: no message," Rodigger replied. "He has to learn."

"Do you have something for me to write the message on?" Catie asked.

The Magiss shrugged and turned away. Catie followed as he went to his office.

"Hey!" Rodigger called after her, hurrying to catch up. "I said we could send a message from Semmedor. I never said you could do this."

The Magiss glanced back at Rodigger, then raised an eyebrow at Catie. She shook her head. They went inside.

"Catie, I absolutely forbid it," Rodigger continued. "We can't let our job be interfered with by this!"

"Rodigger, you're an idiot," she said calmly.

The Magiss placed a parchment and quill at the edge of his desk and glanced at Rodigger. "Should I make you wait outside?" he asked.

As Catie bent and grasped the quill, Rodigger strode forward and seized her arm. She turned suddenly, pouring all her fury into her gaze, like she had never done before.

The blood left his face as his pupils dilated so wide his irises nearly disappeared. His hand on her arm trembled and she saw his legs shaking. In the last moment, she feared suddenly to see a spreading stain on his trousers.

The door crashed open. The Magiss protested as Deuel strode in, grabbed Rodigger by the collar and dragged him out, never once looking at Catie.

When the door closed again, the quill in Catie's hand shook. She brought a hand to her mouth, trying to calm the corners and remember how to breathe.

"Seems like a right bugger," the Magiss said. "Ma'am?" he asked, noticing her trembling.

Her lungs opened, and she took a deep breath. "Sorry," she said, turning away for a moment. "He can be aggravating at times, but I probably went a little too far, there."

The Magiss snorted. "Seemed like he deserved it."

"No," Catie said, finally turning to the page. "No, he definitely did not."

She calmed herself enough to write a message, then rolled it and handed it to the Magiss. "It would be in everyone's interest if this made its way to Sheppar," she said. The Magiss started to grin, until he looked in her eyes. She broke contact as quickly as she could. "Something is going wrong, and he needs to know about it."

"Right," he said. "And do you want that dagger?"

She shook her head. "We don't have time to wait for it. I'll just have to get it from the source," she said with a smile.

The Magiss grinned and gave her a slight nod. "I'll get this out," he said.

She thanked him, and left. Deuel was waiting when she returned to the road. Rodigger was nowhere in sight.

"Wait here," Deuel said, striding quickly into the office. Catie stood, hands folded together. Deuel quickly reappeared.

"Walk with me," he said.

She swallowed. "Deuel, I know—"

But he had already continued past her. She followed, trying to keep her head high.

"No," he said finally, as the last inn dropped behind them. "You know, perhaps, because I have told you. But you do not understand."

"Understand what?" she pleaded. "I didn't mean to do it. And I promise I won't do it again. Deuel! You know how Rodigger can get, and he was worse than ever."

Deuel turned so suddenly, she halted by bumping into his chest. He grasped her shoulders and looked into her eyes. "I don't know what's happening with you," he said in a fierce whisper. "You can feel and radiate more than anyone should. Every dragon and behamian in all Oren felt your fury, just as they would have felt Kaoleyn's. They will not know why such anger is burning, and it is contagious, Catie. They will feel they are being threatened—first in Burieng, and now Andelen, and next...anywhere else it arises. And when behamien and dragons feel threatened, they behave just as humans do: they see danger everywhere, and feel hate everywhere. It is too late for you to never do it again! *I* know it was Rodigger, an utterly insignificant human being. But they will not. Our existence was tenuous when we were thriving. But now humans expand their settlements, and we cannot thrive."

Tears were running great tracks down Catie's face. "I'm sorry, Deuel," she mumbled through a sob. "I really, really didn't mean to."

Deuel drew a sigh, then held her close. "I know." One of his hands slid to the base of her neck, then across to her shoulder, pausing for a moment before sliding down her back and falling away.

"Do I have to explain anything to Rodigger?" she asked, her voice muffled against his chest.

"Yes," Deuel said. "But I believe you will have time to think about it."

"He's terrified of me."

He pressed a cheek against the top of her head. *He should be. Men like him are not worthy of you.*

Catie's sniffle stopped, but she stayed against his chest. *How do you do that?*

Deuel's head shifted a fraction. *All behamien can do that. The question, Catie, is how can you do that?*

I blame you. I couldn't do this before you came around.

Deuel shifted again, then held her at arm's length, gazing into her eyes. *There is probably more truth to that than you know.* "And we should not encourage your connection, I fear."

"Probably too late now, isn't it?"

"That is what I fear," he responded.

"What about Rodigger? Doesn't he have the sense, too? He understood my anger."

"No. He can understand when a dog is angry or happy, too."

"Thanks," Catie drawled, smiling to take the edge off.

"It has nothing to do with you," he replied. "It does not matter how clearly you speak if the person listening does not want to hear."

"Why do you think he's like that?"

"In Rodigger's case, he probably believed a lie and was, at some point, disillusioned," Deuel said, letting his hands finally slide from her shoulders. "But he still does not trust himself to discern fact and fiction. So instead of deciding truth for himself, he found a person to trust and accepted everything they said. It was probably whoever exposed the first lie."

"But isn't he still risking belief in a lie?"

"Of course." Deuel drew a sigh. "But he has to believe something. Now he no longer risks disillusionment."

Catie hugged her arms. "I couldn't do that," she muttered.

"You believe truth is foundational, and can always be found—that lies will eventually be revealed and fall away."

Catie glanced away for several long moments. "If we keep looking for it, yes," she said finally. "Which means we have to keep questioning even what we think is right. Which is a lot of work, I guess."

She felt him snort. "Sometimes you humans think too much about effort and too little about consequences," he said. "It is a wonder the fortified inns were ever built."

Catie grinned ruefully. "Yes, Andelen is much safer now, with those inns. Safe even for nomads to cross the Tevorbath without resistance."

"Because the truth we believed was never again questioned," Deuel replied. He gazed northwest, where, eventually, Balnath Agrend lay. "Let us hope Sheppar still risks disillusionment."

◄O►

Rodigger stood at the window in their room on the second floor of the inn, looking down the road as Catie and Deuel embraced. He swallowed hard. She had wanted to kill him—would have, if Deuel hadn't arrived and plucked him from death. Yet now he held her tenderly. Which was disgusting, really: she was twenty-three, he was three hundred? And behamian.

He both dreaded and longed to return to Roth. How could he face his mentor after so long in the presence of these two, allowing it to continue? But how much longer could he stand to be with them? If only he could trust solving the riddles of the next two Berkarfor.

He scratched at his bandaged arm as Catie and Deuel finally put some space between themselves. He wondered, briefly, what they were talking about. Probably better not to know. He could, possibly, ride out without them and get to the goblet first. Then if he couldn't solve it, they would catch up, he would apologize, and Catie would have to take him back because he was her link to Roth.

His scratching ceased. He would be rid of them, at least for a while—maybe forever. Catie would never even come close to Roth again. There was every chance for reward and almost no chance for failure.

But could he get a whole day ahead of them?

His arms dropped to his sides. There was a way. It would take even more forgiveness if he failed to decipher the riddle. But what choice would Catie have? And Deuel, he felt sure, would follow Catie. He watched as Deuel's hands slid down her arms and hesitantly drop away.

There was a way.

⋯⋯◇⋯⋯

Rodigger lay awake with his eyes closed for what seemed like hours, waiting for Deuel to fall asleep. Something seemed to keep the...*it*...up, not tossing and turning, but breathing like he was awake. Once or twice, when Rodigger dared to glance over, he swore he could see Deuel blinking. Rodigger had never seen him blink in daylight, but he seemed to at night.

Finally, when there was surely no way the creature could be awake, he peeled the blankets off and sat up gingerly. He watched Deuel for a few moments, waited for the dragon-spawn to look at him or say something, then stood as quietly as he could. He picked up his boots and saddlebags, and with no shuffling footfalls made his way out the door. The lamps were trimmed low in the hallway, he was relieved to find, so there was no violent light to intrude into the room and wake the thing.

He glanced toward Catie's closed door and felt a twinge of guilt just as his forearm twinged with an awkward twist of the saddlebags. She had helped him, earlier, and had even been nice.

But then her blazing eyes and murderous intent flashed to mind.

Rodigger's eyes narrowed, and he made his way out into the night.

Gared did not appreciate being woken, and made it known several times before he was saddled. Catie's and Deuel's Midlands, he was delighted to find, were steadfast animals who didn't complain about work no matter what the hour. They took bit and bridle without question, and thought nothing of being led out of the 'vilt without their masters. If they were going to be this cooperative, Rodigger began to wonder just where he should let them go.

——◆——

Catie's eyes opened and she was awake, as if she had only blinked and the night had gone. The thoughts she had fallen asleep with were still with her. Only the sun coming through the window told her she had indeed slept.

Rodigger.

She wasn't sure what to think about having that man on her mind so much. She certainly would have liked to avoid it, but there he was—which, she realized, was just like him; making himself known no matter how much she didn't want to know.

You should wake up, now.

I thought we weren't going to encourage this?

Perhaps I just enjoy being lazy.

I find that hard to believe. Rodigger, perhaps, but not you.

Then this morning is full of events hard to believe.

Catie paused, brow furrowed, one foot in a boot, the other not. *What did he do?*

Will you control your emotions?

Her furrow smoothed, and she drew a breath. He got shot again—no, she might be sad or sympathetic, but not angry. He kept her letter from being sent? He sent a second letter? She sighed. He was capable of anything. *I have to find out sometime.*

He left in the night.

Catie closed her eyes. *Alone?*

For the most part.

Her eyes slitted open. For the most part? Who would he take with him? *Deuel, tell me he didn't...*

He did.

Catie's other foot thudded into the boot and she stood. *Where are you?*

Meet me in the common room.

When she arrived, she found the room mostly empty. Two sat at a table finishing their breakfast, one sat in a corner and seemed to have spent the night there. One serving girl sat behind the counter cleaning mugs. The keeper was nowhere to be seen.

Deuel entered, the sounds of the street waxing and waning behind the swinging door as daylight intruded, then retreated. Then it was dim and silent, with one bright square of sunlight through a window and dull lamplight, and occasional rubbing squeaks of the barmaid's rag in a mug. Catie drew a slow breath as she watched Deuel cross the room to a table away from the others. She sat, but still said nothing, listening to the stillness and enjoying the gloom, wishing they could cover the window and keep out the bright sun.

Deuel's eyes were intent on her, she realized. She returned the gaze and, after a few moments, seemed to surface from a deep lake.

"I guess I shouldn't have told him where we were going," she said.

"Perhaps." His gaze had not lost its intensity, but something in him, too, seemed to come back to the present. Catie wondered vaguely where they had both gone.

"Did he forget you can fly to him and catch him?"

"We still must retrieve the horses and bring them back here. He left most of the tack. He may let them drift after half a day, too."

"Kelsie will come back here on her own," Catie said firmly, putting her hands on the table in front of her.

"That may be worse, trailing her reins."

Catie cocked an eyebrow. "Kelsie can handle herself, I'm sure."

"You know her better. There is still the question of why he wants to delay us."

"Probably because I wanted to kill him yesterday," she said, and shrugged one shoulder. "He's already afraid of you. Now if he's afraid of me too...he's probably trying to escape."

"We might discuss if we should let him."

Catie sat in the stillness again. The sunlight was very bright, streaming through that window. It wasn't natural, putting windows in walls. If you built a cave, you must live in a cave.

"Why do you seek the Berkarfor, Catie?"

"To bring justice to Roth," she said absentmindedly. Silence. Stillness. Coolness. Caves were wonderful places, once you got used to them.

"Why do you need to bring justice to him?"

"He killed...someone," she said, barely conscious that she wasn't really paying attention anymore. "A lot of people, actually." There wasn't the stress and helter-skelter of life, in a cave. Just silence, stillness, coolness, and slow change.

"What would you do if you were free from bringing Roth to justice?" Deuel asked quietly.

Silence. Stillness. Coolness. Peace. That was it: complete and utter peace. No hurry, no fuss or bother.

But she couldn't. Kelsie was gone. She could walk. Walking wasn't the best. But it wasn't the worst. Or run. She was strong. Her hands clenched, her eyes bored into Deuel. "Balnath Agrend," she whispered, and wet her lips. And yet, when she said it, it wasn't right. It was a hollow resolve, a cave: firm and sturdy on the outside, empty on the inside. It would not fill her. But she had to get there! Run. She could run. She nearly stood up.

"Why there?" Deuel asked, his gaze boring back into hers.

"Silence. Stillness. Coolness. Peace," she heard herself saying. Why was she still sitting there? Why was he? He wanted to go too. He could fly. He could be there before she could, even if she were on horseback.

"Catie, you do not know what you're saying."

That was true. She didn't care. Walk. Run. Steal a horse. She had to get there. Her shoulders ached. She wished she could fly like Deuel!

Why?

Silence. Stillness. Coolness. Peace.

Was he keeping her there on purpose? He could get there first. He couldn't. She couldn't let him. Her jaw tightened, and her palms lay flat on the table.

"Catie."

She leapt up, her eyes afire. He *was* keeping her here! To get there first. She took a step away from the table. The room rocked and reeled. The floor became the wall and she leaned against it as the sun went suddenly black.

◆

It was warm and soft, but still quiet. Blankets. And a bed. But quiet. Catie felt air drawing through her nose, and she breathed out a sigh. Her eyes opened and she saw the ceiling. A shadow in her periphery caught her attention: Deuel sat beside her, watching her.

"What happened?" she asked, her voice surprising her in strength and clarity.

"I think that answer will come when you answer my questions."

She looked at him, only blinking.

"When did your father die?"

"When I was very young," she said.

"Be specific."

"Late winter, 1305."

"Haschina," he suggested.

"I think so."

"Your mother left?"

"Haschina 33."

"That date means something to you," he noted.

"It means something to you, too."

"You can speak to me in your mind, and feel the emotions of dragons."

She looked at him long and silently. She could see the path of his mind, but it made no sense. She was not like him. For one thing, she didn't have wings. "Yes, but..."

"What is your earliest memory?"

She blinked. "That's not an easy question to answer."

"Try."

She closed her eyes, nestling back into the pillow. Grandmother's? It seemed like. Her baking in the kitchen, rolls or cookies. Grandmother made the best cookies. Catie was on the floor, playing with a doll? No, she was too high to be on the floor, because she dropped it and couldn't reach it. A chair? The floor seemed so far away, but she was reaching. Then Grandmother came over. No, she got down and got it. So she was old enough to get up and down from a chair. Then father came in to ask her to help, he'd just brought a deer.

Her eyes opened. Stillness. *No.* "Deuel, I don't know—" *Coolness.* She gritted her teeth against the thought.

"Try," he said again, his voice firm but his emotion calming.

"It seems like I'm too young for a clear memory, but old enough to help my father skin a deer," she said. "Which doesn't make sense."

"That's not it," he said. Now his emotion was firm and his voice calming.

"I don't want to pass out again," she said with a whimper.

"At least this time you won't hit the floor in front of other people," he said wryly.

"It's a little early to be drunk, isn't it?"

"A little."

"A cave," she said. "It kept running through my head, downstairs. Silence, stillness, coolness, peace. I thought you were trying to keep it from me, to reach the caves outside Balnath Agrend before me."

Deuel's brows furrowed—actually furrowed. She almost laughed, but the fact that her response troubled him that greatly stopped her. "What is it?" she asked.

The furrows disappeared. "The destination is correct," he said, "but not the early memory. Dragons—behamien—are not born or raised in caves."

"Well of course I'm not behamien, "Catie replied. She flexed one of her shoulders forward. "No wings."

"I noticed. But you are *something,* Catie, something I've not seen before. Everything else fits, except the cave."

"But how? I thought you said I couldn't be anything like that?"

Deuel sighed. "You must forgive me that: it was an idea impressed...forcefully...upon us as children. No behamian I know would mate with a human, but behamien have mated with each other before becoming dragons. It was more frequent when we were many. Now it is greatly discouraged."

"But why?"

"Because we cannot change after giving birth in human form. I do not know why," he said as her mouth opened. "The teaching is that by so doing we are choosing our human forms over our dragon forms. In early times this was not seen as a bad thing. But as I said we are far from thriving, and behamien removed permanently from the pool threaten our survival."

"So my parents were behamien but I didn't know it? I don't remember my mother having wings either."

"No. If they were, you would be less advanced than you are." *We would not be able to speak like this, for one thing. Feeling my emotions, yes. But not complex communication.*

This doesn't seem that complex. We're just speaking.

You interpret what I'm saying because your mind knows Rinc Nain. If you spoke Cariste, or Isan, or Clanason, I could still speak to you this way and you would understand me. Because I am not speaking Rinc Nain, truly. And neither are you.

That seems very complicated.

I told you so.

"Oh, hush." *That doesn't help me know what I am.*

No, it does not. That may come later.

I'm not sure if I like that answer.

Good. It means you will keep seeking.

Catie paused and drew a breath. "Am I...do wyverns start as humans?"

Deuel gazed at her for several very long and uncomfortable moments. She wished, just this once, that he would let his emotions out just a little more than he did. Finally he took a deep breath. "I think we must assume they do," he said. "Perhaps that is why wyverns do not have arms. Yours will become wings, if you change."

She hadn't expected him to agree with her. Now that he did, there was nothing left to hold on to and she whirled away in the flood, an autumn leaf down a raging waterfall. Now more than ever she needed the silence, stillness, coolness, and peace. Especially the peace. But questions pounded down the door of her head, and fear and despair obliterated her heart.

"I don't want to be a wyvern," she managed to say.

Deuel was with her, holding her close and smoothing her hair. He had to know that made it worse. Well, it made her heart worse. So she allowed herself to cry that part out, clinging tightly to him and trying to gain some footing with her head. Questions could be answered. Emotions only did what they wanted.

"Do I have to change?" she asked, plucking up the first question that swirled through.

"No," he said. "I was committed to Gabriel the first time the Call came, and I stayed with him rather than answer it. It is...difficult, but with disciplined focus it can be done."

"Will you be able to help me?"

"Of course."

"So will I live a long time, too? As long as you?"

"I do not know. I think perhaps you have already lived longer than you realize."

There were more questions, awkward ones that she refused entrance into her conscious mind lest Deuel accidentally hear them. She drew a breath. Time to disengage. She squeezed once, then slowly sat back. He let her go, but continued looking at her. She didn't want to look at him, so she closed her eyes and rubbed them.

"I'm sorry," she said.

"I am sure you should have heard that from someone else, someone...wyvern," he added cautiously. "I know very little, but I will do what I can."

She smiled. "Thanks." With another deep, steadying breath she was able to look up at him. "So, what do we do now? About Rodigger."

Deuel paused. "Rodigger probably does not intend to keep our horses. I can go get them, or we can let them return alone. After that is up to you."

"We still need to retrieve the Berkarfor," Catie replied. "You know Rodigger won't be able to, and it will make him more pliable if we don't punish him once we catch up. But I would like Kelsie back here sooner, especially with nomads strangely loose." Her eyes went wide at the thought. "You don't think they've already gotten her?"

Deuel shook his head. "Rodan and I have been together long enough, I would feel, faintly, if he were distressed. But I agree: we should not increase the chance. I will return as swiftly as possible."

14

CHANGING REASONS

"This one here, now."
"You can still change your mind."
"It is still a patriarchal society."
"We can be agents of change, Teresh."

25 Halmfurtung 1320 — Spring

Rodigger glanced up, then backward. The sun had reached its height, and the Midlands still followed dutifully, their reins slack. He almost wished they would give him trouble, make him angry. But instead they kept pace kindly, gazing at him without a hint of consternation.

His mouth twisted, and he stared resolutely ahead. They would just see. He'd let them go tomorrow, get a really good head-start. He was already working on a story to tell at the inn as to why he had two extra horses, that's what he was doing! He certainly wasn't thinking about letting them go so soon.

One of them—Deuel's—whinnied shortly. When he glanced back, its head was up, eyes skyward.

Rodigger's Therian stopped just as his own heart did. Rodigger's eyes shot to the clouds as he searched for any faint but swiftly-moving specks against them. Of course Deuel would fly out to retrieve the horses! He was so stupid! He threw down the reins as if they scalded him. Gared responded to the urgency of the motion, starting off at a trot before Rodigger gave him heel or command—and when the frantic command did finally leave Rodigger's lips they broke into a gallop.

He needed to be far, far away from those horses. He glanced back, saw them turning away and heading back down the road to the 'vilt.

Good horses, he thought, his nerves leaping about under his skin. *Get away, now.* He couldn't tell whether to laugh or to cry, so he muttered and let the wind sting his eyes.

Several miles passed below Gared's hooves before Rodigger finally eased back in the saddle. Gared snorted and blew, and shook his head as if knowing how close they might have come to a violent death. Up ahead, a convoy heading toward the 'vilt appeared. *Could have sold the horses to them,* he thought. But then, he might have been hunted down as a horse-thief. *No saying that still won't happen. But Catie and Deuel wouldn't do that, would they?*

Catie might.

Rodigger shivered. What had he done?

Survive.

Rodigger sniffled, but his jaw set. He did, didn't he? He recognized a threat, and acted boldly and without thought to personal comfort or safety to avert it. Wasn't Roth always talking about that? He knew when Roth was disappointed in him the most—the two times: when he didn't think the same way Roth did, and when he acted out of selfish comfort rather than strength and courage.

Well. He had just stolen a behamian's horse, and the horse of a woman who wanted to kill him, in order to leave them far behind and retrieve Roth's Berkarfor on his own.

And yet, something stifled his joy. He studied the approaching convoy as he tried to figure out what it was. It was the glance up the road that gave him the clue: usually he would see Catie, either directly in front of him or in close periphery. Now there was only brown road and green grass. He had previously managed a way to look near her, but not at her, and yet focus so she was all he saw. Despite her rage and her intent to kill him, his heart still reached out after her.

He cared for her, he realized, more deeply than he had ever cared for anyone before. He wanted to know more about her, where she had come from and where she was going. He could smell her, as he thought about her—slightly floral just after leaving a city, or more like the open plain if they'd been traveling a while. Like cold grass and clean air, and a little bit like sunshine, too.

He blinked. There was also the cusp of mystery. The breathless anticipation of being at the beginning of the story, not knowing how it would end, but knowing they two would be companions through it. It was the threshold of the open door, on the other side of which lay a life with her, the first step of a long adventure, wondering what each new step would bring. He wondered what it would be like to hold her hand, to kiss her, to...

But she was back in Dagget's, and he was here, and her horse closer to him than her. She would be forever a day behind, at least, if she did not just go to Sheppar as she wanted to. He might never see her again.

He gripped the reins tightly, taking deep breaths through his nose despite the horse-stink as he met the convoy and passed through it. The wagoners eyed him, most of them, but no one asked him a question. Because he was a lone traveler, and they were merchants or drivers—surely nothing held in common. He would have been a messenger, perhaps, or some Magiss' son out for a ride on a warm day.

Rodigger ground his teeth as the last wagon clattered past. Not one "hello" or "good day." No recognition they were all Andelian, and could exchange pleasantries along the road.

And no warning of bandits ahead—or whatever those marauders were. Yes, marauders would be a good word. Maybe not marauders, that sounded too concerted, too planned. Sneaks. Thieves, most likely. Thieves, they would be, little raiding parties from little nomadic bands from their little, pathetic deserts. Certainly nothing to be overly concerned about. And not worth killing someone over.

He did miss the sight of her, though.

⬥

Kelsie whinnied happily to see Catie again as night fell. Deuel handed her the halter as he swung off Rodan, and she quickly set about checking her Midland mare.

"She seemed well," Deuel said. "They were browsing, but alert. He did not run them hard."

"At least that," Catie said, still running her hands over the mare, for her own conscience and to show Kelsie she cared. She was barely even dusty.

They led their mounts to the stalls and prepared them for the night. "Have you decided for certain to continue pursuing the Berkarfor?" Deuel asked.

"I think so," she replied as she brushed Kelsie. When Deuel remained still, she paused. "Is there some reason I shouldn't?"

Deuel resumed brushing Rodan. "No, not for you."

"But there is one for you?"

The brush slowed, hesitated, then resumed. But Deuel said nothing.

"Deuel, you know I can sense your feelings," Catie said. She paused, too, stretching her shoulders before resuming the task.

"With Paolound gone, behamien will be going to their *veythya* to await—"

Catie cut him off. "Deuel, I don't know what that word is."

"*Veythya*. It is...to summon change...to become..." He trailed off this time.

"A dragon. And you should have joined them months ago," Catie said, feeling his uncertainty. "But even if you tried now, it might not matter?"

"So I should not try?" he asked quickly.

"Deuel, I just reminded you I can sense your feelings, and that's all I have to go by. I don't know how all that works."

He drew a breath. "Of course not. *Veythya* takes time, different time depending on many things, some unknown. But if several behamien enter it, and one comes out first, the rest will remain in their states until the next dragon dies—then their process resumes."

"So one might have already become a dragon?"

Deuel shook his head. "The Calling all behamien feel would cease. No, Paolound's successor has not yet been born."

"And you want to go enter your *veythya* in case your process is shorter."

"The first time the Call came in my lifetime was during Sheppar's campaign. Gabriel was young, and deeply involved. I could not leave him—I had not learned enough about humans anyway."

"In a hundred years, twenty made a difference?"

She felt him smile. "His family was *aloik,* but they were not my first *aloiken.* But yes, twenty years has made a difference. When this Call came at the start of another journey important to Gabriel, I thought again I could not answer it."

"Now, perhaps, you can," Catie finished, continuing to brush Kelsie, to keep from looking at the dragon-son.

Deuel stepped away from his horse. He looked at Catie for several moments, until she paused to glance at him. "The Berkarfor were important to Gabriel because he was paid for them. Your mission is important to you for...more human reasons, I sense."

Revenge? Catie wondered. That was probably more human, though she wasn't sure Deuel should learn too deeply about that. Maybe if she called it 'justice'—but usually, if one sought justice outside of the law, it was just called 'revenge' again. *I'm not sure if that's reason enough for you to deny who you are.*

"Not for the Berkarfor," Deuel said as she realized she sent that last thought to him. "You seek to find out who you are. I believe that answer will inform who I need to be."

"I thought I was a wyvern."

"That may be the vessel in which you reside. But it does not mean that's who you are."

"Oh," Catie said. "And what if you're wrong?"

Deuel hesitated, and she could feel his mournful sigh. "Then I will need to know even more what it means to be human," he said. "I believe this is the first time the Call has come twice to one generation. I cannot assume it will come again before I die—so if I miss this one as well, I may never know what it means to be a dragon."

⸻◆⸻

Taferk came and went, despite every merchant and inn thinking they had every reason to charge double what their wares and spaces warranted—"might not get much in, but we see a lot going out. Yes sir, Andelen could barely support itself 'thout us. At the head of the Tevorbath, and rightly so! It's the head as most necessary part, isn't it?"

At first Rodigger thought they finally had the right of it, seeing themselves as an integral part of a unified Andelen. By the third person he spoke to he realized they considered only themselves to be Andelen, and the rest of the country as babes on its teats. It was actually the fourth merchant who had used that exact phrase. Rodigger barely kept from shaking his head as he walked away, telling himself it wasn't just because he didn't have enough coin. There the road split, one arm heading west toward Fathistokset in the Rigarbod marsh, the other—the road Rodigger took—still north and slightly east toward Ravverbit.

As he rode one morning, Halmfurtung winding to a close as Spring settled in to stay, a wind came south through the canyon road to Ravverbit. On its eddies lay fragrances and spices which Rodigger had never smelled or sensed, and yet had some peculiar memory tucked in them too scant to blossom. When he tried to sniff deeper, he got mostly cool spring air that stung his nose and made his eyes water.

Ravverbit had only two man-made walls, one each to the south and north. To the east and west were the walls of the canyon, rising sheer and red till they gradually curved away, topped by spires that resembled stacked river-stones, and whatever rock *was* flat was gouged deep and rough—no cart or ballistae could traverse that terrain close enough to bring any destruction from above.

Not that the defenses were necessary, Rodigger noticed as he entered the streets: Ravverbit seemed to let anybody in who wished, without the need for violence. The spices grew thick and heavy, and now the peculiar memory was buried by overabundance. Men, women, and some children moved through the streets in both Andelian and Beltrath garb—and sometimes a weaver's nightmare of both. Simple homespun wool or cotton paired with light silks of every color including some, Rodigger was sure, didn't exist in the natural world. Horses and donkeys made way for taller, four-footed animals with long, U-shaped necks and two great hillocks on their backs, between which someone in even more layers of dazzlingly bright silk usually wallowed. He even heard some people speak in something other than Rinc Nain.

Vendors stalls were a similar hodgepodge of bright colors and strange scents and unusual wares. The shops, he was relieved to see, sold more typical fare—so at least the strange things were temporary. And, as he began to feel a little dizzy from the overwhelming assault on his senses, he realized the inns would likely be more standard fare as well. Unless there was some strange silk-swaddled creature pushing around rooms on wheels, he thought with a smirk—a smirk that caught the unblinking attention of one of the vendors. As the man glared at Rodigger, Rodigger couldn't help but stare back and let his smirk grow a little wider. What could the man do, attack him in broad daylight when he was clearly the interloper?

Distracted by the vendors and passersby in noticeable garb, Rodigger didn't see the man in dun and brown step away from a nearby building and follow after him.

He discovered the inns as he neared the center of town. He passed several where the noise of the common room might as well have not had a door between it and the street, and one or two others whose signs had script he did not recognize and images that did not evoke a sense of Andelen. Finally, at what seemed to be the precise center of the town, he found an inn that looked strangely familiar. As it was surrounded by the rest of the city, several moments passed before Rodigger realized it was a fortified inn, still there from when Ravverbit didn't yet exist. He smiled, and led his horse to the stable at the back, exactly where it belonged.

The evening passed quietly enough: Deuel didn't come swooping in and demand retribution for stealing his horse, and Catie didn't come running up demanding the same. The inn was well tended, but not well patronized. And by the second song of the sitting minstrel Rodigger thought he knew why. But it suited him anyway.

That night, several nightmares came to him, mostly of being shot with an arrow and men in strange clothing surrounding him. Once, the man changed into Catie just as the knife thrust forward, and her hate-filled eyes sparked with joy as she ripped open Rodigger's gut. In another, he defended himself, and watched the gleam in her eye fade as her own blood spilled. When he woke from that one, he wasn't sure which ending he preferred. But it was in that moment, as the early morning scents from the kitchen wafted into the cot-room, that he realized what fragrance it was he was remembering: it was the smell of those bandits, the thieves—what did he decide to call them?

What did it matter? The town reeked of those creatures! They were stealing across Andelen, killing some people and taking others, and shooting him with arrows. And now he was in the middle of them.

Slowly and quietly, he peeled off the blankets and reached down toward his locked chest. He cracked his knuckles on the lid, and in horror realized it was already open. He swallowed, his mind racing. Were they here, then? He turned his head slowly. The morning sun didn't come into the windows, now that there were buildings in the way, but there was light enough to see shadows and shapes, if they were there. But he saw nothing.

He got out of the bed, stepping quietly in his stocking feet. He checked the chest—his things were definitely gone. But his boots still lay at the side of the cot where he left them, so he picked those up and made his way into the common room.

One man was already there. Rodigger almost didn't see him, dressed in tan and brown clothing that fit more tightly than the flowing silks of the foreigners—Beltraths, they must be—and looked more utilitarian than the Andelian clothing. He was sitting behind a table on which lay Rodigger's things.

"I hoped you wouldn't sneak out the back," the man said, his accent such that he made 'd' sounds at every opportunity. For a brief moment Rodigger thought maybe the man had a cold. His hand strayed to his belt before he saw his knife lying front and center of his effects.

"It is a very nice knife," the man said, his eyes never leaving Rodigger's yet somehow seeing his every move. "But you should not have it back yet. Why are you alone?"

"Why, uh, why shouldn't I be alone?" Rodigger asked, working some of the sleeping thickness out of his throat.

"Because you were not alone one month ago."

"And you know this, how?" Rodigger's stomach—already a shriveled apple—tightened.

"I was told this by one who had seen this; do I need to convince you further?"

Rodigger shrugged, a motion intended for himself and the flurry of questions and fears running through his own mind. But it sufficed for the other man, as well.

"Where is the wingéd man?"

It took Rodigger a second to recognize the stress on the 'e', and he shrugged again.

"He has left you?"

"If I'm lucky," Rodigger muttered.

The man looked puzzled. "This is a strange thing."

One of the myriad questions finally popped out: "Who are you?" Rodigger asked. Blurted, really, though he didn't mean to.

"Sharéd Dusslin."

Now that one question had come out, the rest tumbled out behind it. "What are you doing here? What do you want? Why do you have my stuff? Why didn't you just talk to me when I woke up?"

Sharéd's gaze never wavered. "I am looking for the wingéd man. I want the wingéd man. I have your things because I will take you as well. And one does not speak to his captive. Normally."

Rodigger swallowed as his eyelids suddenly couldn't open as wide as he wanted them to. "What about now that the wingéd man isn't with me anymore?"

"Now I think you and I, we will spend much time together, and it could become boring if we do not speak."

And yet, Rodigger and Sharéd remained silent for a time—Sharéd's eyes relaxed but considering, Rodigger's eyes tight and thoughtless.

"Do we wait here—?"

"We wait for the wingéd man."

"His name is Deuel," Rodigger said.

Sharéd hissed, and the knife-point gouged the table. "He is the wingéd man and you will call him the wingéd man in my presence."

Silence again, for a time. Rodigger tried breathing, finding it noisy in the empty common room.

"Can I sit down?" he asked faintly.

Sharéd was silent. He began twirling the knife, point against the table and drilling mildly into it. Rodigger took the silence as acceptance and sat down. The bench scraped back and forth like the tolling of church bells without the echo—but just as loud and attention-arresting. The silence grew again.

But as the silence stretched on, Rodigger's mind began miraculously to move. "He might not come here," he said, as if there had been no break in the conversation.

The twirling stopped. "Why would he not do this?"

"Well, I stole his horse. He may not exactly give me another chance—or the one with him."

"The girl?" he asked, pronouncing it 'girrel'.

Rodigger nodded, trying to keep his lower lip from protruding just a little. "She'll probably be just fine with you keeping me captive."

"This is not to do," Sharéd replied. "Why are they your enemies?"

"Don't you know about the revolution?"

The twirling and silence resumed. Sharéd's eyes glinted as he studied Rodigger for some time. Finally, he said only: "yes."

"Oh. Well, they're on the other side."

"So of course they are your companions," he said drily.

"Well it wasn't my idea," Rodigger said, slouching a little.

"Where will they go, if not here?"

"We were headed to Kavlen. They may go straight there. Maybe not. But I think if you let me continue my mission, we'll definitely run into them again somewhere along the line."

"Why would they not go straight there? They have another mission?"

"Uh-mmm, no, I don't think so. Can't think of one," he said, shaking his head and forgetting to stop.

"You said 'maybe not' with some significance, I think," Sharéd replied. "Enough to assure me it would not matter if they did not."

Rodigger's voice started high and went low: "No! I just mean, I mean, you can't tell with those two. A wingéd man and someone who seems to want to please him more than those of their own kind? She wants to find, um, to continue the mission, with me, at least at the end. Dey—a—he, I mean, there's no telling what he wants." The shaking continued.

Sharéd's hand rested on the pommel of the knife, still driven point-down into the table, as he considered Rodigger sideways. "You are a very bad liar," he said, "and yet you tell some truth. What is this you seek at Kavlen?"

"Just something Roth sent me to do. Talk to the people there, try to gain some sympathizers." It helped that was partially true, as well.

"It has nothing to do with this?" Sharéd asked, raising his other hand:

in it was the first Berkarfor.

Very few people could have resisted the urge to startle noticeably when one of their greatest secrets was revealed, and Rodigger was not one of those people. To his credit, he didn't say anything at first. But then the shaking head resumed, mute.

"It is a very nice cup," Sharéd said musingly, turning it over in his hand. "Perhaps I shall drink from it whenever we stop."

"I don't think that's a good idea," Rodigger said, his voice quivering.

"But surely it is not important? Why do you carry it?"

Rodigger shrugged. "Just something we found along the way. But it's very old, and we found it deep underground and it's probably been there forever. And I haven't washed it."

"That can be relieved."

"Wash something that old? I'd be afraid of damaging it myself. Which is why I haven't washed it yet. Obviously."

"I have said you are a bad liar, and yet you still try," Sharéd replied, setting the cup on the table and continuing to drill with the knife.

"I'm trying to practice," Rodigger replied in a rare attack of wit.

"You should have practiced long ago. But we will go to this Kavlen and wait for the wingéd man," Sharéd said, and then smiled. "And his friend."

⧯

The Beltrath's smile and last words stuck with Rodigger as they left Ravverbit, the infrequent silence that marked their conversation falling utterly now. Rodigger led, Sharéd close behind. His mount was clearly the purer physical specimen, and could give short chase if Rodigger tried to flee.

Fairly assured he was not going to die—and even feeling oddly safer, now that one of the thieves was his escort—Rodigger kept playing those words and that smile in his mind. The words could have meant one thing, which would mean Rodigger would be that much safer with one less person in Andelen who seemed to want him dead. Or the smile could have meant something else, in which case there would be one less person from Beltrath who potentially wanted him dead: there was no doubt in his mind that if Sharéd tried what that smile indicated, Catie would kill him, and probably have no trouble with it. Not that Sharéd seemed incompetent, but he probably wouldn't be ready for her. And yet...

"Sharéd, what do you want the wingéd man for?" Rodigger asked that night as the thief was binding his wrists and ankles.

"You will learn this when he comes," Sharéd replied with a few grunts as he made the knots tight.

"I mean, do you intend to kill him?" Rodigger tested the ropes. They were tight.

Sharéd sat back, studying Rodigger in the firelight. "Do you think

I could?" he asked, almost as if wondering to himself. Rodigger's eyes strayed aside, then snapped back. Sharéd blinked. "I do not think this I could, if I wanted to."

"Then you definitely don't want to kill me?"

Sharéd's head cocked sideways. "Do you want me to? It is a long road to Kavlen, and you are not in the position to resist, right now."

Rodigger's eyes went wide as he tested the ropes again. Still tight. "What would you want to do that for?"

Sharéd stared into Rodigger's eyes. "Because you annoy me. Because you are a burden. Because you are not part of the plan." He shrugged. "The reasons are many."

The plan? Rodigger's mind began to turn, concocting reasons for wanting Deuel. It was difficult, since he wanted him for nothing, and more so after stealing his horse. But what plan could include such a creature? He tried to think like Roth, the best planner Rodigger knew.

He closed his eyes, and barely kept a curse behind his teeth. "Sharéd," he said quietly. "If you want to find the *winged* man, he is usually in the sky."

Sharéd's face went slack. "Why you did not say this earlier?" he asked flatly.

Rodigger glared at his captor. "Because you stole my things and made me think you were trying to kill me! Because it's *winged,* not win-*ged,* you wandering idiot! Now release me before I pelt you with all Roth's coin until it sticks in your skin and poisons you, and we find someone else to lead your people's part in this mission!"

15

TRUE COLORS

"I'm not sure how you manage this."
"Actively."
"It seems a difficult balance."
"Balance is easier if you are moving."

1 Fimman 1320 — Spring

Samdar glanced over the rolls of parchment in front of him with a sigh. *Join the kinnig's closest advisors and read all day.* Samdar knew Sheppar wanted to be a king for all people, not just the rich and powerful. But did he realize how many people wanted to write notes to him and tell him how to be a better—and sometimes worse—king because of that? *Rulers and people in authority should be unreachable* Samdar thought. Maybe not truly a good idea. But right now, when it was his job to read what had come for Sheppar's...edification...it was the best idea.

As he reached for the one to his farthest left—may as well approach it methodically—he noticed a piece of script on the side of another one closer to him. *I know that hand.*

He did: it was from Deuel. How many updates had Samdar read from Deuel during the campaign? Had tried not to read between the lines, but had been too close to the behamian not to see it—had known it would be there as soon as the order went out... Anyway. Deuel had never brought it up, so why should he?

Unless the dragon-son was bringing it up now. Samdar picked up the roll. It was addressed directly to him. And why wouldn't it be? He broke the seal and rolled it open.

It was a different script inside. Shakier. Someone who was not comfortable writing, but at least it was legible. As he read, his eyes first grew wide in amazement and horror, then narrowed in skepticism.

But at the end, there was Deuel's confirmation in his script. The report was true. A few details were added by Deuel concerning more accurate numbers...

By the God—and where? West of the Tevorbath?

The rest of the letters would wait. Sheppar needed to know about this immediately.

And yet, as Samdar stood quickly and threw on his cloak, he could imagine what the aging kinnig might say. *Maybe not if it was from Deuel. Surely Sheppar realizes how much he owed the behamien who had served him in the campaign.*

Samdar found the kinnig in the gardens. A few early tulips were blooming already, and buds were on many of the others, but it was certainly not yet the vision of a garden it would be. There was something hopeful about it, he realized as he approached. And he hoped Sheppar had one more season in him as well.

"My lord?" he called as he neared, also imagining Sheppar's response to *that*.

"Samdar, we have been together too long for that," he said. As was foretold.

"That time has only reinforced the status," Samdar replied with a bow as Sheppar turned.

Sheppar's smile was easy, but mixed. "What is it?"

"I've received a very troubling letter from Deuel, my lord," he said. At Sheppar's dark grimace, he hurried on. "He's reporting movement in the Tevorbath, my lord. The Beltraths are coming out of the Waste in some very large numbers."

Sheppar stood motionless for a few moments. "What large numbers?" he asked finally.

"Deuel estimates five hundred in one encampment alone, that he saw."

"Five *hundred?* Does he say what they are doing?"

"He did not have time to investigate fully, my lord. He was unclear as to what, but something else has his attention right now. He reports that the nomads had not hesitated to kill anyone who observed their movements."

Sheppar closed his eyes. "The day is coming," he said softly. "I had hoped others would not pay my due."

"My lord?"

Sheppar's eyes opened. "You know as well as anyone else, we could not have done what we did in the campaign without making some enemies."

"I would have thought those enemies would have come from somewhere...nearer by," Samdar replied, then pressed his lips together and dropped his head as he realized what he was saying.

Sheppar laid a hand on his shoulder. "So did I, old friend."

"My lord, what are we going to do about this incursion?"

Sheppar sighed. "Did the message come through one of the 'vilts?"

"It did, my lord."

"Then the magiss will need to handle it. It is their duty."

Samdar kept his sigh short. "My lord, the 'vilts are not made for that—you designed them! They are for trade only. And any of the villages or towns in the area have not had to stop an incursion in more than a generation. You've heard about Kavlen, how that village alone has changed. We cannot leave this to them."

"On the contrary, dear friend," Sheppar replied, moving along the paths of the garden as slowly as he spoke. "If what you say is true, then they need, more than anything else, to handle this incursion and learn from it, and stop relying on an old man to always come save them. It is the future."

"My lord, they may not have a future if we do not stop this."

Sheppar laughed hoarsely. "Five hundred Beltraths will not do so much devastation as that," he said. "Besides, they're probably coming for me and Balnath Agrend. It's been said: 'strike the head and kill the body.' Well, they can strike this head if they want. Why do you think I've been drawing back for the past twenty years?"

"You saw this coming? That long ago?"

"Samdar, I saw it coming when I made the decision. I knew I needed to strike, and then fade away. And when I'm gone, Andelen won't miss me." He paused his stride, looking out over the budding garden, nearly ready to explode in summer blooms. "No, each village and town will go on as it has. Andelen may even be better for it, you know?" His deep blue eyes settled on Samdar, and the aide saw in them the glint of a man old and tired, yet victorious in a fruitful life ripening exactly as he'd meant it to.

But Samdar still only saw tenuous buds, nothing yet ready to pick. "And what about Roth's rebellion in the south?"

"Is there a rebellion in the south?" Sheppar asked, beginning his walk again. "I've heard a lot of Roth doing things on his own, of gaining support for ideas. But where's his army? Where is his power?"

"But if he does come—"

"Samdar, you still don't understand," Sheppar said with a chuckle. "Killing me will do nothing. Why do you think his ideas have stopped in the Fallonvall? After twenty years of great autonomy, all the towns in Andelen will not suddenly bow under Roth's yoke just because he talks to them about it. And any show of force he attempts will turn the people away, people too accustomed to keeping their blood in their veins, not letting it upon the ground for an idea. They will, however, let it out for the sake of protecting their future from Roth, or the Beltraths, or anyone else of violence—and they will do that without me, whether I'm living or dead."

"Yes, my lord," Samdar replied with a shallow sigh. He turned and started back through the garden paths.

"Samdar?" Sheppar called. He bent over a lily and breathed it in, then straightened. "Send letters to Kostet's and Fathistokset—and Merneset too, if you would. Find out what they know and what they don't." He grinned. "I would be there at Fathistokset to see how the Beltraths handle the Rigarbod, but..." He shook his head, and glanced at his aide. "Let them prepare themselves as they must."

"Yes, my lord," Samdar replied. It was more than he expected, at least. And, maybe his lord was right.

Summer neared, and for Rodigger and Sharéd, so did Kavlen.

Their pace had slowed since reaching the Nagrath Highlands, as the road curved and curled around rolling hills and bluffs, and sometimes went straight up the side of the less-steep mounds. Mostly it was sandy dirt and scrubby grass. But here and there rocks outcropped or broached the tan shocks, giving hint to the hard soul of the land underneath.

Then, between two hills and down in a sudden but broad valley, spread Kavlen. At this distance, there was something shimmery about it. The houses were not packed together like a proper town, but much of it seemed to be part of the land. Here and there chimneys stood up from the middles of small mounds, and thin tendrils of smoke went skyward. As they neared, it seemed to Rodigger that perhaps there had been jewels in the rock, and that the people here had carved the walls of their home from that rock and left smears of crystals.

But as they drew closer, he realized what it was he saw. Kavlen was largely carved from the hills. There were only a few standing houses or buildings, things two or three stories high and made of brick. For the rest, a face had been cut in the hillside, a door mounted, and he could only imagine rooms hollowed out inside. And every door of every house was a different shade than any of the others. It was a cacophony of colors, most of which he couldn't name: every shade of purple, green, red, yellow, orange, blue, brown—warm brown like roasted pecans and cedar and chestnut, not the brown of the grass everywhere else. There was a low stone wall surrounding the town, only about chest high, and every several paces, to Rodigger's horror, the sockets that would have been drilled to mount a palisade in time of war were instead filled with soil, and flowers grew inside them in another dizzying display of plants and color that he couldn't name.

What had the poem said? Something about rainbows, and being dashed slap-dash on doors. It fit better than he could have ever imagined. So, Catie hadn't lied, and now he was in the right place. The question was where to start looking.

They made their way to the inn—one of the tall, brick buildings, it had a door of a red hue that Rodigger had seen maybe once, in a sunset—and prepared their horses for the night before going inside. It was busy enough to mask guarded conversation without needing to shout.

"What is it we do now?" Sharéd asked. "We are going the wrong way, it seems. Balnath is west, you have brought us east."

"Where the *wingéd* man will come, we can be certain," Rodigger replied. "Now we find the Berkarfor, in case that mission gives us the greatest advantage. If not, we still have the first, and they'll have to come to us for the complete set. And we can deal with them then."

"Where is it we find this thing?"

"Underground," Rodigger replied with a smile. "At least, it was the last time. And the clue said it was hidden beneath the floors."

"So we dig up the floors?" Sharéd asked skeptically.

"No, not literally, it just means it's underground. Probably a cave we need to find."

"Where?"

Rodigger's mouth twisted. That was a good question. The keeper was on his way by, just then, and Rodigger snatched at his sleeve.

"Where might we find a cave?" he asked.

The keeper gazed at him blankly for several moments. "You know this town's name means 'Land of Caves' right?"

Rodigger's crest fell, and he swallowed. "How many, though? That haven't been made into homes." That might narrow it down, at least.

"A couple hundred. This place is lousy with 'em," he replied, glancing back and forth between the two. "It's the land—"

"Of caves, yeah, thanks," Rodigger interrupted with a sigh.

"Sorry pal. But if you want a home, we've got lots of options." The keeper shrugged, and went on his way.

Rodigger glared after him. Why on Oren would he want a home in this ridiculous place? And have to have the color of his door approved to make sure it didn't match anyone else's? He shook his head.

"So the first question comes back," Sharéd said off-handedly. "What do we do now?"

Rodigger set his jaw. "We'll start looking tomorrow. First thing."

"At these hundreds of caves?"

"No, not at hundreds of caves. At a lot of them," Rodigger replied, folding his arms. "Something will come to me. Something will be wrong, won't fit the riddle. I'll figure it out."

⊰•⊱

But after the fifth cave, nothing was coming to him. They paused for some water, and Rodigger tried to think as he sat on a rock in the sun.

"They're similar," he said finally. "We've been choosing caves at random, but they're similar, don't you think?"

"They are small," Sharéd replied, and took a drink of water. "Good for you, they do not take a day to explore."

"Yeah, they're small. And none of them go down. They're on one level, for the most part, right? If it's supposed to be below the town, it would have to be deeper." He capped his own water skin and stood.

"How does this help us?" Sharéd asked. "We have at least one hundred ninety-five more caves to search."

"Let's look at a few more—fifteen. Each: we'll split up. Let's see what they look like."

Sharéd said nothing, but they walked on. Rodigger's feet were getting sore. Very few of the cave floors were even, and he'd gotten used to riding.

By the tenth, something else was nagging at him. By twelve, he knew there was something obvious, staring him in the face—and it wasn't the town with its garish portals, he thought with a grimace as he exited the thirteenth. Fourteen and fifteen went by, and he stopped and waited for Sharéd as the sun topped its zenith and headed west.

As the Beltrath finally approached, Rodigger realized it *was* the garish portals staring him in the face.

"Every cave points away from the town," he said as Sharéd looked at him. "If it led 'under the floors' it would have to point at the town, or double back on itself."

"So we have spent half a day on this search, and now we must keep looking at caves that enter on the other side of the hills? They are hard enough to see sometimes when we look at them."

Rodigger chewed his lip. There had to be an easier way, a guide. They'd had one in Attelek—two, technically. "We need to find the Grandmother," he said. "She might know the old stories, and help us find it more easily."

The third person they asked knew who they were looking for, and, for the first time, the colored doors helped: "it's a little darker blue than the sky is right now"—and it was. Rodigger knocked. Apparently it was customary for Grandmothers to keep a young girl in the house to do odd jobs. This one looked about nine, hair in a single braid behind a heart-shaped face, and green linen summer dress over a strong frame. She narrowed her eyes when Rodigger introduced Sharéd, but apparently attendant-girls everywhere were also taught not to speak, and she brought them in without question.

This Grandmother appeared a bit younger than the one in Attelek. Her eyes, too, darted every now and again to Sharéd. "How may I help you?" she asked. Her voice, at least, was steadier than her gaze.

"Do you know of the Berkarfor?" Rodigger asked.

"I have told the story many times," she replied with a smile. "Do you seek a recitation?"

"We found the first under Agirbirt Lake," Rodigger said. He glanced sideways. "Well, I did. Sharéd joined me later. But a riddle came with it that spoke of Kavlen. It mentioned two Wendol who battle beneath the floors. So I believe it's underground, under Kavlen itself. But I don't know where."

"Have you looked in the caves?" Grandmother asked, with another fitful glance at the Beltrath.

"Some of them," Rodigger replied. "They all head away from town. I was hoping you might know something of the old stories to narrow our search."

Grandmother was silent for some time, glancing every now and again at Sharéd, at the young girl, outside, and back at Rodigger. "I'm sorry, young man," she said. "I'm afraid nothing jumps to mind. You may just have to keep looking. If they're as fantastic as the stories, I'm sure it's worth the search, though?" Her tone went up in suggestion. Rodigger sighed, and nodded.

"I suppose they are," he admitted.

"I am sorry I can't help," she said again. "Would you like something to eat?"

Rodigger waved her away. "No, thank you. We have a lot of work to get to."

As they left, Rodigger glanced at the lowering sun as it headed for the road that Catie and Deuel would ride in at any moment. No doubt they would come straight to the Grandmother, and when another group arrived looking for the Berkarfor, she would undoubtedly tell them of Rodigger and Sharéd's presence.

Rodigger muttered a curse under his breath.

"What is it?" Sharéd asked.

"We've unmasked ourselves, is all," Rodigger replied. "We shouldn't have gone to Grandmother, I think. She'll tell Catie and Deuel that we're here, and looking for the Berkarfor, and they'll find it first, and our advantage will be gone."

"I thought we were supposed to meet the wingéd man? I told you I wanted to."

"I'm just not sure how good an idea that is," Rodigger said. "Like I said, I don't know what kind of mood he'll be in—him or Catie—because I stole their horses."

"That is not my fault. I had the plan before you came. I should just follow the plan even though you came."

"Tell me this plan, then, and how I'm supposed to help," Rodigger said.

"Roth has not explained it to you?"

"Just that I was to meet you, what the key phrase was supposed to be, and that we would be working together. It doesn't involve the Berkarfor?"

"No."

Rodigger blinked. "Oh. Okay. So..." He raised his eyebrows expectantly.

Sharéd hesitated. "Without the wingéd man here..."

"Let me worry about that," Rodigger interrupted. "I've spent time with him. I may be able to help."

Sharéd glanced around the village. He took Rodigger by the arm and guided him away from the bustle of the main streets.

"We need to find the wingéd men—the ones not dragons yet," he said quietly.

"I thought it was just the one *winged* man," Rodigger said, emphasizing the proper pronunciation. He was weary of being reminded of how he had been made a fool.

"We need to know where they, ah, *veythya*—the *wingt* folk," he said, trying to mimic Rodigger's pronunciation and somehow using a 't' sound where he rarely did otherwise.

Rodigger shook his head a fraction. "Where they what?"

"*Veythya*—change into dragons."

"Why?"

"To take them prisoners."

Rodigger blinked, trying to imagine Deuel being taken prisoner. On the one hand, it was a pleasant sight. It just seemed a little too far-fetched. If he tried to imagine it, the wings fanned and Halm and Ro Thull... He closed his eyes and shook his head.

"I'm not sure Deuel can be taken prisoner," he said. "And if there are more like him at this place..."

"No, no," Sharéd waved his hands. "When they *veythya* they are like...worms in the cocoon. Not butterfly, not worm. Not awake. My people surround them, we get wingt folk—the ones not *veythya*—to break their *aloik* bonds and serve Roth."

Slowly, Rodigger's gaze dropped. Roth wanted to *use* the behamien? Something was wrong here. Well, Roth used Deuel because he had to—he had come with Gabriel as a set. Right?

He thought of the army, stalled at the northern end of the Fallonvall. Thought of this journey to acquire ancient goblets meant to transfer power to the one who drank from them. Thought of Gabriel abandoning the mission in Attelek—had that been part of the plan? Had Roth paid the mercenary to leave them, so that just he and Deuel would go on?

Rodigger shook his head. This was getting him nowhere. Only Roth could answer those questions, and he was far away. But surely Roth didn't know Deuel the way Rodigger did—didn't truly appreciate what Deuel was, what he represented. This plan wouldn't work. It might *work*, technically, but it wasn't a good plan. Rodigger's father, long ago, had taught him how to spot a bad plan: they didn't follow the rules. Plans that didn't follow the rules made for dilapidated houses.

"So where do they...change?" he asked. He didn't want to use what was probably a behamian word.

"We don't know," Sharéd replied. "Roth only told us where to hide, he would come to us. That is why we need—"

"Right." Rodigger cut him off with a raised hand. More answers that he probably couldn't find. He chewed his lip as the streams of passers-by flowed toward homes, or to the inn. The sun was low now, the shadows long. Darkness—and, at one time, danger—would be on them soon. People always sought shelter when they thought danger was near.

Not awake. People sought shelter when they slept. Surely the wingt folk would too? He liked that phrase, now: wingt folk—better than behamien. But the wingt folk had been around for a long time, maybe longer than inns. And people would have come to inns, people who might want to kill them. So they would need a different shelter. Shelter that had been around for a long time, and wasn't easily found.

"A cave?" Sharéd asked.

Rodigger's eyes flicked to the Beltrath. He really needed to stop muttering his thoughts aloud. Rodigger shook his head. Caves were perfect, but where? The ones here were too shallow; they were no hiding place, none of the forty-some they looked at today. There were several mountain ranges in Andelen—would they go to some other country to change? They could, but why would they? And he wouldn't be able to help if they did. No, they needed to be in Andelen somewhere.

The noise in the streets grew as more townsfolk met and greeted one another. Rodigger shook his head. He needed to figure this out before the clamor hindered his thinking.

What about the Dragonsbacks? It would make sense, they wanted to be dragons. But the road wound up from the south all the way through most of the 'Back, and the Tevorbath filled another part. So that left...

The Eye. And hadn't Gabriel and Deuel been in Agrend before Roth called them? It made sense they would be close to where Deuel needed to change. Rodigger drew a breath. Should he tell Roth? Most likely. Not that he was defying orders, but that, under current circumstances and what he knew of Deuel, hostages might not be the best idea.

"We'll send a hawk south in the morning," Rodigger said quietly, below the gabble. "I want to tell Roth what's happened the past several months—that my company has changed, and things may not be what he thinks they are. And then we go the Balnath Agrend with your people."

Sharéd cocked his head. "You know it is there?"

No. "Yes," Rodigger replied. "But in fairness to you, I'll tell you that our mission once we get there is going to change. I just wish we hadn't talked to the Grandmother. She's going to alert Catie and Deuel that we were here." He paused for a moment, then shook his head. *And the Berkarfor? Let Deuel and Catie go after them. If it works out, Roth will have everything he needs. And I'll be there to stop Catie from doing whatever it is she plans after handing all the power in Andelen to Roth.* "We'll stay off the road for a few days, so we can avoid those two. He will kill us both too easily if we don't," he added before Sharéd could argue. "Where will we meet your people?"

"I do not know all your names. North of where there is water like jewels across a plain."

Rodigger thought for a moment. "Okay. And west of the Tevorbath?" Sharéd nodded. *If Roth told them to hide there, then he was probably on the right track with The Eye.* "Okay. We'll make for there as fast as we can."

"What are we doing when we get there?" Sharéd asked quietly.

"We're not going to use the behamien," Rodigger said. "We're going to kill them." And as the words left his mouth, he knew it was the right thing to do.

———◆———

The next morning, Rodigger rose from several bad dreams with the vague sensation that he had awoken at some point during the night and saw Sharéd entering the room clothed and preparing to go to sleep. But the Beltrath lay now where he had the evening before—on the floor with barely a sheet. He had claimed the nights here were too warm. Rodigger didn't want to believe him, after hearing enough stories of how hot it was in the desert. But he didn't think about it much. By now he had gotten used to the strange habits of his strange companion, and strangely didn't care anymore.

After breakfast, he went to the message hall and sent the hawk to Roth in Akervet. When he came out, there was a loud procession making its way along the streets. Horns and long flutes sounded a slow and almost wailing song, it seemed to him. A knot of people in billowing white encircled some sort of bier, atop which lay a prone figure surrounded by white and yellow flowers. Behind the group, Rodigger recognized the braided young girl who walked with eyes downcast. He glanced again at the bier: it was the Grandmother, and she lay perfectly still as the bier rocked back and forth in the grasp of the swaying carriers.

People lined the street, touching their faces in some sort of reverent gesture as the procession passed. Rodigger swallowed hard. The hawk's clerk came up behind him, and moaned a sigh.

"I'd heard she passed in the night," he said, bringing his hand up flat, palm toward himself, and pressing the tip of his middle finger into his forehead. "Kierssa isn't ready—wasn't supposed to be." He paused and sighed again. "Times might be a little tough, without a Grandmother."

"I'm...I'm sorry," Rodigger said, glancing briefly at the clerk before striding quickly away, back to the inn.

"Sharéd, we need to leave immediately," he said when he entered. "The Grandmother has died. We might have been the last to see her."

"I heard," Sharéd said quietly. His things were already gathered and packed for the road. "Our fortune: she will not be able to alert the wingt man and the girl."

"Yes," Rodigger said, a little distantly. "Good fortune."

As the procession continued its winding path, Rodigger and Sharéd left Kavlen, heading west as quickly as the terrain allowed.

Before they could see the town, Deuel and Catie heard the music. "That sounds sad," Catie said. "We should be careful."

"Very much," Deuel replied.

As they rounded the bend and Kavlen came into view, Catie knew she had been right about the Berkarfor. She had heard about the dazzling colors of the homes there, but it hadn't prepared her for the resplendent beauty of the place. It seemed odd, now, to come upon it with such a dirge echoing among the hills when the town itself seemed so vibrant and alive.

They passed the walls decked in tulips, marigolds, lilies, chrysanthemums, geraniums, irises, and dozens of other flowers she couldn't make out as the stone stretched away across and between the little hillocks. They rode down streets strangely deserted, but followed the music believing the townsfolk were probably gathered where it played.

A final turn, and they came upon the assembly. Up ahead, double stone doors opened into a hillside near the eastern edge of town—the only doors, it appeared, that were unpainted. They opened inward, and were lost in shadow but the very corners. It seemed the whole town was turned out, and arranged in a half-ring facing the cave. Beside the doors stood a young girl with a dark brown dress and her hair pulled into a single braid, her face lost in its own shadow as a bier was carried inside. A wizened man in white flowing cloak stood on the other side of the doors, chanting what sounded like a poem in an old tongue of Rinc Nain.

Deuel and Catie paused a respectful distance away; Rodan and Kelsie mimicked the quiet mood of their riders, settling themselves so as to not even dance a hoof. The poem went on as the bier was swallowed by the darkness. At a pause, the people raised their voices in a response. The man called again, and the people responded. He called a third time, and the people were silent.

That silence continued, until those who had carried the bier came out once more. The doors were pushed shut—none on the outside worked them, and they were clearly too heavy to swing shut on their own. Once they were visible in the light, Catie could see there had been carvings on the door, but time and weather had washed most of it away.

The crowd dispersed. A few startled when they saw the two riders, then canted their heads in acknowledgement of the respect the two had shown.

"Who was that?" Catie asked quietly as one of the folk came near.

"The Grandmother," she replied. "She died suddenly in the night."

Catie glanced at Deuel, her heart falling. "And the girl who stood outside?" she asked, dreading the answer.

"Kierssa," was the reply. "Far too young a Newmother. She'd only been in the Grandmother's home a few years." The woman shook her head. "I'd have more wisdom than that poor girl. Dark days indeed, for Kavlen."

"Yes," Catie said, breathlessly. "I'm very sorry. No village should be without a Grandmother."

The woman nodded thanks, and turned a glance back toward the stone doors. "She's in good company though," she said. "My own mother is in there, on the third floor. She and Grandmother had tea almost every day, near the end." The woman turned back and smiled at Catie through glistening eyes. "Now they can meet again every day until eternity."

"I'm sorry, there's that many rooms in there?" Catie asked.

"Oh yes, most of Kavlen is buried there," she replied. "It's the oldest and deepest of the caves, with many levels. Enough room for many generations to come."

"I had wondered about the doors, being without color," Catie said with a glance at Deuel. "It makes sense. Thank you. And, again, I'm sorry."

"Thank you, girl," the woman said, sketching a slight bow before walking away. After a few steps, she turned her head as if to glance back, her pace slowing, but she quickly shook her head, and continued.

Catie watched her a moment, then turned Kelsie toward Deuel. *Wars rage far beneath the floors,* she said. She felt his agreement.

"But how do we get in?" he asked.

Catie paused, shrugged, and looked again at the doors. They remained firmly shut.

16

ANGER HATE

"This is getting out of control."
"I think things are coming together quite nicely."
"You must not be looking."
"I look to the future, not the present."

14 Monzak 1320 — Spring

A violent knocking banished Roth's dreams, and he awoke clutching his blankets. There was no light in the room, so dawn had not yet arrived. Yet someone knocked, again.

"What is it?" he demanded. Not that they had been particularly pleasant dreams, but this was surely uncalled for.

"My lord, a message arrived. From Rodigger."

At this hour? "Give me a moment," he replied, pulling the blankets aside. He was not expecting a message, especially here in Vatenhal. And at night? Did the boy send an owl?

He pulled a robe around himself, then opened the door. "Give it to me. Bring the light," he added quickly. One of his guards entered, bearing a torch. "Here," Roth gestured, "get a taper, don't even think of trying to light—good. Thank you." He glanced quickly at the script and seal. It was from a message-hall in Kavlen—Kavlen! By the heavens, if his followers ever reached there...Surely this was good news, then.

He sat down, opened the scroll, and began reading. His eyes widened. "Worthless mercenary," he breathed. "And double worthless that boy! He was there to make sure the mission continued!" He kept reading. "Ah, I see. Well, at least that." The guard stood tentatively nearby.

Suddenly, Roth's hands were shaking. "The God curse that worthless, stupid boy!" he roared, smashing the parchment into a ball and slamming it repeatedly against the table. "What does he think he's doing?" he asked, shaking the crumpled message at the guard. "Ruining years of work and planning! Years!" He ripped the ball apart and cast the pieces across the room. He rose and paced, scratching his head with one hand and making fists with the other.

"Gabriel," Roth said suddenly, snapping his fingers as he turned toward his man. "Gabriel may not care about the Ber- the, uh, goblets, but he'll care about the behamien." He sat down again, taking fresh parchment and a quill. "Send this immediately," he said, scrawling frantically. "Get it to Gabriel in Attelek, and prepare our horses—perhaps ten men." He held the scroll toward the guard, then snatched it back and melted wax for a seal. "Leave our colors. You do not ride with Roth Kamdellan, but with Durla Fest, merchant lord." He held the scroll out again, now sealed. The guard received it smoothly. "We ride for Balnath Agrend to stop a disaster."

⸻◦⸻

Catie sat looking at Deuel. Deuel watched the door.

She hadn't realized how empty the common room of an inn got, in the middle of the day in a village where everyone worked. Usually she was busy herself—or, lately, she was traveling from one destination to the next. It was their fifth day in Kavlen, and she liked it.

She had thought about how to get into the catacombs to try to find the Berkarfor, but not as often or as hard as she probably should have. Maybe she would have found it by now, and they would be on their way to the next. Maybe that was why she tried not to think so hard about it.

But then there was Deuel. He never said anything, but of course she could feel him: he thought they wasted time for no reason, that Catie was clever enough to have figured out a solution by now.

"Why don't you try to think of something then?" she asked suddenly.

Deuel's gaze turned to her. "I do not know humans as well as you do, especially as it concerns death," he said. "I would think your race would be far more accustomed to it, as often as it occurs. And yet you seem to hold it more in awe than any other creature for whom death is a natural cycle."

"Oh." They would be sensitive, most likely, to someone wanting to explore their dead. Even Catie was a little nonplussed by the idea. Maybe that was why she didn't think too hard about it.

She sighed. No. She liked it here, and didn't want to leave just yet. She was singing and playing her Tamis flute again, to supply them after Rodigger had taken all the coin. She was connecting with people, again, making them laugh, and *care*.

She felt a tension in her head, almost a headache but not quite. That had happened a few times since arriving in Kavlen, and she didn't know why. She looked again at Deuel. She was sure he felt it too, though of course he hid it.

She took a deep breath to calm herself. The keeper had opened a window to the warm spring air, and she could hear birds, the faint wash of the wind through some leafy plant—and raised voices. Someone was arguing. That had happened a few times, too. In the middle of one of her songs only two nights ago, two men had suddenly stood up shouting at one another about some argument that sounded like an old hate long buried. Their wives had appeared, it seemed in order to take them each home, and instead ended up joining the argument. Finally the keeper had them all tossed out. But Catie hadn't been able to restore the mood to the common room the rest of that night.

The raised voices outside died down. Deuel gazed at her. "There was much in the riddle about anger, war, and hate," he said, reading her feelings again. "It would not surprise me if the battle the Wendol fight makes its way to the townsfolk's consciousness." He paused as she returned his gaze, conflicted herself. "You know we must face the Wendol and find the goblet," he said gently.

"Then we need to talk to Kierssa," she replied with a resigned sigh. "As Grandmother's heir, she would be allowed to visit the sepulcher, with an escort if she chose."

It took them some time to find her. She would not be left alone, and so she was handed from house to house until a way of succession was decided. Once they found the family she was staying with, it took greater effort to convince the wife to allow them to talk to the young girl aside.

"Hi Kierssa, my name is Catie," she said gently. "This is Deuel. We saw the end of Grandmother's funeral when we arrived in Kavlen. I spent some time with my Grandmother, in Attelek, too. I was not to succeed her. Still, I can imagine some of what you're going through."

"Did you disappoint everyone, too?" Kierssa asked.

Catie sat back. "They're not disappointed in you, Kierssa," she said. "They may be disappointed, but it's not your fault."

Kierssa's lips compressed, and she said nothing.

"Please understand, this is very hard for me to talk to you about," Catie continued. "Like I said, I was very much like you at one time. But we are in desperate need. Will you help us, if you can? If you can't, that's okay though," she added hurriedly.

Kierssa let out a small sigh, but nodded.

"Kierssa, Deuel and I need to get into the crypts for a little bit," Catie said. "Would you take us into them? They'll let you."

"Why?"

Catie leaned forward, her gaze wary but determined. "Kierssa," she said in a near-whisper. "Did Grandmother ever talk to you about the Berkarfor?"

Kierssa's eyes went wide and she leaned back. "No, I don't know anything about them. She never taught me anything about them."

"Okay, it's okay," Catie said hurriedly.

She knows, Deuel thought.

I know, but she's terrified. It'll do no good to press her about it, and we don't need to, anyway. "We were sent to find them, and we're certain one of them is in there."

"I don't think it is," Kierssa said. "I don't want to go in there."

"Is something bad in there?" Catie asked.

"No, dead people aren't bad, they're just—but I don't want to. Find some other way, if you have to."

Catie sat back again for a moment. "Kierssa, have you ever seen people suddenly start arguing, for no clear reason? Or fighting?"

Kierssa glanced from Catie to Deuel and back. "Sometimes," she said. "I just thought people were like that, though."

Catie grinned and gave her head a brief shake. "Not usually. Deuel and I both believe the things down there guarding the Berkarfor might be causing people to act that way."

"I'm sure they don't mean to," she said.

"Sometimes things happen even if people don't mean it to," Catie said with a gentle smile. "You know?" Kierssa looked about to cry, but she nodded her head. "If we go down there," Catie continued, "we might be able to get it to stop."

Kierssa's voice became a hoarse whisper. "I don't want to go down there," she said.

Catie blinked, and smiled again. "It's okay. You don't have to," she said. *Something is wrong,* she thought to Deuel. *She should be sad, of course, but she feels more guilty than seems right. We shouldn't force her.*

Then we still need to find a way down there.

I'll think of something. "I understand, Kierssa," she said. "I'm sorry for your loss. And remember, it's not your fault."

Kierssa didn't reply, only turned and left. Catie thanked the family, and she and Deuel returned to the inn.

⚫

After dinner, while they were still in the common room, the woman who had told them about Grandmother entered and approached their table. Her gaze was on Catie, except for one glance and smile for Deuel.

"I'm sorry," she said when she stood over them. "But you've been on my mind a fair bit of the day. I thought maybe you were familiar to me. My name is Wendeya." She held out her hand.

"I'm Catie," she said. "This is Deuel. I'm sorry, I don't think I recognize you."

She shook their hands. "It was some time ago, you were probably only a little girl. Which is why I didn't think...well really, I don't think it was you."

Catie smiled uncertainly. "Then..."

"Was your mother named Kerlyn?"

Catie's heart froze in her chest. Her mouth worked soundlessly for some moments. "Um, yes."

A smile bloomed on Wendeya's face. "I thought so! How is she? Is she well? I haven't seen her...well, not since she left, I guess." She sat down next to Catie and folded her hands on the table.

Catie continued to stare at her, mouth agape. "I...I don't know. I mean, she left me fifteen years ago. No, it was for my sake—oh...well." She laughed nervously as Wendeya's expression changed dramatically. "It wasn't like that. Someone was after her, and she knew I wouldn't be safe with her so she left me to be Newmother in Attelek."

"Oh," Wendeya said, clearly wanting to believe. "I didn't think—she didn't seem the type, I wouldn't have thought. So you haven't seen her? I guess not, you just said so. Hmm." She smiled and nodded, looking at her hands.

Deuel's glittering eyes went from Wendeya to Catie.

"Did she say...how long did she stay here?" Catie asked.

Wendeya brightened. "Oh, she was here for, I don't know, a few years I think? She was...I think she liked it here. She helped around town a lot. Actually helped with all the flowers!" She gestured a circumference. "On the walls?"

"Oh! Those were really beautiful," Catie said with a small laugh. "She...really, my mom did that?"

Wendeya nodded. "Mmm! She had...I think she had a little shop, for a while. Sold it to Timan...or, left it to him. They left very quickly, actually." She cleared her throat.

Catie blinked. "They?"

"Um, it was after she had been here for a year—two years?—A man came to town. You know, he reminded me of you a little!" she said, pointing at Deuel. "Isn't that funny? That's probably why it awakened my memory so much. Why, you two...Well, they got along, let's say that." She laughed a few peals, then seemed to remember they were talking about Catie's mother and stopped. "It was all..." She made a smoothing gesture. "I mean, he was a very good man. He was in town almost a year before they were really seen together. Things seemed to be going really well for them." Her head was bobbing again, but her eyes were distant.

"But then they left?"

She focused again. "Yeah. Just, almost in the middle of the night. They left a signed paper, leaving her shop to Timan—oh, her hand was very distinctive. Eight of us verified it with letters she had written to us. And then they were gone."

"Do you know where they went?"

"I'm afraid not. We didn't have a roving watch, so no one really saw her leave. A few saw her sort of packing, and that man was with her. Oh, what was his name? Legule? Ledorn? Le-something. Very nice, just...unobtrusive. Sometimes it's worse if someone's name comes too easily to mind, right? But..." She shook her head and shrugged. "We don't know where they went. I'm sorry. I had hoped you would tell me more than I would tell you. I'm so sorry."

"No, it's..." Catie paused with a wave, and smiled. "Not your fault."

Wendeya stood, smiling and in a sort of hunch that maybe was supposed to be another bow. "I'm sorry. Good night. I'm...sorry." She turned and left.

Catie swallowed, and looked at Deuel. His fathomless pools gazed back at her. In them, somehow, she found comfort and smiled. "Well, then," she said, and couldn't help but laugh. It trailed off too quickly, though, as she drew a breath and muttered: "how about that," as her eyes unfocused.

———◆———

Later that night, Catie awoke with a start.

Anger. Hate. Fear.

She sat up, and felt in her mind for Deuel. It wasn't coming from him, and didn't seem to be coming through him, as Kaoleyn's feelings had before. But it was strong, far stronger than the feelings had ever been before in Kavlen.

"We need to go down there. Now," Deuel said, and Catie yelped in surprise.

"Would you use your thoughts when its dark and quiet? And when you're not supposed to be in my room?" she demanded.

"I'm sorry. But you know it's true."

"I know it's true, I just don't know how."

"You may have to convince the guard."

"Deuel, it's not that it'll be guarded," Catie said. "It's that it's sacred."

"So is peace," he replied. "And with anger that strong, it will not be peaceful here for long."

Catie sighed. Of course he was right. Already dogs were barking a storm, and at least one owner was trying to match his hound's volume. "Okay, let's go," she said.

As soon as they stepped outside, she saw a figure walking toward them. Despite the gloom of the night, she recognized Kierssa.

"What are you doing here?" Catie asked in surprise.

"You're right," Kierssa said. "Things happen when we don't want them to, and it's not our fault, not always."

"What are you talking about?"

"Please, can we just go to the shrine?" Kierssa asked. Catie nodded, and let the young girl lead the way.

As they approached, the guard called out: "Kierssa? That you? Who's with you?"

"Just some friends," she called back. Both of their voices were competing with the dogs' now. "I needed to put something in Grandmother's alcove, and they agreed to escort me."

Catie tried to emanate peacefulness, but also a hint of danger. It may have been unnecessary, but the guard rang a little bell. In short order one of the doors swung open, and they entered.

"You know, once we get down here, we're not sure how to get to where the goblet is," Catie whispered as they made their way down the halls.

"I think I do," Kierssa replied quietly, with a tiny glance backward.

"Did Grandmother talk to you about it?" Catie asked.

Kierssa's head shook. "She had a drawer she told me never to look into," she said softly.

Catie smiled. "My Grandmother had one of those, too," she said. "I think Grandmothers tell us that so we'll find exactly what they want us to."

Kierssa's head bowed, then straightened again. Catie could feel her smile, and yet there was still that deep sadness that felt deeper than it should have been. Catie hoped Kierssa would let it out soon. She knew it would need to be.

Lanterns lined the walls of dressed stone that arched overhead high enough for Deuel to walk upright. Every several paces, a doorway opened off to the side, and casks were tucked in alcoves in the walls in great rooms. On the floor of each room was a unique mosaic—Catie thought perhaps it related to the family interred there. Soon she began recognizing the exact hues of some of the doors in the village, and her head gave a satisfied nod.

They descended the floors quickly. There seemed room for five or seven families on each. Kierssa led them through even the third floor, past what Catie was sure was Grandmother's tomb. Finally, on the fifth floor, Kierssa turned into one of the rooms. The walls here were lined with alcoves too—all empty. "Grandmother said once this was for a family yet to come," she said.

Catie glanced at Deuel, who glanced at the floor. The mosaic here contained depictions of cups, and a white bear-like creature whose head more closely resembled an ape of some sort. *Wendol,* Deuel thought.

Isn't that a little obvious?

Only if you've found the first Berkarfor.

Catie turned to Kierssa. "How do we get in?" she asked.

Kierssa turned to the alcoves, pointing to each one across a row and counting to herself. "Eight, nine, ten: one, two three..." Now counting down the column. She stepped forward, reached inside...

And a *thunk,* and a door off to the side swung open. Catie and Deuel turned swiftly to face the opening. Growling could be heard echoing up from the dark hole. Catie was keenly aware of how light she was: no weapon weighed down a scabbard. Deuel alone had Halm and Ro Thull for whatever they found down there.

We didn't need them last time, though, came his thought. Catie took a breath.

"Here," Kierssa said, holding out a lantern. "I'll be here when you get back."

"Thank you," Catie said. "If you decide you want to leave, though, we'll be able to find our way back."

Kierssa did not reply. Catie turned toward Deuel again, and he led the way into the dark door.

His lean shadow speared through the globe of light cast by the lantern as they descended a flight of stairs. Catie's shadow climbed back up the stairs, reaching for the receding rectangle of light at the top. The growling and...barking, it almost sounded like—but more like a human barking than a dog—grew louder, and seemed to echo longer the closer they approached.

They reached a landing. After a short hall, the path turned and descended again. At the bottom of this flight they could see a strange light again, not blue like the first time, but a warm brown. The hall at the bottom was lined with lanterns, but these were encased in an earthy shell, as if someone had managed to take a slice of rock thin enough to allow light to come through. They did not flicker as if a flame were behind the panes, but emitted a steady glow.

Catie set her lantern down. As the light shifted, Deuel glanced back at her. "I still don't necessarily want them to know we're coming," she said, feeling a little foolish, and fairly certain it showed through her smile.

But Deuel only nodded, and continued to lead the way. Ahead, the hall let out into another large cavern. Here, again, a ceiling that matched the style of lanterns along the hall soared overhead with the same steady glow emanating down. It illuminated two Wendol standing a few paces apart, fierce gazes locked upon one another, as they growled and barked at each other. Talons were out and arms held wide as if ready to leap.

Behind them, tucked in an alcove similar to the tombs above, sat a leather bag about the size of a goblet.

"Do you think it's as simple as walking past them and taking it?" Catie asked.

Deuel's gaze swung slowly to face her, and she shrugged.

"It was just a suggestion," she said. "I notice you're not going for your swords, though."

"Neither are they," he replied.

Her gaze snapped to them, and saw they too had turned to look at her and Deuel. She looked in their eyes, seeing there the spark of something more than mere animal. Likely because they weren't real.

Were they? They still felt real. It had been real anger—
ANGER!

Catie blinked and looked at Deuel. He shook his head. It had come from them, not him.

Angerhate.

Catie blinked again. Those emotions had come almost on top of one another. *But why anger and hate?*

Painjustice. The Wendol turned and snarled at one another.

Both of their feelings are coming through at the same time, she thought to Deuel. *I think they're trying to tell us what's wrong.*

Try something else, he suggested.

Why pain?

SelfishpunishmenthateANGER!

The Wendol faced each other again with growling, barking, and gestures coming close to tearing each other with gleaming ebony talons.

"Deuel, we need to separate them somehow," she said. "We aren't going to get anything out of them like this."

In a swift motion, Deuel drew Halm and Ro Thull and strode toward the Wendol, emanating authority and pushing respect and reverence toward the beasts. When they finally turned toward him, his wings punched sideways, spreading to the utmost of their glorious length. He pointed a blade at each of the Wendol, gesturing them apart.

Still growling, one Wendol moved left, while the other positioned itself directly in front of the alcove with the goblet. That made sense, and Catie didn't really care at this point, as long as she could separate them and find out what was wrong.

Deuel turned to face her, keeping sideways glances on the separated Wendol. *Go ahead.*

She turned her gaze on the left Wendol—she called him "Vensi" in her mind, and the other would be "Skald"—and said: *why pain?*

Selfish.

Quickly she looked at Skald. *Why punishment?*

Selfish.

"Great. They're both selfish," Catie muttered. Deuel tried to hide his amusement behind his authority.

Why selfish?

Pain, said Vensi, a hand near his stomach. *Lack,* with a gesture at his mouth.

Hungry? she tried, imagining the feeling of being hungry.

Vensi looked at her a moment. *Hungry. Satisfaction,* Vensi continued, holding up a hand. *Satisfaction,* he said again, shaking the hand. He brought up his other hand, made a grasping motion, then held it toward Skald. *Steal!*

More growling and barking, until Deuel glared at each of them in turn.

Why steal? she asked Skald.

Selfish, Skald said with a glare at Vensi. *Hungry,* he said, putting a hand near his stomach as well. But then he raised his hand as Vensi had done, shaking his head: *lack.*

"One of them had food and the other didn't, but they were both hungry. But surely this hasn't been going on for centuries, right?" she asked. "Or however long the Berkarfor have been hidden."

"It doesn't make sense," Deuel agreed.

She turned to Vensi. *Divide, share,* she tried to project.

Vensi looked at her blankly. *Not ask.*

"Well their vocabulary is improving," Catie said with a grin. *Ask share?* she sent to Skald.

Vensi growled before Skald could answer. *Not equal. Take more* he said with a sideways glance at Skald.

Her glance flitted from Vensi to Skald. *Why take more?* she asked Skald.

Skald's glance darted sideways, then down. *Hate* came softly. *Always anger. Always...sad...not satisfied. Always punishment.*

Vensi's head turned to Skald. *Always anger,* he said, gesturing to the other Wendol. *Always need, always sad.* He put a hand on his chest. *Never enough.*

Anger, Skald said, with a low growl.

Hate, Vensi muttered in response.

Pain, Catie pushed at the both of them.

They looked at her. *Painpain.* They paused, and looked at each other. *Sadsad.* They turned and faced each other fully.

Deuel sheathed Halm and Ro Thull, and folded his wings back under his cloak. He took several steps away and turned again to face them. After several moments of looking at each other, the Wendol turned to face the two companions. Their images shimmered, thinned, almost like a reflection on glass. The two images slid toward each other, joined, and became as one Wendol, solid again as they had looked before.

They seem to be back in harmony, Deuel thought.

Then the image bowed, and shattered into sparkling dust. "They had me going there, for a moment," Catie said as Deuel stepped forward and took the bag from the alcove. "I wonder why they aren't real?"

"Because they would be dead, and not able to guard anything, by now," Deuel replied, handing her the leather pouch. She untied the top, and pulled out the Berkarfor. This one was porcelain, perfectly smooth to her touch, with colors dyed in brilliant, unfaded hues in patterns she had never before seen. No chip or crack was evident. It was flawless in every respect she could think of.

Inside was another rolled parchment. She pulled it out, glanced over it, and handed it to Deuel. "It's not in Rinc Nain," she said.

He looked over it. "It is," he said. "But an older form."

"Oh, right," Catie said. She drew a deep breath. "So, where are we off to next?"

Deuel lowered the parchment, his gaze shifting by degrees to look at her. "Ethfirlaf," he said suddenly. He glanced at the parchment again, and nodded. "Freckled bark and shadowed spark," he said.

"Emerson tree, and..." she trailed off.

"I am not sure," Deuel replied. "But I have heard several times, long ago, of the shadowed sparks in Ethfirlaf."

"I hope you're right," Catie said, turning back for the stairs. "I mean, I'd be surprised if you're not, of course." Deuel said nothing as they walked. "It just...seems too easy," Catie said.

"Only if you have someone nearby who reads older Rinc Nain."

"And someone who can communicate their feelings through thought," she realized. She paused to look at him. "The Berkarfor are supposed to be found by either a behamian or a...wyvern."

"It would seem so."

"I feel like that should be significant."

But nothing came to mind. They shrugged at each other and fell silent.

When they reached the upper chamber, they found Kierssa had gone. "I guess she got tired of waiting," Catie said.

"You did say we could find our own way out."

They wound their way up through the floors. On the third, Catie stopped suddenly as she heard sniffling. She glanced in, and saw Kierssa near Grandmother's alcove.

"Kierssa? It's okay, honey," Catie said, coming in and kneeling beside the young girl. Deuel remained in the doorway.

"Are you leaving?" Kierssa asked, wiping a sleeve across her nose.

"Yes, we'll leave first thing tomorrow," she replied.

"So they're real?" She glanced at Catie and saw the goblet in her hand. "Where's the next one?"

"Ethfirlaf, it sounds—Kierssa?"

Kierssa turned swiftly, her eyes wide, and she pressed back against the bier. "I didn't mean to," she gasped. Then, desperately, she repeated: "I didn't mean to!"

"Didn't mean to, what?" Catie asked.

"He just asked where the Berkarfor was, but I promise I didn't know! Grandmother never told me!"

"Who asked?"

"The man who...who killed Grandmother," Kierssa said.

Catie's eyes went wide. Deuel's boots sounded across the floor and he knelt beside Kierssa, projecting a strange and heady mix of peace, safety, and imminent, terrible justice. "Tell us what happened," Catie said, trying to mimic Deuel's emotions for Kierssa's benefit.

"Before you came, two men came to Grandmother, looking for the Berkarfor," Kierssa said. "Grandmother didn't want to tell them, she said she didn't know anything about them except the stories. I had been in her secret drawer so I knew she knew. But she didn't want to say, so I was quiet too."

Catie smiled. "That's very good, Kierssa," she said. "Never speak of something unless Grandmother does first."

Tears started coming again. "I didn't, even when the one man came back later that night," she said. "I woke up and heard them talking in the other room. Grandmother sounded scared, so I stayed in bed. He kept asking where the next Berkarfor was, but she wouldn't tell him. Then there was a lot of noise, scraping and shaking and it sounded like Grandmother was kicking." Kierssa began crying again. Catie reached out and gripped her shoulder.

"It's okay, Kierssa, you're safe now. Did you get out of bed?"

"Y-yes," she said. "I wanted to see what was happening. I went into the room, and Grandmother was on the floor and wasn't moving. The man was there, the second one who was quiet when they were together. He looked at me and asked me if I knew where it was. He said he would do the same to me if I didn't tell him." She looked up earnestly. "But I really didn't know! I just wanted him far away, so I said Ethfirlaf because I knew it was far away. And then he left."

"Kierssa," Catie said, her stomach turning cold. "What were their names, the two men looking for these?"

"The one who did most of the talking said he was Rodigger," she replied. "The second had a strange name. He didn't look like Rodigger, he had dark hair, more like...yours," she said, looking at Deuel. "But he didn't look like you," she went on quickly.

"Did he look like he spent a lot of time in the sun?" Catie asked, thinking of the nomads they encountered on their way through the Tevorbath. The gloom she felt at learning Rodigger was involved felt more like the beginnings of fear from Deuel—which made her even more afraid.

Kierssa's nod affirmed Catie's suspicion. Deuel's grip became tighter on her arm.

"Kierssa," he said. "It's very important you remember the second man's name," he said.

Deuel, Catie said gently, but he ignored her.

"It was... 'Sha'-something...Sharéd—that's what Rodigger said."

Deuel released her, and terror washed over Catie from him. "Deuel, what is it?" she asked, her own voice shaking. What could terrify Deuel?

"Sharéd Dusslin?" Deuel asked, his voice barely above a whisper.

Kierssa shook her head. "I never heard him say."

"Are you sure they went to Ethfirlaf?" he asked. His voice was calm, in complete contradiction to the emotions she felt whirling from him.

"I don't know," Kierssa replied, appearing on the edge of tears again. "I told him that's where it was, and I never saw them again."

"Thank you, Kierssa," Deuel replied, standing. "You've been a very brave girl. I do not know your custom of titling Grandmothers, but if bravery is important, you will be a very good one."

"Th-thank you," Kierssa replied, turning to look again at Grandmother's alcove.

Catie stood as well. "Will you be okay?" she asked as Deuel exited the room.

Kierssa nodded, wiping her nose again and sniffling. "I'll go back to

Wendeya's soon," she said. "She's watching me now. I just want to be alone with Grandmother for a little bit longer. I'm sorry I didn't..." She trailed off.

"Kierssa, you did very well," Catie said. "I don't think I would have handled it as well as you did, in the same situation."

Kierssa smiled, though her eyes still shimmered. "Thanks."

"Okay," Catie said, patting the girl's head.

We must go, now!

Coming, Catie said hurriedly. She found Deuel just outside. "What is it?" she asked, his fear returning to her again.

"We have to get to Ethfirlaf," Deuel said, striding quickly toward the stairs to the next floor. "I should have recognized those Beltraths we found in the Tevorbath. If it is Sharéd, if he's here..."

"Who is Sharéd? How do you know him? Deuel, please slow down, my legs aren't as long as yours."

Deuel sighed. "During Sheppar's campaign, he decided he wanted to get rid of the dragons too, because people were afraid of them."

"Eck wasn't."

"Most people were. But it was late in the campaign and he didn't want to lose more men getting rid of them." Deuel was silent for a time. "So he forced the few soldiers with *skalderon* to deal with it, thinking the behamien would kill a dragon if ordered to by their *aloik.*"

"But you might be murdering your own parents!" Catie said, aghast. She had never thought Sheppar capable of such a thing.

"It had been a long campaign," Deuel replied. "He just wanted it to be done. In some ways I understand. But no," he continued, shaking his head, "none of us would kill a dragon, even if our *aloik* told us to."

"But, the dragon is gone. Garedardan isn't in the Tevorbath anymore."

"You are right, Garedardan isn't in the Tevorbath anymore," Deuel stopped, and faced her. "He's in the Wastes."

"But..."

"A dragon accustomed to the fertility of the Tevorbath does not easily move to the Wastes," Deuel said. "We found an oasis—one held by Dusslin's tribe. But it was not big enough to support both."

"Deuel..."

"I am not proud of it," Deuel replied. "I have wanted to go and make it right more than once. But the bond of *aloik* was strong enough to prevent that. We forced Dusslin's tribe to move. It was all but a death sentence to them, in the Wastes. I thought, by now, they *had* died." He paused, shook his head, and turned away. They continued on. "But now he's alive, and he's outside the Wastes with a force of over five hundred men. And with Rodigger, who might hate behamien more than Sharéd, even with less reason, and maybe involved somehow with Roth..." He trailed off as they approached the door to Kavlen. "There is no way to look at this that does not make me fear for the behamien on Andelen, and for Garedardan in the Wastes." He paused again, and sighed. "If we don't find Rodigger and Sharéd quickly," he said, glancing at Catie, "I have to find the others and warn them."

Catie skipped a step. "You..." *You'll leave me?* she managed to keep to herself. Of course he would: wouldn't she, if Attelek were in danger? Besides, everyone else had. She pushed that emotion aside. "You should," she said instead. "You should fly up the road. They have five days' head start." *Because I got distracted and wanted to settle down here, with...*

Deuel shook his head. "I will stay with you for a little while longer," he said. "There is little they can do on the road to Ethfirlaf." He drew a heavy sigh. "And I..." He stopped, his eyes glittering as he looked at her.

But he said nothing else, and they returned to the inn for the night.

17

MEMORY SPARKS

"Will you tell me one day what it is you see?"
"We each see things differently, Teresh. You must learn what you see."
"I see chaos."
"Then start with that."

15 Monzak 1320 — Spring

Gabriel awoke to someone knocking on his door.

He blinked, trying not to count the areas of his body that were sore. He had thought that, as a mercenary, he had kept decently limber. The 'simple' life here in Attelek had taught him differently. Yesterday had been his first foray into fishing.

"Gabriel?" came a young voice. At that age, he could never figure out what gender they were. In this town, it seemed not to matter as much as elsewhere.

Maybe that's why Catie turned out the way she did.

Gabriel grunted. A strange thought, even if it were true. "Coming," he called, surprised at how tired and gravelly his voice sounded. He cleared his throat a few times as he rose and threw on a rough shirt and plain trousers.

"What is it?" he asked, opening the door. It was a boy. Tyafor? Maybe his little brother. He held a small scroll out in front of him.

"This came for you, sir," the boy said.

Gabriel stared at it for several moments before remembering he was supposed to take it and read it, at least at some point. "Oh," he managed, finally. "Thanks."

He held it as the boy smiled uncertainly and left. He continued to look at it, remembering when he had held a similar small scroll with a similar seal in Balnath Agrend. No, not similar. The seal was identical. Several thoughts flashed through his mind of how the mission might have gone awry, how Rodigger and Deuel and Catie might have ended up.

I want to leave that behind. Why couldn't they continue on their own? Rodigger had all the coin anyway, he could have returned my share to Roth.

It's been months. Too many things might have happened in such a rapidly-changing world.

Gabriel sighed, closed the door, and broke the seal. As he read, his gloom and despair settled even deeper. *I wanted to leave this behind.*

You know you can't. Deuel needs your help.

The letter says Roth wants my help.

That is not for him to decide. That is for you.

And how will I do that?

Get to Balnath Agrend first. Take it from there.

Gabriel re-rolled the scroll and tossed it into the embers from last night's fire. Then he began packing his saddle bags for a long journey.

———◆◇◆———

Catie lay in her bed that morning with no desire to get up. To get up would mean to get back on the road, and quite frankly she was tired of traveling. To get up would mean chasing after things she was losing faith in:

A boy who would never grow into a man if he never left Roth's apron-strings.

The barest chance of some sort of delayed justice or revenge.

Possibly the success of the rebellion.

In bed, under a layer of blankets, eyes closed, she didn't have to choose. Each moment that passed was another moment not following a choice she didn't like.

But it would be worse. She never was one to avoid a choice, or to sit and make no choice. She took the time to think, to reason, to ask questions. Sometimes she went on instinct. But she always made a choice.

She thought of the Berkarfor. Everyone wanted her to find them: Roth, for his own power. Rodigger, to see his hero win. Deuel? Well, Deuel didn't anymore. He wanted her to figure who she was, though probably now without him.

And yet, who she was had brought her here, hadn't it? Her sense that first night, when Paolound died, had told her she would return home, but not stay. And when they had come to her village, she knew without being asked that their mission was why she would not stay home, that she was to go with them. What was it about those goblets, though? Why were they hidden, guarded supposedly—though, so far, they hadn't been truly guarded.

Except they never would have gotten past if they had tried to just fight the creatures. A real *byor* Deuel likely could have handled, with Gabriel's help. But that one hadn't been real. And clearly Deuel could have handled the Wendol if they had been real, too. But they weren't. They were magic of some sort—an illusion. So if not to physically guard the goblets, they had been there for...what?

Catie rolled over. The Berkarfor weren't there to be taken, they were there to be pursued. Just something to get the pursuer to encounter the guardians and interact with them.

But what might happen if she didn't act the way she was supposed to? What if she did outright attack the next one? She contemplated several scenarios. Most ended with her dying, blown to dust the way the guardians were. But she would never try such a thing. She felt victorious approaching the guardians the way she had been, trying to understand them and work through whatever problem they presented.

What she did not know, and could not begin to guess, was what would happen once she had all four Berkarfor. And she wanted to find out.

She sat up, and took a breath. And what about Deuel? She didn't want him to go off alone. Well, she didn't want to go off by herself, if she needed to be honest. She could follow him afterward.

But, after what? She still needed to decide what her own plan was.

Deuel thought his fate was somehow tied with yours. What if it's the other way around?

So I abandon Dannid's justice and pursue my own future?

No one said those were mutually exclusive.

Catie slouched a little in bed. Was that it, then? Let Deuel go if they couldn't find that *boy* and his Beltrath friend. Find the last Berkarfor. Then try to find Deuel again. But would he tell her where he was going?

If I were a dragon-son, where would I go to change?

Change happens first in the eye.

Catie held her breath. Had that last thought come from Deuel? She didn't recall pushing that one. She reached out gently, trying to sense him. She pulled back with a faint yelp: he was awake, and she was surprised she could actually tell. But he wasn't aware of her.

Are you ready to leave yet? he asked suddenly, causing her to yelp a little louder this time.

Can you warn a girl before you do that?

Last time you told me to use my thoughts. How exactly would you like me to get your attention?

Last time you were IN MY ROOM. Try standing outside and knocking, and calling softly, like normal people!

There was silence. So the first thought had not come from him. But what did it mean? The eye? Whose eye? What eye? A dragon's?

Catie stood, reaching for her clothes. A dragon's eye. Of course there would be hidden caves all through that region, plenty of places for be-hamien to go away from prying eyes. All she had to do was find two more centuries-hidden goblets guarded by magically-created creatures, and then travel across the country and find a hidden cave outside Balnath Agrend.

How hard could that be?

•

As the days passed on their road eastward, Catie kept waiting for Deuel to leave. She could feel him getting more concerned: at every inn they asked, none of the keepers could remember anyone like Rodigger or a Beltrath, especially traveling together. At first, Deuel reasoned that the inns were large, numerous, and busy with traders going between Ostflir and Agrend. Two individuals could easily slip through unnoticed, especially if they were trying. But by the end of the week he had begun flying ahead while Catie kept the horses, trying to spot them unaware on the road.

At Finstaff, early in the night, there came a soft knocking on Catie's door. She blinked, reached out and sensed Deuel, and smiled.

"Come in," she said. "That was perfect," she continued as he entered. "Do it like that from now—" But she could tell from his expression that would be the last time he would need to get her attention. At least, he believed that was so.

"They are not on the road," he said. "Whatever happened, they have chosen not to go to Ethfirlaf. I can only think, after what they did in Kavlen, they have abandoned the Berkarfor. And what we know of Rodigger and Sharéd, it is likely they are pursuing the behamien."

"How would they know where to find them? *I* don't even know."

"Because Roth knows many ancient things that were supposed to have been lost," Deuel replied. "And there are only two roads out of Kavlen. I do not know how, but they know."

"I want you to go, Deuel, I do," Catie said, then paused a moment. "I'm asking this for your advice, not to try to make you stay: what if I need someone in Ethfirlaf? Or wherever the next Berkarfor is supposed to be hidden? What if I can't figure out the next riddle?"

"You are resourceful, Catie," Deuel replied, a spark of respect in his eyes. "You will find a way, as you always have."

"And what about after? You said you wanted to see who I was, that you felt it would help you understand humans better. How do I find you again?"

Deuel looked at her a long moment. "I cannot be sure you will need to," he replied finally. "If I enter the change, or if Rodigger and Sharéd get there first..." He trailed off. She felt his smile. "You must focus on your journey, Catie. If you are meant to find me, you will. I must focus on my journey."

Catie grinned sadly. "Are you leaving tonight?"

"I am."

"But, I mean, where will you stay?" Then, she wasn't sure why, but she just noticed he did not have on his customary thick cloak, and what he wore clearly showed his wings.

He must have seen the recognition in her eyes, for he nodded solemnly. "I have, for so long, kept hidden who I was," he said. "I have given Rodan to a respected hostler. If I need him again, I will come for him. But from now on, I fly."

Catie nodded, pleased with that choice, at least.

———◆———

Two days after they parted, she could no longer sense him in her thoughts.

She continued north and east, trying to get used to Deuel's absence. Kelsie soon stopped shifting when Catie did, thinking they were turning when Catie only wanted to make some comment to the dragon-son.

She talked to caravaners on their way inland, talked to innkeepers, played her Tamis flute for guests, and sang songs. And for moments she was happy. But eventually the day would end, she would lie in her bed, and reach out for Deuel's awareness. And find nothing. They had never shared less than a cot-room, never shared a bed. And yet that connection, that ability to talk without speaking had created a space that—now bereft—was a void that no mere conversation could fill.

She tried enjoying the road. It wound through the Brithelt Forest, a landscape of towering trees and fern-carpeted hillsides. Little streams trickled through nearly every valley, and with summer upon them the birds of the deep forest made song heard nowhere else. Her respect for the Tamis flute increased, and she studied their music to create her own melodies for the inns at night.

From a map she had studied at the inn just inside the border of the Brithelt Forest, she knew one day that she was nearing Tarkusnaab. She started earlier in the morning, pushed Kelsie a little harder through the day, and continued riding later than she otherwise might have. Tarkus-naab was the halfway point to Ethfirlaf, and she was ready for this journey to be over and to find Deuel again.

Torches ahead, blearing through her half-closed eyes, alerted her to her arrival at the hilltop village. Stifling a yawn, she guided Kelsie along the roads without thinking. Tarkus was not a large village, just enough to have a fair share of cross-streets. She passed several, then turned her mare right. Past another few buildings, then left.

And she was lost. She blinked at a house-front, its windows dark, looking for the swinging sign announcing the inn and not seeing it.

Kelsie sat patiently while Catie turned a few times.

"It was here," she said. "It was..." She trailed off, nudging Kelsie to the next cross-street and glancing down it both ways. "There's the forge," she said aloud, where a banked fire still sent a diffuse orange glow onto the street. "Past is the tannery." A riffle of wind and she could almost smell it. She turned the other way, noting the signboards for potter, woodcarver, candlemaker, seamstress—but there was no inn.

Suddenly, she sat back and blinked. *I've never been to Tarkusnaab,* she realized. *How am I supposed to know where the inn is?*

But as she turned and looked each way, and back the way she came, she felt it was too familiar. Not familiar like it reminded her of Attelek—the trees weren't so thick there, and emerson trees did not exist beside Agirbirt. More like, if she took away that house, that one, maybe a few others, it would fit the image perfectly in her mind. Except where the inn was supposed to be.

It was slightly different, yet it's exactly the same. I've been here—but when?

Grandmother had said my mother brought me to Attelek when I was small. She didn't say how small.

She turned Kelsie back down the road, retracing the steps that brought her there. She recognized more of the houses, knew the miller had lived in that one, that the watermill was past the west end of town at a natural waterfall.

But as far back as she could remember, she had been in her parents' house, then Grandmother's after that.

And yet, somewhere, there was Tarkusnaab.

She finally found the inn—left, not right—but the building appeared newer than some of the village, as most of the ones on this street also did. And it was bigger, she thought.

She put Kelsie in a stall, settling her for the night before going inside.

The common room was empty and quiet. A cat lay on the bar. It snapped its head up as she passed, purred, and laid back down.

"I hope there's no nocturnal mice," she said wryly.

"What's that?" called a voice on the other side of a door behind the bar.

"Sorry I'm late," Catie replied, her voice at half-volume.

The door swung open, and a middle-aged, thin woman with dark hair in wisps from beneath a hastily-donned bonnet stood in the doorway. "You aren't kidding," she replied. She glanced down at the sleeping cat and clicked her tongue. "Get five, ten patrons in here with their drinks, she's everywhere at once," she said, gesturing. "Five, ten mice are around, she's fast asleep. I suspect you need a room?"

"If you have one," Catie replied.

"Two coin a night. Breakfast and dinner is extra. I'm Scearon."

"Catie," she replied. She dug in her purse and pulled out the proper coin. "I'll just be the night. Maybe breakfast."

"Whatever you need, my dear," Scearon replied, taking the coin. "Rooms are in the back."

"Um, do you mind?" Catie asked, as she was about to turn to leave. "Has the inn always been here?"

Scearon blinked. "No. It used to be other side of the village," she replied.

Catie nodded. "I had thought so."

A smile crept onto Scearon's face. "Did you indeed? You talk like you remember the old place."

Catie smiled tentatively. "I thought I did," she said slowly.

"Ha!" Scearon laughed. "Then I'll need your secret. It hasn't been there since my grandmother kept it. So you're...fifty?"

Catie managed a chuckle. "Must have been somewhere else, then," she said as lightly as she could. *Why do I have a memory from over fifty years ago?*

I think perhaps you have lived longer than you realize, Deuel had said, once.

"Is there a Grandmother here?"

"Surely," Scearon replied. "Couple houses down from where the inn used to be. Got witch hazel out front."

"Thanks," Catie said with a smile.

As she lay in bed, she realized she and Deuel hadn't spoken about her strange abilities and memories, and what they might mean, for some time. Now it was staring her in the face again. And she couldn't talk to the dragon-son about it. *How am I supposed to figure out what it means to be a wyvern if the only person who seemed to know is heading to the other side of the country?*

The void in her heart—far from healing with time—grew larger.

⬤

The next morning, she found the house easily enough. She paused out front, looking at the windows, the doors, the gambrel roof—familiar in shape, if not color. She closed her eyes, trying to remember. All she could summon was a vague notion, and that might have been from trying too hard. She blinked, walked up, and knocked.

The Newmother answered, gazing at her silently, eyes and hair black and skin whiter than her linen dress. She turned and led the way into the house, pausing only to hold a hand toward the Grandmother before padding off.

"Hi," Catie said with a small wave.

Grandmother gazed at her, brown eyes considering. She was a thin woman, yellowed skin sunken against vein and bone. Gray hair was pulled tight into a braid. Her dress matched the Newmother's, though iller-fitting. When her inspection of Catie seemed complete, the barest of smiles finally touched her thin lips. "Hello," was all she said.

"I seek your wisdom," Catie continued, clasping her hands in front of her and inclining her head a notch to appear demure.

It didn't seem to help Grandmother's mood. "I assumed."

Catie took a measured breath, listening. The house was silent, empty: a dust mote falling through the air. None of the sounds of morning made it in, and the room was windowless and lit only by candles.

She hesitated. "Do you...remember me?" She looked up.

A deep frown. It seemed more comfortable. "A name might help."

"Catie," she said. "Caytaleane."

Grandmother's sniff seemed to echo, her shuffling steps shook the house. "Named after your mother? I was only Newmother at the time."

"Kerlyn?"

The shuffling stopped. "No. Caytaleane. Kerlyn was her sister."

The emptiness of the house loomed around her. "I don't understand..." She faltered.

The shuffling resumed, and suddenly Grandmother was in front of her, gripping her chin and gazing into her eyes. Grandmother's shoulders relaxed as she took a breath. "Well, then," she sighed as she took a step back. "You're not what you appear, are you?"

Catie shrugged. "I guess not. You do know me?"

Grandmother shuffled toward a chair, beckoning Catie. "You're taller, and you look a little older." She grunted as she sat. "But you've done better by far than I have. Better than I've ever seen. But," she continued with a tired smile, "I have heard of such things, even here in the Knob."

"What things?"

"Women who don't age," Grandmother replied, her eyes sparking just a little. "Well, you aged, that's plain. But the fact you don't remember it?" She shrugged.

"Why don't they age? Why don't I remember?"

"And why do you say Kerlyn was your mother?"

"She said she was—she *was*. She raised me in Attelek, with my father." Who had not been her father. She set her jaw a moment before changing tack. "You said 'one of my sisters.' Were there more?"

"Five of you showed up, one day. We thought you were lost. You certainly didn't talk much, except to say you were sisters and give us your names. Strange by far, you were—off in a clutch talking to each other low and quiet. And not in Rinc Nain, at least not a lot. Sometimes, when I tried to sneak up and listen you all went quiet, but by your looks back and forth I always wondered if you were somehow still communicating."

We probably were. "How long were we here?"

"A few months, I think. Then you left by twos, except the last. She stayed around a little longer and avoided all our questions. Seemed she wasn't sure what to do, on her own. Finally one morning she was gone too. But you weren't here long enough for us to notice you as one who doesn't age." Grandmother leaned back into the chair. "Why they don't age, I've never heard, or why you don't remember. I've never seen any like you since."

"Do you know anything about wyverns?" Catie asked.

Grandmother sat still for several long breaths. "No, I don't," she said finally. "Like miniature dragons, though? Wings instead of arms? Why do you ask?"

"I'm not sure," Catie said with a smile. "I'm just wondering if I am one."

The sparkle in Grandmother's eye only made it to one corner of her mouth. "Well if that's your secret," she said, "I'll let you keep it."

She rode for Ethfirlaf the next morning. Every building was where she remembered it, but the road outside of Tarkus was completely unfamiliar. Now that she thought about it, the road in had been unfamiliar as well. Somehow, she had been in Tarkusnaab long enough to memorize where nearly everything had been, but could not remember one step outside of it.

Kelsie plodded on as Catie rode in a daze, calling up alternating memories of a cave, and Tarkusnaab, and trying to see around them. The cave was still more sense than visual: the cool, the peace, the silence and stillness. And Tarkusnaab was much more visual than sense. She remembered where each of the buildings were, remembered a fair number of people who were probably all now dead—that didn't help her contemplative daze. But she couldn't remember what it *felt* like to live there. Couldn't remember knowing any of the people, just where they lived and what they did. And she reached out to sense Deuel countless times before she realized she was doing it.

As she neared Ethfirlaf, she began to see the pockets of clearings. Most of northern Andelen got its lumber from the region. Deep within the Brithelt, the idea of running out of trees was absurd, and so they were harvested almost constantly, with wagons heading south along the road every day laden with either raw logs, logs stripped of bark and smoothed, or cut lumber—a wheeled stream delivering every type of wood to Balnath Agrend, to Ostflir, to Taferk. Ironwood, oak, maple, chestnut, hickory, ash, mahogany, emerson—a lean tree of tough fibers useful for anything from archer's bows to Tamis flutes and lute necks, depending on how it was prepared. Sycamores in the valleys and firs on the heights.

And, somewhere outside the village, a Berkarfor.

Catie pulled out the slip of parchment Deuel had given her, reading over the riddle. It was much shorter than the other one. One line, it seemed, for the general location: Ethfirlaf. One line for the specific location, but she would have to ask where to find 'shadowed spark.'

And one for what she should expect to find there, guarding the goblet. Given what she had faced so far, this sounded rather tame: wolves. And not necessarily a very large pack. But a white wolf would be involved somehow.

The inn at Ethfirlaf was very near the southern entrance. There were scattered patrons in this one—benefit of arriving at a decent hour, she chided herself. But though she sang that night, she was uncertain about pulling out the Tamis flute here, where she was fairly sure it had been created.

When she had finished, and had some dinner, she mentioned the shadowed spark to the keeper. He looked at her warily.

"I don't remember seeing you here before," he said slowly.

She shook her head with a smile. "Just arrived," she replied.

"And you want to know where our rarest resource is," he said.

Her smiled slipped. *Resource?* "Yeah, I guess I do."

He returned a thin smile, said nothing, and moved to the next table.

Well, it's a spark, right? And a figurative one, probably. Should be visible. Maybe more so at night.

The moon is nearly gone, though. Tough to see where I'm going in the dark.

It might not be as hard as you think. Deuel sees pretty well in the dark, doesn't he?

What does that have to do with me?

Try it.

As Catie went out into the night, she felt as though her vision...rippled. Was it a trick of her mind, or just that she paid attention now? The watch roved with torches, but Ethfirlaf was not quite large enough to boast lit streets. And yet, as she made her way through town she saw details just as clearly as if they were. Maybe when she exited the town and was under tree canopy...

She suddenly remembered Kavlen, that she had been able to recognize Kierssa even in the dark of night. She looked up: the sky was overcast. No starlight, no sliver of moonlight. Yet she could see.

She could see at night, like Deuel. Sense the feelings of dragons, like Deuel. Project feelings and thoughts, like Deuel. Would being a wyvern be so different from being a dragon? Apparently he would not be able to communicate with her anymore, would not understand her speech if she changed. Neither would she understand him, if he changed. Just basic emotions—or so it seemed. What if they both changed?

She sighed and shook her head. Questions she would not be able to simply puzzle out the answers for. Time to start looking for a 'spark' somewhere in the middle of the largest forest in Andelen. Perhaps by the time she found it, she would know why she could see in the dark as clearly if it were a full moon.

By the end of the third night, she had walked wide circles north, east, and south of Ethfirlaf, and found nothing. She would wake sometime before dinner, sing for a shift or two, eat, and head off into the woods until nearly Morning. She felt she walked far enough to be just outside what should be associated with Ethfirlaf—though, except for the road south where the region of Tarkusnaab lay, any land elsewhere could only really be considered 'outside Ethfirlaf,' but she tried not to think about that.

She had to look west tonight before she could truly start losing hope. But it was summer, and nights were short. Maybe she should wait until winter when she would have fistfuls of night-shifts to walk in the endless woods.

She forced a smile, and began to hum one of the songs that the patrons here preferred the most—'Hatchlings in the Dale' they called it. She thought she had created it after hearing the birdsongs in the woods on the ride into town. But, then, probably a lot of folks had heard the same birdsong, so it shouldn't have surprised her that someone had put words to it as well.

The west side of Ethfirlaf, unlike the other quarters, had a carpet largely of fern, quieting her steps. The previous nights' walks had been through accumulated dead leaves and twigs crackling and crunching underfoot. Every few steps, she could glance to her right and see a wavering torchlight in the direction of Ethfirlaf, peering between the maze of trunks. After Night-Fall, the insects of the forest went to sleep, and there was left only the barest *shush*-ing of ferns against her boots. Even the wind was calm, and the trees themselves seemed to settle in for the night.

So it didn't surprise her as much as it may otherwise have to see a wolf, ahead and to her left, slinking in between the trunks of oak and maple. It was not looking at her, but only ahead to where it was going. She paused mid-stride to watch it, and continued once it had put her firmly behind its tail.

If there are to be wolves guarding the goblet, she thought, *it makes sense this one would lead me to the others.*

Perhaps a quarter-shift later proved her right. Ahead, a pack of wolves had gathered in the night, looking for all the world like people gathered for a speech and awaiting the head speaker. Mother wolves tended bickering cubs. The males conversed about the days' business, or attended their mates. A few apparently un-mated wolves tried to look momentarily busy but relationally available. Catie put a hand to her mouth, keeping in a chuckle. She could even see Rodigger, sitting next to an important wolf and acting as though the importance was shared, though he was a little bedraggled and didn't appear too bright.

Catie sobered. She hadn't thought about Rodigger in some time, she had been so caught up with Deuel leaving and her continuing the job alone. Of course, she hadn't really thought of it as a job from Roth in so long either. She shook her head, returning her attention to what was going on ahead.

She noticed, then, a large stump in the middle of the pack that seemed to be alight with fire. And just as she noticed it, a massive wolf, snowy white, leapt out of the darkness and onto the top of it. As if a whip-crack signal, all the rest of the wolves' gazes came immediately to attend who was clearly their leader.

Catie's brows knit. Likely, then, the Berkarfor was hidden in the stump, or was somehow connected to it. She continued to watch the pack. They made no sounds, but as the white wolf glanced around those gathered she felt he was somehow imparting something to them all.

The last two times, the 'guardians' needed us to react to them in a certain way, to solve some issue or let one sort itself out, before they would leave and give us access to the goblet. So what is supposed to be going on here?

Catie stood and watched until her legs began to stiffen. But nothing up ahead changed. If it was a speech, it was an interminable one. She saw, occasionally, one of the other wolves shift. Snow-white would gaze at it and shift a little, and they would seem to go back and forth for a time. Then another would shift, and snow-white would turn to it.

Perplexed, Catie reached out, trying to sense any feelings or thoughts coming from the wolves—but there was nothing there. She took a few steps closer, quietly, and tried again. But still there was nothing. Maybe a faint sense of an almost tangible vastness, but that might have just been her.

Catie frowned. Standing still seemed to be accomplishing nothing. Maybe these guardians required her to walk up on them before something else would happen. She took several more steps, until her foot finally landed on a rare twig that broke beneath her weight.

Snow-white's head snapped up and it stood, hackles raised and a deep growl echoing through the night. The entire pack turned and assumed a similar position. A few circled to her flanks.

Maybe this goblet requires courage? she thought—hoped. She stood firm, gazing into Snow-white's eyes and pushing calm and curiosity. But the wolf on the stump took no notice. It raised its head and let out a deep, long howl. The wolves on the flanks leapt suddenly toward her.

She paused for a brief moment. *I think this Berkarfor requires me to run!* she thought. True to her thoughts she turned and bolted for Ethfirlaf.

The soft ferns were a trap, now, snagging her feet as she dodged between trunks. She could see the flickering watch's lights ahead, so impossibly far away. Growling and barking closed in behind her. The ferns seemed not to hinder her pursuers.

"Help!" she shouted into the night, hoping the guards would hear. She ducked beneath a branch, and around a trunk. A wolf launched sideways, its snapping jaws just missing her arm. She wished she had brought a weapon of some sort. The wolf landed to her right-front, turned, and leapt again. But its feet slipped, and it fell short. She twisted around another tree. She could see a few buildings, now.

"Help me!" she cried again. Something hit her back and knocked her flat. She twisted quickly, elbow out, knocking the wolf's head sideways just before its jaws lunged for her neck. She brought a knee up swiftly, and the wolf pitched behind her. But a second was right behind it, eyes shining and teeth dripping. She gripped the fur of its throat, arm stiff. It twisted its head, trying to bite her arm.

Another appeared beside her, and fangs sunk deep into her left shoulder as she screamed. She tried to bring up her left arm to keep that one away, but her muscles refused to work. The wolf wrenched and tugged as she cried. She couldn't let go with her right hand, for it would allow that one to finally reach the prize of her throat. She tried to bring a knee up, but the wolf skittered sideways.

It yelped, suddenly, releasing her arms as a halberd's point drove it to the ground. The wolf in her right hand twisted to get away. A sword came for that one, and she released it just quickly enough to keep her flesh away from the blade.

She sucked in ragged breaths, her eyes squeezed shut as fire consumed her shoulder. A torch lit her eyelids, and a voice called out to her. But she was not yet ready to answer questions.

18

Healing Wounds

"That wasn't my fault."
"You cannot retract that claim, if she grows from this."
"Are they on their way yet? Perhaps they can help her."
"You still do not realize her potential, do you?"

4 Savimon 1320 — Summer

Catie awoke the following morning, but did not open her eyes. Someone would be there looking at her. They would ask how she was, if she was okay. And she didn't want to fake a smile and lie through it.

She had refused to watch or speak as the doctor sewed up her wounds. Fortunately, around so many woodcutting saws and axes, the doctor here was familiar with cut and torn flesh. Her shoulder in the morning actually felt better than she thought it would. So, in a way, she would not be completely lying. But she knew that wouldn't pass a Grandmother's scruple.

Her first real test since being on her own again, and she had failed—miserably. Had to run for help, and almost didn't get it. They had asked how she had come across the wolves, and the only explanation she could give them made her seem like more of an idiot, some empty-headed girl who only worried about clothing and hair and whether or not she was beautiful, and had no business being on her own in a sawmill town.

The room, though, was silent. So here she was, alone. Everyone had abandoned her yet again, because they had more important things to attend to. Gabriel had chosen life in her village. Rodigger, his own hate for Deuel. And Deuel? At least Dannid hadn't had a choice: Roth took him from her. Deuel, who shared thoughts and feelings, who had seemed to care about who she was and what was happening to her—of his own freewill had left her because his own desires were more important.

Part of her knew that wasn't fair, but it was a far smaller part of her than the part that felt alone and incapable. She shouldn't have been surprised: she was a woman. A girl. Rodigger had known she wasn't capable, and had only retreated from her when she tried to assert otherwise. But until that point, he had seemed interested in her. Maybe he hadn't abandoned her, she had pushed him away with her delusions of competence. Maybe if she'd felt a little less capable, Deuel would still be here, too. And if she'd felt a little less capable, she wouldn't be in this bed in the aftermath of a wolf attack with stitching in her arm. Stitching done, by the way, by a man. A *capable* man.

And so she stayed in bed with her eyes closed, waiting for someone more capable to feed her and tell her it was okay, that it wasn't her fault because she shouldn't truly expect to be successful anyway, that she should just stay in bed and get her rest. One day she could go back home with a caravan filled with capable people. She could get married back there, and have children, and do all the things in life that were expected of her. Nothing difficult, things people were okay with her doing, as a woman. A girl.

But no one came to feed her. She peeked once, and no food was by her bed. There was a pitcher of water, but no glass. Dangerous, probably, for her to try to get her own drink or feed herself. Better wait for someone to come.

The shifts dragged by. She blinked her eyes open wide and glared at the ceiling. She glanced again, managed to raise herself up a little. There was definitely nothing to drink from except the pitcher. Where *was* everybody? She cocked an ear, but she heard no sounds outside the door.

She managed to rasp a faint "hello?"—her throat was so dry!—but no one answered. She needed a drink. This was ridiculous. She rolled to a sitting position on the edge of the bed, still glancing toward the door. She flexed her shoulder. It hurt, and she couldn't move her arm easily, but it moved. She stared at the pitcher, rose, and walked over to it, and took a sloppy drink from its wide mouth.

The water was so *cool!* She had never tasted water so pure and cool. She raised the pitcher again, not caring as water spilled off the sides of her mouth and onto her shirt. She paused to breathe through her nose when she needed to, but drank half the pitcher in one shot. Well, maybe a third of it, with the rest of a half spilling down her front. Even that was refreshing.

She took a deep breath, and sighed. The house sat on the edge of town, and the Brithelt Forest stretched away outside the window. It was

Evening, at least: orange eve-light lit the trees and ferns in sporadic shafts that flickered in a breeze. And when the dancing leaves parted just right, a thin beam made its way to her eye. Her window faced west, toward last night's debacle.

Why had the wolves acted that way? The white wolf fit the riddle. The 'shadowed spark' was evidently some sort of glowing lichen, and had been there. What had changed? *Should* she have simply stood her ground?

Or was she meant to find the location only by the wolf and the lichen, but approach in daylight? Should she try to find out?

I thought you weren't capable?

Catie snorted. Capable of fighting wolves by herself? Who was? She had misunderstood. A failing, perhaps, but one she could repair. Maybe if more people weren't afraid to misunderstand, they would admit when they did, and move on to understanding instead of straining violently to cling to their misunderstanding as truth.

Like you misunderstand Gabriel, Rodigger, and Deuel?

Let them pursue their own desires. Deuel, she knew, did what was right. At least, what she would do if faced with the same fear. Gabriel, too. Rodigger? No, he was one who clung to misunderstanding, and she would never be like him. She couldn't force him to change, but neither could she think he did what was right, what could set him free to become the man he might be capable of being.

And Roth?

She paused. The Wendol in Kavlen fought and argued because each had been hurt by the other. Did Roth, too, fight and argue because he had been hurt? Did he simply hide that hurt under anger and hate, because it was easier than admitting the hurt? She didn't know—couldn't know unless she could talk to him.

And she couldn't talk to him without bringing him the Berkarfor. If she did that, then maybe he would listen to her.

She drew another deep breath. Time, then, to put her theory to the test.

But first, she wanted a bit more information on wolves. Just to be safe.

⸻◆⸻

The keeper glanced up as she entered, looked her up and down.

"You don't look too much worse," he said. "How do you feel?"

"Foolish," she replied.

The keeper chuckled. "Thrad said you did okay, for having two wolves at you," he said. "Said he couldn't imagine facing more than one, and that without a blade."

"Tell him I don't recommend it," she replied with a smile. "Speaking of which, where might one get a blade around here?"

"Going sawin'?" he returned with a grin.

"Actually I was hoping to find a Nagrath dagger," she said.

The keeper had the good sense to look in her eye before laughing, and didn't. He acknowledged her sincerity with a respectful frown. "Seems—most often—folks that know how to use one of those don't look much the part," he said. "Kiel'll have one. Two shops up from the south sawmill." He paused to wipe a mug and place it under the counter. "Going hunting for the wolves that got you?"

"I assumed the two that got me were killed by the watch," Catie replied. "And I don't hunt things I don't understand." *Except Berkarfor.* "Much."

"Smart lass. You might ask Eidemon," he said, gesturing with another mug toward a patron Catie hadn't noticed. A quick glance told her he was old and wore thick pelts, even in summer.

"Does he know the ones around here?" she asked, glancing again at gnarled fingers and thin russet hair that looked only slightly better-kept than Gabriel's had been.

"I don't know. Newer in town, only showed up a month or so ago," the keeper replied. "Not sure what he does with himself either. But you don't get a coat like that without learning a thing or two."

"Oh?" She looked again, recognizing now the thick wolf pelts. As if sensing their conversation, the man named Eidemon looked at them. He frowned. Catie looked back at the keeper. "Thanks," she said. "I'll see what he has to say."

She put on her most reassuring smile as she walked toward him. His frown only deepened as he looked her up and down, but he said nothing.

"Hi, my name's Catie," she said as she neared. "The keeper told me to talk to you about the wolves around Ethfirlaf."

"Catie, eh?" he said, his visage relaxing a little. "You almost look familiar to me. At least your outfit does. Do I know you from somewhere?"

Catie shrugged. "I don't think so. And I'm from a long way from here."

"And what would bring a young girl like you a long way from home?"

She smiled, a spark in her eyes. "The wolves of Ethfirlaf," she replied.

"I told a mercenary friend of mine, once, that folks needed to learn what dangerous beasts was, and what wasn't," Eidemon replied, his face stern. "I think you need to learn the same lesson."

"What do you think did this?" she asked, gesturing to her shoulder.

"Your stupidity," he replied swiftly. He turned his gaze resolutely down and ate.

Catie regarded him for a moment, then sat down. He still refused to look up. "You care about them," she said finally. He paused a moment to swallow, and take a drink. His gaze softened, but still did not rise. "And your coat," she said, glancing at the many hides. "Found them left to rot?"

"A wolf doesn't deserve that," he rumbled, his words still not wanting to leave his mouth.

"I saw a pack of them, led apparently by a white wolf," she said. "They were intelligent, self-controlled, and respectful." She paused to let a wry grin surface. "I'm afraid I may have snuck up on them."

"I doubt that, lass," Eidemon said, his eyes finally coming to meet hers. "There's nothing can sneak up on a white wolf. She would have known you were there."

"She certainly seemed surprised. She was holding some sort of—council, it seemed like, with the other wolves."

Eidemon gazed at her, seeing if she was making fun. But her walnut eyes were honest. "Most would find that hard to believe," he said.

"Most don't care about wolves," she replied.

"Why do you?"

"I think they protect something that I'm looking for," she said, leaning closer as she lowered her voice. "I tried to get it last night, but the wolves were there. I need to know how to get past them to get at it."

He looked at her, then glanced around the room. "I've been away a long time—long enough that keeper doesn't recognize me anymore," he said wryly, his voice also quiet, but firm. "But I know they don't want strangers finding what I think you're looking for."

Catie considered him a few moments, then smiled. "Oh, no. I've already found the 'shadowed spark'—"

"It's called gnotglow," Eidemon said.

She cocked her head. "But it does glow," she said.

Eidemon chuckled. "No, *gnot* glow," he repeated, enunciating. "It means 'night glow.' I think the name used to be *nochtglow*, but..."

"Oh. Well, you can keep all that. I'm looking for something a little older and a lot more rare."

"How rare?"

"There are only four of them."

Eidemon whistled. "That is rare. Why do you want them?"

Catie couldn't help but laugh a little. "Because I'm the sunniest girl in Andelen," she replied. Eidemon cocked an eyebrow. She shook her head. "Never mind. I'm just trying to understand wolves, so if there's a way to get around them, I can do it."

"I would find it strange that the wolves are there all the time," Eidemon replied with a shrug. "Just go when they're not there."

Catie drew a breath. "I'm not sure these are normal wolves," she said. *Even though they acted like it last night.* "And I don't want to wait until tomorrow morning. Would you come with me, this time? Then you'll get to see what I'm looking for," she offered.

Eidemon took a last bite, his gaze considering her as he chewed. "Why do you think that will make a difference?"

"What will?"

"Me coming with you."

Catie shrugged. "Because you know them, or it seems like you do," she said. "I tried understanding them last night, and it didn't work."

"They're just animals. You can understand a mountain, but that doesn't make it easier to climb."

"But taking someone with you that knows how to cross the mountain can keep you from dying," Catie replied.

Eidemon smiled. "I'll go with you," he said. "But I think you might do just fine on your own."

They rose. Catie watched as he threw his cloak over his shoulders. When he turned back, she managed to put on a smile. She *had* seen him before, long ago in Aresmak. She couldn't help but wonder if his mercenary friend had been Gabriel. *That would be a coincidence for the ages,* she thought as she led the way out of the inn. Even if that weren't the case, he had lived here, but had also lived in the south, and she could not know how he felt about Roth or Sheppar. Either way, he might misinterpret her seeking out the Berkarfor—want her either to give them to Roth, though she intended no such thing, or not want her to, even though she intended no such thing.

The further I go, the more I step right in it.

Give him a chance.

Without a weapon of some sort. And with an injured shoulder.

He is weaponless too. And you don't want to approach a wolf with a bared blade. They don't understand that.

Catie sighed, heading west. The sawdust smell of the mills gave way to the paler scent of leaf and wood, both living and decaying. Breezes today were light. She looked around the darkening wood, suddenly unsure if she could find her way back. She had roved a circle last night, starting from the south, and she couldn't quite remember how long she had followed the wolf before reaching the council.

But Eidemon was beside her, making no comment. Surely if she was going the wrong way, he would say something. He glanced at her, and something in his look confirmed it.

"You know a lot more than you let on, don't you?" she asked, her voice hushed, though the sawing and felling of trees by lumberjacks using the last of the daylight was loud enough to mask it.

"No," he replied, eyes twinkling for a moment before going flat again. *Caution to the wind.* "Do you know what I'm looking for?"

"No," he said again, with the same brief twinkle.

"But you know why I'm looking for it."

Eidemon was silent, his eyes roving through the trees. "I once heard someone in a green hood speak out against a powerful person, in the presence of his followers. I thought they were stupid." His roving eyes came to rest on her. "But I also thought it was a man. There's your wolf," he said, flicking his eyes forward.

Catie looked up, seeing the wolf paused in mid-stride as it regarded the two of them. The sounds told her the lumberjacks were in far off other-reaches, almost as if they knew to stay away from this place. Which made sense, if they were so protective of their gnotglow.

The wolf considered both of them for a moment before continuing on its way. Eidemon followed, and Catie followed him. The wolf would pass behind a tree, stop to see if they still followed, and continue on.

Then, as they entered a nearly silent part of the woods and night fell, the white wolf appeared, sitting on the same gnotglow-covered tree stump.

You came back.

Catie blinked in surprise. *You* can *talk to me? Why didn't you do that last night?*

You didn't ask, you only pushed. And I didn't know you. But I knew if you returned unarmed, you were to be trusted. I didn't imagine you would bring The Hunter with you.

Catie swallowed. *I didn't know he was a hunter. I'm sorry.*

The white wolf's mouth opened in what seemed to be a smile. *He doesn't hunt us. He hunts with us.*

Is he...I mean, I've read stories...

Too many stories. No, he is human, which is why he looks at the both of us with such curiosity.

Catie glanced quickly. Eidemon indeed looked perplexedly between the two of them, as if realizing there was a conversation going on that he could not hear.

And why can I talk to you?

White's mouth closed, and her head cocked. *If you do not know, I do not believe I am to tell you.*

Because I'm a wyvern?

White glanced her over, and Catie felt amusement coming from her. *You do not have wings, scales, or claws. No, I do not think you are wyvern.*

That's not what I meant.

A low growl came from the wolf. *Are you abandoning, then, what you came out here for? What your shoulder was torn for? What two of my sons died for?*

Catie's gaze dropped. *I'm sorry,* she said again. *I didn't want them to be killed—not really.*

White settled herself a little. *They were not supposed to. But they did not do exactly what they were told. Even wolf younglings are often wise only in their own eyes.*

We are almost always wise only in our own eyes, Catie replied. *I'm out here because someone sent me who thinks he is wise. Maybe I'm only here because I think I am wiser.*

And why is that?

Catie sighed. *I think, because Roth attacks Sheppar because he believes he is right to; but Sheppar, in doing what he thinks is right, attacks no one. Violence may sometimes need to be met with violence. But I don't understand meeting peace with violence.*

Then you have learned something that many animals know, White replied. *And for that, I will teach you what no one else knows. Come to me, and look in the hollow of this stump.*

Catie hesitated, then walked forward. The white wolf, she realized as she drew nearer, was *massive,* even recognizing she was elevated on a stump. Had Catie seen her running through the forest, she might have feared for her life. But now, Catie glanced down as she drew near, looking only for the hollow White had spoken of, and not at the great shaggy beast towering over her.

At the base, directly below the great wolf, was a dark hole a little bigger around than Catie's fist, black in the middle of the effusive gnotglow that lit the stump as if it were on fire. She glanced at White, then back down.

Inside.

Catie knelt down as White watched. Reaching inside, she felt only earth. Her fingers searched, and she worked her arm farther in, until…

There. She felt the round hardness of the goblet, though the surface was rough. Found the stem and gripped, and pulled it from the stump. In the light of the lichen, she saw the cloth wrapped around the cup, and removed it. This was carved from Tiger's Eye, polished smooth with crystalline white lines between the brown and refracting even the faint orange glow of the lichen. Inside its cup was the rolled parchment she expected.

She looked again at White. *Thank you,* she said, bowing her head.

White bowed her own. *Thank you,* she replied. Catie felt her amusement again. *Now I can go back to a normal life, without protecting this stump for all time.* With that, the great wolf turned and bounded away. As she faded from the light of the gnotglow, Catie could see the rest of the pack detach from the trees where they had hidden, and follow.

Catie unrolled the parchment, reading it in glow-light as Eidemon approached.

"Why do you bother?" he asked. "Even with the lichen it's too dark."

She glanced quickly at him, then back down. She could read it clearly enough. She just couldn't understand it:

"Where a man could starve surrounded by food;
another die of thirst surrounded by water;
below, there mirrors the dancing rings;
the line is drawn between the kings:
the urchin and the otter."

Eidemon looked at her, eyebrows raised. "You have to figure out where that is to find the fourth?"

"This one is harder than the rest," she admitted, frowning at the parchment.

"You sure you read it right?"

"I can see pretty well, Eidemon," she said.

"And speak to wolves, if I'm not mistaken."

"It seems so." Catie rolled up the parchment, the words still etched into her mind's eye, and tucked it into the goblet. She took a breath. "I wish Deuel was here," she said, turning toward Ethfirlaf with a glance at Eidemon.

"Is this what Roth sent those three out to get?"

She nodded.

"I don't understand Gabriel leaving his mission," he said as they walked back to town. "How many years I've known him, he's always finished the job."

"And Deuel was probably always with him, right?"

Eidemon cocked an eyebrow. "Do you mean they're not?"

Catie shook her head. "Gabriel is in Attelek. Deuel is headed to Balnath." She stopped suddenly, not sure if she should have mentioned *exactly* where Deuel was going.

"Off to see the Kinnig, is he?" The old wolf man chuckled. "I suppose it was about time."

"You knew about that, then?"

"Gabriel and I served together, back then," Eidemon said. "Not always side-by-side, but we kept up. I got to know Deuel pretty well, too, and if he's headed to Balnath to see Sheppar..." Eidemon shrugged. "Do you plan to join him there, once you've found the fourth?" he asked suddenly.

Catie bit her lip, her gaze on the ground in front of her. "I think, if I can," she replied quietly. "He may need my help."

Eidemon stopped, casting a glance toward Ethfirlaf before leaning in close to her. "How much help do you think he'll need?" he asked.

Catie hesitated. She knew Deuel didn't want everyone to know what was near there—wasn't sure *she* was supposed to know. But if Eidemon knew him, and Gabriel, if they had been close, at all? "I think there is a very serious threat against Sheppar," she said. "Deuel may get caught up in it. That's all."

Eidemon's eyes searched hers for several long moments. Finally, he nodded. "You do well," he said. "That is a very close secret, one which I've kept for years as well." He paused, his eyes growing distant. He straightened, and focused. "The ocean," he said, with a smile.

Catie blinked. "What?"

"Where a man can die of thirst, surrounded by water."

She looked at him and drew a deep breath. "Well, that makes it easy," she said, easing her tone with a grin. "Anything else?"

Eidemon shook his head. "Never much cared for the ocean, so I didn't visit it much. You'll be okay. It's probably in a port, not just out in the middle of the water. Try Ostflir, it's closest."

Catie groaned a chuckle. "Thanks," she said. "It's probably in Satost, to teach me patience."

He laughed, and she laughed too as they continued into Ethfirlaf.

19

LIGHT SONG

"I hope I'm not being too obvious."
"You must learn by doing."
"I'm not sure that helps."
"We guide them, Teresh, not each other."

5 Savimon 1320 — Summer

Rodigger shifted in his saddle, trying to not cast another glance at Sharéd. They were in another of their long silences—days long, this one. Sharéd spoke, certainly, but only to innkeepers, and only when Rodigger refused to. They exchanged few words.

It didn't help, either, they were on the exact same road they had traveled to get here. If he had to spend another month in northern Andelen, they might have gone through the Brithelt, just to see it. But no, Sharéd always wanted to make time. Rodigger shuddered to think what would happen when his Therian reached the mountains.

"Are all your people gathered here already?" he asked, striking upon another idea.

Sharéd glanced at him, almost startled he had spoken, then looked away. "Enough."

"Are more supposed to be coming, though?" he pressed.

"They might."

Rodigger could tell the Beltrath was getting testy. "I just mean, I mean, better more than enough, than less, right? Can we be sure these behamien will be easy to take?"

"If they are in *veythya*—"

"But what if they're not? I think we should get everyone ready, and keep training until some more come," Rodigger said in his best Roth voice. "Really go after their stronghold in force."

Sharéd said nothing as they continued to ride. Rodigger thought he saw a shadow move quickly in the corner of his eye. But as he turned to look, Sharéd's stare distracted him. "What?" he asked.

"Why delay now? A week ago you were..." He gestured a flapping motion with his hand. "*Pamdras.* Now..." He sneered and went silent.

"The mountains are difficult, Sharéd," Rodigger replied. "They might be able to watch us approach from a hundred different directions."

"What do then suggest?" Sharéd asked, facing forward again.

"We approach from a hundred different directions," Rodigger replied with a grin. "We should send out some scouts, first, and find where they hide. Then bring our troops up through as many avenues as possible, until the last possible moment."

Sharéd sniffed. He reached down and took a water skin, uncapping it and drinking a few sips. When he capped it again, he glanced quickly at Rodigger. "I think this is a good plan," he murmured.

Rodigger smiled. He thought it was a good plan, too.

—◆—

Catie rode out of Ethfirlaf, saddlebags repacked for another week on the road. That would get her back to Finstaff. Then it was the longer road east to Ostflir, the great port of northern Andelen. Anything from overseas making its way to Balnath Agrend, and almost everything leaving Andelen for the Clanaso Islands and eastward, went through that port. It was a broad ocean between the continent and the Islands, and she hoped somewhere in that expanse of water to find a cup. She almost never could believe the tasks she set up for herself.

And yet, as she glanced down, she remembered that she had already found three goblets that had remained hidden for centuries. It was not the first time they had been hunted. In fact, they had been hunted enough that most were convinced the Berkarfor were legends—for surely nothing hidden could be so hard to find. It almost didn't bother her that she had lost one to Rodigger. He would be easier to find than a cave hidden beneath a lake, right?

And yet here she was, loathing the long journey to Ostflir for the last one. How many before her would have done backflips of joy for finding three of what everyone said didn't exist? To have faced down a *snehr-byor,* two Wendol, a massive white wolf... She wondered what waited ahead of her. The riddle didn't quite say. Unless it was a massive otter that would break her over whatever it meant by 'urchin.' No matter the guardian, history suggested she would overcome that, too. And she had her dagger, now. *Saferd* might have been a better word—longer than a dagger but smaller than a short sword, with saw teeth along the back edge from tip to about half-way back, and a hook for sword-breaking. It was called a Nagrath dagger because, according to legend, no one could survive the Nagrath Highlands with anything smaller. Her father had taught her to use it because it was wieldy from a young age, almost as if he had known he would leave before she was old enough to be taught by him on a true sword. She remembered asking Grandmother about that, long ago. But Grandmother had only smiled a sorrowful smile and said sometimes folks knew, without knowing.

Catie picked up her reins and clicked Kelsie into a fast trot. It was a beautiful day for riding through the trees, and she intended to enjoy it.

⸺◆⸺

As the month closed, Catie found herself atop a small knoll, finally look-ing down the long road into Ostflir below. After so long on the road and at inns, the size of the port surprised her. Tall square buildings crowded the wharf, spreading out and up a broad bowl like sheep bedding down for the night. Great arms of land, bristling with more shops and homes, held the flat, gray-watered bay in a loose embrace. Far out on the points, barely visible at this distance, were look-out towers. Beyond that lay green, unsettled ocean, and a ship full of sails making its way in.

The breeze gusted, overflowing with salt and spices and animal and people smells, and, fainter, the cry of barterers and a white bird she didn't recognize. Clattering wagons and lowing oxen, eager for rest, passed her by on their way into town.

As she gazed between land, sea, and sky, she thought she might actually prefer looking for the last Berkarfor on the sea, rather than in Ostflir. One of those ancients could easily have stuck it in someone's house, and it would never be found by someone actively looking for it.

She pulled out the parchment—it had become a daily habit since Hyalendel—and looked over it again, then up at Ostflir. *Where a man could starve surrounded by food. An expensive inn?* She grinned. Probably not that. Somewhere food was visible, but not attainable. She glanced down again. What if two lines referred to the same place? *Surrounded by inaccessible food and water...fish, and saltwater.* As she gazed out over the vista, her grin faded. If it was actually in the sea, she could swim, she knew that. But what was she supposed to do, dive down over and over again until she found it? More likely it would be so dark she wouldn't be able to see it. But then, strange lights attended every other Berkarfor: blue light in Agirbirt, brown light in Kavlen, orange light in Ethfirlaf. Maybe light wouldn't be a problem, but a clue.

She would still need to breathe, somehow. And she would need to know where to dive. For now, the sun was failing behind her. She tucked the parchment away and began riding for town. *The line is drawn be-*

tween the kings: the urchin and the otter. So, she would find a boat to take her out into the ocean until she saw an urchin and an otter, dive down between them, there would be some magical light, and a goblet. And a guardian, of some sort. Then she would travel back across Andelen, find Deuel, and...then...do something else with her life.

Simple. It was always so simple.

She found an inn, and sat in the common room trying to overhear conversations. Each goblet also was tied to the history of its hiding place, and she assumed Ostflir would be no different. But most of the people here were foreigners, only passing through, and most of the conversation seemed to surround trade and trading routes. She finished her dinner—fish, of course; there was abundant supply just on the horizon—and went to bed. Staying at one inn would probably not serve her well.

The next morning she went out to the docks. Clouds hung low and threatened a drizzle that never quite formed, but always seemed like it did. Even the birds—seagulls, someone told her with a grimace—didn't seem to want to go into the air today, bouncing in their fast-footed walk and peering at the interlopers who carried boxes and bundles and sacks and jars and hopes for a brighter future.

Well, most of the interlopers seemed to carry those hopes. As After-Noon came, Catie began to discern another group of people. These went about the docks quiet, reserved, undistracted, usually in light linens and heavy-soled sandals, and deep tans. Fishers. Men whose home would be Ostflir. Men who would have their own boats.

"Excuse me," she said to one with a beard as white as foam and more wrinkles on his face than Agirbirt on a windy day; "My name's Catie. I might need a boat ride one day. Soon," she added hurriedly as his face scrunched in puzzlement. "Would there be a boat I could pay to ride out on, just for a day?"

"Will it stop me fishin'?"

Catie thought a moment. "Not necessarily, but I would need to go to a specific spot."

"Which spot?"

Another thought. "Between the kings?" she said.

A grin split his face. "Lots of those, dearie." He gestured a hand loosely indicating the waters behind him. "Magiss a hunnerd years ago set up kings at every compass of the bay."

She craned her head, looking along the wharf wherever a ship didn't block her view. She could see the statues, now, standing at the ends of prominent piers and gazing across the water at one another. At least it meant she shouldn't need to leave the bay.

"What's an urchin?" she asked.

"Sea urchin?"

She shrugged. "Sure."

"Spiny things, 'bout yea big. You hungry?"

She shook her head. "Not really. You can eat them?"

"You can. Not very filling, so they ain't cheap usually. And they're harder and harder to find, anymore. Otters always seem to get 'em."

"In the bay?" Simple. It was always so simple.

The fisher laughed. "Not anymore, too many ships chased 'em out, I think. Further down the coast, though. Is that where you want to go? See you some otters?"

She smiled faintly: not that simple. "No, I don't think so. I'm not sure yet. But I'll come find you whenever I'm sure. What's your name?"

"Pag," he said. "If you get here early enough, I'm usually at Gart's dock, that way," he said, gesturing.

"Perfect. Thanks," she said with a smile. "Oh! How much will you want, if I want you to take me somewhere you can't fish?"

"A day's catch brings me twenty, thirty coin, most days."

"Oh," she said, managing to keep her hand from straying to her coin purse. "Thanks. Hopefully I'll see you again soon."

She returned to town, to a different inn this time: Fishers and Crowns, it named itself. It was closer to the docks, where Catie hoped sailors who lived in Ostflir might patronize on their way home at night. After paying for her room and dinner, she tucked her purse away and pulled out her flute.

In Ostflir, it became apparent, patrons paid the musician directly, instead of through the keeper. Also in Ostflir, people were tighter with their coin than in most of the villages where she had tried this before. She played everything she could think of, as lively as she could manage. But as Evening wore on she still had only a few glints in the cloak she had placed on the floor to catch the thrown coins—the first few had bounced away and into untold recesses of the room before she thought of putting something down to catch them.

Finally, late at night when the patrons were sufficiently drunk, one shouted out: "play one we know, already!"

"What would you like?" she asked. He laughed lewdly, joined quickly by the others equally drunk as he. "What song!" she groaned over their racket.

The first drunk glanced around, an evil light coming to his eyes. "Liebast!" he said suddenly, and the laughter started again. "Sing the one about Liebast!" The others quickly joined him, hoisting their mugs.

"Ho hey! Liebast!"

They began singing, then, a shanty about someone named Liebast, apparently known for his exploits with women. Catie sighed, looking toward the keeper. He was talking aside to a man with a lute-case on his back, and presumably a lute inside the case. They both glanced at Catie, then to each other and nodded.

Catie glanced back to the patrons. She didn't know the song—happily, she thought—but she hadn't made nearly enough yet. Fortunately, it was a shanty, and she had already picked up the tune.

She raised her Tamis flute and joined in, following the melody with the deep reed and highlighting the jokes with peeps and whistles on the short reed. The patrons howled with laughter, and a few more coins arced her way.

At first she tried to ignore the words, suggestive as they were, but the more she tried to anticipate the wordplay, the more she had to pay attention.

Liebast had been a king of Andelen, apparently, who sired an untold and untellable number of children as he copulated his way through the breadth of Ostflir to the ocean. There he died, drowned in ecstasy, beer, and seawater, so worn out from his activities that he couldn't keep his head up for breath or women as the tide came in. Though history named him one of the greatest kings, and elevated him to the very pinnacle of the heights of Ostflir, true natives knew him—as the song ended—as a man "so prickled out from ten days of nights, that he lives in paradise *kal-fites.*"

Catie smiled faintly as the laughter galed over her. She had no idea what the last term meant, but they seemed to think it was hilarious. She glanced down at her cloak. There were enough shiny bits gleaming in the folds to last her, so she gave the stage to the lutist, gathered up her things, and went to her room.

She went again to the docks the next morning, hoping to find something on the statues of the kings, or maybe pick up more conversation about Ostflir itself that might help. Down in the heart of things, the incessant noises common to the sea seemed to fade into the background. The sailors shouting, feet running along the wooden piers, the various creaking and thumping of boats that rocked together, avian cries—all became part of a music so prolonged it faded as if into silence. Catie focused instead on making her way to each dock, studying the plinths and statues for some sort of resemblance to the riddle-poem.

As Noon approached, she saw another great ship as she wandered, coming into the bay through the watchtowers. This one looked a little different, somehow. More aged, perhaps, and the cut and number of its sails were different from what filled the rest of the wharf.

Smaller boats went out to greet it, and guided it toward the dock where she stood. She realized it might get very busy very soon, but she hadn't made it to the king standing at the end yet, so she backed as hard as she could against a stack of boxes and tried to stay out of the way. Dock-men moved past her, preparing to receive the ship. She startled as something slippery brushed past: it reminded her of a fish, a little, or maybe a frog except it was upright and only a little shorter than her. It wore only a loincloth, and a band of blue wire on its left arm. It seemed to move a little less surely than the others on the dock, and kept its head down. She wondered what it was, but didn't have the time to ask as the ship drew nearer, catching her attention again.

Sailors scrambled through the rigging, drawing sail and letting the oared boats move their ship. A few folk gathered along the rail: apparently a cargo ship that also took passengers—she had seen it before, but it was uncommon. Most of the passengers lining the rail were not Rinc Nain. They had black or brown or yellow-white hair—she had no idea what nation had yellow-white hair. Lots of strange things to see in an international port, she thought absently. There were two, though, that were Rinc Nain: a lady, it appeared by her rich blue dress and posture. And her attendant, though the poor man was missing his left arm below the bicep.

Ropes leapt from the side, and dock-men hurried to tie off the ship. Gangplanks ran out, and the passengers offloaded first. Catie kept her eyes on the two Rinc Nain, watching as they descended but didn't seem to know where to go. The lady spotted Catie and approached.

"Do you know where we might stay for a night? And we'll need horses."

Catie smiled. "I'm sorry, I'm new here too. Well, newer. Just don't stay at Fishers and Crowns, lady. I don't think you'll appreciate it there."

The pair smiled, and glanced at each other as if sharing a joke. "I'm not a lady," she said. "But I thank you for your advice."

They turned and moved away, their heads together in conversation that looked closer than a lady and her attendant. Catie wondered what the joke had been. Maybe she was called a lady despite her protests for the entire journey from whatever port she had come from. Catie smiled as she remembered Geezer's words.

"Ready to go yet?" came a familiar voice. Catie turned, and glanced down toward the water. Pag sat in his boat gently rocking, squinting up at her. He had been one of those guiding the ship in.

"I thought you were only a fisher?" she asked.

"I take what comes," he said. "They were headed my way, and it's easy coin. Where to?"

Catie grimaced. "I still don't know," she replied. "And even if I did know, I'm not sure I can get to it."

Pag continued to squint. "But you know it's by boat."

"Well, it might be in the water. Deep, in the water."

"And you can't swim?"

"No, I can. I grew up in a small fishing village on a lake."

Pag drew a breath. "I've been on easier fishing trips than trying to get answers from you, girl," he said. "You know you need to get somewhere on a boat, but you don't know where. You know you might need to swim, and you can, but you can't. No wonder you young kids never get anything done."

"It's a very long, very complicated story," Catie said. "And the answers might bring more questions than they solve."

"Well, you dodged that net," Pag growled. "It's a large bay. Get in, and you can tell me all about it while I row."

Catie blinked. Why not. She squatted onto the dock and sat, then lowered herself into his boat. He seemed to eye her praisingly as she kept the rocking to a minimum. "I said I grew up in a fishing village," she said as she sat down.

Pag said nothing, but pushed them off with the oar and slipped it into the lock in one smooth motion. He pulled them away. Catie unlocked the tiller, looped her arm over it, and steered as a smile came to her face. It had been some time since she'd been on the water, and she had forgotten how it felt.

As he pulled, he began muttering a song in time. Catie cocked her head. "What language is that?" she asked. It wasn't Rinc Nain.

"Old Clansmen," he said. "I guess we picked it up on our way through those islands, and some of it stuck."

"And what does *kal-fites* mean?" she asked.

Pag chuckled. "Again with the sea urchins?"

Catie stared hard at him. "Which one is King Liebast?" she asked, gesturing to the statues.

"Ah, him. Poor man never had a chance. Well, most folks coming into port don't even know their kings, so I guess it doesn't matter. He's the one on the left," he said, jerking his head toward the twin arms making the mouth of the bay.

"Who's on the right?"

"King Tareddor. Longer ago than Liebast. Swam the bay around in one go, because someone said he couldn't."

"So he was a good swimmer?"

"Could you swim around this?" Pag asked with raised eyebrows.

Catie's head swiveled. She didn't even want to *walk* around it. "As good as an otter?"

Pag frowned. "Now you mention it, they did call him The Otter. How about that?"

"Yeah," Catie said, glancing toward the watchtowers, on which stood The Urchin and The Otter. "How about that."

"That's where you want to go?" he asked.

Catie nodded, adjusting the tiller. It was still a broad mouth, even if you drew a line between it. That left one more line: *below, there mirrors the dancing rings.* Somewhere along that line, she hoped, would be something of an image of dancing rings.

Pag rowed her along the line, then patiently across again. But she saw no rings, and certainly no dancing. She sighed, looking out to sea. The sun was high overhead. It was a clear, hot day, and though she did the least work, she was beginning to sweat. And it was lunch time. *Surrounded by food,* she thought, and looked down into the water again. It would be supremely foolish to just start diving down, hoping to see something under the waves.

"Are there any sunken ships down there?" she asked.

"Probably," Pag said. "This harbor mouth looks wide, but come at it in the night, in a storm, maybe one of the watchtowers' lights has snuffed out?" He shrugged.

"But none you know of for certain," she said.

Pag shook his head, resting on his oars. They sat without speaking. The locks clicked and groaned as the boat rocked. The waves slurped against the side of the boat. But it was otherwise a sort of silence, as if the world waited for her to solve the riddle.

"I'm hungry," she muttered at length. She rarely could think while she was hungry, and she had been growing tired of the silence, too.

"You didn't bring anything?" Pag asked. Her gaze was so close on the water she didn't see the sparkle in his eyes.

"I didn't know I'd be out here right now," she replied, a little snappier than she had meant to.

"Here," he said. "I always bring extra." He held out a cloth wrapping. She sat up and looked at him warily.

"Fish?" she asked. She'd had more than she thought was enough, the past few days in Ostflir.

"Imagine it's chicken," he said, giving the wrap a quick shake.

She took it. "Thanks," she said, pulling back the layers. It did look like chicken, but it smelled...fishier. "What is it?"

Pag held a finger to his lips, and leaned forward with the same finger held pointing upward. "It's seagull," he whispered.

Catie glanced up. Gulls were circling overhead, their cries blending with the rest of the music so she had forgotten they were there. She smiled. Most people would be so concerned with the food so obviously below them, they wouldn't think there might be food above.

Her smile froze. Surrounded by food. Music meant dancing, and circles were like rings. She glanced away. The gulls swooped above the boat, but not above the water anywhere else. She looked down into the boat, expecting to see the Berkarfor there, maybe dredged up in a net and forgotten.

"I told you to imagine it was chicken," Pag said defensively.

"No, it's..." she trailed off, looking down into the water. How deep was it, here? Deep enough to let ships pass. Too deep to dive?

"Going in?" he asked, beginning to understand.

"I think so," she said, trying to calm her breath. She needed to relax, if she wanted to hold it for any length of time. But something held her back, seemed to tell her the goblet wasn't there.

Below, there mirrors the dancing rings.

Mirrors weren't the object, they reflected the object. Below mirrored above. She looked up, squinting as the sun dazzled her with its brilliant white.

Blue light. Brown light. Orange light...white light?

She blinked, sitting back a little. What did the colors mean? Why would white come after orange?

It wasn't the color. It was the light shining through: water, earth, fire...and air.

She shaded her eyes and looked up again. The gulls still circled, still cried, but something wasn't right. They weren't looking for food, weren't landing on the water or flying away. They were just there—had seemed to be there without warning. And they were definitely too high to grab.

She reached out, trying to sense their little bird brains. Maybe she needed to communicate with them, like she did the other guardians. But it was as if nothing was there. Not that there wasn't something to communicate with, but literally as if the gulls didn't exist. Like she was imagining things.

To come this close, and yet seem so far, to have spent so many months searching, solving puzzles, learning, growing, sympathizing, forcing herself far, far outside the places she felt comfortable. Allowing herself the concept of forgiving Roth, of letting go of what happened, because she wanted to be *better*—better than she was yesterday, and better tomorrow than she was today. And to reach this point, and be stuck yet again? What was it all for? Catie sighed. She truly believed the Berkarfor were to be sought, not acquired. But how was she to know if she had actually found it, unless she saw it? She needed to know. She needed to see it. If only she could bring the birds down closer. Call them, somehow.

Catie pulled out her Tamis flute almost reverently. She looked up at the gulls, and began to play like the birds in Ethfirlaf, in the Brithelt. After all, Tamis had created the flute to attract the birds back to the devastated forest. Maybe she could use it to attract the seagulls lower.

She listened to their cries, tried to mimic them but more soothingly. Still they circled, not looking, not even seeming to exist except Pag had seen them, too. She continued playing, trying to ignore Pag's look as if she were losing her mind. She knew that what she sought was there, and didn't care how she looked trying to attain it. It had to be there. Right?

After a few more moments, just as her hopes splintered, one of the gulls swooped lower, drawn by the music. It came down, wings spread, landing perfectly on the gunwale, its eyes piercing Catie's.

On its back it carried a goblet of a crystal so clear it seemed invisible but for the occasional swirl of rainbow light across its surface, or the refracted sparkles reflecting off the water's surface as if it were encrusted with a thousand diamonds. Lowering the flute, she reached out, and grasped it.

Blinding white light struck her. Or, it seemed like it should have been blinding, but it didn't hurt—it seemed rather to heal. It seeped into her like water into a cloth, spreading along every fiber, into every corner of her mind, soul, and body. It flashed, *becoming* her mind, soul, and body. She drifted away, above Ostflir, above Andelen. She could see the Clanaso Islands like dots, Gintanos farther south like a god's smoke-pipe. The Pal Isans. Rinc Na like a two-headed beast. Carist south like tussling kittens. She could see the breadth of Oren, stars, great clusters of stars, thin clouds of brilliant green and red and orange with more stars in them—drawing further and further back until even those seemed tiny and insignificant. And then there was only the great ponderous bulk of time, shrinking and wrapping and crumpling up until a thousand years ago was yesterday, and two thousand years into the future was only tomorrow.

She paused there in utter stillness. She would have fainted except for the brilliant light becoming her and keeping her together. The great expanse of world and stars and clouds and time began drawing a breath, slowly, as if fearing that too sharp an intake would shatter everything. A hum grew, the beginning of a note of music too sweet to release. She wanted desperately for that note to release, to sound across the world and across time, knowing it would begin the purest melody ever created. The bow was on the string; the hairs drew across it in anticipation.

But the bow lacked sufficient hairs to vibrate the string. The note could not be made. To strike now would be to destroy everything with a pitch-less keen. In the stillness she knew the light that had become her had created her first, could shape her into an adjoining hair. That when enough others joined her and the time was fulfilled, they could start the note that would start the tune. But she had to let herself be shaped, drawn tight, and pressed hard against the other strings. As she imagined the note that might be sounded, realized her wildest imaginations did not even equal the fourth part of the hum she heard now, she yearned for it. Begged for it. Pleaded for the chance to be part of the making of the melody.

The drawing breath ceased. The note retreated from the cusp, and Catie fell from the stillness. Great thin clouds, and stars, and continents, and Andelen, and Ostflir, and Pag's boat, and the 34th day of Savimon rushed toward her.

Suddenly she held the goblet. The seagull and the light were gone. And Pag looked at her closely as she wept without restraint.

20

THREADS GATHERING

"I didn't know they could do that."
"She is definitely the first to do it while alive."
"What does that mean?"
"...I'm not sure."

1 Fulmatung 1320 — Summer

Catie sat on her bed, trying to remember yesterday. She knew it had felt real, as if she had truly been there, had seen Oren and stars as if from an unfathomable height. Now, reaching back in her memory, it felt more like remembering a dream. Which, truly, made more sense.

The Berkarfor were real, though. She had three of them arranged on her trunk. They could have hidden them in houses, nondescript as they were, just clay, wood, and steel. She thought for a moment the first had been silver, wondered what it looked like now. She hadn't looked at any of them that closely lately. Maybe that had been the steel one. No, that was the one she had just found. A mirror, like the riddle had said. Wood from a stump, clay from a cave. Just cups. Perhaps someone would have thrown them away, if not hidden.

She sighed, scratching an itch on her foot. She still wanted to find Deuel.

The thought, innocent as it had seemed, surged through her. She needed to find him. There were things to be done—too many things. Deuel, Roth, Sheppar, Rodigger, Gabriel: so many people she knew, so many that needed to join the song.

But even as she considered them, she felt it wasn't right. She needed to go...somewhere. But why? She paused, one leg swung off the bed. She didn't know. It was the same sense she had gotten in the grass outside Akervet. There had been a voice, she thought, while time was unfolding and uncrinkling and flattening back out to normal and depositing her into yesterday again. What had it said? She closed her eyes, trying to remember the dream. *Remember the Ekllar?* And yet, it was not her who heard it, it was someone in the future. Was she going to say it to someone? What was an Ekllar?

There had been another memory too, one she did not try so hard to remember. A memory of wyverns in the sky, of her flying with them. She was not settled on that life, just yet. There seemed too much to do, first.

She shook her head. Maybe something had been in the seagull she ate. She stood and pulled on her shirt. When her head came out the top, she saw the goblets arranged on the trunk. No. It had been real, and it had something to do with seeking—not finding; seeking—the Berkarfor.

And now she needed to find Deuel, and then go...somewhere. Time was...she almost thought *of the essence,* but time was not the master. She would move with purpose, not impatience. *I have a purpose.* She smiled with a mix of joy and duty. She had a purpose, and she would fulfill it. Whatever it was.

As she rode out under blue skies, she passed a convoy on its way down Great Merchant Road. The sun was rising clear of the watchtowers, the two kings, light filling the harbor.

"Are you following us?" a pleasant voice asked.

Catie startled forward, a quick denial on her lips that never left. It was the lady and her attendant from the ship.

"Oh, no!" she said brightly. "I'm just leaving the same time as you, I guess."

The lady—woman—smiled. "So are a lot of people, it seems."

"Well, a lot of cargo comes into Andelen through here."

"I've been cargo for far too long now," the woman said. "It could have been made a little faster a trip," she added, with a sidelong glance at her attendant-companion.

"If I had known it would be so hard for you to give up, I would have left you to it," the man replied. Though his voice rumbled, Catie could tell he wasn't in earnest. She felt like playing along anyway.

"Seems like men never leave women to it," she said lightly. "We always have to give things up for a man's demand."

"Oh I didn't do it for him," the woman said, her voice now sincere, and low. She took a breath and smiled. "He just happened to be right, this time."

"My name's Catie," she said. "If we're going to be traveling together a while."

"Sarah," said the woman.

"Geoffrey."

"What brings you to Andelen?"

"A friend asked me to come," Sarah said. "Geoffrey decided to come with me."

"I'm sorry, I was trying to figure out if he was your attendant, or someone," Catie said.

"Just a long-time and very good companion," Sarah replied. "We've been through a lot together."

"Oh." Catie managed to hold her smile in place. "I had one of those, not too long ago."

Sarah's smile faded. "I'm so sorry. What happened?"

"Oh, that sounded bad! He's alive, I think. I'm pretty sure. He's..." She trailed off and laughed. "He's very good."

Sarah looked at her with an arched eyebrow and chuckled. "Is he indeed?"

"He just had something he needed to do, east. In Balnath."

"Are you headed there to meet back with him?"

"I hope so. I'll have to find him, though."

"Then perhaps we *will* be traveling together a while," Sarah said. "We're headed there as well."

"With the convoy?" Catie asked.

"Well, it's been some time since I've been here," Sarah replied. "Unless Geoffrey remembers the country better, I'd like to stay with people who know it."

Geoffrey shook his head. "I did not explore very much," he replied. "When I was here, I was mostly concerned with heading south."

"Well, I'll be taking a different road when we get to Corsred," Catie said. "The convoy will head down Gathering Road—there's more to trade along the way, and it follows the water. But there's a faster route for riders on Forest Highland Road toward Mihrlandhen we could take, if you're interested."

Sarah glanced at Geoffrey, who shrugged and nodded. "We've been awhile at sea," Sarah said. "It might be well to make up some time. We're not sure how quickly Sheppar needed me to come."

Catie's eyes went wide as Sarah's mouth went thin. "Shep—" Catie cut herself off, glancing at the wagoners they rode among. She eased Kelsie a little closer. "Your 'friend' is the kinnig of Andelen?" she whispered fiercely.

Sarah sighed. Geoffrey rolled his eyes and gazed at her expectantly. Playfully. "Not exactly," she replied quietly. "One of the rulers in Burieng is, and I am his friend. He asked me to come and see what I could do."

"What can you do?" Catie's hand went to her mouth. "I'm sorry, that sounded mean."

Sarah laughed. "I understand. When I was asked, I had...other abilities. Now?" She shrugged. "Geoffrey and I have been through a lot. We might be able to give him counsel."

Catie sat back. "He probably needed it more, about a year ago." She glanced between the two companions. "Is that what you gave up? Your wind magic?"

Sarah glanced at her, a new light in her eyes. "It was. How did you know?"

"I guessed. Wind magic would have helped you sail here faster, you're wearing a blue cloak like I imagined a wind-user would, and you look..." Catie trailed off, but was plainly looking at her face.

"I'm a little older than Geoffrey," Sarah affirmed. "Maybe you'll be able to give counsel to Sheppar as well."

Catie gave a thin smile. "Could be," she said. "I've been through a lot, too."

◆

Sheppar glanced up from the lilies as Samdar approached, a scroll clutched in the aide's hand. It was the third, and the latest, so it must have come from Merneset. If he was honest, he was a little more than curious about the relationships between the peoples represented there. Even twenty years ago, at the height of tensions, it was commendable that a Rinc Nain town within the Wastes managed to survive. If this recent incursion was in retaliation for the campaign, he would have thought Merneset would have been the first to go.

"Yes, Samdar?" he asked.

"It's from Lukens," he said. "Captain of the guard there after Jochavel retired last year. They've had no problems, have not seen any marked increase or decrease in gate passes to Beltraths. Prices on the streets are a little higher than normal, but there's rumors that a few of the springs have failed, and maybe some sort of blight on goats."

"So he believes everything is fine," Sheppar asked. Samdar nodded. Sheppar sighed. "How old is Lukens?" he asked.

"Oh, his father served with you in your campaign, my lord," Samdar replied. "He was a good man. Led the 4th Heavy in the Tevorbath."

"Ah yes, General Lukens," Sheppar said, smiling at his lilies. "I thought the name sounded familiar. His son's a good man?"

"I haven't heard any bad reports, my lord."

"Hmm. Beltraths in Merneset are charging more, and their water is scarcer in a land already made scarcer by us. They probably don't have milk, and less meat, because their goats are dying. And Guard Captain Lukens—son of General Lukens who helped drive Garedardan, whom many people worshipped, out of the Tevorbath—Captain Lukens doesn't perceive there to be a problem." Sheppar bent down and breathed deep of the rich, sticky scent of the lilies.

"Um, my lord..." Samdar began, spreading a hand wide.

Sheppar stood. "Send a message back to relieve Captain Lukens at once. Order patrols around Balnath Agrend, and especially into the Dragon's Eye itself. And send one detachment to Kostet's." He paused and squinted up at the sky. "And please request Fathistokset, Taferk, Ravverbit, Semmedor, and Narpont keep a look-out, would you?" He glanced at Samdar, a gleam in his eye that had faded almost twenty years ago. "The Beltraths are coming, if they're not already here, and we are going to help protect the behamien the way they helped protect us."

"Yes, my lord," Samdar said, bowing low.

<hr>

"West!" Roth hissed. "We're going west, Stethen, because we cannot have five hundred..." He broke off quickly, glancing around the still-crowded market. "Five hundred *kettles* sitting in town," he finished in a moderately lower tone. He shook his head. "Do you know there was a time I enjoyed the catch-phrases and speaking in riddles? Especially when teaching that worthless, stupid boy who now threatens to ruin everything!" He pounded his thigh with a fist. "I hate catch-phrases and riddles. I should have taught the boy plain so he would not *wreck it all* in some ridiculous attempt at piety. I cannot remember what I saw in him. If there was anything before, it is gone now. And if there is still breath in him when I catch up to him, I'll make sure that's gone as well! I told them to make camp west of Fathistokset, far out into the plains where they would not be easily found, until I could come to them and tell them where all the little hiding places were, in the Eye. So, do you understand why we're going there now?"

"Of course, sir," Stethen replied. "I misunderstood. I thought Durla was our cover, and it was all we needed."

Roth glared at him. "Durla is not a large enough cover for *five hundred kettles*. Durla could not cover *ten* kettles this far west of where kettles are made."

"I'm sorry, sir," Stethen said.

"This is why Durla can rarely come out of the Fallonvall," Roth continued to seethe as they rode out of town. They had brought a few wagons north with them, and had them sitting outside of town also as cover. Supposedly, that's how Durla Fest preferred doing business. "Because Durla is surrounded by very sorry people."

"Yes sir," Stethen replied tiredly, letting Roth ride up to the wagons ahead of him. There was a time—it was a while ago, now—that Steth had admired Roth, admired what he stood for and proclaimed. Then Roth had started to change. A few months ago, the change had become severe and pronounced. Close as he was to the man, Steth still did not know what happened. It was almost overnight, Roth had suddenly begun violent temper swings. The army was falling apart around him. The southern villages had started slipping away, returning to their own ideas and lives. Maybe that was it. Suddenly, Steth couldn't remember which had come first.

Whatever Roth hoped to find and accomplish here, Steth wasn't sure it would be in time. Lately, he wasn't sure he *wanted* it to be in time.

Gabriel entered Taferk, tired and sore.

It had been a long ride through the Tevorbath, as it always was. At least there had been a few days he was able to push to a second inn, and made the ride a little shorter. Now, he felt it in his muscles. Usually, he had only felt it in his conscience.

It was not that long ago, by his reckoning, that he could catch at least one glimpse of Garedardan on any given ride through the valley. A great, black-scaled dragon, Gared had always jealously protected the Feast, and kept a keen eye on it. Gabriel suspected that, as behamien, Garedardan had lived in the Tevorbath, had somehow had a closer connection to it than it being simply his nest.

It had taken a lot of persuasion to get him to leave, more than Gabriel was strictly comfortable with. Harder still to find a place in the Wastes, and convince him to stay there. Deuel had been helpful in that: flying at height, he had been able to see the glint farther off where the sun struck water. Deuel had been able to fly to it and scout, to see who protected the oasis and whether it was large enough—of course, he had the dragon's eye for it. And it had been Deuel, with a little prompting from Gabriel, who had talked the great, magnificent dragon into seeing it for himself.

The rest had been relatively painless. Except now, spending days and days riding through the valley, looking for the great, graceful blackness, constantly remembering it wasn't there, remembering where it was instead.

Still, it was like riding a saddle for a long day. It ached and pinched in the evening, but given enough time the pain was eventually forgotten. At least, until you had another long day in the saddle. That's what he told himself as he lowered himself to the ground with a grunt, and handed the reins to the young boy who waited with outstretched hand.

The clouds below him passed, and Deuel could see the peaks and sharp valleys of the Dragon's Eye. From this height, it truly resembled an eye, a circle of peaks near the center as pupil and iris, great valleys stretching away east to west giving the illusion of a lidded ball, the foothills themselves the lids.

It was also easy, from this height, to see where the caves lay. From the ground, he knew, the valleys forced most on foot or hoof to traverse right by the place of *veythya*. But from here?

He pitched forward and folded his wings, a stooping falcon in man-size plummeting from the blue skies. He hurtled past the highest peak before snapping his wings open, muscles straining to slow him down. He banked, circled, rose, and landed on a stone porch before a great black opening. To the right, jagged rocks like stairs led to the valley floor. He shuddered his wings—they were trying to fall asleep after the sudden release of strain—unsheathed Halm and Ro Thull, and entered the cave.

His eyes adjusted quickly. There appeared to be no danger, no one hiding. He had passed Rodigger and Sharéd still on the road sometime back, he was fairly certain. He had known that didn't mean Sharéd's men might not have already scouted and found the cave. But everything appeared as it should have.

He drew a breath and walked deeper inside. There would be many rooms. Each dragon-son was to have his own, if he needed it, to have space to grow. With one sense testing for residual Calling—even if another had already entered *veythya*, the Calling might persist, as growing times varied—and another sense reaching out for sentient life, he quietly entered the next room.

He stopped. Lying on a shelf against the back wall was a behamian. His gray wings were folded around himself and had already hardened into a chrysalis. Deuel stood at the entrance, angling Ro Thull to catch the light of the cave opening and reflect it into the room. It shone through the semi-translucent wings and onto the face of the behamian underneath.

Deuel's breath caught. He knew he might recognize him, but this—this was still unexpected.

———◆———

Rodigger entered the camp with Sharéd, eyes wide as he looked at the gathered tents. They were low, and situated in the surrounding terrain so that he hadn't seen them till they had come around a low hillock. Even now, the further they wound into the camp, the more he could see them stretching away.

"This is five hundred of you?" he asked.

"More have come," Sharéd replied, without looking around. "Perhaps delay is not needed."

Rodigger glanced around, and behind him, then shook his head. "No, I agree. But we still need to scout the Eye to find where they are staying, before we move in."

"Roth does not know this location?"

Rodigger pursed his lips. Probably Roth did know that. But if Sharéd didn't, and Rodigger himself didn't, that meant Roth or a messenger was on their way with that information, and might convince Sharéd to stick to the original plan when they arrived.

"We should already be in position, though. If we can," Rodigger said. "And since we'll be waiting, we can spend that time scouting. Here." Rodigger dismounted his Therian, scuffing the ground to clear the grass. It took him longer than he wanted, and he began to feel foolish continuing to kick the ground, but he was committed by then. More Beltraths gathered around, glancing between their leader and Rodigger.

"Keff ka duuli geyrda dana shah?" asked one of those gathered. Intent on the ground, Rodigger missed Sharéd's half-smile and shake of the head in response.

Finally he had a space of dirt large enough to draw a map, and knelt. He pulled out his dagger. "Balnath Agrend," he said, sticking the point in. "Dragon's Eye," he continued, tracing a line. "Us. I want scouts, four teams of four, going into the Eye, dividing it in quadrants. I want our forces split into four groups and camped here, here, here, and here," he continued, pointing to each side of the Eye as he went. "When one scouting team finds where the behamien are, each member returns to the four camps and leads everyone in."

"Might I suggest the scout teams are larger?" Sharéd asked, gesturing. Rodigger looked up. "Dangerous things in the mountains, not good for one man to walk alone."

"Sure, fine," Rodigger said, glancing back down. "Whatever size you think is appropriate—but divisible by four, so equal teams can go to each camp."

"And the other three scouting teams?"

Rodigger shook his head. "We'll have to count them a loss. Besides, the behamien may have more than one lair, so it will be better for my purposes—our purposes, rather, if they keep looking and make sure there's nothing there. Once one lair is cleared, the camps return to their original position, until all scouting teams have reported back."

"Good," Sharéd replied with a nod. Despite being contrary to Roth's original message, it was a good plan that allowed Sharéd his justice. Most of it. "If we find the wingt man," he continued with a significant nod at Rodigger, "he is left for me. I must meet with him alive."

Rodigger glanced at his hen-scratched map for a moment, then nodded.

⸺⬦⸺

Catie shifted in the bed, rolling onto her side with a sigh. Twisting her neck, she could see through the window the half-moon over Mihrland-hen. The night was past its zenith and headed toward morning.

For months—most of her travels, really—her shoulder blades had not ached like they did in the Fallonvall. Now, suddenly, they decided to keep her awake again.

It was no use. Even on her side, they still bunched and hurt. It wasn't stress. Traveling with Sarah, if anything, relieved her stress. Geoffrey was not even that bad, considering he was nothing like either Gabriel or Deuel, and especially not like Rodigger.

She eased herself upright. Sarah was on the next bed, breathing deep and evenly, but she doubted it would take much to awaken the former sorceress. Catie slid on her pants gently, pulled her shirt over her head but only snugged the laces at her neck a little, picked up her boots, and stole into the hallway. There she tied the laces and tugged on her boots, creeping past Geoffrey's door before walking normally to the end of the hall, and entering the common room.

She was eager to find Deuel, to be rid of the Berkarfor if she could, though she knew it would do Roth nothing to hold them. She opened the door and stepped out into the cool night air. Autumn was definitely approaching, now. She began walking toward the forests around the edge of town.

She was a little concerned with how she might find Deuel, and what, if any, predicament he might be in. She couldn't imagine many. The dragon-son was certainly capable of handling himself. She wasn't sure what Rodigger might have planned, but didn't think it could be much. But that wasn't why her shoulder blades hurt.

She entered the woods proper, outside the edge of town. She still gave a brief shudder as her vision rippled, despite slowly getting accustomed to the uncontrollable shift. Here as in Ethfirlaf, she could tell her vision was better than the moonlight should have allowed. It had not been like that in the Fallonvall, or even out of it that she could remember. Not until Kavlen. But then, until Kavlen, she had not been outside at night that often either.

She breathed deep, drinking in the smell of the forest—of growing, woodland things. She could hear, faintly, the trickling of a small stream over rocks. She moved toward the sound, picking out the fold of ground where she knew she would find it.

The shadows gathered in the valley, and even here her sight was not perfect. Here and there the moonlight glinted off the water like scales of a fish rolling in shallow water as it pursued its prey. She breathed again, expecting the cool, liquid smell of the stream.

But something else was there. It took her a moment to realize she was not alone in her mind. There was a presence, mammoth and ancient, between her and the stream—that the glint was not from something *like* scales, they actually *were* scales. And for a moment, she was terrified.

Then she saw the eyes, all warmth and sunlight and inviting like flames from an unexpected campfire on a freezing night. And then her terror was replaced by the kind of joyous surprise that only fits in a void left by banished fear.

Who are you? she asked; the 'dragon' part was obvious.

I am Lamendaretha.

I am Catie—Caytaleane, she corrected, remembering the old ways.

Did you summon me out here?

In part. The rest was you. And Deuel.

You've heard from him? Is he okay?

He has reached the Eye. But so, I fear, have many others.

Catie took a step forward. *Is he in grave danger?*

It is likely. He is strong, but he is only one.

True. But what can just the two of us do?

More than you can believe, Lamendaretha said with an enigmatic smile. *For one, you understand humans better than our son.*

I thought he was Kaoleyn's son?

Lamend chuckled. *The sons are more concerned with parents than parents are with sons. While he was in Burieng, he was Paolound's, and Kaoleyn's who gave him birth. Here he is mine and Garedardan's.*

I think Garedardan needs to return from the Wastes, Catie thought. *The danger Deuel is in is because of that.*

That is yet to be decided. For now, you must go to him. Lamendaretha's head snaked forward a little, and she breathed on Catie. As Catie drew the warm air into her lungs, it seemed her sense of the dragon heightened. *You will now be able to sense Deuel more keenly,* she said. *The Eye is formed to keep the unlearned lost. Take this, as well.* Suddenly, images flashed through Catie's mind of great valleys and passes and peaks and a cave. She blinked rapidly. When it was done, she could not recall the images to mind.

I think I've forgotten them already, she said with some alarm.

You will remember when you see it. Lamend's nostrils suddenly flared, and she looked up. *One comes.*

Catie's head whipped around as someone crested the rise behind her. She thought she recognized the form—Geoffrey perhaps? Yes. His left arm.

It's one of my companions, she said.

He smells of death.

Catie turned back. *I'm sure he's not that dirty.*

Lamend's head dipped. *He has killed,* she clarified. *Dragon.*

"Geoffrey, I'm here," Catie called as she stood. "It's okay. This is Lamendaretha, she protects the Brithelt."

"Well that is gratifying to hear," he replied. "I was not prepared to die just yet."

Tell him to put his weapon away, Lamend said with disgust.

"Geoffrey, your sword?"

"Right." He sheathed it quickly. "What are you doing out here?"

"I wanted to go for a walk," Catie said. "My shoulders were sore and I couldn't sleep." *Why are my shoulder blades sore so often?*

Deuel desires veythya, Lamend replied. *It is how his Calling affects you. But only when he dwells on it too much.*

"Did you kill Paolound?" she asked Geoffrey as he drew near.

He skipped a step, glanced between the two, and bowed his head slightly. "The second time, we did—four of us did. Sarah and I and two other companions. We did not know his spirit was being controlled by another."

"Controlled?" Catie asked, the same time as Lamend. *I could sense something was wrong,* the dragon continued. *I have never heard of this, though.*

"Yes, a mage in Burieng, Lasserain. He had killed Paolound some fifteen years ago, revived him with Life magic—" he paused as Lamend snorted her anger "—and Lasserain's spirit was able to manipulate the dragon to attack us."

"Is he—this mage—is that why you left Burieng?"

Is he still free to make war against dragons?

"We left after we killed him," Geoffrey replied. "Haydren, another of our companions, was able to fight and kill him this autumn."

Catie blinked. "Geoffrey, it's not autumn yet."

He paused. "Of course, I forget how far south Burieng is. It would have been your spring—the end of Halmfurtung."

"Paolound is avenged, then," Catie relayed from Lamend to Geoffrey. "She is grateful. She wants to know if there is anything she can do for you."

"We each had our reasons for what we did," Geoffrey replied. "The reward was in the success."

Catie cocked an eyebrow at Lamend, feeling her joy welling up. *What is it?* Catie asked.

Ask him to remain still, and to trust me, she said. *Tell him that some of the rules that humans are meant to abide by have not been emplaced on dragons.*

Catie relayed the message. Geoffrey held still as Lamend approached. Her great green head, sparkling like a thousand emeralds, bowed toward Geoffrey. The light behind her eyes grew till they pierced the night. As she breathed, her tongue flicked out, touching the stump of his arm, and he gasped as if sunk suddenly into cold water.

The lights in her eyes dimmed as Lamend retreated.

"She says to rest," Catie said, watching the dragon settle herself once more into the valley stream. "And then to hurry toward the end of our journey."

"Very well," he said quietly, his glances between his arm and the dragon.

As they walked back toward town, Geoffrey kept glancing down at his arm. "It's cold," he would mutter. "Her breath and tongue were warm, but this feels cold."

Catie was able to make her way into bed without waking Sarah. The next morning, she awoke to a terrific pounding on the door. She and Sarah both leapt up, throwing on their clothes quickly.

"What *is* it, by all things?" Sarah demanded as she opened the door. She stopped, her hand flying to her mouth.

Geoffrey stood outside, holding up both hands, his left arm completely restored.

21

ARRIVES TEN

"Things are about to get very complicated."
"They have been for some time."
"And the Islands?"
"Difficult to say."

10 Nuamon 1320 — Summer

After helping Geoffrey explain to Sarah what happened—several times—Catie spent the rest of the morning riding in relative silence. The two companions rode ahead, Sarah holding Geoffrey's restored hand as they spoke only by touch and glance. She was happy to see them that way. The love they had for each other was plain, even from the back. And she could not imagine losing something that significant and then receiving it back in such a manner. After all, she never actually had Deuel.

It wasn't the same, and she knew it, but it didn't help. Lamend's breath on her had changed something. Even now she could sense Deuel, though nascent and distant. But even if he rode beside her, would it be any different? He would always be behamien, and she would always be not. And what kind of relationships would wyverns have? Could she have if she could choose not to become one? Dannid had been fun, had been exciting. But he was a pale spark next to what Deuel had been able to offer her—*had given* her, right before he went away so she would have to chase him down again. Half of her screamed to dig in her heels and make Kelsie fly. The other half wanted to turn and run the other way, to pursue what the wretched, incomparable Berkarfor had shown her.

Either prospect was exhilarating and impossible to even dream of, and yet she would have to pick only one. If only Deuel had been a terrible person, like Rodigger.

Autumn approached as inexorably as the Dragon's Eye, and by the time they left the Brithelt it had arrived. Another week, and the mountains themselves rose pale and gray on the horizon. The road ran obliquely to meet the corner, the Eye Fold—thus, Agrend.

One day's ride from the great capital city, Catie rose in her stirrups and gazed south at the mountains. It may have just been a trick of the morning sun...

No, it was the pass. As she gazed at it, she realized that even Kelsie would struggle on those slopes.

"What is it?" Sarah asked.

"I need to go into the mountains," Catie said. "I don't think Kelsie will make it through, though." She glanced back at the two. "Would you mind taking her with you to Balnath Agrend? I'll come back and find her when I'm done."

"Sure," Sarah said with a quick glance at Geoffrey. "Do you need anything?"

"I should just need a small pack," she replied, reining Kelsie to a stop and dismounting. She repacked the saddlebags as Kelsie and the others watched, moved her Nagrath dagger to her hip. Then she went to Kelsie's muzzle.

"Be nice to them," she said with a grin. Kelsie was always on best behavior. "I'll see you again in a few days. And thank you, both," she said with a smile for the other two.

"Be careful," Sarah replied. "We'll leave a message with the tower guards, to let you know where to find us. It was a pleasure riding with you."

"You too." She gave Kelsie one last rub, and turned for the mountains as Geoffrey and Sarah continued down the road.

It had been some time since Catie walked, and she'd forgotten how much slower things got closer. As the sun continued west toward the horizon, she entered the foothills—sharp, rugged hillocks here, as if long ago the mountains had punched through the surface of the land and showered great blocky boulders on the plain.

Darkness approached. She reached out for Deuel, but instead of finding his deep presence she felt a hundred small ones—several hundred, even. She paused, feeling deeper: they were men, banded together, and not too far away.

She continued forward quietly and carefully, keeping below the hills as much as possible. She wanted to get as far along as possible, and with her improved night vision decided to continue after it got dark.

She reached the base of the pass. The ground veered suddenly upward, not too steep to climb but steep enough that if she fell she likely wouldn't stop until she hit the bottom. Craning her neck, she thought she could discern a little shelf about fifty paces up or so. She took a deep breath and began to climb.

Using her hands to grip little tussocks of grass, she managed to reach the shelf. It cut back maybe two paces before the hill went up again. She paused to catch her breath, and looked down.

Below her and to the northeast, she saw faint glows as of coal-fires, kept low. But if that were so, it would mean at least two hundred fifty men—probably more if they cut down the number of fires, which she would have done if she were trying to remain hidden. She glanced along the shelf, but saw that it disappeared precipitously only a few paces that direction. She looked up again. Maybe she would see more from up higher.

She continued climbing as the moon rose, full and silver, lighting up the night for her like morning. The pitch grew less steep, until she could walk almost completely upright. She paused and looked down once more, chest heaving. Whoever they were, they hid themselves well. Even now she could only barely make out that there were, indeed, several hundred men, fires, and tents pitched below. Surely it was Rodigger and Sharéd's army, coming after Deuel and the behamien.

The sight gave her new energy, and she pressed on into the night until she had reached the summit and scrambled a few hundred paces down the other side. The valley below ran east to west, with another ridge directly in front of her. She looked back and forth. East was the way to go.

Her legs were on fire, and her knees didn't want to stay in one position. But Deuel was in danger, and might not know it. She reached out again, probing deeper into the interior of the Eye.

He was there! No longer a wisp, but solid and real as if she could reach out and grasp his arm, feel his flesh and bone beneath her hand. She closed her eyes and sighed. How would she ever see him face to face and leave him again?

She took a few breaths, turning her mind toward the great vastness she vaguely remembered from her dream in Ostflir. It *was* real. It was *real. It* was real. She had been there, had seen worlds and stars as small as sand. She was part of that, now.

She reached out again. *Danger,* she sent. Somehow she knew that anything more wouldn't translate. She felt him respond.

Catie?

I'm coming.

She continued scrambling down the slope. It was so much easier on this side. A few times she was able to just sit and slide. But the Eye was large, and she knew it would be another day or more before she would find him. Yet, somehow, she wanted to keep going, as if she could reach his cave any moment now. She continued up the valley, looking for the next pass to register in her memory as the moon climbed.

It was long after nightfall when Sarah and Geoffrey were finally ushered into Sheppar's study. The room was small, with a few plain wooden chairs and desks littered with papers, some loose and some in tight stacks. Sheppar sat back in one of the chairs, scanning a document by the light of the forlorn candles that emitted almost as much black smoke as flame. He had undone a few of the top buttons on his cloak, revealing a dirty-white tunic underneath.

"Twenty years since I gave them authority," he said as the steward shut the doors on his way out. "You would think they would know by now what help I give, and what I don't."

"But you still read their messages," Sarah replied.

Sheppar glanced over the top of the parchment. "Sometimes they're right. Have a seat, please. It hurts my neck to look up at people."

"Thank you," Sarah replied. She moved a small stack of papers off one chair and arranged her dress as she sat. Geoffrey took another nearby. "You do not have aides to read them for you?"

Sheppar barked a laugh. "They don't usually know what help I give either. It doesn't matter," he said, putting the parchment down and sniffing. "It gives me something to do. Sorry for not seeing you more formally, but by this time of night formality is usually tired and looking for a bed to sleep in, too. What can I do for you?"

"Earl Durdamon sends his regards," Sarah replied with a smile, "and his regrets: with recent events in Burieng he was quite busy. But he asked if I could come and offer my services."

Sheppar gazed at her blankly for several long moments. "Services for what?"

Sarah glanced at Geoffrey, then back. "I believe he said you were facing a rebellion."

"Oh, that," Sheppar said, leaning back with a wave of his hand. "I *thought* it was too prescient for the Beltrath incursion, no matter how much Durdamon knows. Well, I hope you have other business in Andelen, because the rebellion is nothing—Roth getting upset and talking to too many people."

"We had heard he controlled the Fallonvall. That seems like a large portion of Andelen to simply be dismissed."

"Well if he controls it, it's because the people want him to control it," Sheppar replied. "If that's what the people want, they shall have it. And he hasn't moved outside the 'vall in almost five years. I assume it is because he can't."

"And the Beltrath incursion you mentioned? They are from the east, right?"

"That matter is all but concluded, before you even arrived." Sheppar shrugged. "I'm sorry, but Durdamon worries too much." Sheppar's eyes slid to Geoffrey, then back. Whatever had been in his glance, Sarah did not understand it.

But it seemed Geoffrey did understand. "My kinnig," he said, leaning forward. "Durdamon knew something—you know he knew something. And for good or ill he sent Sarah as his emissary. I asked to come along, but she is the one you should be talking to, not I."

Sarah managed to keep her composure as Sheppar sighed. "Very well," he said. "I'm still not sure how much harm there is in him, but I've been hearing...troubling things, out of the south. There was sent from Roth some time ago a mercenary group looking for four goblets of legend."

"The Berkarfor?" Sarah asked with a raised eyebrow. At Sheppar's sharp glance, she smiled. "I had heard something about them a number of years ago when I lived in Andelen for a short time."

"Yes, well. Those. I'm not as worried about the goblets themselves as what it signals from Roth. He always had been a little over-eager for power, but to chase such a legend is absurd even for him."

"You know him?" Sarah asked.

Sheppar frowned. "You are intelligent, at least. Yes, he was one of my—no, he *was* my top general during the campaign twenty years ago. I relied on him for so much of the success. But then it was he who championed killing Gared. And he never quite forgave me for being so hesitant about the whole thing. Then, once I began handing control over to the magiss'..." Sheppar shook his head. "He resigned within the year. Said the people of Andelen owed us for their safety, and we should exact as much as we could from them. I think he believed that was the whole point of the campaign—not that we did it *for* the people. I don't know to this day how he missed that, but..." He shook his head again. "I suppose I missed it in him, too."

"And why do the Beltraths invade?" Sarah asked.

"I sent some of our troops into the Wastes, trying to do an especially good job of keeping Andelen safe—Rinc Nain Andelen, anyway. After I made them kill the dragon, the same people who wanted Garedardan dead, including Roth, wanted all threats pushed away from Merneset. It required far more violence than I had wanted. But I also wanted it done with, and quickly. So I don't blame them, those who wanted it done. I wanted it done as well."

"We're not here to weigh in on that," Sarah said. "But with the incursion coming so close to the mission for the Berkarfor—are they related?"

"I doubt—"

Sheppar was cut off by a knock at the door. He looked up. "Come in," he said. "Ah, General Piembry. News from the patrols?"

"Yes, my lord," he said with a bow. "The patrol south reported: they discovered a Beltrath camp between here and Kostet's, approximately two hundred fifty men. We suffered approximately ten percent casualties, but we took most of them."

"And the rest?"

"They fled east my lord. My men pursued them as far as they could, but they quickly disappeared into the Eye. We broke off at that point and continued south, to garrison the 'vilt."

"Very good. Thank you, General."

"Sir," Piembry saluted, and exited.

Sheppar sighed, then glanced at Sarah. "You see? All taken care of."

"But something else troubles you."

Sheppar was silent for some moments. "I would have preferred they didn't enter the Dragon's Eye," he said quietly. "It's too easy to…" He trailed off, then closed his eyes for a moment. "I think that will be all for tonight," he said finally, looking up again. "I will take care of a few things in the morning. Please come see me again after lunch, and we'll discuss how you might help me."

"Thank you, my lord," Sarah said, standing. Geoffrey echoed her words and actions, and made for the door. Sheppar stood as they exited. Sarah paused, glancing back as Sheppar stood over one of the candles, studying it wearily. As it guttered, he took a shallow breath and blew it out, then bowed and shook his head. "Too easy," he muttered again.

Sarah shut the door and followed Geoffrey down the hallway.

⬥

Where are you?

Catie glanced up. He was far closer now than he had been. Was his cave so near? She gazed at the mountains, at every detail of the peaks, and sent it to Deuel. *There are men—Rodigger's men in the walls outside the Eye,* she said.

She paused, waiting for the response, but nothing came. Hesitantly she started forward again, her boots crunching on the stone that frequently breached the surface. She took a breath and shook her head. Surely he had heard her.

A wind rose in the west, rustling through the trees behind her. Except, there hadn't been trees. She turned quickly just as Deuel landed, his wings folding with a few shakes.

"Hi," she said. Her brain at this moment would only allow her a few letters at a time.

"Come with me," he said.

Anywhere, she managed to keep to herself.

He stepped forward and picked her up very suddenly, and she gasped as her arms went reflexively around his neck. "What are you—?"

She broke off with another gasp as his wings unfurled and shot them into the air. "What about the soldiers?" she shouted as the air whipped past them.

Who? he asked with amusement.

Well it's not like I'm used to this! she retorted, swallowing as she looked at the ground now far below, and then the peaks still far above them. *The soldiers. Rodigger and Sharéd have their forces outside the Eye.*

Very well. We'll stay below the peaks a little bit.

Are you sure you can carry me? she asked.

I surely won't drop you. You could hold on a little less tight, though.

Sorry, she said, loosening her arms. Deuel rotated his neck a few times, then suddenly pitched right and up, taking them swiftly over a saddle of the mountains. Catie's stomach, though, stayed for a moment in the valley behind them.

She swallowed, and rested her head against his shoulder. The beat of his heart and wings lulled her. She closed her eyes and let her momentum shift as it needed to. She wasn't sure how long they flew, and she wasn't entirely sure she stayed awake the whole time, though she couldn't imagine how she would have let herself sleep at a time like that.

Eventually, though, he was in her mind again. *Get ready to run a little bit.*

Um, what?

I'm going to let you down quickly. I may be more tired than I realized.

Oh. Okay.

She opened her eyes, seeing now that they were headed toward a cave opening halfway up on of the cliffs. She let her gaze wander. They had to be near the middle of the Eye. Suddenly, movement in the valley to the south caught her eye.

Deuel, she said.

I see him. It's too late, now. I'm going to let your legs down. I'll be right behind you, so keep running.

Have you ever done this bef— she cut off suddenly as her legs dangled in mid-air. She took a few deep breaths through her nose, tried to poise herself as the cave approached. When his wings flared, she slipped a little and his clutch choked her throat. Then she was falling. She flailed her arms as she tried to right herself. Her feet slammed into the ground and she ran, smacking her palms against the hard stone to keep from sprawling flat.

But she did it. She kept running, hearing Deuel's feet behind her. Finally she slowed and stopped, her heart racing as she was panting.

Are you okay?

Her palms burned, but she felt fine. There was a faint light from further in. *Do you have a fire?* she asked, a little alarmed, but also a little cold.

She felt his amusement. *Yes, you may warm yourself.*

She continued into the next room, then stopped as she looked at the wall.

Yes, Deuel said, coming in behind her. *That is what our chrysalis looks like.*

Do you...is it... She trailed off, glancing from the hibernating form to

Deuel.

Yes, he said, and she could feel a somberness she didn't understand. *It is my brother.*

She reached out and put a hand on his shoulder. "Is that...isn't that good?" But then she thought of herself as she watched Sarah and Geoffrey, seeing what they had that she could no longer be happy with. "I know you wanted it, too."

But Deuel shook his head. He pulled a stick from the fire and held the flame closer to the head. It was still clearly human, but had also changed dramatically. The dimensions and form were almost canine, she thought, if dogs had smooth, reptilian skin instead of fur.

"I don't..."

"He's becoming wyvern," Deuel replied, his gaze locked onto Catie.

She knew her gaze spoke volumes; Deuel's did not. "But if he is behamian," she wondered, "what does that mean?"

Deuel was silent for several moments, and only the crackling of the flame broke the silence. "I don't know," he said finally. "We were raised together, taught together. But I have not seen him for over two hundred years. I do not know what may have happened to him during that time. I did not even know he was in Andelen."

Catie winced as he gave evidence of his true age, but turned her mind quickly onto the...wyvern...before her. She wanted to help, but she didn't know wyverns even existed until she had met Deuel. She was sure she had never heard any stories about them.

But she had heard plenty of stories about dragons. Deuel's brother, then, was likely to be buried into anonymity, an unknown race that even those who could communicate with their minds couldn't understand, according to Deuel. "So this is what I will become?"

"I cannot be so sure, anymore. It would seem wyvern and dragon are not as different as I thought."

Her chest heaved as she drew a sigh. "I do know. The guardian of the third goblet told me I was. And then... It's a very long story, but I have some sort of future memory of me flying with a whole group of wyverns. But I don't know if I can..." She shook her head as he stared blankly at her, as if he didn't know where her thoughts were going. "I thought, when you left... Have you changed your mind already?"

"You do not understand the effect of the Call. And now to be here, and see this... To be so close. Would you prefer I deny it? Are you sure you can stop from being a wyvern? If you had this 'future-memory' then am I to remain as I am while you become what you are?"

"I'm not certain that's what it was! Deuel, I don't know anything about this. I don't..." Her lips pressed together. "I don't know how you feel about this. You never talked about your brothers very much. You know more than me about wyverns and dragons and behamien and I don't even know why I can sense you and talk to animals and dragons, but I thought—"

"When did you talk to a dragon?"

"We met Lamendaretha in the Brithelt," she said. "She gave me the ability to sense you at longer distances, and showed me how to get here." Deuel went still. "What?"

"This...this..."

"This is where I come in!" said a new voice behind them.

Catie whirled, her dagger flying from its sheath. Deuel took a few steps sideways to stand out from behind her as Roth entered the chamber.

"How perfect!" he said, holding his arms wide. "I have a behamian and the woman who had better have my Berkarfor, all gathered together in one place."

"You'll have to—" She cut off as four soldiers entered behind Roth, arraying themselves in a line behind him.

"I'll have to what?" he growled. "I paid out good money for those goblets and you *will have to* give them to me—I wouldn't do that!" he said, pointing at Deuel. Catie glanced at him, saw his hands going for Halm and Ro Thull where they leaned against the back of the cave. One of the soldiers approached, sword held in front. He made it until one hand rested on the pommel of Ro Thull before Deuel swiped the out-stretched sword aside, grabbed the soldier by his throat, and flipped him backwards.

A bow creaked, and Catie looked up again to see the arrow aimed unwaveringly at Deuel's chest. The soldier on the floor groaned as he climbed to his feet. Roth chuckled.

"I didn't tell you to do that either," he said to the soldier. "What *idiot* would get that close to a behamian? But no matter. Unless this behamian is immune to arrows, he won't do that again."

"Do not touch that which isn't yours, again," Deuel said.

"He's really, very good," Catie said, still staring down her blade at Roth. "I wouldn't be surprised if he is immune to arrows—or at the very least able to swipe them out of the air with a wing."

"Possibly true," Roth agreed with a smile. "Still, might not want to risk it, just in case you're wrong. Besides, all you have to do is give me what I know you have, and we'll all be on our way."

"I don't think it's that simple," Catie replied.

"Let me try," Roth replied, taking a step forward. "First, you get that knife *out of my face!*"

She lowered it a little, in surprise if nothing else. Roth had been so controlled last time she met him.

"Next, you give me the goblets which I assume are in that bag. Then I leave, and take the country back for myself." He smiled, arms wide again. "What did I miss?"

"First, I only have three of them. You'll have to talk to Rodigger to get the fourth."

Roth waved his hand. "That child would give me his throat if I asked him."

"More importantly," Catie continued, "I don't think the Berkarfor do what you think they do," she said. "I was with them for the finding of each one, and...it's hard to explain."

"Fortunately, you don't have to, little *girl*," Roth sneered. "I've read more about the Berkarfor than you've read about everything. But we needn't have this little argument here. Instead, you just give me the goblets, and let me worry about what I know and what you don't."

"And you'll leave the behamien alone?"

"Of course I will. They were...just in case," Roth said, his smile returning.

"Catie," one of the soldiers said. She glanced at him, her brows furrowing, then going wide in recognition.

Roth turned on him slowly. "It was you, wasn't it?" he said. His fist lashed out. The soldier ducked, his out-flung arm striking the bowman. With a cry the bowman twisted, tried to catch his balance, and released the string. Catie shouted a warning. Roth roared anger and pain as the arrow embedded deep into his thigh.

"You imbecile!" he roared, collapsing onto the ground. "I'll kill you all! Get me to my horse this instant! Get me a sage! A wizard! Not you, conniving, usurping, witch-spawn! Stay with them or I'll gut you and everyone you love! Bring me my Berkarfor or I'll gut your Grandmother like I gutted your husband! Put me down until she gives them to me. Kill the behamien if she doesn't!"

As Roth continued to curse and splutter, Catie shook her head at how far gone this man was over something he didn't understand. He had only read about them, made them in his mind to be something they weren't, and went mad with desire. She suddenly was not sure if it would help him more to keep them, or show them to him. If seeing them would shatter his expectation, destroy him, let him heal—or if he would continue to see them as he thought they were, try to wield them in a way they weren't designed, to who knew what end.

Before she could decide, she heard the tramp of many feet outside the cave, and she shuddered.

"No one move!" came a voice, this one far more familiar, though marked with greater authority than Catie had ever heard him muster. She quickly understood why. Behind Rodigger came ten or fifteen men armed with drawn blades, and it sounded as if even more were gathered outside.

"How dare you!" Roth shouted. "Do you even understand—"

"More than you know!" Rodigger said overtop of him. "To think I believed in you and what you *said* you stood for. And here you are making *treaties* with these...these..." He turned and looked at Deuel, his eyes sparking with hatred. His gaze turned to Catie, softening a little into a sort of regret, though it turned her stomach. Then the gaze slid to the wall behind them.

A torrent of emotions washed across that gaze, then: betrayal, hate, disgust, violence, a tinge of fear that was quickly squashed as he strode forward with a growl that became a roar. Catie wanted to step in front of him, but something in her chest vibrated, something that knew Rodigger was not himself.

"Rodigger," she managed weakly. He did not even hesitate. He passed her, and his hand jerked swiftly.

"Rodigger!"

"You—!"

"No!"

The last from Deuel, who leapt in too late. Rodigger, fueled by rage, kept Deuel away long enough to drive the blade home, in between the translucent wings. The wyvern inside shuddered and shook, squirming away from the steel as blood ran out and filled the chrysalis. Its mouth opened wide in soundless, writhing screams, then finally went still.

Deuel stared at his brother, dead in the cocoon. Three Beltraths came forward, blades outstretched to protect Rodigger, who backed away a few steps with a mixed look of horrified triumph on his face. Catie stared at Deuel, feeling the swirl of emotions coming from him and blending with her own.

"This is only the beginning," Rodigger whispered fiercely. "My men and I are going to continue through these caves and dispatch with every filthy vermin we find—starting," he continued with outstretched finger, "with you. And then," he pointed at Catie, "with those who sympathize with them."

"The wingt man is Sharéd's!" one of the Beltraths said, glancing at Rodigger.

"Sharéd isn't here!" Rodigger spat back. "He hasn't lived day in and day out beside this...thing! You'll tell him you couldn't help it, that Deuel attacked you."

"I do not serve you," the Beltrath replied, turning to face Rodigger.

Catie lashed out, catching the second Beltrath's sword in her dagger and wrenching it from his grasp. Deuel leapt forward, taking down the third.

More came forward. Roth's soldiers joined in, assuming Roth would be taken as well by someone entering who did not know who was who.

Rodigger tried to skirt around it all, parrying with a small sword as best he could as he pressed against the wall of the cave, edging toward the entrance. Catie pursued, but more nomads came in from outside.

Deuel came around behind her, Halm and Ro Thull ringing. He hadn't had on the bracelets to lend magic to the fight, but he was very good with just the blades. The shadows dancing from the fire confused the Beltraths. Deuel's and Catie's skill and advantage of being on the other side of a small opening kept them from surging in the numbers they hoped.

Suddenly a hand grabbed Catie's foot and pulled. She fell with a shout. Roth laughed, kicking her with his good leg. Stars exploded in her vision, and her ears rang. She rolled away from him, losing track of the fight for a moment. One of his soldiers, nearby, stabbed downward. She squeezed her eyes shut, and heard a terrific ringing right in front of her nose. When she looked up, she saw the soldier she recognized crashing a fist into the one that had tried to kill her, knocking him senseless.

There was a prolonged shout from outside, and Deuel was back in the room. Catie rolled to her feet, miraculously still hanging onto her dagger. Her ears still rang, though the pitch had changed. She came in beside Deuel, drawing some of the Beltraths away.

Suddenly she heard growling, and men shouting, but their speech was not Rinc Nain so she didn't understand what was being said. The fighting in front of her slacked.

What's happening?

I think there is another force outside.

She managed to reach the arm of the soldier in front of her, slicing it. He yelped and backed out of the cave, leaving her, Deuel, Roth, and the other soldier. She glanced around. The other three in Roth's entourage had fallen.

"I'll go out and see," she said. She exited the cave into pre-dawn light. The mountains hid the sun but the sky was already turning blue. She turned on the cliff, looking down the stairway as the backs of a few more Beltraths receded.

In the valley below, a pack of wolves were loose among the remaining fighters. The men were huddled together, trying to keep a circle, but the wolves too easily dodged blades and got inside. As she watched, suddenly Catie grinned.

"It's Eidemon!" she shouted back into the cave. "He's brought wolves with him! That innkeeper said he knew something about them!"

Below, the Beltraths were breaking, running southward as if trying to get out of the mountains. But there was a steep climb ahead of them, which surely the wolves could ascend more easily—

As her eyes continued upward, Catie frowned. "Eidemon!" she shouted suddenly. "Bring them up here!"

She pointed, where at the top of the ridge a new force of Beltraths were forming and preparing to descend. Eidemon glanced where she pointed, then at her with a nod. A few whistles and shouted commands in a language she didn't recognize, and the wolves and Eidemon were making their way up the natural staircase.

"It won't be perfect," she said when he neared the top, panting twice as hard as his wolves. "But it'll be more defensible than the open valley."

"I thank you," he managed. The wolves looked between the two.

Thank you, and be welcome, she said. A few cocked their heads, and seemed to nod in respect.

"Deuel's inside, as well as Roth," she said. "We seem to be holding him for now."

"Well, let's go," he said. Catie nodded, glancing again at the south ridge top. There were another several hundred men gathering as though waiting for those fleeing to bring them news on the forces they faced. In her mind's eye, Catie could see them laughing with their superior numbers.

"I'm not sure we'll be able to hold them," she said as she came into the cave. "Or outlast them, if they simply sit outside and wait."

"I'm bleeding," Roth said, petulant now that he held the lower hand.

"You could tie it off," Catie replied. "Or let someone do it for you. You're not going very far."

"Of course I could," he said, veritably spitting at her feet. "Those are my Beltraths out there. They're not going to kill me if I tried to leave."

"You *did* bring them out?" Catie asked. "Why?"

"I needed to get out of the Fallonvall. I needed Sheppar to take me seriously."

"Why not use the troops you already had?" Catie asked.

I think I can guess, Deuel muttered wryly.

"Because I'm the last one," said the soldier.

"You be silent!" Roth roared.

"Or what? There never was an army," the soldier went on.

"There never...then, how? Why?"

"He had heard the story of a lieutenant in Burieng overthrowing an entire province on the rumor that he had an army poised to strike. A long time ago, during the Age of War. Roth thought he would try it here. The problem was, the Province back then was united under a common heritage. Andelen isn't."

"It could have worked!" Roth spat. "If Sheppar hadn't demanded that everyone be different, everyone worry only about themselves and no one else—he should have united them instead of letting them divide."

"Like you did?" Eidemon interjected. "By force?"

Those soldiers will be here any moment, Deuel said. *We either need to let him go, or begin preparing.*

I say we let him go.

And the Berkarfor?

"I tried persuasion," Roth replied. "I tried it for years. People were too stubborn and too selfish. With the threat of the Beltraths, and the power of the Berkarfor, they would have loved to follow me. I could have given them the world they didn't know they needed."

Catie took a breath to cut in, then paused. Something was changing, she could feel it. At the edge of her consciousness was something vaguely familiar, but fresh. "I'm inclined to let you return to wherever you need to go to get help for your leg," Catie said, finally. "I'll keep the Berkarfor for now, and give them to you later."

"Absolutely not!" Roth said. "You're going to die here, and I'll never see them."

"Then I'll hide them in here. You can come back after we're dead and retrieve them."

Roth glared at her. She raised her eyebrows, waiting for his decision. "Fine," he muttered finally. "I'll go to the 'vilt, south—just in case you manage somehow to make it out of this alive. But don't think I'll request it of the Beltraths. They can have you and your...*friend.*"

"Thank you. Steth, wasn't it?" she asked, turning to the soldier.

He smiled. "I'm pleased you remember," he said.

"It's been a long road since you brought me Kelsie," Catie replied, smiling. "Help him south, will you? And keep an eye on him until I get there?"

"Are you sure you will?"

"I've made it this far," she said with a shrug.

"Why aren't we keeping him as hostage?" Eidemon asked. "We could use him to barter with the Beltraths."

"Oh, I don't think we'll need to," Catie replied. "And I'd rather he didn't die just yet, actually."

With Steth's help, Roth got to his feet. They had been able to stop the bleeding, and had trimmed the arrow down to a nub just long enough for the surgeon to grasp, when that time came. As he hobbled out of the cave, he laughed.

"Something must be working in my favor," Catie heard him cackling to Steth. "Here I have my turncoat soldier helping me away from a lunatic of a woman, too silly to dispatch her enemies when she has the chance."

"I'm not sure I disagree with him," Eidemon said in a low growl. The wolves were laying down and resting, but now they looked toward the mouth of the cave expectantly.

"Would you mind helping me get these bodies out of here?" Catie asked. She went to the nearest one and picked him up under his armpits.

Eidemon turned to Deuel, keeping his voice low. *"Has* she gone mad?"

Deuel only looked at him, then went to the next body and picked it up. Eidemon watched him go. When he turned back, his wolves only looked at him. Muttering under his breath, he grasped one near him by the collar and began to pull.

"They're still at the bottom of the valley," Catie said from the cliff. *Would you mind helping too?*

After a pause, the wolves got to their feet as well, and began dragging the dead out of the cave. Eidemon glared at them, then at Catie.

"Would you kindly mind telling me what we're doing this for?" he asked.

"They'll want to honor their dead," she replied, entering the cave for the next fallen soldier. "I thought we could do the same."

"And you think they won't still kill us after they've honored them?" Eidemon said. "They may not, you. But they'll still be furious with Deuel."

Catie paused, cocking her head as if listening for something. "No, they won't kill us," she said finally. "But we should still hurry. Make sure to leave the entrance clear," she added, dragging out the next one.

The procession continued until all the Beltraths were laid out to the side of the cliff, near the stairs, just as the living Beltraths reached the bottom and began their ascent. "Back inside," Catie said, swinging her arms in a herding motion. Eidemon glanced down the cliff-side, then at her.

"You must know something I don't," he muttered.

She smiled. "Oh, I do. Stay just inside, and stay calm." *Everyone in the cave is friendly.*

Eidemon obeyed, looking outside. Shortly there came a light whistling, like wind among the crags. A sudden flap, as from a massive bird, and his eyes doubled in size as Garedardan, shepherd of the Tevor-bath, exile to the Beltrath Wastes, settled on the cliff outside and waited for the soldiers below.

22

DEPARTS FIVE

30 Nuamon 1320 — Autumn

As the Beltraths reached the top of the climb, they froze. Catie stood next to Gared, her hand on his shoulder. "Take your dead," she said. "Garedardan is leaving the Wastes. Roth has abandoned his purpose," she continued, gesturing with her free hand to where Steth and Roth were making their way out of the Eye below. "There is no need to decimate your people further."

They paused, looking at one another. Finally one turned back to Catie. "What about the wingéd man?" he asked.

"He is not your enemy. It was not his fault alone that Garedardan was put where he was. Punishment is coming to those who were truly responsible for that decision. As I said, no more of your people should die because of this thing. But know that *this* place is sacred, and critical..." She trailed off, realizing what she was saying. "I'm sorry," she said, bowing her head. "I know your oasis was sacred too, and critical to your survival. And I know nothing can replace having that taken from you for a generation. But nothing, not even killing a dragon and his children, can return that time to you."

"But their death is safety for our children's children," their leader replied.

"They were a tool," Catie said. "Used by others to hurt you. Roth tried to use them as well—and you—to hurt his own people. Would you have Andelians come again to your land to destroy you, because Roth promised you vengeance in return for your destruction on this land? Would you have them seek to kill all Beltraths for the safety of their children's children? Or would you ask their forgiveness for acting because of how someone made you feel, instead of what was peaceful?"

"You ask this as you stand beside our enemy, in front of our dead? You ask us for peace?"

"I ask you to think of your children's children. When they hear about how many died in order to kill two or three; when they hear that you had a choice to depart from the path of your past onto a new road, and you didn't take it; that they do not have a grandfather because he sought vengeance for *his* father—will they care? Or will they see the children with grandfathers, and only feel the lack? Nothing done before now has been right. Your choice now is to start down the road of what *is* right. You may not be able to forget the past. But if we are ever to leave this cycle of war, you have to forgive the past."

"You do not know what you ask."

"My husband was killed by that man," she said, gesturing again to the dwindling form of Roth. "He tried to kill me. And yet he goes, still living. And I will do nothing to kill him. I only ask you to do as I have done—to make your decision not from bitterness at the past but in hope for the future. Please take your dead, and honor them. And then return home and honor the living by *going on* living."

Go inside, Gared said. *You have said enough, and they will make their decision. But they will not be presided over by a Rinc Nain Andelian.*

Catie bowed to them, and turned. It was only then she noticed, at the back of the group, a young man standing a little taller, and who had seen far less sun. *I wondered where he had gotten to,* she thought. She went into the cave, wondering if Rodigger had thrown his lot completely in with the Beltraths.

"I think you did well," Eidemon said as she entered. "I hope you did, anyway. I'd like to be on my way."

"I'm going to explore more of the caves," she replied tiredly. *Have you looked for any others in here?*

No, Deuel replied, similarly weary. He stood beside his brother, again. The blood had run out of the chrysalis and stained the wall, puddling on the floor and adding a metallic smell to the wet stone. She paused beside him.

I'm sorry, Deuel, she said, resting her cheek against his shoulder. *I guess I have to hope you won't seek revenge, either.*

It is a difficult position, he agreed. *So is mine. He was my brother, whom I have not seen. I mourn his death, but I do not need fear for our race. I think that would make it worse. But I cannot say it makes it better.*

I know, she said. She embraced him from behind, and he reached up and put a hand on her arm as they stood silently for several long moments.

Thank you, Caytaleane, he said finally. *Go, see if anyone else has entered veythya.*

Okay, she said. *I'll be back. Garedardan, have they decided?*

They are gathering their dead. I will come in shortly—we must trust them to keep their word.

Thank you. Catie turned to the dark opening leading deeper into the caves, wondering how much her vision could adjust.

It rippled, but she still struggled in the dim gray. The next room was empty, and she could make out a long, winding path to the third, but few details. She entered, and everything settled into a haze. Halfway across the floor, a shape on the wall to her left caught her eye. She squinted, then took a few steps forward. There was definitely one there, but it was different from Deuel's brother. The chrysalis seemed...fuller. But then, as the dragon grew, she realized it would have to. She took another step closer...

And gasped. Drawing closer to the changing form, her sight brightened, confirming what she saw. There were two bodies inside, curled back-to-front as if cuddling. She didn't recognize the face of the form in the back, but in the front, her body melding with the form behind, was Catie's mother.

Deuel, could you come here please?

Garedardan is coming as well, he replied.

She waited, shaking a little, as she heard footsteps—small and large—coming down the tunnel. When they entered, she felt a love coming from Garedardan that she hadn't felt in a very long time.

"I don't understand," she said, somehow knowing Gared did.

Lamend told me about you, about your meeting in the Brithelt. Knowing it might come to this point, we agreed to tell you some things that normally are not told.

"Why is my mother here?"

She is actually your older sister. You two spent a number of years growing up in the Brithelt. A great number of years.

"Why don't I remember being there?" Catie asked.

It was a long time ago, Caytaleane. And, you are supposed to forget.

"What am I supposed to forget?"

That you are behamona.

Catie's eyes went wide, unsure if that meant what she thought it meant. *Behamona?*

Dragon-daughter.

She sat down. She couldn't help it. *But I don't have wings,* she thought faintly.

You are female, Garedardan replied, still chuckling but also as if appalled. *Females do not have wings.*

Why didn't Deuel tell me? She looked at him. He was only a little less surprised than her.

I didn't know, Deuel said. *I only realized a few moments ago that you were not wyvern, but indeed dragon-kind, when you said you had spoken to Lamend. I knew only dragon-kind could do more than sense the emotions of dragons. I still don't understand how.*

Garedardan glanced between them, his eyes kind. *It is for behamien to forget they are human. It is for behamona to forget they are dragon. In this is balance. Deuel has probably never considered the fact that all his siblings were brothers.*

His expression told all.

There is an age where your memory begins to fail. It is this age you are sent out among humans, to be raised with them, and to believe you are one of them for a time. It was Bahamut's way of ensuring compassion.

"Did my...sister know, then? Or find out?"

When several of Sharéd's tribe came seeking revenge, and the man you called father died defending you both.

Catie pressed her lips together, hoping a similar walling-off took place in her mind. Perhaps her sister had done what she thought best, but wouldn't she have been able to help Catie as she got older? Help her understand what had been going on with her?

Your Grandmother did that, whispered a thought that was not from Deuel or Gared.

Had she? It was not custom to let a Newmother wander off into the world, as she had been allowed to do. Had Grandmother let Catie leave in hopes that she might figure things out better than staying in Attelek? Catie thought back to their conversations when she had returned to her village, had started preparing to leave with Gabriel, Deuel, and Rodigger. She knew that was exactly what Grandmother had done.

Deuel glanced from Catie's sister to Gared. *What about wyverns?*

Wyverns are born when a dragon-child enters veythya alone. There is not enough flesh and bone in one child to grow into dragon. But for you, Deuel, understand this: do not think of wyvern as 'not-dragon'; they are wyvern. They are not defined by what they lack. There is much that wyvern can—and do—that dragon cannot, and do not. Their story in this age is yet to be understood. One day it shall be told. Spare yourself shame on that day by honoring them now.

Catie shook her head. "I still don't understand why this knowledge is hidden. Why not tell the children that, to become dragon, they must enter veythya with a mate?"

It seemed as though Garedardan smiled. *And shall I also tell you that you will marry someone with dark hair, so that you look past all those with light hair? Ages ago, too many dragons entered veythya with a mate because they knew they must. Within a few years, those dragons died of inner torment because their two halves were at war with one another. Only those who truly love—who are willing to sacrifice themselves to see the other become who they were made to be—will survive as dragon.*

"I still..."

Paoloūnd has died. A male dragon must be born to replace him, Garedardan replied. *Were it the other way—had Kaoleyn died—Ledogar must be willing to live as female dragon to replace her. Some of Kerlyn's traits will survive, as they must to make the dragon complete, as I carry in me many of the things that made my wife who she was. But to the world, I appear as male. To the world, Lamendaretha is female, though it took a complete male to make her as well. What we appear to be on the outside is dictated by the needs of the world, and the time in which we are born out of veythya. But what we are on the inside will always contain parts of both.*

"So, if Deuel wanted to become dragon..." Catie broke off, and her face went red. From Deuel she felt very little emotion. From Gared she felt rolling laughter.

This is why Lamend and I decided to give you some knowledge that is not normally given at this early time. Deuel would be with you, gladly—he has demonstrated that, as you have demonstrated you would take him. Gared paused for another chuckle. *But Lamend and I both believe dragon-kind will be best served if you wait until a female must be replaced.*

Catie's hand went to her mouth, and she closed her eyes. *I'm sorry. I've just been on my own for so long, I had to...I'm used to making decisions for myself, and acting on them.*

Do not be ashamed about this, Gared said. *Among humans, perhaps, Deuel should be ashamed for acting as what they perceive is 'not-man'—but that is only because male is considered supreme, and female as always lacking. Deuel is himself; you are yourself. What you each may lack in your character has nothing to do with your sex, but because you are young and still selfish. There are times where you still do not look beyond yourself, or this age, to understand and do what the Great Harmony requires.*

Is the Great Harmony... Catie trailed off, and tried to call up the memory from Ostflir. Garedardan's gaze sharpened.

Even I have not been allowed to see that much, he replied. *The God has blessed you, Caytaleane. But for what purpose I do not know.*

I have spent more time with her than you, Deuel said, his gaze much softer. *I have seen her prepared to do whatever was necessary, despite risk or lack of understanding, than anyone. If the God has some great purpose for her, his guidance would not be wasted.*

Gared glanced between them. *And does he guide you, Caytaleane of Brithelt?*

Catie considered for a long moment. The memory of the Ekllar, that strange future-memory—but she also knew it was not meant to guide her. Beyond her plan of finding Roth again...

Maybe that was enough. She had promised to bring him the Berkarfor. Perhaps after she kept that promise, her next step would become clear. "I will find Roth," she said. "After that, I do not know."

I will take you to him, Garedardan said. *Deuel should see to the honors of his brother. After, I will bring her back?* He said it as a question, looking at Deuel.

That will be fine, he replied.

A memory exploded in her mind. "Oh, Rodigger has the first Berkarfor, though!"

"Was he one of the dead?"

"No, I saw him outside."

I saw him as well, Gared said. *If he was carrying it, he hid it well.*

What do you mean?

Let us return to the first chamber.

They walked through, and when they reached the room they found that Eidemon and his wolves had already departed. Catie's gaze swept the room, lighting quickly on a small pack near where the fight had begun.

"Is that his?" she asked, trotting forward. She retrieved it, and peered inside.

She pulled out an iron goblet. *I don't understand,* she said. *I know when we found these they were very exquisite, some of the finest craftsmanship...*

Charmed, Gared said. Deuel broke his gaze from his brother's corpse to look at the great black dragon. *There is an ancient dragon-charm on all the Berkarfor to make them appear more valuable than they are.*

"Usually when you want to hide something, you make it appear common," Catie said.

You also put real guardians around them, to prevent anyone from taking them, Garedardan replied. *Everything about the Berkarfor are designed to frustrate the plans of those who would take them for easy power, and only truly bless those who retrieve them realizing the important thing is who you become in the journey, not what you get out of the pursuit. You see them for what they are because they hold no power over you, Catie.*

"So, Roth?"

It will be as it should, Gared replied. *Whatever his intentions with these goblets, we must let him make his decisions, and abide by the consequences.*

Deuel returned to tend to his brother, and as Catie and Garedardan continued outside they found the Beltraths were gone too. The sun was well over the mountains, then, and a hawk circled below for prey. Taking a deep breath, Catie climbed Gared's offered foreleg and onto his back.

He won't have gone far, Catie said.

I know. I can see them.

You all are very good, she said with a laugh. *I keep forgetting that.*

You are very good, as well, Gared replied as he dropped off the cliff and soared out across the valley. *But I think you've never believed that.*

Who me? The sunniest behamona in Andelen? she asked, and they both laughed.

Roth and Steth stopped as Gared's shadow swooped over them, craning their necks. He settled in the valley ahead of them, and Catie dismounted.

"Let me down!" Roth shouted. "She brought them to me—miracle of heaven! Get me on the ground!"

Catie strode forward as Steth struggled to comply. Though he cried out several times, Roth finally made it to the ground, and lay down.

"Bring them! We don't have much time!" he said hoarsely, laying a hand on the tourniquet Steth had applied. "You do have them?"

Catie shook her head slightly as she held the bag out in front of her. As he gazed inside it, she knew Roth wasn't seeing them as they were, but as what he expected them to be—knew by the glint in his eye and light in his face, that he was seeing the jeweled, sparkling Berkarfor. She feared for what he was about to do.

"What order did you find them in?" he demanded, pulling them out. Catie gestured to and numbered them each.

"Perfect! Excellent!" He took the first cup, undid the tourniquet, and began filling the goblet with his blood.

Nothing prepared her for that. "What are you doing?" she demanded, taking a step back.

"The legends say, to gain the power, you must drink blood from the Berkarfor—there is life in the blood! Life, with new power." He began filling the second goblet.

"I don't think that's how they work—I *know* that's not how they work," Catie said, taking the step forward again. "Roth, you must listen to me!"

"No!" he shouted. "I know what you think—you who would see me die! *And* you!" he said with an accusing glare at Steth. "You are working together, I know you are, and I will deal with both of you when I am done." He let his blood into the third goblet.

"Roth, I don't care anymore," Catie said. "I've given up on that. But I have actually made the effort to find the goblets, and I can assure you the finding is the most important part."

"*You* found them? Ha! You would never have begun looking if I hadn't found out they existed to begin with." The fourth went near his leg and blood stained the cup. "I am certain I had the harder task."

Gared, help me stop him.

They are said to grant great power, Gared replied. *He may be right.*

"You know he's not," she said, turning to face the dragon fully. "You know this will kill him."

He will not be stopped. Whether this way, or some other, he will kill himself. Do you see?

Catie whirled. Roth had already downed the first goblet. She stepped toward him. He snarled blood at her, lashing out with surprising strength, a small dagger in his other hand. She jerked backward, too slowly, as blood oozed from the small cut.

Steth came forward, pulling her away from Roth as he slurped down the second goblet.

"Please, stop it," she said, tears coming to her eyes, and not entirely from the fire in her arm.

Roth laughed, more blood spraying from his throat, before lifting the third. Catie buried her head in Steth's shoulder. *Why do we do this?*

Because we believe we have the ability to judge for ourselves.

Roth drew a deep breath and smiled, setting down the fourth goblet. "Now, it is time," he said. He tilted his head back, spread his arms, waited for the power to infuse him. "No one will ever know anyone as great as Roth Kamdellan."

Catie drew a breath, looked at Roth, almost hoped he *would* receive whatever power he thought he would.

But instead he became pale. He shook feebly, as if with chills, and his lips turned blue. His eyes widened in disbelief and horror. He bent forward suddenly, vomiting. Shaking and gasping, he fell backward, his breathing in swift gasps as his limbs twitched.

"No...can't...be..."

Catie looked at him more intently as he tried to speak between coughs. His eyes locked onto hers, and rage filled them. "You...did..." He coughed again, his body writhing. His head snapped backward, he arched away from the ground as he twitched.

Suddenly he went slack. His voice, when he spoke, was deeper. *"The way south is open,"* he said, as though confiding in someone else, someone Catie couldn't see. *"After centuries..."*

Coughing wracked him again. He cut off in the middle of a wheeze, frozen as if unable to draw strength to inhale. He stayed like that, heels and fingernails wrenching at the ground, as all the color left him, and seemed as if his flesh withered in on itself.

Catie drew a shaky breath, and pushed herself away from Steth. She glanced at him, could tell by his expression that he hadn't heard Roth's last words.

"He never was himself, lately," Steth said, also sighing. "When I first followed him, it seemed he had a wonderful vision for Andelen. Probably most of us felt the same way. But ever since this spring..." Steth trailed off, shaking his head. "Something changed. He was almost always angry. The more time went on, the more he would fall into fits, like you saw him today. I guess I assumed it would be the end of him soon. How is your arm?"

"Oh, it's fine," she said, waving him away. Her sleeve was stained, but no fresh blood was evident. "Can you do something for me? Go to Agrend and let Sheppar know what happened? I need to get back to Deuel."

"Of course," Steth replied. He stepped away, but did not turn. "It was good to see you again," he said. "However briefly."

"You too," she said with a smile. "It was your fault," she continued lightly. "If you hadn't brought me Kelsie..."

"That was a long time ago," he said with a dismissive wave. "I wouldn't presume there weren't a great many things you've overcome since then. I will bury Roth. He probably still deserves that. And I will deliver your message. Fare well, Catie."

"You too, Steth," she said. She turned and climbed onto Garedardan, waving one last time as the dragon leapt into the air.

Did you hear him? she asked as they winged toward the cave once more. *'The way south is open, after centuries'?*

It sounds like Gintanos, Gared replied. *Cariste landed there long ago, but have stayed north of the mountains, believing it was impossible to make their way south. Perhaps they have found a way.*

I think that is where I am to go, Catie said slowly. The next step.

And Deuel?

He will have to make his decision, first.

⚬

"You could perhaps head south," Sheppar said, gesturing on the map as if he had not suggested it three other times earlier in the conversation.

"My lord, the Beltraths here suggest Roth may be here," Sarah replied—also as if she had not used the same rebuttal at least twice. "By the time we travel all the way south, learn this for certain, and come all the way north again—"

"I have said that Roth is not the concern," Sheppar said, seating himself. "The state of the settlements in the Fallonvall *is*. We must know how much sway he holds, because removing him from that power may not be enough. If he is here, it is because he has the Berkarfor already, and is preparing an attack of some sort against Agrend. If we make him a martyr, then the rebellion will not die. But if you go south, you might undermine his support there—cut out the heart, instead of removing the head."

Sarah drew a breath, then glanced at Geoffrey. That actually made some sense. The problem was cutting out the heart before the head struck off Andelen's head. "How fast can we get down there, though?"

"The fastest route would be by boat," Sheppar said. "There is a private port, to the west. They would be suspicious of people traveling south on foot, anyway. If your ship docks at Satflir, you can say you are from Burieng."

"Are you up for another boat ride?" Sarah asked with a twinkle in her eye.

"Of course, lady," Geoffrey replied.

She glowered at him playfully as a knock sounded on the door.

"Come," Sheppar said. When Samdar entered, he smiled. "Ah, Samdar, perfect timing. These two need to go by boat to Satflir."

"My I ask my lord's purpose?" Samdar asked, also smiling. "It does not regard the rebellion, does it?"

"Why shouldn't it?" Sheppar asked.

"Roth is dead," Samdar replied. "A messenger came with it a few moments ago."

"What happened?"

"Apparently the Berkarfor are not what we believed them to be. Roth drank his own blood from them, and died."

"Oh! Well, then..." Sheppar glanced at Sarah and Geoffrey, his smile tinged with a little sadness. "I'm sorry you came all the way here," he said.

Geoffrey glanced down at his arm. "I'm not," he said quietly. Sarah gripped his hand, smiling as well.

"This is such sudden good tidings. What will you do now, though?" Sheppar asked. "I still might have a use for an advisor—two advisors," he amended quickly, smiling at Samdar, who appeared properly concerned.

"Carist?" Sarah asked, glancing at Geoffrey. "I left my father on bad terms. I hoped to make it up to him."

"Rinc Na, first," Geoffrey replied. "I have work to do there." He shrugged. "And we might find Haydren."

Sarah smiled, and nodded. "Did the messenger mention anyone named Catie?" she asked Samdar.

Samdar cocked his head, shaking it. "No, but I could ask him."

"She is supposed to meet us here. We'll find out then."

"Very well," Samdar said with a bow.

⚬

Garedardan landed with Catie, on the cliff outside the cave. Catie drew an unsteady breath, wondering if Deuel had decided. She almost wished he had not, that he would go with her. She had to follow her decision, she knew that. But, thinking of the time in the Brithelt away from Deuel, she did not enjoy the idea of leaving him again. She knew, deep inside, she would if she had to.

Sometimes, that felt worse.

She walked into the cave. *Deuel?* she asked.

I am here, he said. She could sense nothing from his words as to what he might be feeling.

She walked in. Deuel's brother was no longer on the shelf. There was a cairn in the room, now, beside which Deuel stood, head bowed. She walked up to him, placing her hand on his shoulder, keeping silence as he did.

Deuel drew a breath, and turned toward her. *Do you know what you must do?*

I know where I must go, she said. *I don't know why, yet.*

That is enough.

The silence stretched on as Catie waited for him to indicate his decision, if he had one, knowing that her previous hope was too much to ask for. "And you?" she asked finally.

"How have you made your decision?" he asked instead.

"Deuel..." She glared at him. He waited patiently for her. *Gared can tell you,* she said finally. *If you don't want to trust me.*

I want to make sure we can decide separately from each other, Deuel replied. *That you can follow the plan for your life, even if it means leaving me.*

"We did that already," she said, taking a step back. "Remember? You came here, and I kept searching for the Berkarfor? I would never keep you from doing what you felt you needed to do, Deuel, and I know you would never keep me from it either."

"I am sorry," he replied, and she felt that he meant it. "I had not thought...I did not think what it would mean for you to go on alone. I knew only that I had to come here. I'm sorry."

"Well, Roth killed Dannid, and I forgave him, so..." Her mouth quirked into a smile.

"I remember another brother of mine, Berygal, went east, when we left Kaoleyn's nest," Deuel said. "I had thought to find him, and tell him about...Marethal," he said, glancing at the cairn.

Catie pressed her lips together to keep the ridiculous smile she felt inside from showing. "How far east?" she asked.

"I believe he went to Gintanos," Deuel said, his eyes searching hers. She knew he could sense it, but didn't care. "He always liked the cold. And you?"

"Something happened as Roth was dying. He mentioned the way south was opened after centuries," she said.

Deuel gazed at her for several moments. "Gintanos," he said. "The way south through the mountains."

The smile started to seep through her determination.

"We will have to be content to spend a lot of time together, then," he said, stepping closer to her. Her smile disappeared as she looked into his eyes.

He pulled her close, wrapped his wings around her to hold her even closer, bent down, and kissed her.

⸺◆⸺

Rodigger lay resting in the sun as it crested the mountains. His Therian stood nearby, reins loose. He wondered, briefly, how Gared would make it out of the Eye. Their trip in had not been easy, even with the scouts to guide them. The Therian was just not made for steep, loose trails.

It had hurt, seeing Catie with those creatures—Deuel, and the one wrapped in its own wings, sickly and gray, and with that *face.* He didn't understand how such a pretty girl could stand that close to something like that. He had really hoped to carry her out of there, to save her from her own delusion. But, here he was instead, fearing for his life again.

There wasn't much left. The Beltraths didn't want him, obviously, even though he was sure he could have made a fine leader. Under Sharéd, of course. He would have been obedient to Sharéd, if he'd had to.

Too late now. His best hope was that Deuel, in a rage, would come and drive Halm and Ro Thull through his heart. It wouldn't have been a surprise, or any less painful.

After all their traveling together, he didn't understand how Catie could have turned the way she did. He coughed. He had never seen this coming—any of it.

A shadow passed over him. Here comes Deuel now, he thought. Come to finish me off. The shadow passed again, and he looked up to see a winged shape circling slowly. It wasn't Deuel, it was too small.

The vulture landed just out of his reach, looking at him. Another shadow passed. Another vulture circling lower.

Rodigger coughed again, looked at the Beltrath arrow pointing skyward from his chest, then again at the pair of vultures. They wouldn't have long to wait.

THE END
of
The First to Forgive

THE ONE KNOWN

Book 3 of The Triumvirs

Daniel Dydek

BEORN PUBLISHING, LLC

CONTENTS

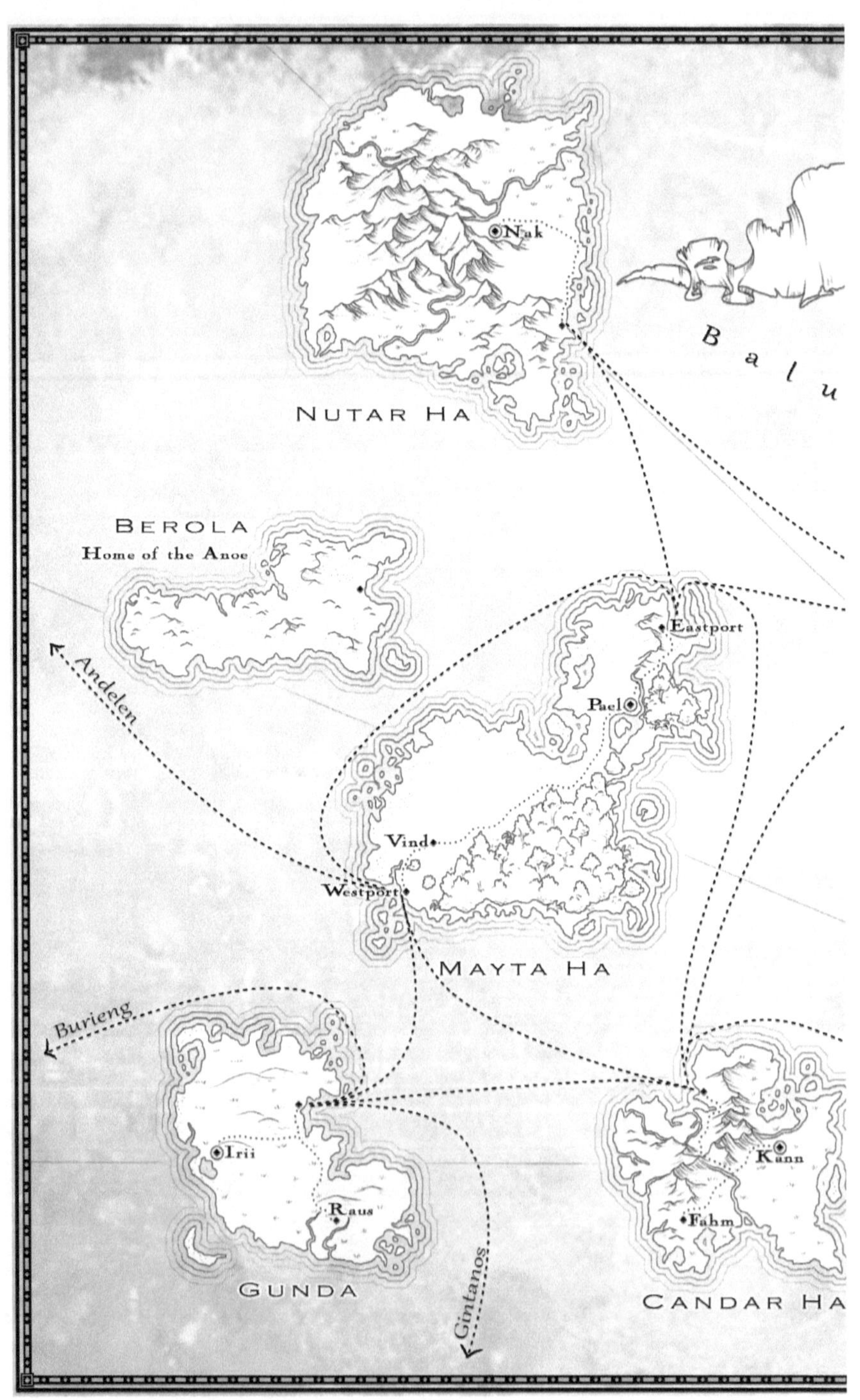

Nak
NUTAR HA
Balu
BEROLA
Home of the Anoe
Eastport
Pael
Andelen
Vind
Westport
MAYTA HA
Burieng
Irii
Kann
Raus
Fahm
Gintanos
GUNDA
CANDAR HA

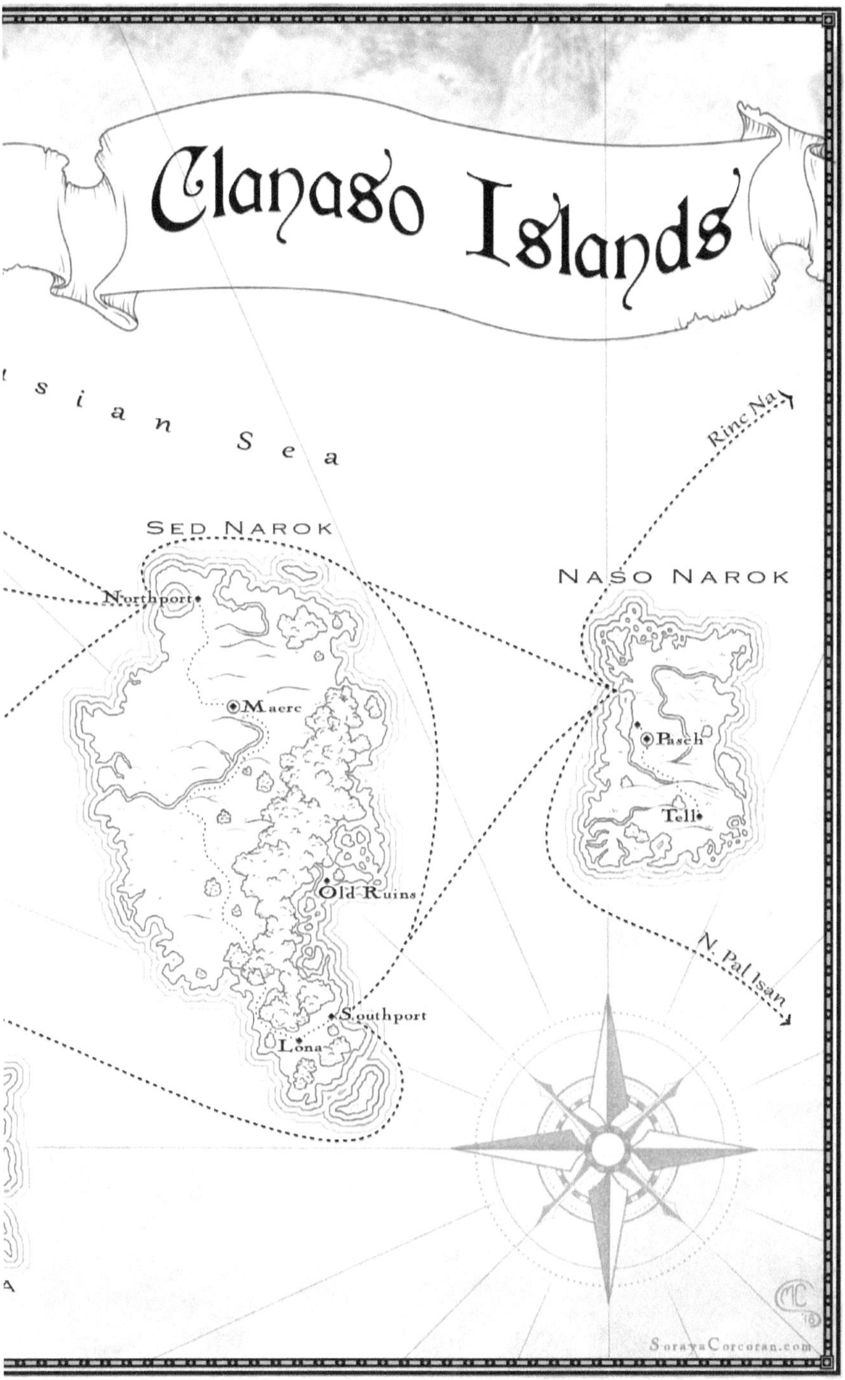

Clanaso Islands
Rinc Na
sian Sea
SED NAROK
NASO NAROK
Northport
Maerc
Pasch
Tell
Old Ruins
Southport
Lona
N. Pal Isan
SorayaCorcoran.com

I

OLD TALES RECOUNTED

"You still watch Haydren?"
"No, I watch the Islands."
"What's there?"
"Do you not have your own war to avert?"

16 Monzak 1320[1] — Rainy

A boat was missing.

Keebo sat back in the hammock, his gaze gliding along the horizon. The gentle curve of the white-sand bay embraced the placid blue waters. The grasses further up the dunes swished in the gentle breeze. Somewhere in the small port-village a street performer strummed a dulcimer, adding some depth to the seagulls' incessant cries. Everything was there that should have been.

Except a boat.

The dock was empty. A limp flag, too heavy to be caught by the light breezes, would have said "Back Soon"; folded, it read "Bac on" which only made him hungry for fried pig. So that was missing, too. And clouds: for being the Clanaso's rainy season, there should have been clouds somewhere, and rainwater almost everywhere.

Keebo sighed, swinging his legs off the hammock and settling brown

---

1. See Author's Note on Calendar for explanation of dates

feet into sand. He groaned himself to standing, bracing one hand against the palm tree while he jabbed himself playfully in his distended pot-belly with the other.

"You don't need bacon, Keebo," he muttered. Nor did he need a boat, really; when he recognized himself in his proper spot in place and time, there was little that he truly *needed*. Life tended to provide for itself. In the present, he was full, the sun was warm, and no one was physically pushing him into the water.

It was only that if he didn't leave Gunda very soon, that man in Irii might remember who he was and track him down. It would be a sticky end at best. Not that Keebo needed to live for any particular reason; he simply also did not need to die either.

Out around the point, sails suddenly appeared; his heart lifted, but only for a moment as he knew there were too many cloths to be the ferryman he waited for. As the ship continued wobbling into view, he guessed it would be from Burieng; deep-water boats from that quarter were almost never made as stable as those from Andelen or the Pal Isans—and those from Gintanos would have rounded the other point.

Lower sails were hauled in, slowing the ship as it neared. Keebo began wandering up the beach toward the dock. It might be making for Sed Narok next, and might be ready to depart before the ferryman returned—"soon" being such a vague notion of time, especially in the Islands. But foreign boats stayed only long enough to restock a few provisions before heading to the interior, as the bay here was too shallow for them to survive the ebb tide.

The ship turned into the wind and dropped anchor. It was the *Sword Dancer,* he saw. Skiffs, already loaded with people and some casks, lowered away; and with outrigged oars they moved like water-spiders, scrabbling their way across the water toward the dock.

Keebo kept out of the way, watching for the mate as the boats were tied up and unladen of sailors and passengers—the latter were helped out of the boat, the former made their own way. He quickly spotted the one man directing the sailors.

Before he could call out, a man's voice beside him said: "excuse me." Keebo turned and looked up into a face that reminded him of a younger Tolma Bergin—chestnut hair, gray eyes, though the skin was tanner. "Can you tell me where I can find something besides fish to eat?"

"I can do even better," Keebo replied, smiling. "I can take you there! Just let me get a quick word—"

"They're not leaving again for at least a shift," the young man replied. "And they won't leave without me."

"You're someone important?" Keebo asked lightly.

The young man gave a resigned grin, saying nothing; his hand, though, strayed absent-mindedly to his sword. Keebo's brown eyes searched the man's face. There was no belligerence or pride to suggest a threat, so there was something else behind the gesture. He glanced down, then looked closer.

The sword-handle was in the form of a dragon, the scabbard in black leather with silver stitching like scales. It reminded him of something, an image he had seen years before. The sword was potent, even if the owner was resigned to using it. He looked up again.

"You saved their lives, somehow?" he asked, quietly.

The young man glanced down, then took his hand quickly off the hilt and folded his arms. "And my own," he replied, as if defending a boat-full of people might be wrong. A strange young man, Keebo thought, not to boast in a heroic deed.

"What is your name?" he asked.

"Haydren," the swordsman replied.

"Well, I am Keebo. Welcome to Gunda. Let me show you some food."

Haydren grinned. "Thank you; that's the best welcome I've ever received."

Keebo led the way to the only shop, fourth hut from the end. Raised on stilts for storm tides, open walls to allow a breeze, and palm-thatch roof were the hallmarks of permanent structures in the Islands' ports, and Jedded's Gundabulous Fare—a particular type of restaurant known in the Islands as a Fire Pit, specializing in smoked meats with tangy glazes—did not disappoint. The scent of sweet vinegar and roasted meats were almost as thick as the smoke trapped in the ceiling. Several of the sailors—undoubtedly the higher-ranking ones—already took up most of the bench-space where Jedded laughed and served mild liquors. Keebo waved to Jedded as they entered, then led Haydren to a corner table. He sat with his back against the corner, where he could see anyone approaching long before he could be seen himself.

He smiled as Haydren glanced around after taking a seat. "I'll let you know if I see anyone suspicious," he said with a wink.

Haydren's grin was curious in return. "Why would I be worried about anyone suspicious?"

Keebo gazed at him a few moments. "You carry a rare sword, and don't want to be famous...or perhaps notorious. I haven't decided which, yet."

Haydren smiled. "That may not be up to me," he replied, then shrugged. "Sometimes fame comes from doing what you must."

Keebo blinked, and looked away. "Or from listening to voices in your head," he said quietly.

Haydren's smile disappeared, but before he could say anything Jedded arrived beside their table. "From them!" he said loudly, gesturing toward the benches as he plonked down two mugs of watery rum. Jedded believed in productivity, and never served full-strength alcohol before the sun went down. He also believed in profitability, with the same outcome. "What else will you have?"

"Um," Haydren said, gesturing toward Keebo.

"Rack and Ruin," he said with a smile. "You'll love it," he continued as Jedded left. "Smoked pork ribs with a glaze you won't believe is good for you, and shredded chicken and bean soup that actually isn't."

Haydren laughed. "How so?"

"Well, let's just say we might be making full use of the forward privies on our way to Sed Narok," Keebo replied, beaming. "But it's delicious."

Haydren groaned. "Even these sailors may not be so eager to have me aboard after that."

Keebo raised his mug, waited for Haydren to match, then took several long swallows and sighed. "Even after a hundred fifty years in this heat, it's still nice to have something to take the edge off," he said.

"You're a wizard?" Haydren asked.

Keebo shrugged modestly. "I do a bit here and there. Moderation is the key; too many wizards try to use too much, end up getting old like normal people."

Haydren grunted. "Or try to take over a country and have to be stopped."

"You came from Burieng?" Keebo asked. When Haydren nodded, Keebo drew a breath. "Your accent was the biggest clue; but I also think you're talking about Lasserain."

"Did you know him?"

Keebo smiled. "Just because we both use magic, doesn't mean we all know each other. But I had heard enough. A lot of refugees went to Gintanos, but some came here, too. How much of the country does he own these days?"

Haydren smiled. "About six feet," he said. "If you can call it 'owning.' He's with Illmali and the Riven, now."

Keebo's eyes went wide. "Is he, now?" he said. "And you did that?"

"Me and two others. Three others," Haydren amended quickly.

Keebo cocked his head. "You lost count?"

"Well, really, there were countless others who helped us along the way; there were three of us physically there when he died, and a fourth was..." Haydren trailed off, spinning his hand in the air. "Around. I'm not sure exactly how, myself," he said with a chuckle.

"And I assume your sword helped too?" Keebo asked.

Haydren paused as Jedded arrived just then with a bamboo plate piled with pork ribs, and a large walnut bowl of steaming, spiced chicken stew. He set them down, along with wooden spoons and forks, and a stack of thin bread almost like parchment.

"Like this," Keebo said, picking up a rib with one of the pieces of bread, tearing off a chunk with his teeth, then wiping his chin with another part. "Helps keep you clean and fills you up extra," he said around the mouthful.

Haydren drew a breath and tucked in. For the next several moments he concerned himself only with thoroughly enjoying the meal. "We don't have anything like this in Burieng," he muttered around one of his eager bites.

"I eat here whenever I'm in Gunda," Keebo said. "The stew has enough seasoning to awaken the tongue, but enough sweet to keep your mouth from burning or puckering. Am I right?"

Haydren chuckled, and nodded. "You've had more time to consider it than I have," he said.

Keebo snorted agreement. They continued without speaking until the final rib was bare, and the bowl empty. Keebo sighed contentedly. "Where did you get your sword?" he asked, sitting back.

"Oh, I found it when I was very young," Haydren replied. "In Rinc Na. But actually, Lasserain had a spell to stop the Bultum from piercing him; I used a dagger made of Cretal to actually kill him."

Keebo's eyes narrowed a little; the young man was sharp, to recognize the true line of questioning. He picked up the last piece of bread and held it toward Haydren in offering. Haydren chuckled and declined; Keebo shrugged, wiped the plate with it, and chewed for several moments longer. "Magic doesn't work that way," he said finally. "At least, not to my knowledge."

"Lasserain did have access to many spell books," Haydren offered. "He even began using Time and Shape."

Keebo shuddered a little. "That confirms a rumor. Regardless, magic commands the raw elements; I know of no shielding technique that would work against one metal and not another."

"Could he command the Bultum in my sword to stop, thinking that he was commanding the Cretal?"

Keebo sat up. "Your sword has both?" he said loudly.

Haydren rolled his eyes and glanced toward the sailors. "They don't know that, yet," he muttered. "I didn't want to draw much attention to myself."

Keebo continued to stare as if he hadn't heard. The image in his mind was knocking on his teeth. "Aerithion," he whispered finally.

Haydren looked at him silently, and did not deny it.

Keebo's gaze went distant. "You have one of the Shadebreakers. After hundreds of years..."

"I hadn't heard it called that," Haydren said. "Not even in Deewan."

"Have any others been found?" Keebo asked.

Haydren nodded. "A man named Aver, from Gintanos, has found Skyalfamold. He was in Deewan when I was there."

"The rest will be found soon, if they are not already. This Aver—he is a bold man?"

Haydren snorted. "He cared more for his goods than helping us defeat Lasserain," he said. "He was a merchant. I believe he was heading back to Gintanos as quickly as he could."

"Gintanos," Keebo repeated. He shrugged. "Something may still come of that." He shivered. "I didn't think it would happen in my lifetime."

"What would happen? What are these swords tied up in? Why didn't the Kesten tell me about these as—what did you call them?"

"Shadebreakers," Keebo replied. "And the Kesten did not call them that. I assume they only made what they were told to make. The name of Shadebreaker is part of a prophecy that cropped up elsewhere—I'm not sure where exactly, or even when. But it foretells some sort of cataclysm from which the world will never return, once all four are found and used."

"Used? Used for what?"

Keebo shrugged. "Not really sure. It might just be that activating the magic in all of them will do it. Or they might have to be used together for some purpose."

"You don't seem to care very much," Haydren said.

"Well, it's prophecy; have you ever tried to stop a prophecy?"

Haydren opened his mouth to reply, then closed it. "I suppose I did, in a way."

"Not very successful was it?"

Haydren glowered, about to retort when one of the sailors called out to them. "Ship's leaving!"

"Ah, just in time!" Keebo said. He dug into a pouch and produced a coin. "I hope you have one of these," he said.

Haydren stood, reaching into his own, much larger pouch to dig out a palm-full of coins. He rooted through, found the proper size, and gave it to Keebo.

"We'll just leave that on the table," he said, placing Haydren's coin down and pocketing his own.

"Hey!" Haydren protested.

"You've got plenty, and this is my last one; besides, I helped you out. I may help you even further, if the opportunity arises; and I won't ask for payment then, either."

Haydren shook his head. "Fine, whatever."

They left the hut, made their way to the beach and into the boats. "You coming too?" one of them asked Keebo. "It's a mark for passage to the next port."

"Yes, of course," Keebo said, looking pointedly at Haydren.

Haydren chuckled in disbelief, but handed over the coin. Keebo sat back with a smile. He had a full belly, and a boat. He didn't miss the rain, or the man from Irii.

When the skiffs were more than halfway to the ship, a figure appeared on shore, running to the edge of the pier. His shout rolled across the bay.

"Keebo Burami! You won't hide from me! I'll catch up with you yet!"

2

THE CLOUDS BURST

"Do you want me to go?"
"I do not think he would be happy to see you."
"Why not?"
"I passed him over for the Triumvirate, in favor of you."

16 Monzak 1320 — Rainy

"You know, you never answered my question."

Keebo looked up in surprise. The wind was fair at their backs, well on their way to Sed Narok, and Haydren had been quiet since Keebo refused to tell him who the man on the shore was. Not that it was anyone's business. "You had a lot of questions; which one didn't I answer?"

"About Lasserain, if he could have stopped the Bultum thinking he was stopping the Cretal."

Keebo's face scrunched up as his eyes went skyward, looking as clouds began to amass. "Technically, he could have commanded the metal in your sword. But he couldn't just create a shield—he would have had to speak the command as your sword came at him. Probably not fast enough."

"He could command Time?" Haydren offered.

Keebo's eyebrows flared, his gaze still in the clouds. It was a nice day, truly. He was in good spirits. But clouds were gathering, and he didn't like it. "Then it wouldn't matter what the blade was made of, would it? Did he say he found a way to stop Bultum?"

Haydren hummed. "You know, he did; he said he was looking for a way to keep magic from piercing him, and found a spell mentioning Bultum and thought he had found it. He didn't know the magic wasn't in Bultum."

Keebo smiled as his gaze finally lowered to Haydren. "Only plain folk don't know that Bultum isn't magical," he said. "Anyone who knows spells knows it's in Cretal."

Haydren looked hard at Keebo. "The Kesten didn't make it seem that way."

Keebo looked surprised. "Really? You would think folk from a remote mountain village with few visitors would know better."

Haydren rolled his eyes. "Fine. But still, Lasserain lied then? Why would he do that?"

Keebo shrugged. "Well, maybe he didn't know. He was only a mage, after all, and self-taught."

Haydren looked across the waters. "I find that hard to believe."

"I guess we can't ask him."

Haydren paused, then laughed. He shook his head when Keebo cocked an eyebrow. "A friend of mine, Geoffrey, once said the same thing about someone else I had killed."

"There *is* a certain amount of finality, around death," Keebo agreed.

Both countenances darkened a shade, and they lapsed into silence, watching the waters slip by. Keebo's thoughts turned again to Sed Narok, to his home. He wished he was there, wished he had never visited Irii and been recognized. He had been mostly honest with Haydren—he didn't know the man. Not personally. Knew enough to understand the hate, yes; but not why it surfaced now. And for the second time.

"Not after so long," Keebo muttered, intending it for himself as he looked cloud-ward again.

"It's only been a few months," Haydren said with a shake of his head. Keebo's brows knit. "What?"

"Since Lasserain died; it was Halmfurtung—less than two months ago."

"Oh, sorry; I was referring to something else, something that happened…" He scratched his belly. "More than two months ago."

The silence fell again. The clouds were turning dark. Keebo glanced backward at the ship captain, who shook his head briefly and waved away port-side: apparently he believed the storm would move north.

"Happy thoughts," Keebo announced, smiling. "Where are you headed?"

"Rinc Na," Haydren replied, trying to match his smile. "Trying to find my sister. Tell her our parents are…dead."

Keebo's smile plummeted, and he sighed. Clouds.

———◆———

For a wonder the rain held off the two days and nights it took sailing to Northport on Sed Narok, each squall missing them north or south. After docking, some few passengers and goods headed inland for Maerc; most, including Haydren and a quarter-hold of crates, stayed aboard for Naso Narok and points east. Keebo bid him farewell and headed quickly inland as well. For what he needed to do, he wanted as few onlookers as possible.

It was one of his newer tricks, but he enjoyed it far more than riding horseback, or walking. About a quarter-mile down the road, he reached out and began gathering clay from the surrounding land, drawing it to himself and molding it into a compact plate. Clay, he found, was more comfortable than dirt, lighter than rock, and took far less energy to manipulate. It also helped to gather bits, rather than lifting it complete; folk didn't like the strange holes it left when he did it that way.

When he was done, a disc of dried clay roughly a pace across and only two fingers thick was before him. Glancing quickly around, he sat cross-legged atop the disc. "Now," he said, looking down; *"Lan eki kohthatka ekikein pif jeu oren."*

The disc took off like a galloping horse, skimming over the ground as Keebo leaned forward with a grin. He always cheered giddily at traveling this way, part because it felt like flying, and part because he knew he must look ridiculous. But not, to him, as ridiculous as he looked on a horse. His legs might be a bit worthless for a while, losing all that energy in a magical casting, but he could eat while he rode to replenish some of his stores.

He thought the clouds did him a favor as the town of Maerc slid by on his left, and he turned the disc west on the road home. But when the rain finally did come it seemed intent on making up for lost time, and Keebo was soaked through before he was halfway along the lonely track. Despite the fat drops pelting his face at galloping speed, at least it was warm.

That the area was farmland was obvious—tilled earth and orderly plantations rose and fell with the landscape. That it was inhabited was less clear. Single-story huts and homes peeked between the rolling hills to the road, though their dark windows and shut doors abruptly ignored any passers-by. It was mostly why Keebo had chosen this area to live—and chose the home farthest from the city. He did not regret his choice, especially now he was the only inhabitant of all the Islands whizzing about on an oversized dinner-plate.

When his home finally came into view, the rain had lessened, though the damage to his mode of transport was already done. The road had narrowed along the last few houses, then became a walking trail, and now ended at his door. The disc—now a muddy shadow in the shape of a cross-legged Keebo—stopped and sank to the ground. He remained seated for a moment, assessing his gardens with a rain-filled glance; they would hold until morning. He stood shakily, then paused, feeling the dirt through his feet. Maybe a little bit of effort was needed there, near the beans...with a few thoughts, he opened the dirt, let water seep through where it had been trying to puddle. There: that would certainly hold.

He went inside, let himself drip for a time. The rain was actually a soothing sound, once it wasn't plonking on his head and shoulders. He closed his eyes and breathed deep. There were moments that made 150 years—and the prospect of 150 more—worth the living. Even if it was far short of the thousand years he had once dreamed of.

It was dark inside, and he did not care to light a candle. He went to a chest he knew by memory, removed a blanket, and dried himself with it before falling onto his cot and drifting to sleep.

The next morning, the rain still fell. He opened his eyes. The clouds were thinner, though, and enough light shone in the far window to light the interior of his house. He lived simply, in one room: the bedroll on which he lay, against the north wall; window on the west, a chest below it with blankets, a few items of clothing, and his books inside; cookstove, one shelf—decked with pot, skillet, tongs, and a fork—and a table and three-legged chair on the south wall; door to the outside on the east wall, and a trapdoor to his pantry on the floor next to it. In the rafters were a few extra chairs for guests, gathering dust because he never had any. That was the point—but he didn't want to seem inhospitable. Baths were taken on days like today; relief was taken however far he made it outside before he felt like stopping. He went to Maerc when he needed groceries, and any of the other islands when he needed to stretch his legs. Except Nutar Ha; there was never good enough reason to go there.

After making use of the outdoors he returned inside, and went again to the chest. This time, he lifted one of the two books and retreated to his table. *Style of the Elements,* written in Cariste (of course), gazed at him blankly for a moment. Neither of them knew why he pulled it out. It was for mages and sorcerers, just arrived at Tamecal with no idea what they were doing, and surely a wizard was beyond that.

And he was. Until Haydren wondered about some sort of shield preventing magic from piercing it.

Keebo read as the rain dripped on. A few of the questions he had one hundred years ago when he first read the book lingered: why could Air and Fire both control lightning? Why could Earth and Air both heal wounds? The words were different, but the spells achieved nearly the same thing (Earth was the better spell, of course). Water, Earth, and Air all had good spells for plant life.

A peal of thunder rumbled, and Keebo glanced up briefly and rolled his eyes. Typical.

Nothing controlled all the elements at once. It went against the nature of Magic. To cast a spell, you had to first call out to the element, get its attention. Like when he got home last night, he had convinced the clay to become more like sand for a minute, stop being belligerent toward the water that only wanted to help his plants grow. Then it went back to clay when he was done. But he did not do one thing to tell the water what to do; it did what it always did, whether anyone was looking or not.

The rain ceased, and Keebo closed the book. Lasserain was a powerful mage, had found spells that no one else had found in recorded history. And he should not have had power equalling a wizard in every element, either. Maybe that's all it was. For now, his garden needed him, and Keebo needed breakfast.

He went out; the sun was shining again, always quick to apologize for the storms that hit the Islands this time of year. The garden was not badly damaged. Keebo walked between the rows, speaking to the earth, making sure the roots were not too sodden, holding water in pockets to be released later. Harvest time was always good for Keebo, and for those whom he visited occasionally throughout the year.

"Good afternoon, my friend," said a voice.

Keebo didn't even look up; he had suspected this visit when the single peal of thunder struck, had been worried when the man from Irii suddenly wanted to kill him, and when he met the one who had killed Lasserain and carried one of the Shadebreakers. "Out for a walk?" he asked.

"As it were," replied the voice with an edge of testiness. The owner of the voice hadn't walked in centuries, and Keebo knew it. "Still using your vast talents to grow lettuce?"

Keebo paused, loosening another area where rain clung too tenaciously, bringing some richer soil up from below and mixing it into the topsoil. "You know, I've found the secret," he said, moving on, knowing his visitor would follow. "One magic user uses no magic, lives an extraordinarily long time, but doesn't get to use his magic. Another uses his energy constantly, dies the same time as anyone else. Moderation is the key! A little bit here and there, minor daily uses, nurturing the affinity and granting the longest life with the most use of magic. At least, as much life as can be had on Oren."

He turned finally, looking on his aging, red-robed visitor. It was a form the man always carried, even among those who knew him better. Perhaps he had to; Keebo didn't care, and likely would never know. "In your Room, though...how old are you now? You look the same as last time I saw you."

Melnor gazed at him. "You know that doesn't matter. Do you know what it takes to come see you? How difficult and dangerous it is to ride a bolt of lightning, make the jump to your mind quickly enough without you noticing?"

"You shouldn't have bothered," Keebo said. "I'm not worth the effort."

"You could at least burn a candle." Melnor knew he would receive this sort of reception, but it still rankled.

"Of course! Then you could come visit me anytime." Keebo turned away and continued tending his garden.

Melnor stood a little taller, towering even more over the chubby earth wizard. "Keebo Burami, I did not come through lightning to bicker with you; I came to speak to you of a matter most important."

Keebo glanced at him. "You don't scare me, Melnor; you're barely real, and you wouldn't do anything to my mind. Speak your piece and move on."

Melnor checked a sigh. Perhaps he should have been more certain before making Keebo think he might be raised to Triumvir. If it hadn't been for that woman...no, it had been Keebo. And Melnor still hadn't found an opportunity to address that. This was not the time, either.

"There has been an...incident," Melnor said. "I was elsewhere, as was Teresh and Kanala. None of us saw what happened. But a messenger is on his way from Maerc, he should be here soon. It is very important that you accept his word."

Keebo stopped, glancing over his tomato plants: none of the fruits were ready. There went that idea for breakfast. "I will see what it says," he replied. He knew Melnor couldn't tell him specifics in advance; only the spirit of his message would remain after he left, some compulsion to do whatever it was Melnor wanted—a compulsion made stronger by the fact Melnor visited him in person instead of just influencing his thoughts. This time, apparently, a compulsion to answer a summons that he otherwise would not want to answer. That alone worried him. There were too many things he might be asked to do that he would not want to. "Will you stay for breakfast? Oh, sorry; concerns of the living."

Melnor wished he could make Keebo forget, make him move on. But that was something the Clansman would have to do on his own. "I'll stay until you light a flame," he said.

3

SONG OF DEATH

"He doesn't seem to like you."
"I once thought he was ready to be a Triumvir."
"What happened?"
"I was wrong."

20 Monzak 1320 — Dry

The messenger arrived before lunch, his horse foaming and his legs stiff. "Keebo," the man said, a little out of breath. "Message from Master Bergin."

Keebo tried to remain relaxed, sitting on the stairs and shucking some early peas, but it was difficult. Tolma Bergin was definitely near the bottom of the list of people he wanted to hear from. "Yes?" he asked.

"He requests you proceed at once to Nobak, prepared to spend an Evening there."

Keebo could tell by the way the man said it that he didn't know what he was talking about. "Where's Nobak?" he asked, as a game.

The messenger would not play along. "I don't know, sir; I assumed you would know."

He did know it. It was the former Anoe capital, between Maerc and Lona if one cared to look for it. No one usually did. "What am I supposed to do there?" Keebo asked.

"I'm not sure, sir. He said to give you this." He held out a letter.

Keebo dropped the pea-pod and held out his hand. It had been a long time since he had seen the seal on the scroll that the messenger handed over. "Peas?" he asked, holding out the bowl.

The messenger shook his head. "I'll take water though."

Keebo nodded once, and flicked a finger toward the well. He broke the seal as the man walked off, trying to ignore the horse's cautious gaze. He began to read, snorting after "My old friend," but sobering as the letter progressed.

"I hope you are well. I'm afraid the Islands are in grave danger. Last week, sometime after we ate lunch on the road to Maerc, Jon went off for a ride. He mentioned the old ruins." (That's what most Rinc Nain called Nobak, pushing away the memory of their genocide.) "That night, when Jon was far too late in returning, a man we sent to look came back saying he had found Jon's body at the ruins, killed horribly. By the time you read this, we'll be on a ship to Nak for safety until you can come and tell me what happened. I know no one else who can do it. I've seen you do it before, and I know you have methods. Please use them, and hurry; I cannot explain much here, but the Islands may truly come apart at the seams if this is not solved quickly.

"Yours,"—et cetera.

Keebo lowered the parchment, his eyes going distant. Nak, on Nutar Ha. Yes, it was safe, and wickedly defensible; Keebo's folly had been to help make it so. And Tolma wanted him to go there, of all places, after doing...*that*...of all things. The man was a villain.

"You're sure he didn't tell you what he wanted me to do?" Keebo asked finally.

The man shook his head honestly. "He only said to tell you to go—"

Keebo waved him silent. At least that secret was safe.

Kin-singer.

He hated even thinking the word. Well, the Steward of the Islands asked him to go, so he should go. The thought briefly occurred to Keebo to ignore the directive, but it didn't stick. *Probably Melnor's meddling,* he thought. As he recalled the name to mind, so too came the memory of his visit earlier. Another limitation on the Triumvirate's power. Maybe it was better... He sighed as he stood, glanced up at the sun.

"Oh, I'm to give you my horse," the messenger replied as if just remembering. "Seemed important. What's happened?"

Keebo shook his head, eyeing the animal. His stubby legs didn't usually fit well on a horse's saddle; much better suited to a pony or donkey. Or a clay plate. But Nobak was a five-day journey—such use of magic would take up nearly all of his energy reserves. It might even kill him. Even if it didn't, he was bound to need those reserves in the coming days, trying to solve this thing. There was nothing for it. "I'll let his Stewardship tell you," he said, using his favorite title for Tolma when he was frustrated with his ancient friend. He appreciated seeing the eyes widen of whomever was nearby. But the messenger and his horse both only looked placidly on, and Keebo's mood fell further.

"Well, help an old man up into his saddle," he said. Together they shortened the stirrups, and managed to get Keebo high atop the horse.

Once there he settled in, turning the mount easily and cantering down the road, eastward.

All things considered, Keebo was impressed that—off his plate—it only took him two days to reach Maerc. As the city rose on the horizon he veered south, deciding to avoid the Noon traffic and the temptations of the myriad vendors' stalls, all with fresh hot food. He dug into the saddlebags, pulling out what remained of a rind of hard cheese and a heel of bread, also hard. His searching fingers also found a small pouch of clinking coins; had Tolma thought even of that? Hopefully, and he had not instead just stolen the meager wages of a poor messenger. Perhaps he should stop—

The road south came into view, and he continued. Late-season clouds massed to the west. These, at least, did not appear to contain lightning. No threat from bolts, and no threat from visiting Triumvirs. What he had to do, he wanted to do alone. Melnor hadn't liked it, when he learned of Keebo's unique ability, likely because he didn't understand it. To be fair, Keebo neither liked nor understood it either, but it was apparently necessary.

When the rains arrived, he slowed to a walk and let the horse stray into the thick grass along the roadside. The road itself would too soon be mud, and short as he was he knew he was still heavy, still a greater burden for the poor animal than it was used to. There was no need to also force it through fetlock-sucking mud. If they kept to the roadside they could keep making good time.

It was a light rain, a cleansing rain, and it helped Keebo relax despite the thoughts hammering for entrance into his primary consciousness. He wasn't sure why, but an old friend kept coming to mind, too. He had not seen Shokalog for many years. He didn't want to, except he suddenly missed the little frog. Kal was a dreamer, like Keebo was once. Full of hope and promise, and...well, motivation. Keebo missed that, too.

He pushed it away. Think on it too long, and it too often came to be. He had no desire to see Kal, especially anywhere near Nobak. No, Kal needed to be firmly in Berola, and for many days before and after last week, with plenty of witnesses. A Clansmen's court would likely need...five Anoe. No, royalty was involved: ten. And that only if the court was mostly made of Rinc Nain; too many of Keebo's kind, and it still wouldn't hold a judgment. A Clansmen Captain, maybe? Yes, one who had taken Kal—or any Anoe—to Berola and left them there.

Keebo shook his head. He did not know what he would find yet.

But surely Tolma had thought of that possibility. Almost any Rinc Nain Clansman would. And he sent a known ally of the Anoe to investigate, and a Pal Isan. Was his sense of justice so keen? Tolma was never particularly fond of the Anoe, would not necessarily care if one was prejudicially accused of a crime. Almost any Clansman wouldn't; and most Rinc Nain certainly didn't.

Maybe it was just because of Keebo's gift—well, talent. It was rarely a gift in the traditional sense.

At least the rain was pleasant. He shut his mind again, enjoying the soft patter of water on his skin, the cool rivulets running under his clothes and carrying with it the salt sweat, returning it to earth.

————◆O◆————

As the sun passed Afternoon and descended through thick but scattered clouds toward Evening, two days south of Maerc, Keebo spotted the pair of hills far to the east that marked the gateway toward Nobak. In his mind's eye, he could still see the trail branching off the road. In the present, there was only grass—plain and unbroken, no indication that a civilization once lay that way. He turned the horse and made for the valley between the hills. He glanced back, judging: the sun should be out again by the time he reached the ancient village. He sighed. He needed the sun, but wished it would have delayed.

No. There was death to solve. Murder. Putting it off would not make it easier.

As the land opened before him, he was reminded once again of why the Anoe would choose this spot: the valley sloped gently away, falling several hundred feet to the floor below, and broadening into the cupped hands of the verdant hills. The valley continued widening south-eastward until it ended in white sand. On a bright day, calm blue seas lapped the shore behind the city, with white breakers rolling on the horizon.

But now the clouds lay over the horizon, a pall over the ruined capital. The city below was broken, fragmented, gray stones crumbled and devoured by vines. The streets some time ago had disappeared beneath the leafmold.

Keebo glanced back once more toward the sun. Hopefully he was not too late. The trick would be finding the spot. Gruesome as it was, and as much as it turned his heart, he hoped to find blood. Otherwise he might be here for days.

He nudged the horse, and began the descent. He passed rotting trunks, former pillars of outlying huts, leaning oddly between the ferns, and entered a palm forest. Despite the intervening years, the hall where the road had once been was still evident and he followed it. Occasionally his horse's hoof thudded dully on nearly-exposed stone. Lovers of nature that the Anoe were, they had not minded clearing land for this, their greatest city. Everywhere else in the Islands, their settlements had long ago disappeared until only Berola was left. To this day, they had kept to their impermanent dwellings and never tried to recreate this hallowed place.

Keebo paused in the square, at the dank water and leaf-filled pool. It seemed odd, to him, to have such a large pool in the city, when the ocean was so near. Strange stone knobs almost like mushrooms encircled it, and he wondered if it was some sort of ceremony place. Maybe a question for Kal next time he saw him.

A few palms rose from within tumbled walls, hushing now in a light breeze from the sea. Why would Jon have come out here? Where would he have gone? Tolma at least could have mentioned specifically where they found the body.

Keebo set his jaw a moment, and sighed. There was nothing for it.

He began singing.

It was a song possibly millennia old, the words of a language long, long lost. At least, that's what he had been able to learn from Melnor; the words and tune came to him long ago in a dream, and knowledge of its purpose came even later. Its rhythm and meter were like nothing sung now. It was not meant for worship, or for pleasure, or politics.

It was meant to see the dead.

As he sang, he dismounted. He walked slowly past the fountain, glancing around the ruins. He continued singing, looking up at the sky as the sun broke through the clouds. The wind stirred a little higher, rustling a few hanging creepers and clattering their woody stalks against one another.

Among the buildings, he stepped off the street through an archway. The stones of this building were still mostly intact, and two hallways ran away from a large foyer or anteroom. Through the song, he thought he remembered Kal mentioning this might have been their city hall, of sorts. Community meetings were held here, and here the ruling officials conducted business with all visitors. It seemed as good a place to start looking for a visiting young lord.

Without knowing why, he made his way down the right-hand hall. After a turn, several rooms began opening to the right, their wood doors long decayed and gone, rusted hinges bolted to thin air.

His voice echoed, now, adding unintended layers to the melody. The wind was coming through gaps in the walls, but the sun had not yet come out and everything was cast in a gray-green pallor. He glanced into a room as he passed, noting the remains of a thick table, stones collapsed into the floor, ferns and palm leaves and vines intruding into the room, and scuff-marks on some dirt that had made its way inside.

He paused, then stepped inside the room. The song faltered, caught; he swallowed once as he saw the rust-stain of blood on pitted stonework. He picked up the song again, waiting.

The breeze rose, rustling the fronds. Sunbeams trickled through the leaves, intensified, lit a million motes as they brightened the room, danced through the waving trees. Where they struck they blossomed into almost ethereal white, like ocean spray frozen delicately in time. Keebo took a few steps further into the room and leaned against a wall. Then, in the midst of the beams, Jon appeared.

Keebo would not hear a voice. He would not see any other actors unless they too were dead. The kin-song would only show the last moments of Jon's life at the time of day they occurred, and as long as the song was sung. Quickly Keebo noted the slant of the rays, in case he ever needed to return. He had such need the last time he had performed the ritual, though not always looking for clues. He blinked the thoughts away, watching the specter of his young friend.

Jon was speaking to someone. At first it appeared to be casual conversation. He was smiling. He usually did, Keebo recalled, when there was not dire need for any other expression. There was a pause as Jon watched someone cross the room.

Keebo knew the expression. Jon had always taken more after his father than his mother. Now, at the oldest Keebo had recently seen him, he appeared more the Tan King by far. The monarch always bronzed deeply in the bright sun, and his eldest seemed to take on this trait; Strake, conversely, kept the paleness of his mother no matter how much time he spent out of doors.

Jon's smile began to fade, became care-worn. Keebo stepped closer. Jon was watching someone, sympathy lining his face.

Keebo tried to stand where Jon was focused, getting an idea of where the killer—if he was speaking to the victim—would be standing. It unsettled him, Jon seeming to look directly at him in such a way. Keebo did not warrant that kind of look. He kept singing, watching; the look was not truly for him, but for whomever Jon had been meeting—someone, apparently, Keebo's general height.

Jon's smile and compassion disappeared. He said something. He glanced away, took a deep breath, shook his head. More words. His face darkened. Keebo followed his eyes, coming around the end of the table. A few words, cut off. Gestures, becoming urgent. His hand reached out, resting in mid-air near Keebo's shoulder; instinctively, Keebo flinched.

Jon flinched, too, his eyes widening. He looked down as blood poured from his midsection. A knife appeared in the image, then—the murder weapon usually did, at this point, but would only last while it touched the body. Swallowing again, Keebo quickly studied it: it was unimpressive, a simple blade with wooden handle secured by several rivets. Almost anyone could own such a weapon.

Jon was on his knees. He looked confused. Betrayed. Tired. His hand went to the knife, pulled it out. His fingers uncurled and the blade dropped and disappeared. He fell sideways, the ghostly image of his blood seeping into the real stain on the floor.

The wind blew, and the image disappeared. Keebo took a deep breath, and a long cry of grief tore from his throat.

4

Heirlooms and Victims

"He didn't take that very well."
"No, Teresh, he would not."
"He knew him?"
"Keebo had sworn to protect Jon after the King died."

24 Monzak 1320 — Dry

Keebo stood, panting, unable to take his eyes from the spot where he watched Jon die. It was one thing to be told—he had experienced a lot of death, in his time. But to see it happen, to make every death he had ever heard of, every death he himself had caused, to give each name spoken, each body he had seen only in peaceful stillness—to give them all animation, an image of what their last moments might have been like...

As the sunbeams shifted, he noticed glittering among the rubble. He stepped forward, reaching down and pulling from between the rocks a silver locket on a fine chain. Patterned scrollwork was thinly etched upon the face; when he opened it, each side held a lock of hair—different colors. One, he thought he recognized: it was the exact shade of Jon's, if he remembered right. The other was jet black, and slightly curled. It surprised him; he had never known Jon to be sentimental. He closed it, noticing among the whorls on the back a thin obelisk. From Pael, then? He would have to ask around.

He tucked the locket in a pouch and turned away. The knife was no longer where Jon had dropped it. Keebo ducked, glancing under the broken table. Nothing. He walked bent, searching among the fallen stones and rotted timbers. It wasn't in the room. Had the killer picked it back up? Or the men who retrieved the body? He would have to ask Tolma if it had been found.

After one last, quick inspection Keebo left the room. His head remained bent on the stones beneath his feet. All that, and almost nothing solid to pursue. Jon had been killed with a plain knife, by someone he cared about, had intended to meet. Tolma had said Jon had ridden off alone, only mentioning the ruins. He would have to talk to his old friend first, then, see what Jon had been doing, who he had been meeting with, in the last few months.

For a Protector, Keebo had been terribly absent from Jon—and Strake's—life for the past...how long had it even been? A year? Surely less.

He sighed. Long enough. He exited the ruined building, glancing again at the sun. It was nearly set, maybe too late to make the next yurt. He had pushed the horse—and himself—hard today reaching the ruins; he disliked the idea of doing it again.

His belly reminded him he had not eaten much today. At his horse, he rummaged through the saddlebags again, but found little—the remains of bread that he had meant to discard on the way down here. He chewed on it, a sour expression on his face. He noticed some ruined barrels nearby; nothing in there would have lasted centuries, so he didn't know why he found himself walking over and removing the rotted boards that had once been a lid.

He paused, blinking, and swallowed. Something long and narrow was inside, wrapped in oiled cloth. He wiped his hands on his vest, and pulled the object out. Perfect weight for a sword. Hesitantly, he unwrapped it.

The sheath was black leather, with silver stitching like miniature dragon scales; the mouth was of a translucent crystal, etched also in scales. The pommel was pale liquid-red in the shape of clawed toes, almost like a hawk's. The handle was the same black leather with silver stitching as the sheath, and the guard was the same pale red metal, in the form of thin wings. Above was a head also of the metal, similar to a dragon's but with shorter snout, almost canine. As he drew the blade, he saw the edges were also of the liquid-red metal, but down its center was a jagged bolt of amber rimmed in orange rust.

Keebo's arms trembled. It might have taken him longer to recognize if he had not met Haydren earlier in the week. He had already suspected when he saw it in the barrel, and now knew it instantly.

Boanerges, Wyvern of the Air, made of Bultum and amber, the amber apparently edged in Cretal. A Shadebreaker. Third of four to be found before the ending of the age.

But why had it come to him? He was no swordsman, had no intention of being one. He certainly didn't have the time now to go all the way to Deewan in Burieng to learn its use.

Maybe he should put it back, wait for someone else to find it. He began wrapping it in the oiled cloth, but the cloth had suddenly become brittle and fell to pieces every time it crinkled. He dropped the tattered remnants, gazing at the sword. This shouldn't be.

A low rumble of thunder brought his thoughts back to the present, as he glanced at a sky darkening toward evening. He couldn't leave the sword here; history and prophecy both dictated that he accept the gift, and do with it what he could. He drew another sigh, turned back to the horse, and left the valley heading south.

As stars appeared in the east, the roadside collection of huts drew near. Andelen, he heard, had its fortified inns; the Islands had their yurts—shelter, if not food prepared by a keeper, and Keebo's favorite characteristic: they were free. If there was damage, you were expected to help fix it. Patrons brought and cooked their own food, made their own fire. And there weren't that many, really: most towns and villages in the Islands were close enough to one another. Sed Narok was one of the exceptions.

Keebo tied the horse; it would eat better than he would tonight. He pulled a thin blanket from the saddlebags, and lay down. Warm as it was, he didn't even need to make a fire. Fires attracted things, like moths, leopards, and Triumvirs. And, perhaps here, a dragon.

As his eyelids drooped, watching the horse gorge itself on the thick grasses, Keebo wondered why he hadn't seen Belaornen for some time. Not like the island was large; and the beast had stayed away from Maerc and Lona long enough that the residents were not even antagonistic toward dragons anymore—so she shouldn't feel the need to hide in the wilds between towns.

Before he could decide, Keebo was asleep.

⸺◆⸺

Lights glittered on the horizon the next evening, welcoming him to Southport. The sun had just gone below the western rim, and early eastern stars already shone. He made his way toward the docks, hoping to secure passage before dawn for the opposite side of Sed Narok.

The gulls had long since gone to roost, and the bay was peaceful. An occasional thump of boat to dock came faintly, and the creak of shifting rigging; but the sailors had all already gone to drink or bed. He sat his horse, looking out over the dark waters, still puzzling over the sword now lashed behind the saddle.

"Ain't no one goin' out this hour—Oh, it's you."

Keebo turned and looked down upon a sailor who had somehow come up right beside him. His eyes darted for a moment, then he smiled. "Brin," he said. "I was hoping actually to secure a ride for the morning. Might you be heading to Northport?"

Barinbar Kerasco, captain of the ferry *Unswift,* grunted. "No. I'm settlin' some things here and going straight back to Nutar." He paused, straightening a little. "I've been asked as personal ferryman for his Stewardship, after this morning."

Keebo and Brin gazed at each other for a few moments, then burst into laughter. "Tolma is a scoundrel," Keebo said, as he dismounted. "And so are you. Did you see him earlier this week?"

"Aye. Ferried him here from Naso. Said he liked my silence and my speed, and hired me permanent. I've just had to finish some business in Candar Ha."

Keebo patted the horse's neck. "To get there and back in that time, you must have had the God's speed," he said respectfully. The Islands were not large; a good Captain and Calderon—a sort of captain-in-training, who sailed the nightshift—with fair winds, could stop at every island and return home within the span of two weeks. Still, business in the Islands rarely went quick. With a gleam, Keebo added: "And a new Calderon."

Brin winked and nodded. "Made most of the time today; you must have noticed the good westerly winds we had."

"Indeed. I'll need to go visit Master Bergin, actually, I've been summoned. Can we make a stop off at Northport tomorrow before continuing on to his Stewardship?"

"Aye, I'll be needing a few odds and ends there myself. Meet me here about Moon-Set; we'll get out before all the rest of these clog the harbor."

"Any room at the, uh..." Keebo trailed off, barely refraining from shaking his head. Melnor had to be behind this.

"Wyvern and Cliff?" Brin supplied with a raised eyebrow. "Aye, I think he's got a room or two."

Keebo smiled faintly. He always stayed at the Wyvern when he was in Southport; somehow it slipped his mind. And he with Boanerges. "Thanks, Brin. See you tomorrow."

He made his way into town, then, following familiar streets through a few twists before arriving at the Wyvern. Southport was a smaller harbor, but sent and received ships to Gintanos—overflow from Gunda. The Wyvern and Cliff was the oldest accommodations in town, and still one of the largest. The owner, Jerreth Detler, received it from—eventually—his great-great grandfather. Kaertan Detler had been a special person, by all accounts, and the Wyvern showed it: a round common room like a great turret, with two wings in a shallow V pointing to the harbor; all the second-floor rooms had balconies without railings—the "cliffs." The whole thing was done in white stucco, with black double doors for the main entrance and two golden windows where you would expect the eyes of a monstrous winged creature.

For all that, rooms were cheap; the materials and labor to build had been paid long ago, and few dared to assume such an august building should pay more than marginal tax. It was also rumored Jerreth sat on an inheritance to rival the King of the Islands, and did not require his inn to make a profit.

Keebo slid off his horse, and handed the reins to a young stableboy still rubbing early sleep from his eyes. The truth of how such a massive inn survived on a small port was not quite as grandiose: Jerreth offered discounts to the deep-water ships' crews—and all their passengers. Forty years ago when trade began increasing between the Islands and Gintanos, most ships bypassed the southern port and docked in Northport instead, where supplies were more plentiful. With Jerreth's discounts, and fabled inn, they began again to dock here. Lona benefitted too, becoming the fastest-growing village in the Islands.

Keebo took the ridiculous sword inside, refusing to buckle it around his waist but feeling equally foolish simply carrying it like a staff. He had re-wrapped it in new cloth—no point drawing even more attention with its unique scabbard—and banged it into several tables and chairs as he made his way across the common room.

He stopped short just before reaching the stairs, staring at a table off in the corner, his eyes refusing to blink. Haydren handled the encounter much better, cocking his head only slightly and grinning. Keebo approached the table.

"Are you following me?" Haydren asked as he drew near.

"Not on purpose," Keebo said, with a faint smile. He sat down at Haydren's gesture. He made to put the sword on the floor.

Give it to him.

Keebo paused with a slow blink. *That might be hard to explain.*

He knows who I am.

"Melnor said to give this to you," he said—quietly, though the nearest patron was several tables away and clearly not listening: a serving girl with a plunging neckline bent over as she took his order. Keebo held out the wrapped sword.

Haydren's grin disappeared, and he went still. "What for?"

"Did he develop a new habit of explaining himself, since I last spoke to him?"

Haydren rolled his eyes. "No, I can't imagine. What is it?" He took it, but did not unwrap the cloth.

"Boanerges," Keebo said, his heart beating a little slower now that he was rid of the thing. "Only one more to find," he said with as much sarcastic cheer as he could fit.

"Am I supposed to be the one to find it?"

"You would have to ask him." Keebo meant it as a joke, but he noticed the slight spacing of Haydren's gaze that Keebo knew meant a Triumvir was talking to him. They thought they were sneaky, that no one outside the person noticed; but Keebo did.

When Haydren refocused, Keebo smiled. "Well?" he asked.

Haydren's gaze dropped, as if caught doing something he wasn't supposed to. "He said it isn't for me, but he wants me to deliver it to someone. I thought I was done with them, after Lasserain."

Keebo cocked his head. "Do you want to be?"

Haydren paused, and slowly shook his head. "I guess, if I'm honest, no."

And if Keebo was honest, too, he would have said the same. It was a little game he played with Melnor to lie, though; sort of a way to rub it in, since he could and Melnor could not. A perk of still being on Oren. "I'm still surprised to see you here," Keebo said. "Weren't you headed for Rinc Na?"

"I am; our captain wanted to make a stop here before leaving for Naso Narok, then overseas."

Keebo's brow furrowed. "Did he say why?"

"I didn't ask."

"What's his name?"

"Mandor. I'm not sure of his first name."

"I am," Keebo said. Another of Melnor's men. He probably didn't know why he was to come here, either. "Most people would have asked more questions when I mentioned they were tied up in a prophecy about the end of the world," he continued. "But not you. I wondered then if you had experiences others did not."

Haydren shrugged. "It also seems a little outlandish. I wonder if it doesn't mean something else."

"What if it doesn't?"

"Like you said, hard to stop a prophecy," Haydren replied, though his mouth was set in a grim line.

Keebo swallowed. "Hmm. I've got an early boat, so I'll bid you good-night."

"Is he okay? The captain?"

Keebo smiled and nodded. "One of the best; you'll be fine. Fair winds, Haydren." He turned, paused, and turned back. "Did Melnor mention how the person was to learn the magic?" he asked.

Haydren's gaze came up quickly. "He was going to teach them," he said, then smiled. "I wondered the same thing."

"Hmm. You'll be fine, Haydren," Keebo said. He turned, and left the common room.

⊷◆⊶

Keebo had found someone to take the horse back to Maerc the next morning, made good time to Northport, and now sat at a small shop munching roasted caterpillars as Brin made a few provisions for the longer journey to Nak. He wasn't sure why he liked them, the caterpillars; they tasted mostly like ash, and not the good ash of a well-roasted Duuge fish, but like burnt hair, and they had no real smell whatsoever. Maybe it was just something to do.

The sun was shining, and clouds were nowhere in sight. A fair wind aired the little shop, just off north-west, but close enough that he was sure Brin could still make good use of it. And his Calderon was indeed a fair sailor, making as good a time from Southport as Brin. Still, Keebo was not looking forward to this next trip, or meeting with Tolma; but if it had to be done, better than waiting with it impending like a slow thunderstorm.

Of course, there were always pop-up showers that weren't noticed until it was too late. The first roll of thunder was a familiar voice in Keebo's ear.

"I told you I'd catch up with you," it said, just above a whisper. The most frightening storms always started quietly, that way. "If you don't want this to be public, follow me."

Keebo sighed, tossing down the last of the caterpillars. Northport was well-made, streets stoned and sealed, and the storm-winds that would have come through yesterday likely cleared out most of the dust. Very little earth to work with, here. He got up, walking down the alleyway where the man from Irii pointed him.

"You know I didn't mean for it to happen," Keebo said. "I've tried to fix it as best I could."

"And you've done a smart job, at that," he said. "Which is why I won't kill you."

"What were their names?" Keebo asked.

There was a slight pause. "Julan, my wife; and Terress my daughter."

"I'll remember them."

"Not as much as I will."

The first blow almost knocked him out; it certainly knocked him down. As the veil drew shut, and the succeeding kicks and blows echoed against his ribs, he thought he saw an Anoe come around the corner and pause.

Then everything went black.

5

THE FIRST SUSPECTS

"Did he deserve that?"
"He thinks so."
"And you almost made him a Triumvir?"
"We all make mistakes."

29 Monzak 1320 — Dry

When Keebo awoke, he was sitting up against the wall. He breathed shallowly; the image of looming mountains flashed quickly through his mind, but he shut them out. It would stop eventually, once everyone got their justice. He was fairly sure he was drawing near the end of the list. He had to be.

But who propped him up? Did the one who beat him do it? Or Brin, come looking?

Brin. How long had he been out? He needed to get to Nutar Ha.

"You should rest a little, first," said a new voice.

Keebo blinked. "Kal," he mumbled. He squinted against the brightness; no matter how accustomed he was to seeing Anoe, they seemed odd outside Berola with their thin limbs and shiny green-and-blue mottled skin—which, of course, they rarely deigned to cover up more than was absolutely necessary. On Berola, they looked like Anoe; in the rest of the Islands, they looked like frogs walking upright. And now they would be hunted again. "You shouldn't be here."

The Anoe squatted down in front of him. "And you shouldn't call me that," he said quietly. His large, glossy black almond eyes studied Keebo for a minute. "How many does this make?"

Keebo waved him off. "Ten? Fifteen? Not enough."

"It is enough; it was not your fault."

"What are you doing here?"

Kal paused for several long moments. Keebo's pulse began to slow before Kal finally spoke. "I was looking for you," he said slowly.

Keebo misunderstood. "I feel fine, Kal; no need to talk so carefully." He tried a grin to prove it, but was only partially successful.

"I just don't know if you're ready for what I need."

Keebo paused and eyed him a moment. "Maybe let's get me standing first."

Kal blinked a few slow times, mouth drawn tight—tighter than normal. Soundlessly he rose and held out his arm, leaning back.

With a loud sigh and grunt, Keebo heaved himself to his feet. He kept a hand on Kal's thin arm, pressing the other against the alley wall. "I can't tell if that gets easier or harder, each time," he said. A few deep breaths—nothing felt broken, just sore—and he stood on his own. After a few more sniffs and snorts, he turned to his friend. "Now; what can I do for you?" he asked with a smile.

"I will likely be accused of murder," Kal said. "And I am innocent."

Keebo's smile faded, becoming a snarl. "I should have stayed seated." He started leaving the alley.

"Keebo," Kal started.

"Seated!" Keebo shot back, glaring. "With a pint! Maybe a quart!"

He turned the corner, heading for the nearest Pit. They would have something stiff this early in the day. Faintly he heard Kal's slapping footfalls behind him, but didn't care. He would hear him out, but definitely over a drink.

He found one—Tully's Fire Pit—in short order, and had a drink in hand even faster. Kal came in behind him, but only wanted water. It's all the Anoe seemed to know how to drink. Keebo was resolutely silent, gripping his mug and gritting his teeth.

"I promise you, I did not do it this time," Kal said quietly. "Last time I was not guilty; this time I *was not there.*"

"But someone will think you were?"

"I was supposed to be there," Kal replied. "It will not take long to find that out. And they will think I have motive—"

"*I* will think you have motive!" Keebo spat. "I just came from there, because Tolma wants *me* to figure it out!"

Kal watched him. "I am sorry," he said finally, as Keebo drank. "You Kin-sang?"

Keebo swallowed and glowered. "Let me see your knife," he said suddenly.

Kal reached down to his waist and drew it out. It was a plain blade with wooden handle, just like he had seen—like anyone would own. He studied it closely, where the halves of the handle met, to see if any dried blood lingered inside. It looked clean. Smelled clean, too. Kal either planned it out, or was innocent. Keebo guessed much of the investigation would go this way. Princes were not murdered by idiots who would be quickly caught.

"Why were you supposed to be there?"

Kal sheathed the knife. "Prince Jonkar wrote me a letter, requesting I meet him in Nobak two weeks ago. When I arrived, there were three horses outside—but he had promised to come alone. So I waited; eventually they brought out the—his body, and left. So I came to Maerc hoping to see you. I grew worried, and decided to just go back to Berola this morning."

"Why did he want to see you?"

Kal sighed, clasping his hands and wriggling the fingers. He glanced aside, then back to Keebo, then down at his hands. "We had been talking for several months, now," he said, almost in a whisper. "He had first come to Berola, disguised, near the turn of the year. He heard me speaking. And...he wanted to help."

Keebo found his eyebrows could not go high enough. "Your people—"

"I know," Kal replied loudly. He drew a long, tired breath, and lowered his tone. "I know. And that's why we're still there where no one bothers us; why we're all living in huts, with barely enough water, little food, thefts and murders—we were a people of honor once! Of pride! We did things well, with excellence, for the sole purpose of doing them..." He trailed off, shaking his head. "Prince Jonkar wanted to help; I knew the elders would refuse, but I trusted him, so I came."

"I've always thought Jon was honorable," Keebo said. "But why did you? You had only just met him. And it's not like the elders are entirely outside their right to distrust a Rinc Nain."

"We have a very bad history, true," Kal said. "And every treaty they've made, they've made in Maerc—always we came to their table, begging scraps. 'Please, master, can we have back some of what was ours.' But without my even asking, when Prince Jonkar wanted to meet, immediately he suggested Nobak. He was coming to *us*, Keebo; he was coming to our table, apologizing for the theft and returning the stolen goods to us, at least as much as he could at first." Kal shook his head. "We cannot have the Islands we once had. I have accepted that; many others have not. But he seemed truly sincere, the first Prince or King I have heard of making such a move."

"So who wants him dead?" Keebo asked quietly.

Kal sighed. "I do not know. I would think, if the elders found out, they would kill me."

"But the rest of your clans would not approve that; you're more of their leader than two-thirds of your elders."

"You give me too much credit."

"No, I don't, and you know it. Between the two, the elders would be much more likely to have Jon killed to stop a treaty they hated."

"Do you trust me to find out where they were two weeks ago?"

Keebo shook his head. "I would; Tolma and the other Rinc Nain would not. You will have to be a suspect, and you will have to stay out of the investigation as much as possible." He shook his head and took several long pulls to finish the mug. "Even talking to me now compromises you, and me," he continued, wiping his mouth. "I will have to talk to Tolma first, find out what I can; I may come to Berola second, depending...oh, do you recognize this?" Keebo fished around in his belt pouch, pulling free the locket.

"It looks like a locket," Kal said.

Keebo shot him a withering look. "I didn't ask you to tell me what it was."

Kal took it, opened it. "This is Jon's hair?" he asked, tapping the one side. Keebo nodded with a shrug; probably. Kal studied the other side. "From what I have heard, this could be..." He trailed off as Keebo's gaze hardened. "Well, not *anyone's;* but certainly any of several...young ladies'."

"I had not known Jon to be like that," Keebo said stiffly.

"You have not seen him for some time," Kal replied, handing back the locket.

Keebo snatched it back, shoving it into the pouch. "Are you saying he was a...a..." He didn't want to say the word.

"No, of course not," Kal said. "He never took it *that* far. But he was fair to look at, and—lately—he took advantage of that. If the whispers are true."

Keebo sighed, gazing out toward the sea, visible here between a few leafy trunks. He should have been around. Maybe then... He waved away a serving maid as she approached with another pint. Brin might be waiting for him, and the morning was growing late. He would need to talk to Tolma before anything else. He wanted this done with.

"Go back to Berola, and wait," Keebo said. "I will go to...Nak, and find out what Tolma knows and what he can tell me. I may have to visit you soon after, so if you can stay near the docks..."

"I will wait."

"Popular opinion is going to be that you did this, Kal," Keebo said, his gaze expressionless. "Especially after the last time. They think I overlooked many things because of my friendship with the Anoe."

"Do you think that you did?"

Keebo's gaze lowered. "If I did, I would not have cleared you. But most don't see it that way. And now that you're under suspicion again..."

"Will Tolma appoint someone else?"

"I'm not sure who else there is."

"Someone from the Island Watch?"

"Ha!" Keebo slapped a hand down on the table, then covered his mouth. "I hope not." His face went suddenly grave, and he rubbed his lip. "I hope not," he repeated more quietly. "Not if you're truly innocent."

"Do you believe I am?"

Keebo drew a breath. "Let's see what my investigation uncovers," he replied.

He found Brin waiting at the boat, and only a little impatiently. Once the captain saw Keebo's face and scuffed clothing, he grunted. "Another one?"

Keebo nodded as he clambered aboard. "From Irii."

"You do take it well," Brin said, slacking a line and letting the sail catch the wind.

Keebo straightened his vest as he sat amidships, facing forward. Ferries on the islands were small boats, only wide enough for two or three fares sitting side-by-side, and a small compartment behind Keebo where a Captain and his Calderon traded places to sleep. Passengers slept on deck, under erectable pavilions. Narrow outriggers on either side kept them stable in rougher seas. Brin took the tiller at his seat aft, making the sails dance via neatly-routed lines and pulleys as he guided them through the crowded port into the open sea. It was calmer today, though a few thunderheads still prowled the horizon. It did not look like they would interfere with the voyage though.

"Will we reach Nutar Ha tomorrow?" Keebo asked.

Brin sniffed. "Likely," he said. He glanced overhead at the sun, then behind at the receding port; he made minor adjustments to tiller and sheet, then settled back. "Very likely," he added with a grin.

They progressed well throughout the afternoon. Keebo broke out some meat and cheese, which Brin received with thanks; the clouds slipped behind them south—Keebo sent up a quick whisper for his garden—and it was clear skies till the sun began to dip toward the west.

About Evening, Brin sat up suddenly, peering westward. "Uh oh," he muttered. He took in the line and steered a more northerly course. "Wes!" he bellowed, summoning his Calderon from belowdecks.

"What is it?" Keebo asked, looking to the west and only seeing another boat. Seemed to be heading for them, though he couldn't imagine why—with two masts, it surely had more supplies than Brin's little gondola, and they weren't out far enough to have news of any import.

"Let's hope we can outrun them," Brin muttered. "They haven't bothered this close in shore yet."

"Why? What would they want?"

"Oh, just a toll of some sort. Maybe burn the boat if they think I make too much."

"Brin, I don't..."

"It's the deep-water guild."

Keebo stared at him. "The *what?*"

Brin glanced at his sail, then at the oncoming ship, and sighed. "The guild that oversees the deep-water ships. You haven't heard? There's a bit of a skirmish between them and the shallow-water boats."

"Why on Oren does it matter?"

"Because my boat makes trade between the Islands more profitable than trade with other countries—Gintanos, Andelen, the Pal Isans. The new captains apparently think they should be more aggressive at encouraging international trade. The princes thought so too, last I heard. His Stewardship has tried to stay out of it until a proper successor comes in, but..."

"This is ridiculous."

"Tell them that. Tell *him* that, if you see him tomorrow."

Wes appeared on deck, followed Brin's eyes and clipped gesture westward; his lips compressed. "Should I row?" he asked.

Brin growled and slowly shook his head. "Maybe if we had more passengers, they could help."

Before long, the ship drew alongside, its captain leaning over the railing. "Why, it's a little skiff!" he said, as his crew guffawed. "Lost at sea! We'll save you, little skiff."

"This is my boat," Brin growled back. "I'm making time just good enough, thank you; and I know where I'm going, too!"

"And where is that; fishing for little fishes?" More laughter.

"I am taking Keebo Burami to see the Steward, Tolma Bergin!" Brin shouted.

The captain's smile faded a moment. He knew both of those names. But, after chewing his lip a moment, the smile returned. "Presumably it's a matter of some importance then! No good arriving in a little skiff; we'll take him, and payment for our trouble."

Keebo glanced at Brin. "I'm sorry I'm not a water wizard," he said. Why *was* he an earth wizard in an island chain? Surely Rinc Na or Gintanos would be better...maybe something to mull over another time. "I'll pay you back," he said quietly.

Brin kept his face drawn in rage, but managed a slight wink. "Maybe I will do some fishing while I'm out here," he muttered. "Won't be a total loss." Wes cracked a tiny smile as well.

Keebo climbed aboard, tossing a few of Tolma's small coins to the captain. His attackers had always seemed satisfied to take their justice from his flesh, rather than his purse. Sails were raised, and the ship leapt northwesterly. Keebo spared a quick farewell for the *Unswift*, then made his way to the bow. He preferred to see where he was going, even if the view just now was mostly water.

The ship did make better time, and was more comfortable overnight, Keebo had to begrudgingly admit. Not long after the sun rose the next morning, the low mountains of Nutar Ha pierced the horizon.

"Such a big island, to only have one little port on it," one of the sailors muttered as he tied off a line near Keebo's hip.

Keebo glanced sideways. The sailor was young; he looked to be about fifteen or sixteen. Before his time. And few talked about it anymore, he supposed. Well, it was what it was, to most people. The maps changed, and time went on. Except for those who lost friends and family. He returned his gaze to Nutar Ha.

"It used to be smaller," Keebo said, watching the all-too familiar peaks continue to grow.

"What made it bigger?" the sailor asked.

Keebo smiled grimly. "Magic."

6

In the Citadel

"With the proper Water spell—"
"That is not the issue."
"But if he forgot..."
"That is a choice still before him."

30 Monzak 1320 — Dry

Tolma was not at the port to receive him, which probably shouldn't have been surprising, late as it was. The Steward would be close to his charge, further inland at the citadel of Nak. He didn't completely abandon Keebo, though; a guard waited with a nice, Keebo-sized pony ready to travel, saddlebags bulging with what appeared to be good food, and even a waxed poncho against the remote chance of rain. The man was thoroughly Rinc Nain, but maybe not so bad after all. Of course Keebo was accustomed to being rained on, sometimes even enjoyed it. But it was thoughtful.

It was a long, twisting track through the mountains of Nutar Ha, and Keebo met no one on the way. Surely Tolma had already cleared out the non-essential staff at the castle, and the soldiers at the head of the road in port recognized Keebo to let him past. It was eerie, and quiet except for the echo of his own pony's hooves, as if waiting with bated breath for the outcry of the Islands like the pounding of surf when they learned Jon was dead—murdered, no less.

Keebo pulled a soft dough-roll from the saddlebags, still slightly warm so it must have come from the garrison's kitchen, and ate. Salted chicken was in there as well, and he found a small skin of—he sniffed—wine. It was a light wine, but still he only took a few swallows. Pony-back riding was still difficult without being drunk. He found water in the other bag, and drained half that skin as he finished the chicken. An apple to top it all off, and he felt better than he had in a while.

He pressed against a rib, holding his breath; then fingered below his eye, where it was still tender. He hadn't bothered to see if he looked as beaten as he felt, and wondered if Tolma would be able to tell, and what he might say if he could. Keebo sighed and took another, very small, swallow of wine.

There were no yurts on the road, as the distance between port and Nak was normally an easy journey. But the dry season was fully upon the Islands, and Keebo was able to simply steer his horse off the road as night fell, hobble it, and curl up in a small corner of ferns.

As the sun reached Afternoon the next day—he had kept the pony at a nice, easy gait on the long track—the road bent, and the citadel poked above a shoulder of rock. A gleaming spike of smooth gray that seemed almost as if it were natural, rather than made of block, it had been one of Keebo's finer achievements of his youth. Barely adequate to make him a master, but enough.

He knew he was drawing close when he spied carefully-hidden siege engines on the slopes—catapults and ballistae ranged for the road to begin decimation of an approaching force. He could sense, too, magic-bound stones that would take the barest nudge to send hurtling downslope. They were his own addition to the defenses, so long ago. In the quiet of the valley, he felt as though he were walking into an ambush. The stones he could handle—pitiful the earth wizard who could not—but flying steel from the ballista would be an entirely different matter. He nudged the pony to a little bit faster canter, eager to be through the gauntlet.

The rest of the castle came into view, as well as the fields on the slopes behind it. Those had been the pride of Queen Rayenne, thirty years ago. Far less stunning, magically, but more significant to Keebo; he had helped the soil there, made it tractable, nutritious enough to provide for the keep, and even surplus for some export, when they had a good year. It had been a joy to plan: on the higher elevations were almonds, pistachios, mangoes, and kiwis; a little lower were the limes and papayas; and nearest the castle were coconuts, pineapples, and bananas. The last had not been planted until near the end. They had taken a little extra work, and some help from Sarah (where was she, these days?) to encourage better rains and more humid air the trees needed. Of course, pistachios had been the queen's favorite, so he had spent extra time on that plot, and they had kept an army of servants to harvest the nuts.

With a grimace, he could tell the expansive garden was less tended now. Tolma had never been keen on it, said the 'natural order' of things was better. Probably why the duskgleam was gone from the queen's tower, too, Keebo noted with even greater sadness. That was a true shame:

unnatural or not, duskgleam's evening blooms, iridescently purple as though creating their own small moonlight within the curved petals, were impossible to forget.

Clearly, Tolma wanted to try. Or, maybe it had hurt Strake and Jon too much to remember the queen mother.

The gates were firmly shut, the guards stolidly suspicious. Only after a private had been sent to the keep and came back was Keebo allowed admittance. He dismounted while he waited, taking exaggerated steps to loosen stiff muscles.

Finally the gates opened, and he was escorted by no less than ten soldiers; his pony was swiftly taken and led away. "It is Master Bergin's, not yours," he was reminded when he protested.

The city inside was also as beautiful as Keebo had been able to make it. While most homes and buildings were quarried stone and wood, a few who had been able to afford it received marble paneling in all sorts of colors—pink, green, black; others had gardens with statues more smooth and detailed than any crafter could manage, and some polished to a high gleam that reflected the sun like a beacon. Flagstone courtyards of the most elite residents displayed mosaics of anything the customer wished—birds, waterfalls, forests, seas, loved ones. The Karekans had a map of Oren laid out; much of it was obscured by creeping plants and benches, Keebo noticed as they walked by, and only the Islands were really visible, centered between the encroaching flora and set pieces. He wondered: Hirem and Jessalon had loved that mosaic, when Keebo arranged it, and their children had as well. Something of that attraction had apparently been lost by the time the grandchildren came along.

The city, like the valley leading to it, was strangely quiet. No one was in the streets, no children played in the courtyards. He thought perhaps once he saw a curtain shift in a window as if someone had stopped looking, but he couldn't be sure.

Keebo had never been around during the time of a murdered heir—wasn't sure what the proper action would be. There had always been quiet, proper succession in the Islands. Nothing like what he heard of from Andelen or Burieng. Gintanos and the Pal Isans were too far away to matter—though a few strange rumors had come from the Twin Lands, things you only heard of in plays. Whenever anyone said 'dark powers' Keebo couldn't help but smile a little. These folks didn't smile, though.

And now Jon was dead, and Nak was silent. He thought to ask one of his escorts, opened his mouth, then shut it. Tolma would tell all.

The spike came into view, now, and as Keebo's eyes couldn't help but loft, he hoped Tolma would meet him on one of the lower levels. Maybe they had installed that contraption, some sort of room they could winch upward or downward—a device from Rinc Na, it was said. But surely he would be able to tell if a new room was added to the spike, even a moveable one.

They entered, and Keebo was passed off to another gauntlet of guards, these in heavier, shinier armor and duller faces. Hands were kept on daggers and swords, and mouths were kept shut. Their heavy footfalls echoed through the chambers and halls, and up the stairs. Keebo closed his eyes briefly, hoping his breathing wouldn't become too loud.

Fortunately, they took him to a room on only the third level. More guards, similarly dressed, ringed the room; the windows were shut. Tolma sat behind a large desk of mahogany; his chair, at least as much of it as Keebo could see around the edges—Tolma was thin; Keebo would have consumed the same chair if he sat in it—was upholstered in dark leather with brass buttons. A similar chair, less well-appointed, sat empty in front of the desk—presumably for him. Shelves with dusty books were to the right; a large tapestry rigged to stir the air was overhead; and a map of the islands was tacked to the wall on the left. Tolma followed Keebo with his eyes as the wizard moved to the chair and sat down. After a pause, he gave a grim smile.

"Difficult times," Tolma said.

Keebo blinked. "Yes." He took a breath. "What's happening here in Nak? The city seems deserted..."

"Most of that is recent," Tolma replied. "I wanted no sleeping assassins to come upon us suddenly. Though, after the King died, the city was not so full of life as it once was, and many families packed up and left. At a time like this, with the remaining heir potentially in trouble..."

Keebo glanced around again. "Where is Strake?"

"Upstairs, and well guarded," Tolma replied, "until we know who did this, and know whether the threat is eliminated."

"You both were together after Jon rode off?"

Even the grim smile faded. "Of course," Tolma said. "You suggest—"

"I'm sorry; silly to ask." He twisted his lips into an attempt at a disarming smile. "Did your men pick up a knife when they recovered Jon's body?"

"They gave none to me. I could ask them about it. Do you know what it looked like?"

Keebo snorted. "Just a knife; dark blade, wooden handle held by rivets. I've probably seen dozens. Hopefully when I find it, there will still be some blood somewhere on it." He spread his hands helplessly.

Tolma took a breath. "What happened to you?"

Keebo smiled genuinely, if a little sadly. "Someone who remembered. Husband to Julan and father to...Terress."

Tolma's gaze flickered over his face. "I can't imagine what that must be like, Keebo," he said. "To have that on your shoulders...even if accidentally..."

Keebo took a breath. "Do you recognize this?" he asked, retrieving the pendant from his pocket.

Tolma's eyebrows drew down; he took it and opened it. He peered at the right side, then the left, and his features relaxed. "Oh," he said. "I thought he had given this back. This belonged to a young girl from Pael, with whom Jon had passing interest." He closed it, handing it back.

Keebo took it, and tucked it away. He was right about the obelisk, then; at least he had an idea where to start looking. "It's probably important, Tolma; she might have had something to do with it—do you think she had reason to?"

Tolma leaned forward. "No, she's dead; killed herself. I believe Jon felt responsible. I think her father agreed..."

"His name?"

"Tirtar. He's a carver—mostly furniture, but some artwork as well. He did a piece for me, for the Citadel, here. His daughter was with him when he delivered it. I insisted they stay for lunch, and Jon...well, Jon was Jon."

Keebo sighed. "I'm sorry I've been away so long..."

"Jon missed you the most, I think."

Keebo's gaze cast downward as he blinked. "I know. Was he like..." Keebo shrugged. "Like what I've been told? Lately?"

"Depends what you've been told," Tolma replied a little stiffly. "He did nothing to impugn his honor as a Terose."

"But enough that a girl killed herself over it?"

"What that girl did was a reflection of her own situation," Tolma replied. "It is no fault of Jon's for being mature and responsible a year from his..." Tolma ceased with a huff. "He was one year away, Keebo; the throne would have been his. He needed to start making good decisions, ones that would affect the entire Islands. Do you fault him for that?"

"I need to know what I'm getting into."

"You're going to see the father? Tirtar?"

"I thought I would start there."

"Not the Anoe?"

Keebo's gaze snapped upward. "Why do you say that?"

"I thought Shokalog would have found you by now, maybe mentioned something," Tolma replied off-handedly. "I thought you two were close friends."

"Tolma...I don't know who my friends are, anymore. Why do you ask about Kal and the Anoe?"

"*I'm* your friend, Keebo," Tolma said, his tone neutral. "Haven't I always been? Even after the incident here on Nutar, I've stuck by you."

"You have, Tolma. Thank you. But I still need to know what I'm getting into. Why do you mention the Anoe?"

"Jon was no real friend of theirs. I tried to teach him to be more diplomatic, especially with them. The Islands are too small to make enemies of those within our waters. But he...I don't know, it was almost as if they had done something personal to Jon. It came on in the last year or so. But I believed he was meeting secretly with one of their people. I know Shokalog is becoming something of a spokesperson—"

"He leads them better than their own elders," Keebo interjected.

"So I've heard. I thought Jon might have been meeting with him, but if all his talk around here was any indication, the meetings would not have been favorable to the Anoe."

"Is that all?"

"Of course not. The only reason I suspect he was meeting with Shoka-log specifically is because he was seen outside the ruins, by the one who found Jon's body."

Keebo tried to keep his expression calm, but assumed he was failing miserably. *He said he wasn't there!* "Then I will definitely need to speak to him as well," he managed. "But I also need to find out how this locket got there. Can you think of anyone *else* who might want him dead?"

Tolma sat back, blinked, and drew a breath. "There is one more item, maybe bigger than all the rest..." he began.

Keebo tried to keep from rolling his eyes. "Yes?"

"I'm not sure how much you've been paying attention, but there is something of a...cultural civil war brewing in the Islands."

Keebo cocked his head. "Between the different ships guilds?" he asked.

Tolma's smile was tight. "You have heard. It's strange—not something people from other nations might understand. It seems so silly, some-times, on its face; but when you realize the implications..."

"Whose side was Jon on? I assume he also would be seeing to that, if he were king."

"I knew you were the right person for this investigation. He favored the shallow-drafts—the inter-Island boats. That was why I cautioned him so strongly about being fair with the Anoe: if he was going to care about the Islands, and only the Islands, he would need them to be strong. He would not want to risk an uprising, and a fracturing of an already-tiny nation. The vulnerability..."

"And Strake? How is he with the Anoe, and the ship guilds? And women?"

"Keebo, please be calm about this," Tolma said. "I know you and Jon were close, closer than Strake. And it grieves me too that he is dead, but we must focus now on finding out—"

Keebo sighed. "I know. It just...Jon seemed more prepared to be king when I knew him. I don't understand how he could have fallen..."

"He didn't take it well, when you...I'm sorry, Keebo; I only want to tell you as a friend. I don't think it's your fault. Jon made his decisions. But you're right, too; something happened a few months back, I never found out what it was. He seemed different, suddenly—as if one night he went to bed the Jon I knew, maybe changed a little since when you visited more. The next day he was—'independent' sounds like a good thing. But he stopped taking advice or counsel, and the ideas he suddenly supported... It was strange. I cannot explain it. But somehow in a very short time it was as if he had read one book he had never read before and applied it irrevocably to his life." Tolma spread his hands helplessly.

"Would Strake know, perhaps? If I could talk to him..."

Tolma shook his head. "I'm afraid not. Not yet; he's still...he's very disturbed by his brother's death. Look into the Anoe, talk to Shokalog; visit Tirtar if you must. Perhaps when you return he will be ready."

"Who leads the deep-water-ships guild?"

"Beroc, on Naso Narok. I doubt he will come out and tell you anything..."

"No one does; most of the time it's what they don't say that is the most telling." Keebo paused. "Do you know, one of their ships thiefed me from the boat I was on, coming here? Barinbar was bringing me, and another ship came alongside."

Tolma sighed. "I had heard that was happening; give my apologies to Brin, if you see him again."

"What of the other ship?"

"I'll handle that. Please say nothing to Beroc; it is not strictly his doing, and will likely only make him defensive."

Keebo's brows knit. "How would it be his doing at all? He does not control the captains of his ships, does he?"

"Well he provides them the boats..." Tolma's lips compressed. "I just wanted to make sure." He brightened, suddenly. "Before you go, I wanted to show you my new horse. It just arrived from Andelen; it's a Therian. I plan to take Strake all through the mountains of this Island—he hasn't seen much of them, you know."

Keebo raised an eyebrow. "I don't know horses, Tolma, except I feel about to fall off them all the time," he said. "Are Therians steady in the mountains?"

7

THE DARK CARVER

"Will you tell him?"
"He has to learn on his own."
"What good are we, again?"
"We can only guide their thoughts, Teresh, or remind them of old ones; we
  cannot give them new ones."

2 Savimon 1320 — Dry

Tolma had given him a room for the night, and breakfast the next morning; the horse looked beautiful, but also tall—its shoulder was at Keebo's chin. While Keebo didn't know horses, he knew his pony's stout legs felt better under him in the mountains than his own spindly ones, and the Therian's seemed even thinner than Keebo's. Maybe there was hidden strength, there.

He returned alone to the port, an order in his hand for the boat there to take him wherever he wished. He stood a moment on the dock, contemplating as the sailor gazed at him expectantly. He was a young man, seemed very eager; his chestnut—almost red—hair was close cropped, and it didn't appear he needed to shave very often. His gray eyes were bright, though, and he tanned better than most Rinc Nain on the Islands. He said his name was Nedley. He said a lot of things, actually. His Calderon, Torin, stood aft with a patient expression.

"I've only been in his lordship's service for a little while now, but I guess he's found me reliable. I can't remember how many times I've ferried his lordship and his little lordship around the Islands—through all sorts of weather, too! Could have taken you as far as Naso Narok even in last night's storm, I could. My boat and I, we've seen it all and come out orchids. So don't you worry, Master Keebo; anywhere you want to go, I'll get you there. You want to come back? I'll bring you back too."

Keebo glanced warily at him. "Ever ferry an Anoe around?" he asked.

Nedley's countenance dimmed slightly. "No, begging your pardon Master Wizard. They haven't asked." He appeared to be ready to say something else, but for the first time refrained.

Keebo didn't want to see Shokalog just yet, after learning of his lie. And he didn't want to be in a boat with this—eager—young man all the way to Naso. So...

"I think just take me to Eastport," he said. His hand went unconsciously to his pocket; despite several allegations, the only real piece of evidence belonged to a grieving father in Pael.

Nedley's smile returned. "Sunny, Master Keebo; climb aboard."

Despite all his chatter, he sailed well and they made good time south to the northern port on Mayta Ha, arriving just before Noon the next day. Keebo amused himself considering that perhaps all the wind coming from Nedley's mouth was what propelled them. They slid into the great bay just as a light rain began to fall, the kind that usually marked the last gasp of the rainy season; not another drop would fall now until the new year.

For fun, as he walked through the streets of Eastport and made for the south road to Pael, Keebo practiced firming up the ground just before he stepped on it, returning it to slopping mud as he lifted his foot. Some of those he passed wore a newer fashion, clogs of a sort with two vertical planks of wood—only about the size of a hand—underneath the sole to help elevate them above the mud. More than one glance cast downward, prepared to boast of their supreme wisdom in buying the clogs, came back up muttering and sneering when they saw his feet were completely dry. And Keebo would just incline his head and wish them a good day.

He thought perhaps of getting hold of a pony or donkey—Tolma had provided him with papers for that, as well; and it was too wet again for his little disc—but the poor beast would have had a time as the rain began falling even harder once he exited Eastport. He was in no great hurry; presumably, if Tirtar was even at home, his grief would not be considerably less in one more day.

When the clouds darkened further, Keebo moved off and stood in the shelter of the forest to his left. Uncharacteristic of even this seasonal last-gasp, great sheets of rain fell, and rivers ran down the road; the water coming off the young redgum under which he sheltered was nearly a veil. He waited, watching the lighter patches of cloud slide toward him. A wagon, pulled by a pair of depressed oxen, came around a bend. Keebo waved, but the driver seemed to ignore him as he slapped the reins across the oxen's backs by habit.

He realized his feet were cold, and glanced down to see he had sunken ankle-deep into the mud. "Now, now," he chided, cocking his head.

"Oren, oren, quono lohr wie juilo deium piku." The ground began firming, and he rose out of the muck.

He glanced up as the rain began to slack. Further down the road it seemed the driver shifted, as if suddenly turning to face forward again. Keebo's smile was thin; he wished folks were more accustomed to magic. Another reason he believed it best to use small amounts frequently: aside from building up the user's affinity, it also made people more comfortable with its use.

Maybe the man was Rinc Nain. They never grew comfortable with its use. And why did Keebo live in the Islands, again? After Nutar Ha especially, and later the Queen's death, it could be so much easier to simply move, and live somewhere else.

But then, perhaps Jon's death would go unpunished. Even with his Kin-song, Keebo had very little to investigate. He gazed down the road south. It felt good to stand out of the rain; and he did not believe his destination would yield much in the quest for justice. A father in grief still rarely murdered a prince. The father that had come after such a lowly wizard as Keebo had even settled for a beating. A son, before him, had settled for as much, too.

When he wondered why the son had come, after nearly two decades, he thought perhaps it was the God's way of reminding him of what he'd done. He had begun to forget it, after all—went whole days without remembering, sometimes. So maybe it was for the best. Still, odd to have no one seeking vengeance for so many years, then suddenly two show up in the span of a few months. Maybe that was just how the world worked.

Keebo sighed; it also worked by raining a lot just before the summer, and he was no closer to Pael just standing here. He moved out of the trees and continued down the slopping road.

The clouds lifted as darkness fell, and a small stand of yurts appeared just off the road. Keebo made his bed, ate lightly on bread, cheese, and dried meat, and fell asleep. He woke early to a bright morning and continued down the road on a small disc he was able to gather from drier parts near the forest. He abandoned it a mile from town to avoid the stares. It wasn't so bad when there were only a handful; hundreds began to get uncomfortable. The disc had quickened his trip, though, and he did not mind walking the last, short leg.

The village around Pael ringed the edge of Lusch Lake—businesses on the north and west sides, farms to the south and east—while the city center was built upon the large island near the western shore. Three great bridges, from the north, north-west, and west, arched over the still waters, and folk in broad conical hats teemed back and forth across them. It was one of the larger cities of the Islands, exceeded only by Maerc; and Keebo came seeking one woodcarver, and no indication in which part of the city the man might live and work. His clue, he hoped, was the symbol on the back of the locket. His first stop would be the Obelisk Quarter.

It was another remnant of the Anoe—specifically, their gods. The

Obelisk had first resided in Nobak, until a few centuries ago when it had been carefully removed from the then-deserted city, moved by ways Keebo couldn't imagine, probably magical, and set up here. A team of earth wizards then altered the stone, and the writing upon it, to change it from the Anoe god Int-hep, god of protection—clearly a false god—to the God of All. The Obelisk had never been part of that canon, but now many in Pael and elsewhere in the Islands wore it as if the God himself had created the pillar.

Nearly fifty feet tall, it towered over the square, casting its shadow over half the buildings in the course of the day—the residents and shopkeepers in those buildings imagined blessings during the time they were touched; Keebo thought being blocked from the light would be a curse. It glistened wetly now; the rains had ceased but the sun was not yet strong enough to dry it. As much as he knew about stone, Keebo did not know—nor did any other, to his recollection—what the Obelisk was made of. It had an appearance like raw granite, and yet had a semi-translucent surface that, on the sun-struck side, gave it an almost quartz-like quality. It was the only example he knew of.

Once he could pry his eyes from the monument, and cast them around the square, he quickly noticed a storefront that must have been what he was looking for, a rusted and useless bow-saw suspended over the door. Tirtar's shop, he noticed, was not on the side of the square that would receive the Obelisk's shadow. It had a suspiciously boarded-up look to it; and yet the short steps were still clean and the awning was bright—blue and orange stripes, reminding him a little of a ringed octopus.

He went up to the door and knocked lightly. The square was beginning to come alive, but not yet clamorous. "Tirtar, I need to talk to you about your daughter," he said quietly; he needed the man inside to hear him, but didn't want to draw attention from the marketplace.

At first he thought it had not carried far enough; but, presently, he heard a leather footfall on the opposite side, and the creak and scrape of wood being moved against itself. He stepped back with a smile, hands clasped in front. The door opened into darkness, the daylight now an intruder only half-heartedly revealing who Keebo assumed was Tirtar.

The shadowed man and his entire wardrobe had clearly seen better days. He was a little taller than Keebo, but stooped to about the same height; gray hair hung limply framing a thin, weathered face with a few days' scraggle on the chin. Black eyes existed below thick eyebrows. His gray vest was rumpled, his brown shorts partially undone at the laces, stained throughout, and frayed at the hem. Bony legs bowed downward into hard leathers like moccasins.

"You know my name, so you must know that I have no daughter," he said in a flat voice.

Keebo's grin faded as he gazed on the disheveled man. "I know," he said; it was no great stretch to put on the same despair Tirtar wore like skin. How many people like this had he produced for the sake of love?

"I'm sorry to refresh the memories, but I need to know what happened. May I come in?"

Tirtar's eyes came up briefly before he turned and shuffled away, leaving the door open. A faint spark of curiosity had been in that glance, and Keebo grasped it like a drowning man a rope. When he had first seen the carver, he worried that no stories would be forthcoming. But that one glance showed the man might still function.

As Keebo shut the door, a lamp flared to life on a small table. The home was a little better furnished than others in the Islands, so Tirtar had done well, at least until recently. He had probably supplied most of his own furniture and ornaments; a few tables were scattered with small figurines—horses, fish, birds, turtles; there were a lot of turtles, from sea turtles to snappers to box to tortoises. One sat half-finished in a corner, appeared it might end up as a small chair, or a large footstool.

The chairs were wicker mesh; solid wood was usually far too hot to sit in, and only royals still suffered them. And since Tirtar seemed intent on keeping all the windows closed, it was already humidly warm inside. Keebo wiped a bead of sweat before it plunged off the edge of his nose, lowering himself gently into a seat opposite Tirtar; the tensile strength of wicker and his weight did not often match. It creaked dangerously, but held.

"What do you think happened?" Tirtar asked first, as Keebo sat stiffly.

"I have heard nothing specifically," he replied, only partially lying. "I wanted—"

"How did you know to come here?"

Keebo shifted ever so cautiously, reaching into his pouch and pulling out the locket. "This belonged to your daughter?"

Tirtar took it, leaned over to inspect it under the light. "Yes." He opened it, gazing at the black lock of hair for many moments. Almost absently, and without really looking, he plucked Jon's chestnut lock out from the other side and flicked his fingers, dusting the hairs onto the floor. He closed the locket, and kept it tight in his fist.

Keebo studied him; something about the way he moved seemed familiar, as though many, many years ago they had been acquainted. But nothing specific stuck out. "You did not like Jon Terose," he said instead.

"He killed my daughter."

"Please tell me how," Keebo asked, keeping his voice mild and slightly curious.

"He wooed her over the course of a month's lunches, ordering hundreds of tiny carvings—small, so I could complete them quickly and she could deliver them. Made her every kind of promise, wrote her things, read her things..." He shook his head. "No man since Jalar did so much to win a girl's heart, and that after she had already given it to him."

Keebo couldn't help but smile a little: Jalar had supposedly filled ten pools with the water from the ten oceans, ringed them in beaches of sand delivered from the eight continents, to allow his love to 'travel' without ever leaving Candar Ha. One of those ballads that people swooned over even though, at its core, was all about jailing someone in invisible walls because they loved them.

"Finally, on the day he was to bring her to Nak to wed, a messenger came instead severing all ties. No more orders for carved figures, no message of explanation. She wrote to him every day for a month asking why, explaining her love. She took a ferry to try to see him, and was turned away at the port. Finally she gave it up, thought to move on." Tirtar stopped, his eyes going even further distant.

Not just Tirtar's mannerisms: now his voice sounded vaguely familiar. Keebo knew he had not actually heard the voice before, and yet a certain word here or there, or a particular depth... Still not enough for bold inquiry. He waited, trying to ignore the sweat tickling paths down his back. It would be insensitive to fan himself, he supposed. But there was more to the story, and he waited quietly for the telling.

"She started noticing strange looks from patrons, several days later. Folks coming up to the shop seemed surprised to see her. At first we thought they assumed she would be to the castle by now. But there was something else; they began to look disgusted, as if how dare she show herself. She began to be refused service at some of the shops; got surprised indignation when she suggested it was out of the ordinary. Finally someone told her, in tones as if she should know: Jon had accused her of charming him, bewitching him, offering her body as bribe to be made queen. Somehow the whole of the Islands seemed to know, though it was a shock to us.

"She tried to make do; but forgiveness was nowhere to be found. Not that she needed it," he added with an angry glance. "But even if she did, she should have found it at least somewhere."

Keebo could not wait any longer. He leaned forward. "Tirtar, forgive me, but—do we know each other? Before this?"

The carver looked at him. His glance, though tired, seemed keen as it went to Keebo's eyes, nose, and mouth. He shook his head dully. "I know you by reputation, a little; but no, I don't know you."

Keebo sat motionless. "Are you sure?"

"Is it important?"

"It could be—that is, if I had known your daughter as well, before...well..." The silence stretched too long, and Keebo sat back with a wave. "Never mind. You knew your daughter best," he said. "You know for certain she could not have done as he said."

"She could not; she was never gone long enough, and always ate lunch with the Steward, and sometimes younger master Terose present, not to mention servants."

"Her letters?"

"She read aloud each one to make sure it didn't sound silly, or bad. She could not understand how a carver's daughter caught the attention of a prince, but she was determined not to ruin it." He paused, his eyes making another rare trip to meet Keebo's. "We didn't know it wasn't up to her."

Had Jon really changed so much? The Jon that Keebo had known would never treat even his worst enemy in such a way. "Is there any chance the letter hadn't come from master Terose?"

"It wasn't a letter, just a messenger. In Terose livery, yes."

Keebo scratched at his belly. If, for some reason, Jon hadn't sent the message, why were there no more orders? Why were there no more visits? Why would she be turned back at the port? Why wouldn't Jon reach out?

Why would he still have the locket?

"Do you have a knife, master Tirtar?" Keebo asked. Tirtar looked at him levelly for several moments before he understood. "Um, do you have a plain knife, wooden handle, held together by rivets?"

"Plain knives break too easily; my tools are the result of years of careful acquisition."

"I should still see them, if you don't mind."

After a breath, Tirtar gestured to a far corner. "You can see my workbench; they are in a roll of leather."

Keebo stood slowly, made his way over to the bench. He found the roll and unlaced the tie; each tool was in its slot, brilliantly clean and oiled. There was one tool that matched the vision, except the blade seemed perhaps darker. He scoffed at himself; the whole room was darker. No help. He returned to the chair, but did not sit down.

"Where were you around mid-Savimon?" Keebo asked, suspecting the answer; Tirtar gestured silently around the room in confirmation. "Can anyone avow that?"

"Sarren looks in on me from time to time," he said. "Baker, across the square; Noon shadow. Why?"

"Did Jon return that locket at any time?" he asked, pointing.

Tirtar gazed at his fist, shifting his fingers only a little. "No," he said quietly. He looked up. "And no, no one can *avow* that," he added with a touch of mockery.

"Jon was killed last month," Keebo said, watching Tirtar closely.

His lips went thin; after a breath, he looked up. "I'm not sure he would have made a very good king," he said.

"Tolma seems to think Jon had to make a hard decision in breaking things off with your daughter; a decision affecting the rulership of the Islands."

"If he believes the story too, that my daughter was a whore, then I'm not surprised."

"A lot of people seem to believe that story."

Tirtar's gaze came up, hard but silent.

"Except you," Keebo pressed.

"The door is behind you."

Keebo turned and shuffled to the door. He paused after opening it and glanced back. "For what it's worth," he said, taking one final look around the room; "I don't believe the story either."

Tirtar gazed at him, then down at his fist once more. After a moment, he turned and blew out the lamp. Keebo shut the door, leaving him to it.

8

FISHING WITH ANOE

"Are they on their way yet? Perhaps they can help her."
"You still do not realize her potential, do you?"
"As you realized Keebo's potential?"
"He may yet grow into it."

4 Savimon 1320 — Dry

Keebo stood outside, looking across the square. He supposed, for the sake of being thorough, he should go talk to Sarren; it wouldn't hurt to buy a few rolls for the road, either. But he knew Tirtar was speaking the truth. That much despair encouraged sloth, not flight, and certainly not murder. Tirtar would be lucky to muster enough motivation to work again. And, if he had somehow exacted justice, he would be brighter. Most likely.

Unless he learned Jon was not who he thought he was, and realized he had murdered an innocent man. Keebo stepped resolutely off the small landing and crossed toward the baker's, oblivious to the calculating eyes that followed him.

He could smell the fresh bread three steps before he opened the door. Baskets draped in lumpy cloth held in heat and steam, keeping the loaves fresh and moist. The proprietor smiled as Keebo entered, surely recognizing a hearty customer when she saw one. Without prompting, she began undoing the cloths, revealing a medley of long loaves and short rolls in every shade from pasty Rinc Nain white to Pal Isan dark.

He smiled, selecting several of the darker ones by pointing. "Sarren?" he asked as he handed over his pouch.

"Indeed," she said graciously, tucking the loaves inside. "Half a mark, my dear. Why do you ask?"

Keebo handed over the coin. "I was asking after Tirtar across the street; he said you've looked in on him these past days."

She dropped the coppers into a jar and put her fists on her hips. "One of these days I'll drag him back outside to remind him the sun still comes out when all the world has passed away."

"He's been there this past month?"

She nodded. "I've seen him all except one day, about mid-Monzak; wouldn't answer. He does that sometimes too; I left some food on the stoop. It was gone before too long."

"Did you see him take it?"

She shrugged. "Who else would have?"

"Someone who didn't want to see him taken care of?" Keebo glanced behind him as the door opened and shut. The man who had entered seemed not at all pleased to be in a baker's store. Maybe he just didn't like waiting.

"Who would that be?" Sarren asked, drawing back Keebo's attention.

"Someone who hadn't forgiven his daughter?" he offered.

Sarren's arms folded tightly. "What a daughter does is rarely fault of the father."

"You believe she did it?"

She shrugged again. "Wouldn't be the first, I don't doubt. I'm sure master Terose has to deal with such things a lot. At least he dealt with it; others before him didn't have the stomach," she added, her mouth drawing tight.

Ah, yes; that story. That one Keebo did believe, having been on part of the receiving end. Well, kings often went un-liked; what did it matter if an earth wizard joined the crowd? "Tirtar seems to disagree."

She drew a deep breath through her nose. "Well, father's blessing I guess, to think the best of his daughter. Aught else?"

"One little thing; has Tirtar always been a carver? I seem to recall him a little, though I can't place him. I've never needed something carved."

"Before my time, dearie; he was here when I moved in. Perhaps, though: he was old then, and his daughter was quite young. He may have done before she came along."

"And his wife?"

"Passed on, oh...ten years ago? Hard times on him then, too, I heard; but he wasn't alone that time."

Keebo glanced sideways at the other patron, smiled, and nodded. "Thank you." He exited, chewing thoughtfully on a roll. Even in the heat, there was something about fresh bread...

Back to Eastport, he supposed, and the difficult journey to talk to Kal and find out why he lied. He made his way through the Obelisk Quarter, enjoying his food. A splatter of water onto the road behind him made him turn, glance up at a housewife giving him a barely-apologetic smile for nearly hitting him with the wash-water. He smiled in return; the sun would dry it soon enough, and he didn't want the patron from the shop to know he could tell he was being followed.

He continued down the street, making a few random but decisive turns. At every cross, the man was still behind him. Surely this wasn't a third, not already.

A fifth random turn, and Keebo was beginning to lose where he was. He thought this was taking him back toward the Obelisk, which also proved the man was not simply returning home. Keebo stepped suddenly sideways, hiding himself in a doorway and peering back the way he'd come.

The man entered the intersection and paused, glancing left and right. It was then Keebo recognized the driver from the road into Pael, who had shifted suddenly as if turning forward. Perhaps, then, he had recognized Keebo as he passed and was double-checking. Which triply meant this was no accident.

"May I help you?" Keebo asked, stepping from the doorway.

The man snorted, striding forward as his hand went across his body, clutched, and extended. Keebo caught a glint of metal in the man's hand, and his smile departed.

"Let's have none of that," he growled. A quick whisper, and he gathered dirt from the corners and coalesced it around the blade. Suddenly heavier than he anticipated, the knife fell from the man's hand, narrowly missing his foot. He jumped a little sideways, glaring at Keebo. He reached down as if to pick it up.

"I said 'no'!" Keebo said; and the stone now around the blade became one with the cobbles of the street.

The man grunted as his back spasmed, unable to pull the knife from its magical sconce, or lift up a whole section of street. "You can do this if you need to," Keebo continued, "but murdering me will accomplish nothing."

As the man straightened, Keebo couldn't help but notice the simple wooden handle of the knife. Everyone *did* have one of those, didn't they?

"What were their names?" he asked, gently now. He truly did want to remember them all; he didn't realize there were so many.

"Why did you do it?" the driver asked, his voice suddenly hollow.

Keebo stood amazed. No one had asked him that, ever. More than anything, right then, he wanted to sit down and cry. In the face of the impending beating, he allowed himself the latter, at least a little bit. "She said she loved the mountains," he said quietly. "Wanted an Island full of them."

——◆——

When consciousness came back, the sun was nearly set, the alley almost completely dark. A scruffy dog left off licking his face and scampered away, pausing once at the intersection to look back before continuing out of sight.

Keebo sat up and wiped away the drool. Caralet, Westburr, Danala, Peythro, Manalein, and Fedrin. That man'd had a large family, to be sure. It was always the sons and fathers that survived. Or the only ones strong and free enough to seek revenge. Maybe the wives and sisters who survived only killed themselves, like Tirtar's daughter had. Surely they were stronger than that, though.

Keebo blinked a few times; he had never learned the daughter's name. For as much as she should have been around the castle, he was surprised Tolma had forgotten it. Maybe he didn't want to remember, after everything that happened. Still, odd; maybe next time he went to Nak...

For now, he still needed to get to Eastport, and find a ship to Berola. He sighed, tilting his head back to gaze skyward: he wouldn't make the port tonight. Hopefully Tolma's missive would work for lodging, too.

The next morning, Keebo departed early, partly because he was eager to be on his way, partly because the innkeeper was more than happy for the event as well. 'Free lodging' did not specify a length, after all.

The clouds were gone, and a deep sapphire sky remained as he skimmed along the road. Nedley was in port when he arrived, and only glowered a little when asked to take him to the home of the Anoe.

"You don't like them?" Keebo asked as the sail bloomed.

"They can keep to their island," Nedley replied, his eyes seeming to search the small sail intently, perhaps for a loose thread or something.

"These used to all be their islands," Keebo reminded him.

"A long time ago; things change, I hear."

"And if someone wanted to change them back?"

Nedley snorted. "Best of luck to them. As if they'd ever get out of their huts and try."

"They might get help."

Nedley's gaze lowered. "Now you sound like..." He trailed off. When Keebo glanced at him, his eyes shifted to the horizon and he bumped the rudder a notch.

"Who do I sound like? Strake?"

Nedley's mouth twisted. "Not my place," he mumbled.

"It is your place to help in the murder inquiry of your prince," Keebo replied sternly.

"Just something I heard, is all," he said, scrunching down in his seat.

"From Strake? Jon? Tolma?"

"I don't know where it was from! The soldiers, probably, at the dock; you know how men chatter."

Keebo held in a sigh, and the boat was quiet. Why had he gone away for that year? If he had kept visiting, he would have known the nature of Jon's character; now he needed to rely on those around the lad, and everyone told differing stories. So he sat and brooded, and wondered what Kal would tell him this time.

They made fair time through the night. "We're close," Nedley said as the sun passed its height the next day. He sneered. "I can smell it."

Keebo glanced up; in truth, the low island was visible on the horizon, a few plumes of smoke rising faintly into the sky. He pulled out one of the loaves from earlier, tore off a chunk and offered it to Nedley.

"Thanks," he said. He nudged a water-skin that was on the deck closer to Keebo.

"And returned," Keebo said with a smile, hefting the skin and taking a few swallows. Spiced, he noted, with a bit of rum; normal for large ships on long voyages, a little more than indicative on a small ship that was never more than a couple days from the next port. But he said nothing, and returned the skin to his captain.

"Do you know how long you'll stay?" Nedley asked as he bumped up to the rickety pier.

"I would say 'not long,' but these visits tend to stretch; the Anoe can be very welcoming." He paused, glancing eastward. "You can return to Nutar Ha if you want; send a boat when you get there. I'll be going to Naso Narok when I leave here."

Nedley paused in furling the sail, looking north-easterly. "It's fine," he said finally. "I can share with my Calderon. It's not that bad," he added, pushing a finger against his nose with a teasing grin.

Keebo nodded, his smile fading to a growl as he turned. He knew the joke: they smelled like stagnant water, just like you would expect of frogs. They bore a passing resemblance, true; but spend a few moments in conversation and you quickly realized they were likely smarter, kinder, and more generous than the average Rinc Nain with all their talk of the God of All. And hadn't they adopted the eastern deity, at least some of them?

He made his way up the beach toward the nearest village. Berola was almost entirely sand: loose and white on the beaches, a little grittier and browner across most of the rest of the island. Thin grass grew in sporadic clumps, and the Anoe deeper in the interior managed some meager fruits. Mostly, though, they fished. The Rinc Nain thought they were lazy because they rarely fished during the day; in the heat, though, it made sense that they fished dusk through nightfall. In fact, Anoe were rarely seen outside until the sun began to sink.

Which was how he was able to enter the village apparently undetected. He moved between the huts, grass mostly, with a few sporting actual wooden walls, at least on one or two sides. Weighted linen blankets hung in the doorways, dyed with family crests—usually orange on brown, but a few blues for the Council Elders. Keebo paused before a door with circling dolphins; before he could knock, Kal pulled it aside.

"I thought I smelled you," he said. "Come in."

Keebo frowned, almost ducking his head to sniff himself before he realized the jest. "You know I never laughed at that joke."

"Well then, you're practically Anoe," Kal said with a little warmth.

"Have I done something wrong?" Keebo demanded; after all, Kal had lied to *him!*

"The door is getting heavy," Kal replied. "Please come in."

Keebo set his jaw, ducking through the opening. Inside he found the entirety of the Council seated around a small fire on which several fish roasted. "I had meant to speak to Kal alone," he said.

A few half-smiles and a snicker puzzled him. "I told you that you should not call me that," Kal growled, puzzling him further. He glanced around them, trying to understand. Kal returned silently to the one empty spot around the fire. "Please join us, and we will speak," he continued, glancing pointedly at a small chair nearly in the corner.

Keebo stiffened. "I had hoped to come as a friend, despite what happened earlier," he said, making no move except to clench his fists. "Instead you look to wrong me further."

"How have I wronged you?" Kal asked.

"You lied to me! You said you came only as they were removing the body; Tolma said the man who found Jon saw you, and you ran."

All eyes swung to him. "Shokalog?" one of the elders asked.

Kal sat quietly, large eyes blinking. He removed a dipper of water from a bucket behind him, poured it over his head and shook the droplets free. "I needed your help," he admitted, replacing the dipper. The next Council member repeated the ritual as Kal continued. "I thought if you knew that, you would assume I had done it—or at least would be less inclined to help."

Keebo stood frozen. He certainly *was* less inclined. "Tolma also said Jon wanted nothing to do with you; that he would rather provoke the Anoe than help them, and that Tolma had to talk him down."

"So I went to him uninvited? Convenient. Did Jon strike you as such a man?"

"Tolma said he had changed, almost overnight."

"When?"

"Some months back."

The fourth elder bathed himself. "Then why would he come here and speak so intelligently to us all only three weeks ago?" he asked.

"What did he say?"

Kal took up the tale. "He wanted no enemies, here or across the seas. Whether we trusted him or not, he would begin lifting the restrictions on where we lived. We were going to be able to take our lands back that his people had stolen. Beginning with Nobak."

"You told me the elders wouldn't want to hear it."

"We didn't," said the sixth as water cascaded over him. "We even thought to ask him to solve a problem as proof of his veracity, but..."

"What problem?"

The elders were silent, introspective. Kal glanced around, then at Keebo. "Some of our people have been going missing, Keebo; just a few at a time, late in the night and those who go out the farthest to fish. We've tried fishing closer, but..."

"Our waters are dying," an elder spat. "There are no fish close to shore. We have to go out. And there aren't enough of us to protect ourselves. We lose fewer if we spread out so far as to be alone. That way, we only lose two or three a week."

Keebo sat thunderstruck. "Two or three of you go missing *per week?!*"

"Only recently; but, in another month..." Kal spread his hands wide. "That's why we thought to ask Jon, because maybe he could help, and it might make steps toward proving him."

"But you didn't ask."

The sixth elder continued the tale. "No. Sent him on his way. Shoka-log, we only learned recently, pursued anyway. It did not surprise us; always he lives up to his name."

Kal look shamefaced, as near as Keebo could tell. He'd have to ask him about his name one day—perhaps someone in Anoe history he was unfamiliar with. Later. "And?"

"And now we will never know. The old laws will stay in place until Strake ascends, and probably beyond that," said the seventh and final member, just in front of Keebo. "Life for us does not change."

Keebo's glance went backward around the circle; in each face was resolute acceptance. They had known no other life, never had hope in another. How many generations had grown up and died in that way? How many generations of stories were about defeat, relocation, oppression? A long march through time, with only faint echoes of far distant glory all but snuffed out. Clung to, still, for without even faint hope they would disappear from the face of Oren; and yet that clutch drove the bitterness even deeper. Jon had come, intentionally or not, and raised that hope beyond a dying ember, despite all their caution to the contrary. With his death, the glower sank deeper toward darkness. Keebo saw the darkness, the hushed return to cages in every slick face, every glistening eye seated around that fire—except the last.

In Kal's was the ill-contained fire of bitter frustration.

9

AN ABANDONED SHIP

"I never met these people, while on Oren."
"Few have."
"How is that possible?"
"They do not call attention to themselves, because they are rarely believed."

6 Savimon 1320 — Dry

"I don't know what's going on anymore, Kal," Keebo said, setting down the empty plate of fish.

The Council had left, letting them talk privately. Keebo had kept silent through most of the meal, aside from complimenting the quality of meat. Fish was hard to prepare well; but, he supposed, Kal and the other Anoe would have had more opportunity to practice.

"Why not?"

Keebo shrugged. "I enjoyed my garden, doing little odd bits of magic for it. No one bothered me. Sometimes it seemed they were happier to see me the longer I stayed away."

"It is not good to be alone," Kal said, showering under another ladle of water. "Thoughts fester, and bad ideas make their homes."

Keebo grunted. "But in the company of others, we take beatings."

Kal looked close. "Another one?"

Keebo nodded grimly. "In Pael. Caralet, Westburr, Danala, Pey...Pey..." He grimaced, trying to recall the name. So *many*.

"Keebo, why do you do that?"

He squeezed his eyes shut, trying to recall the names. "To remember."

"Remember what? A mistake?"

"Peythro," he said suddenly, and sighed. Manalein, and Fedrin. "To remember the innocent, Kal. You don't seem to mind how much I care for your people."

"You do not take it as personally as you do these others," he said. "It was a mistake, one I know you will not make again. You need to leave it behind you. You do no one any good by being alone."

"Name someone I do good by being around," he muttered.

"Me," Kal responded immediately. "You will do Jon well to be around, doing exactly what you are doing. You will do the whole Islands well to properly solve his murder."

"Hmph. Right."

"What have you learned so far? Who has done it?"

"Assuming you didn't," Keebo said with a jesting smile, "that leaves Tirtar, and anyone from the deep-water ships guild." Keebo's brow furrowed. "What did you say Jon said to the elders when he came here?"

"That he would give us back—"

"No, about enemies."

"He wanted none here or across the sea."

Keebo's hands went to the floor, his body tensing for the effort it was about to make. "You are sure?"

"Of course; those words."

"Hoo-kay!" he grunted, climbing to his feet with many a groan. He arched his back until he heard a faint pop. "Ahh. Kal, I need you to come with me."

"Where are we going?" Kal asked, rising easily—and without groaning.

Keebo glared a moment. "Young toad," he muttered. "Pasch, is where we're going, to see the head of the deep-water ships guild. Tolma also told me Jon favored the intra-island boats. But if that were so, he wouldn't care about enemies across the sea. Then we're going back to see Tolma, and find out why *he* is lying to me. Oh, and I'm sorry about Nedley. You'll see," he finished with an apologetic smile.

⸺⬗⬦⬖⸺

"It seems like I'm going to run all over these Islands," Keebo said, enjoying the sun on his face as Nedley steered them toward the inlet at the entrance to a long, narrow bay, deep inside which lay the port of Pasch. "You don't mind, do you?" he said to Kal; Nedley had been strangely quiet the entire five-day trip to Naso Narok, a feat he suspected unlikely to be repeated.

Kal lifted his arm from the sea and splashed the water on his face. "No. Though I'm not sure why you need me."

"Because you were the last one he spoke to privately, it would seem. You and Tolma seem to be the only ones to know what he was like—what he was up to the last few days. And you're telling very different stories."

"Why do we not go to Nutar Ha and see Tolma first?"

Keebo looked at him. "Because it may not be necessary, if our murderer is here on Naso. I follow the clues that seem the likeliest first, then the ones that are...less so."

"It is not because you believe Tolma is your friend?"

"Tolma is my friend, Kal," Keebo said, leaning back again with a sigh. "He's a good friend; stayed there with me in that whole..." he gestured with his hand. "Aftermath. Not many did."

"He helped you move on?"

Keebo opened his eyes and pursed his lips. "I don't know about that, necessarily. He's helped me to remember."

"Remember what?" Nedley asked, suddenly breaking his silence.

Keebo looked across to Kal, then twisted to look back at Nedley. "Well, I cast a spell a long time ago. Long, long time ago. It had some...unintended consequences. Very bad ones. I hurt...a lot of people. So I've put away the big spells; just do little things now."

"What spells?"

"Earth magic stuff; changing soils. It helps in my garden. No chance of going horribly wrong, again."

"Huh. I crashed my boat onto a reef once; it survived, mostly. One of my passengers was thrown overboard."

"Did she drown?"

"She split her head on the reef and a shark came and ate her before we could haul her back aboard."

Keebo looked again at Kal, and shifted. "Um, Nedley..."

"Still sailing though."

The sail luffed a little, snapping against the line as the wind shifted; rope buzzed around a pin as Nedley slacked the line to bring the sail back into the wind, and the boat slapped through a few choppier waves as they passed into the bay.

"Accidents happen," Nedley continued in the renewed silence. "Doesn't mean you stop everything; just avoid the reef the next time."

"It's a little diff—" Keebo cut off as Kal suddenly leapt over the side of the boat. Keebo scrambled over, ready to grab a line; he looked into clear waters, saw his friend keeping pace underwater with powerful kicks. There was a pod of dolphins below, weaving in and out of line with Kal's heading. Keebo smiled; must be nice.

Suddenly Kal drew near the surface. He leapt out of the water in a spray, landing back in the boat. He shook himself with a smile. "That feels better," he said.

"Did you see the dolphins, or...?"

"I was interrupting your nonsense," he replied casually. "The question ultimately comes down to this: did Master Terose change his mind? Was he going to favor the shallow ships, or the deep-water ships? Does Master Nedley have any opinion or knowledge of this?" They both turned to him.

"I only ever took Steward Bergin and Master Strake, and only a few times. I didn't get to know Master Jonkar."

"They traveled separately that much?" Keebo asked, finding his seat again, this time facing sternward. "That seems strange for a Steward to leave off his charges like that."

Nedley shrugged, but Kal answered. "Jon had to grow up sometime. Perhaps it was his own suggestion that they travel separately, and allow him to begin living the role of King. Strake was too young, yet. Who brought them to Northport last month?"

"Wasn't me," Nedley said. "Steward Bergin had sent me south to Gunda, a sort of spiced punch only made in Raus and he wanted some gallons. When I came back he was off; port guards said they had gone on to Sed Narok, so I followed to see if they needed a ride back."

"Any ideas who he would have gotten?"

"Seemed to me this hiring of specific ferrymen was new. Time was you just took whoever was there, way my grandad tells it. Steward or not. Maybe this time he didn't care."

"But you wanted to be sure it was you?"

Nedley shrugged. "I wouldn't mind. He gives me a daily wage whether I end up sailing him or not."

"Funny thing," Keebo said, picking at his shirt. "When all this started, Brin told me that Tolma had chosen him as a permanent ferryman." He pulled a fraying thread, inspecting it before tossing it into the waters. "Would he suddenly need two of you?"

Nedley kept his eyes on the horizon. "Can't say what he needs. I do what I'm told, until he stops telling me it."

"That seems like a nice..." Keebo trailed off as Nedley continued staring intently over his shoulder. Ahead of them, the bustling port at Pasch was steadily coming into view.

Despite the comparatively small size of this island, it was one of the most populated. On the northeast side, the city of Pasch was third-largest of the islands and home to every trade available. On the northwest side, tucked into the hills, was the village-almost-a-city of Tell, home to artisans, philosophers, even a few magicians. It was believed by most that the only reason it had not become a city was lack of revenue. The harbor where they docked was almost naming size, and ships from North Pal Isan and Rinc Na came and went here, and—the object of Keebo's desire—was home to the shipyard of all deep-water boats built in the Islands. Scattered farmlands could be seen ranging across the flats and up onto the hillsides. A few of those farms sported terraces, the rice paddies carved there hidden in their little hollows; the rest were the usual mixes of fruits and nuts and vegetables as could be had. On the south sides were pig farms and chicken runs, as cattle needed too much acreage to be profitable in the limited land-space. Beef was an almost nonexistent commodity throughout the Clanasoes; what did show up was the thickly smoked, salted, and imported variety, so most settled for pork, poultry, or fish.

"I'll stay here," Nedley said, not looking at either of them.

"Thank you," Keebo said. "We shouldn't be long."

They moved along the docks, ducking around men, women, and carts laden with boxes, bundles, sheafs, and rarely arms and armor. Keebo couldn't imagine wearing some of that thick, heavy stuff in this heat; closer glances at a few faces told him they couldn't believe it either.

"It's been too long, Kal," he said as they walked, feeling the familiarity of those feet slapping behind him. Years and years ago, he and Kal had been nearly inseparable, except at great need. "What happened, anyway?"

"My people needed me," Kal replied. "Your farm needed you, or so you said."

"You should try it sometime," Keebo said, side-stepping a pile of fish guts that someone thought belonged there. 150 years on these Islands and Keebo still sometimes found himself holding his nose. "No one bothers you, it's peaceful, time almost..." He paused with a beaming smile, waving his hand across the sky. "Disappears."

"For some, time is a great anchor around their neck, dragging them into the deep."

The smile left. "Wonderful."

"It is only reality; growing vegetables only for yourself does not change it."

Keebo stopped and turned. Kal blinked at him, then shook his head. "I am sorry, friend," he said. "My words were unfair, and meant more for the whole Islands than for you."

Keebo cocked his head. "What do you mean?"

"You know the conflicts. Some here would see the Clanasoes draw tight around themselves, shut others out; others would expand, increase trade of goods, people, ideas to the rest of Oren."

"But for how long it takes..."

Kal looked past him, then back. "I think it does not take so long now as it used to; but the Guildmaster can explain better."

Keebo nodded, turned, and continued walking. "And why do you want to see the Islands expand?" he asked, glancing back with a raised eyebrow.

Kal was silent a moment. "Because I have heard that in North Pal Isan, the Rinc Nain and the natives live in better harmony than we do here." His voice lowered. "I would like to know how. And I would like the Rinc Nain here to know, as well."

"Maybe I could teach them," Keebo said, trying to keep his voice light. He felt something vaguely profound in the silence following his words, but when he glanced back Kal was looking away, watching something happen down the streets.

They continued on, soon coming upon a road that ran down again to the sea, where half-finished boats sat in berths; great scaffolds and ropes were lifting a mainmast into place while builders' shouts competed with the gulls' cries and creaking tackle. The mast settled, suddenly, and a moment later the thud of it reached their ears. As little as he knew ships, and despite how early in the building process this was, Keebo could tell this one was different—sleeker in hull, obviously, but the masts themselves looked different.

They approached the building signed "Office" while the builders scrambled along ropes and knots, the palpable tension gone now that the heavy lift was settled. Keebo led the way inside.

"Are you the Guildmaster?" he asked of a middle-aged man at a desk inside.

The man looked blankly up for several moments, then suddenly shook his head. "No, he's supervising the work. Sorry," he added with a pale grin. "It's been a long morning. Look for a head of bushy white hair. Bigger than yours," he finished, his grin a little healthier now.

Keebo thanked him, and returned outside. Almost at once he saw that head of hair, just off to the side, bent now in discussion over a sheaf of papers with a younger, more muscled man. As he approached, Kal in tow, he thought perhaps the younger was a son—they had matching, broad noses and some stippled tattoos around their eyebrows.

"Guildmaster?" he called as he approached.

"Make sure those beams are still—be right with you—make them tight; don't count on that rain we just got."

"Pap, this ain't my first boat."

"It's the first one like this! No chances, unless you're going to put all your livelihood and your family's on a safe journey through storms. Now git, and check 'em."

The young man left, and the Guildmaster squinted at the two. "Beroc," he said, offering his hand. Keebo shook it. He glanced at Kal, and made some sort of sign Keebo didn't recognize. "I welcome the Anoe and their wisdom of the sea," he said.

Kal looked properly surprised, and returned the gesture. "It pales in the face of one who practices the most," he replied.

"Hnn. We'll see."

"New kind of ship?" Keebo asked, ignoring the previous greeting for a moment and turning to the boat.

"Very. Came from Rinc Na—they've got some interesting ideas. It might cut travel time between countries by a third."

"Kal mentioned something like that on the way here. How so?"

But Beroc was looking at the Anoe. "You let him call you that?"

"I have asked him to stop," he replied with a dismissive gesture.

"Should I leave you two alone?" Keebo asked suddenly, beginning to feel hurt, if he was honest with himself. Kal had been his friend, and now this Beroc... He let it pass. "I'm sorry," he said instead, before they could speak. "I'm here looking for a murderer, and you two are...I'm sorry. Please, tell me about the ship."

Beroc glanced between the two, then quickly up at the hull. "Well, you can see it, uh, the hull is narrower. The keel, too, it...I'm sorry, a murderer? Who? Who was killed? Why do you look for him here?"

Keebo closed his eyes and sighed, then looked at the Master. "I need your discretion," he said. "We don't want word getting out too far just yet." He paused when Beroc nodded emphatically and shrugged. Keebo lowered his voice. "Prince Jonkar Terose," he said.

Beroc's eyes went wide, and the sheaf of papers slipped from his grasp. "By the God." His eyes ticked sideways as his jaw lowered. "Uh...When? How?"

"Almost a month ago, in Sed Narok; I would rather not say how, just yet."

"But this..." Beroc's eyes went to the construction, and he gestured wearily. "This was to be his ship."

Keebo glanced at it, then back, his gaze hard. "Since when?"

"The order came in," Beroc said, bending to pick up the littered sheets, still moving slowly. "Oh, months ago. Three months ago? He was here! Only early Monzak, to check on the progress! He was delighted..." Beroc set his jaw and shook his head. "Should I still finish it?"

Keebo folded his arms and gazed at Kal—*Shokalog,* he thought firmly; the Anoe returned the look blankly, but with a mild *I-told-you-so* set to his jaw.

"Is it possible Master Terose was changing his mind?" Keebo asked, turning back to the Master.

Beroc turned away and shrugged. "I suppose anything's possible..." he said, as though it didn't seem very possible.

"Steward Tolma suggested a very sudden change in Jon's—Prince Jonkar's mind; as though he had read a book and in one night changed everything he believed."

Beroc turned back. "If he did, it would have been a great loss to these Islands when he became king," he said firmly.

Keebo's brows rose. "Perhaps Strake would do better?"

"I don't know the younger prince as well as I knew Master Terose; prince Strake was very quiet when they came around, seemed to never be outside Steward Bergin's shadow."

"Did you ever speak to him? Prince Strake?"

"I tried, once or twice; mostly smiles and nods in return. Friendly enough; nice enough; but King?" Beroc shook his head. "Whoever would have been his closest advisor likely would have been king."

"Carefully, Guildmaster Beroc," Keebo said. "He may indeed be your next king."

"Begging your pardon," Beroc said without sincerity. "I can't help I would have preferred Prince Jon."

"Well, if he was to favor this ship—and more like it—that would put you in good stead, wouldn't it?"

"Doesn't give me much reason to kill him, does it? I mean, that *is* why you're here."

"It is; and that holds only so long as Jon still favored this ship. If he had suddenly changed his mind... How much do you have invested in this boat? And others like it?"

"This came straight from the King's coffers," Beroc replied, folding his arms over the sheaf of papers.

"But how much of your life, the lives of these men, the future of the guild..."

"I was here, working on this boat since plans were laid, with barely a moment to go to my own home here in port—much less all the way to Sed Narok and back."

"And your men?"

"They've been here..." He trailed off, looking over the boat.

"You don't sound so sure, Master Beroc."

"Larrince," he muttered, then sighed. "I did lose a man," he continued, turning back. "Larrince; defected to the shallow-water ships."

"'Defected'?" Keebo echoed.

"We're in a war, Master Keebo," Beroc said. "It may not seem like much to the outside, but deep-water boats are in short enough supply. Not wanted until they're needed, is usually how it goes. Well you can't just up and make a deep-water boat at a whim, and you can't support a Guild on crusts. So yes, when one of my men leaves my shipyard and finds work in the other's yard, it's a defection and a betrayal of all of us. If Prince Jonkar was *not* changing his mind—as I believe he was not—the timing of Larrince's...re-employment...is convenient for such a murder."

"He left...?"

"Seventh of Monzak. Just after Prince Jon's visit."

IO

AN ANOE OVERBOARD

"Did this Prince change so much?"
"Some people do."
"I never understood why."
"They are afraid to make a mistake."

11 Savimon 1320 — Dry

Keebo and Shokalog made their way quickly back to Nedley's boat. "We need to go to Candar—"

He cut off as a sudden clattering of armor sounded down the docks. He turned to look, saw a detachment of two of the Island Watch's Tri-guard striding swiftly away from a larger vessel that seemed preparing to sail. Keebo might have paid no attention, except the apparent leader of the detachment was gazing at him.

They turned swiftly down the pier. "Keebo Burami, and Shokalog?" the leader called out.

Hesitantly, Keebo stepped back out of the ferry and onto the dock. Now he recognized the sergeant's insignia on the shoulders. "Yes, we are."

"Orders just came in; you're to report to *The Wanderer* to be brought to Steward Bergin on Nak." He extended his hand in a chopping motion toward the ship Keebo noted earlier. He paused, Keebo felt significantly, and said with a hard gaze at Shokalog: "Both of you."

"Are you coming with us?" Keebo asked as Kal joined him on the dock.

"Captain Belltash will keep you well. Captain," he continued, looking at Nedley and softening his voice. "The Steward thanks you for your service, and requests the usual order from Raus, if you would."

Nedley smiled brightly. "Orchids; I'll sail immediately."

The sergeant turned back. "If you both will kindly follow me," he said.

As Keebo followed, he wondered if Kal's placement between the pair of Tri-guards was an accident; he didn't assume so. They soon arrived at the gangplank, and were left as the sergeant made his salutes to some of the men on board. Though they departed quickly, Keebo couldn't help notice at least one surreptitious glance back.

Two men in particular towered above them, exuding authority Keebo assumed rightly belonged to them. He approached steadily, aware of Kal's feet padding behind him; this time, he wished his friend were not here.

"Did Master Tolma say why he needed us to return so urgently? We were on our way to question someone else," Keebo said.

"I usually leave that for the Steward; but in this case, he said outright to tell you Strake is feeling better—his words—and that you should hear him."

"You may still call him Master Strake, even if Tolma doesn't," Keebo returned. He shook his head. "This is most inconvenient."

"The Steward doesn't care about your convenience. I am Belltash, captain of *The Wanderer*. You may both call me Captain Bell. Kesh here will get you into quarters." He gestured to a young boy nearby. Keebo glanced back a moment.

"Your son?" he asked.

"Grandson," Bell replied with a broad grin. "His dad's the first mate. He'll make a fine mate too, if he ever learns to go aloft."

Kesh's grin faded as he glanced up. The sails were turning as the ship backed clear of the docks. Over the side, Nedley's sails were refilling; he spared a smile and wave as he pulled away from his own mooring and shot north toward the head of the bay.

"Well, thank you for that, then," Keebo said. "Quarters," he clarified. He gestured for Kesh to lead the way; the boy's grin returned as he scampered for the nearest companionway.

"Dinner in my quarters," Bell called after them. "The boy'll bring you."

They made their way belowdecks, Keebo a little more stiffly. Deck prisms diffused a soft glow, showing a first deck of swaying hammocks, a few of them full of night-watch. Behind was the galley; it appeared the cook was on a break. Two hands glanced up briefly from a game of Dice and Bones, squinted at Kesh, and returned.

"What's below?" Keebo asked quietly.

Kesh opened his mouth wide, paused to glance at Kal, then slowly shut it. "Cargo," he said. "Mostly. Grin-da—Captain Bell carries stuff between the Islands, whatever people need. You can have these two," he continued, reaching out to shake the indicated hammocks. "Boxes underneath if you need to secure anything." He glanced at the two up and down. "Captain Bell doesn't like any guests to go into the hold, um, without escort, so...don't. I'll find you when it's dinner time."

"Thank you," Keebo said with a smile. Kesh glanced between them, lingering on Kal as the Anoe's large almond eyes blinked once, then turned and went back up the companionway.

"Need to store anything?" Keebo asked with a grin. He hauled himself into the hammock and stretched out with a sigh. "I could get used to this. More comfortable than Nedley's boat, fast as it was."

Kal padded to the other hammock and sat down gently. "I do not like the smell of this ship," he said.

Keebo wrinkled his brow, sniffing deeply. "It smells like...wood, a little bit of tar...salt water..."

"There is something else," Kal said; his toe tapped the planking. "Below." He glanced sideways as the two sailors quickly turned back to their game.

"All we're doing is being taken back to Nutar Ha and talking to Tolma," Keebo said.

"And trying to solve a murder."

"That's the plan."

"You do not think it is important to talk to that man...Larrince?"

Keebo shrugged. "I'm sure it is. It's probably more important to talk to Strake though, and Larrince can wait."

"Strake cannot?"

"Strake will not." Keebo gestured around them. "Unless you intend to jump off and swim for Candar Ha. *You* could make it, I don't doubt," he said, cutting off Kal's intake of breath. "I could not. We'll come back. And you're still a suspect, so don't seem too eager to cast suspicion on certain people."

"Why would I have done this?"

"Same reason as Beroc: because Jon was suddenly changing his mind, and upsetting everyone's world. If you had thought he was taking you to Nobak to discuss terms and suddenly told you that it was quite impossible, that life must go on for the Anoe as it had—tell me you wouldn't be upset by that."

"*With* his death, it is quite impossible, and life will go on for us as it has, and I am upset by that."

Keebo chewed his lip. "I know. That's the problem, Kal; *if* Jon was changing his mind, it would be to you as if he were dead. Maybe by holding the knife, you felt some sort of...release."

"Do you think Tolma believes so?"

Keebo sighed. "I don't know what Tolma believes. I don't know what Tolma knows; I'm assuming Jon was changing his mind, becoming someone he hadn't been."

"Because Tolma said so?"

"He suggested it, but only after the necklace; Jon didn't used to keep things like that, and he didn't treat people that way, the way he treated that poor girl. He was certainly different from when I knew him. Maybe he was beginning to make decisions he felt were best for the Islands, and that upset a girl and her father, a guildmaster, maybe an apprentice, and an Anoe."

"But so far, only one of us was near the ruins when it happened."

Keebo frowned, and nodded.

"But you don't believe I did it?"

Keebo's gaze searched, and he drew a breath. "My first instinct is no; my second is that I just *want* to believe that. My third goes along with my first." His frown deepened as he looked away. After several moments of silence, Kal stood.

"I'm going on deck," he said quietly. "At least you know I won't go anywhere until we reach Nutar Ha."

Keebo closed his eyes as the boat rocked around him.

⎯⎯◈⎯⎯

Dinner with the Captain was an experience, for Keebo, a real treat: thick, moist, dark bread; two kinds of shellfish and three kinds of fish to choose from; as well as a little chicken sprinkled with a crumbled green leafy spice that Bell called 'parsley' that he had shipped special from northern Rinc Na. Apparently it would not grow in Keebo's garden, and preferred the cooler climes of that region. The unwatered rum came out after dinner, along with sweet rolls with cocoa powder and cinnamon.

Despite the sumptuous spread, the conversation was strained. More than once it seemed Bell had to force himself to remember Kal, and offer him the same foods and drink he gave to Keebo. Topics were avoided, sometimes neatly but more often with stutters and hard glances. The first mate simply stopped talking somewhere right before the sweet rolls, and left before the last snifter of pure rum.

"He's too often about his duties," Bell said with a thin smile. "A good hard worker is fine, but if one can't relax…" He settled back with a broader grin and sipped his rum. "You, master Keebo, seem quite capable."

Keebo smiled. "I have my moments," he said. "Especially with a belly full of such wonderful foods."

"Many don't take to the eel," Bell replied, raising his glass in quiet salute.

Keebo's eyes widened. "I thought that was salmon!"

Bell laughed, shaking his head. "Saltwater eel, and a cook who knows how to prepare it."

"Have you never had eel?" Kal asked Keebo.

Bell laughed again. "Well, your people probably have it all the time—not like this, though, right?"

Kal's smile was tight. "A little different," he said.

"A little? You eat it almost raw, don't you?"

Kal grimaced. "Of course not. We season it a little differently—"

"You're Anoe! The day the Anoe teach me how to prepare food..."

"I would think they would have some practice," Keebo offered. "Yours is very good; but surely those who introduced the meal..." He trailed off as Captain Bell's face darkened. "I mean no insult, Captain; will we eat like this every night? I don't think my bruised palate—"

"Maybe your friend can cook our eel next time, since he does it so well."

"That is not what I meant, Captain."

"And that's not what he said," Keebo chimed in. "He only said they season it differently."

Bell upended his cup, and wiped his mouth. "I've a ship to tend," he said. "If you'll please excuse me."

They rose unsteadily. "Thank you for the meal, Captain," Keebo said. Kal murmured an echo, and they exited. They found the companionway as the sun lowered behind the sails; Sed Narok was a thin, hard smudge on the western horizon.

They took to their hammocks. "What do you suppose that was about?" Keebo whispered as sailors began filling their berths.

"It appears he has some ideas about the Anoe that he prefers to keep," Kal replied.

Keebo's lips compressed. "Right. I'm sorry, Kal."

Kal blinked and sighed. "He probably doesn't even realize it. Maybe one day he will, but clearly not yet."

"We could eat with the crew, if you want."

Kal shook his head. "I find sitting down to dinner changes people more than arguments."

Keebo hummed. They lay in their hammocks and let the gentle sway of the boat on the calm waters swing them to sleep.

⊷◦⊶

Keebo awoke suddenly in the night to shouts on deck, and sounds of scuffling. He thought he heard a wet slap of feet on the boards above his head; he turned and saw Kal's berth empty.

He leapt up, making better time up the ladder than ever before in his life. He turned right, then left; near the railing, three men held Kal tightly as Captain Bell glowered at him with folded arms.

"Captain?" Keebo asked, striding forward.

"I needed—" Kal cut off as one of the three men struck him.

"Captain!" Keebo shouted, wishing he could sense dirt somewhere to hurl at the sailor; Bell kept too clean a ship.

"Your friend was caught attempting to escape," Bell said.

"Escape how?"

One of the sailors spoke up. "He was going over the side; had a rope let down and was in the water when the night-watch caught him. We hauled him up, though."

"Escape implies he is a prisoner; are we prisoners, Captain?" Keebo asked with as much righteous anger as he could fit into his stature.

"You are under my charge, to bring yourselves to the Steward," Bell said levelly. "This one appears to want to be free of that fate."

"Captain, I'm sure—"

"I am not so sure," Bell said firmly. "Take him below and secure him until we reach Nutar Ha."

II

THE ANOE ONBOARD

"Can we help them figure this out?"
"Perhaps this once..."
"I could get used to this."
"That is what I fear."

12 Savimon 1320 — Dry

"Captain, you must let me speak to him."

Bell looked at him long and hard. "It is not customary for friends of the accused to investigate their crime. There tends to be bias."

"But it is common for friends of the accused to defend their case," Keebo replied. "I don't know if he was trying to escape, or just wanted to go for a swim. He does that, occasionally. At least let me find out his side of the story before you keep him locked in a cage in your hold."

Bell tapped his fingers together, glancing out the window to the gentle sea. "Tesh!" he barked suddenly. He glanced over as someone entered the cabin behind Keebo. "Assign two men to take our distinguished guest below to visit the Anoe. Keep him well guarded, please."

"Thank you, Captain," Keebo said. "I will keep myself from prying into your precious cargo."

Bell's eyes flashed as Keebo turned to leave, but he said nothing.

Tesh, a tall, broad man who appeared to be Bell's adult son and thus the first mate, led Keebo to the companionway, sliding down the rails on his hands with the experience of one who has gone up and down a thousand times. Keebo said nothing as he followed at his own comfortable pace. By the time he reached the lower deck, Tesh was standing with two other sailors, equally broad but shorter and with a keener gleam in their eyes. Keebo marked them as purer Rinc Nain than even Nedley had appeared, and their eyes upon him bore flickering traces of disgust.

"Pulwin and Derako will go with you," Tesh said. "Keep him close, and take him only to the Anoe in the cage," he said aside. "Bring him back up swiftly and to me when he is finished."

They gave him wide berth at first, and he fell in behind them as they led him aft. Another stair, less steep, led down into darkness. A faint smell wafted from below, presumably the one Kal had noticed last night. Keebo drew a breath. It seemed faintly familiar, at first like over-ripe banana but changing in his nostrils to brackish water. He tried to keep from sneezing.

"Watch your step," one of them said—he could not see to know who. "Follow directly behind me; there's gaps in the floor. You won't fall far, but you might break an ankle still." The other muttered something Keebo missed, and both chuckled.

Keebo listened closely to their footsteps, staying behind them. Occasionally he tested with his foot; their way was perhaps a pace wide before he felt the lip of some pit. He wondered briefly what cargo they possibly carried, and then the footsteps before him stopped.

"Here," said one. A hand grasped his shirt-front and guided him forward. He reached groping arms, his hands falling on bars of cold steel.

"Kal?" he said.

"Keebo," Kal's voice rasped in whisper. "Thanks for coming. Do you have water?"

Keebo stood a moment, feeling the stuffiness of the lower deck, the still, humid air like a hot wet blanket through which he tried to breathe. His grip on the bars tightened. "One of you go get a pitcher of water," he said. He turned his head slightly when neither of them made a sound. "How often do you clean the deck down here?" he asked quietly. "I think I feel some dirt in all the corners; very useful dirt, to an earth wizard."

They moved, one only a few steps backward, the other hurried along the beam toward the steps. Keebo sighed as he turned back, and slid into a sitting position. "I am sorry, my friend," he said quietly, twisting so he could sit with his back against the cage. There was rustling, then a weak squeeze on his shoulder.

"I will live."

"Why were you going overboard, Kal?"

The hand left his shoulder, into silence. Keebo blinked as the faint light from above lent a gloom to their deck. It was cross-hatched with beams, and that scent came back to him. Why was it so familiar?

"Kal?"

"I need water."

Keebo glared away. "I sent him for—"

"Keebo, think," Kal rasped. He gave a short sigh, and made some sort of mewling and clicking sound in his throat. Something in the darkness thumped. "You are dear to me, my friend, but you do not love the Anoe as well as you imagine."

Keebo's back stiffened. "Of course not; that's why I'm down here trying to hear your reason, to try to defend you to the Captain. That's why I kept you from a mob last time, and am trying to keep you from a mob this time. I'm probably the worst friend you have, Kal—"

"What do I look like to you?"

"What do you mean?"

"If you had to compare me to something else."

Keebo shifted. "I'm not...I mean...Well, everyone is unique, it doesn't always say something about a person because they look a certain—"

Kal's sigh cut him off. "What does the Captain think I look like?"

"A...frog, I imagine."

"I imagine," Kal echoed. "It might have something to do with the fact that I look like a frog, Keebo. There is no shame in it, I cannot help it. The problem is not that I look like a frog, but that people assign me lesser value because of it."

"Okay, fine; so what?"

"Where do frogs live?"

"In—" He cut off again as Derako descended the steps with a small bucket, and approached. "He's bringing the water," he said.

"I can smell it," Kal said, rising.

"Here, and hurry up," Derako said, spooning out a ladle and holding it toward the bars.

"May I have the whole bucket, please?"

"You get a spoonful, and no more!" Derako growled. "Far more than you usually get." It sounded as if he tried to cut himself off at the end, but too late.

Keebo glowered, forgetting his stares were useless in the dark. "I am sure, on such a short voyage, you can spare—"

"Oh, fine! You try to escape again, I'll throttle you." He fumbled at his belt, and Keebo heard jingling of keys. A rusty squeak as the prison door opened, then slammed shut again.

"Thank you," Kal said, and he poured the bucket over himself with a grateful sigh.

"You hump-headed parrotfish!" Derako exclaimed. "What was that for? Wasting our clean water!"

"I did not ask for water to drink," Kal responded calmly.

"Kal, what *did* you do that for?" Keebo asked wearily. It would not help his defense if Kal annoyed everyone on the ship that way.

"I am a frog, Keebo," he replied, wiping his body upward to keep the water from running down too quickly. "Or near enough; I need water. We cannot swim without breath like fishes, but we dry out very quickly and it hurts. Did you not wonder about our rituals in the huts, when you came and spoke to me on Berola?"

"I thought it was just that, some sort of rit—" He stopped suddenly. That smell. The smell of sweating Anoe. A *lot* of sweating Anoe. "Derako," he said, his voice low. "What is your cargo?"

"None of your business, is what it is," he sneered. The sneer turned to a strangled cry as Keebo wrapped a collar of dirt around the sailor's neck and drove him against the bulkhead. Pulwin's shout was similarly drowned out.

"I told you it felt dirtier down here than topside," Keebo growled. He moved to one of the spaces between beams and gazed at the lid; it was locked, as he assumed it would be.

"Keebo, what is happening," Kal asked.

"We'll soon find out," he replied. As the sailors gripped at their restraints—they would not choke, he made sure they were not that tight—Keebo picked up the keys Derako had dropped and undid the lock. He grasped the ring and wrenched upward.

He still was not prepared for the smell that wafted up suddenly, though he anticipated the mewling and clicking, and the writhing mass of bodies. Four Anoe were huddled in a space that would barely fit him alone. "We've found some of your missing people, Kal," he said. He glanced up, and in the gloom could see Kal's hands wrap tightly around the bars of his cage. "Slavers," he said heavily. "They've been stealing your people and selling them—probably overseas."

"Let...us...out!" Derako rasped, finally allowing himself to relax enough to speak.

"I'm sorry, did you say, 'let them out'?" He shrugged. "I'm sure that's what they want, too." He glanced down again, noticing the Anoe there had not made any effort to climb out of the hole.

Derako must have known, for Keebo saw a faint flash of teeth. "They're Anoe," he spat. "They know their place."

"Because you've stolen them and beat it into them?"

"We were not taken," said one below.

Keebo's head snapped downward. "What?"

"At least, not most of us; the first ones—but, once we heard what was happening, we wondered...would it be so much worse?"

"Keebo," Kal said. "He may have a point, twisted though it is." He shook his head and his hands dropped from the bars. "In slavery they have a chance at life elsewhere. At least, so they believe; they may submit for the sake of escape."

"So I should leave them in there?"

Kal remained silent.

"Of course you should leave them in there," Derako said, grinning again. "Even if they decide to clamber out, the crew will put them right back in as soon as they're topside. What do you expect to happen to them? That we should up and let them go? Long-faced loach! Captain will kill you first. And throw your friend in with them, where he knows he belongs."

"They may have lost hope, coward; I have not," Kal said, standing taller. "You will not find me so pliant a prey."

"He makes a difficult point, Kal," Keebo said. "We can't take over the ship with just the two of us; and if they won't help us..."

"Do you think Steward Tolma approves this?"

A sharp sound drew Keebo's attention suddenly to the sailors, but they now only gazed at him. "Does he?" They only blinked.

"It's bright," said a small voice. Keebo glanced down; one of the Anoe turned away. "Please shut the door; it's bright."

"What's your name?"

The Anoe huddled closer, and were silent.

Leaving the lid raised, Keebo went to Kal's cell and unlocked it. "See if you can talk to them," he said. "I'll have a word with the Captain. Let's go!" he said sharply, turning to the sailors. He detached the collars from the beams, but kept them wrapped tightly around their necks, guiding them up the stairs against spluttering cries.

Getting them up the steep companionway was the most difficult, but on deck both Tesh and Captain Bell arrived quickly.

"What by the deeps are you doing?!"

"I could ask the same thing, *Captain*," Keebo replied, biting off the title. "I found what was in your hold. The smell should have given it away much sooner, but here we are at least. Who permitted you to take slaves?"

"No one *permitted* me—now let them go! If you continue to restrain my men—"

"And if you continue to restrain those Anoe, it will not go well with you when we reach the Steward! Does he know you have them?"

"He has never said anything against it."

Keebo stared hard at him. Suddenly, Derako stumbled toward the railing and nearly pitched over the side, his fingers still flailing at the earthen collar. "I could easily release him and take the next," Keebo said. "Are you sure you want to play games with an angry wizard?"

"He doesn't know about it," Bell replied, glowering. "I asked the Guildmaster for the modifications after the Steward signed the build permit."

"Did Beroc know what the modifications were for?"

"I doubt it."

"Did Jon know about it?" he pressed. Bell's lips thinned. "Strake? Kal? Tirtar? His daughter?" Tesh's glance flitted to Bell and back. Keebo straightened. "You know, Tolma never told me what Tirtar's daughter's name was. Do you remember?"

Both men remained silent. By now a few sailors had gathered around Derako and had taken hold of his shirt and trousers, though they continued to keep wary eyes on the exchange. Keebo sighed, and set the poor man back on his feet. They did not have the true argument, and holding him for ransom was unfair.

"Captain, someone killed Prince Jonkar, the heir to the throne of these islands, and no one so far has seemed too worried about it."

"Steward Tolma does a fine job," Captain Bell replied. "He doesn't interfere—"

"Of that, I'm sure," Keebo retorted. He released both Pulwin and Derako, and drew the dirt back into a tight ball in his hand. "I'm going to keep this, for now. You are going to get water down to the Anoe in your hold; and when we get to Nutar Ha you will wait until I can report to Tolma on your actions, and he can pass judgement. Do you know about Nutar Ha? How it got its mountains?"

Bell considered him for several long moments. "Yes," he said, finally.

"Then you should assume I can keep you detained at the dock at my leisure."

Shokalog appeared at the moment, though no one was with him. Keebo's gaze became harder still. "Worthless, despicable..." he muttered. He ground the ball between his fingers, keeping the dust suspended in the air between himself and the captain. "You will do as I said?" he asked.

Bell glanced at the men still gathered, watchful. He tried to brush the dust from the air, but his hand struck it as though it were a mountain cliff. Keebo's gaze never wavered. "Tesh, get the Anoe some water," Bell said quietly, his eyes never leaving Keebo's face. As the first mate moved away to comply, Keebo turned toward Kal and strode toward him. "I will need this deck clear for my men!" Bell protested.

Keebo turned back, an eyebrow cocked as the cloud of dust expanded, pushing the captain and one of the nearest sailors away. "Ay, ay! Fine! If they can't keep this ship moving, though, or hurt themselves running into something they can't see..."

The dust disappeared suddenly, and a small sculpture of an Anoe appeared on the deck where everyone would be able to see it. Bell growled, and turned to walk away. "I thought wizards weren't supposed to be strong enough to move mountains?" he said with a backward glance.

"I am very special," Keebo said without levity. "And very angry. You would quail in the face of what I could do right now."

12

THE FIRST ARREST

"I do not understand why this is a bad thing."
"This? It is not."
"But other times..."
"They are not to rely on us."

17 Savimon 1320 — Dry

Acontingent of guards and two saddled horses waited at the dock
for Keebo and Kal, this time, and they were able to make their way
to the fortress by nightfall. Rather than the brightly-polished guards at
the entrance, Keebo was surprised to see Tolma himself waiting on the
steps to the keep.

"My friend," he said, stooping slightly to grasp Keebo's hand. His eyes
flicked sideways, losing a hint of their warmth as they settled on Shokalog. "Welcome to you, as well," he said, turning and bowing slightly. Kal
inclined his head in response.

"Tolma, how much do you know of the ship that you sent to bring
us?"

Tolma straightened, his eyes sweeping over the guards arranged behind them. "Come inside, please," he said, turning aside with a gesture.
"Strake is waiting."

"You may need your guards to return to the dock—"

"Keebo, it is so good to see you," Tolma said, his eyes darkening. "I
have tea waiting, and we will speak at length."

Keebo set his jaw, glanced at Kal, and climbed the rest of the stairs. A
man in white livery stood by the doors, his face as blank as the motionless

guards. Kal's fleet slapped against the stone behind him, followed by Tolma's crisp step. As the doors boomed shut, Tolma strode up beside Keebo.

"Is it not enough, *friend,*"he hissed, "that I come out to you and welcome you, without you discussing all matters in front of my servants?"

"I deemed it important, my friend," Keebo replied evenly. "Did you know that many Anoe had been going missing from Berola?"

"Probably running away from a harsh situation."

"Interesting you should say so, for they were indeed—though their people thought they were being abducted; but they are finding themselves in a situation much worse." He paused until Tolma acknowledged him with a raised eyebrow. "Captain Belltash sails a slaver; we found almost fifty Anoe locked in his hold, four to a pit that wouldn't fit me comfortably, with no water. They had a blue wire wrapped around their upper arms to mark them as slaves, of a metal that could not be easily cut. One decision made in a harsh situation, and they would be bound forever unless their master set them free—and even then, removing the wire would not be simple, or without scars."

Tolma's pace slowed, and he lowered his head. "Keebo, I didn't know," he said. They kept walking. "I will send someone down immediately to bring him here. Are they still in the hold?"

"Yes, but better cared for now."

"And you're sure Captain Bell hasn't just turned and sailed out?"

Keebo grinned. "No, he's still there." Another raised brow appraised him. "I brought up some parts of the sea floor, under his ship; he's...in dry dock, let's call it."

Tolma's jaw set. "Very well. He'll be secure there for now, then. Oh, meanwhile, I questioned my men: no one found a knife like you described when they recovered the Prince."

Keebo nodded; it would have been nice if the killer had used something unique.

They ascended several flights up into the keep, Keebo slowing with each successive landing. Kal stayed close behind, still silent. Tolma paused at each one, waiting with hands clasped. Finally, at the fifth, they turned and passed through a tapestried hall lined with guards. No shiny, ornate armor on these; their dress and bearing were practical and terrible, their blades already drawn. Every one seemed prepared to kill instantly and without question.

"I see you keep him very safe," Keebo muttered.

"Of course," Tolma replied. "These are my Brightblades—while on duty, their swords are never sheathed." They stopped before a thick oaken door braced and studded with iron. A small table sat nearby with parchment, ink, and quill. Tolma stooped and signed his name. "Now both of you," he said, stepping back. As Keebo bent over the desk, Tolma continued: "Each person signs their name upon arrival, and strikes it out when they leave. No one—not even I—can enter without first doing so."

Keebo grunted, scanning quickly up the parchment. "You seem to be his most common visitor," he said. He stepped back as Kal stepped forward and scratched his name in as well.

"I've been keeping an eye on him," Tolma agreed. "For his sake, and to send for you as soon as he seemed well."

The guards stood aside—no halberds here, practically worthless in close quarters—and a sergeant unlocked the door. Keebo peered close as he went past; the sergeant's eyes were wary, but they did not seem to have a target. At least, they did not often look down the hall. Keebo gave him a tight smile.

Sunlight streamed through tall windows that faced west, lighting thick carpet and tapestries of vivid colors. A tall canopy bed draped in white stood to the left, a fan waving back and forth above it. Strake sat on the edge, his back to the windows, his face cast down. He did not look up as they entered.

"Young master?" Tolma called gently. "I've brought some visitors."

He looked up slowly, eyes hooded. His features softened only slightly upon seeing Keebo. "Hello," he said quietly. "I haven't seen you in a while. You, I haven't seen ever," he added to Shokalog. For the briefest moment he appeared to smile.

Keebo smiled back. He had never felt toward Strake the way he had felt toward Jon. He wasn't sure if it was the age difference, or something in their personalities; but now, sharing the loss, his heart tugged toward the young boy. He wanted more than anything to go and hug him, tell him it would be better, try to let him know somehow that he could still go out and change the world and that Keebo believed in him.

He settled for sitting beside him on the bed. "Your brother was a great loss," he said. Strake's eyes went back to the floor, and then beyond. "But many are the losses of the world, and yet hope and greatness come again in the morning, and often from places un-looked for."

This time Strake did smile, earnestly, though his gaze did not waver.

"I do need to talk to you about your brother," Keebo went on. "We need to find out who killed him, and why, to make sure there's not continued danger for you or anyone else, okay?" Strake nodded. "Do you know whether your brother was...changing his mind about things? Things that he had been certain of only a few months ago?"

"He always had ideas," Strake murmured. He shook his head. "I think so. Like he had..." He trailed off, squinting his eyes shut. "It was sudden. We used to talk all about his plans for the Islands, for trade and relations with..." He opened his eyes suddenly, looking directly at Kal. His features drooped until they were blank. "And then suddenly he wasn't."

"Wasn't what?" Keebo pressed.

"Wasn't going to go through with them. He came in one morning, just as I was waking up, and almost ran down a list of what he had given up on. It was like...like he read a new book before bed—he used to do that—and in one night, whatever it was he read, changed his ideas."

Keebo glanced at Kal, compressing his lips. "How did you feel about that?"

"It didn't really matter to me," he said. "Jon was always assured of himself; he didn't really listen if I thought he was wrong."

Keebo frowned. "He used to listen, didn't he? Did that change too?"

Strake looked up, eyes darting. "Maybe. I think so. Maybe it was just about his new ideas..." He trailed off, shrugged, and sniffled.

"It's okay," Keebo said calmly. "I've been gone a while. What about the girl Jon was seeing? Did she get upset when he started changing his mind?"

"Elandra? No, I think she was okay. I think she defended his ideas."

So that was her name. Keebo glanced at Tolma. "Are you sure about that? You're sure he talked to her about them, and she agreed?"

Strake looked up, his eyes earnestly searching Keebo's face. "I—yes, we were at dinner one time. I remember. I was trying to say he shouldn't say the things he was saying—"

"We had a lot of dinners together," Tolma cut in quietly. "I think maybe you are confusing—"

"No!" Strake said, rising suddenly. "I remember the words—every one of them! Why...?" He trailed off again, looking at Keebo. "Why wouldn't you believe me?"

Keebo smiled faintly. "Because according to everything people are saying, Elandra was gone before he started changing his mind."

Strake stared at him, chest heaving. He turned slowly away. "I can't do this," he muttered.

"Can't do what, Strake?"

He breathed deep in the silence, and sighed. "Maybe I am confused. That happens sometimes. Maybe with a little more rest, I can order things better in my mind." He turned and walked to the desk, and sat down.

Keebo watched him, then turned a cocked eyebrow on Tolma. Tolma grimaced.

"Very well, Master Strake," Tolma said, gesturing toward Keebo and Shokalog. They moved to the door, and Tolma opened it.

"Tolma?" Strake called, still facing the desk. "Could I please have back my other knife? This one doesn't cut very well."

Keebo shifted; Tolma shook his head. "I've told you this new one is a magical knife, Master Strake; it cuts only when and what it's supposed to."

Strake said nothing, and they left the room.

"I didn't want him to have something sharp," Tolma said as they struck their names out of the log book. "I gave him something more ornate and very useless, just in case."

"Can I see the knife you took from him?"

"Of course," Tolma replied, beginning to lead them back to his study. Once there, he closed the door and went to his desk. He unlocked a drawer and pulled out a plain, dark-bladed knife with wooden handle and held it out. Keebo took it, turning it over several times; it was what he feared. It matched the knife in the vision—and Shokalog's, and one of Keebo's assailants, and every other utility knife in the island.

"Where do these all come from?" he muttered, handing it back.

"It's one of the first things apprentice blacksmiths make. Cheap, but they serve. What have you found out?"

Keebo sighed and sat. "Well," he began, gesturing. "Jon had endeared himself to many with his ideas and plans for when he became king. Then, several months ago orders a young girl, who he seemed to admire, to stay away from him. To ensure she did, he slandered her name and ignored her pleas to the point she killed herself, leaving behind a grieving father. He made promises that became known to an entire race of people, then appeared ready to break them all. He also made promises and commissioned work for a large, fast ship, with potential for a whole fleet—and suddenly no longer wants them. Supposedly, everyone was so busy working on the ship that they wouldn't have had time..." Keebo shrugged.

"So you have no idea, and essentially nowhere left to go."

"I had hoped for more from Strake," Keebo admitted. "And I have one more question to pursue. I knew Strake and Jon were close, but I'm still surprised he's been affected so...deeply."

"I think perhaps because they were not doing so well lately," Tolma said heavily. "Or maybe he, like you, believes it was Jon's changing attitudes that led to his death, and since he was unable to help him see the truth..."

"That sounds like a bit of a reach," Keebo said. He shook his head and turned. "You haven't said much," he said to Kal.

"I am not sure why I'm here," Kal replied.

Tolma sighed. "There is one aspect you seem to be neglecting, Keebo," he said. "I was a little worried when I asked you to investigate, but there was no one else who can do what you can—"

"What aspect?"

"The Anoe," he said with a flickering glance. Kal shifted. "As you said, Jon had made promises to a whole race of people, and appeared to be breaking them. We know an Anoe was near the site of Jon's murder. And now we have a ship full of runaway Anoe who are about to be sold as slaves. Perhaps someone who knows much about the goings-on of his people had found out?"

Keebo was suddenly aware of the number of guards stationed around the room. "You didn't know that when you asked us to come here, though," he said.

"Correct; I added that just now."

"So why did you want him here before?"

"While you were gone, I had a few men go to Berola to see what they could find," Tolma said. "I know you trust the Anoe and trust Shokalog, but in a case like this we must pursue every possibility."

"I thought you trusted me to do that."

"I did. And to a degree I still do, even though you seem to be fighting the obvious. But this isn't the point; the point is they found this, hidden in one of the tents." He reached into another drawer and pulled out a dark-bladed knife with wooden handle, covered in dried blood.

Keebo blinked, trying hard not to look at Kal. "Kal had his knife—"

"Keebo, there are hundreds of these, as you've already noted. How hard to have two, and keep one hidden?"

"Why keep it at all?"

"A trophy; the Anoe are seeking a new history, aren't they?" he asked, turning to Kal. "They want to redefine themselves, bring back some of the pride of years past. What better way to start than the assassination of one of their oppressors?"

Keebo didn't let Kal answer. "They said that Jon had come to them more recently, still promising the same things—had come after you say he had started to change."

"I'm sure they did," Tolma said drily. "And no one to confirm it. Either way..." He gestured, and three guards stepped forward, two seizing Kal while the third stood with his weapon ready.

"I don't think this is necessary," Keebo said, rising from his seat.

"It is necessary," Kal said. "For they cannot stand to think it was one of their own."

"Did you do it?" Keebo asked.

"I would not have come here if I did."

"Perhaps he did not," Tolma allowed, still seated calmly. "But perhaps his imprisonment will loosen some tongues." He gestured again, and the guards led him from the room. "You had best decide on your loyalties, Keebo," he continued after the door had shut. Keebo turned back slowly.

"Oh?"

"You, perhaps, do not mind wasting days chasing down the wind. I cannot abide another day without knowing who murdered Master Jon. Go back to the Anoe, ask more questions. Surely even you can do this simple task?"

"'*Even*' I?" Keebo echoed.

"You have not been yourself since the incident here. I had hoped perhaps this might awaken you from your stupor, but it seems I was wrong. However, I will give you one last chance; find this murderer among the Anoe or my men will."

"Will you let me speak to Kal first?"

"You do not have time. Five days, Keebo. Bring me someone in five days, or Shokalog will be sentenced. And since it has already been a month, I would imagine his execution will follow swiftly."

13

A Common Knife

"Can we—?"
"Not this time, Teresh."
"Do you not even care to know?"
"We must one day answer for our choices, too."

18 Savimon 1320 — Dry

Keebo stood at the dock. Captain Bell glared as he went by, wrists locked in iron chains. Keebo hardly noticed. He looked eastward, but his mind drifted westward toward Berola. Despite what Tolma had said, he was fairly certain the murderer was not among the Anoe. But that shipbuilder that Beroc had mentioned, Larrince, was a loose end that desperately needed picking up.

Five days. He could make it to Candar Ha and back in five days, if the wind was fair; but he could not delay. He chewed his lip.

But if Tolma was right, and another of the Anoe *had* killed Jon, then he might waste his time in Candar Ha and Kal would be imprisoned or killed unjustly. Maybe if the tribal elders knew that, they would turn in their own.

He took a deep breath as Nedley approached. "Needing to go somewhere?" the sailor asked.

"I'd prefer Candar Ha, but...do you know anyone who would take a message to Berola, for me?" he asked.

Nedley paused. "We might be able to divert someone on our way," he said slowly. When Keebo cocked an eyebrow, he continued. "If not, I know a captain in Candar Ha."

"I didn't realize you had that sort of authority."

"I do now," Nedley replied, a contented grin blooming. "Royal Ferryman, just assigned. Official," he said, holding up a scroll. "Orders from Master Tolma; my Calderon and I are retained—that's what it says—for whatever the Steward needs, and only what he needs."

"Wonderful news," Keebo said, wishing he sounded happier; it was good news, for Nedley. But he could not share in the rejoicing just yet. *Five days. Kal's life in the balance.* He hated decisions like this. His gut was a poor guide, only useful for finding a good place to eat. *Melnor?* But he expected the silence that followed. They didn't often help in times like these. Maybe that wasn't fair; they would not know who killed Jon either. Probably.

This wasn't hastening his decision. "Candar Ha it is, then," he said. "As quick as you can."

⸺◈⸺

When Keebo awoke on the boat two days later, Nedley nodded toward the southern horizon. Almost near enough to touch was the port on Candar Ha. Great mountains ensconced the bay, the rumpled blanket of forest draping to the water's edge on left and right. Behind the piers was a medium-sized collection of huts. A few people stirred on the beach; one whisper of smoke marked kitchen or forge—they would have to be closer before Keebo's nose could decide which.

"That was quick," he grunted. He dipped a hand into the water, feeling the tug, then splashed some on his face.

Nedley tossed him a wooden cup filled with cut pineapple. "Too early for good food here," he said. "I can find the captain while you search for your man."

"Mmm, wonderful," Keebo replied, sucking down a few of the chunks. "Where should I start looking, do you think?"

Nedley pointed wordlessly west; a small shipyard was evident near the farthest end of the bay, a few boats under construction. Men like insects already stalked around them, but they did not appear particularly busy, yet.

"Perfect. You remember the message?"

"Shokalog to be tried for murder of Prince Jonkar unless the real murderer is found, and brought to Steward Bergin," he quoted.

"Thank you, Nedley," Keebo said. "And you're sure you can find someone to handle the Anoe?"

"Long as they can secure him, and as long as he don't mind being tied up in the bottom of the boat for a day."

Keebo smiled. "I don't think he should expect much choice."

Nedley grunted. "You said these elders respect Shokalog, right? Think the highest of him?"

Keebo shrugged. "Yeah, I think so. Seems like it, at least."

"Hmm. How do you know they won't just hand over someone who might be innocent?"

Keebo pursed his lips as Nedley began reefing the sail. "I guess I don't," he admitted slowly. "But I hope to still question whoever it is they bring."

"But then if you prove him innocent, Steward will just lock Shokalog back up, won't he?"

Keebo arched his back, rocking a little as the boat bumped against the pier. "Let me worry about that, okay?" he said.

As he stepped on shore, his nose told him the smoke was from a Pit; his head told him it didn't matter, so he turned right and walked along the shoreline. He glanced back as he neared the shipbuilders, saw Nedley shaking the hand of another Captain whose Calderon quickly prepared their boat to sail. *Let them be on time.*

Let me be on time, too, he realized, quickening his pace up the beach. As he approached, a large, squat man exited one of the shanties near the water, and all the workers suddenly tried to look busy—except one, Keebo noticed, who stood leaning against a rail while trimming a nail with one of those cursed, common knives.

He approached the large man. "Are you the Guildmaster?" he asked.

The man turned, glanced him up and down. "I am," he rumbled. "Palak. You're Keebo?"

Keebo cocked his head. "I am. Though I'm surprised you know that."

"Aren't many earth wizards around, and I've heard of you."

Keebo looked at him cautiously. "Have you?"

Palak gestured. "My son, Larrince, heard about you somewhere. Told me you might be coming."

At the mention of the name, the young man trimming his nail stood up, sheathing the knife. Keebo glanced back. "Why should I be coming?"

"Ask him, I suppose; but be quick, we've got work today."

"As do I," Keebo assured him. As he approached, a smile spread across Larrince's face. "You are Larrince?"

A quick nod. "I am; good to see I was right."

"Why were you right?"

"My job to know these things, if I'm going to be the Royal Ferryman."

Keebo blinked. "Why would you do that?"

"I took the Steward and young Master Strake home, after what happened to young Prince Jonkar."

"You did? I didn't realize you were a captain."

"I wasn't; but I was in the area when their need was desperate; Steward Tolma himself promised, I get them to Nutar Ha timely and I'd have a new job. Me! Can you imagine, taking royalty wherever they want to go, whenever they need to get there?"

"I've seen you sail," his father growled in passing. "A miracle you didn't end up in Rinc Na."

Larrince's face darkened. "Well I did it," he muttered, trying to let

Keebo hear but not his father. He glanced furtively back to check his father far enough away, then turned back in confidence: "Said I did a fine job. I've wished for it all my life; no more scraping about here, working sun-up to sun-down for no thanks and only scraps at meals. Always: 'aren't you Palak's boy'? Ha! They'd start asking if he was my dad after that. I'd be somebody!"

"Very fortunate of you to be nearby when they needed you, wasn't it?" Keebo asked.

"That's how it works, sometimes; being in just the right spot when the opportunity's coming by."

"What were you doing there? I heard you were working for Beroc over on Naso Narok."

"Well, I was; no more use there, though, not after Prince Jonkar canceled all his orders."

"When did he do that?"

"He came by, early Monzak; after he left, Beroc told us mates work would be scarce for a while, to leave off the ship—can you imagine? Dead stop, hull half-built on the water—how foolish does he look, then?"

"Beroc told me when Jon visited, he approved of the building and was looking forward to seeing the fleet ready."

"Of course he did; went to see Beroc after the murder, did you? Bet he had all his crews working hard on the boats when you got there? Sure; have to look busy like nothing's changed. I suppose I just up and left for no reason?"

Keebo's hesitation was answer enough. "So Beroc told you to leave?"

"Not as much; but if the Prince don't want Beroc's boats he'll likely need my father's. Ever been caught waiting for a ferry?"

Again, Keebo was silent.

"Sure, we all have. I was, on Sed Narok a week later when Steward and Master Strake show up—they were stuck, too, till they mistook me for a Captain. Asked me if I could take them with all haste to Nutar Ha. I figured it was my chance, but I had to be bold; a boat was there, Captain and Calderon were ghosts, so I jumped aboard and took him where he needed to go. When he left me off port, he asked where I was headed; I told him, and he said wait there because he was going to send for me to be his personal ferryman so he'd never have to wait on a boat again."

Keebo took a deep breath. "That's interesting," he said, glancing across the water to where he could make out Nedley's boat bobbing on the water. "Because a captain named Nedley brought me here; and he has orders in his pocket making him the Royal Ferryman."

Larrince's eyes followed Keebo's gesture, but the smile barely faltered. "Must be a mistake; those orders are probably for me, and he was supposed to deliver them."

Keebo shook his head, unsure. "He seemed fairly certain about it; had talked about the possibility before today."

Larrince's smile remained fast. "Let's go talk to him; I'm sure we'll get it cleared up."

"Before we go, can I see your knife?"

Now the grin slipped. "Why?"

"Because you were on Sed Narok very near the time Prince Jonkar was murdered, happened to be right where Steward Tolma and Prince Strake needed you, and at that point you had lost your job because of Jon and were headed back here for thankless work with your father. Let me see your knife."

Larrince gazed at Keebo, calculating; he must not have liked what he saw, as he quickly handed over the blade.

Dark blade; wooden handle. Keebo sniffed it; it smelled of oil, and a little bit of tar...probably from Larrince's fingernails, he realized too late. "Everyone has one," he muttered under his breath.

Larrince's smile returned. "Not likely," he said smugly. "This one was crafted special—only a handful made, as I'm aware."

Keebo glanced at him warily. "It looks like every other knife I've seen."

"That's because you're an earth wizard, not a man who uses knives. Look," he said, holding it in his palm. "Malgus blade; olive wood handle—you've probably seen apple wood, usually from pruned limbs; three pins in the handle, not just two if it has any. Only one man makes these: Master Blacksmith Grinbar, in Pael. That's how I know you're wrong about those orders: Steward Tolma himself gave me this one, as promise of making me his man."

In a daze, Keebo stared at the knife; now that he looked closer, he saw the wavy lines across the blade almost like wood grain, the three pins through the handle where others only had two. What knife had been in the vision? He couldn't recall now, though he thought it had three rivets.

"I have need of great haste," Keebo said. "Can you trust me to take up your matter with Steward Tolma? Right now I need Nedley to take me somewhere."

Larrince glowered. "He better make me a good offer, and quickly, for having to stay here longer."

"I'll make sure he does."

After Larrince nodded begrudgingly and turned away, Keebo hastened back to port.

"Back to Nak?" Nedley asked with a quirking smile.

"Eastport," Keebo said. "I've got to get back to Pael, and find Grinbar."

"You won't make it back to Nutar Ha in time," he replied as Keebo clambered aboard, quickly raising sails anyway.

"I know; I'll need you to go ahead, tell the Steward I may have our best clue yet and he needs to delay sentencing until I can run it down—at least, wait until I've questioned the blacksmith. I will come straight to Nak no matter what he says, and report to Tolma."

"As you wish," Nedley replied. He turned the boat north and skimmed it across the calm waters of the bay. If ever Keebo wished he were an Air wizard, it was now.

14

IN THE BACK

22 Savimon 1320 — Dry

Nedley barely stopped the boat in time for Keebo to clamber out before he was turned and back out to sea. As Keebo strode inland, he could not help but think Nedley had been a wiser choice for Royal Ferryman. But those thoughts quickly faded as he gathered dirt into a plate: he needed to be in Pael yesterday. He built it perhaps a little too swiftly, and worried about the drain on his energy; he paused, eyes closed as he breathed deep and sent his consciousness inside. His imagination passed through his stomach and into his mind like water through a reed, gently as though fountaining into his skull. As the water dripped in rivulets down the inside of him to his toes it raised to his conscious mind how every part of him felt, how much energy there was. It was yet another trick he doubted Melnor knew, and one he did not care to share. It also made him wonder if part of him did carry affinity to water.

But this was not the time. When all the water finally drained out of his soles, he opened his eyes: the disc would not carry him all the way to Pael without killing him, though it could get him most of the way. He steadied himself, and breathed the command. The energy rushed out of him as if a sluice gate had opened, and he slumped forward over his stomach as the plate took off beside the road.

He allowed himself to sleep. An hour would not be much, but it would restore him enough to walk the final mile into Pael. He dreamed of riding a great dragon—which seemed odd, when he awoke: he had never dreamed such before, despite sleeping on his flying disc more than once. But it was pleasant, and he felt refreshed as he clambered off the disc and began walking; before long, the villages of Pael rose up before him.

The sun was low, but night was still far off as he entered the city proper. How to find the blacksmith? He noticed a roving Tri-guard of the Island Watch, and put on his easiest smile.

"Any of you know where to find Master Blacksmith Grinbar?" he asked lightly as they passed.

The three soldiers stopped as one body, though only one turned toward him. "Obelisk Quarter, good sir," he said, a brief raise of his right hand to his temple. "Any disturbance?"

Keebo blinked until he realized it was probably a standard question. "No, thank you." *Why there, of all places?* It was too convenient. The soldiers rattled off on their patrol, and Keebo turned to his goal.

The Obelisk now stood silent and dark, the shadows of the clustered shops beginning to touch its base. The square, too, was quieter—most trade for the day was concluded. He stood a moment, feeling the wind, and a middle-aged couple exited a shop nearby and made their way to a far alley. Keebo glanced at Tirtar's awning, the ringed octopus; it still looked deserted. On the breeze he smelled freshwater; then, faintly, heard the ringing of a forge.

He glanced away and began following the sound. Finally, as evening began creeping through the streets, he saw the faint orange glow across the road of a great but contained fire. The dull thwacking of iron on iron cascaded among the buildings, punctuated only occasionally as the smith lightly rang hammer to anvil, keeping the time of his strokes while he paused to inspect the piece. Above the door of a great-beamed building, crossed tongs and hammer hung above the metal print of an anvil.

He went inside; it was a simple shop, with a few implements on display. A bench near the back appeared to be where trade actually occurred; and to the right, a broad doorway led into the forge itself. Steam hissed as hot metal was quenched.

"Master Grinbar?" Keebo called, taking a few more steps into the shop.

A slide of metal being thrust into coals sounded, then a tall, broad-shouldered man with dark skin and stubbled beard peered out at him. "Yes?"

"I am Keebo, earth wizard from Sed Narok, sent by Steward Tolma—well, in general. I'm here specifically because of some knives I've heard you make."

"I make many knives," Grinbar replied, disappearing back into the forge.

Keebo approached until he could watch the Master about his work. It appeared to be a simple farming implement, perhaps for a plow or some such; Keebo never really used those things. "This was a very special knife, I'm told: olive-wood handle, Malgus blade, three pins."

Grinbar grunted, hauling out the strip of iron to observe the tip, then pushing it back into another section of the coals. "Does the Steward want another shipment?" he asked, working the bellows.

"Is he the only one who ordered them?"

Grinbar was silent as he pumped the levers a few more times. He turned and wiped his hands briefly on a towel hung on the wall. "Not sure where he got the design, but it is a fine knife. He had ordered four made, some time ago—three months, perhaps? Provided the materials and all, so I shipped them back quickly. Does he want more?"

Keebo gaped. *Four? For whom—and why does Larrince rate one of them?* "Are they expensive?"

Grinbar shrugged, worked the bellows again. This time he removed the metal and began hammering. When he paused to inspect it, he said: "I only did the metalwork; but he paid me two thousand marks for it." He continued hammering as Keebo continued gaping. Finally he turned and quenched the metal.

"Did that seem a fair price?" Keebo asked.

Grinbar shrugged again as he clamped the metal onto a workbench and inspected a file. "Any other customer, I may have asked that for everything—work and materials—but I also would not have had the order done in a week, so..." He trailed off with another shrug, then turned and began working the file.

"And...would you happen to know who he wanted them for?"

Grinbar's glance said enough. After another few strokes, he paused and turned to Keebo. "You could ask Tirtar, across the way," he said.

"Why would he know?"

"He delivered them; I had brought him a new paring chisel and we talked. I mentioned the knives, and he said he would soon be making a delivery of figurines, so he would take them. So if you need to know right now, you could ask him. Seeing as how you were here for the Steward himself, though, I assume you could ask him." He gave an exaggerated shrug, then turned back to his bit of metal with an air that told Keebo he was done with conversation for the evening.

"Thank you very much for your time, Master Grinbar," Keebo said sincerely. It had been a most informative conversation—he wished he had more of those, these past weeks.

Keebo exited into deepening gloom, the orange glow from the forge the only lighting in this alley, now. Daylight still lit the wide-open square, and a bit of sun still struck the very top of the obelisk so it looked almost like a beacon. In the gloom, the orange and blue awning fairly blazed; some chinks of light were evident through cracked shutters on the windows. Tirtar was home, and apparently not in the dark.

Keebo strode across the square and knocked. Inside remained silent. "Tirtar?" he called. "I saw your lights; I just have one or two more questions, if I can have a few moments of your time."

Still silent. He stepped back a pace, glancing at the shutters—but now there was no light visible. He leapt forward, banging on the door. "Tirtar, please open this door; you will not be in trouble, but someone else may die—"

A door slammed, and leather footfalls scattered down a back street. Keebo ran to the side of the house; far down the alley a hooded figure ran.

"Oren, oren—Bah!"

The figure ducked sideways down another street; why did spells have to take so long to cast? Hopelessly Keebo went to the spot where Tirtar had turned. Down that street, five others branched off within a hundred paces. He waited for a few breaths, listening, but the night was silent.

Keebo returned to the square, listening at the door to the carver's shop, but inside was stone quiet. Tirtar was gone, and in such a way as made him seem terribly guilty. Only good news for Shokalog and the Anoe if Keebo could return to Tolma in time—if Tolma had agreed to wait the extra day.

Too late now to return to port, Keebo glanced around the square; most shops were closed up, but in the corner one man was only now at his door sweeping debris into the street. The shop sign told he was a weaver.

"Sir?" Keebo called out as he approached. "Where might I find lodgings for the night?"

Pausing for only a moment, he gestured down a street northward. Keebo nodded thanks, and began walking with his thoughts. By the time he found an inn, however, nothing had come to mind.

"Room for the night?" he asked, pulling out the scrip from Tolma. When the innkeeper glanced it over, she snorted.

"Good thing you're not here in a couple days," she said. "Otherwise, steward's demand or no, you'd be out on the street."

"Why so?" Keebo asked, following her to a room.

"Do you think we're called the Juggler's Row for nothing? Show's in town for next week, and here's where they stay."

"Are they indeed?" Keebo asked. "I love the show; of course, I haven't seen it in..." He trailed off as a thought blared in his mind. Had it been?

The innkeeper mistook his pause. "You should stay, then—not here, but there's plenty others that have rooms."

"I wish I could," Keebo replied distractedly, his brows knit. A traveling troop not only performed juggling and tumbling, but plays as well. Back when Keebo used to see it, they had a leading man—oh, he was very good. Keebo always got lost in those plays, this actor played his part so well. What had been the man's name?

"Well, shame then. Sleep well. One night only?"

"Mmm, mmhmm." Keebo barely noticed as the keeper shrugged and left. The actor's voice then would have been pitched and raised to reach the audience; but his mannerisms, facial expressions... Tirrin Tarabar. The man was genius with dress and hair to play any part. Keebo suddenly wondered if he had helped with props for the stage as well, the little wooden bits that transformed it into the scene wherein the actors played. It would explain his ability to turn his trade from acting to woodcarving after his wife died. Luceanne Tarabar—she was very nearly as good, and playing next to her husband only elevated her.

Keebo sighed, and stretched out on the bed. He could take some comfort in the fact he had been fooled by no less a talent than 'Tirtar,' as he evidently styled himself now, to be so convinced he was mourning his daughter instead of seeking revenge on the man who ruined her. He hoped Tolma would take similar comfort, but he doubted it. His friend was very exacting.

⚬

When he reached the port on Nutar Ha, guards there scrambled to get him a horse, and send a messenger ahead of him to let Tolma know he was coming. Keebo noticed Nedley's boat tied up at the dock, and hoped it was a good sign. "When did Nedley get here?" he asked one of the guards, as another brought his horse.

"Two days ago. Get on."

"Why thank you," Keebo said blandly; it was a big horse, and his legs were going to lever out awkwardly. "Any word on—"

"I just do my job. But I suspect the Steward is waiting, as you were supposed to be here yesterday. Hopefully he'll receive you."

Of all his trips into the interior of Nutar Ha, this one took the longest. It seemed days by the time he started to see the mountainside defenses, and at least a week before he actually approached the citadel. The sun was low and his stomach grumbled loudly as he fairly fell off the horse onto his wobbly legs.

The great doors swung open, and Tolma approached. His face was unreadable—but then, he wouldn't want to give anything away in front of his servants. "Good to finally see you," was all he said.

"I'm looking forward to many meetings," Keebo replied. "I saw Nedley's boat—he and I have become quite good friends—"

But Tolma had already turned and began walking inside. Keebo hurried to follow. When the doors boomed shut behind them, Tolma spoke. "He is here, as is Shokalog."

"Thank you," Keebo said in relief.

Tolma's stride checked. "For what?"

"For giving me the extra day. I think I've found—"

"We did not wait," Tolma said, stopping suddenly. "The Anoe you sent back confessed, and was executed at sunset yesterday. I found no need to wait for additional clues."

Keebo gaped at Tolma; but as his anger rose, his mouth snapped shut. Tolma turned and continued down the hall, and Keebo's rage finally spilled over. "You didn't think he might have confessed simply to save Kal's life?" he thundered.

Tolma turned back, and Keebo couldn't help but shake his head at how calmly the Steward spoke. "I cannot imagine that was the case—who would think to let themselves be killed like that? With the shame of guilt forever on their name?"

"Someone who cares about another person more than themselves, I suppose."

"I assumed they would care about the truth."

"No one cares about the truth whenever Anoe are involved; apparently not even you."

"I'm not sure you should speak to me that way," Tolma replied, bristling. "I am still the Steward of these Islands—including Berola and the Anoe—until Strake ascends."

"And a fine—"

"Your services are no longer required, Keebo," Tolma grated, taking a step toward the wizard. "I suggest you leave, now."

"You do not even care what I have to say? What I've learned?"

"It will do no good, now. Would you rather I execute another? Messengers have already gone out with the news, and the Islands will want to move on from this, I think." He turned again to leave, and two guards came up behind Keebo to escort him out.

"What did you do with the Malgus knives you ordered from Grinbar?" he called after his old friend. "Why did you have four of them made?"

Tolma turned again, held up a hand to stay the guards. "One for myself, Strake, and Jonkar; the fourth I had not yet decided what to do with it but knew it would be a gift. I gave it to Larrince in oath to make him the Royal Ferryman."

"He's still waiting to become that."

"When I gave it to him, I assumed he was a captain," Tolma replied with a sneer. "Instead, he will be a shipbuilder with a very nice knife."

"I need to see those knives, Tolma. One of them killed—"

"No, it didn't," Tolma replied with a foul grin. "An Anoe did." With a wave, the guards gripped Keebo by the arms and hauled him away; Tolma turned and continued up the passage.

"Go that way," the guard said, once outside and Keebo was mounted. "Don't come back unless you've been summoned."

Keebo paused to glance up at the towering walls. What had happened? He thought Tolma would be fair—would actually be concerned about who had killed Jonkar. Never in his friendship had he thought Tolma would only care about placing blame.

Perhaps that was not entirely fair; never before had Tolma been required to guide the Islands through an assassination. Keebo nudged his horse down the road, careless this time for how long it took. When darkness fell he moved off the side of the road, hoping one of the rocks might break loose from their magical perch and come crashing down—

He did not care to live in these new Islands.

Before lunch the next day he stood at the docks; Nedley was there, preparing his boat. As Keebo stared listlessly at the calm waters of the bay, a thin-fingered hand fell on his shoulder.

"I know you tried, my friend," Kal said quietly.

Keebo shook his head. "Not hard enough. I chased too many questions. I should have paid more attention to the knife in the vision, should have asked about it instead of assuming—"

"It is done, and not by your hand," Kal said firmly. "You asked for another day—Tolma told me so. Kadelkay did not have to sacrifice himself for me, either. And Tolma did not have to take his word for it."

"I never thought he would do something like that. Tolma."

"He needs a story to tell the people, so they will feel safe that there is still a stable rule in the Islands—especially with the conflict between ships' guilds, and your culture that fears the change of outside influence."

"What of your people, though? Do you have any hope left that things will change? Can you?"

Kal was quiet, looking out to sea. After a moment, his eyes glistened. "No."

Keebo swallowed, bent his head down; he nodded, then shook his head. "I'm sorry, Kal."

Kal snorted lightly. "I know."

Keebo watched his friend climb into another boat, and slowly drift away. How had it come to this? Had he not taken the task seriously enough? He had hesitated, certainly; too many bad experiences in the past. And what of Tolma? Keebo would have sworn he would never have done such a thing—regardless of the culture of the Islands. Had it changed that much while he was tucked away in his gardens?

"Excuse me," said a woman behind him. "Are you here to see the Steward?"

Keebo didn't look up. "I've already seen him," he said. *For all the good it did.*

"Are you a friend of his?"

Keebo grunted; a week ago—a day ago, that would have been an easy answer. Now? Could he be friends with someone who murdered—that's what it was—murdered an Anoe so easily? And yet, Kal was gone now when Keebo needed a friend most, something Tolma had not done twenty years ago. As much as this hurt, surely it was in everyone's best interest. "I suppose I am," he said. It didn't seem wrong— "Ah!"

Keebo's eyes bolted open as he gasped; terrible, piercing pain shot through his back and into chest, as though someone reached through with pincers and tried to pull a rib out through his lung. He took a stumbling step forward. The immediacy of the pain faded, reduced to a pumping ache. Something wet ran down his back.

He turned slowly, his eyes drawn sluggishly to the blade covered in his blood. Curiosity flowed dully through his mind; he was stabbed? *Another victim of the mountains of Nutar Ha...wonder what kind of knife...* The blade was hidden, but between the gaps of the fingers holding it he could see an olive-wood handle. *Bet it has three rivets,* he thought as darkness began to veil his vision.

"Keebo!" He heard a far distant cry. *Kal? But who...?*

His eyes finally traced upward as he began to fall. Before the veil closed entirely he thought he saw jet black hair, slightly curled. *Elandra...*

He hit the water with a terrific splash, and quickly sank.

15

DARKNESS TO DARKNESS

"Will you speak to him?"
"Not directly, no."
"But he is not finished."
"He is not finished; but neither is he ready."

2 Fulmatung 1320 — Dry

He awoke in darkness and silence except for his own shallow breathing. Once, he had been taken by Melnor into the interior of his mind; he wondered if this was the same place. Some middle-ground between death and life?

Except, in the interior, he did not have his other senses; he felt the humid warmth of the air, the thin, tight canvas of a cot; he could hear, now, the rustling of palm thatch in a light breeze. He turned his head.

"Melnor?" he called, softly, cautiously.

There was a stirring. "Keebo," said Kal's voice, nearby. The Anoe's thin hand rested on his arm.

"How...where..." Too many questions wanted answers at once.

"I was able to bring you up from the sea, though I wish you were as light then as you are now."

"Am I?" Now Kal mentioned it, Keebo was ravenously hungry. "How long?"

"Ten days."

Keebo tried to bolt upright, struggled, and failed. Kal's hand moved to his shoulder to hold him down.

"I have something here for you; but eat slowly or you will make it worse."

With his friend's help he sat upright, and a warm bowl was put into his hands, then the thin blade of a spoon. "It would help if you lit a candle, or something; I have flint in the case over there." He gestured, realizing too late that in the darkness it would not be seen.

"Eat some of this soup," Kal said, working Keebo's hand and spoon. "You must get back your strength; you nearly died three times."

"I can feed myself," Keebo protested, though he felt his arm shaking as he tried to lift the spoon of broth. "At least until you light—"

"Keebo," Kal said gently, helping him with the spoon. "I am afraid to tell you this: but it is mid-day."

In the silence, Keebo knew Kal would be watching him closely. *Interesting. All from being stabbed.* "Well," he said. "My hunger, I can control." He continued struggling with the spoon, and Kal helped him.

⚬

"You know what it was," Keebo said quietly, leaning on Kal as he walked unseen lines around his hut. "I used too much magic; I kept riding those discs instead of walking. The old ways are always best."

"I am not sure how that would have helped."

"I would have had more strength." They had apparently reached the cot again, as Kal stopped walking and let Keebo slide downward. He reached a hand out until he felt the canvas, and lowered himself into it. "Or I might have kept more in reserve, to have made it back to Eastport in time to get to Nak by the original deadline."

"I am not sure Tolma would have listened, anyway."

"Then I could have had more energy to stop him," Keebo replied, his fists tightening on the edge of his cot.

"Keebo," Kal said quietly, his voice suddenly coming from below; he had sat on the floor. "I am thankful that you seem to care so much; but this one event is not the entirety of the Anoe story, and you know it. Kadelkay is not the first Anoe to die unjustly, and he will not be the last. Nor is that one ship the only one carrying Anoe slaves."

"It wasn't?"

"Nedley told me another had been discovered, this one empty and returning from Andelen. It had been doing so for some time. Others have gone eastward."

"How many?"

Kal sighed. "We are not sure; some of our clans in west Berola have stopped coming to the *wandhpa* for many years; we don't know how many they have lost, and they will not say."

"I didn't realize the Anoe were fractured, like that."

Kal snorted. "My own elders are fractured," he said.

Keebo sighed. "So are mine."

———◦◦◦———

Keebo awoke, and blinked. He rubbed his eyes hard, squeezed them shut, then blinked forcefully a few more times. "Well," he said. He turned his head, waiting in the silence. "That's interesting," he continued, louder this time.

Bamboo squeaked as his door opened, then shut. "You are awake?" Kal said.

Keebo smiled. "I can't see you," he said. "But it got brighter in here when you opened the door."

A green shape grew large in front of him. "That is incredible news, my friend," Kal said; his thin fingers found Keebo's and squeezed. "Perhaps you will get better as your strength continues to return. I have brought some vegetables from your garden."

"How is it doing?" he asked, confounded he had forgotten it so long. "Probably a mess."

"When one learns how to grow vegetables among sand, those in loam are not so difficult."

"Thank you, my friend," Keebo said; he rubbed his thumb across the smooth skin of a tomato, sniffed it. "The stalks must be doing well to not let these drag in the dirt."

"I remembered you had propped them up; I found your...trellises" —he hesitated slightly over the unusual word— "and set them up as I had seen you do it before."

"Oh; very well." He bit into the tomato, savoring the juices and that clean, still slightly earthy flavor in its flesh. "I forgot where I had put those, to be honest."

"I discovered them under your trap door."

"Of course." Keebo hurriedly put the tomato to his mouth, wiping his chin as the fruit exploded at his harsh bite. He chewed silently, his eyes still roving about, hoping to suddenly see clearly.

"I found your letters, Keebo; I thought I should tell you."

Keebo swallowed, dropped his head as if inspecting the tomato. "I imagine you read them, too?" he said, trying to modulate the anger in his voice. He did still want some of his displeasure to come through; those had been private letters.

"I did not," Kal replied. "But I noticed you had not sent the final one to her."

So he knew with whom Keebo corresponded. It could have been worse. "She asked often about her garden," he said, only partially lying. "She knew I was good at it." Pure truth.

"Your gardens would be legendary, if more people saw them," Kal replied. "Even in the abundance the Islands provide, your plot is alive. Why did you not send the last one?"

Keebo ground his teeth, then relaxed and took another bite. When he finished, he said: "I wrote that long after she was dead, when it was too late to tell her what I wanted to, and too late to do anything to me if it was found."

"Did anyone else know?"

Keebo shook his head, bit the last piece of tomato away from the stem. "Shall we walk?" he asked, holding out his hand.

Kal grasped it, and helped him to his feet.

⸻⬦⬦⬦⸻

This time, when Keebo awoke, the gloom was a true result of the pale morning light. He gazed up at the roof of his hut, at every line etched between the palm leaves. Kal had clearly also done some roof-work while he slept. He looked around the simple room, drinking in every detail—the pale yellow of the bamboo walls, the tight latticework of the woven chest containing his magic books, the hard and pitted iron of his cookware, the stark black charcoal ends and gray ash of last night's firewood, the bulbous white onions almost luminescent hanging from the wall.

He glanced down; Kal was still asleep on the floor, breathing evenly. He lay on his stomach, his arms straight down at his sides as though he were drifting through the water. They were strange creatures, the Anoe, if Keebo thought about it—not human, anyway. It shouldn't have mattered—horses were not human, but were well cared for regardless—but for some reason it did. It didn't help, probably, that they were short and easily dominated, out of water, at least. The strongest Anoe he had seen could barely lift a full-blooded Rinc Nain onto his toes. Get them in the water though, they could out-swim a boat.

Kal blinked suddenly, arched himself backward until he could shift onto his feet; strange creatures indeed.

"I can see clearly, now," Keebo said quietly, simply.

Kal's head swung over, his large almond eyes gazing. "That is welcome news." Though his lips didn't move, Keebo could tell the Anoe was smiling.

"I suppose you'll be leaving now?"

"My people still need me," he replied. "You, I think, no longer do."

Keebo swung his legs off the edge of the cot and settled them on the floor. He rested his hand on his belly—no longer distended, as it had once been—and stood without groaning. He walked over to the window and looked out. "I guess not." He continued to gaze as the pre-dawn landscape came slowly into clarity. Near mid-summer, now, the grasses and ferns stretching to the wood-line up the slope were as rich and vibrant as they would ever be. Another few months in sweltering heat, they would positively need the rains that would begin to pour down at the turn of the year. For now, they were nearing their peak, oblivious, it seemed, to what lay ahead.

Keebo could relate.

"I am still sorry about Kadelkay," he said quietly. "And the whole event. Even with justice believed to have been served, the people of the Islands would look even more harshly at your people. Some—probably not a few—will believe he had help. There will even be those who will say the entire nation had a hand in the murder of Jon. And without the Steward backing me on bringing Tirtar and Elandra to questioning, I see no way to change it." His vision, once clear, blurred again. "Do you want me to find them anyway?"

"They may have left the Islands; Elandra fled when I came back. Nedley said he saw her get into a boat further down the docks. Her father was there waiting."

"So nothing happens, then; except now you are in danger everywhere you go."

Kal was silent. Keebo finally turned to look at him. "My friend," Kal said tiredly; "It burdens my heart that you say 'now' as if this had not been a reality for the Anoe for a very long time."

"Kal, I don't—"

"I told you to stop calling me that, and many others have as well," Kal said harshly, turning away. "And yet, oh great friend of mine and the Anoe, you persist."

Keebo gaped. "I call you that because I like you."

Kal snorted.

"I thought we were close, that—"

Kal turned back on him sharply. "Do you know what my name means?"

Keebo paused at a creeping sense of dread and shame.

"Why, perhaps, I keep telling you not to call me 'Kal'?"

The dread grew. "I—"

"In the language of our people, my name is better said as *Sho kal'Og*. 'Sho' is our word for sunlight, but also means the rays that pierce through clouds, or the reflection of those rays on mirrored surfaces. 'Og' means water, but especially water that is clear, rippling, alive. 'Kal,' when used to modify a word like water, means 'on.' As a whole, my name can be several-fold, for sometimes the sunlight reflecting off water is a beautiful thing, an entrancing thing. Sometimes it goes through the water, illuminating the depths of the mystery. It reflects brilliantly off clouds, and in a hundred shades in the evening. It can also be a harsh glare, blinding the watcher. But out of that context, 'kal' connotes something so low and firmly placed it cannot be lifted. It means the part of the water that is reflective, which cannot be separated from it. By calling me Kal you say, over and over, I am low, firmly attached to my low position, unable to be removed, or lifted away. As Kal I am never better than I am now—of a people once glorious but now banished to an island of sand and rock; the only time our word is taken as honest is when we admit to blame, savagery, or stupidity. You call me how you think of my people, according to one issue—our race; you deal pitiably with us because of one problem, reducing us to our struggle with the Rinc Nain. The Rinc Nain could go to the deeps, and we would still struggle; with them or apart from them, we live, we love, we strive, we have dreams, goals, friends, enemies—we are more than simply Anoe, we are beings."

"I—" *I didn't know;* he almost said. *But then, I never asked.* Keebo went to his cot and sat down. Shokalog was right, and he knew it. He did pity them, but he did not empathize with them. "I had meant to ask you, once..." He trailed off, shaking his head. *It hadn't been important enough.*

"You do far better than most," Shokalog said gently. "I am glad you listen to me most of the time, and pay attention to some of our lives. I am not angry with you for that. But if anything is ever to change, it is not enough—and you are not enough. If we despair, it is because the mere acceptance by one man only gives us the faintest glimmer of what could be, but never will. Prince Jonkar—he sat in on our ceremonies; he asked hundreds of questions, never once offering an opinion; and finally toward the end he was saying simply he would allow us free movement off of Berola. He did not say where we were to go, never talked of 'giving us back our land'—only saying we would be free to reclaim it, resettle it, without his defining it."

"Do you think the people who live in your old lands would let you come back and live there?"

"No. But then, it has been a long time since we have lived there, and our people have grown as well. I do not think we could reclaim the old ways anyway. So we would do as we had, centuries ago, when we came here: we would fit in where the land would take us and sustain us. At least, that is what I was trying to counsel my clan. That part of our heritage, we could retain if the restraints were finally taken away."

"Now they will come down even harder."

"It is very likely. At least, there will be fewer Captains willing to ferry even a single Anoe; and fewer ports who will let us dock."

"What will you do?"

Shokalog sighed. "I do not know. For now, return to my people and discuss what we do next."

"Do you have a way back?"

"Nedley has agreed to pass nearby your shore, in the event I need a boat; he will take me back when next he comes by. What of you? What will you do?"

Outside, the sun had risen behind a cloud, and the gloom in the little hut deepened. Keebo's head was still bowed, and he was silent. After a time, Shokalog placed a tender hand on his shoulder, squeezed, then walked to the door. He paused to look back at the huddled figure, the once-stout earth wizard now thin and rickety. It saddened the young Anoe, but he believed perhaps finally Keebo might begin to understand the attitude of his people. "Be at peace, Keebo," he said. "It is not the end, yet."

Keebo sighed, but did not look up. "Maybe not," he said. "All the same, I think I'll stay here for a while, see about regaining some of my energy. Maybe a few months. I could use the rest."

"If I can, I will come back to see you, then."

Keebo said nothing, and Shokalog exited, leaving him in the dark.

16

A Little Magic

"How will you know when he is ready?"
"I must make him ready."
"When?"
"Right now."

19 Haschina 1321 — Rainy

After four months, as the dry season ended and the rainy began, Keebo still did not feel rested. The year turned, and almost another full month was gone. His crops had long been harvested, dried, smoked, or pickled, and stored. He sat in his cot one morning as Haschina slid closer to Mantaver. A storm had swept through last night and soaked the land, though now it only dripped off the roof.

As the months had passed, he made himself go out daily and do little bits of magic. He started with his own soils—Shokalog had done a fine job, but still not what Keebo could do, sensing each bit of soil as he worked it. But soon it was as good as he could get; knowing he needed to do more—though not why—he began sneaking to other farms, working their soil as well. It was pleasant, even though he never heard from any of the tenants how they felt about their crops. For him, it was enough to do it.

It wasn't entirely selfless: he needed to restore his reserves, and he knew this was how to do it. Perhaps he could have stayed on his own land, simply built furrows and smoothed them out again, or worked a rock from one depth to another and back. Maybe it was something Shokalog had said—that part about his gardens being legendary, if anyone knew about it. He still didn't want anyone to know about his own, but no harm in letting his distant neighbors grow famous with theirs, was there?

But those days had passed. All the crops were in, not just his. So he sat now at the edge of his trapdoor, one leg dangling while the other he pulled up and tucked against his chest. While he read, he would sometimes stretch down a toe and fiddle with some light magic. He knew his efforts at reviving his stores was paying off as he ground two rocks against one another almost half a mile away and two hundred feet down. And that while he was slightly distracted.

It seemed so silly, now, almost thirty years distant—his illicit relationship. It had been hard to justify, in the early days. Then it had been only letters; but suddenly the King abandoned their bed; spoke to her only at meals and great need. She claimed he never spoke harshly to her; but he had apparently grown weary after so many years without an heir. She needed more comfort than ink on a page; and, since Keebo had loved her first, it had felt only fitting and proper... At the time, it was almost all he lived for; that, and the visits from Melnor. He snorted. Times changed. For him, they changed in the span of a week: she wrote to Keebo to tell him she had finally convinced the King back into their blankets and produced an heir. She wanted him to stay away, disdaining his love the second time. In desperation he gave her the mountains she said she had wanted, to catastrophic result. Melnor rejected him then too, and all he had left were his gardens.

After twenty years, he had made peace with it, relished it, defended it to the end. Until someone assassinated the prince, and he dared leave...

He folded the letter, tucked it with the rest, stopped pushing rocks a half mile away. With a sigh he brought his leg up and stood. Enough for one day; time to prepare dinner.

He went to his hearth, struck flint on tinder and started his cookfire. A pot dunked in the rain barrel that would not run dry for another several months, and quickly-chopped garlic and peppers, handfuls of beans, a little salt, and smoked ham and paprika—imported, purchased in Maerc—were all he needed for a good soup.

While it was never truly cold in the Islands, not like what he heard from Andelen or Gintanos, sometimes the heavy rains cooled it well below normal; so tonight he let his fire burn while he ate, just enough to add some warmth to his hut. As he finished his dinner, a knock sounded on his door.

Furrowing his brow, he stood and opened it; outside was an old man in red robes. Startled at first, Keebo froze; then rolled his eyes.

"Really, Melnor? We know how unnecessary that is for you."

"And yet you were surprised to see me."

"It's been months," Keebo replied, shutting the door. When he turned back to the fire, Melnor was there peering into it.

"I appreciate you letting me arrive normally, instead of by lightning bolt."

"We all make mistakes. What do you want?"

"I was just wondering if you ever intended to finish what you started."

"There's nothing left for me to do; haven't you heard? The Steward has settled his mind, and the only other two I could question are gone."

"There used to be a time you could change Tolma's mind even after it had set."

"Times change. Besides, I thought *you* were in the mind-changing business." Keebo stalked over to his table and gathered bowl and cup. He went outside, where another rain barrel became a wash pot. As he wiped down the cup, Melnor appeared again beside him.

"I am in the mind-changing business, and I'm here to change yours."

"No, I mean changing your mind," Keebo replied with a glare. "Remember? You changed yours twenty years ago, just late enough to allow me the greatest hope possible before shattering it. Tolma changed his so that I became powerless to prevent an innocent Anoe from dying. Jon changed his and started this whole mess to begin with. Rayenne changed hers, and—" Keebo uselessly clamped his mouth shut, then frowned.

"No need to finish that sentence. For your information, Keebo Burami, it was never my intention to change my mind; you were not ready."

"I'm sorry; I wasn't ready? At what point was I not ready? You said you had watched me—which is a little creepy and annoying, by the way—for a long time before even entering my conscious; and even after you first came to speak to me, you said you watched even longer and were—I think you said 'very impressed'. So at what point was I 'not ready'?"

"Everything I had observed showed you were ready. But I was not able to see until later that you were not strong enough—that your grasp of magic was not deep enough."

"My grasp..." Keebo trailed off, his face hardening. He thumped the bowl onto the half-closed lid of the rain barrel. "I think you have no idea how strong I am, or how deep my knowledge runs. I think there are things..." He cut himself off again, this time in his mind as well. Melnor looked at him warily, as a fierce grin twisted Keebo's lips.

He closed his eyes a moment, letting his sense run down again from the top of his head to his toes. His preparations the past months had been more successful than even he anticipated, and he shook with excitement. His eyes snapped open as the grin disappeared; the line of his mouth flattened in determination.

He let his sense of the ground spread from his feet. But what type of display might be useful?

He began whispering quickly; he did not even need to try very hard, and he knew the element heard him. Across the field, perhaps a hundred paces away, columns of earth about man-shaped suddenly sprang up, mats of grass like hair. He conjured an image in his mind: the man-shapes grew to various sizes, five hundred of them—an army made of earth.

His words flowed faster, clearer, the images precise—they had to. From the ground all around them dust rose up, not billowing or blowing like natural dust would on a dry day, though there were still puddles after last night's storm. But thousands of fine particles rose slowly from the ground, evenly spaced, and once it reached over their heads blotted out the faint sun shining through a thin overcast.

Fast as a hundred horses, the dust collapsed into a rock in front of the army; he spun it, faster and faster until it seemed a blur. A whine rose to almost a shriek, and the the ball burst asunder. Spikes of earth arrayed in a line, each spear pointed at one of the earthen soldiers, each matched perfectly to the varying heights of their heads. They held, quivering, as the day grew silent. Keebo watched Melnor, who watched the army.

With a faint flick of his finger, the spears shot through faster than any arrow, and the dirt heads exploded; but instead of raining down, the remains floated upward and coalesced into a broad, flat stretch of dirt. When the spears had passed through the entire 500 they turned upward, somersaulting; they drove down onto the top of the suspended remains, and the table of rock crashed to the ground, flattening the columns in a spray of loam that fell just short of where Keebo stood.

He closed his eyes; plenty of energy left for one final show. He reached out through his feet as he took long, slow, deep breaths, feeling for anything living—worms, moles, pigs, ground-nesting birds, even leopards. The earth told him where each was—thousands of them—and he quickly painted in his mind the spaces between, ensuring they would not be touched with this final spell.

He reached out further and further; he sensed an edge, a point past where his powers could not extend. He smiled, then, and looked again at Melnor. The triumvir now faced him with deep concern.

"Strength and knowledge?" Keebo said with a sneer. He declared the words of the spell in a ringing cry; Melnor's face blanched.

With the roar of a thousand thunders, the ground around them began to shift. Great valleys split wide; granite and basalt thrust skyward into new, soaring mountains—far more beautiful, he realized, than those on Nutar Ha. Great new rifts of shadows and shafts of sun cut across the land as the peaks climbed higher. His hut was cast suddenly into darkness, though the sun still shone on his garden. As it settled into its new arrangement, the earth sent him word that everything living of the earth survived, held securely in soil that did not move; new instincts were imprinted on every creature so they would not become lost in this new island.

The thunder echoed away, rolling across the island to the sea. Keebo heaved a great breath, willing his legs not to collapse beneath him as he gazed at Melnor. "What were you saying before?"

Melnor gazed hard at Keebo for several moments as if looking for something. He stepped back finally with a thoughtful grunt, then swept his eyes over the landscape. "You're certainly making something of your home; it's even more beautiful than last time I was here. And you've learned some neat tricks." His gaze came back and settled mildly on

Keebo. "How did you know it wouldn't kill you?"

"The earth tells me," he replied. "As I imagine the spell, it lets me know if it can obey what I want."

"Hmm. Fascinating. Your affinity, then, has grown essentially into a friendship."

"I...it seems something like that, yes," Keebo replied. "But that's—"

Melnor cut him off. "And how did you come by that much power? You should not have that much in you—or does the earth, like a good friend, do all that work on its own?"

"Hardly," Keebo replied. "It cannot break the rules."

"But you seem to have."

Keebo crossed his arms. "Truly? Is there knowledge I have that the great Triumvirate does not?"

"Very important knowledge, that I wish you wouldn't hide from me; it may answer a great deal."

Keebo compressed his lips, then shrugged. *When you use little bits at a time, just some little spells daily, it seems to build up energy within you—in the smallest parts that make up the body. I don't know more than that, I'm not a physician. But it stores it in places I cannot take from for normal effort.*

"Hmm. Interesting."

"And how now have I helped the Triumvirate, while still receiving nothing in return?"

"We have long wondered how Lasserain was able to do the things he did," Melnor replied. "Until him, we assumed certain limits applied to mages and wizards; after him, we thought maybe he had broken some of the rules. But perhaps, as you did, he was able to build friendships with all the elements, allowing him access to spells normally thought reserved for wizards. Then by storing energy the way you have, he was able to carry off a level of magnitude we assumed unattainable by anyone. Magnitude like...well, this," he finished, gesturing around the mountains.

"Fascinating. And a little late to be useful."

"Time moves on, Keebo; and knowledge applies itself to more than just one age."

"Indeed. Well, even if you have only done it obliquely, I appreciate your acknowledgement of my strength and understanding of magic. I feel a little awed that I was able to change the mind of a triumvir. Perhaps that knowledge, too, will apply itself to more than just one age," Keebo said with a satisfied grin.

Something like compassion glistened in Melnor's eyes. "I am sorry, my friend; but you have not changed my mind in the least. You have power, for certain; but what I said was strength, and grasp of the use of magic. I meant strength of character, and grasp of the reality of being a magic-user—and what it means to be a Triumvir."

"Then the Triumvirate also has very important knowledge, that I wish you wouldn't hide from me," Keebo replied, not caring to temper the bitterness in his voice.

"Even if you may never again have the opportunity to join us? I cannot guarantee that, you know."

Keebo took a moment to gaze around his home. It actually looked...rather nice. Certainly a fine place to live out the remainder of his life. "Fine. Yes."

"As a Triumvir, my choices—some of them mistakes—have cost the lives of thousands, Keebo. Thousands died in Burieng because those I sent pushed Lasserain over the edge; hundreds more before that, when I didn't understand the threat he posed. Within the first five decades of being assigned, my mistakes in North Pal Isan and Rinc Na cost thousands more. And those are choices I made to act. Sometimes we must not act, and watch as whole nations are wiped out. If we punished ourselves the way you did after the mountains you raised in Nutar Ha—though I'm glad to see you've gotten better at that—we would have ceased to exist millennia ago. That is the true cost of using magic—not that you die earlier, but that others do—sometimes because of what you've done and shouldn't, but sometimes too because you did exactly as you should. Once I saw that in you, that inability to move on, I knew you could not be one of us. Even Teresh understood it, yet he still struggles sometimes."

"So I should stop letting the survivors beat me up?"

"I wish you would. But it's more than that; it's this life of seclusion you've forced yourself into, to avoid the possibility of another accident. Well, more are dying and will die because of your inaction, here in the Islands."

Of course Jonkar's death would ripple out. And if Keebo had been around he might have cared what was happening and been able to help. "Why did he start changing? Had you any part in that?"

"Unfortunately, no; we were not around. Perhaps our mistake was focusing on the guild masters themselves. The struggle with the Anoe had not yet ripened enough for us to act. I don't always know why," Melnor said, silencing Keebo's planned retort. "Many times we are instructed by the God of All; in this case he said it was not yet time—or, at least, we were not to interfere."

"Did he tell you to interfere with Jon's death? I assume he saw it coming. He is supposed to be all-knowing."

"He is; but we—like those on Oren, though we have been given far higher capabilities—are still given our free will. He has drawn our boundaries, let's say, and told us to act as best we can within them. Occasionally we embark on a path we perceive as best for a person, or country, and he calls to us and says that way leads outside the boundary—we almost never understand why. But we have seen him work things out without us in most cases."

"What of the other cases?"

"We trust that it remains to be seen. He has never proven faithless."

"What are my boundaries?"

Melnor smiled. "Far beyond your garden, impressive as it is. There is still a murder to solve; I suggest—" He cut off abruptly, wheeling to look over the mountain southeastward. "I have to go. Good luck."

He winked out suddenly, before a shrieking cry echoed across the ranges. Keebo's eyes widened as a great winged shape cleared a nearby pass.

It was the dragon, Belaornen; and she was angry.

17

COMPANY OF DRAGONS

"That was a near thing; what's next?"
"He must survive."
"I fear for Rinc Na."
"I will go there next."

19 Haschina 1321 — Rainy

When she saw Keebo she screamed again and tucked her wings, exceeding even the speed of his earthen missiles. Why would she be angry with him? It didn't make—

Lightning forked from her mouth, blasting the ground where his army had been crushed. He ducked inside the hut as she streaked overhead, the thrusting wings battering the thatched roof ten times over the strength of the storm it had recently endured. Keebo peered through a window as she slowly arced, turning back to strike again.

He considered quickly; surely she had not missed that wide accidentally. So she likely did not actually want to kill him. Hopefully. If she did, he would not have enough energy to stop her. But, maybe...

As she descended on his home again, he crawled quickly to the south window, looking at his mountains. They were so beautiful, he really did want to keep them. But, if he died because Belaornen did not like them, it wouldn't matter, would it?

Another ragged bolt of lightning, this one in his garden. *"Kiet fior thoi!"* he called.

Amazing how easy it was to undo what he had done. Energy rushed back into him—that little bit that always returned to the user when a spell was ended, now multiplied exponentially by the magnitude of this spell. Earth roared again as valleys were raised and mountains brought low. Still the pockets where living creatures lived were protected as all the land flattened out to its original, natural shape.

When he had made his disastrous mistake on Nutar Ha he had left it as a reminder to never do so again—and especially never for the reasons he had done it. He had good precedent: there were many monuments in Carist—eternal spells left going because they had destroyed the magic user who cast them. So it had seemed a good idea, to him. Perhaps...perhaps it was not.

He skittered over to the other window, craning his neck in attempt to see Belaornen again. She was up in the sky, waiting as she watched the land reform, her flapping wings echoing even so far above. Keebo hoped the nearest farmers were not watching—or cowering—as she hovered like some beacon of doom.

The echoes faded away again, and Keebo could see clear to the horizon across sunny plains; the clouds, for now, had gone. Belaornen's head swiveled as she surveyed the land, then her gaze came to rest on Keebo's hut. She descended slowly, this time; her anger appeared to have spent. He stood shakily, and went outside.

Belaornen landed lightly, though the gusts from her wings whipped through Keebo's hair. He squinted, until she settled herself. But she did not sit: she stood still on all fours, tail extended behind her and wings raised in pavilion. He took a step toward her, but she fixed him with such a glance of consternation that he stepped back.

She lowered her head, herding him away from his hut. "I am sorry," he said over and over. "I didn't mean anything by it; the earth told me its creatures were—well, okay, as you wish." He scuttled away, giving her wide berth.

She turned her back to his hut, looking at him with utter patience and serenity as she lifted her tail, then slammed it down onto the middle of the roof, flattening it instantly with a spray of splintered bamboo. Two, three more times the tail came up and back down; then whipped back and forth, scattering every bit of his home to the four winds.

When she had finished she settled back, raising her head to regard him...rather smugly, he thought. For all his power as a wizard, she had strength to alter his home as well, without training at the legendary Tamecal and the pride that inevitably followed.

"I—well, I suppose I deserved that. Sorry I disturbed your home; I had not seen you for some time, you know."

If she understood him, or forgave him, he could not tell as her great wings thrust her back into the sky, southeastward. He marked her flight, reminding himself never to go that way unless he needed a dragon for something.

He turned again to his shattered abode. He walked through the remnants, observing the tattered shreds of his cot, bent and mangled cookware—even the chairs he reserved for guests who never came were broken in two. As he kicked aside a small section of lashed bamboo, a sudden wind caught stacked parchment and lifted it spinning out of his reach. He watched it go, too numb already to care that his letters from Queen Rayenne were now gone as well. At the far side he found what he sought: though the chest was no more, his books and a blanket were intact.

"So, then," he muttered. "I suppose I have enough. Although, with the chance of rain..." He trailed off, squinting into the cloudless sky. "Hmm. Fine for now, I suppose."

His gardens, too, had survived some of the onslaught, except one large blackened crater where the lightning had struck. But no food had been destroyed. He unearthed his cellar and took out what could be tied up in the remains of his cot.

While rummaging, he also came across his tinder and some bits of wood that had been the fire. Melnor had not quite finished with him, and besides, he needed to know what to do next. For him the trail of Jon's killer had overgrown, the thickets of time obscuring even what clues he had originally found. So he set up a small bundle of sticks and wood in the protective bowl of the lightning blast, lit it, and waited for Melnor to arrive.

"I am glad to see you made it," Melnor said, standing suddenly on the other side of the flames. "And thank you for helping me come back."

"You're welcome. What am I supposed to do next?"

Melnor smiled. "I had intended you to go back to Tolma; but this arrival of Belaornen and her...apparent anger, changes things. Remember this time, Keebo, for the God is working outside our boundaries here again. Go to Gunda and wait until you see the winged man." Melnor paused and chuckled. "The wingt man. Ha." He shook his head, then became serious as Keebo cocked an eyebrow. "Some other time, perhaps. He'll be traveling with a young woman with chestnut hair. Ask them why Belaornen may have attacked. I'll try to meet you after that, but if I cannot—well, you should be able to figure out what you need to do. Retrace your steps, if you must."

"I made a lot of steps—oh, fine," he cut off as Melnor suddenly disappeared. "Better things to do, I suspect. Well. Gunda. Off we go, then."

⸺⬥⸺

Keebo found a boat easily enough, securing passage without coin by promising to help clean the boat. He didn't intend to trick the Captain, but when he cast a simple spell and watched the dirt and dust whirl off into the ocean, his triumphant smile was not returned. Still, the captain carried him there in fine time and left him at port pleasantly enough. Keebo wandered to Jedded's Gundabulous Fare and sat.

"What will it be, old friend?" Jedded asked with a smile.

"Should I warn you that I don't have any money?"

The smile disappeared with a groan. "Keebo, you should know better. I can't keep you from sitting on my steps, but the tables are for *paying* customers."

"Thanks, old friend," Keebo replied behind his vanishing smile. "No spells I can perform for you? How about cleaning—?"

"My floors are clean," Jedded responded, turning and walking away.

"Of course they are." He got up and wandered outside.

Well, if he was to wait for two arrivals to Gunda, he should do that closer to port, most likely. He wandered down the beach, settling into the same hammock he had found the last time he was in Gunda. It was not as pleasant a day—it was not raining, at least, but the sun was not shining either and the white sands were morose and the sea dimmed. The boat was still missing, but the flag unfurled in a steady east wind and clearly said "Back Soon."

"I'm right back where I started," Keebo muttered. He closed his eyes and set the hammock swaying. No one from Irii was trying to kill him, now, as far as he knew. And rather than trying to leave, he was supposed to stay and wait. "I hope I don't have to retrace every step," he continued to himself. "That would seem rather disheartening. And I could definitely use some bacon right now."

Don't get too comfortable.

Keebo's eyes popped open, and he looked out to sea. A tall ship was entering the harbor, just then; this one was steady, and the sails held tight in the wind. A good, proper Andelian ship, it appeared. Keebo wondered if the winged man—*wingt man?*—was aboard, with his female companion.

He stood again, wandering down to the docks. Surely those weren't still his footprints from the last time...couldn't be.

The boats lowered away, and as passengers clambered down the short ladders into them Keebo spied the man—thin, his movements precise, and dark hair; followed closely by a young woman equally precise, with reddish hair. He kept his eyes on their boat as it was rowed to the dock. They disembarked, talking together and smiling—well, she smiled; he appeared happy though his face showed no obvious emotion. An interesting pair. The winged man saw Keebo's gaze and paused. The woman followed his eyes, smiled at Keebo, and waved.

"Hello," she said brightly. "You're looking at us very intently."

"I'm sorry, but I was told to find you," Keebo replied. "I had an incident with..." He glanced at the other passengers streaming past, then mouthed: "a dragon."

"Oh," she said, casting a knowing glance at the man beside her. "We should talk, then. Do you know somewhere...?"

Keebo grinned widely. "Indeed I do. My name is Keebo; let me show you some food."

"Nice to meet you Keebo; I'm Catie," she said. "This is Deuel."

He quickly led them up the beach and back into Gundabulous Fare. "Paying customers," he said with a waggling finger as Jedded looked at him in consternation. "Jedded is really very nice, just cheap," he explained quietly as they went to a lonely table near the back. "Please, sit." He took up his own seat against the wall out of habit. "Are you coming from Andelen?"

"We are," Catie said, a curious look in her eyes.

"Your ship," Keebo replied. "It doesn't look like a Burieng ship, or from the Islands, so... What news from there? Sheppar still king?"

"Yes—well, kinnig, I guess. He wants the towns and villages to rule themselves, so he got rid of the title of king. Upset a few people," Catie added with a thin smile.

"How so?"

"Well, Roth Kamdellan wanted a king. He claimed a king was necessary to unify the Andelians under common experiences, or something. I think he just wanted power."

"That has a way of driving men mad," Keebo agreed.

"He started a rebellion to get rid of Sheppar—well, he did and he didn't. I think he started out with one," she explained hurriedly. "But at some point he started just making up the size of his forces and what land he had taken over. Created a pretend front line, and had 'scouts' guide people through it as though Sheppar's forces were gathered there."

Keebo sat back with a disbelieving chuckle.

"Oh, it gets worse," Catie said somberly. "He started to make deals with Beltrath nomads to invade the rest of Andelen, and promised they could destroy the—uh, people like Deuel, all of them, if they helped him win his rebellion. 'Revolution,' sorry." She rolled her eyes. "He had hired Deuel to find these supposed goblets of legend that were supposed to give him power if he drank from them." She glanced down, picking at the edge of the table. "I didn't know he meant to drink his own blood from them."

"He seems to have gone well beyond the normal madness for power," Keebo said quietly. "You were there when he died?"

"I gave him the goblets," she said. "I didn't know what he had planned. He wasn't like that when I first met him. Still not a good person, but...Steth, one of his soldiers, mentioned something happened to him last spring, that his madness seemed to get worse. He wasn't sure why."

"Had he been fighting his cause for a while? Sometimes people just get tired, desperate..."

"He had been stuck for some time, true."

"And he was willing to pay my partner and I an extraordinary sum to find these goblets," Deuel said. "He was most assuredly becoming desperate, as much as he tried to hide it."

"Anyway, after that Halmf—oh, yes; um..." She broke off as Jedded suddenly appeared at their side. She extended a hand toward Keebo. "Whatever you recommend, I suppose."

"The usual, Jedded," Keebo said with a smile.

"For three?" he asked warily.

"I have no way to pay," Keebo said.

"Oh!" Catie said. "You've been so nice, though. We'll take care of it: three, and thank you."

"Thank you so much," Keebo said as Jedded walked away. "Last time, I may have tricked my guest into paying for me. Anyway, you were saying how this Roth Kamdellan went quite mad."

"Oh! Yes." Catie's hands went back to her side. "According to Steth, it happened suddenly, almost overnight, as if something had happened to change him."

Keebo stared at her. "As if he had read one book and it changed him irrevocably?"

Catie shrugged. "I guess so? Why do you say it like that?"

Keebo shook his head. *What in Oren was happening?*

18

CHANGE OF ROLES

"I did not touch Roth."
"Perhaps you should have."
"You didn't tell me to."
"I've tried everything; go to South Pal Isan and see what you can do."

24 Haschina 1321 — Rainy

Keebo sat brooding even as Jedded brought their Rack and Ruin; Catie and Deuel fended for themselves for a while. *The leader of a rebellion in Andelen changes suddenly; Jon was leading a kind of rebellion here in the Islands—rebelling against the Rinc Nain oppression of the Anoe, and changes suddenly. The Andelian grew more zealous; Jon grew less? What was the connection? Triumvirate business?*

I told you we are not yet fully involved in this, but we are looking. Find his killer first.

Keebo blinked, suddenly noticing his guests struggling with their food. He grinned, and showed them the way.

"Ohh!" Catie exclaimed with a smile. "That's fun!"

Deuel gave her a glance while Keebo chuckled. They continued, much as Keebo and Haydren had, in silence until the last bit was cleaned from the bowl.

"So; what happened with this dragon?" Catie asked when they all sat back.

"Oh, right; well, she attacked me," Keebo said. "Flattened my home and brushed all the bits to the wind—well, most of the bits. I was able to salvage some belongings." He nudged the bundle at his feet.

"Unprovoked?" Catie asked.

"Well..." Keebo hedged. "I thought it was—I mean, I didn't think I would do anything to her. I cast a spell to raise a few mountains around my home," he explained. "But I reached out beforehand and asked the earth if anything was out there that might get hurt, so I could protect it."

"Who was it?" Deuel asked.

"Belaornen?" Keebo replied.

A mild grin flashed across his face and was gone. "Belaornen is of the sky, not the earth; it would not have recognized her. However," he continued, his face stilling again, "if her nest was protected she should not have destroyed your home. When did this happen?"

"Five days ago?" Keebo offered, wiggling his fingers. "The 19th."

Another long glance exchanged between the winged man and his partner. "Strange," he said, turning back finally. "I had felt something shift, five days ago—something in the consciousness of the dragons, or at least some of them."

"You can do that?" Keebo asked. Deuel ruffled his wings in explanation. "Oh, of course; continue."

"We don't know what it is, though," Catie said. "Belaornen herself doesn't seem to know—he asked her," she explained. "She did say it has happened before."

"Is it a permanent shift? Will I ever be able to rebuild my home?"

"Oh yes," Catie replied quickly. "I mean, no. She didn't want to do it, destroy your home; she said a strange compulsion took her—not a compulsion," she amended quickly after Deuel's swift glance. "But she recognized that what you did upset her more than it should have, and she couldn't seem to shake it."

"This sounds like bad news for dragon-kind, at least in many places."

Deuel nodded gravely. "It is. If these events become more frequent, there is greater chance of this mood and some offense occurring at the same time. Anything gained since Bahamut will be gone."

"Could you please tell her I'm sorry, then? I hadn't meant to disturb her. At first I was glad to see her, actually; I had missed her."

"I certainly will," Deuel replied warmly.

"Did this change affect you as well?"

"Not in exactly the same way," Deuel replied drily as Catie turned a slightly redder shade.

Keebo politely ignored her reaction, and sat a few moments in silence. "I'm not sure what else to ask," he said. He spread his hands. "I believed it was important to come talk to the two of you about this incident. I had hoped to understand something more about what's been going on here, but...maybe your story of Roth Kamdellan was enough. But, that's for me to work through."

"Who told you to find us?" Catie asked.

"Oh, uh, a wizard—fellow wizard, sort of, named Melnor?" He posed it as a question, unsure if they had any interaction with him. By their glances and Catie's shrug, they had not. "He's not as well-known as some others," Keebo continued smoothly. "I think he prefers it that way."

"He is some sort of prophet or seer?" Deuel asked. "There are few with that gift."

Keebo ignored the mild knowing on Catie's face. "Something like that. Perhaps I was mistaken as to his intentions. Where are you going next?"

"Gintanos," Deuel replied. "I have a brother there, and Catie has heard something out of there that she must pursue."

"I've not heard much news from that area," Keebo said. "Perhaps if you come back through this way..."

"Of course we will. What about you?"

"Oh, I've got a murder to solve," Keebo said with a nod. "Well, the murder happened some time ago—you know, it's a long story. Thank you for lunch! I always enjoy being able to eat here."

"I can understand that," Catie said appreciatively as they stood. Keebo hefted his bag and slung it over a shoulder. Catie looked at him with concern. "Are you sure you'll be all right? Nothing else you need?"

"Oh, I'm fine," he said with a nod. "I've got a full belly, I can earn enough keep to take the ferry back home, and the nights here aren't cold enough to absolutely need shelter."

"That doesn't seem like a lot," she said.

"It's enough for now. It's only because we can look ahead to tomorrow, and worry about it, that we think we need anything else. I have enough food for now; I have enough shelter for now," he said, placing a hand first on his stomach, then tugged at his clothing. He shrugged. "It's all the animals have, and they don't seem too concerned about it. Do you believe they are better-provided for than us?"

"I suppose not," Catie said with a faint smile. "It's hard to think that way, though."

Keebo grunted. "After enough lifetime, it becomes easier, when you see provision day after day."

"That is true," Deuel agreed.

They walked together back down to the docks; stores were still being loaded into Catie's and Deuel's ship for the long voyage southward, so they stopped at the hammocks to wait. Keebo glanced toward the ferry dock, then blinked as he recognized the sails. He paused and turned to the two companions. "Can you do me one last favor?" he asked. Catie nodded. "If you hear of anyone else suddenly going mad, could you let me know, somehow? Have Belaornen visit me again, but just communicate through winks and nods or something, rather than with her tail?"

Catie laughed. "We can only do as we're told," she said.

Keebo nodded, forcing his smile until he turned away. A leaf spinning away in a flood, that's what he was. He frowned and went down to the docks.

"Hello, Nedley," he said.

The Royal Ferryman glanced up quickly. His smile was reserved. "Keebo."

"I don't suppose you could take me to see the Steward?" he asked.

"I don't have no orders."

"Are you headed there now, or soon?"

Nedley glanced away, then back. "Suit yourself. Climb aboard. But might be you'll be turned away at the port, and don't complain to me then."

"Why would that be?"

"Tolma wasn't much taken to you, the way things played out. The only reason I'm taking you now is that he has never exactly told me not to," Nedley said, stooping to coil some rope below a pin.

Keebo climbed aboard. "Why has he not spoken of me well?"

"He said you took too long, found no answers, then questioned him when he tried to put the matter to rest." Clattering and squeaking, the mainsail lowered and soon caught the wind. The Calderon came on deck to help maneuver the boat out of the narrow port.

"I had hoped to find the truth. I still hope to find it. That's why we're going to see the Steward."

Nedley held his silence as they slowly turned the ship into the main channel. The Calderon gazed around the bay, cast a glance at Nedley, then went below.

"If you go looking for truth," Nedley said quietly as they quartered to the wind; "then I wouldn't expect to make it past the guards."

⸺◆⸺

In a sense, Nedley was correct: he had not made it 'through'—the guards at the port now encircled Keebo tightly as they approached the castle of Nak. A runner had gone ahead to announce Keebo's approach, but no one yet waited outside for them. The captain lifted a small horn and sounded it; after an instant, the doors swung open and they continued wordlessly through the abandoned town.

Inside the keep, a short man in purple and gold silks sat at a long desk, two more guards in silver armor attending him. "Welcome, Keebo," he said in a high voice. "I see you don't have an appointment. How can I help you?"

"You're new," Keebo commented.

The man smiled. "Dorran, attendant to the Steward. I keep his schedule. I started a few months ago. How can I help you?"

"I need to see Tolma—The Steward," Keebo amended quickly as Dorran's eyes turned to saucers. He suspected he could no longer get away with the jests he once did. "It concerns the murder of Prince Jonkar."

The smile became patronizing. "That incident has been put to rest."

"What about the suicide of Elandra, daughter of Tirtar?"

"I assume it was ruled a suicide."

It was Keebo's turn to smile patronizingly. "She's still alive, and I saw her on this Island."

Dorran's smile disappeared. "The Steward is available now. Take him straight up, please," he said to the guards at Keebo's side.

They tramped through the familiar halls, up the familiar stairs—easier, now that he was lighter—and to the familiar door. The guards there took over, opening the way for him and announcing him to Tolma Bergin.

Inside was far from familiar: gold, bronze, and silver accents were everywhere; new tapestries rich with reds, yellows, and purples, the colors of Terose and Bergin, draped along every wall and bunched in every corner. Keebo already felt uncomfortably warm. Tolma's desk was new—heavy, rich mahogany, with silver accents on it as well. His chair back was higher, with padded wings encircling his head like a three-quarter halo. Tolma himself appeared a little brighter—compliments, partially, of rich silk in gold and deep blue.

"You're looking much better," Keebo remarked, forgetting that perhaps he should tread more carefully.

Yet Tolma grinned widely. "As are you, in some respects. Still not a care for that mossy fuzz around your head, though?"

Keebo shook his head, suddenly feeling the expanse of hair he had not trimmed since—well. "Why so much change since I left?"

"Oh, this? Turns out when your royal heir has been assassinated, the nations send envoys of regret. Hoping for better terms, I imagine the true reason. I've yet to decide if they'll receive them. Please, sit."

Keebo took his seat, and the guards were dismissed. As soon as the door clicked shut, Tolma's face darkened. "What do you want?" he spat. "I thought we were done with you months ago."

Keebo didn't even blink; this was more like what he had expected. "I thought I was done with it too. But something keeps bothering me about this murder."

"Let it bother you; the threat is eliminated."

"I think you know it's not, Master Bergin," Keebo said. "You know that confession was false. Much more likely the assassin is still out there, and until we know why she killed Jon we cannot know she won't come after Strake."

"She?" Tolma sneered. "As if a woman—"

"Elandra," Keebo said.

Tolma rolled his eyes. "She's dead, Keebo, remember?"

"No, she isn't; she tried to kill me—where do you think I've been the past several months?"

Tolma's face sobered, then went hard. "Hopefully tracking her down!"

"Recovering, Tolma; I nearly died. But I tried to tell you last time that her father might have had something to do with it."

Tolma spluttered a few moments. "Well, then...Surely they're gone from the Islands, if they've done nothing since then."

Keebo shook his head. "They're here. I don't know where."

"Then why aren't you looking for them now?!"

"I thought you should know—"

"Messengers! You could have sent Nedley, rather than coming all the way here with him."

"I wasn't sure you'd be ready to listen, Master Bergin; you certainly didn't want to the last time."

"The last time, a girl who was supposed to be dead, still was, as far as we knew."

Keebo was silent a moment. "Might I talk to Strake? I'm hoping—"

Tolma shook his head. "He is not well; you know how the weather changes affect him."

Keebo nodded once; he was always the more frail. "I'm still curious how you forgot the name of a woman who had been all but betrothed to Jonkar. When I first came to you, you said you had forgotten her name."

Tolma waved him off. "Perhaps I had other things on my mind, like how to keep the Islands from destroying themselves in the face of assassination of their prince?"

"Information about her and her father might have been important."

"It's easy to say that now. Now if you don't mind, would you be so kind as to investigate this threat to the Islands?"

Keebo rose, and bowed. "I serve at your pleasure, Master Bergin," he said. "Do I have the pleasure of the services of the Royal Ferryman?"

"Of course; and everyone else, as before." Tolma removed a piece of parchment from a drawer and scrawled on it quickly. He rolled it up, placed his seal, and handed it to Keebo.

Keebo raised it in salute, turned, and left.

Back at the dock that Evening, he handed the scroll to Nedley. "Any idea where they might be?" Nedley asked, not yet laying hand to line.

Keebo pursed his lips; an excellent question. Nothing from the Triumvirate. "We should probably rule out their home," he said. "I cannot imagine they would hide there. But how could they even hide—? Hmm. Tirtar is a trained actor." He nodded when Nedley raised an eyebrow. "So they could be anywhere, and we could walk right by them and not know it." He sighed heavily.

"Was he in that traveling show, led by Klaggen Bontifar?"

"Yes, why?"

Nedley uncoiled a rope, let it slide around a pin; the mainsail lowered, catching a light evening wind. "Torin!" he shouted. "Get up here and oar; this wind is no good." As his Calderon came on deck, he furled the sail a little to not work against the efforts to row. "I know where Klaggen lives, over in Vind. He may know something. Folks tend to go back to people they trust when they're in trouble. And if Tirtar needed costumes, Klaggen would be the most likely to still have them."

They docked in Westport several days later, and Nedley led Keebo inland to the town of Vind. The town had outgrown its boundaries many years ago; outside the wall the streets ran sloppily, connecting houses that had been built around former farms. Inside the wall was far more ordered, and was where most of the businesses would be found, as well as the older homes. "Been in his family for a few generations," Nedley explained. They had left his Calderon with the boat, so Nedley could guide Keebo straight to the man's house.

A doorman answered their knock, bowing stiffly in a garish juggler's costume. He carried himself like a proper servant, incongruent with his outfit. Still, Keebo held his peace, and Nedley had the presence of mind to follow silently as well.

They were shown into a large room, carpeted, with walls of a pale wood Keebo couldn't identify; candles set in sconces on the walls lit the interior well. A large, dark man in plain silks stood next to a fireplace where coals glowed; a drink was in one hand and a pipe in the other, and he gazed at his guests from under bushy eyebrows. Bald up top, he compensated with a thick beard underneath. His voice, when he spoke, was a bit wheezy.

"Ah, welcome, I suppose. Hmm. To my home," he said, then clamped his teeth onto his pipe. He nestled his chin even closer to his chest as his eyes darted between Keebo and Nedley.

"Good afternoon, Mr. Bontifar," Keebo said; the surroundings seemed to call for formality. "I am—"

"Keebo Burami, yes, I've been told. And expecting you, to be sure. Hmm. And Nedley. Sit, please." He swept his arm at the couch in front of him.

"Thank you, very much," Keebo said. As they sat, Klaggen remained standing. "Why did you expect us?"

"Just you, I suppose. Hmm. Makes no difference. The show goes on, as it were; all sorts stop by, share some news. Far easier in the old days, just pulled up a chair around the spittoon, to be sure. Hmm. Not so much now, so spread out. But still they come by."

"Has Tirrin come by?"

"Of course not." He clamped down again on the pipestem, puffing almost angrily.

"Why, 'of course not' Mr. Bontifar?"

"He knows you're looking for him. If he wanted to be found, he would be at home, or he would come to me."

"Who told you that he knew I was looking for him, then?"

"The one who used to handle our itinerary, made sure we got from show to show," he replied with a twinkle in his eye, then pointed with his pipe. "Nedley, of course."

"Nedley?" Keebo exclaimed, turning just in time to see a blur of movement before lights exploded in his eyes, and the world went dark.

19

WELL AND BACK

31 Haschina 1321 — Rainy

Keebo blinked his eyes, unable to discern a difference between closed and open. *I've been blind before. It wasn't fun then, either.*

Somewhere, water plonked. It smelled of wet stone and moss. But he was not hungry, so he had not been unconscious very long. He was on folded blankets, but under that was stone. His searching hands groped out; circular walls surrounded him. A puddle stood in one corner; he wiped his hand on his vest, craning his neck upward.

Dimly, he could see a circular opening above him, a hard dark edge between the pit he was in and the roof overhead. *Not blind; just dark.* "Excuse me?" he called, standing up. "I think there's been some mistake."

There was movement overhead, a rustling of clothing perhaps. Padding feet, fading away. "Hello?" Nothing. Door hinges creaked and light shot across the opening; a ceiling of wooden beams was overhead, and the top of the opening was rough-hewn stone. *An old well? Hopefully filled in...*

Shadows running. The padding footsteps returned double. A broad, dark shape appeared over the well.

"Sorry for this, to be sure. Hmm. Had to be certain, you know. I understand rock is very hard to manipulate?"

Keebo reached out; hewn rock certainly was, torn from the bosom of its natural mother. "To be sure," he replied drily. He could not even sense dirt outside the well.

"Nedley warned me some time ago you might be coming. We prepared this for you. I do apologize, I suppose. Had to be sure."

Keebo sat down. "Sure of what?"

"My troupe is conducting an investigation of their own, you see. Into you, and Tirrin. Need to watch out for ourselves, I suppose. Nedley worried you cared more for the Anoe than your own kind, might pin something on Tirrin he didn't deserve."

"The Steward has pinned something on the Anoe that they don't deserve, though."

"To be sure. Hmm. A right sticky mess all around. Can't be helped."

"How is your investigation going? Mine has been terrible."

"Nearing its end. To be fair, yours may be as well. No, it wasn't Tirrin; he's got good reasons for all that's gone on—why things appear as they have, you see. We did need to make sure he didn't play the turncoat, to be sure. Hmm. But if he didn't do it..." Klaggen trailed off.

"Then I've got nothing," Keebo muttered. He raised his voice to be heard: "How much longer will I be down here?"

"Not long, couple days I hope."

"I hope so, too."

"Jenzi should be arriving shortly with the results of our last inquiry. If the answer is positive, you'll be let out, to be sure."

"What if it's not positive?"

"Oh. Well. We've prepared for that, too, you see. But, I'd rather not dwell on the unpleasant."

Keebo sighed. "May I ask of the nature of your inquiry?"

"You may, but it won't help. It concerns you—specifically, your honor."

"Any insight I can offer?"

"None that we would trust, wizard. Just be patient."

Klaggen's ponderous bulk left the opening; his heavy footfalls departed, and the light cut off by the closing door. A few moments, and once again all he could see was the dim opening of the well.

———◆———

Keebo tried to track the days by when they lowered in food, but he never felt a particular schedule was kept. The light would flare, footsteps and shadows approaching, then bread and cheese—sometimes some hunks of salted meat—would tumble over the edge to patter and splat onto the floor. The first time, he was also smacked in the neck by a skin of water; after that, he waited to dive upon the victuals until that had fallen in as well.

Sometimes he was famished; other times it seemed as if he had just eaten. So the eleventh time the light came on and the feet approached, he merely looked up to make sure and avoid the falling provender.

This time, though, Klaggen appeared. "Jenzi has come back. Hmm. Quite a tale he had to tell."

Keebo stood; he did not like the sound of Klaggen's voice. "How so?"

"Told me a tale, to be sure; of a young wizard and a young married woman. Hmm. I may have traveled much as a youngster, but I had never heard of such a thing."

"People change," Keebo said, running his hands over the wall. He just needed a bit of natural stone, or maybe some earth…

"Perhaps. Hard to tell though, isn't it? Maybe they just twist the truth better. Normally it isn't up to me."

"I'm not sure circumstances have changed," Keebo said, his hands becoming frantic despite the calm in his voice. "Perhaps you should just give me to the Steward, let him decide my fate."

"I had considered that too. But then, he may like you more than I do. Hmm. My way is better."

"How do I know you aren't just covering for yourself? Or Tirrin?"

Klaggen's voice was quiet, directed at someone else. "Bring it over here," he said. Chains clanked above, and something was rolling. He called down toward Keebo. "Well indeed, I might be, you have a point. But then, it's too late for you to tell. Hmm. I know I cannot trust you, though; and that's enough for me. Sorry this is the only way to do it." His voice changed again as the dimness ahead went out; he was no longer speaking to Keebo.

Here. Suddenly, his hand found a stone that had not been hewn; likely, during the building of the well, it had fit without alteration. The words buzzed through Keebo's mind hurriedly, and he pressed himself against the wall.

"Release it," came muffled from above; there was a snapping sound, then a rush of air and a terrific crash. Pain blasted through Keebo's left big toe; he had not been quick enough to get all the way inside the little chamber he had made, and now a great millstone sat atop part of his foot. His eyes went wide the instant before he stuffed a fist into his mouth to silence the cry trying to escape: squashed wizards made no cry. Blood thundered through his ears, drowning out any noises from above.

He forced himself to take slow, steady breaths as the throbbing in his foot slowed. The opening above remained dim. A few final, steadying breaths, and Keebo looked down. In the darkness he could see nothing; when he tried to move his foot, slicing pain lanced through the toe. *It could be worse; it could be worse; it could be worse.* He bent forward, straining down and trying to get fingertips beneath the edge of the millstone. If he could lift it even a little, he might be able to slide his foot out.

Noises again came from above; he recognized Klaggen's heavy footfalls departing. He straightened quickly and pressed into his alcove. His toe could wait. Firelight wavered, then spilled down into the pit. *Are they just making extra sure...?*

"What would you expect to see down there?" a new voice asked, one he had not heard since waking up down here.

"I wouldn't mind some blood or bone dust," replied another. That one he recognized from the first day.

A muffled strike, as if someone hit the back of another's head. Keebo rolled his eyes.

"Just fill it up," came the first voice. Keebo cocked his head; it suddenly sounded familiar, somehow... "You know he can't control cut stone! What do you think he did?"

"I'm just careful, I guess."

"You weren't so careful about Jenzi; you should have told him what I said, not try to make something up on your own."

Keebo strained hard, now, trying to place the voice; pitched low, it was difficult. But it was definitely a memory from before coming to Klaggen's.

A clink and scrape as if of metal on stone. "What you said to say was stupid." A light rattling sounded in front of Keebo's face, almost like... He dared not hope. "I had to improvise."

More clinking, and then rattling. Careful of the light, Keebo reached out and grabbed a fistful of the dirt being shoveled in from above. He pressed it to his lips and smiled through the pain still pulsing in his foot. He would make it out of here alive.

"Well your improvisation is terrible," the first voice said, louder now. Keebo's smile disappeared as he recognized the speaker. *Larrince?! What is he doing here? And what does he have to do with this?* "Next time you want to improvise, don't."

"Klaggen believed him, didn't he?"

"Klaggen is a fool; he wanted to believe it. If anyone comes asking, they'll see through it in an instant."

"And all they'll find is a well that's dried up and filled in. Unless you think they'll dig?"

"Hurry up down there!" came shouted from somewhere even further away.

There was silence except for rapid shoveling and sweet, life-giving dirt raining down on top of the millstone. After long moments dragged by, the light flared again; it revealed a smooth mound of dirt, and not one visible speck of millstone in the hole. Keebo had even magicked a little in front of his alcove to help hide it from view.

"Let's go."

Silence dragged on, and still Keebo waited; too soon and he might spoil it all. Finally, he tore a small piece of his vest near the hem and readied it to staunch the bleeding. Several deep breaths, then a command; dirt fled down the side of the millstone and wedged itself under the rim. Keebo blinked as the energy left him; it seemed more than it should have, but he was, after all, trying to lift a ponderous rock.

He pulled his foot free and ceased the spell; stooping, he jammed the rag against his toe and sucked through his nose. He allowed himself a little groan, then, and waited several more long moments.

Finally, gingerly, he removed the rag and touched his toe with a finger. Scowling, he fluttered his finger around the edges. "Hmph." It was still there, and seemed intact. There were two parallel cuts, but surely...

He reached out a hand and touched the top of the millstone, below the dirt; it was smooth. The cutting edge, then, was on the bottom. He stooped again, running his finger on the underside; sure enough, he felt the grooves. His toe must have ended up between them. If he had been the same size he was five months ago, or if they had dropped it upside down...

"Well, then," he whispered, straightening. He clambered out on top of the dirt-covered stone, checking his toe one last time; no fresh blood, though it throbbed inconsolably. "Quit whining," he admonished it. "We're all alive, and we're going to get to the bottom of this." He glanced up, rubbing his hands. "Well, to the top first; then the bottom—oh, *Oren, Oren...*" Chunks of dirt lodged themselves against the side of the well, making a ladder—a less-expensive spell than carrying him bodily upward.

At the top he paused, pulling himself carefully over the rim of the well and peering about. All remained silent, and still no lights were visible. After being so long in the bottom of the pit, he could feel slight currents of air against his face. He pulled himself slowly clear, and stepped out.

The currents were now at his feet. He followed them carefully to the right, hands groping. He found a stone wall, a corner, then a hinge; he continued across hewn boards, then finally fell upon a latch. *Please don't be locked from outside...* His other hand found a bolt; he turned it and slid it cautiously open, then pulled.

But the door stuck fast. He pulled again, then felt around the edge for a second bolt—nothing. He paused, breathing slowly. Would it be locked from outside as well? With a faint sigh, he pressed his head against the wood.

The door moved slightly. Looking up, he grasped the handle again and pushed. The door swung outward easily, onto cobbled streets washed in moonlight. He peered around, seeing no one. The nearest cross-street was to his left; he darted there, then right, away from Klaggen's home. He continued as swiftly as he could, taking as many random turns as he could while working himself generally northward. He could not risk going back to Westport, in case Nedley was still there. He would have to take the long road to Pael, then Eastport, and then...where?

At least he would have time to think. He had never thought Nedley would be part of this. Larrince was less a surprise, though how he was connected with Klaggen and Tirtar was also a mystery. He seemed too young to have had two careers. Maybe Keebo would have to go back to

Naso Narok, speak to Beroc and find out when Larrince had come to apprentice, if Beroc knew what he had done before that.

Or he could go to Tolma and report this latest. At the very least, Klaggen was taken to deciding cases and pronouncing judgment outside the knowledge of the Steward. Tolma would want to know that. But if Keebo took all the time to get there, still without actual knowledge of who the assassin was, or where Tirtar and Elandra were...

And how was he supposed to find that out, now? He was back to the beginning, no idea where they might be and now no clue as to how to find them. Well, he was passing through Pael; maybe that baker—what was her name? Or even the innkeeper, she had remembered the troupe—they might have overheard some of the names of Tirrin's co-actors, and know where they could be found. It was slim, but a chance.

But then, they clearly were all watching out for one another. And it only took one of them to learn Keebo was alive, and know that he shouldn't be, for everything to go sideways again. One thing was for sure, he would start carrying a bit of dirt with him. Sad, he thought as he scooped a bit out of the ground and put it in his pocket, that for 150 years he had felt perfectly safe. Now he was forced to carry a weapon with him, something he had never even considered before. People got hurt carrying weapons around with them.

Or they hurt others. Like with knives. His mind kept coming back to that fact. He tried to recall again the knife in the vision that had killed Jon, but it slipped away. At the time he thought it had been a plain knife. Now there was a chance it was one of only a few.

All the knives that he had seen, since this case started, flashed through his mind. Shokalog had one; the man in Pael had one; Strake; Tolma; Larrince. Even Elandra had one.

Keebo's brow furrowed as he lay awake in the yurt, partway to Pael. Where had Elandra gotten hers? Tolma had said the four were for himself, Jonkar, Strake, and a gift. Keebo had only seen two that he could verify: Larrince's, and the one Elandra had gotten—from where? Tolma had showed him the knife he had taken from Strake, but Keebo had only labelled it as another plain knife—had it been one of the Malgus blades? But if Tolma had Strake's, and Jonkar had his when his body had been recovered, that left Tolma's that he had not yet seen.

But where would Elandra have gotten hers? It made the most sense that Jonkar would have given it to her, but then he wouldn't have had it on him. Perhaps Tolma or Strake had gifted theirs, to either Elandra or Tirtar; and Strake's knife that Tolma had shown him was not one of the Malgus blades.

But all of this rested on questioning Elandra or Tirtar, whom he could not find; and Tolma, whom he was not yet ready to see—not without better evidence. He sighed and rolled over. And all this depended on what knife had actually killed Jonkar. As sleep finally came, he knew: he would have to return to Nobak and watch the murder again. He also knew he had fallen asleep with happier thoughts.

20

A Dead Suspect

"I've found Tirtar."
"I do not recall asking you to do that."
"It was an accident? He's in—"
"Keep it to yourself, for now."

36 Haschina 1321 — Rainy

As Keebo's boat neared Northport on Sed Narok, he peered through the misting rain. He had been cautious at Eastport, scanning warily for Nedley's sails. He could be anywhere on these Islands. But Keebo had fairer weather that first time; now he could be almost on top of it and not see it, especially if Nedley was docked with furled sails.

Many boats were in port, today; not many Clansmen traveled on soaking days like this. Hopefully the Captains and Calderons would be below decks or holed up in town. Keebo had no intention of sticking around. He paid his own captain a little extra in return for memory loss, and hurried inland. The port itself was buttoned up tightly; once, passing a ramshackle tavern, a door had opened suddenly and Keebo had a spell on his lips an instant before he knew the man was too large by far to be Nedley.

In short order, Keebo was outside the port and heading inland toward Maerc. He hoped the rain would hold, and he could pass through quickly and sleep outside of town in the folds of the hills. He had gotten far more limber on his feet in the past months—his toe had finally quit complaining just outside Pael—and distances like this were not as daunting as they once were. Still, he vowed to himself that once this mystery was solved, he would go back home, rebuild, and rest and eat until he got back to proper girth. If nothing else, he was tired of cinching his belt so tightly.

Ten miles down the road, the mist cleared and the rain became a sparse drizzle. Fifteen, and even that stopped. He hurried his pace, to no avail; as Maerc came into view the clouds departed, and an evening sun shone gloriously down upon the city.

He could not pass by without stopping for supplies; it was a long road to Nobak, two days at least, and no wild fruit would yet be ripe. He pulled a little at his hair, snugged his vest a little closer, and grumbled. Winter in Andelen or Gintanos, one could wear thick cloaks with hoods, and hide; not so much in the Islands.

The streets were comparatively teeming when Keebo entered the town. Small children splashed in puddles while their parents haggled with vendors, and dogs bayed after each other. It felt almost festive, but Keebo could not join the celebration. He tried to appear calm, but jumped every time a door slammed, and turned suddenly at every quick patter of feet.

Finally he found a vendor selling cured goods, and purchased enough for four days. He thanked the man, tried to convince himself the look he got in return was not suspicious, and darted down a side street when that failed.

He wound his way through the back streets of the city, only getting lost twice. Finally he could see fields ahead of him, and he smiled in the gathering gloom. In short order he would have darkness and valleys to protect him until he could continue his journey to the old ruins.

Then, ahead of him, a man walking by a cross street glanced, then skidded to a stop. He squinted as Keebo's steps faltered, then his eyes widened.

"Keebo?" he asked, beginning to turn.

Keebo didn't recognize the man, but neither was he taking chances. As the man strode toward him, Keebo turned back and ran. With a glance and quick words he cast the dirt from his bag into the man's face, plastering it over the man's eyes as a blindfold. He kicked up some of the dirt from the alley for good measure, then turned right as the man cried out. He pushed himself to run faster, turning again; he had to make it to the open fields.

His heels began to ache, but another quick glance showed him no one was following. Still he pressed faster, breaking away from the city. The cool grass and earth felt good beneath his feet. A low hill to his right beckoned him; he ran behind it, then fell to the grass, panting. He allowed himself only a moment, then looked back: the man was nowhere to be seen.

A few more short gasps and Keebo pushed himself to his feet, running at a low crouch with the hill between him and Maerc. More and larger hills loomed out of the dusk, and he wove between them. He paused at the road south, glancing quickly, then dashed across. A great forested valley opened beneath him, and he descended rapidly. Halfway down, his exhausted legs fell behind and he tumbled. He came to rest, mostly unscathed but his chest still heaving. He lay there, facing up the hill, for long moments as he caught his breath. No one followed.

Finally he rolled himself over and stood: not what he intended, but effective. The sound of trickling water drew him on, and he soon found a spring and drank. He sat and dunked his legs, appreciating the cold waters on his minor cuts. As he sat, he looked around the trees; there was not much undergrowth here, but some, and probably enough to hide at least until morning. But he would want an early start, and dawn likely came late down here.

He took another several drinks, then heaved himself up and began climbing the southern slope. The night was quiet, and he moved slowly—partially from caution, mostly from fatigue. As he neared the top he found a tree that had nearly fallen, opening a small bowl behind it in the ground. He drew in some ferns for bedding, magicked a few pits around him for traps, and fell asleep.

Dawn still came late, even on the edge of the valley. Keebo awoke, listening carefully, hearing nothing but birds and a sounder of pigs far down below. He ceased the pit spells and left the forest, still keeping to the hills as he made his way south. Clouds scudded in as Noon wore on, and shortly after lunch rain began to fall that did not let up through the night. Still, he made better time than he thought; as he turned east next morning to make for the ruins, his only concern now was whether the sun would return by evening.

By dinner, he knew it wouldn't matter; weariness caught up with him, and as he stood at the head of the valley leading down to Nobak, the sun was almost set behind him and the ruins were cast in shadow. He descended slowly, watching his footing in the gloom and the wet. As darkness deepened, the ruins seemed even more menacing and he decided to pass through them and stay on the beach. Woody vines still clacked, echoing among the walls, and drops of rain found pools so their plonking sometimes sounded like feet on stone.

With a shiver, Keebo hurried away until the sound was overwhelmed by surf on the beach. The clouds began to thin, and the moon shone on the white sands. He wanted to go down to the waters, but knew his dark shape would stand out against the foam, visible to anyone out to sea or at the top of the valley. A small chance, but tonight, one he was not willing to take. He moved back into the shelter of the palms and slept fitfully, hopefully for the last night until he at least had some answers.

The next day dawned bright and clear; the clouds' rearguard moved south-east, still trailing its attack against the ocean. Keebo enjoyed a quick breakfast of sausage and cheese, but decided to stay on the beach, for now; nothing would be happening at the ruins for most of the day. He tried putting the murder far out of his mind, having no new answers anyway; but the looming potential behind him made it difficult. He tried to imagine scenarios—if the knife was plain, what then? And what if it was indeed the Malgus blade? He would certainly need to talk to Tolma then, and try to account for each knife. But he also still needed to find Elandra and Tirtar regardless, and finding them would be impossible without help, or absurd luck. Maybe he would go back to Beroc, see if he could turn up anything there.

He swam a bit in the warm surf, then came back for lunch, his gaze still across the ocean. Far out he thought he saw white sails—but those could be headed for Southport. Though he was an earth wizard, and appreciated it above all else, there was something about the ocean that still drew him. Probably why he stayed on the Islands.

He dusted his hands and stood. He determined to search a bit through the ruins as Evening drew on. He checked the sun; he had one or two Shifts before he would need to be in the room, singing.

In the sun, though fading, the ruins were not quite so scary. And since this time he knew what he was here for, he was not so apprehensive as that first trip last year. Now, as he wandered with a little less purpose, they only seemed sad. If one could only clear out the vines and ferns, it would be quite beautiful. Clean up those stones and repair the house wall, and that bench could once again seat two folk in close conversation. From it, you could watch the sun set over the bay. Rebuild the tower and hang the bells—though, Shokalog mentioned they didn't use bells. Great, deep horns, he'd said—something that reminded you of the breadth of the ocean, or surf pounding from far away. Those would sound across the town to call Anoe to pray, or ceremonies at the water's edge.

He had wondered, the first time in, why the fountain pool was so large; now he guessed it was practical, a place for Anoe to douse themselves when feeling dry. All the little blocks of stone like toadstools ringing it were perhaps to rest at its edge.

Wherever he looked, he saw not only the crumbling remains of a settlement, but broken reminders of community. Clansmen towns were not like this, and as he looked about now, he missed it.

He caught himself standing long at one square, gazing sightless at what appeared to be a stone arbor, now overshadowed by palm. He awoke because the duskgleam there had begun to open its flowers. He glanced worriedly at the sun, then turned and raced for the chamber where Jonkar had been killed.

He slowed as he neared, catching his breath. The disturbed dust at the doorway had been mostly smoothed by the intervening winds and rain, but he remembered the hinges and the table inside. The sun's rays broke through the leafy branches and holes in the walls just as it had before. With one final, long breath, he began to sing.

Jon appeared almost instantly, already part-way through the conversation. Keebo moved forward, studying Jon's face more closely. Whoever he was speaking to, he clearly cared for them. And yet, he grew frustrated. His demeanor changed subtly, but quickly. Perhaps Tolma had been right about the prince's attitudes of late; perhaps he had been taken by the same madness as the Andelian. But why? How?

Keebo did not flinch this time as the knife appeared; he inspected it closely: the images conjured during these songs were always slightly translucent, so he could not make out any particular coloring. Yet the three pins on the handle were evident. When Jon pulled it free, Keebo leaned in: there were faint markings on the blade almost like wood grain.

It was a Malgus knife. He needed to locate all four. He would have to go to Tolma, even if he could not yet point to the exact killer. If only he could find Elandra or Tirtar along the way! Questioning them could reveal everything.

Keebo straightened, unconsciously still singing the song. There seemed nothing else to see; he turned away from the scene, then fell back with a yelp.

But the man in the corner disappeared as soon as the song left his lips. Panting, Keebo glanced wildly about the room. It was empty; even Jon's image had gone. Cautiously, curiously, Keebo picked up the song again.

In the sunbeams, the man re-appeared, gazing at Jon—no, just in Jon's direction. Keebo stood, moving to the side; the man did not follow him. But, if he was there only during the singing, he would be dead. A second victim he had missed the first time?

The man was tall and thin, with black hair. He wore a cloak that didn't move; strange attire for the Islands. But there was something wrong with his face. Keebo moved closer, cautious but in haste before the man disappeared.

He was burned, his face scarred horribly. As Keebo studied him, a curious thought came to his head. Stepping quickly, he moved around behind the image. The back of the man's cloak was torn, his skin punctured as though by several short spikes. All at once, questions pounded though Keebo's mind.

When had the survivors of Nutar Ha begun attacking him?

When had Jonkar begun changing?

When had Tolma purchased the knives?

When had Deuel and Catie said Roth began going insane?

When had Haydren said he had killed Lasserain?

The answer in his head echoed like bells rung:

Halmfurtung.

Halmfurtung.

Halmfurtung.

Halmfurtung.

HALMFURTUNG!

The song died on his lips once more as his breath caught in his throat. As the image of Lasserain faded away, Keebo turned and ran. Outside, he cast about wildly for pieces of wood, whispering desperately that they would be dry. He gathered fallen leaves, sticks, bits of rotted cloth, shattered timbers—anything he could find that would burn, and piled them high. His hands shook as he fumbled with flint and steel from his pouch; one, two, three strikes and a bit of tinder caught. He snapped his fingers waiting for the flame to catch enough to coax larger, without blowing it out. Finally the little flame spread, and Keebo put his breath to work, hoping also to calm down a little.

Soon enough the fire was raging; it reached high into the sky, a blazing bonfire. *Melnor, Melnor, Melnor...* he repeated. Supposedly it did not help conjure the Triumvir, but Keebo thought maybe he only said that to avoid being distracted.

"May I be of service?" a voice said beside Keebo.

He turned; Melnor was looking at him patiently. "By the God, I hope so."

Melnor's expression became sober. "Have you found out who murdered the prince."

"If I were you, I would stop worrying about the world here and look after your own," Keebo said. When Melnor's brow furrowed, Keebo continued, chilled by his own words.

"There's another Triumvirate, manipulating people to do evil; and Lasserain is part of it."

21

THE ONES UNKNOWN

"About time you've come, Kanala."
"I came as swift as I could, Teresh. Where is Melnor?"
"Below; we are in trouble."
"You have said that before."

3 Mantaver 1321 — Rainy

Melnor shook his head. "Not like this," he muttered. His gaze came back to Keebo. "How do you know this?"

"I find it suspicious that the same month Haydren kills Lasserain, a series of strange events occurs at the same time, events that look very much like your own manipulations. And during my kin-song just now, I saw Lasserain in the room at the time Jonkar was killed."

"But why now? Surely such a—an entity would have existed alongside the Triumvirate for centuries now."

"Are you sure it hasn't?"

"We have seen..." Melnor trailed off, his eyes tracking sideways. "I do not recall seeing evidence, but perhaps it was; we never thought to look for it. Surely if we occupied the same mind...maybe they have been lucky. Unless they know about us when we don't know about them? How could it happen?"

"Lasserain knew about you, didn't he? You told me once you sent men after him."

Melnor's gaze lowered. "He does know about us. Perhaps he brought the knowledge to them. And we can assume, as we serve the God of All, they serve Illmali—this is very bad. Why would not the God have told us?" He said the last more to himself, but Keebo shrugged.

"You'll have to ask him, I suppose."

Melnor's eyes burned. "I will. For now, we will have to focus more on finding this...what should we call them? The Black Triumvirate?"

Keebo slowly folded his arms and gave Melnor the grumpiest look he could twist onto his face.

Melnor smiled tightly. "Forgive me; the obvious opposite to the White, I did not think it through. Perhaps if we put a plain face on it, we will have the proper fear: the Unknown. Surely their plans are grander than just toppling governments. Lasserain's plan certainly was. Now that I look back on it, perhaps it should have been clearer."

"How so?"

"When Haydren killed him, the last thing he said was 'thank you.' I assumed he hated what he had become and was grateful it was over. Clearly we have underestimated how evil he was—what his true dreams were."

Keebo shook his head. "I'm still not sure I understand."

"Think of it: when we seek to replace one of our numbers, we scour the continents for worthy wizards. How might the Unknown prove themselves? Perhaps by causing so much destruction, and being killed only by a great warrior—perhaps one of our chosen—hopeful wizards or mages prove themselves worthy of being raised to their ranks. Lasserain also seemed very adamant that Haydren had to be the one to fight him." Melnor paused and shook his head. "I believe I have chosen a proper name for them: Unknown defines every thought I have, except that they exist. And perhaps they have existed right alongside us since the beginning; perhaps they began the Age of War, though the God redeemed that time in his own way." He shook his head again. "I must return. There is much my brothers and I must discuss, and some questions I have for the God of All, as well."

"What should I do?"

Melnor hesitated, mouth opened part way. He pressed his lips together quickly, then spoke. "Tirtar and Elandra are hiding in a house in Maerc. Ask for Buras; then search the bedroom for a false floor."

"You should not have given me that information."

"We too are allowed a certain amount of free will, remember? Until I understand the mind of the God on this matter—well, it's too late anyway. Besides, I do not know what they will say, or if it will sort out this mess." He turned as if to walk away, then turned back. "Oh, and Keebo?"

Keebo raised his eyebrows.

"Don't ever summon me again that way; I am not yours to command."

"I deemed it important."

"I check on you frequently; anything you know can wait until then. Just light a flame occasionally, in case I need to visit." He smiled, then disappeared.

Keebo glowered. "But apparently I am yours to command," he muttered, turning away. "We should have called Lasserain and his brothers the old cranky Triumvirate."

He turned the corner of a building, surprising himself and three men who waited there in a crouch. Keebo leapt back, beginning a spell.

"Wait!" One man stood, arms outstretched. "We mean you no harm!"

"Where did you come from?" Keebo demanded, holding soil suspended in front of himself.

"Our boat," the man continued quickly, pointing toward the bay. "We saw your fire and thought someone might be in trouble. We thought this land uninhabited."

Keebo sighed. "It is, usually. I am Keebo, an earth wizard sent to solve—" He cut himself off; they would think it was already solved. "To resolve, rather, a possible threat to the Islands."

"The death of Prince Jonkar," the man said. "It happened here, did it not?"

"It did, but the threat is bigger than we anticipated." *So, so much bigger.* "Who are you?"

"Corl," he said. "First mate on *The Starling Spray.* These are some of our men, Marun and Deas. Can we take you somewhere? We were headed to Southport; but, for a threat against the Islands, I'm sure the Captain would be eager..."

"I would thank you if you could take me back to Northport, actually; I must get to Maerc."

The man relaxed with a smile. "Of course; come with us."

⸺◦⸺

The Starling Spray sent Keebo ashore at Northport the next morning, keeping the boat at sea ready to turn again to the south. Keebo thanked them and headed inland for Maerc.

It was nearing Evening when he arrived, but most shops were still open. He made his way through the market, asking vendors for Buras. Finally, an old toothless woman behind five mounds of spices directed him to Korless Street; there, he found a young man just departing who directed him to a home of moderate size just past the next cross-street. Much like Klaggen's, it was one of the nicest homes on the street. Being a performer in the Clanaso Islands clearly paid much handsomer than being a wizard. Keebo shrugged it off and knocked on the door.

After a long pause, he knocked again and readied some dirt; something felt off. The street was growing darker, and he did not like the silence before him. He startled, turning as shutters clattered closed behind him. As he turned back, he caught movement at the corner of the row of houses. He sighed, knocked again, and waited. Finally, he turned and walked away from where he had seen the movement.

At the cross street he turned left, then waited, counting silently. At thirty, he turned and went back the way he came. A thin man in dark clothes halfway up the street paused mid-stride, and his shoulders sagged.

"I suppose that was too easy, even for you," he said. "Although, you *are* supposed to be dead. Should I try to run?"

Keebo smiled and held up his fistful of dirt. "Only if you can run faster than five horses," he said.

Buras shook his head and continued toward his home. "Come on in, then," he said with a wave. "Just out of curiosity, how did you survive that?" He produced a key and unlocked the door.

"One of the stones lining the well had not been cut," Keebo replied, following the man inside. "I was able to reach through and create a depression behind it to hide in. Still nicked my toe, though."

Buras paused before lighting a lamp, and grunted. "Clever."

"And lucky," Keebo said.

"You're here to see Tirrin, I presume?"

Keebo smiled. "And Elandra."

Buras grunted again. "Of course. Follow me." He led the way down a long hall, then into a room on the right. He shoved the bed sideways a few feet, then lifted and twisted a small metal ring in the floorboards. With a heave, a door opened and steps descended into a lighted room, of which only the facing wall was visible. Leaving the lantern, Buras led the way down the steps. "Tirrin?" he called. "Visitor; I think we need to sort this out."

When Keebo reached the bottom of the steps and turned, he saw Tirrin standing at a table as though interrupted. Elandra sat across from him, her expression resigned.

"Well," Keebo said, placing his hands on his hips. "Imagine my surprise at finding you two here. Miss Tarabar, you look in very good health for one who has died. And, *Tirtar*, your expression does not match one whose daughter has come back from the dead. Shall we reset the stage?"

Tirrin smiled nervously, and sat back down. "This isn't what it appears."

"You lied to me during the investigation of a murder, and now you're hiding in the secret room of a friend, with whom you once worked as an actor."

"We did not kill the prince."

"Of course you didn't," Keebo replied, his smile widening and becoming more false. "No one did. He stabbed himself with his own knife."

Tirrin glanced at Elandra and Buras. "Do you know, that might not be far from the truth?"

Keebo folded his arms. "Buras, would you mind taking a seat with them? Thank you; now, let's start from the top. Elandra, why are you not dead?"

"We faked my suicide, trying to figure out who might be a threat to Prince Jonkar."

Keebo stared at them. "Okay, perhaps you tell me where the top is, and work your way down."

She sighed, clasping her hands on the table. "Almost a year ago, Jonkar began to worry that someone might be trying to kill him—he was nearing the age to inherit the throne, and he knew his policies were not going to be well-received. Just showing interest in deep-water boats had already brought envoys from several quarters questioning the wisdom and, from some of them, warning of ramifications if he pursued the path."

"He received death threats? Was this near Halmfurtung last year?"

"No death threats, they were not that forthcoming," Elandra said, as the others shook their heads. "And it *was* Halmfurtung; how did you—?"

"Doesn't matter. Proceed, please."

"Okay. He didn't trust any of his usual advisors, so he turned to me." She paused, stilling her quivering lip. "We were already deeply in love, and when he knew who my father was and how he was connected, he set up his own information network. Many of us came from outside the Islands, so we obviously would not share some of the prejudices of those threatening him."

"Sounds like a good plan," Keebo commented.

"It worked the first month or so," Elandra replied. "But soon he began to worry about us. Many who knew did not approve of our courtship, and he worried that those opposing him might become suspicious of our relationship and look at it more closely. If nothing else, if we ever ascended the throne together, my history would certainly come up."

Keebo nodded. It was customary in Clanaso inheritance to conduct a full investigation of inheritor's lineages.

"He worried that such an investigation would reveal his secret network. So he came up with this idea of appearing to spurn me because of that lineage, and spread a rumor that I was a whore. I would commit suicide and disappear for some time—until after he assumed the throne, and until he could uncover what, if any, plots might be against him. After that I could return, and we could be married."

"Why suicide? Why couldn't you just have left the Islands?"

"That was Jon's idea, I'm not sure I fully understood it," Elandra replied. "Something about not wanting the possibility that I could return—I never understood if it was for my safety or...someone else's."

"Fine. Did you uncover any plots before he was killed?"

Buras glanced at Tirtar and took a breath. "Nothing definitive," he said slowly.

"I'll take something indefinitive," Keebo said drily.

"The strongest threat came from the shallow-water ships guild," Buras said. "We never quite found the head, but rumors were circling of what might happen if more and more deep-water ships were built."

"Does your network know why deep-water ships are pirating the passengers of shallow-water ships? I was picked up several times, and relations are certainly...strained."

"As far as we can tell, that's unrelated," Tirrin replied. "Although, it's likely that the deep-water captains are aware of the threat to their trade now that Jonkar is dead, so..." He spread his hands wide.

Keebo chewed his lip. "Why did your network try to kill me?"

All three shifted uncomfortably, and it was Buras who finally spoke. "Well, we are sorry about that; but we were told your loyalty to the Anoe was above all else and your sole purpose would be to shift the blame off of them. We could not trust that you would treat Tirrin fairly. With you gone, perhaps we could find an investigator with a fairer mind."

Keebo glowered. "Who told you that?"

Buras shook his head. "I was not part of that investigation," he said, and glanced at his companions. "None of us were. But word of the judgement went out after the fact."

"Fine. Where do we stand, now? Why did you say the thought of Jonkar killing himself might not be far from the truth?"

Tirrin shrugged, and Keebo could sense some exasperation. "Because we can't find anything out about who might have. We even questioned those traveling with Jonkar—everyone says he was the only one who rode away that day."

"Who was the man the Steward sent after Jonkar when he was late coming back?"

Glances again, as everyone hesitated. "Well," Tirrin said. "It was Torin, actually; he's my youngest brother, used to run the backdrops of our plays, just before Klaggen decided to disband the troupe."

"Why did he do that? Klaggen, that is."

Tirrin shrugged. "We had a good run; he was growing tired of the travel. He had his home by then, and said he wanted to settle there. No one wanted to continue without him, so we all found new jobs."

Keebo's brow furrowed. "Fine, so you said—who was with the princes? Torin? I feel like I know that name..."

Elandra smiled weakly. "I'm sure you do," she said. "He's Nedley's Calderon."

22

A Surprise Visit

"Kanala has returned to Gintanos."
"Good. There is still much on Oren we must handle."
"What of this new Triumvirate?"
"It seems that is for us to discover."

4 Mantaver 1321 — Rainy

"Please don't be mad at Nedley," Elandra said quickly, holding up a hand as Keebo's glower became a fire.

"Why not? He hit me over the head with a giant..." Keebo trailed off, fuming: he had not actually seen what Nedley hit him with.

"We were acting in what we thought was the best interest of the Islands—the Islands that Prince Jonkar wanted," Buras said.

"I don't even know what he wanted, anymore," Keebo muttered. "But I doubt it was to have highly-respected earth wizards bashed over the head, thrown into a well, with a giant millstone to follow."

"Klaggen's methods are...unique," Buras allowed. "But he has always gone about things his own way. Nedley should not be blamed for that, either."

Keebo shook his head. "How does Larrince fit into all this? I would have thought as a member of the shallow-water ships guild, he would not be trusted."

The three exchanged puzzled frowns. "We didn't know he did fit into this," Tirrin said, turning back.

"He was there, helping fill in the well with dirt after the millstone had been dropped in. It seemed he had influenced someone named Jenzi?"

Tirrin's and Buras' faces hardened; Elandra's looked guilty. "Jenzi was responsible for investigating you," Buras growled. "Master Keebo, if what you say is true I must apologize—we all must. We must also look into this; what exactly did Larrince say?"

"He reprimanded the other shoveler, said that he should not have improvised when speaking to Jenzi, and should have only said what Larrince had told him to say."

"How could he have done so?" Buras asked Tirrin. "If this other man had been anyone Jenzi knew, he should not have taken only his word for it." He turned back to Keebo. "Do you know who the other man was? Did you recognize his voice, too?"

"No, Larrince was the only one I recognized. But it would seem your little network is not as full-proof as you would ask me to believe."

"But now that we know this, we will look into it. Perhaps this other man had not been with us as long, did not hold the same loyalties as we would like. Without knowing who he was..." Buras spread his hands.

"And you trust Torin? Trust he could not be bought? Likely, this other man was."

Tirrin glared at Keebo. "Torin would not; for one thing, he is doing quite well as Nedley's Calderon, now they are Royal Ferrymen."

"Yes, that's something else curious, isn't it? Before this all started, a friend of mine and Captain had been told he would be Royal Ferryman; Larrince had been told he would be, as well; and yet Nedley and Torin end up with it. Trying to get into the Steward's good graces for some reason? Maybe to be available once Strake can leave Nak again?"

Buras settled back. "I can only say that no, that's not what we're trying to do. Jonkar trusted us, and we loved and trusted him to do what was right."

Keebo sighed. "What about when he began changing his mind?"

Elandra furrowed her brow and shook her head. "He wasn't changing his mind."

"I was told by several people he was. When did you last speak to him?"

"At No—" She cut herself off, shaking her head with a short sigh.

Keebo's eyes went wide. "At Nobak?" he asked, his voice rising. "The day he was killed?"

Elandra bowed her head, and nodded. "It wasn't—"

"What I think—it never is what I think, is it." Keebo ground his teeth. "Is that when you got the knife? Did he give you his?"

"He was getting worried; he said he had heard rumors that people were suspecting I was not actually dead. He gave it to me to protect myself."

"How did you come to meet him at the ruins?"

"That's where I was staying, in hiding. He would meet me there on occasion—whenever he was on the island and could get away."

"And why did you try to kill me with it, last year?"

Elandra's eyes dropped as Tirrin's jaw set. "Yes, about that mistake," her father said, looking at her pointedly.

"I guess...I've blamed Tolma for Jon's death since the beginning. Not on any evidence; but he is the Steward—he's supposed to protect the heirs until they can ascend the throne." She looked at Keebo sorrowfully. "When I saw you, and you said you were his friend, I just..." She held out supplicating hands. "I'm sorry, something just..."

Keebo was unmoved. "Something seems to always 'just,'" he said bitterly. "That doesn't explain why you were there in the first place, if you're supposed to be hiding. So here's what's going to happen; Elandra, you are coming with me to Nak to be presented to the Steward. He can make use of your little network if he chooses to, or he can destroy it."

"Keebo, wait—"

"I will not," Keebo said, hating the little bit of pout in his voice. "I've been lied to since the beginning, and I tire of it and the questions that are always answered by lies. You and your little group were the last to see him alive on numerous occasions, and I have nothing but your word that you were worthy of his trust—promises that, in the light of all other evidence, mean absolutely nothing to me."

"Wouldn't we have lied about our involvement, if it would have incriminated us?" Buras asked.

"That will be for Tolma to determine," Keebo replied.

"The Steward?" Tirrin asked. "The one who executed an Anoe out of convenience?"

Keebo set his jaw. "Let's go. Just Elandra," he continued coldly as all three began to stand. "If it suits you, I would rather you other two stay here for now."

"I'm not sure you can make—" Buras choked off as Keebo bound them to the chairs with loops of stone.

"Don't worry," he said; "I've added a time limit to this spell—just enough to let us be on our way before you're free. You won't starve. Elandra?" he said, magically binding her hands behind her back and drawing her forward. "I will do my best to protect her," he assured Tirrin as they began climbing the stairs back to the bedroom above.

"Cold comfort," he heard Tirrin mutter as he shut the trapdoor. Keebo shook his head, casting a thin smile at Elandra.

"I hope you can appreciate my position," he said as he led her through the house.

She sighed. "I can. I know exactly how it looks, especially for you. I hope you can appreciate my fears as well."

Keebo was silent for a few moments as they walked down the street in the dark. "I can," he said finally. He let go a frustrated burst of air. "But I don't know what else to do."

He led her outside Maerc, out again into the hills. After a few hours he turned off the road, finding a spot in the brush to hide them in case Tirrin or Buras decided to try to rescue her. He gently but securely bound her in earth, and they slept without incident.

The next morning they were heading west toward the port; Keebo kept them off the road, fearing ambush. Shortly after a brief lunch they reached the docks. Keebo paused just south of the port, scanning the ships tied up there. Among the bobbing masts and occasionally blooming sail, he saw Nedley's boat.

Keebo chewed his lip. He probably needed the Captain and his Calderon to report with him to Tolma. But if their loyalties lay with their community rather than the Islands, it was a sure way to die. He cocked his head; perhaps there was a way to use that loyalty.

"I'm sorry I have to do this, Miss Tarabar," he said, turning to her. She gazed back with patient anxiety. "I'm going to need you as a sort of hostage, until Nedley sails us safely to Nutar Ha."

Impressively, she made no sound—just gave a short, resigned nod. He led her down to the docks and approached Nedley's boat.

Word traveled fast within this group, for Nedley did not even seem surprised to see them. "Ah, Master Keebo," he said. "Come aboard. Nutar Ha, was it?"

"Indeed it is—unless there's something you can say now that will immediately absolve your Calderon."

Nedley shrugged. "Afraid not. He was in and out of my service those past months; I can't say what he might or didn't do."

"You also know I may have trouble trusting you not to kill me in my sleep, or at least dump me overboard."

"I promised you when we first met I could take you safely anywhere."

Keebo barked a short laugh. "That rang true until Klaggen's home."

"Those were—"

Keebo held up a hand. "Special circumstances, yes; ones which, according to you, have changed. Forgive me if I don't see it that way."

Nedley spread his hands. "I'm listening."

"You, of course, recognize Elandra Tarabar," he said, turning to her. Nedley nodded assent. "Well, here's how we do it—please turn around, dear. I have cast a magical binding around her wrists—not too tight, of course, I'm not that kind of man. You'll notice though—" He paused to whisper a few words. This time, Elandra did make a small noise of surprise. "They are now made of rock. Still, not too tight?" He asked it of her; she shook her head with a tremulous smile. "Good. Now, I can free her from these quite easily. But if you would try to break them, however—" He paused again, spreading his hands with an apologetic smile.

"Orchids. I get you to Nutar Ha safely, she's released from her rocky bonds, we go see the Steward."

"And get your good names cleared, if they are so now." He sobered. "And may you rot with The Riven if they are not."

As they sailed, Keebo would occasionally and without warning free Elandra from her bindings for a brief time—never so regularly that they could plot against him and overthrow him while she was free. Though she was grateful, their attitude remained patient as though they had never thought to fight back. Maybe they did not. But it was with no small relief to Keebo when they raised the mountains of Nutar Ha after lunch the next day.

The guards on the docks appeared distracted by an earlier arriving boat, and when they recognized Keebo flew into a flurry of activity.

"Master Keebo," one said, huffing; he was wearing the pins of a Captain. "We did not expect you; are we to escort you to Nak to see the Steward?"

"I wouldn't mind," Keebo said placidly. "Is there some news?" he asked, glancing at the other ship, where soldiers paused with their necks twisted to watch the Captain as if anticipating contradictory orders.

"No, of course not; just—usually we receive word, is all, and prepare a better greeting." He flapped his hands at his soldiers, who immediately turned back to work. "If you don't mind, give me a few moments to gather a squad together to take you inland. Will you require horses? Or a cart?" He glanced meaningfully at Elandra, who remained bound.

"Oh, of course not—not a cart," he replied. He muttered, and Elandra's restraints turned to sand and blew away.

The Captain swallowed. "Very well; please, follow me."

As he turned, Keebo thought he caught some faint movement of the Captains fingers. He might have thought it nervousness, except a soldier further up the docks immediately turned, mounted, and galloped up the road.

"He seems to be in a hurry," Keebo commented as they made for a small squat building just up the beach.

"Of course," the Captain said, failing to hide the nervous shake in his voice. "The Steward will want to know you're coming."

"Will he indeed," Keebo mused. It might be funny to surprise his old friend. They reached the building, and the Captain held open the door. Keebo stood aside, allowing his charges to proceed ahead of him. "After you, Captain," he said graciously, bowing.

"Oh, um, thank you." The Captain stepped inside.

Keebo slammed the door, running toward the road. He heard the door bang open and the Captain shout orders, but he didn't stop. Soon the sand turned to dirt, and Keebo hastily assembled a plate. Still running, he hopped on as he commanded it to skim inland as quickly as he dared make it go. It shot forward, seeming eager to be off. The Captain's voice, and the ensuing pounding of hooves, receded quickly behind him as the wind flattened his hair against his scalp.

It was an exhilarating ride—faster than any he'd done previously. Strangely, he didn't feel the drain on his energy he thought he should. He wondered briefly if being 'friends' with the element did have some hidden benefits. But those thoughts fell away behind him as well, and he simply enjoyed the ride, laughing giddily as he whipped past the rider who had been sent ahead.

As the road began to wind familiarly, another thought struck him: what if the defenders perceived him as a threat, and loosed the traps guarding the way?

Before he could decide, he was past the first one. He needn't have worried: moving as quickly as he was, he skimmed through the line of attack before anyone on the hills would have been able to react. He saw one boulder begin to move, glancing behind as it crashed onto the road by the time he was a hundred yards beyond it.

The fortification loomed ahead of him; he had made it in half a Shift, when walking it would have taken a whole day. Again his eyes went to the bare walls of the queen's tower. It had been so beautiful, once, especially near this time of day. It appeared to be dying now, as she had when Strake was being born. Keebo wondered if that's where the boy's weakness had come from—perhaps he had come too early, or had not gathered the strength he would have from a healthy mother, the way Jonkar had.

The disk slowed, then stopped and sank to the ground. Keebo sat another moment, then slowly got to his feet. He should be almost out of energy, and yet he felt no lack. Another curiosity of magic to be pursued, but not now.

Those at the outer wall had seen him arrive, and apparently under-stood the futility of attempting to restrain him in his current mood. The gate remained open, and the guards did not even pretend to acknowledge him as he walked by. He kept some dirt handy as he strode along the darkening streets, but the city had continued abandoned.

The guards at the citadel looked at him bewildered. He approached calmly, mounting the steps but staying just out of weapon's reach. "I need to see the Steward," he said. His voice echoed against the walls; he hadn't meant to be that forceful about it. Maybe he had.

"Um..." one said.

Before the guard had a chance to find his words, the door behind him opened. Tolma was coming out, his head down. He glanced up, caught sight of Keebo, and froze.

"Burami," he said. "I had no word you were coming." He glanced around quickly as if looking for an errant messenger.

Keebo smiled. "I took other means of travel," he replied. "You should try it sometime, it's breathtaking."

Tolma's smile seemed forced. "You will have to show me," he replied. "But not right this moment; I was about to head to the docks. I received word about a ship...but, I suppose that can wait for another..." He trailed off, looking around as if only just realizing how dark it was getting.

"I would think it could wait until morning," Keebo said. "No use traveling by night, is it?"

"It is, actually," Tolma replied, his smile fading but becoming more assured. "Unless the road is suddenly dangerous at night? I had hoped to be there in the morning."

"Then it can certainly wait another shift; I have news of my investigation, and several suspects that you will need to question. They should be on their way shortly. You can question them in the morning, if you would like."

"Hmm. Perhaps. Well, if it's that important—"

"It is," Keebo replied. "This may go much deeper than we realized."

"Well." Tolma breathed deep as he drew himself up into a more regal bearing. "Please, come inside, then."

"Thank you," Keebo replied with a wide smile. Tolma ushered him in, then led the way up to his chambers on the third floor.

23

BLOOD AND TEARS

"When did Rinc Na invent such technology?"
"Apparently some time ago. May we finish in the Islands first?"
"I merely thought you would want to know."
"I thought the same of you."

6 Mantaver 1321 — Rainy

"Who is on their way?" Tolma asked as Keebo watched an attendant pour a glass of water.

"Nedley, and his Calderon, Torin," Keebo said, raising the glass. "Tirtar's youngest brother."

Tolma's folded hands dropped as Keebo took a drink. "You are wasting—"

Keebo swallowed. "And Elandra."

Tolma stared blankly at him, then folded his arms. "You found her."

Keebo nodded. "Yes, I did."

As the silence stretched on, Tolma's eyes grew steadily wider. "Continue, please," he said finally.

"Oh, I'm sorry," Keebo said, setting down the glass. "After so long of your not listening to me, I guess I grew the habit."

"Well, when you truly bring me something important—"

"The innocence of an Anoe isn't important?"

Tolma's eyes flashed. "Keebo, you gain yourself a little of my patience—"

"Do you know, we were friends, once," Keebo said, hardening his own features. "But lately I've grown weary of your kind of friendship."

"The kind that sticks around when no one else—"

"And why *did* you stick around?" Keebo asked, ignoring Tolma's increasingly-reddening face at every interruption. "I used to appreciate that, possibly to my detriment. Because all you ever do is remind me of my errors—almost as if you don't want me to move on from them, to stay crippled by fear and self-doubt. That does not strike me as much of a friend." Keebo held up his hand to forestall Tolma's open mouth. "But I'm not here to discuss our friendship; I'm here to tell you a story."

Tolma sank a little deeper in his chair, glowering. "I had hoped you would."

"This is the story of a young prince who was trying to change the world—or at least his little corner of it. But because so many feared what he wanted to change, he came to believe there might be some grand conspiracy to assassinate him. And so he set about building his own information network—spies, in his own domain, to look after his interests. He feared so many people so much, that he even hid it from his advisor and Steward. He had a young woman fake her suicide, in order to keep her safe, and arranged secret meetings to find out what his network learned as he neared an age to take the throne.

"This is also a story of a young prince who was lied about—who had it rumored about him that he was changing his mind, turning to appease those who might threaten to dismantle his change—to feel safe from those who might kill him in order to keep things the way they were. But that same secret network who had met him the very day he was killed assures me he was not changing his mind. Isn't that a most interesting story?"

Tolma rolled his eyes. "Keebo, you are still a plain, simple man," he said. "Isn't it more likely he *was* changing his mind—perhaps even threatened to disband that network, and that's why they killed him?"

"I am not that simple," Keebo replied flatly. "Of course I thought that, which is why Elandra is on her way here to be questioned by you. But I did hope to prepare some things beforehand. Would you mind showing me the other two Malgus knives?"

"I only have the one—mine, that is," Tolma replied. "I gave Strake his, again."

"You deemed him well enough for that?"

"I did."

"Then I will need to speak to him—if you don't mind."

Tolma shook his head. "I'm afraid I do mind; he is unwell." He gestured vaguely toward the window. "The weather."

"Tolma, he has never been that fragile."

"He had recovered from the first illness, or so we thought; when he went out into the mountains on his Therian—terrible horse, by the way—he fell back into his illness. I don't want him disturbed."

Keebo pursed his lips. "Tolma, I'm afraid I'm going to have to insist."

Tolma stared darkly at him. "Keebo, I understand your position, but—"

"I am not asking!" Keebo thundered, rising from his seat. "If Strake killed his own brother, he is not fit for the throne. I am not doing this for your sake or mine but for the Islands. Take me to him, or I will find my own way."

"You think you can get past the guards?" Tolma hissed, rising as well.

Keebo's gaze was steady. "With ease," he said quietly. "Don't forget where you are, or the power of the one who made it how it is."

Tolma faltered a little, his eyes darting as if to look outside at the mountain ranges Keebo had raised so many years ago. His glower quickly returned. "Have it your way," he said. "Let me prepare the way. Guard!" The door unlatched behind Keebo and footsteps approached. "Please go up and let my Brightblades know I will be bringing a guest, and to have everything ready."

"Sir," the guard replied; his voice to Keebo sounded uncertain.

"Now!"

"Sir!" came the far-surer response, and a clatter of armor as the guard retreated.

Keebo kept his eyes on Tolma during the exchange; the man was perplexed, that was evident. "I do not mean to bark orders, Tolma," he said. "But it feels as if I have had no help since the first letter you sent me."

"I have helped you, though you choose not to see it," Tolma seethed. "I have given you every accommodation, making sure your expenses were paid, giving you far more time than I should have to look into this matter. I assumed you would be the best man for this job; I'm sorry to find I was wrong."

"I have information now, don't I?"

"You have tiresome meddling."

"Because I'm trying to track down every one of the possible murder weapons?"

"It was Elandra!" Tolma fairly screamed. "She killed him with his own knife after he gave it to her, because he threw her away when he had no more use for her—tried to buy her off with a gift, and failed."

Keebo paused, and slowly nodded. "You may be right," he allowed. "We may find out when she arrives later tonight. For now, may we go and speak to Strake?"

Tolma's lips twisted as he tapped the desk with a finger. Finally, he drew a deep breath and nodded. "We will find out what happened, though I am already quite convinced."

Keebo's smile was not genuine. "I'm sure you are."

Tolma rose stiffly, holding his hand toward the door. "After you, Master Keebo; you do already know the way."

Keebo rose, bowed, and turned for the door. He mostly remembered the way. He closed his eyes briefly as he approached the door, recalling which way they turned. He paused. "He is in the same room as last time?"

he asked—for assurance, but also to take another moment.

"Yes," Tolma replied quietly, following him.

Left. Keebo continued down the hall, noticing the guards' sometimes sideways glances. It was strange for a visitor to be leading the Steward through his own halls, but Tolma seemed in a foul mood. Keebo couldn't blame him, after how roughly he had been treated. Still, certainly no rougher than he deserved.

The way came back to him as they walked, up stairs and down various halls. In short order the Brightblades lined the next hall they turned down. Footsteps quickened behind him as Tolma moved to the front; Keebo glanced at him in some surprise.

"It is expected," Tolma whispered aside to Keebo as he passed. He stopped before Strake's door and waited beside the logbook, gesturing to it. "We do still ask visitors to sign in and out, just as a precaution."

Keebo smiled, and glanced down at the page. "I see not everyone seems to like it, though," he said, indicating the page with the quill as he bent to sign.

"Anything to keep the remaining heir alive," Tolma replied. "Even if it may sometimes seem a burden."

Keebo straightened, and nodded with a smile. "I tried to sign mine a little more legibly, just to be sure."

Tolma did not respond, but opened the door. He held his hand open, indicating Keebo should go first. With another nod, he entered, glancing around for the heir-apparent.

The room was in a certain amount of disarray; the bedclothes were shoved mostly to one side, and Keebo counted at least four different outfits strewn across the rugs. A desk near the window was littered with parchments, more stacked on the chair, and others strewn onto the floor. All appeared to have writing on them. The window itself stood open.

"Strake?" Keebo called out; where was the boy? He hurried over to the desk, twisting himself to look out as Tolma entered the room behind him and closed the door. There was no moon tonight, and from this height Keebo could not make out the ground. "Why would you keep him in here with a window open? I thought he was ill?"

Keebo turned back to face Tolma, who had crossed the room to stand near him. "I thought we had locked it; he must have opened it himself, somehow."

"Well, with a desk right by the window, I can't imagine how he reached it. Strake?" Keebo called out again. One of the tapestries had been cut, he saw; an image of the Teroses standing together had been shredded. "I suppose this is what he did with the knife you gave back to him?" Keebo asked as he crossed over to it.

There, huddled behind a box, was Strake. The knife was still in his hand as he hugged his knees and rocked a little.

"Strake?" Keebo said gently. "It's Keebo. Are you hurt?"

Strake looked up, his face softening into a grin. "Keebo," he said softly.

"So good of you to come. Is Jon with you?"

"He's not, Strake; can you come out from behind there? We should talk about what happened. Can you give me the knife?"

Still smiling, Strake handed it over. Keebo took it gently, glancing at the markings like woodgrain along the blade. Reversing it, he held it out to Tolma handle first. The Steward took it as Strake stood and held his hand out to Keebo. "What do we need to talk about?" Strake asked.

"Where did you get that knife?" Keebo asked.

"Tolma gave it to me once I was feeling better."

"After he took it from you? But where did you get it before that?"

Strake pointed a shaky hand. "F-from Tolma. He's always giving it to me." His face split wider as he laughed. "Not that I mind, of course; it's quite an elegant blade, for certain. Fine craftsmanship."

Keebo glanced at Tolma; the Steward bore a patient smile. "Strake, why did you cut up the tapestry?"

Strake twisted to glance at it, then back at Keebo. "It seemed proper," he said, walking suddenly to the desk. He lifted several parchments and began to read. "I'm the last Terose, so no use pretending we're all together," he continued distractedly. He paused and held out the documents. "Tolma, I do think we need to send a letter to Beroc—tomorrow. Strongest wording possible. I'll draft something tonight, and have the scribes work over it first thing in the morning, would you?"

Before Tolma responded Strake dropped the parchments on the floor and gazed out the window. He began to hum to himself, something bittersweet, it sounded to Keebo's ear.

Keebo turned to Tolma, his voice low. "When you said he was ill, I assumed it was a stuffy nose!"

"I have not seen him like this bef—"

"Well I'm going to!" Strake said loudly, turning away from the window. He looked not at Keebo or Tolma, but over toward the bed. "I've done just fine so far, I think." A pause, and his face darkened. "Easy for you to say; but keep watching, I'll do even better." He turned again, this time toward Tolma and Keebo. His hand gestured toward the bed. "Honestly, I don't know how you stand having this man around."

Keebo took a step forward. "Why do you say that? Sometimes hard truths are necessary."

Strake laughed. "Oh yes, his honesty is refreshing. But look at him! He could at least cover those burns—well it's not like they can't see them as well!" His voice grew loud again as he turned toward the bed. He paused, and took a step backward, a hand to his mouth in shock. "I-I'm sorry," he said quietly. "No, I'm always pouting. I'm always doing the wrong thing. I thought you liked it though, the blood." Strake cowered again, slumping into the chair.

"What blood?" Keebo asked.

Strake scrubbed a fist in his eye and sighed. "So much of it. It was supposed to be on the ground, he said so. Blood on the ground, Islands in safety. Safe from outside threats. We couldn't let our people go across the sea; they would become sick, and come back and bring the sickness with them. It had to stop, and blood on the ground would do it. He said so." His eyes flickered toward Tolma, then Keebo. "He said so."

"Strake, was it Jon's blood that had to be on the ground?"

"Blood and tears; tears and blood. Blood for food, tears for drink. It's how we grow the people of the Islands."

"Did you succeed? Did Jon's blood get on the ground?"

Strake looked up, smile shining through his tears. "I succeeded. I did what I had to. Now our Islands will grow strong. I wish Jon could be here to see it."

"Oh, Strake," Tolma whispered; he gave Keebo a heavy glance, then turned for the door.

Keebo stood in silence while the Steward summoned a few of the guards. Strake stared at his hands, sometimes glancing again toward the bed where Keebo imagined Lasserain stood—or at least had. He didn't feel like singing now. What was the goal of this Unknown? Illmali's goals were always isolation and self-obsession; well, the Islands that Strake would have governed would have been that. Perhaps it was as simple as the Unknown manipulating minds for the purpose of Illmali. Of course, they would not see it as manipulation, just as the Triumvirate did not.

Tolma re-entered with three guards. "Keep an eye on him," he said. "He is responsible for the murder of Prince Jonkar. I have no concept of how he should be punished," he continued with a heavy sigh. "I will assemble our scholars of law in the morning on how to proceed."

"Who will govern the Islands?" Keebo asked. "He obviously cannot inherit the throne in his state."

"I will," Tolma replied. "I've been doing so for twenty years, now; may as well continue."

Keebo nodded. "May I speak to some of your Brightblades, outside? There is more we need to do, at least immediately."

"Come," Tolma replied, leading the way back into the hall. "We'll continue with the visitor log," he said, gesturing to the book as the door shut behind them. Keebo nodded, striking out his name as he remembered. "To whom would you speak?" Tolma asked.

Keebo looked up and down the hall, noting the three empty places where those now guarding Strake once stood. They had been picked apparently at random from various places along the hall. He went to the nearest spot, and stopped in front of the guard still there. He stared hard at the man.

"What is your name?" he said suddenly, making his voice hard.

"Dromir," the guard replied curtly.

"Hmm." Keebo gathered some dirt from the corners, sending it whirling around Dromir's head. The man lost a little bit of his bearing, but not much. "Dromir, under the authority of Oren and in fear of the fates, whom do you serve? The throne, or the king? If you lie, Oren will know and it will pierce your skull."

"The throne," he replied instantly, pride in his voice.

"Among the Brightblades gathered here, whom do you trust? Call three by name."

Again, he did not hesitate. "Suldur, Grithwild, Kalatan," he said loudly.

"All of you, follow us please. Tolma, may we return to your chambers?"

Tolma hesitated, looking warily at Keebo. "May I ask what your plan is?"

"To protect you," Keebo replied, glancing at him. "We want men around you who will not be swayed by the same power that swayed young Strake. There is a new fear in Oren," he continued. "Called the Unknown. They are able to enter folks' minds and whisper to them, trying to convince them to do the will of the Unknown." He paused, then decided to make it clear. "To do the will of Illmali."

24

THE ONE KNOWN

"The world is changing."
"That is not new."
"Where should we focus our efforts?"
"For now, everywhere. The God of All has yet to make his plan clear."

6 Mantaver 1321 — Rainy

"I still struggle with this new turn," Tolma muttered as he poured a glass of water. He offered the pitcher to Keebo, who declined. The four Brightblades stood near the door, swords still bared.

"Do you know who would succeed Strake if he were killed?" Keebo asked.

Tolma shrugged and sat down heavily. "With two possible heirs, it was never discussed. The Teroses were a dying house, but perhaps some relative still exists. Once we determine what to do with Strake, I'll look into it."

Keebo's eyebrows flared. "I'm not sure you will."

Tolma studied him curiously. "Are you saying I will not do my duty? Have I ever failed in twenty years?"

"Yes," Keebo said. "You failed last year, at least, when you killed Jonkar Terose."

A metallic clatter told Keebo the Brightblades noticed the comment. Tolma stared hard at Keebo. "I'm waiting for you to smile," he said. "As a joke. You heard Strake just now admit to it."

"He admitted to doing the actual stabbing, yes," Keebo said. "But I don't think his turn of madness is new to you."

"Keebo, I swear—"

"Don't you dare sit in that seat, dare to claim the title of Steward, and continue to lie to me!"

Tolma's face twisted; he took a deep breath and collected himself. "Don't you stand before this seat, and bring wild accusations, Keebo," he said, fairly spitting the name.

"How did you know that Jon gave Elandra his knife?"

"I—you..." Tolma trailed off then sat back silently.

"You knew because Strake told you. So at the least you knew he had killed Jon long before you sent me to the ruins."

"I did not know then how to proceed," Tolma said. "Yes, I knew about it afterward. That's a far throw from knowing about it beforehand."

"And you continued to cover it up—very elaborately, I might add," Keebo continued. "Keeping Strake 'safe' and even keeping a logbook of every visitor, including yourself. But then, you always knew when I was coming; until tonight. I surprised you, didn't I?"

"I was not prep—" Tolma cut himself off.

Keebo smiled grimly. "No, you were not. Which was why you had to send a guard up before us to 'make everything ready'—including entering a list of new names into the logbook, something you had not bothered to keep up after murdering the Anoe. Your name was on that list, Tolma; but scribbled in haste, and in the same handwriting as every-one else's."

"You still speak only of a concealment, which I admit to. I'm waiting to hear how you think I committed the murder that Strake admits to."

"Then there is the matter of the Royal Ferryman," Keebo continued as if Tolma had not spoken. "Three Captains had been told they were to get the job; only one of them did. The first made no fuss about losing the position; I know him, he didn't truly want it. Another inquired after the fact—a man named Larrince who did truly want it, but instead got only a knife. He tried to ensure my death, you know? At the hands of Klaggen, and Jon's secret network. I wonder how he knew about that? And what would motivate him to do such a thing? Perhaps he had been promised the position if he helped secure the Islands?"

"What other men do is no concern—"

"Then there's the matter of why the position eventually came to Ned-ley. A neat coup for the network, who could use such a position to learn all manner of interesting things, things important for the security of the Islands."

"He was a trustworthy Captain," Tolma replied. "I may have been rash with some of my promises, but in the end he was the best sailor."

"He is indeed, a very good Captain," Keebo said. "I have tested his wares and they are excellent. But you didn't give the position because of Nedley; you gave it because his Calderon promised to lie for you about who had come and gone when Jon went to the ruins."

"He did not lie for me," Tolma said, sitting forward.

"Did he not?" Keebo mused for a second, studying Tolma's smug gaze. "Then perhaps Strake had left the party the day before; after all, what did Torin vow? 'No one left *that day* except Jon,' I think they said." When Tolma's face fell for an instant, Keebo knew he'd hit his mark. "Hmm. Then there is the story of Jon suddenly changing his mind, creating all these enemies who might have killed him. And yet those who were closer to him than you have assured me that his mind was adamant until the day he was killed. So where might one get such an idea, unless it was Strake's mind that was 'changing'? Very handy, I would say: with one lie, suspicion is cast on Prince Jonkar who was perfectly sane; and off Strake, whose true madness you began guiding toward assassination. And it began in Halmfurtung, quite some time before Jon's assassination."

Tolma's eyes widened. "How did you know—?" He stopped himself too late.

Keebo's mouth set a grim line. "So there it is. I knew, because that was when you ordered these special knives made, and because that was when Lasserain was killed in Burieng and joined the Unknown. And Lasserain was at the ruins when Jon was killed, nudging Strake toward it, making him angry. You may not have known who was behind it, but you had started to see that Strake could be manipulated, that his heart was turning away from his brother's policies. I'm afraid you, too, were the object of manipulation."

"Speculation," Tolma muttered, though it was clear his heart was not in it.

"And just now, when Strake said he was told that blood on the ground would save the Islands, he looked at you, not toward Lasserain. You knew he faltered into childishness as part of his madness, and during those times, you told him a nursery rhyme about killing his own brother."

Tolma said nothing at first, only stared at Keebo. "That's why you brought my own Brightblades," he said, his eyes flicking toward the door. "So I could not order them to seize you and kill you. How did you know who to pick?"

"When you went to fetch guards for Strake, you took your time, and you didn't just take three men nearest the door," Keebo replied. "You went to men especially loyal to *you*. I assumed you passed over those nearest to them, because you knew you could not trust them. Which is why I conducted the little spell. See, Tolma? You did choose the right man to find out who killed the Prince."

"I *thought* I had," he replied venomously. "I thought all the fight had gone out of you. Gods know I tried my best."

Keebo nodded sadly. "You should have just let Jon take the throne. He would have been a good king."

"He would never take the throne!" Tolma spat, standing suddenly. "No bastard heir would ever inherit the throne while I lived!"

Keebo took a step back. "What do you mean, 'bastard'? He was—"

"No, Master Keebo, he was not," Tolma seethed, his smile twisted. "It was fortunate the King Terose tanned so easily; it hid Jon for many years. Until Strake came along, anyway."

"But...then..." Keebo faltered, his heart failing. His sins were coming back to haunt him again.

"He was yours, Keebo," Tolma replied. "Why do you think she named you Protector so quickly? And a fine job you did, too. It was well she never named you true father; you would have shunned that duty as well."

"How do you know this?"

"I told you: Strake. It seems the good King Terose was incapable of fathering children. Rayenne confirmed it when she became pregnant."

"How did she do that, if...?"

Tolma's wild grin became dark. "Strake was mine. And since I stayed here as advisor, a far better protector than the one she named, it was natural for the king to name me Steward after she died. What a fool he was," Tolma laughed, but it quickly faded. "You both were. Foolish, and easy to manipulate. Taking the Stewardship was one of the easiest things I had to do; making the Islands the way I wanted them was almost easier, until Jon started meeting those wretched Anoe."

"What would you have done if he hadn't?"

Tolma shrugged. "I would have found something. Or made something up. One way or another, the Bergin name will ascend."

"Well, it would have..." Keebo trailed off as Tolma's grin widened. "You do not expect to go unpunished, do you?" Keebo asked, glowering.

"Save it for your friends the actors," Tolma snarled, "while I tell you how this will actually play out. These Brightblades will take me into the dungeons; Strake, undoubtedly, will follow shortly thereafter. In the morning, the scholars of law will be assembled; they will declare the two of us unfit for rulership. They may debate this for some time, but no doubt the end will be the same. I do intend to put up as good a defense as I can. But when I lose, they will search the rolls for other heirs. This may also take some time, while you tend to your garden. Finally they will come upon a name from seven generations back—all the others have died off; seems the lineage generally is only good at birthing girls, or no one at all. This name they find, they will trace back down the generations to one Larrince, shortly of Candar Ha, and—wouldn't you know it?—a distant nephew of mine. I'll be very proud of Larrince Bergin, whose mercy to me will be swift, I'm sure. And do you know? I think his hatred of the Anoe, and loyalty to true Islanders runs even deeper than mine. He was most interested to learn about this secret network of Jon's, let me tell you. I don't believe Elandra will have to fake her death this time."

Keebo's mouth tightened as he struggled to see some way past this. If Tolma was right about the lineage, there would be nothing he could do—unless he murdered Larrince. As Tolma began to laugh, Keebo turned on his heel and walked out, casting a quick glance to the Bright-blades as he did so. Dromir appeared to be in as much despair as Keebo. It was small comfort—almost none—but at least there were still men of honor in the Islands. They might persevere, despite the Unknown.

The door shut behind Keebo, muffling Tolma's laugh as it faded to chuckles. Well, he would not stand idly by while this threat loomed against the Anoe, and Jon's network. He could warn them. And then he would need to flee for his life, too; surely Larrince would want him dead.

Keebo left the castle into the night. He paused just outside, gazing at the thousand peaks black against the stars. There was one other thing he could do, that might come in handy before too long. He stretched his senses into the mountains: it was time to tear down a monument.

"Oren, oren, kiet fior thoi."

The ground shattered in the night, rock rumbling and echoing like a thousand landslides—landslides that poured energy back into him. He walked calmly away as the guards at the entrance stared about wildly, most of them too young to remember that Nutar Ha had been that way before. Cartographers and sailors would be upset too, at the change; but, so it sometimes went.

At the entrance to the long canyon, Keebo formed his plate again. He would not go so swiftly this time, but it was still much more pleasurable than walking. With his newfound energy, he might even be able to pick up Nedley and Elandra on the way down, return to the boat and run for safety.

But where? Oren was a big place. It sounded as though peace had come to Burieng and Andelen. Not Gintanos: its troubles were only starting. Further eastward? He wondered how things fared in the Pal Isans. Rinc Na was large, and he could hide...

But there would be no hiding from the Unknown. Now that he had discovered the threat, he felt he needed to help do something about it. But where?

There were still some questions about magic that he would have liked answered. And maybe some information on the Triumvirate. But the last time he had seen anything remotely referencing the Triumvirate and the Age of Magic had been at Tamecal, in Carist. Perhaps there, then.

He heard hooves, and slowed his disk. He stopped, hovering, just off the path as guards bearing torches approached. They stopped quickly at the sight of him.

"You need to come with...us," the Captain said as his horse stamped its foot nervously.

Keebo smiled. "I am glad you grasp the absurdity of your assumption," he said. "But actually it's unnecessary; Strake has gone mad, and Tolma is responsible for the death of Prince Jonkar. A few of his loyal Brightblades have taken him into custody, but it likely won't go well for the Islands in the near future. I need Nedley to take Elandra and I to safety. And his Calderon. If you don't mind," he finished, widening his smile.

The Captain took in a deep breath, held it as he glanced again at Keebo hovering on a plate of earth, then sighed as he gestured to his soldiers. They stepped quietly away from the three 'prisoners', gathering instead around their Captain. "We'll continue to the stronghold," he said. "See if we can be of service. I'll send my lieutenant back with you to ensure your safety getting into the harbor."

"Thank you, good Captain," Keebo said. Without further ado, he led his entourage down the road into the darkness.

25

TO LANDS EASTWARD

"Another end is upon us."
"Indeed."
"It is no longer satisfying."
"Even if a thousand yet remain, we are still one step further along the path."

9 Mantaver 1321 — Rainy

Rain fell in great sheets across the ocean as Nedley busied himself preparing to sail. The Calderon, too, lent a hand; if he noticed Keebo's lingering gazes, he did not acknowledge them.

Finally Nedley moved fore while his Calderon was aft. "Good captain," Keebo said, keeping his voice low. "Are you able to sail to Berola without the aid of Torin?"

Nedley glanced at him, aft, then out to sea. "We wouldn't make good time, wizard," he said. "I'm not sure my sea anchor is serviceable, anyway." He shook his head. "I think he'll need to stay."

Keebo nodded. "Just beware; he betrayed the network—he lied for Tolma's sake to help cover up the murder of Jonkar."

Nedley tied off the line, yanking the knot tight. "That should hold," he said with a grin. "Don't want no accidents at sea, do we?"

"Of course not," Keebo replied, settling back. The temporary shelter was up, and he and Elandra reclined in the passengers' chairs. As Nedley went aft, Keebo looked at Elandra and shrugged. "I suppose—"

He broke off as a splash sounded behind them. Whirling quickly, they saw Nedley near the railing, hand to his mouth as he looked overboard.

"Oops," he muttered. He glanced up as the sails began to fill, and the boat began sliding away from the dock. "Well," he said, cheerily now. "Good thing that happened in port." He shook a finger at his passengers as he took the helm. "Don't want no accidents at sea, right?"

"No, of course not," Keebo replied, craning his neck to port as Torin splashed in the shallow waters toward the dock. As the disgraced Calderon heaved himself on deck he flashed a rude gesture at the ship; but Nedley and Keebo only laughed as Elandra rolled her eyes.

⸺◦⸺

By the time they reached Berola the next day, the clouds had gone and a bright sun shone on the rough sand. "Just give me a few moments," Keebo said as Nedley dropped the sails. "I want to warn Shokalog, then we'll be on our way."

"On our way to where?" Elandra asked.

Keebo shrugged. "I'm heading east, to Carist; you are, of course, free to go where you wish. But remember the threat of Larrince."

"If he's as bad as you say, the network may be more necessary now than ever."

"Rebellion?" Keebo asked, shaking his head. "That did not go well for Andelen, or so I have heard."

"We must do what we can."

The boat nudged to shore, and Keebo stepped off. "I'll be right back," he said. He made his way up the beach, the gentle lap of the surf fading away and leaving him in silence. With each step, the cheer of the sun faded from his mind as the silence grew ominous. There should be some movement in the village—surely they did not all go fishing at once, did they?

Keebo hurried on. Could Tolma, or Larrince—? He reached the first hut and pounded on the doorframe; silence from within. He peered through the flap, then stuck his head all the way inside: empty. He ran to the next, and the next—all empty.

"Shokalog?" he shouted. More empty huts. "Shokalog!"

He made it to the village council; here the door hung slightly askew, and the wind and yesterday's rain had not yet washed away hundreds of footprints. His hand trembling, he pulled aside the curtain.

But inside was empty. Charred logs remained in the central fire, and pots of water sat still around the circle. Keebo's brow furrowed as he turned slowly in place, trying to figure out what happened here. He went to the fire: stone cold. Inside was a similar confusion of footprints, but no indication of why they were so scattered. At least there was no blood; unless, of course, they surrendered willingly.

Bending closer, Keebo examined the prints. Every one was of webbed feet—if they had been captured, surely there would be shoe prints from Larrince's soldiers.

A shadow suddenly fell across him; with a yelp, he turned, preparing a spell.

"Shokalog!" he shouted, now in relief. "Where were you? Where is everyone?"

"Who has brought you?" Shokalog asked.

"Nedley; it's all right, he's okay. His Calderon, Torin, is another matter, but we threw him overboard at Nutar Ha."

"You have discovered who killed Prince Jonkar?"

"Yes; it was Strake, but being manipulated by Tolma—and others, we're calling them the Unknown. It's...these are dark times, Shokalog. Larrince will take the throne, and put Tolma's plans in motion—including eradicating the Anoe from the Islands. I came to warn you—"

"We have been warned already," Shokalog replied. "A vision came from the Spirits yesterday."

"To your elders?"

Shokalog shook his head. "To me. Our people will be safe for the time being, I have ensured it. It was not easy, but..."

"Where are they?"

Shokalog looked sideways, then shook his head. "It is better if I do not tell you, in case you are arrested by this new king."

"I'm leaving as quickly as I can," Keebo replied. "The Islands won't be safe for me—really, nowhere will be safe. But I intend to learn as much as I can, see if there is a way to defeat this new threat."

"Where will you go?"

"Carist," Keebo said. "Tamecal. I need to learn about—well, it's complicated."

"So we both will bear secrets with us."

"Shokalog...I'm sorry. I'm sorry for how terrible a friend I've been; I'm sorry I disappeared for so long. Perhaps if I had cared sooner, we would not be in the situation we are in."

"Or perhaps Tolma would have killed you, too," Shokalog replied. "Is Nedley taking you eastward?"

"To Naso Narok, at least; I think he and Elandra are staying behind to see how they might be able to frustrate Larrince and Tolma's plans."

"Elandra? The one who tried to kill you?"

Keebo smiled. "A misunderstanding. She thought I was in league with Tolma, whom she rightly blamed before knowing why. All cleared up. But..." He trailed off, sobering. "Thank you for caring."

Shokalog only blinked. "I am your friend," he replied. He took a breath, then glanced toward the beach. "Do you think Nedley would mind taking me on board as well?"

Keebo shrugged. "I imagine. Where are you going?"

"Naso Narok, then the Pal Isans," he said.

Keebo glanced at him quizzically. "Why there?"

"Part of the deal I made with the Elders, and my people," he said. "I do not want us to fight against the Rinc Nain here. I have heard that the natives of Pal Isan and the Rinc Nain and Carist do not fight with each other." He shrugged with another sigh. "I hope to find out how they do it, and come back here."

"They may not fight because the land is bigger; or because Tolma and Larrince aren't there. What if that's the case?"

"Then I will return, and we will fight for our freedom."

"How long can they wait, though? This journey will take some time. How can you be sure they won't be found before you get back?"

Shokalog smiled. "Because Tolma and Larrince cannot hold their breath that long." He shook his head at Keebo's glance. "It is a long story; but, since we are friends and will be sailing together for a long time, I will tell it to you one day. For now, let us quickly be away from here."

Keebo squinted suspiciously, finally shaking his head with a smile. "And perhaps, since we are friends and will be sailing together for a long time, I will tell you about the Unknown. I think things that have been well-hidden for centuries will finally be coming to light, now that they are here."

Ignoring Shokalog's strange gaze, Keebo led him back to the boat.

◆

One week later, under low gray skies, Keebo and Shokalog stood watching on the dock at Naso Narok as a constant stream of sailors went up and down the gangplank with stores for the voyage to North Pal Isan. Beroc, now turned a sort of privateer, stood on deck shouting orders. It was the boat he had been building for Jonkar; now complete, Beroc intended to make a profit—or so he had informed Keebo when asked for passage.

"Thank you for paying my way," Shokalog said, glancing along the sleek lines of the new boat. "It looks fast, and I do believe you are right; time will be important on my journey."

"As it will be on mine," Keebo replied.

Shokalog shook his head. "It is still difficult to imagine," he said. "What if one of the Unknown is in our minds right now? They could know everything we have planned."

Keebo pursed his lips. "I guess that's possible," he said. "Thank you; now I won't be able to sleep—ever."

Shokalog shrugged. "I suppose we all must do what we can, for as long as we can."

"Indeed." Keebo continued to watch as the last several crates were heaved onto shoulders, and the sailors staggered up the narrow plank. "You know," he said suddenly; "I kept my end of the bargain, but you have not kept yours." He turned, raising an eyebrow. "How are the Anoe staying hidden?"

"Oh, yes. Well..." Shokalog trailed off, glancing around. "Sea caves."

Keebo turned to him, both brows now raised. "Sea caves?"

"Under Berola," Shokalog continued, glancing around warily. "It turned out it was perhaps the best place to exile us. Deep under the northern shore are hundreds of caves, that can only be reached by diving down two hundred feet, then swimming through another several hundred feet of tunnels. Once inside, the caves themselves are dry, and narrow vents make their way to the surface for air." He shrugged with a smile. "Even if Tolma or Larrince learn of them, it would take years of digging through rock to reach them."

Keebo gaped. "How long have you known about them?"

"Actually, only a week." Shokalog smiled grimly. "They were part of my vision the day before you came to Berola."

"And you convinced the Elders to attempt such a crazy plan?"

Shokalog shook his head ruefully. "I convinced the people; hope, it seems, has not entirely left them."

"Maybe once those Anoe we freed from Belltash returned..." He trailed off as Shokalog's eyes darkened. "What, they didn't talk about how terrible the conditions were?"

"They were not returned, Keebo; the Captain and his men were all freed, and they loaded the Anoe right back on board and sailed for Andelen."

Keebo sighed and closed his eyes. After a time, he looked again at his friend. "The rest of your people are safe, then? They agreed to wait in hiding?"

"They are. I spoke to them of the conditions of the slavers, and once they spoke up to their Elders, they could not easily turn away."

"I have seen them do it before, though," Keebo said.

"Yes. Well, the people also made me their chief."

Keebo's eyebrows rose to new heights. "And the Elders stood for that? The Anoe haven't had a chief since..."

"Long before your lifetime," Shokalog confirmed. "They opposed it vehemently; they only agreed when I thought to go to the Pal Isans to learn what I can there."

Keebo glanced back out to sea. "You know they'll bring the Anoe back under their control while you're gone," he said quietly.

Shokalog sighed. "Probably. But when I return, hopefully, I will bring them news that will return them to me, and return the Islands to peace."

Keebo said nothing, but he wondered if peace would ever be found while the Unknown roamed Oren.

As a light rain began to fall, a sailor approached the wizard and the Anoe. "Masters Keebo and Shokalog?" he asked, hunching slightly as the drizzle became a deluge.

"Yes?" Keebo shouted over the rain.

The sailor smiled, holding a hand toward the dock. "Your boat is waiting."

Keebo smiled, too. "It's about time," he said.

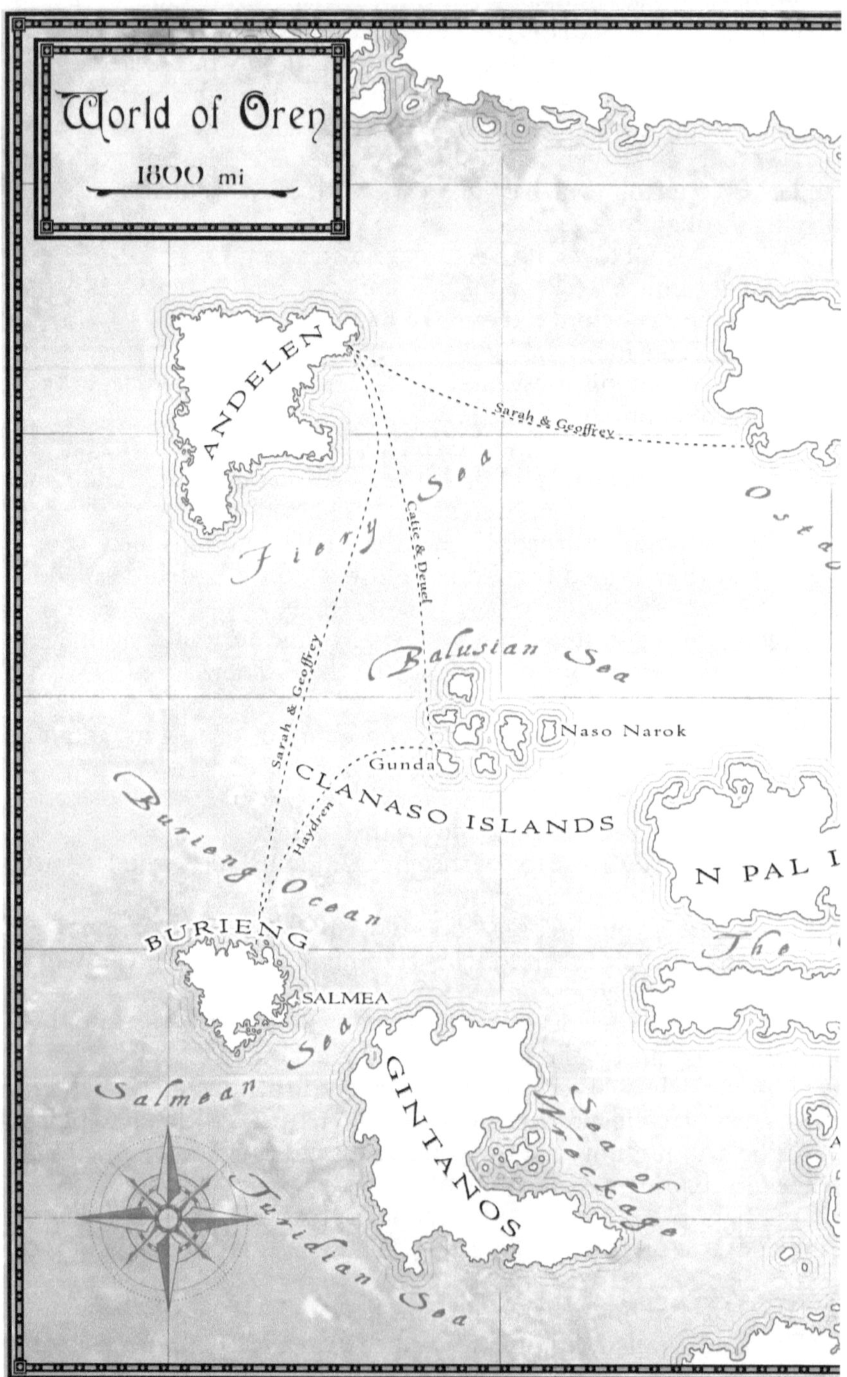

World of Oren
1800 mi
ANDELEN
Sarah & Geoffrey
Calie & Deuel
Fiery Sea
Ostea
Balusian Sea
Naso Narok
Sarah & Geoffrey
Gunda
CLANASO ISLANDS
Haydren
N PAL I
Burieng Ocean
The
BURIENG
SALMEA
Salmean Sea
GINTANOS
Sea of Wreckage
Juridian Sea

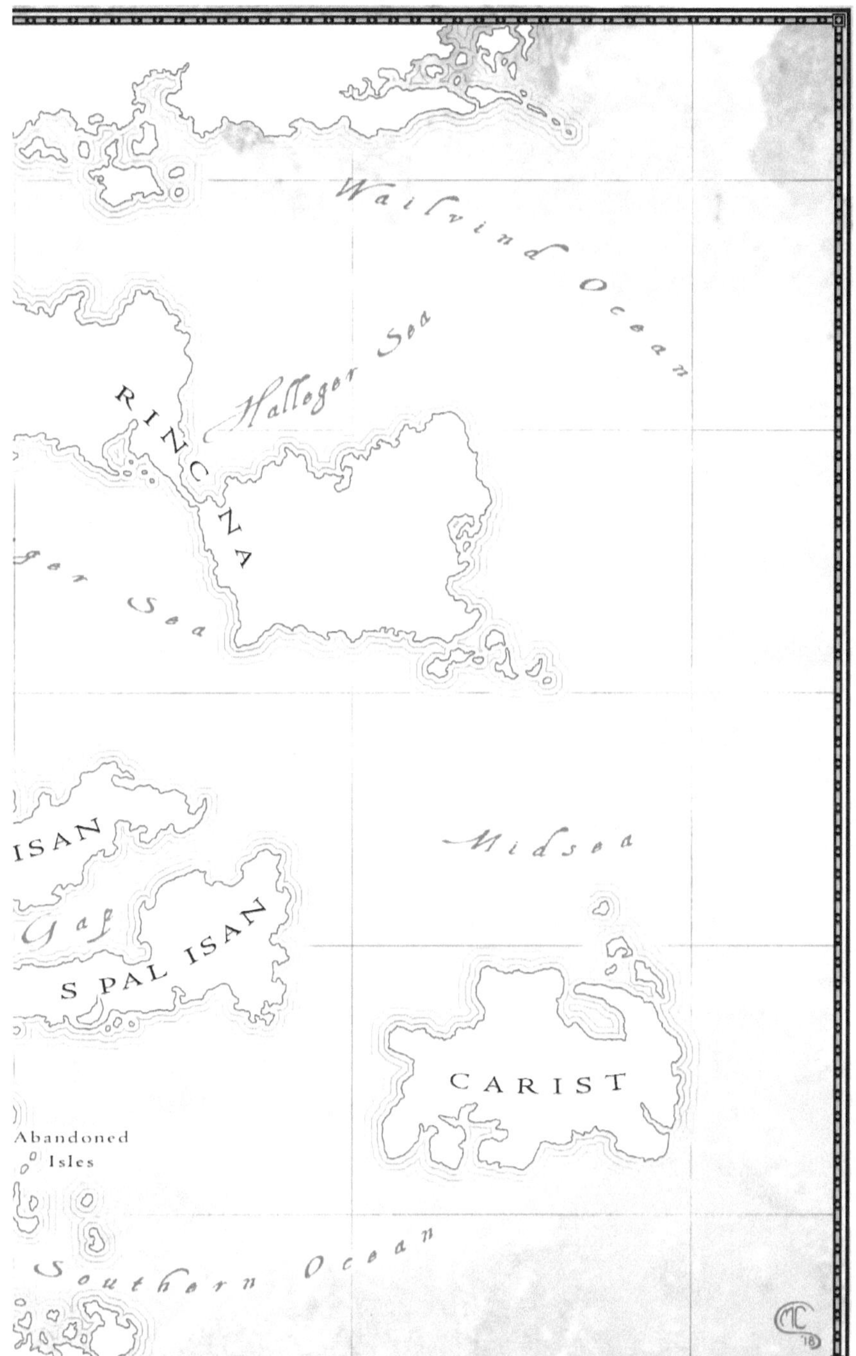

Wailvind Ocean
Halleger Sea
RINCNA
ger Sea
Midsea
ISAN
Gaf
S PAL ISAN
CARIST
Abandoned
Isles
Southern Ocean

Author's Note on Calendar

I provide here a brief description of the history of Oren, its Ages, and Calendars.

As conquerors, Oren history is told mostly by the countries of Rinc Na and Carist, and the Ages and Times as they understand them are assumed.

The First Age, the Black Age (B.A.), is an unknown age. Some few documents remain in fragments, and there are none who know when it began or how the world looked when it did. Every culture's Creation Myths are guesses at this Age, but little more.

The Second Age, the Magic Age (M.A.), is defined and known as the year when magic was first discovered in Carist, and began to be taught by those who used it best. From start to finish numbers 1,095 years as the knowledge and use of magic grew exponentially. Discoveries were made by many great men and women, daring souls who spoke a language they did not know or understand, and many died in the pursuit. The Age ended with the terrible conclusion of the Wizard War, or War of Magics, that had wrought so much devastation to the lands it touched.

The Third Age, the Age of Discovery (A.D.), began as Cariste and Rinc Nain began to pick up the pieces and embark on a new pursuit: that of sailing to all parts of the existing world. Over the succeeding 2,060 years these two competing countries settled all the known world, either living with or displacing native peoples on the Pal Isans, the Clanaso Islands, Andelen, and Burieng. Cariste found none living on Gintanos at first, though in the current Age that is soon to change drastically (the first hints of this can be found in *The First to Forgive,* and will come to full fruition in *Sacrificing All Pain).* The Age ended when the settlers on eastern Burieng sent a missive to Carist declaring their autonomy from that home country, and was the first stroke in the most tumultuous age of history.

The Fourth Age, the Age of War (D.W., or During the War) was not a time of constant strife, though strife indeed pervaded every year. In Burieng, Cariste and Rinc Nain fought over the country and were overthrown suddenly by the native Endolin under King Burieng. News of rebellion against the home countries of Rinc Na and Carist spread, and each country in turn declared and fought for their own autonomy from the lands where they had originated. After 896 years all was settled once more, and with only minor exceptions the countries look now as they did then.

Finally, the current Age, after the eight continents solidified, (A.E., or After the Eight). A common calendar was formulated and agreed upon by all Rinc Nain and Cariste, and eventually by the natives as they conducted business with those two peoples. The calendar was conceived and developed by the Rinc Nain, though only those people know it as "the Rinc Nain calendar." It consists of 400 days across 11 months of varying lengths. It begins with **Haschina** (named from legend), on the Winter Solstice in Rinc Na and countries north of the equator; or the first day of Summer in southern latitudes. It continues with **Mantaver** (Month Two), **Thriman** (Third Month), **Halmfurtung** (Half Four Moon, as four Full Moons have come and gone), **Fimman** (Fifth Month), **Monzak** (Month Six), **Savimon** (Seventh Month), **Fulmatung** (Full Eight Moon), **Nuamon** (Ninth Month), **Tetsamon** (Tenth Month), and **Elfumon** (Eleventh Month).

ABOUT THE AUTHOR

Daniel Dydek is a multi-genre author with his sweeping epic fantasy series The Triumvirs, and his supernatural suspense series, Spirit Wind, has already garnered two Finalist awards from Realm Makers. Besides writing, he also enjoys a personal relationship with Jesus Christ, mountain biking, reading, coffee shops, book stores, and Durango Colorado. He lives in Canton Ohio with his wife and son and two cats.

Support for the Author

First, thank you for reading this story on whichever medium you chose—Kindle, KU, or paperback. Your support means dreams come true! If you loved the story, there are a lot of ways to continue supporting the author FOR FREE. Here's a few:

    1. Subscribe to the newsletter on danieldydek.com

    2. Tell your friends!

    3. Leave a review on Goodreads, Amazon, Barnes & Noble, or on your social media. (This is probably the greatest support of all, because we love hearing what people enjoyed about the book! Plus, you know, algorithms...)

    4. Request your local library to get a copy

All these things help promote the books, and encourage the author to keep writing stories you'll love!

—The Beorn Publishing Team

The Triumvirs epic fantasy series

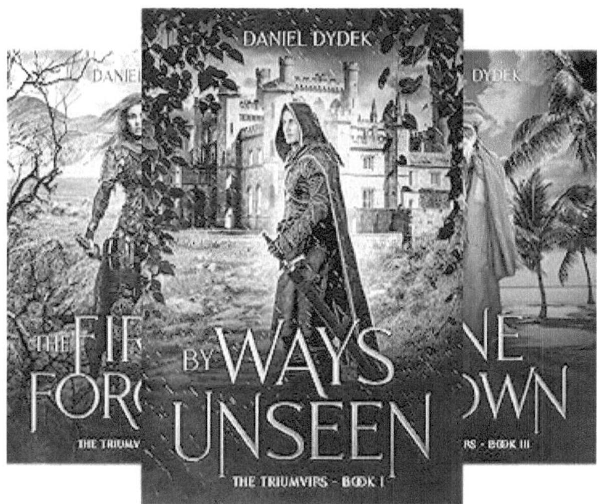

Centuries ago, the world of Oren was ravaged by uncontrolled magic during the Wizards War. In the wake of such devastation and evil, the God of All took three wizards and established for them a Room, of darkness and consciousness, and placed before them a great table whose appearance is of translucent slate, through which they might call up visions of the lands, entering when needed. Few even know these former wizards exist, and their work will always be credited to brave men and women of the world who were faithful in their obedience.

These wizards' task is keeping the peace, of prompting action against the forces of evil. They answer still to the God of All, but retain autonomy. He named them The Triumvirate, and over the centuries twenty-two Triumvirs have guided Oren through wars, famines, pestilences, and the rising and falling of countless empires.

Now, in this current Age of men, will come their most difficult battle.

Amazon search: The Triumvirs Dydek

Spirit Wind Christian suspense series

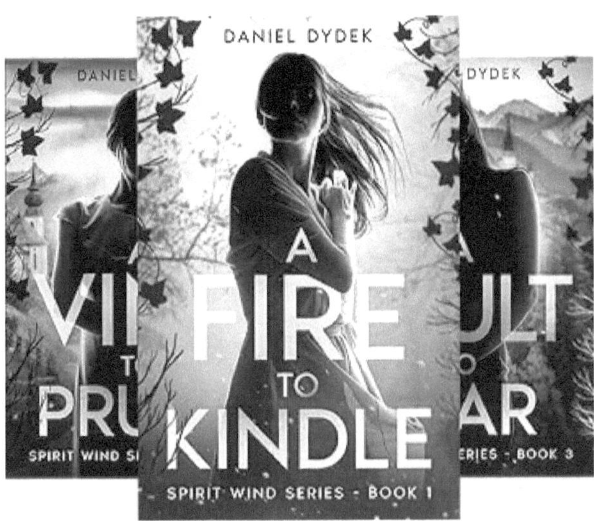

Cursed with left-handedness, then cursed with fire.

Except the fire seems to comfort, to strengthen, to speak wisdom. Wisdom like:

"The wind bloweth where it listeth, and thou hearest the sound thereof, but canst not tell whence it cometh, and whither it goeth: so is every one that is born of the Spirit."

And so Rae-Anna is borne on itinerant winds, never knowing what danger she'll be asked to face. But she knows this: it will always be demonic. And she will never be alone.

Amazon search: Spirit Wind Dydek